PENGUIN  CLASSICS

ORLANDO FURIOSO: PART TWO

LUDOVICO ARIOSTO was born in 1474, the son of an official of the Ferrarese court. He first studied law, but later acquired a sound humanistic training. His adult life was spent in the service of the Ferrarese ducal family. Essentially he was a writer; his lifetime's service as a courtier was a burden imposed on him by economic difficulties. His fame rests on his major work, *Orlando Furioso*. The poem was probably begun about 1505. It was first published in 1516. The most important of Ariosto's minor works are five comedies, written for production in the Ferrarese court. Ariosto died in 1533.

BARBARA REYNOLDS was for twenty-two years Lecturer in Italian at Cambridge University and subsequently Reader in Italian Studies at Nottingham University and Honorary Reader at Warwick. Her first book was a textual reconstruction of the linguistic writings of Alessandro Manzoni. The General Editor of the *Cambridge Italian Dictionary*, she was created Cavaliere Ufficiale al Merito della Repubblica Italiana in 1978. She has been awarded silver medals by the Italian Government and by the Province of Vicenza and the Edmund Gardner Prize for her services to Italian scholarship and to Anglo-Italian cultural relations. She has been Visiting Professor in Italian at the University of California, Berkeley, at Wheaton College, Illinois, and at Hope College, Michigan, where she has been awarded Honorary Doctorates, and at Trinity College, Dublin. Barbara Reynolds has translated Dante's *La Vita Nuova* and *Paradiso*, left unfinished by Dorothy L. Sayers on her death in 1957, and Ariosto's *Orlando Furioso*, for which she was awarded the Monselice International Literary Prize in 1976, for Penguin Classics. She is the author of *The Passionate Intellect: Dorothy L. Sayers' Encounter with Dante* and *Dorothy L. Sayers: Her Life and Soul*.

ORLANDO FURIOSO
(THE FRENZY OF ORLANDO)

A Romantic Epic by
Ludovico Ariosto

PART TWO

TRANSLATED
WITH AN INTRODUCTION BY
BARBARA REYNOLDS

PENGUIN BOOKS

PENGUIN BOOKS

Published by the Penguin Group
Penguin Books Ltd, 27 Wrights Lane, London W8 5TZ, England
Penguin Putnam Inc., 375 Hudson Street, New York, New York 10014, USA
Penguin Books Australia Ltd, Ringwood, Victoria, Australia
Penguin Books Canada Ltd, 10 Alcorn Avenue, Toronto, Ontario, Canada M4V 3B2
Penguin Books (NZ) Ltd, Private Bag 102902, NSMC, Auckland, New Zealand

Penguin Books Ltd, Registered Offices: Harmondsworth, Middlesex, England

This translation first published 1977

024

Printed and bound in Great Britain by Clays Ltd, Elcograf S.p.A.
Set in Monotype Garamond

ISBN-13: 978-0-14-044310-3

www.greenpenguin.co.uk

MIX
Paper | Supporting
responsible forestry
FSC
www.fsc.org FSC® C018179

Penguin Books is committed to a sustainable
future for our business, our readers and our planet.
This book is made from Forest Stewardship
Council™ certified paper.

CONTENTS

INTRODUCTION

I. THE STRUCTURE OF THE POEM

THE present translation, for purposes of convenience, is divided into two volumes. This does not correspond to Ariosto's intention. Unlike Boiardo, he chose not to split his poem into individually numbered books. The madness of Orlando occurs at the end of Canto XXIII. In respect of the number of cantos, it occupies a central position; in respect of the number of stanzas, the mid-point is reached where Isabella, about to kill herself in grief at the death of Zerbino, is persuaded by a hermit to dedicate her life to God.[1] This is characteristic of the way in which the focus of emphasis appears to shift throughout the work. Unlike Dante's *Commedia*, Boccaccio's *Decamerone* and Petrarch's *Canzoniere*, Ariosto's epic is not arranged in accordance with any precise numerical plan. The cantos themselves range in number of stanzas from 72 to 199. Ariosto apologizes for the length of some which are relatively short, while for the two longest (XVIII and XLIII) he makes no excuse whatever.

The absence of structural divisions, the interweaving of varied themes, the frequent interruptions, the lack of unity in the Aristotelian sense incurred the condemnation of late sixteenth-century critics and poets, notably of Tasso and of Ronsard, for whom the *Orlando Furioso* was 'a deformed and monstrous body'.[2] The principles of literary criticism after the Counter-Reformation were weighted against the likelihood of

1. XXIV.89-90.
2. '. . . *le corps est tellement contrefaict et monstrueux qu'il ressemble mieux aux resveries d'un malade de fièvre continue qu'aux inventions d'un homme bien sain*' (*La Franciade. Oeuvres Complètes*, ed. Paul Laumonier, Marcel Didier, Paris, 1950, XVI, p. 4). Nevertheless, Ronsard imitated Ariosto's combats; e.g. the battle between Francus and Phovere, Livre II, 1233-1468.

discerning structure in the poem. Theorists looked for what
was not there and failed to see what was.

There is some danger among modern readers of erring in the
opposite direction and of assuming that the absence of an
obvious control of form signifies a willing surrender to a
dream-world of surrealism and confusion. This view of the
poem is reflected in the film version directed by Luca Ronconi,
a work in marked contrast to his theatrical production which
captured more convincingly Ariosto's mastery of his complex
material.

There are fundamental things still, even after four and a half
centuries, to be discovered about the poem. Professor C. P.
Brand considers it is 'still essentially undefined and un-
categorized'; the intermingling of the serious and the light-
hearted, he says, 'gave a stimulus to what was essentially a new
genre'. Professor Brand is the first to have pointed out the
thematic design which emerges from the grouping of stories of
constancy and inconstancy in love round the central motif of
Orlando's madness.[1] Professor Robert Griffin also recognizes
what he calls the 'structure of vision' and 'the larger patterns of
the poem', but he considers that Ariosto loses control in the
second half:

The porous memory, ignorance, and general fallibility that plague
[Ariosto] in the second half of the poem are consonant with the
differentiation he establishes between his folly and God's wisdom
and with the parallel he stresses between himself and Orlando.[2]

There is, he thinks, 'madness in the author's method'. Nothing
could be farther from the truth.

Ariosto many times assures the reader that he knows what he
is doing. He may seem to have lost his way, but he knows which
thread he is weaving into his fabric (a favourite metaphor with
him); he knows the value of variety, not only of subject but of
tone; and he sees more artistry in managing a swirling complex-
ity than in designing a predictable symmetry.

The celebrated interruptions in *Orlando Furioso* are usually

1. C. P. Brand, *Ludovico Ariosto*, Edinburgh University Press, 1974,
p. 194, p. 189.
2. Robert Griffin, *Ludovico Ariosto*, Twayne, New York, 1974, p. 150.

recognized as an inheritance from the narrative tradition of the *cantastorie*, whose intention was to arouse suspense in their listeners and an eagerness to return on another occasion to hear more. Thus Ariosto ends his cantos, and occasionally even episodes within a canto, at a moment of crisis. His intention is sometimes to produce a humorous effect, sometimes to heighten a dramatic situation or a tragic event, and always to beguile the reader with variety.

This, though true enough, amounts to little more than the technique of any competent writer of a serial. Something else is here involved, something of greater subtlety, which goes to the very heart of the problem which has always confronted a narrator: the problem, that is, of time and the sequence of events. When and where is an author to begin? Involved in this is his relationship with what he is narrating: is he to tell his story in the first or the third person? For some events, the viewpoint of the third person may be satisfactory; for others, especially those which antedate the main action, an evocation in the first person by one of the characters, usually the protagonist, has often been preferred. Homer and Virgil adopted this method of narration-within-the-narration, whereby events preceding those with which the story begins are related not directly by the author but, in the *Odyssey*, by Odysseus to King Alcinous and, in the *Aeneid*, by Aeneas to Dido.[1] This change of viewpoint, though it provides first-hand participation, sacrifices the immediacy of direct action, of something happening here and now before the reader's eyes. Whether the author uses past or present tense is not important; the effect of immediacy is achieved by the fact that the narration is made direct to the reader. Other effects of great beauty and solemnity are achieved by Homer and Virgil by the interplay of two planes of time; the solution they chose was in accordance with the totality of their poetic aims.

Although Ariosto learnt much from Homer and Virgil, he chose not to sacrifice the immediacy of direct narration. For all the major events of his poem he is himself the narrator. That is why he has to move so frequently from place to place ('Now I must go in search of Astolfo', 'Now let me follow Angelica', 'Now let me see how Bradamante is faring'). He has to be there,

1. *Odyssey*, Books ix–xiii; *Aeneid*, Books ii–iii.

to tell the reader at first hand what is happening. These are not interruptions for interruption's sake; they are displacements of the author rendered necessary by his decision to sustain direct narration.

There are of course several exceptions and it is important to notice two things in connection with these. First, the stories related by one or other of the minor characters are always subordinate to the main plot. Secondly, these inset narrations are never interrupted; in other words, Ariosto always refrains from intruding into a function from which he has temporarily withdrawn. The reader has become a third party, an observer listening in, and so he remains until Ariosto takes over once more and re-admits him to the intimacy of direct communication. In fact this is never interrupted in any important sense.[1]

These considerations, though basic to the structure and unity of the poem, do not account for the arrangement of the material. From a deliberately contrived impression of random sequence, certain patterns of order emerge. The most significant of these can be grouped under three headings: Balance, Totality and Intricacy Resolved.

PATTERNS OF BALANCE

These are achieved by juxtaposing episodes either of similarity or of contrast. The most striking example of the latter is the placing side by side in succeeding cantos (XXVIII and XXIX) of the most extreme instances of female inconstancy and constancy. The bawdy tale of Fiammetta's skill in deceiving two men who lie one each side of her, and the heroic tale of Isabella's sacrifice of her life in order to remain faithful to Zerbino, offer the most violent contrast in the entire poem. A previous instance of immediate proximity had occurred in Cantos X and XI where two women, naked and helpless, are rescued from death by two knights; here Ruggiero who, on parting with the magic ring of reason, is fired with lust, is contrasted with Orlando who behaves with perfect decorum. He is a trustworthy escort also of Angelica and Isabella; his attack on Angelica at the height of his frenzy is consequently all the more startling. Orlando's mad-

1. The inset narrations are almost invariably amorous or erotic.

ness, caused by Angelica, is balanced by Rodomonte's madness, caused by Doralice; later they are grappled together, wrestling on Rodomonte's bridge, and pitch headlong together into the river. Both Angelica and Doralice find refuge with their lovers in a shepherd's hut. Ginevra, condemned to be burned to death for unchastity, is balanced by Ricciardetto, condemned to be burned to death for sleeping with the daughter of the king of Spain. Rinaldo rescues Ginevra, Ruggiero rescues Ricciardetto; later they are brought face to face in combat. The siege of Paris is balanced by the siege of Biserta. Alessandretta, the city of men-hating women, is balanced by the kingdom of Marganorre, the woman-hater, and Marfisa plays a part in destroying them both. Orlando throws the cannon of Cimosco into the North Sea; Ruggiero, with a comparable concern for the ideals of chivalry, throws his magic shield into a well. The tone of burlesque in Orlando's combat with Mandricardo when they fight with sticks and fists is echoed when Bradamante and Marfisa also are reduced to fisticuffs. Characters, as well as episodes, are balanced and paired, or joined by kinship. Rinaldo and Orlando, who are cousins, both love Angelica; both are cured. Bradamante has a twin brother; Ruggiero has a twin sister. All through the poem, such doublets and correspondences, sometimes in immediate vicinity, sometimes occurring at a distance, serve to stitch the material together.

PATTERNS OF TOTALITY

It is evident from his choice of episodes that Ariosto desired to present a complete range of the three main subjects of his poem: war, chivalry and love. Chivalry, or the lack of it, is manifested from the extreme treachery of the Maganzans to the heroic self-sacrifice of Leone and Ruggiero, rivals at first for Bradamante's hand, later outvying each other in mutual courtesy. His tone varies appropriately to suit the different aspects of war, from rumbustious zest to elegiac pathos and epic solemnity. It is to be noted, however, that only with reference to the Carolingian battles does he adopt the humorous or exaggerated style of the *cantastorie*; his allusions to contemporary war are always grave.

The range of the erotic episodes, too, is comprehensive: love with honour, fidelity, infidelity, infatuation, obsessional desire, primitive lust, multiple sex, homosexuality, depravity, transvestism, voyeurism, cruelty, bawdy innuendoes and frank voluptuousness. Ariosto associates himself with the irrationality of love and counsels against surrender to extreme emotions. He is particularly good on the theme of jealousy and on the anguish of lovers separated by war or death. The laments of Bradamante while she is waiting for Ruggiero to arrive at Montalbano are among the most tender and imaginative of his stanzas. In many ways such set pieces seem to anticipate the appeal of an operatic aria.

Ariosto not only warns against extreme emotions: he also conveys disapproval of extreme demands and expectations. The end of the story of Fiammetta (Canto XXVIII) is a splendid instance of humour and good sense triumphing over an arbitrary refusal to accept reality: the picture of the two duped men falling back helpless with laughter on the bed, tears of merriment running down their faces, is like a gust of sanity. It is followed by the moderate, balanced observations on marital fidelity by an elderly man at the inn, to whom no one pays any attention, least of all Rodomonte, sunk in his injured self-esteem. Ariosto's own experience of love was not always joyful, if we are to take his asides on this matter at their face value.[1] Perhaps his most convincing self-portrait is to be found in the opening stanzas of Canto XXXV where, having shown that the wits of lovers are on the moon, he asks who will ascend there in search of his. Then, returning from this flight of fancy, he indicates the source of his own equilibrium: solace in his Alessandra's arms.

It can be seen that the patterns of balance and the patterns of totality are aspects of one another. The poem swings like a pendulum across an arc, of which the extremes and the segments are thus brought into an increasingly emphasized relationship; or it may be thought of as describing a full circle, coming to a position of rest only when fulfilment is reached in the marriage between Bradamante and Ruggiero and in the conclusion of the conflict, with its epilogue of the death of Rodomonte.

1. See, for instance, XXX. 1–4.

PATTERNS OF INTRICACY RESOLVED

This category is proclaimed by Ariosto from the first stanza of the first canto. The poem is to be about love, war and chivalry, and about their interactions one upon the other. This promise is maintained. Not only is the action of the war continually interrupted by chivalrous adventures and by amorous entanglements, but war, chivalry and love become intricately intertwined.

The most elaborate instance is to be seen in the fortunes of Bradamante and Ruggiero. Having pledged their love and vowed to meet at Vallombrosa, where Ruggiero is to be baptized, they are separated by a series of events relating to the war. Ruggiero, gravely wounded in combat with Mandricardo, is unable to join Bradamante at Montalbano as he had promised. News reaches her that Marfisa is tending him in his convalescence and, tormented by jealousy, she resolves to challenge him to a joust. When the moment comes, she is unable to strike him. A reconciliation occurs, but the complications have scarcely begun. Bradamante's parents wish her to marry Leone, the son of Constantine, Emperor of Byzantium. Rinaldo, her brother, has in the meantime given his consent to her betrothal to Ruggiero. An impasse is reached, which Bradamante tries to solve by asking Charlemagne to decree that only a knight whom she cannot defeat in combat shall marry her. Charlemagne agrees. Bradamante is confident that Ruggiero will accept the challenge. Meanwhile Ruggiero has gone to Bulgaria with the intention of killing both Constantine and Leone. After winning great glory in defence of the Bulgarians[1] and inspiring the devoted admiration of Leone, he is betrayed and held captive in a dungeon. While awaiting death, he is rescued by Leone. Ruggiero's identity is unknown to him, for he has assumed an emblem not his own. Ruggiero swears undying loyalty to Leone; thus, later, he cannot but agree to fight Bradamante, impersonating Leone, when requested to do so.

Bradamante, believing her opponent to be Leone, does her

---

1. Since Bulgaria was in the power of Islam in Ariosto's time, this extension of action and terrain strengthens the relevance of the poem to contemporary Christendom.

best to defeat him. Ruggiero, striving not to wound her, is obliged in loyalty to Leone not to surrender to her. He is declared undefeated and a worthy husband for Bradamante, who has no option but to accept him, believing him to be Leone. Ruggiero receives Leone's fervent thanks and goes off into a forest to die of grief. In the meantime, Marfisa asserts Ruggiero's claim to Bradamante's hand and insists, in the presence of Charlemagne, that Leone shall fight Ruggiero to test his prowess still further. Leone has no doubt that the unknown cavalier will again fight in his place with equal success and he goes off confidently to look for him. The intricacy has now reached a point of insurmountable illogicality: Ruggiero has to fight Ruggiero. Supernatural aid is enlisted. The good sorceress, Melissa, leads Leone to where Ruggiero lies near to death. His identity is revealed. Leone, amazed at his chivalry, renounces all claim to Bradamante, and brings him to Charlemagne's court, dressed as the unknown knight, come, he declares, to claim his bride. Marfisa challenges him to a duel in (as she believes) Ruggiero's absence. The unknown knight's helmet is removed. Ruggiero is revealed and all is explained.[1]

Of all the stories of mistaken identity, misunderstandings and inflexible rules of chivalry which the work contains, this is the most complicated. The fascination resides, as in a detective story, or as in any game or puzzle, in watching the knots becoming more and more entangled and finally untied. The art resides in the embellishment of the verse by which the reader's emotional and aesthetic responses are evoked.

INTRICACY OF COMBATS

Ariosto felt particular delight in devising and resolving intricate conflicts. His *chef d'œuvre* in this category is undoubtedly the siege of Paris, which has been analysed in detail in Volume I of this translation.[2] The siege of Biserta balances this as an event but comes nowhere near it in complexity. The minor combats of the second half of the poem are, however, remarkable for their ingenuity and precision. If the laments of anguished lovers

1. cf. the intricate fortunes of Ariodante, Cantos v–vi.
2. pp. 474–7.

seem to anticipate operatic arias, there is much in Ariosto's management of combats which is akin to choreography. It is likely that Ariosto worked from models of knights on horseback in planning the movements. Certainly if the reader will try the experiment of following them through with models or chessmen, it will be found that every detail is clearly accounted for. To do so, greatly heightens appreciation of the verse and also reveals the three-dimensional nature of Ariosto's art.[1]

Ariosto surpasses himself in the intricacy he devises for a series of quarrels which spring up among the pagans as a result of Dame Discord's renewed efforts, urged on by the enraged Archangel Michael. The multiple combat near Merlin's fountain in Canto XXVI[2] is left unconcluded: Ruggiero has not regained Frontino from Rodomonte, Mandricardo and Ruggiero still deny each other's right to the Trojan eagle, Rodomonte and Mandricardo are still rivals for the hand of Doralice, and Marfisa has still to avenge the affront she has suffered from Mandricardo. After slaughtering many of the Christians encamped outside Paris, where they are joined by Sacripante and Gradasso, the disputants go before Agramante to obtain a decision as to the order in which they may settle their various claims and resentments. Agramante decides that they must draw lots.

> Taking four slips of paper, the king wrote
> First 'Mandricardo–Rodomont' on one;
> 'Ruggiero–Mandricardo', he next put;
> 'Ruggiero–Rodomonte', he went on;
> 'Marfisa–Mandricard' was the fourth note,
> And to the goddess Chance, when this was done,
> He left the choice; and she that day decreed
> That Rodomont and Mandricard should lead.[3]

Mandricardo and Ruggiero are to fight second, Ruggiero and Rodomonte shall fight third, the fourth combat shall be that between Marfisa and Mandricardo.

In one pavilion Rodomonte is arming, with the assistance of

1. See diagrams of two combats, pp. 674–8.
2. See stanzas 132–7.
3. XXVII. 45.

Sacripante and Ferraù; in the other, Mandricardo is being
assisted by Gradasso and Falsirone. Gradasso is about to hand
Mandricardo his sword when he sees from the lettering
engraved upon it that it is Durindana, Orlando's sword which
Mandricardo seized and to which Gradasso has long laid claim.
He challenges Mandricardo for it, requesting him to ask
Rodomonte to defer the present combat. Ruggiero refuses to
consent to a change in the battle-order unless he himself is
moved to first place. Mandricardo, enraged, strikes the sword
from Gradasso's hand and is prepared to fight Gradasso,
Rodomonte and Ruggiero simultaneously. Ruggiero and
Gradasso fight for precedence; others unwisely intervene.
Only the entrance of Agramante with Marsilio halts the com-
motion. As Agramante tries to reason with the disputants, a
clamour breaks out in Rodomonte's pavilion: Sacripante has
recognized Frontino, the horse which was stolen from him by
Brunello; he claims it but tells Rodomonte that he gives him
leave to ride it in the coming combat. Rodomonte refuses to
admit Sacripante's claim to the horse and they begin to duel.
Those standing by join in and so great is the uproar that
Agramante leaves Marsilio to hold the situation in Mandri-
cardo's pavilion and goes to try to resolve the matter of the
horse. Marfisa joins them and recognizes Frontino as the horse
which Brunello stole on the occasion when he also stole her
sword. Brunello is pointed out to her and she at once asserts her
right to deal with him as she thinks fit. Agramante is put out by
this and is on the point of challenging her, but is dissuaded by
Sobrino and allows her to depart.

There now remain five cavaliers who desire to fight one
another and who clamour for precedence: Rodomonte,
Ruggiero, Mandricardo, Gradasso, and Sacripante. Ariosto's
pleasure in this complexity is clearly seen in the following
lines:

> There are five cavaliers whose minds are set
> On fighting first, although the battle-list
> Presents a tangled skein more intricate
> Than all Apollo's wisdom could untwist.[1]

I. XXVII. 102. 1-4.

Agramante begins by trying to bring about a reconciliation between Mandricardo and Rodomonte, the rivals for Doralice. They will not budge. At last he asks if they will be content to let Doralice choose between them. Since each is confident of being chosen, they agree. Doralice chooses Mandricardo. Rodomonte, in deep dejection, rides away on Frontino; Sacripante rides after him in an attempt to regain the horse.

This leaves Ruggiero and Mandricardo who contest each other's right to the Trojan eagle, and Gradasso who claims Durindana which Mandricardo has seized from Orlando. Agramante suggests that these two disputes shall be settled as one: let it be decided by lot whether Ruggiero or Gradasso shall fight Mandricardo and let the victory or defeat count for both. They agree, and Ruggiero's name is drawn. Mandricardo is killed. Durindana is awarded to Gradasso; Brigliadoro, Orlando's horse, which Mandricardo was riding, is given to Agramante. Ruggiero keeps Mandricardo's armour.

The tangle is thus untied. The transference of horses, swords and armour continues to be significant. In the final combat between three Christians and three pagans on the island of Lampedusa, Durindana is wielded by Gradasso, who rides Baiardo (Rinaldo's horse); Frontino is ridden by Brandimarte; Ruggiero's sword, Balisarda, is wielded by Orlando; and Ruggiero's armour (once Mandricardo's) is worn by Oliver. The vicissitudes by which all these displacements come about are clearly accounted for. It is as though Rinaldo and Ruggiero are represented at this crucial and conclusive combat; and since, as Ariosto continually reminds us, Mandricardo's armour was originally forged by Vulcan for Hector, the victory of the Christians can be seen also as a final vindication for the Trojans.

Overriding all the minor patterns of intricacy resolved is the master pattern of the entire poem. By the end of Canto XXIII we are left with three main stories which appear to be developing in different directions: Orlando's madness, the love of Bradamante and Ruggiero, and the war between the Christians and the Infidel. Their resolution appears to be impeded by a whole series of subordinate stories: Rinaldo's love for Angelica, Astolfo's journeys on the hippogriff, Fiordiligi's quest for Brandimarte, Isabella's grief at Zerbino's death, Rodomonte's fury on being jilted by Doralice, Marfisa's discovery of her identity, the discord among the pagans described above, to mention only a few. In reality, it is these other strands which serve to bring the complexities of the poem gradually and inevitably to a point of convergence, rather as the many ropes cast about the body of the frenzied Orlando serve to bring him under control and thus capable of being restored to sanity. Gradually too, as the stories come together, more and more prominence is given to the surmounting of obstacles which impede the marriage of Ruggiero and Bradamante, the ancestors of the House of Este, as Aeneas was the ancestor of Augustus. The abrupt conclusion of the wedding feast, and of the poem, with the death of Rodomonte is a final echo of Virgil who ends the *Aeneid* abruptly with the death of Turnus.

II. THE DEVELOPMENT OF THE POEM

It is often said that as the poem progressed during the twenty-five years or so which went to its composition the later cantos took on an increasingly sombre tone.[1] Marganorre's savage treatment of women, Drusilla's melodramatic revenge and Theodora's determination to put Ruggiero to a cruel death are three examples which are cited. There is some truth in this, yet the evil machinations of Pinabello, Polinesso and especially Gabrina bear comparison with later lurid interludes. It could probably be shown that there is, blow for blow, rather less violence in the second half of the poem than in the first. Not even the atrocities committed by the deranged Orlando approach the ferocious deeds of Rodomonte in his attack on Paris.

Yet a development does occur and it is one which affects the poem in all its aspects. Whatever the nature of the episodes, tragic or comic, heroic or romantic, there is a gradual heightening of style. The stanzas become richer in texture, revealing the hand of an experienced artist. The senses are regaled with ever more colour and splendour, emotions are evoked more keenly and over a wider range, the imagination is held by increasingly elaborate allusions and comparisons.

1. See, for instance, C. P. Brand, op. cit., p. 78.

These mature qualities of Ariosto's later style are already evident in the story of Olimpia, especially in the description of her beauty.[1] They are to be seen also in the expression of Isabella's grief (of far greater depth than her earlier laments to Orlando in the cave); in the relentless attack on Rinaldo by the monster symbolizing jealousy (Ariosto's masterpiece in this genre); in the imagery of precious stones by which Bradamante expresses her fidelity to Ruggiero; in the midnight battle between Gradasso's fleet and Agramante's escaping ships, illumined by the glare of flames; in the complex and sustained debates; in the dramatic intensity of the dilemma of Ruggiero; in the playful fantasies of boulders which change to horses and of leaves which, cast upon the water, turn to ships. Everyone who reads the poem will come to have a private anthology of favourite passages, but whatever selection is made a deeper awareness of life and of art will be found to characterize the later cantos.

There is an important exception: religion continues throughout to be treated with the lightest possible touch. The prayers and fasting of both armies before the siege of Biserta are related with a levity which recalls the bargaining of Charlemagne with God before the siege of Paris. Three pagans are converted and baptized in the course of events: Marfisa, Ruggiero and Sobrino. Only one ceremony of baptism is described, that of Marfisa, which is performed at the court of Charlemagne by Archbishop Turpin, no less. In this brief scene, ecclesiastical and imperial splendour somewhat overshadows the spiritual. Ruggiero is brought to Christ by the hermit who awaits him on an island where, like Odysseus, he scrambles ashore after being shipwrecked. This episode is related with a simple devoutness which is almost convincing, except that the reader cannot help suspecting that Ariosto is smiling. This is clearly the case when Sobrino is converted on witnessing the miraculous repair of Oliver's broken ankle and the instant healing of his own wounds. Miracles are treated in the same spirit as magic, the palace in the Terrestrial Paradise is not more splendid than Logistilla's or Prester John's, and St John the Evangelist himself is more

1. Cantos IX–XI. This episode was inserted into the early part of the poem in the last edition; cf. Vol. I, Introduction, pp. 45–8.

interesting on the subject of writers and patrons than on religion.

Ariosto loses none of his philosophy of humour with advancing age. The word 'irony' is often used in this connection, but it seems a heavy-handed term for the irrepressible laughter which bubbles forth at incongruous moments. His zest for life remains undiminished; it is manifest in his delight in the absurd, in his witty and subtle double meanings, in his joy in friendship and above all in the pleasure he takes in shaping his eight-line stanzas to suit the requirements of his vast and varied themes. *'Parva sed apta mihi'* is how Ariosto described his house in Ferrara.[1] The words are also appropriate to what he ultimately made of the *ottava*.

III. REALITY AND FANTASY

One of the most remarkable features of the art of Ariosto is the precision with which he represents the real world in which he sets his other world of legend and fantasy. This is particularly relevant to the geography. A pattern of totality is in evidence here also; it seems to be Ariosto's desire to take the entire earth as a stage for his events, with the moon as an extension. Just as he may have used models to plan the moves of the combats, and possibly a table mock-up for the sieges of Paris and Biserta, so it is highly probable that he used maps to plot and keep track of the journeys by land, by sea and by air. So precise are his indications that an Ariosto world tour could be organized by an enterprising travel agency. Every important event can be pinpointed: Orlando's attack on Angelica on the shore of Spain, just north of Barcelona; Rodomonte's bridge across the river Hérault, near (it seems likely) the village of Aniane; Bradamante's journey from Montalbano past Quercy and Cahors, along the valley of the Dordogne; Rinaldo's journey by boat along the Po to Ravenna, every ramification of the river (as its course was then) charted and described; Astolfo's flight on the hippogriff over Spain and along the north coast of Africa, south over Cyrenaica and into Ethiopia to the kingdom of Prester

1. 'Small but suited to my needs.'

John. Even Alcina's island, unnamed, may be Japan, as shown on Contarini's map.[1]

Ariosto delights in geographical precision, as he delights also in versifying the chronicle of Italian history represented by the prophetic paintings in Tristan's castle. Historic personages, contemporary rulers, acquaintances and friends are met with again and again, on the marble surround of Merlin's fountain, as caryatides supported on the shoulders of admirers gracing another fountain, and as a reception committee gathered on the quay to welcome Ariosto back from his long journey. Some of the real characters even wander into the world of fantasy.

This framework of reality and precision constitutes a structural device of great originality. It provides unity and relevance to the multifarious episodes and lends verisimilitude to the incredible. The uncertainty of life, man's helplessness before forces he cannot control, the illusions and self-deceptions of human relationships, the capriciousness of Fortune, conflicting motives and desires, irrationality, violence and insanity are imaged in the wanderings, the quests, the search for adventure, the mysterious forests, the sea-journeys, the storms, the sorcery, the monsters, the large-scale conflicts and the duels, the anguish of frustrated love. But though life is chaos, man has rational powers; on his varied and disparate material, Ariosto imposed his vision of order and the patterns of his art.

BARBARA REYNOLDS

Nottingham and
Berkeley, California
16 March 1976

---

1. Giovanni Matteo Contarini published his map of the world in Florence in 1506. It shows the ocean extending continuously from Europe to China. The islands discovered by Columbus are shown about half-way between, with South America near by and Japan lying somewhere to the west of Cuba.

PRINCIPAL NEW CHARACTERS
AND DEVICES

MEN

Aldigiero, bastard son of Buovo
Viviano, son of Buovo
Malagigi, sorcerer, son of Buovo
Aymon, Duke of Montalbano, father to Bradamante
Guicciardo, brother of Rinaldo
Ricciardo, brother of Rinaldo
Astolfo, King of Lombardy
Fausto Latini
Giocondo, brother of Fausto
Greco
King of Gothland
King of Norway
King of Sweden
Marganorre
Cilandro, son of Marganorre
Tanacro, son of Marganorre
Olindro, husband of Drusilla
Prester John (Senapo)
Alcestes, suitor of Lydia
King of Lydia
King of Armenia
St John Evangelist
Folvo, King of Fers
Bucifar, King of Algaziers
Branzardo, King of Bugia
Anselmo
Adonio
Bardino, guardian of Brandimarte
Constantine, Emperor of Byzantium

Leone, son of Constantine
Vatran, King of Bulgaria
Ungiardo, ruler of Novigrad

WOMEN

Fiordispina
Fiammetta
Ullania, messenger of Queen of Iceland
Clarice, wife of Rinaldo
Drusilla, wife of Olindro
Argìa, wife of Anselmo
Lydia, spirit
Theodora, sister of Constantine
Galerana, wife of Charlemagne

PERSONIFICATIONS

Old man, representing Time
Fates
Scorn

MONSTERS

Black bat-like bird
Harpies
Many-headed female, representing Jealousy

SUPERNATURAL BEINGS

Demon sent by Malagigi into Doralice's palfrey
Manto, sorceress:
        transformed to snake
        transformed to dog

HORSE

Batoldo, Brandimarte's steed, owned by Barigaccio in
  Orlando Innamorato

ANONYMOUS CHARACTERS
IN ORDER OF APPEARANCE

Landlord of inn at La Rochelle
Surgeon who tends Corebo
Shepherd interrogated by Zerbino
Hermit who befriends Isabella
Envoy who appeals for help for Agramante to Rodomonte
    and Mandricardo
Envoy who appeals for help for Agramante to Ruggiero
Hermit who cuts Bradamante's hair
Messenger who brings news to Aldigiero
Envoy sent by Aldigiero to Rinaldo
Giocondo's wife
Lover of Giocondo's wife
King Astolfo's wife
Dwarf, lover of Astolfo's wife
Woman rescued from the Seine by Sacripante
Landlord who tells the story of Fiammetta
Man who defends the reputation of married women
Two woodcutters attacked by Orlando
Shepherd watering his horse, slain by Orlando
Physician who tends Ruggiero
Gascon knight who brings Bradamante news from Arles
Knight who encourages Rinaldo to test his wife's fidelity
Ethiopian who tempts Anselmo
Castellan at Tristan's castle
Shepherd who directs Bradamante to Tristan's castle
Two damsels who accompany Ullania
Woman who tells story of Marganorre
Greek cavalier
Lady loved by Cilandro
Drusilla's serving-maid
Pilot who brings Christian captives to Algiers
Hermit who baptizes Ruggiero
Nephew of Constantine

Cavalier from Romania
Gaoler
Squires, attendants, soldiers, guards, pilots, shepherds,
    courtiers, crowds, etc., *passim*

ORLANDO FURIOSO

ORLANDO FURIOSO

CANTO XXIV

1

Who in Love's snare has stepped, let him recoil
Ere round his wings the cunning meshes close;
For what is love but madness after all,
As every wise man in the wide world knows?
Though it is true not everyone may fall
Into Orlando's state, his frenzy shows
What perils lurk; what sign is there more plain
Than self-destruction, of a mind insane?

2

The various effects which from love spring
By one same madness are brought into play.
It is a wood of error, menacing,
Where travellers perforce must lose their way;
One here, one there, it comes to the same thing.
To sum the matter up, then, I would say:
Who in old age the dupe of love remains
Deserving is of fetters and of chains.

3

You might well say: 'My friend, you indicate
The faults of others; yours you do not see.'
But I reply: 'I see the matter straight
In this brief moment of lucidity,
And I intend (if it is not too late)
To quit the dance and seek tranquillity.
And yet I fear my vow I cannot keep:
In me the malady has gone too deep.'

4

My lord, in my last canto I had said
That Count Orlando, of his wits bereft,
Scattered his armour and his clothing shed,
Even his trusty Durindana left.
He tore up trees, and noise to wake the dead
Resounded as caves, caverns, rocks he cleft.
To meet their fate or to atone for sin,
Shepherds ran forth, astonished by the din.

5

First, from far off they watch the madman show
A strength unheard-of; next, they draw too near,
Then turn to run, but where they do not know,
As happens when a man is gripped by fear.
The madman to pursue them is not slow.
He seizes one and is as quick to tear
His head off as a man might easily
Pluck blossom or an apple from a tree.

6

He swings the heavy body by one leg,
Using it as a club to beat the rest.
Two of them have no time or chance to beg
For mercy: until doomsday they will rest.
The footsteps of the others do not drag.
Of policies, they judge retreat is best.
The madman is diverted from the chase
And turns upon the flocks, which he now slays.

7

The peasants who were working in the fields,
Leaving their scythes, their mattocks and their ploughs,
Clamber to roof-tops or whatever yields
A vantage-point (not trusting to the boughs
Of trees) and watch the madman as he wields
His grisly weapon, or kills oxen, cows,
Tearing the hapless creatures limb from limb –
And swift indeed are those which flee from him.

8

A pandemonium one might have heard
Reverberate from every near-by town,
Of voices, horns and rustic trumpets, blurred
By bells which every other clamour drown.
With bows and clubs and spikes and slings, a herd,
About a thousand, from the hills leaps down,
While from the valleys many hundreds vault,
Resolved to take the madman by assault.

9

As when a wave rolls gently to the shore,
While playfully the south wind blows at first,
And as a second follows and then more,
Stronger and stronger, till at last they burst
With all their volume, and the sandy floor
Is lashed as though the sea would do its worst,
So now against Orlando mounts and swells
The hostile crowd which pours from hills and dells.

10

He slaughtered ten, and then another ten,
Who in disorder fell beneath his hand,
And from this demonstration it was plain
That safer farther off it was to stand.
His body none can injure and in vain
Their weapons strike him; God on high had planned
That he should be preserved inviolate,
Defender of the Faith decreed by fate.

11

Orlando ran a mortal risk that day
(Had he been capable of death, that is).
Just what it meant to throw his sword away
And then, unarmed, join in hostilities,
He would have learned, and what the price to pay.
The crowd retreats, and when Orlando sees
That nobody his movements now opposes,
He strides towards a little group of houses.

12

There not a single soul is to be found,
For all in terror of their lives have fled;
But humble viands everywhere abound
Which rustic folk find fitting for their need.
Unable to distinguish, I'll be bound,
Between the vilest acorns and good bread,
He fell upon whatever food he saw,
And ate it ravenously, cooked or raw.

13

Then, as he roamed about the countryside,
He hunted animals, and humans too.
The nimble-footed creatures, terrified,
Goats, stags and does in vain before him flew.
With bears and with wild boars his strength he tried,
And many with his naked hands he slew;
Their flesh, quite raw, and innards, all complete,
With savage relish he would often eat.

14

Here, there, up, down, the length and breadth of France
He goes, till to a bridge he comes one day.
Beneath, a river flows, of broad expanse;
Steep, rocky banks its swirling waters stay.
Beside it is a tower, whence the glance
The land in all directions can survey.
But what he did there you will learn elsewhere,
For now about Zerbino you must hear.

15

After Orlando left, first for a while
Zerbino waited; then he took the route
Marked by the paladin; in leisured style
He rode, more at an amble than a trot.
He had not gone, I think, above a mile
Or two when he observed, bound hand and foot,
A knight upon a nag; and on each side,
Like guards, two cavaliers in armour ride.

16

Zerbino recognized the prisoner,
And so did Isabella, from close to,
For he was Odorico, in whose care
She had been placed. A wolf a tender ewe-
Lamb would protect as well, but trustier
Zerbino thought him and more staunch and true
Than all his friends, and so believed he could
Rely on him to guard her maidenhood.

17

Exactly what had happened, Isabel
Was vividly describing to him then:
How, when the vessel sank, as it befell,
She had survived, together with three men,
How Odorico tried to force her will,
How she was carried to the pirates' den.
She had not finished all she had to say
Before they met the villain on their way.

18

The two who lead him captive know the truth.
They recognize the damsel instantly.
The knight beside her must be he who's both
Her lover and their lord; and when they see
The markings on his shield, they'd take their oath
Those ancient signs betoken royalty.
When they come near enough to see his face,
They have no doubt at all about the case.

19

Dismounting from their steeds and kneeling down,
They clasp him where the humble clasp the great.
They bare their heads and, visible from crown
To chin, for his acknowledgement they wait.
Zerbino, staring with a puzzled frown,
Beholds thus paying homage at his feet
Corebo and Almonio, whom he
Had sent to bear his lady company.

20

Almonio spoke: 'Since it has been God's will
That Isabella should be here with you,
I understand full well, my lord, the ill
Report I have to give you is not new,
Of how this felon sought to wreak his will,
Whom as a prisoner between us two,
Fettered upon a nag, you now behold,
For she who suffered must all that have told.

21

'How by this traitor I was tricked when he
Despatched me off to La Rochelle, you know,
And how Corebo, for his loyalty,
Was wounded by what seemed a fatal blow;
But what occurred when I returned to see
Your lady vanished and my friend struck low,
She could not tell you, for she was not there;
So now to tell you this, falls to my share.

22

'From La Rochelle I galloped back again,
To bring the horses I was quick to find.
I gazed ahead, intent on the terrain,
Eager for signs of those I'd left behind.
Onward I ride, I look about in vain,
I reach the shore, now here, now there I wind;
Of my companions I can see no trace,
Save that a trail of footsteps marks the place.

23

'I followed them; they led me to a wood,
Fearsome and dark. I'd gone but a short way
When from a sound of groans I understood
That therein someone sorely wounded lay:
It was Corebo, weak from loss of blood.
"What has become of Isabel?" I say,
"Of Odorico?" When the truth I knew,
After the traitor through the woods I flew.

24

'In vain all the surroundings I explore,
Wherever labyrinthine pathways lead.
Then I return to where Corebo's gore
Has stained the earth around so deep a red
That, had he lingered there a little more,
A grave he would have needed, not a bed,
And priests to bury him with solemn prayer,
Having long passed beyond a doctor's care.

25

'Help came and he was borne to La Rochelle.
The landlord of an inn, who was my friend,
Summoned a surgeon, old and of great skill.
The wounds in a short time began to mend.
Clad in new arms and on new steeds as well,
We scoured the countryside from end to end
In search of Odorico; in Biscay
We came upon him at the court one day.

26

'The justice of the king (who a free field
Allows), the truth, which the Almighty sees,
And Fortune also, who is wont to yield
The victory wherever she may please,
So aid me that the traitor scarce can wield
His lance against me; and I captive seize
The felon. When the king his crime had heard
He let me deal with him as I preferred.

27

'I had no wish to sentence him untried,
But, as you see, to bring him to you, chained.
It is for you to judge him and decide
If he deserves to die or be detained.
News that you rallied to King Charles's side
Brought me from Spain to seek you in this land.
Now I thank God, who led me to this place,
Where I least hoped to meet you face to face.

28

'I thank Him also that your Isabel
(I know not how) is safely in your care,
Of whom good tidings, after what befell,
And at whose hands, I never thought to hear.'
To everything Almonio has to tell
Zerbino listens, fixing with a stare
The villain, Odorico, less in hate
Than sorrow for their friendship, and regret.

29

And when Almonio his story ends,
Zerbino stands perplexed for a long while:
That one whom least of all his many friends
He would suspect of treachery and guile
Should have betrayed him for his lustful ends,
With what once was he fails to reconcile.
He sighs and, from his stupor coming to,
He asks the captive if these things are true.

30

The traitor fell at once upon his knees
And said these specious words in his defence:
'My lord, each one of us a sinner is.
Between the good and bad the difference
Is only that the latter is with ease
Defeated by desire and then repents.
The other takes up arms against the foe,
But he too by one stronger is brought low.

31

'If you had trusted me to guard a fort
And I had yielded at the first attack,
Hoisting, without defence of any sort,
The banners of the foe, you would not lack,
On hearing tidings of such ill report,
Terms of abuse to heap upon my back;
But if I long resisted, I am sure
My fame and glory would for long endure.

32

'The more redoubtable the enemy,
The more acceptable is the excuse
Of him who has to cede the victory;
And, like a fortress ringed about with foes,
I knew that I must guard my loyalty;
And so, with all the prudence I could use,
With heart and soul I tried, but to my shame
My passion my resistance overcame.'

33

Thus Odorico spoke, and added then
Still more which it were lengthy to relate,
Showing how sharp his sufferings had been,
How fierce the lash, how agonized his state.
If ever prayers the wrath of angry men,
If ever humble words the heart placate,
Then surely Odorico must succeed,
So skilfully and ably can he plead.

34

Revenge for such an injury to take –
'Twixt yes and no Zerbino's will is hung,
And difficult he finds the choice to make:
Only the felon's death would right the wrong,
And yet he hesitates for friendship's sake,
That bond which had united them so long.
The water of compassion in his heart
Quenches his rage and counsels mercy's part.

35

And while Zerbino hesitated still
Whether to take as captive or to free,
Whether to castigate, or yet to kill
The miscreant for his disloyalty,
The horse which Mandricardo, as you will
Recall, had left unbridled, rapidly
Approached, bearing the hag who not long since
Contrived to bring such peril to the prince.

36

The palfrey, hearing hoofs, had pricked its ears
And galloped at full speed across the plain
To join its kind; the harridan, in tears,
Shrieked all the while for help, but shrieked in vain.
Zerbino, when he sees her, offers prayers
Of thanks that Heaven so benign has been
As to deliver in his hands those two:
For them alone hatred from him was due.

37

Zerbino first detains the evil crone
Till he decides what he will do with her.
Cut off her nose and both her ears is one
Good method evil-doers to deter;
To let the vultures pick clean every bone
Would be another: which does he prefer?
On punishments of many kinds he muses
And one solution finally he chooses.

38

He turned to his companions and declared:
'I am content to let the traitor live;
Although he does not merit to be spared,
Yet neither does he merit to receive
The final penalty; I am prepared
To let him be released – this boon I give.
I see his error was the fault of love
And this the guilt in great part must remove.

39

'For love has many times turned upside down
A mind more stable and more sound than his.
Greater excess is laid to love's renown
And greater outrage than our injuries.
Not Odorico is to blame; I own
I am the culprit, mine the error is.
I should be punished, having been so blind.
That fire burns straw I should have borne in mind.'

40

Then, fixing Odorico with his eye,
'The penalty for your misdeed shall be
That for a year you shall be followed by
This agèd crone and on your company'
(He said) 'both night and day she shall rely,
At every hour, wherever you may be;
And with your very life you must defend her
Against whoever threatens to offend her.

41

'And I decree that you shall undertake,
At her command, with whomso'er may chance,
To engage in mortal strife; and you shall make
From town to town this quest throughout all France.'
Such was Zerbino's judgement; for the sake
Of mercy he had spared the miscreant's
Unworthy life, but dug a ditch too deep.
Across it (save by luck) he'd never leap.

42

The evil crone had injured and betrayed
So many men and women in her time,
Whoever at her side a journey made
Would meet with challengers in every clime.
Thus equally they both would be repaid,
She for her evil deeds, he for the crime
Of having pledged to champion the wrong,
Whence he was bound to meet his death ere long.

43

Then Prince Zerbino made the traitor swear
A sacred oath that he would keep the pact;
But if he should break faith, let him beware,
For if by any chance Zerbino tracked
Him down, no pleas this time would make him spare
His life: a cruel death let him expect.
Then to Corebo and Almonio
Zerbino turned, and bade them let him go.

44

Reluctantly obeying, they untied
The traitor finally, but not in haste,
For both of them were vexed and mortified
So sweet a moment of revenge to waste.
Then through the forest the two villains ride,
Passing together from the scene at last.
What next befell them, Turpin does not say;
I read it in another book one day.

45

I will not tell you who the author is.
He writes that ere a single day went by,
Breaking his oath, to rid himself of his
Encumbrance, quickly managing to tie
A rope about her neck with expertise,
He left her dangling from an elm near by;
And a year thence (the place I do not know)
He met the same death from Almonio.

46

Zerbino, who was following the track
Of great Orlando, which he must not lose,
Now saw the chance to send a message back
To reassure his troops; for this he chose
Almonio and gave him too (I lack
The time to quote his words) the latest news.
Corebo with Almonio he sends
And thus he parts with both his faithful friends.

47

His love for the brave paladin was great
And Isabella loved him too no less,
And for this reason he resolved to wait,
Eager to hear the tale of his success
Against the Tartar knight, whom soon or late
He would be bound to meet; he'd soon redress
The outrage of being hoisted off his horse.
Zerbino lets the three days run their course.

48

During this time for which Orlando bade
Zerbino wait till Mandricard should come,
Along no pathway and along no glade
The Count had travelled did he fail to roam,
And he arrived at last beneath the shade
Of trees on which the faithless damsel, whom
Orlando loved, inscribed Medoro's name,
And to the broken cave and fount he came.

49

Glimpsing an object shining on the ground,
He recognized it as the Count's cuirass;
And next, a little farther off, he found
A helmet (not Almonte's, but of brass).
Then, startled by an unexpected sound
Of whinnying, he sees, cropping the grass,
Its bridle from its saddle hanging loose,
The famous Brigliadoro he well knows.

50

He searched for Durindana through the wood.
He found it lying there, without its sheath;
And next he saw Orlando's surcoat, strewed
In countless pieces; both the lovers, with
Their faces woebegone and pensive, stood
Amazed; these did not seem the signs of death.
Over all possibilities they ranged,
Save that Orlando's wits had been deranged.

51

They might have thought Orlando had been slain
But for the fact that nowhere could they see
A drop of blood nor any gruesome stain.
Along the stream a shepherd hurriedly
Approached; pale and distraught, he had seen plain
The tokens of the victim's malady:
How he had torn his clothing, strewn his arms,
Killed shepherds with their flocks, and ravaged farms.

52

Zerbino, who interrogates the man,
Receives a true account of what has passed.
He tries to credit it, but scarcely can,
Though everywhere the signs are manifest.
Dismounting from his charger, he began,
Filled with compassion, tearful and downcast,
To gather up the remnants where they lay,
Scattered some here, some there, as best he may.

53

And Isabella leaves her palfrey too
And gathers all the weapons in one pile.
As they are thus engaged, a damsel who
Is tearful and forlorn draws near meanwhile.
If you should ask to what her grief is due,
And who it is who sorrows in such style,
Her name is Fiordiligi, I'd reply;
She searches for her loved one low and high.

54

When Brandimarte left the city gate
Without a word to Charles or to his love,
She waited for him some six months or eight.
Resolved, when he did not return, to rove
Through France from coast to coast to learn his fate,
The Alps, the Pyrenees, below, above,
She searched, looking in every place except
The one where as a captive he was kept.

55

If she had visited that hostelry
Created by Atlante's magic spell,
She would have seen him wandering aimlessly,
Gradasso, Ferraù, the Maid as well,
Ruggiero and Orlando, even he;
But when Astolfo blew that terrible
Loud blast, to Paris Brandimart returned,
But this, fair Fiordiligi had not learned.

56

As I have said, she happened now by chance
On those two lovers in their deep distress.
She recognized Orlando's arms at once
And Brigliadoro too, left riderless,
His bridle hanging free; and at one glance
She understands the signs, for she no less
Has heard the story from the shepherd lad
Of how he watched Orlando running mad.

57

Zerbino gathers all the weapons there
And hangs them up in order on a pine.
On the green bark this legend, brief and clear,
He writes: 'Arms of Orlando, paladin',
By this inscription meaning to deter
Whoever saw the splendid trophy shine,
As though to say: 'Hands off, all who pass by,
Unless Orlando's strength you wish to try.'

58

His pious labours being completed then,
Zerbino was preparing to remount
When Mandricardo came upon the scene.
He asks Zerbino for a full account:
What does the splendour on the pine-tree mean?
The Prince relates the truth about the Count.
The pagan monarch, wholly undeterred,
In joyful triumph takes Orlando's sword.

59

He cried: 'This, nobody can take away.
Here on this spot I seize it rightfully,
For I laid claim to it before today,
And will again, wherever it may be.
Orlando feigns his wits have gone astray,
Rather than stand and hold his ground with me.
If thus he thinks he can excuse his fright,
That is no reason to forgo my right.'

60

Zerbino shouted, 'Do not touch that sword,
Or think that you can seize it undefied.
The blade of Hector does not well accord
With such a thief as you!' At once they ride
Against each other with no further word,
Two paragons of prowess, each well-tried.
The wood already echoes with the din,
Almost the very moment they begin.

61

Twisting and turning like a living flame,
Zerbino dodged where Durindana fell.
As nimble as a doe his horse became,
Leaping now here, now there; and it is well
It yielded not one jot in such a game,
Else were the prince despatched at once to dwell
Among his fellow-sufferers in love
Whose mingling shadows haunt the myrtle-grove.

62

Just as a hound will rush towards the boar
Which in the fields has wandered from its herd,
And round it run in circles, ever more,
Until to a mistake the prey is lured,
So, as the weapon flashed above him or
Below him, Prince Zerbino never erred,
Striving his best to see, in all the strife,
How he might save both honour and his life.

63

But when the pagan plied his sword, the sound
With whining, whistling winds might well compare
Which through the mountain peaks in March resound,
Or seize the forest by its tangled hair,
Bending the tree-tops down to kiss the ground,
And whirling broken branches through the air.
Although the prince avoided many blows,
One finally was sure to come too close.

64

One mighty stroke at last achieved its aim.
Between his sword and shield it reached his breast.
His mail was thick, his corslet was the same,
His metal apron too was of the best,
Yet through them passed that sword of cruel fame.
They being unequal to this crucial test,
Nothing resisted the descending blow
Which slashed from mid-breast to the saddle-bow.

65

If Mandricardo's stroke had fallen true,
It would have split Zerbino like a cane;
But as it scarcely penetrated to
The living flesh, the wound was in the main
Inflicted on the skin; a span or two
Perhaps in length, it caused a shallow pain
And in a crimson stream the blood ran hot,
Streaking his shining armour to the foot.

66

Thus have I often seen a scarlet band
Of ribbon on a silver dress, with art
By such device divided by that hand,
Whiter than alabaster, which my heart,
Alas! divides. Zerbino's courage and
His skill in war play now but little part.
That Tartar monarch, as his strokes evince,
In strength, as well as sword, outdoes the prince.

67

This blow of Mandricardo's had appeared
More deadly than it was in its effect
And Isabella, looking on, had feared
The worst (nor could she otherwise suspect).
It froze her bosom and with horror seared
Her heart. Zerbino's daring is unchecked.
Enraged, he takes his sword in both his hands
And on the Tartar's head a blow he lands.

68

Down to his charger's neck the Saracen,
For all his pride, was bowed by such a stroke.
Only his magic helmet saved him then;
So mighty was the crash it almost broke
His skull; not waiting to count up to ten,
Or to defer revenge, the pagan took
His sword and raised it high above the crest,
Hoping to split Zerbino to his breast.

69

Zerbino called both eye and mind to aid
And turned his charger quickly to the right,
But not so fast as to escape the blade,
Which caught his shield and through the centre, quite
From top to bottom, two half portions made.
The thong beneath was severed, and the knight
Received upon his arm the blow, which passed,
Piercing his armour, to his thigh at last.

70

Now here, now there, Zerbino tries to break,
But all in vain, through his opponent's guard,
For not one blemish all his blows can make
Upon the armour of King Mandricard;
But *he* can now a good advantage take,
And presses back his enemy so hard
(Whose shield and helm are broken) that his blade
Has seven or eight relentless gashes made.

71

But though the prince was weak from loss of blood,
Of his condition he was unaware.
His vigorous and valiant heart withstood
The strain and he was able still to bear
His body upright; meanwhile in the wood,
His lady, pale with terror, to the fair
Young Doralice turns, and begs her end
The deadly strife in which the two contend.

72

Being courteous as well as beautiful
(And being uncertain who will win the fight),
She gladly now persuades her love to call
A truce; and Isabella, too, her knight
Beseeches so successfully that all
His anger from his heart is put to flight.
Letting her choose the path, he rides away
And unconcluded leaves the bitter fray.

73

And Fiordiligi, who has also seen
The trusty sword of the unhappy Count
Plied to such ill effect, feels woe as keen.
She weeps and strikes her brow at this affront.
Ah, would that Brandimart had present been!
And if she ever finds him, she'll recount
The whole, and when he learns what has occurred
Not long will Mandricardo flaunt that sword!

74

She went on searching night and day in vain
For Brandimart, for whose embrace she yearned,
But he, who could have healed her grief and pain,
Unknown to her to Paris had returned.
She wandered over hill and over plain,
Till, as she crossed a river, she discerned
And recognized the frenzied paladin.
But let us say what happened to Zerbin.

75

To leave the sword so shames him as a knight,
It pains him more than any other ill,
Though he can barely sit his horse upright
For all the blood he's lost, and loses still.
Heat, by his anger kindled, has now quite
Departed, while his grief increases till
It rushes through his veins and, as it grows,
He feels his life-force ebbing to its close.

76

Too weak to travel farther, with a sigh
He stopped beside a stream and down he lay.
To help him Isabella longs to try.
She knows not what to do, nor what to say
And, failing proper care, she sees him die.
All habitations are too far away
Where to a doctor she might find access,
Invoking pity or his worldliness.

77

So she can only call upon the skies,
Reproaching Fortune and her fate in vain:
'Ah, why was I not drowned, alas!' she cries,
'When first my ship set out upon the main?'
On her Zerbino turns his languid eyes.
Her lamentations cause him greater pain
Than all his wounds, which no respite allow
And to the point of death have brought him now.

78

'My only grief, dear heart,' Zerbino said,
'Is that I leave you helpless and alone.
If you will love me after I am dead,
I'll have no vain regrets when I am gone.
If in some safer place my life were shed,
These few last moments had serenely flown:
Contented, happy and entirely blest
That, dying, in your loving arms I rest.

79

'But since I am condemned to leave you here,
A victim of whoever first goes past,
By this sweet mouth, by these sweet eyes, I swear,
And by these tresses which have bound me fast,
Though I go down to Hell in my despair,
Yet every punishment will be surpassed
When thoughts of you arise whom I have left
Abandoned here without me and bereft.'

80

And Isabella, infinitely sad,
Bending a tearful countenance to his
And touching with her own his mouth, which had
The languor of a rose whose season is
Gone by, whose beauty, paling in the shade,
No passer-by has plucked and no one sees,
She answered thus: 'My life, do not believe
Your spirit shall without me take its leave.

81

'Of this, I do beseech, my love, doubt not:
I'll follow you to Heaven or to Hell.
Our souls, from one same bow together shot,
Still fly as one and thus will ever dwell.
As soon as I have seen those dear eyes shut,
My grief all suffering will so excel
That I will die, or else, I give my word,
Into my breast today I'll plunge this sword.

82

'And for our bodies I at least have hope
That better dead than living they may fare,
For someone passing by perchance may stop
And in one sepulchre, with pious care,
May bury them.' Her welling tears now drop
Where with her lips, ere Death the Plunderer
Has done his worst, his fleeting breath she drains
While yet some vital sign of it remains.

83

Exerting his now faltering voice, he spoke:
'Belovèd, I entreat you by that love
You showed me when for me you once forsook
Your father's shores, live out your life enough
To reach the time allotted in the book
Of destiny, as God has willed above.
This I command you, if command I may.
How deep my love was, ne'er forget, I pray.

84

'God may perhaps provide a means to save
You from all villainous attack, as when
He sent Orlando to the pirates' cave
To rescue you from those rapacious men.
Thanks also to His aid, the ocean wave
Did not engulf you; by His help again
You managed Odorico to defy.
But if all fails, then be content to die.'

85

I do not think this final utterance
Could be distinctly heard; as fading light,
For lack of wax or other sustenance,
Subsides and is extinguished, so the knight
Expired. Who can the sorrowing desolance
Of Isabella in her wretched plight
Convey, as pale her dear love lies, and cold
As ice the form which now her arms enfold?

86

Upon his blood-stained body she then flings
Her own, and bathes him with her streaming tears.
Her shrieks awaken distant echoings.
Neither her bosom nor her cheeks she spares,
But rends the tender flesh, the curling rings
Of her gold tresses, in her frenzy, tears
Unjustly from her head, while in her pain
She cries, unceasing, the loved name in vain.

87

So deep her rage, so wild her ravings seem,
Which sorrow has induced, the maid might well
Have plunged the sword into her breast, I deem,
Thus disobeying her Zerbino's will,
But that a hermit, who the crystal stream
Was wont to visit from his near-by cell,
Arriving at that instant, her intent
Was able, by persuasion, to prevent.

88

This venerable hermit goodness joined
To natural prudence and was well endowed
With charitable feeling; every kind
Of precept he could quote, if time allowed.
On the afflicted damsel he enjoined
Patient endurance, and good reasons showed,
And many virtuous women instanced too
From the Old Testament and from the New.

89

And then he showed her that true happiness
In life was to be found in God alone.
All other hopes, all other earthly bliss,
Were transitory, fluid and soon flown.
He urged so justly, from her pitiless
Intention he dissuaded her quite soon,
And she resolved, so well she understood,
To dedicate her life henceforth to God.

90

But she has no intention to abjure
Her love, or to neglect her lord's remains,
For, to protect the body and ensure
Its safe interment in due course, she plans
To keep it by her, night and day; the pure
And holy man, still strong in back and reins,
Helps her to lay the prince upon his horse,
Which stands dejected, and they take their course.

91

The prudent hermit did not deem it wise
To take the young and lovely Isabel
To the wild mountain-cave, wherein there lies,
Not far away, his solitary cell.
He thinks: 'A conflagration will arise
If in one hand I bear a torch as well
As straw.' He does not trust either his age
Or prudence in such trial to engage.

92

So he resolves to take her to Provence.
Close to Marseilles, he knows a castle where
A sisterhood, in holy abstinence,
A convent has established, rich and fair.
And at another castle, which by chance
They come upon, for the dead cavalier
Is made, at their request, a coffin which
Is long, capacious and well sealed with pitch.

93

They travel many miles for many days.
Since war is raging everywhere they turn,
They choose the rough and least frequented ways,
For to be unobserved is their concern.
At last a knight obstructs their path and says
Ignoble words of insult; you shall learn
His name when later I return to him;
But now King Mandricardo is my theme.

94

When he had ceased from battle, the young king
Sat down to rest a while in cooling shade,
Taking his ease beside the crystal spring,
And from his charger reins and saddle had
Removed, letting it go meandering
To graze at will. Not long like this he stayed,
Ere his attention was aroused again
On seeing a knight descending to the plain.

95

As soon as Doralice raised her brow,
She recognized the cavalier and to
The king she said, 'Proud Rodomonte now
Approaches down the hill to challenge you,
Unless my eyes deceive me; and I vow
All valour and resolve you must renew.
He holds the loss of me, his bride, a great
Outrage; his claim he comes to vindicate.'

96

As when a well-trained hawk a duck or quail
Or dove or partridge or like bird has seen
Winging towards it from some distant trail
And its bright head has reared, alert and keen,
So now the king, like one who could not fail
To slaughter Rodomonte, and has been
Awaiting this encounter, with delight
And confidence remounted for the fight.

97

They rode towards each other and from where
The haughty interchanges could be heard,
Waving his trusty weapon in the air,
The monarch of Algiers, by fury stirred,
Tossing his head in menace, cried: 'Beware!',
And vowed, his frenzy mounting with each word,
His rival would repent the outrage shown
To him, and the rash deed which he had done.

98

And Mandricard replied: 'He tries in vain
Who tries to frighten or to threaten me.
Children or women take alarm, or men
Who never battle know or weapons see:
Not I, who love all combat and would fain
Spend day and night in strife, whether it be
On foot, on horse, unarmed, in arms arrayed,
In fields of battle, or in the stockade.'

99

They pass to oaths, with insults interspersed,
To swords unsheathed, to clash of blade on blade,
As when a wind, which softly blew at first,
The ash and oak-tree back and forward swayed,
And day, by clouds of dust, to night reversed,
Uprooted trees, and houses flattened laid,
Vessels submerged at sea, and in the wood
The scattered sheep destroyed by storm or flood.

100

The pagans, who no equals have on earth,
With their last ounce of strength, from their brave
To fearful blows and battle now give birth,   [hearts,
Befitting foes of such ferocious parts.
The globe reverberates in all its girth
Soon as the clamour of the combat starts.
Sparks from the clashing blades to heaven rise,
Lighting a thousand lanterns in the skies.

101

Taking no rest, nor stopping to take breath,
The kings no respite have in their travail.
Now on this side, now that, above, beneath,
They try to pierce the armour and the mail.
Though they pursue the battle to the death,
In gaining terrain neither can prevail
(Perhaps the ground there costs too much an inch),
Nor stir beyond the compass of a trench.

102

Among a thousand blows, the Tartar king
One blow now deals on Rodomonte's head,
Both hands upon the sword, such as to bring
A myriad of lights, whirling at speed
Before his eyes, more than the stars that ring
The world; then backwards on his startled steed
He bends and from his saddle, all strength gone,
He dangles, with his lady looking on.

103

As when a sturdy and well-fashioned bow,
With finely tempered metal reinforced,
By winches and by levers is bent low,
The heavier the weight by which it's forced,
The greater is the fury it will show
On its release, nor does it come off worst,
So Rodomonte rises instantly
With doubled strength to strike his enemy.

104

And where he had been struck, in that same place
He likewise hit the son of Agrican,
And yet the weapon failed to cleave his face.
His helm protects him as none other can.
The Tartar was so stunned he lost all trace
Of what o'clock it was; the African,
Who now was so enraged that he saw red,
Brought down a second blow upon his head.

105

The charger, flinching from the deadly sword,
Which whistles as it menaces on high,
Now, to its own undoing, saves its lord,
As, backing a few steps, it means to try
To leap well out of range, but in reward
Receives the impact on its skull, which by
No Trojan helm (unlike its master's crown)
Defended was; stone dead it tumbles down.

106

No longer stunned, the king leaps to his feet
And brandishes his blade, burning inside
And out with fury that his horse should meet
Its death. The African intends to ride
Him down and spurs his charger; no retreat
The Tartar makes, nor does he turn aside.
A rock does not withdraw before the flood:
The charger fell and Mandricardo stood.

107

Feeling his charger sink beneath his thighs,
The African has grasped the saddle-bow.
Letting his stirrups dangle, he relies
On his dexterity and leaps below.
On equal footing now, and in no wise
Placated, they resume; with every blow
Their hatred, pride and anger are increased:
But suddenly an envoy comes in haste.

108

This envoy was among the messengers
Sent by King Agramant throughout all France
To rally all the private cavaliers
And captains, for, with deadly arrogance,
The fleurs-de-lis, inflicting dire reverse,
Had ravaged all the camp; and if at once
Help is not mustered and despatched, says he,
The slaughter of the Moors will certain be.

109

He recognized the foemen straight away,
Not by their surcoats or their crests, as much
As by the swordsmanship which they display;
No other hands were capable of such.
He does not dare to intervene that day,
Nor as an envoy with his baton touch
Their blades; though he's a king's ambassador,
He does not trust immunity so far.

110

Approaching Doralice in their stead,
He says King Agramant and Stordilan
And King Marsilio, with few to aid,
In their encampment by the Christian clan
Are sorely pressed; he begs her to persuade
The valiant warriors, as best she can,
From their ferocious combat to desist
And hasten back to Paris to assist.

111

The lady, with great courage, stands between
The combatants and says: 'Stop, I command!
If you both love me, let it now be seen.
Put up your swords; save them to put an end
To the great peril which the Saracen
Now faces; ringed by foes on every hand,
Our people, lacking all defences, wait
For help – or ruin, if help comes too late.'

112

And then the fate to which they'd all succumb
The ambassador outlined; when he had done,
He duly handed letters-patent from
Troiano's son to Ulieno's son.
The warriors cannot refuse to come.
On this decision they agree as one:
To call a truce to last until the day
When the besiegers have been chased away.

113

And they resolved that without more ado,
Once they secured the safety of their side,
Their former enmity they would renew,
Forgetting comradeship, and then decide,
By cruel tests of arms, which of the two
The more deserved the lady as his bride.
Upon her hands this oath they swore, and she
For their good faith as knights stood guarantee.

114

Dame Discord by this plan is much put out,
Being a sworn enemy of truce and peace.
And Pride likewise begins to sulk and pout.
She cannot bear such rivalry to cease;
But Love is also present, who can flout
Them both and put an end to their caprice.
All-conquering, his arrows are enough
To drive Dame Discord and her ally off.

115

The truce was duly sworn, as I have said,
As she desired who had command of them.
They lacked one horse, for Mandricard's lay dead
And nothing further could be hoped of him.
But Brigliadoro came to meet their need,
From where he cropped the grasses by the stream.
My lord, this canto is concluded now,
So I will make a pause, if you'll allow.

CANTO XXV

1

In youthful minds how great the contest is
Between love's impulse and desire for praise!
And which of them prevails, none ever sees,
As to and fro the tide of battle sways.
Honour and duty the advantage seize
In both the knights, in whom, it seems, love plays
A lesser part, since now a truce they've made
Until their stricken allies they can aid.

2

But love was stronger, for, had it not been
Their lady who had thus commanded them,
The cruel battle would no end have seen
Until a victor's laurel one should claim;
And Agramante long had looked in vain
Ere help from two such valiant warriors came.
Love is not always evil, truth to tell;
Though harm he does, he serves the good as well.

3

And so, deferring now all thrusts and parries,
The cavaliers set out upon their course,
And with their lady travel on towards Paris,
To save the Africans from death or worse.
The dwarf, who witness of the whole affair is,
Goes too; when Sarza's king to find a horse
Had left, he followed him from place to place
And saw him meet the Tartar face to face.

4

By chance a meadow they soon came upon,
Where cavaliers close to a fount reclined.
Two had their helmets off, two had them on;
A damsel sat beside them, fair and kind.
You'll learn just who they are, but later on,
Not now, for first Ruggiero I must find,
The good Ruggiero who, as you heard tell,
Has thrown his magic buckler down a well.

5

He'd barely gone above a mile or so,
When, riding fast, a messenger drew near,
One of the many Agramant bade go
And summon help from pagans everywhere.
This courier now lets Ruggiero know
The peril of the Saracens, who fear
(So great the danger), if no help arrives,
They'll either lose their honour or their lives.

6

Reduced by his conflicting thoughts to doubt,
Ruggiero pauses: which course is the best?
No time, no chance he has to think things out,
On every side by urgent matters pressed.
The lady wins; he turns his steed about
To face the way she came; taking no rest,
Together through the wood they gallop off.
For all their haste, their speed is scarce enough.

7

The route they chose (by then the sun was low)
Had led them to a citadel at last,
In central France, which King Marsilio
Had lately captured from King Charles; he passed
Across the bridge and through the gate; and no
Resistance does he meet, no doors shut fast,
Though at the barricades and on the mounds
With men-at-arms the garrison abounds.

8

Knowing the damsel who had brought him here,
They saw no reason to suspect the knight.
They did not challenge him, nor ask him where
He came from; on he went, as if of right.
It did not take him long to reach the square
Which, thronged with people, was ablaze with light;
And in the midst, his face an ashen gray,
There stood the youth condemned to die that day.

9

Ruggiero gazes at his face, held low,
Eyes fixed upon the ground and filled with tears.
He seems to see his Bradamante, so
Astonishingly like her he appears.
The more he looks, the more he seems to know
That semblance and that face. Transfixed, he stares,
And to himself he says, 'It must be she,
Else, though I'm called Ruggiero, I'm not he.

10

'Perhaps she rashly went to the defence
Of one who was condemned, so young, to die,
Eager to rescue him, and, as events
Turned out, was taken prisoner. Ah! why
Did she not wait? Alas! that I, far hence,
Could not assist in her emprise! But I
Will save my Bradamante from this fate.
Thanks be to God, I have not come too late.'

11

Without delay, Ruggiero seized his sword.
(His lance, in his last combat, had been split.)
His steed against that unarmed crowd he spurred,
Their chests and bellies ramming; many a hit
With scythe-like movements of his blade he scored
On foreheads, cheeks and throats; the mob, no whit
A match for such as he, in terror fled,
Or limped away, or nursed a broken head.

12

Birds winging in a flock perhaps alight
Beside a pond; intent upon their food,
They forage, unafraid; but from a height
A falcon drops and seizes one; the brood
Is scattered, every bird in single flight
Abandons its companion; so you would
Have seen that crowd disperse, soon as Ruggier
His weapon drew and laid about him there.

13

The heads of four or six he neatly lopped,
Of some who were too slow to run away.
His sword sliced through another six, nor stopped
Until it reached their chests; I cannot say
How many to their teeth or eyes were cropped.
I grant they wore no helmets on that day,
Though many metal caps were to be seen;
But not much use would finest steel have been.

14

Ruggiero's strength is now beyond compare.
No modern cavalier could fight as well,
No lion could compete with him, no bear,
Nor any beast however terrible.
Only the Earthquake is perhaps his peer,
Or the Great Devil – not the one in Hell –
I mean my lord's, of which the fiery blast
On sea, on land, in heaven is unsurpassed.

15

One man at least went down at every blow.
Sometimes a couple fell, or four or five.
A hundred soon Ruggiero had struck low.
Against his mighty strength in vain they strive.
Through armour made of tempered steel, as though
Through curdled milk, his sword appears to drive –
The cruel sword which Falerina made,
To slay Orlando in Orcagna's glade.

16

She later wished she had not made so fine
A sword, when all her garden was laid waste.
What death, what slaughter, must it now combine,
In such a hand of such a warrior placed!
If force, if fury, ever were the sign
Which made Ruggiero's valour manifest,
Here it was seen, here in full evidence,
As he moved forward to his love's defence.

17

And as a hare delays when dogs are loosed,
Just so that rabble stand their ground with him.
Already a vast number he'd reduced,
While others fled in an unending stream.
Meanwhile the lady the occasion used
To set the young man free in every limb,
And soon he stood (her eager hands being quick)
Girt with a sword, a shield about his neck.

18

His honour being outraged, as best he can
He seeks for vengeance for his injury,
And soon his former captors, to a man,
Good reason have to judge his gallantry.
Already now the golden wheels which ran
Towards the West had dipped below the sea,
When brave Ruggiero, and the youth as well,
Restored to freedom, left the citadel.

19

And when that comely youth, alive and well,
Faces his rescuer outside the gate,
His heartfelt words of thanks unending spill
In courteous phrases, gracious and ornate;
To save him from a death so terrible
This gallant cavalier had tempted fate,
Not knowing who the man he rescued was.
The youth then asks to whom so much he owes.

20

Ruggiero said, 'I see my lady's face,
Her features beautiful beyond compare,
I see her lovely aspect and her grace,
The sweetness of her voice I do not hear.
These words of gratitude I cannot place.
Such thanks to me, her lover, strange appear.
If this is Bradamant, how can it be
That she forgets my name so soon, and me?'

21

In order to be sure, he shrewdly said:
'Have I not seen you somewhere else ere now?
I've turned the matter over in my head,
And still I can't remember when or how.
Tell me if you remember it instead.
Your name might be of help, if you'll allow.
Reveal it, then, that I may know whom I
Have rescued from the death you were to die.'

22

'It may be you have seen me once before,'
The youth replied, 'when, where, I do not know,
Since many different regions I explore;
Seeking adventure, through the world I go.
You may have seen my sister when she wore
Full armour and a sword; we two are so
Alike (for we were born on the same day)
That who is which, our parents cannot say.

23

'You're not the first; it causes us great mirth
That many folk commit the same mistake.
My father, brothers, she who at one birth
Produced us, the same error often make.
Short hair I have, my sister once no dearth
Of tresses had which for adornment's sake
She twisted round her head in a long braid;
And this between us some distinction made.

24

'But she was wounded in the head one day
(How this occurred would take too long to tell),
And when a holy hermit passed that way,
He cropped her hair so that the wound might heal.
Now which of us is which no one can say,
If we our names and sex do not reveal:
I Ricciardetto, Bradamante she,
Born of the Montalbano family.

25

'Such joy at first, such torment in the end
My likeness to my sister brought me to,
I could relate, if you an ear would lend,
A strange event that would astonish you.'
No history or tale could more commend
Itself, no anecdote, Ruggiero knew,
More please him than a narrative wherein
His love appeared; he begged him to begin.

26

And thus he did: 'My sister, not long since,
Was riding through these woods, unhelmeted,
And, overtaken by some Saracens,
By one of them was wounded in the head.
A passing hermit, using his good sense,
Observing how extensively she bled,
Cut off her golden hair; then on she rode,
Close-cropped as any man, about the wood.

27

'Thus wandering, she reached a shady fount.
Her wound had weakened her, so she drew rein,
And when she had descended from her mount
She pulled her helmet off and on the green
Young grass soon fell asleep. I'll now recount
The most delightful tale that's ever been:
Out hunting with her friends that very day,
Fair Fiordispina chanced to pass that way.

28

'She saw my sister as she rested there,
In armour fully clad, save for her face;
A sword was at her side, where women wear
A distaff; as she views the manly grace
Of one she takes to be a cavalier,
Her heart is vanquished, and to join the chase
She first invites her, then contrives ere long
To separate her from the merry throng.

29

'Alone with her, where no one could surprise
Them in that leafy, solitary nook,
Her anguished soul reflected in her eyes,
The damsel then began to show with look
And words and gestures and with ardent sighs
Her passion for my sister, whom she took
To be a man; she pales, then, blushing red,
She steals a kiss, so greatly she's misled.

30

'My sister understood the maid believed
She was a man, and it was evident
Such burning love could never be relieved
By her. "Better" (so ran her argument)
"This damsel should at once be undeceived
Than she should think me so indifferent.
Better a woman I should prove, and kind,
Than seem a man for love so disinclined."

31

'And this was right, for base it were and weak,
And worthy of a statue, not a man,
When such a lovely maid her love should speak,
So sweet and melting in her languid pain,
To sit inertly by, as mild and meek
As a young owl by day; so she began
To tell the maid she was a woman, not
A manly cavalier as she had thought;

32

'That, like Camilla and Hippolyta,
She went in search of glory in the life
Of arms; that in Arzilla, in Africa,
She had been born and bred for martial strife,
And trained from childhood in the arts of war.
No spark of love is quenched; it is as if
The remedy has been applied too late.
The damsel's wound is deep and desperate.

33

'That face on this account is no less fair;
That glance, that grace of manner are the same.
The damsel's heart does not return from where
It sunned itself in the belovèd beam
Of those entrancing eyes; seeing her wear
That manly armour which has earned such fame,
Her longing may be yet fulfilled, she thinks,
Then sighs and into deepest sorrow sinks.

34

'Whoever heard her mourn and weep that day
His own lament would have combined with hers.
"What cruel torments", she began to say,
"Have ever been, than which mine are not worse?
Of any other love I could allay
The pain by hope of solace in due course;
The rose I'd gather which sharp thorns defend.
Only my present longing has no end.

35

'"Love, if to torture me was your intent,
If you so envied me my happy state,
Could you, as is your wont, not be content
With many another lover's wretched fate?
In all the world of nature, you invent
A female lover for a female mate!
Women their hearts to women do not lose,
Nor doe to doe, nor ewe to other ewes.

36

'"On land, on sea, in heaven, I alone
Must bear a blow of such severity;
You mean by my example shall be shown
The last extreme of your authority.
The wife of Ninus, who desired her son,
Your victim was; Myrrha with infamy
Desired her father, Pasiphae the bull,
Yet mine the maddest folly is of all.

37

'"The mother, hoping to seduce the boy,
Succeeded in her scheme, so I have heard,
And Pasiphae achieved a lustful joy
Inside a wooden cow among the herd.
If Daedalus should all his skills employ
And fly to my assistance like a bird,
This knot would be too intricate for him.
The master-hand of Nature is supreme."

38

'So bitterly she grieves in her despair,
No solace can she find in her laments.
She beats her face, she twists and breaks her hair,
And on herself, herself revenge attempts.
My sister, looking on, cannot forbear
To weep at what such sorrow represents.
She seeks to turn her from her vain desire,
To no avail; she cannot quench the fire.

39

'Not comfort Fiordispina needs, but aid,
And, unconsoled, she grows the more distressed.
The daylight now would soon begin to fade,
As redder flamed the sun towards the West;
The time had come for them to leave the glade.
Since both considered this was for the best,
The damsel to her home near by invited
My sister, lest they both become benighted.

40

'She could not find it in her to refuse
And so together they approached this town,
Where I by burning was about to lose
My life, had you not mowed the rabble down.
All courtesy the gracious damsel shows
To Bradamante; and a woman's gown
She gives her, so that everybody can
Observe she is a woman, not a man.

41

'For, understanding that she would obtain
No solace from my sister's virile air,
She judged it would be ill-advised to gain
A name for dalliance with a cavalier.
She also hoped that it would dull the pain
Which armour had inflicted on her fair
Young, unsuspecting, palpitating breast,
To see her thus in women's garments dressed.

42

'They lay together in the selfsame bed,
But not the same repose; for while one sleeps,
The other groans and, still uncomforted,
With longing is on fire, the more she weeps;
And if she slumbers, by her dreams she's led
To Fancy's realm, where promises Love keeps,
Where Fate's decrees fond lovers do not vex,
And where her Bradamante has changed sex.

43

'As when a sick man with a raging thirst,
If he should fall asleep, will toss and turn
And, with his lips as fevered as at first,
Will dream of drinking deep at beck or burn,
So in her dreams, when grief has done its worst,
Her longings gain the boon for which they yearn;
But on awaking, with her hand she gropes,
And finds once more that vain are all her hopes.

44

'What vows, what prayers she uttered every night
To her Mahomet and to every god,
That, working wondrous miracles, they might
To manhood change her love from womanhood!
But all in vain; the heavens mocked her plight.
The long hours passed and Phoebus from the flood
Now slowly lifted up his golden head
And on the waking world his radiance shed.

45

'The day arrived when more reluctant yet
Fair Fiordispina from her couch arose,
For Bradamante said, with feigned regret,
She must depart (from this impasse she knows
There is no other exit than retreat).
The damsel offers her before she goes
A Spanish horse, with trappings all of gold,
A surcoat also, broidered gay and bold.

46

'The damsel bore her company a while,
Then, weeping, to her castle went her way.
My sister galloped on, mile after mile,
And Montalbano reached that very day.
Our mother once again began to smile;
Her brothers gathered round to hear her say
What had befallen her, for we had feared
The worst, no tidings of her having heard.

47

'We gazed astonished at her close-cropped hair,
Which formerly was wound about her head.
Her strangely-broidered surcoat made us stare.
She told us everything, just as I said:
How she was wounded in the forest, where
A hermit passed who, seeing how she bled,
Cut off her tresses that the wound might heal;
And now no more discomfort did she feel.

48

'And how, while she was sleeping by a fount,
A beautiful young maid came riding by,
Who took her for a knight and bade her mount
And join the huntsmen's merry hue and cry;
And how the maid then drew her from the hunt.
No detail did she spare us or deny.
The story stirred us to our very souls,
To think how nothing the poor maid consoles.

49

'Of Fiordispina I was well aware,
In Saragossa I'd seen her and in France.
Her lovely eyes, her rounded cheek, her hair
Were to my taste and often drew my glance;
And yet not long I let it linger there,
For hopeless love is folly; now that Chance
Provided access to an open door,
The flame leapt up as ardent as before.

50

'So from new strands of hope Love weaves his net.
(No other threads at present can he use.)
He catches me and shows how I may get
My heart's desire, how by a simple ruse
I may succeed; if I'm content to let
My likeness to my sister so bemuse
Beholders that they think I am my twin,
The damsel also may be taken in.

51

'Shall I or shall I not? I ponder well.
To follow pleasure where it leads seems good.
But no one of my secret plan I tell:
To seek advice on this I am too shrewd.
My sister's arms I found when evening fell
(Those she had worn when riding through the wood);
I put them on and rode her horse away,
Not waiting for the light of the new day.

52

'That very night I leave (Love being my guide)
To find fair Fiordispina once again.
I reach the end at last of my long ride
Just as the sun is rising from the main.
The eager servants one with th'other vied
To carry the glad tidings to their queen;
Hoping to curry favour and earn grace,
They hurried off to her at a great pace.

53

'They all mistook me, as just now you did,
For Bradamante, being deceived the more
By her apparel and the Spanish steed
On which she galloped off the day before.
And soon towards me Fiordispina sped;
Such joy and happiness her visage wore,
So festive was her welcome and so fond,
No one in all the world was more jocund.

54

'Throwing her lovely arms about my neck,
She clasps me sweetly and imprints a kiss
Upon my mouth (I swear it was no peck!).
Imagine if Love's arrow now can miss!
Straight to my heart, its flight receives no check.
Then to her room (no harm she sees in this)
She hurries me and there, from helm to spurs,
Disarms me and no help allows but hers.

55

'Then ordering a robe, ornate and fair,
She spreads its folds and in it dresses me
As if I were a woman; on my hair
She puts a net of golden filigree.
The modest glance, the bashful look I wear,
My every gesture femininity
Proclaim; and though my voice too manly is,
I use it so that no one notices.

56

'A hall we entered next, where many folk
Awaited us, ladies and chevaliers.
They paid us honour and respect, and spoke
As when great ladies or a queen appears;
And up my sleeve, as at a secret joke,
I laughed at some who (this is for your ears),
Not knowing what I hid beneath my gown,
With languid glances looked me up and down.

57

'The night was far advanced, the hour grew late;
The servants long ago had cleared the board,
At which the guests and household always ate
The choicest viands, fit for any lord.
The lovely Fiordispina did not wait
For me, who longed for her, to speak the word,
But, as she rose from table, graciously
To sleep with her that night invited me.

58

'When all the waiting-women moved away,
And pages who escorted us to bed
Had left the sconces flaming bright as day,
"My lady, do not be surprised", I said,
While we in night-attire together lay,
"Though on my homeward path you saw me sped
(And when I would come back God only knew),
To see me now so soon returned to you.

59

'"I'll tell you first just why I had to leave.
Next, why I have returned will be explained.
If, lady, I'd had reason to believe
Your ardour would have cooled had I remained,
No greater joy or sweetness than to live
And die in serving you could I have gained;
But as my presence caused you grief and woe,
I judged it best at last that I should go.

60

'"But Fortune made me wander all about
Among the tangled branches of a glade;
And suddenly I heard a piercing shout
As if a frightened damsel called for aid.
I did not hesitate for long in doubt:
Beside a crystal lake, a bare-limbed maid
Who dangled from a rod-and-line I saw.
A cruel troll prepared to eat her raw.

61

'"I rushed towards the monster, sword in hand
(Nor could I help the damsel otherwise).
That evil fisherman will never land
Another catch; the maid, to my surprise,
Leapt back into the water from the strand.
«You'll be rewarded handsomely» she cries,
«And anything you care to ask, I'll grant;
I am a nymph; this crystal lake I haunt.

62

'" «I am possessed of wondrous potency:
The elements and Nature I can bend.
Ask what you will and leave the rest to me,
If you would know how far my powers extend.
The fire to ice, air to solidity,
Will change, the moon above to earth descend
To hear my song; with simple words alone
The globe I can dislodge and stop the sun. »

63

'"No treasure did I ask, no gold require,
No wish had I to dominate mankind,
Nor to a superhuman strength aspire,
Nor fame in military conquests find.
Only the means I ask that your desire
May be fulfilled; and so whatever kind
Of spell or influence she needs to use,
I do not specify, but let her choose.

64

'"No sooner had I uttered my request,
Than once again she dived beneath the lake,
And put her magic talents to the test:
The only answer she would deign to make
Was to splash water at me, as in jest!
At once I see, I feel – there's no mistake –
I know, though credit it I scarcely can,
I'm changing from a woman to a man.

65

'"If it were not that here and now straightway,
You can confirm it, you would doubt it too.
As female once and now as male today,
My pleasure it will be to pleasure you.
Command me, for I long but to obey,
And gladly will I serve the whole night through."
And, taking then her hand in mine, I made
Her test and prove the truth of what I said.

66

'Like one who, lacking hope, for long has pined
For some loved object, lost (or found too late),
Who, sighing, cannot put it from his mind,
And moans and groans and rails against his fate,
Who if he unexpectedly should find
What he desires, having been desperate
So long and by ill fortune so ill-used,
At first incredulous, would stand confused,

67

'So Fiordispina, when she feels and sees
What she has been desiring for so long,
Her touch, her eyes, can scarcely trust; she is
Afraid that after all she must be wrong
Or sleeping; to dispel these fantasies,
Good proof I gave her, adequate and strong.
"Dear God," she said, "if this is dreaming, make
Me always dream and let me never wake."

68

'No roll of drums is heard, no trumpetings
These love-opponents forth to battle send,
But dove-like kisses and sweet murmurings
Give signal to go forward or ascend.
Our weapons are not arrows, nor yet slings.
No scaling-ladders here assistance lend.
I leap upon the fort and am not slow
To plant my standard and subdue my foe.

69

'If on the previous night that bed had been
A vestibule of sighing and laments,
Tonight, although unaltered is the scene,
Sweet games and smiles and joy are the events.
The sinuous acanthus ne'er was seen
To twine on columns and on pediments,
As we, who clasp each other face to face,
With arms and legs our breasts and thighs embrace.

70

'At first the secret stayed between us two.
For several months our pleasure was secure.
But someone then observed our rendezvous
And after that it was not long before
The king, her father, heard of it; and you,
Who rescued me, require to hear no more.
You saw the flames; you understand the rest.
God sees the pain which leaves my heart distressed.'

71

This was the story Ricciardetto told
As on they rode together through the night,
Breasting a rising terrain, sheer and bold,
Surrounded by ravines to left and right.
A narrow, rocky pathway, like an old
And rusty key, turned slowly to the height
To reach a citadel, called Agrismonte,
Guarded by Aldigier of Chiaramonte.

72

This governor was Buovo's bastard son.
Vivian and Malagigi were his two
Half-brothers; do not put reliance on
The rumour that Gherardo (it's untrue)
His lawful father was. Brave deeds he'd done,
And he was prudent, kind and gracious too.
Custodian of his brothers' citadel,
He laboured night and day to guard it well.

73

He welcomed Ricciardetto courteously,
As between cousins, to the manner born.
He loved him like a brother; equally
He paid the brave Ruggiero, in his turn,
All due respect; and yet not joyfully
He sallied forth, but with a face forlorn.
That very day a message he has had
Which grieves his heart and makes his aspect sad.

74

Without formality he said straightway,
'Brother, there is bad news; a messenger
On whom I can rely disclosed today
That Bertolagi and Lanfusa were
Negotiating terms: he is to pay
Rich loot and costly merchandise to her,
And she to sell my brothers to this man,
Our Malagigi and our Vivian.

75

'When prisoners they fell to Ferraù
He gave them in his cruel mother's charge.
She hid them in a dungeon, waiting to
Conclude her evil pact. She will discharge
The bargain with that vile Maganzan who
(On his iniquities I'll not enlarge)
Tomorrow near Bayona the price agreed
Will pay for two such knights of noblest breed.

76

'I have informed Rinaldo; only now
An envoy at the gallop I sent off;
But for the life of me, I can't see how
He can arrive in time, so long and rough
The journey is; my means do not allow
Me to set forth, I have not troops enough.
My soul is willing but my strength is weak.
I know not what to do, nor how to speak.'

77

Young Ricciardetto finds these tidings grim.
Ruggiero too is downcast for his sake.
Since both the cousins, standing silent, seem
Unable any rescue-plan to make,
Ruggiero sees that it is up to him:
'Do not despair, this task I'll undertake.
This sword against a thousand will prevail
And liberate your brothers without fail.

78

'No men-at-arms, no troops do I desire,
For single-handed I'll perform this deed;
But someone who can guide me, I require,
To where this vile exchange is planned; indeed,
I'll make them keep their contract, but the hire
In shrieks by both the parties will be paid.'
To one, Ruggiero's words said nothing new,
For he had seen what this bold knight could do.

79

The other scant attention to him paid,
As one of many words but little sense.
So, taking him aside, his cousin said
How this brave knight had come to his defence:
No idle boast was this which he had made,
As would be shown in time and by events.
Then Aldigiero pays more heed to him
And holds him in respect and high esteem.

80

At table, where the cup of plenty flowed,
He honoured him as if he were his lord;
And then and there arrangements they conclude
Whereby the brothers, cruelly immured,
May be set free. The dying sun bestowed
The boon of sleep on all who left the board
Except Ruggiero; though repose he sought,
His heart was pierced by a tormenting thought.

81

The message which the envoy brought that day
Concerning Agramante's grievous plight
Has vexed his heart; he knows the least delay
Will be to his dishonour as a knight.
What scorn he will incur if he now stay
With his lord's enemies, whom he should fight!
And as a coward how he'll be despised
When news leaks out that he has been baptized!

82

At any other time they might believe
True faith had moved him to conversion thus.
But now that it behoved him to relieve
His monarch from a siege so perilous,
No word of his would ever undeceive
His allies, who would hold him treacherous
And cowardly, in spite of evidence
Of his good faith; this thought all sleep prevents.

83

And to depart without his lady's leave!
That is another cause of his distress.
Many such thoughts his troubled bosom grieve.
Some urge him this way, others that way press.
No comfort, furthermore, does he receive
When he recalls their plan had no success:
They were to meet each other, they'd agreed,
To rescue Ricciardetto, as I said.

84

Then he remembers he has pledged his sword
To meet his love at Vallombrosa's shrine,
And he imagines her by wonder stirred
At his delay. Would he might send a line
At least to let her know what has occurred!
She has good reason to lament and pine:
Not only has he failed to do her will,
But he departed ere they said farewell.

85

Thus, turning matters over in his mind,
He thinks that he will write to her straightway.
As yet he's formed no plan of any kind,
But he will write the letter, come what may.
Perhaps upon the morrow he will find
Some trusty messenger along the way.
So, leaping from his bed that very night,
He calls for paper, ink and pen and light.

86

The servants hasten, ready and discreet,
To bring Ruggiero all that he commands.
His first words (as is customary) greet
His love; then, passing onwards, he expands
Upon the message from his king: how it
Requests his aid, else capture at the hands
Of enemies, or death, will be the fate
Of Agramante if help comes too late.

87

And, he continues, since to such a pass
His king has come that he has called for aid,
She must agree that nothing would surpass
The shame he would incur if he delayed;
And more than ever it behoved him, as
The husband (as he hoped) of such a maid
To keep his honour as a knight unsmutched
So that her own, so fair and true, it matched.

88

If in the past an honourable name
By noble deeds he'd laboured to deserve,
So, having won the recompense of fame,
Its cherished lustre henceforth to preserve
Now more than ever it must be his aim,
To seek renown, by straining every nerve,
For henceforth she would share it as his wife –
One soul within two bodies, all their life.

89

As he had said already, face to face,
He said to her in writing once again:
When from the service of his king release,
His bond being terminated, he should gain,
The Christian faith he would in truth embrace,
As he had long desired to do; and then
He'd ask her father Aymon for consent
To marry her, that they might be content.

90

'I wish', he added, '(and this wish pray grant)
To raise the siege which menaces my lord,
And quell the slander of the ignorant,
Whose scorn on me would otherwise be poured:
"As long as Fortune smiled on Agramant,
Ruggiero's loyal service was assured;
Now that success has veered to Charlemagne,
He rallies to the victor, it is plain."

91

'Give me but fifteen, twenty days', he prayed,
'That once for all it may be clearly shown
Those Africans, besieged in their stockade,
Their liberation owe to me alone.
Our union will not longer be delayed.
I will return, soon as this deed is done.
Grant me, for honour's sake, this one request.
I give you then, of all my life, the rest.'

92

These words and others similar he wrote,
But everything he said I cannot tell,
For he continued until every spot
Was covered of the page and covered well.
At last in careful folds he closed the note
And stowed it in his bosom, under seal.
He hoped to find a traveller next day
Who'd take his message to the Maid straightway.

93

The note being closed, his eyes he also closed,
And Sleep, beside the couch he lay upon,
Sprinkled him with a branch, as he reposed,
Dipped in the waters of oblivion
Of Lethe's quiet stream; nor was he roused
Until the joyful East with flowers shone,
Crimson and white, by lavish hands bestowed,
And Morning issued from her gold abode.

94

When little birds on the green boughs began
To greet with song the light of the new day,
The hospitable Aldigier (whose plan
It was to guide Ruggiero on his way
With Richard to the spot where, if they can,
The cruel Bertolagi they will slay)
Was first afoot, and when they heard him stir
The other two arose and ready were.

95

Then, being dressed and fully-armed once more,
Ruggiero and the cousins all set out.
In vain did he beseech them and implore
To let him undertake this task without
Their help; but they, being eager to restore
Their kin (and to avoid the charge, no doubt,
Of churlishness), as obdurate as stone,
Refused to let Ruggiero go alone.

96

When Vivian and Malagigi are
To be exchanged, that day the trio reach
Bayona; this is an arid region where
No cypresses, no ash-trees and no beech
Protect the naked land from the sun's glare;
No laurel-trees, no myrtle-bushes which
Give shade are to be seen amongst the scrub,
But only sparse, uncultivated shrub.

97

The three brave warriors at last drew rein,
And where a narrow path could be discerned
They saw a knight in armour cross the plain.
A banner with a golden border burned;
It bore as emblem on a field of green
That long-lived bird, the phoenix. I have earned,
My lord, a rest; this canto's at an end.
My song, with your permission, I suspend.

CANTO XXVI

1

Women of chivalry in olden days
There were, who valued manly valour more
Than wealth; quite other now are women's ways,
For most of them on gain set highest store.
Those women in whom virtue rightly plays
The greater part such avarice abhor,
Content to follow truth and righteousness
In hope of glory and eternal bliss.

2

Praise everlasting Bradamante earned,
Who loved not riches and not power desired,
But for Ruggiero's martial valour burned
And to his noble excellence aspired.
And he, as she deserved, her worth discerned;
His bosom by her loveliness was fired.
To please her he performs heroic deeds.
All other knights in prowess he exceeds.

3

Now with the Clairmonts, as you are aware,
Ruggiero rode; these cousins thought it right
(I speak of Ricciardet and Aldigier)
To save two brothers from a gruesome plight.
Across the plain they'd seen a cavalier
Approach – an arrogant and haughty knight,
Flaunting the bird which rises from the flame
Renewed, unique and of undying fame.

4

And when the oncomer observed the three,
Each poised for combat, ready to set off,
This seemed a welcome opportunity
To test their worth. When she was near enough,
She challenged them: 'Who dares to fight with me
With lance or sword? I'd like to see what stuff
You're made of; and the one who stays upright
Shall be declared the winner of the fight.'

5

'Gladly', said Aldigier, 'I'd try my skill
Against you, wielding either lance or sword,
But with another task, which, if you will,
You can observe, such test does not accord.
No time to joust, nor even to stand still
In parleying with you, can we afford.
Six hundred men who'll reach the cross-roads soon
We have today to try our prowess on.

6

'Two of our kith and kin it is our plan
To rescue, whom their captors here will bring.'
And he goes on to tell, as best he can,
The story of the cruel bartering.
'If this excuse is true,' the knight began,
'Which I cannot gainsay, then everything
You tell me makes it plain that there can be
Few knights who are the equal of you three.

7

'I hoped I might exchange a blow or two,
To test your valour and your expertise;
But if your skill you are prepared to show
At someone else's cost, then, as you please.
I only ask that I may fight your foe,
And with a shield and helmet such as these,
If you accept, I hope to demonstrate
That no unworthy ally you have met.'

8

Someone, I think, would like to know the name
Of him who offers to assist the three
Who to the rescue of the brothers came,
So I will say the cavalier is she
(Not he or him henceforth), that very same
Marfisa, who a toll of chivalry
Exacted from Zerbino, binding him
To do the vile Gabrina's every whim.

9

The Clairmont cousins and the good Ruggier
Welcomed Marfisa gladly as a fourth,
For they believed she was a cavalier,
Not knowing her true sex nor her true worth.
A banner was soon spied by Aldigier,
Which fitful breezes fluttered back and forth.
Alerted, his companions watch the train
Of men-at-arms who wind across the plain.

10

And as the hostile column closer drew,
Their Moorish dress could plainly be made out;
So they were Saracens, the allies knew,
And in their midst they saw, beyond all doubt,
Pinioned, each on a little nag, the two
Defenceless brothers. Then with a great shout
Marfisa cried, 'What are we waiting for?
This party offers merriment galore!'

11

Ruggiero answered, 'But not all the guests
Have yet arrived; many are missing still.
Such preparation for a ball suggests
A gala day; we must use all our skill.
So let *us* choose the festive games and jests,
And with our partners frolic as we will.'
The traitors of Maganza now advance
And it is almost time to start the dance.

12

The Maganzese from one direction ride,
Leading their mules weighed down with merchandise –
Rich garments, gold and precious goods beside,
While from the other come, with downcast eyes,
The captive brothers, hemmed in on each side
With lances, swords and bows, a costly prize;
And cruel Bertolagi could be heard
As with the Moorish captain he conferred.

13

Neither Count Buovo's nor Count Aymon's son
At sight of him can any more delay.
Couching their lances, at their foe they run.
One lance the traitor's paunch is seen to splay,
First piercing the front saddle-bow, and one
Splits both his cheeks. Ah, would that in this way
The world of evil-doers might be rid
And traitors die as Bertolagi did!

14

And at this signal, waiting for no blast
Upon a trumpet, both the other knights,
Marfisa and Ruggiero, follow fast.
Each with the foe with lance unbroken fights
Till from the saddle three of them are cast:
Ruggiero first the Moorish leader smites,
A worthy enemy, and next, with him,
Two more are sped to regions drear and dim.

15

From this, confusion in the ranks arose
Which brought about their ultimate defeat;
On the one side the Maganzese suppose
That they have been betrayed; the Moors, who meet
With like affront, the Frankish side abuse
As vile assassins, and the noise and heat
Of battle now begins, as weapons clash,
As lances hurtle and as arrows flash.

16

Between the lines Ruggiero alternates,
Killing now ten, now twenty, at one swoop.
Likewise Marfisa's weapon decimates
Now first the one and then another troop.
Touched by the blade the victims meet their fates
At once and from their saddles sag and droop.
Helmets and breastplates vanish all around,
Crashing like burning timber to the ground.

17

If you recall that you have ever seen,
Or if report has ever reached your ears,
How when a swarm of bees has risen in
A warlike cloud, a swallow then appears,
Skimming among them greedily with keen
And snapping beak, so the two cavaliers,
Ruggiero and Marfisa, seemed to be
Two swallows swooping on the enemy.

18

But Ricciardetto and his cousin chose
To trip a measure less diversified.
Leaving the Saracens to the others' blows,
They now bore down on the Maganzan side.
The prowess which Rinaldo's brother owes
To knightly training is now multiplied,
Till he is brave and strong enough for two,
By hate for his hereditary foe.

19

And the same hatred makes the bastard son
Of Buovo seem a lion in his rage.
Without a pause he lays his weapon on,
Splitting the helms like eggs with its sharp edge;
But who such daring would not then have shown,
Or seemed a Hector born in a new age,
Having companions like Ruggiero and
Marfisa, unsurpassed in every land?

20

Marfisa, never pausing in her fight,
Glanced round at her companions now and then.
Seeing such proof of prowess and of might,
She was amazed to see the number slain;
But most of all she marvelled at the sight
Of him she deemed unequalled among men.
This must be Mars himself, she thought, come down
From his fifth heaven, lending us renown.

21

She marvelled at Ruggiero's deadly blows.
She marvelled, too, at their unerring aim.
When Balisarda struck, you would suppose
That iron, paper suddenly became.
However thick the armour of the foes,
In twain the weapon sliced them just the same,
Down to their very steeds, and sent them flying
Till here, there, everywhere the dead were lying.

22

Sometimes the selfsame stroke would follow through,
Killing the horse together with the man.
From shoulders, heads in all directions flew,
Torsos were severed where the hips began.
Five at one blow and even more he slew.
Did I not fear to go beyond the span
Of what can be believed, I would say more,
But here the truth the face of falsehood wore.

23

Turpin, relating marvels such as these,
Knows that he speaks the unvarnished truth and leaves
His hearers to accept whate'er they please.
He says (you may consider he deceives)
Almost as though Marfisa's enemies
Were ice, they melt as, like a torch, she weaves
Among their ranks, causing no less surprise
Than he on whom she turns astonished eyes.

24

If she the god of war considered him,
Ruggiero in his turn could equally
Bellona this amazing damsel deem,
Did he but know the truth, so contrary
To what her skill and courage make her seem.
Between them then arose keen rivalry.
Alas for their poor foes, upon whose flesh,
Blood, sinews, bones they now compete afresh!

25

The valour and the skill of four suffice
To put both armies in the field to rout.
The legs of horses are the best device
For those who flee, of that there is no doubt.
They have a value now beyond all price,
The gallop being better than the trot,
And he who has no steed soon notices
That war on foot a sad profession is.

26

Victorious, the four survey the plain.
The field is won, the booty now is theirs,
For neither Moors nor Maganzese remain;
Gone are all men-at-arms and muleteers,
Who'd fled in two directions from the scene,
Leaving the prisoners and precious wares.
They set the brothers free with joyful hearts
And many a willing hand unloading starts.

27

Not only silver in great quantity
They found, fashioned in divers plates and bowls,
And women's clothes with rich embroidery,
And, fit for palaces, long, precious rolls
Of gold and silken Flemish tapestry,
Of which the beauty all the world extols,
And many other rich and costly things,
But also wine and bread and victuallings.

28

When all have drawn their helmets off, the three
Observe to whom they owe such timely aid:
The golden, curling tresses they now see,
And the fair features, of a lovely maid.
They greatly honour her and beg that she
Will not conceal her name, which she has made
Deserving of such glory; she replied
With courtesy and with their wish complied.

29

They gaze their fill upon her countenance,
Remembering her valour as a knight.
Upon the others she scarce deigns to glance,
But keeps Ruggiero only in her sight
And talks with him; the servants now advance
And all the gallant company invite
To take their places in the hill's cool shade,
Beside a fountain where a meal is laid.

30

This fountain, made by Merlin (one of four
In France) was girdled by a fair surround
Of polished marble, white as milk and more;
Figures, exquisitely inlaid all round,
Witness to the magician's handwork bore.
You would have said they breathed, save that no sound
Escaped their lips; each one appeared to live,
So wondrously did Merlin's art deceive.

31

They saw a loathsome beast depicted there,
Cruel and ugly, with a wolfish head
And fangs, and asses' ears; its body, spare
And fox-like, looked as if it seldom fed,
Despite its lion's claws to rend and tear.
Through England, France, Spain, Italy it sped,
Throughout all Europe and through Asia too,
Till all the world its fearful havoc knew.

32

It killed or wounded everywhere it went,
No less the highest than the lowliest,
For those who suffered its most violent
Attack were kings and princes and not least
The Roman court, where with malign intent
Prelates and Popes were murdered by the beast.
Infinite scandal it had brought upon
The Faith, contaminating Peter's throne.

33

Before its onslaught, crumbles every wall;
No rampart but must yield at its approach;
There is no citadel which does not fall;
All gates of castles open at its touch.
Worshipped as if divine by fools who call
It prudence, it will further yet encroach,
For to itself it abrogates as well
The very keys of Heaven and of Hell.

34

Crowned with imperial laurel now appears
A knight and at his side another three;
All are of royal standing, each one wears
A surcoat woven with the fleur-de-lis;
And with a banner similar to theirs,
A lion moves with awesome majesty.
And on their garments or above each head
Their names and titles may be plainly read.

35

That one who in the monster's belly plants
His sword up to the very hilt is named
In marble script: Francis the First of France;
And Maximilian is next proclaimed,
Of Austria, and Charles the Fifth, whose lance
Pierces the monster's throat; of one who aimed
An arrow at its heart, the English king,
Henry the Eighth, a future age will sing.

36

'The Tenth' is written on the lion's back.
Sinking his fangs into the monster's ears,
He shakes it; others run to the attack
And gone, it seems, are all men's doubts and fears.
That former errors may be kept in check,
An army, moderate in size, appears
And soon it rids the world of the vile beast,
And mankind now it ceases to molest.

37

Marfisa and the cavaliers desire
To know who all these warriors may be
By whose stern hands they see the beast expire,
That cause of sorrow and iniquity.
And so, of one another they enquire
(For though the names and titles they can see,
These have no meaning in those far-off days)
What is the story which the fount displays.

38

Viviano looked at Malagigi, who
Stood listening, but had uttered not a word.
He said, 'This marble story is for you
To expound, for you are learnèd, I have heard.
What men are these, who divers arms imbue
In that beast's blood which has their wrath incurred?'
And Malagigi said, 'This history
Is no part yet of any memory.

39

'For you must know, all these who, each by name,
Are indicated here, are not yet born;
But seven hundred years from now, their fame
The temples of the future will adorn.
Merlin the sorcerer from Britain came
In brave King Arthur's time and one fine morn
Gave orders for this fountain to be made
And by the finest craftsmen thus inlaid.

40

'This monster issued from the depths of Hell,
When weights and measures in the world were new,
When property was made divisible,
When pen and ink recorded what was due.
At first not every land, as I heard tell,
The monster ravaged; some, exemption knew.
The harm it does today, although widespread,
To men of low degree is limited.

41

'From its beginnings to the present age,
The monster has been growing and will grow,
Until, of all the beasts which havoc wage,
No larger, no more vile, the world can show.
The famous python, which on many a page
Has been described, was large as pythons go,
Yet was not half so large as this will be,
Nor was it so detestable to see.

42

'Much cruel slaughter will this beast commit.
There'll be no region it will not infect,
No country which will be immune from it,
No town it will not damage or affect.
And of such torment longing to be quit,
The world will cry for help, and these elect,
Shining like oriflammes, whose names we read,
Will save the nations in their hour of need.

43

'The beast will have no more relentless foe
Than Francis the French monarch, of that name
The First; such skill and valour he will show
That many who seem valiant he will shame.
No equal and few rivals he will know.
His royal splendour and heroic fame
Will others' deeds eclipse, as by the sun
All lesser lights are instantly outshone.

44

'In the first year of his auspicious reign,
The crown being scarcely settled on his brow,
He'll cross the Alps, where he will render vain
The plan to hold the pass, revealing how
His heart is stirred by wrath and just disdain
That the disgrace is not avenged ere now
Which frenzied herdsmen on the French will bring
With savage and ferocious battering.

45

'To the rich Lombard plain he will descend,
Surrounded by the flower of all France,
And Switzerland to such submission bend
That checked for ever is her arrogance.
The Church and Spain and Florence will defend
A fortress, but in vain, for he'll advance
Upon it and will storm the citadel
Which they had deemed to be impregnable.

46

'The weapon that will serve his purpose best
Will be that honoured sword by means of which
He will have previously slain the beast,
Corruptor of all regions and of each
Community; no standard makes the least
Resistance; not a rampart, not a ditch,
And not a wall, however thick and strong,
Will keep a citadel secure for long.

47

'This prince in all the virtues will excel
Which any conqueror has ever shown:
Great Caesar's courage, and that prudent skill
Whence Trebbia and Lake Trasimene were won,
And Alexander's lucky star as well,
Without which every plan is overthrown.
Such liberality he will possess,
There is no measure he will not surpass.'

48

Thus Malagigi read the marble screed,
Inspiring in the knights a wish to know
The names of other figures who, instead
Of slaying the infernal monster, show
How best to set about the noble deed.
He said, 'That one whom Merlin places so,
Bernardo, will confer upon Bibbiena
Renown eclipsing Florence and Siena.

49

'And to the forefront, each a paragon,
Are Sigismond, Giovanni and Ludovic
(Gonzaga, Salviati, Aragon),
Who the destruction of the monster seek.
Francis of Mantua, likewise his son
Who follows in his footsteps, Frederick;
Two dukes, Ferrara's and Urbino's, stand,
Brother and son by marriage, on each hand.

50

'And Guidobaldo, son of one of these,
Does not intend to linger at the back.
Eager as Ottobono Fieschi, he's
As quick as Sinibaldo to attack;
And Luigi of Gazolo's arrow is
So swift, the metal burns the creature's neck.
Phoebus, the archer-god, will grant him bow
And quiver, Mars himself a sword bestow.

51

'Two Ercoles and two Ippolitos
Of Este; and of these names another two
(A Medici and a Gonzaga, those)
The traces of the weary beast pursue.
Giuliano with his offspring level goes,
Ferrante with his brother; near by too
Andrea Doria stands vigilant.
No passage will Francesco Sforza grant.

52

'Of noble, generous, illustrious blood,
Two of Avàlos carry as their sign
A mighty rock, like that which long has stood
Holding Typhoeus helpless in confine.
No injury against the monster could
Exceed the blows which these two will combine.
Francesco of Pescara one is named,
And one Alfonso of Vasto is proclaimed.'

53

But what of the great commandant of Spain,
Consalvo, who was held in such esteem,
Whom Malagigi praised and praised again?
Few in that band there were to equal him.
And last, of all those who the beast had slain,
William of Monferrat not least I deem.
Few were those heroes in comparison
With those the brute had wounded or undone.

54

In games or converse, after their repast,
Together they beguiled the heat of day,
Or else beside the fountain took their rest
'Mid shady shrubs, or on fine carpets lay.
While the two brothers, in full armour dressed,
Kept guard lest any should approach that way,
A lady, unescorted, soon they see,
Who rides towards them with rapidity.

55

It is Ippalca, who set out to lead
Frontino to Ruggiero, as his love
Desired, and was obliged to yield the steed
To Rodomonte; all that day she strove
To follow him; in vain she tried to plead,
Or curse: the miscreant she could not move.
Then on her way she learned (I know not how)
Ruggiero was with Ricciardetto now.

56

And since she knew the territory well,
For she had been there many times before,
She rode towards the fountain without fail,
Finding Ruggiero and the others (for
They'd rested there a while, as you heard tell).
And she, who was observant and still more
Discreet, when she saw Ricciardetto there,
Feigned not to know or recognize Ruggier.

57

She turned to Ricciardetto straight away,
As though her message were for him alone.
He rose to welcome her without delay,
Asking her where she went. Her eyes still shone
With tears, and sighing she began to say
(Though speaking audibly in a clear tone
In order that Ruggiero, who stood nigh,
Might hear how sorrowful she was, and why):

58

'I was conducting on a leading-rein,
As Bradamante had commanded me,
A splendid destrier, with flowing mane;
Frontino he is called, a horse which she
Most dearly loves; my orders were to gain
A region near Marseilles where she would be
Ere many days had passed; I was to wait
Till she should come where we arranged to meet.

59

'My heart was confident, I had no fear
That anyone would try to take the steed.
Its owner's name I deemed enough to hear –
Rinaldo's sister, famed for many a deed;
But yesterday an African drew near;
He was on foot and of a mount had need.
I told him Bradamante owned the horse
And yet he seized the rein from me by force.

60

'I followed him, beseeching him in vain.
Throughout all yesterday and all today
I cursed and menaced and besought again.
I left him finally not far away,
Fighting, hard-pressed, with all his might and main,
Against a warrior whose prowess may
Bring down revenge for me upon his head –
A retribution just and merited.'

61

Ruggiero at these words leapt to his feet,
And scarcely could he wait to hear them all.
He turns to Ricciardetto to entreat,
If he considers he has served him well,
That he may leave without delay to meet
This unknown knight, and that Ippalca shall
Go with him to point out the arrogant,
Importunate horse-stealing miscreant.

62

Although it seems to him unchivalrous
To leave to someone else an enterprise
Which thus concerns a member of his house,
Yet Ricciardetto with this wish complies;
And so Ruggiero takes a courteous
Farewell of his companions, whose surprise
And wonder know no bounds when they observe
His resolution and unfailing nerve.

63

When she had led the knight some way apart,
Ippalca then revealed the true account –
How she was sent by her upon whose heart
His image was engraved to bring the mount
To him, and she proceeded to impart
(No longer feigning now, as at the fount,
When she saw Ricciardetto standing near)
All that her lady bade her tell Ruggier.

64

She added that with overbearing pride,
On learning who Frontino's owner was,
The Saracen had straight away replied:
'What you have told me gives me greater cause
To take the horse; my name I will not hide.
Throughout the world its splendour overawes
Whoever hears it. Should Ruggiero want
His steed, tell him to seek out Rodomont.'

65

Ruggiero's rising colour soon reveals,
As he lends ear to what Ippalca says,
The wrath and indignation which he feels.
Frontino's dear to him in many ways;
This noble horse which Rodomonte steals
He nurtured with great love; if he delays
He sees his honour is in jeopardy.
This outrage straight away avenged must be.

66

Ippalca willingly Ruggiero guides,
Longing to see the offender make amends.
She brings him soon to where the road divides.
One branch goes to the plain, and one ascends
The hill; but to the valley, from both sides,
Each of these paths returns at last and ends.
Though steep, the upward route, Ippalca knew,
Was, strange to say, the shorter of the two.

67

Ippalca's eager longing to regain
Frontino and to bring revenge upon
The African leads her to turn the rein
Towards the hill; but Rodomont has gone
Along the slower route towards the plain,
Together with the three who follow on;
And so he does not meet the angry pair
Who search for him – Ippalca and Ruggier.

68

The enmity between the other two
Had been deferred till they could help their king.
With them (you know) was Doralice who
Had caused their strife. Now hear me while I sing
The sequel of their history to you:
As to the fountain they come cantering,
They see the brothers, Aldigier, Marfise,
And Ricciardetto, who recline at ease.

69

Marfisa, in response to the request
Of her companions, in the jewellery
And feminine apparel was now dressed,
Which the Maganzan in his treachery
Intended for Lanfusa; so from crest
To spurs, Marfisa doffed her arms, though she
Was rarely seen without them, and arrayed
Herself, to please the others, as a maid.

70

As soon as Mandricard set eyes on her,
He planned, with overweening confidence
(For, in his view, she and his lady were
A fair exchange), that he would recompense
The Sarzan monarch and to him transfer
This damsel, having first removed her hence:
If Love, he thought, arranges matters thus,
The African will not lament his loss.

71

So Mandricardo, scheming to provide
His rival with the damsel who appears
As comely as the lady at his side
(Whom he desired to keep), the cavaliers,
Whom he approached, now formally defied,
Claiming the lovely maid as his, not theirs,
And, challenging them all to joust with him,
He called them forth to battle fierce and grim.

72

The brothers, who had kept their armour on,
To guard the company from all affray,
Ready and eager, had at once begun
To move to the attack, believing they
Were challenged by both knights; but of these, one
Remained immobile, nor in any way
Gave sign of joining in this joust; and so
Two combatants opposed a single foe.

73

Viviano moved towards him with high heart,
His heavy lance couched low; towards *him* came
The Tartar king, whose prowess in the art
Of combat earned for him undying fame.
Each seeks to strike the other in the part
Which least can stand the blow. Viviano's aim
At Mandricardo's helmet fails to make
Him fall: he is not even seen to shake.

74

But Mandricard, who has a stronger spear,
Shatters Viviano's shield as it were glass,
And from the saddle sends him flying clear,
To land among the flowers and the grass.
Then Malagigi spurs his destrier,
His brother's setback eager to redress.
He goes to keep his brother company
The sooner, sharing his indignity.

75

Next, Aldigiero, having quickly put
His armour on, was mounted on his steed,
Not waiting for his cousin, and full out
Rode off against the pagan; at top speed
He struck the helmet in the centre, not
An inch below the sights, and yet no heed
Does Mandricardo pay, while to the sky
Four fragments of the shattered weapon fly.

76

The pagan struck him now upon the left.
The weapon's impact was so violent
That Aldigiero's shield in two was cleft,
And his cuirass as much protection lent
As plaited straw, or bark; the cruel shaft
Through Aldigiero's snowy shoulder went;
Amid the grass and flowers fell the knight,
His armour gory red, his visage white.

77

With daring, Ricciardetto follows on.
He couches, as he comes, a mighty lance,
Showing once more, as he has often shown,
He is a worthy paladin of France.
As though the conflict were already won,
He gallops onward, but by some mischance
His charger falls and Ricciardetto is
At once unhorsed, though by no fault of his.

78

Then, since there is no other cavalier,
The pagan thinks that he has won the joust,
And to the fountain goes to claim the fair
Young damsel, and he says: 'Lady, you must
Concede that you are ours, since it is clear
No one is left to champion you. I trust
You'll not demur or make excuses, for
This custom has been long observed in war.'

79

Raising a haughty face, Marfisa said,
'The premisses of your remarks are wrong.
Right would be on your side, I will concede,
And you could justly claim me, if among
These cavaliers, who on the ground lie spread,
Were one who is my lord; but I belong
To no one but myself; and so you see,
Who wants me must do battle first with me.

80

'A buckler and a lance I too can wield
And many a cavalier I have unhorsed.'
Then to the squires she said, 'Bring me my shield,
Bring me my arms and steed.' Away they coursed.
Stripped to her doublet soon she stood revealed.
Save for her visage, valour, reinforced
By combat and the hardihood of wars,
Had formed in her a replica of Mars.

81

When she was armed, she girded on her sword
And lightly leapt upon her destrier.
Putting him through his paces on the sward,
She rode him three times round, now here, now there.
And then with many a defiant word,
Aiming her lance, a gallant challenger,
Against the Tartar king she galloped on,
Bold as the Troy-defending Amazon.

82

Then both their lances to the very butt,
At that first, fierce encounter, broke like glass.
Yet neither foe had yielded by one jot,
Nor did they sit their steeds upright the less.
Marfisa, eager to discover what
The pagan's prowess is, resolves to pass
To combat at close range and *corps à corps*;
So, sword in hand, she faces him once more.

83

Cursing the heavens and the elements,
The pagan raged to see her still upright;
She too blasphemed with no less violence
To see his shield intact; the chilling sight
Of naked steel each cavalier presents.
In turn, the blades the magic armour smite
In which both combatants that day are clad,
And greater need of it they'd never had.

84

Enchanted armour nothing can assail,
No sword can penetrate, no lance can pierce.
They could prolong the fight to no avail
That day and all the next, from dawn to tierce.
But Rodomonte now begins to rail.
Flinging himself between them, proud and fierce,
He shouts: 'If you are eager for a fray,
Let us conclude our fight begun today.

85

'We called a truce, do not forget, and made
A pact to bring assistance to our side.
No other battle, till we lend such aid,
Should be begun, no other foe defied.'
Then, bowing to Marfisa, he displayed
The message they received, and does not hide
The story of the courier who came
To ask their help in Agramante's name.

86

He asked her then if she would please defer
The inconclusive combat here begun,
And without more ado invited her
To fight with them for King Troiano's son:
This is a nobler cause and worthier,
For which there's greater glory to be won,
Than in a quarrel of no consequence
Which such heroic enterprise prevents.

87

Marfisa, ever eager to contend
Against the knights of Charlemagne with lance
And sword, and having had no other end
When from so far away she came to France
Than to observe their valour at first hand,
Hearing the pagan's words, jumped at the chance
Of helping Agramante in his need,
And with the plan she readily agreed.

88

Ruggiero in the meantime has in vain
Followed Ippalca on the mountain route,
For when they reach the summit it is plain
That Rodomont, of whom they're in pursuit,
Has gone the other way; so once again
Ruggiero turns, and at a spanking trot,
Knowing the miscreant has not gone far,
Reaches the fountain where the others are.

89

But first Ippalca he has wisely sent
To Montalbano, a distance of one day;
For, had she come with him, this would have meant
An even longer journey and delay.
He bids her be of cheer and not lament.
He'll win Frontino back and in some way
Get word to her, wherever she may be,
That she may hear the tidings speedily.

90

He gives to her the letter which he wrote
In Agrismonte and has ever since
Kept hidden in a fold inside his coat.
Ippalca on her memory imprints
His word-of-mouth additions to the note.
The loyal messenger no effort stints.
Without a moment's pause she gallops on
And comes, when evening falls, to Montalban.

91

Along a well-marked trail Ruggiero chased
His quarry; not until he reached the fount
Did he catch up with him for all his haste.
And there he saw him on the stolen mount.
The Tartar had just promised not to waste
More time – an oath confirmed by Rodomont:
They'd perpetrate no further hostile ploy,
But save the camp which Charles's troops annoy.

92

Ruggiero knew Frontino, and thus knew
Who the thief was who sat his horse astride.
Over his lance his shoulders rounded grew,
As loudly he the African defied,
Who showed more patience then than Job could do;
For in response he quelled his mighty pride,
Refusing this new challenge, he who fought
So willingly and ever battle sought.

93

This was the first and last occasion when
The monarch of Algiers refused a fight;
But Agramante now needs all his men
And Rodomont acknowledges his right
To summon aid; and if Ruggiero then
Were at his mercy like a hare held tight
Between a leopard's paws he would not so
Delay as to inflict a single blow.

94

To add to this, the Sarzan is aware
This is Ruggiero come to claim his steed,
The one whose valour he would gladly dare,
And whose renown all warriors concede,
Whose feats are celebrated everywhere.
He longs to test his mettle and his breed,
Yet he refuses – an amazing thing –
So greatly he prefers to aid his king.

95

A thousand miles and more he would have gone
For such a fight, had this not been the case;
Yet nothing else that day would he have done,
Were it Achilles in Ruggiero's place.
Of all the many sparks which flew, not one
Caught fire and of a flame there was no trace.
He tells Ruggiero why he will not fight
And begs him aid their monarch in his plight.

96

For as a loyal cavalier he must
Defend his lord and rally to his side;
Let them conclude their duel when this trust
Has been fulfilled. Ruggiero then replied:
'I am quite willing to defer our joust
Until the Frankish king has been defied
And from his clutches Agramant is free,
If first Frontino is restored to me.

97

'That you have greatly erred I'll prove by force
Of arms; it ill became you as a knight
To rob a gentle maiden of my horse.
But if you wish me to defer our fight,
Dismount Frontino; it will be the worse
For you unless you yield me up my right.
For then no earthly power will induce
Me to delay, nor grant you one hour's truce.'

98

So these, then, are the terms Ruggiero makes:
Frontino, or a combat then and there.
While Rodomonte neither offer takes,
Unwilling yet to yield the destrier,
Or further to delay, for all their sakes,
The Tartar from the other side draws near
And on Ruggiero's banner sees the bird
On whose account new conflict now is stirred.

99

An eagle, argent, on an azure field
Ruggiero bore, the noble Trojan sign,
Being descended, as I have revealed,
From mighty Hector and his royal line.
This fact from Mandricardo was concealed,
And, not permitting that this bird divine
Should be by any other knight displayed,
A challenge to the newcomer he made.

100

He also bore upon his shield the bird
Which from Mount Ida snatched up Ganymede.
This shield on Mandricardo was conferred
At Castle Perilous for a brave deed.
I think, among the stories you have heard,
You will remember how the fairy maid
Gave him those weapons which Jove's armourer
Had forged for Hector in the Trojan war.

101

These two, Ruggiero and the Tartar king,
For this same cause had often fought before.
How they had parted and gone wandering
Is known to you: of that I'll say no more.
And now their fates these knights together bring.
Seeing again the shield Ruggiero bore,
On all his strength and rage the Tartar drew,
And to Ruggiero cried: 'I challenge you!

102

'That emblem which you rashly bear is mine,
And this is not the first and only day
That I have seen you flaunting that ensign
Which still, despite my warnings, you display.
Madman! no threats, it seems, can I combine
To turn you from the folly of your way:
I'll show you it were better to have paid
Due heed to me, and my commands obeyed!'

103

As well-dried kindling quickly catches light
At a small puff of wind, and leaps and flares,
So now Ruggiero's angry pride burns bright
As soon as Mandricard's first words he hears.
'You think' (he said) 'because this other knight
To pick a quarrel with me rashly dares,
That I must yield? But I will take the two –
Frontin from him and Hector's shield from you.

104

'I fought with you before, not long ago.
And for this selfsame cause; I did not slay
You then, for I would scorn to kill a foe
Who has no sword, and you had none that day.
Now let us pass to deeds (that was but show).
For that white eagle you shall dearly pay.
That emblem from my forebears I inherit.
You have no right to it: I justly wear it.'

105

'*You* have usurped that emblem, which is mine!',
The Tartar king retorted, and drew sword,
The one which he had found beneath the pine
With all Orlando's other weapons stored.
Ruggiero's sense of honour is so fine,
By him no rule of chivalry's ignored.
Seeing the Tartar draw his sword, at once
Upon the ground beneath he casts his lance.

106

Then, grasping Balisarda in his fist,
His shield upon his arm he firmly takes.
But Rodomonte plunges in their midst.
A sudden dash Marfisa likewise makes.
Each urges one opponent to desist
And forces them apart, for all their sakes.
The African in his complaint is loud:
Twice Mandricardo broke the truce he vowed.

107

First, thinking he could win the maid as his,
He'd stopped and jousted more than once; and now,
To take away Ruggiero's emblem, he's
Prepared once more to violate his vow:
A poor concern for Agramante, this!
'Let us conclude *our* fight: you will allow,'
He said, 'if dilly-dally here you must,
Our combat is more suitable and just.

108

'A truce was sworn between us and agreed,
And our dispute must thus be settled first.
When I have dealt with you, I shall proceed
To answer him who in his folly durst
Contest with me the right to mount this steed.
Then for his shield, against him do your worst.
But I shall give you so much work to do,
Ruggiero will not find much left of you.'

109

'The part of me you think you can defeat',
The Tartar king replied to Rodomont,
'You'll not subdue; but I will make you sweat
From head to foot and on this you can count.
More than you bargain for in me you'll meet.
Like water springing from a living fount,
My strength will last me for a thousand fights,
With you, Ruggiero and all other knights.'

110

Their anger mounted and the insults flew
Now from the one, now from the other, side.
King Mandricard would like to fight with two
At once, so fierce he burns with rage and pride.
Ruggiero, who is not accustomed to
Endure abuse, will not be pacified.
Alone Marfisa turns now here, now there;
In vain she tries to calm each cavalier,

111

Just as a farmer, when a swollen stream,
Topping its lofty banks, new outlet seeks,
Will hasten where the rising waters seem
To menace his green pastures, and there checks
Their onrush, or where next they'll overbrim
The hoped-for corn, he blocks and dams the leaks
As best he can, and yet, for all he does,
Elsewhere the water, ramifying, flows.

112

So, while Ruggiero, Mandricardo and
Fierce Rodomonte are at odds, all three,
Each being resolved to win the upper hand
And show the others his supremacy,
Marfisa does her best to gain command.
Yet all her efforts end but fruitlessly:
If one of them she does at last restrain,
She sees the other two begin again.

113

'Brave knights,' Marfisa said, hoping to bring
Them to agreement, 'heed my words, I pray:
Defer all single combat till our king
Is out of danger; and if then for fray
Among yourselves you are still hungering,
Let us resume our fights begun today.
With Mandricard my combat I'll renew,
To test his boast and see the matter through.

114

'But if King Agramante needs our aid,
Let him *be* aided and our strife deferred.'
'I'm willing to depart', Ruggiero said,
'When I regain my charger; in a word,
Either this thief surrenders me my steed,
Or else I claim it back with lance and sword;
Either I die in combat *sur-le-champ*,
Or else I ride Frontino back to camp.'

115

And Rodomonte answered, 'To obtain
The second of your two alternatives
Will be less easy than the first to gain.'
And he continued, 'If our king receives
Insult or injury, it will be plain
The fault is yours, not mine.' This protest gives
Ruggiero not a moment's pause; no heed
He pays but grasps his sword and spurs his steed.

116

And with the impetus of a wild boar
He hurls himself against his enemy,
With shield and shoulder battering the Moor,
Who slips his stirrup, so put out is he.
The Tartar shouts, 'Defer this battle or
You'll have to settle your account with me.'
Dishonourably, even as he spoke,
He dealt Ruggiero's helm a cruel stroke.

117

This bows Ruggiero to his charger's neck
And when he tries to raise himself upright,
The blows of Rodomonte serve to check
All his attempts; such deadly onslaughts might
Have cleft his helmet, splitting cheek from cheek,
But, adamantine, it protects the knight.
Ruggiero in dismay flings both hands wide.
The rein hangs loose, his sword falls at his side.

118

The charger bears him off, and on the ground
His Balisarda lies. She who that day
Companionship with him in arms has found,
Watches with burning wrath the ignoble way
Against one, two in enmity are bound.
Since she is valorous and brave, straightway
Against the Tartar she directs her horse
And strikes him on the head with all her force.

119

After Ruggiero Rodomonte speeds:
Another blow will make Frontino his.
But Vivian and Richard place their steeds
Between the two and check hostilities.
One hurtles Rodomonte and succeeds
In blocking him from where Ruggiero is.
The other, Viviano, hands his sword
To his good friend, Ruggiero, now restored.

120

Soon as Ruggiero to himself returns
And in his hand finds Viviano's blade,
Eager for vengeance, all delay he scorns
And on his foe he rushes unafraid,
As when a lion, tossed on a bull's horns,
Feeling no pain, is driven, undismayed,
By frenzied rage to re-attack in haste,
The quicker its desired revenge to taste.

121

A rain of blows on Rodomonte's head
Ruggiero strikes, and if he had the sword
Which by a breach of honour, as I said,
He was obliged to drop upon the sward,
I do not think, if I am not misled,
That helmet much protection would afford,
Though for the king of Babel it was fired
When to wage war with heaven he aspired.

122

Dame Discord, thinking nothing could reduce
The strife and turmoil which had broken out,
Seeing no prospect of a peace or truce,
Assured her sister they need have no doubt:
Their work being done, their bonds they now might
And to their monks, so pious and devout,   [loose,
Return; so let them now depart; we'll stay
And watch the progress of the bitter fray.

123

Ruggiero hit the other with such force
Upon the brow, that Rodomonte struck,
With back and helm, the cruppers of his horse.
From side to side, three and four times he shook,
Dangling head down; and in the frantic course
Which, uncontrolled, the startled charger took,
He would have lost his sword, had not a twist
Of leather tied it firmly to his wrist.

124

Meanwhile Marfisa makes the Tartar sweat.
He also for his part so shrewdly hits
That she, like him, pours like a rivulet.
The hauberk of each one so closely fits
That through no chink can either's weapon get,
Thus in their duel so far they are quits;
But at a sudden turn made by her steed,
Marfisa of Ruggiero's help has need.

125

The charger of Marfisa, making a swift
Leap sideways where the grass was soft and moist,
Slipped and went down; straightway it strove to lift
Its heavy bulk, which was no sooner hoist
Than Brigliadoro hurtled from the left
(The steed in which Orlando once rejoiced),
Spurred by the Tartar with a total lack
Of honour, and Marfisa's horse fell back.

126

Ruggiero, when he sees the damsel lie
Thus disadvantaged, help does not defer.
His foe being stunned, there is no reason why,
Since he is free, he should not rescue her.
He strikes the Tartar's helm a blow whereby,
If but that sword his Balisarda were,
That head he'd sever like an apple core,
If Mandricard another helmet wore.

127

And in the meantime the Algerian king
Comes to himself once more and gazes round.
He sees young Richard and, remembering
How he had helped Ruggiero hold his ground,
He makes for him, a harsh reward to bring
For his brave deed; but Malagigi found,
With his great skill and using a strange spell,
A means by which the pagan's wrath to quell.

128

For Malagigi knew the secret art.
Compared with any other sorcerer,
He was no less accomplished and expert.
And though his book of magic was not there,
He had the special formula by heart
Whence by long usage demons conjured were.
He sends one into Doralice's horse
Which drives it forward on a frenzied course.

129

Into the body of that humble hack
Which bore the daughter of King Stordilan
Upon its docile, uncomplaining back,
The sorcerer (brother to Vivian)
By words alone sent one of Minos' black
Angels; the nag, which never walked or ran
Unless encouraged, leapt into the air
Sixteen feet high and thirty long, I swear.

130

The leap was high and wide, yet it was not
The kind to make a rider lose his seat.
Thus flying in mid-air, the damsel thought
That her last moment she would surely meet,
And in great fear began to call and shout.
The nag, just as the devil urges it,
After a second leap runs off so fast
The speed of every arrow is surpassed.

131

And from the combat Ulieno's son
Withdrew at the first sound of that loved voice,
And where the palfrey bore his lady on
He raced to rescue her; and the same choice
The Tartar made, and straightway he was gone;
Without requesting either peace or truce
Of either foe, he chases Rodomont
And Doralice on her frenzied mount.

132

Meanwhile Marfisa rose from where she lay,
Burning with wrath and rage and ire and scorn.
She longs for vengeance but too far away
She sadly sees her enemy is borne.
Ruggiero at such ending of the fray
As lions roar in rage (not when they mourn)
Bellows in fury, for he knows indeed
They cannot now catch up with either steed.

133

Ruggiero, far from willing yet to cease,
The matter of his charger still contests.
Marfisa does not want to leave in peace
The Tartar till she further probes and tests
The limits of his skill and expertise:
To leave such things unsettled, each protests,
Would be a grievous breach of chivalry,
And so to follow them they both agree.

134

In Paris they decide to seek them out
(If they should fail to come upon them first),
For there they will have gone without a doubt,
Where Charlemagne prepares to do his worst,
By putting all the Saracens to rout;
And so to satisfy their unquenched thirst
For vengeance, they resolve to leave straightway.
But now Ruggiero, his farewells to say,

135

His horse's head has turned where to one side
The brother of his lovely lady waits.
He vows they shall be friends, whate'er betide,
No matter what shall be their several fates.
Then in his name (and this no harm implied)
Remembrance to his sister he entreats.
This part he did so well and with such tact
That Ricciardetto nothing could suspect.

136

Of him, of Malagigi, Vivian,
Of wounded Aldigier, his leave he takes.
All of them proffered friendship, every man,
For all that he had done for all their sakes.
Marfisa, to defend the Saracen,
For Paris her departure quickly makes,
Without farewells; the brothers wave goodbye,
But cannot catch her up for all they try.

137

And Ricciardetto too went on his way,
While stricken Aldigiero tarried there;
Against his will he was obliged to stay.
Then, taking the same path as the first pair,
The two remaining followed on that day.
My lord, in my next canto you shall hear
What superhuman deeds against Charlemagne
Those four achieved, whose marvels I'll make plain.

CANTO XXVII

1

The advice of women, if spontaneous,
Is better than if pondered well, and weighed.
This is their special gift which bounteous
Heaven, with countless more, to them has made.
But men's advice (and this is curious)
Which a mature reflection does not aid,
Is rarely good, but must be long thought out,
Each aspect studied, sifted every doubt.

2

The plan which Malagigi formed seemed good
And yet was not; although (as I have said)
The danger in which Ricciardetto stood
Was thus removed, the stratagem had led
To the departure of two foes, who would,
To Charlemagne's discomfiture, be sped
To Paris all the faster, there to smite
The Christian cavaliers with all their might.

3

If he had had more time to think it out,
He could have helped his cousin equally,
As he was bound to do, and yet without
Causing the Christians any injury.
He could have sent the damsel round about
The world, eastwards or westwards, so that she
Would vanish from their ken and never more
Be heard of in all France, from shore to shore.

4

The two who loved her would have followed her,
Just as to Paris, so to any place.
This obvious truth escaped the sorcerer,
Who had reflected for too short a space.
The demons who from Heaven banished were,
Of blood and fire and slaughter go in trace;
And so, being free to choose, this demon went
Where he could bring King Charles most harassment.

5

The palfrey which the fiend has thus possessed
Carried the frightened damsel on and on.
No stream, ditch, wood or marshland could arrest
Its course; up hills, down valleys it had gone
Till, where the French and English troops were massed
With other Christian forces, it had won
Its way through all those hostile ranks to bring
The damsel to her sire, Granada's king.

6

The rivals, Rodomont and Mandricard,
Pursued their lady for a while that day,
Keeping her still in sight by riding hard.
She disappeared from view at last and they,
Like well-trained bloodhounds which their pace retard
And closely track the footprints of their prey,
Followed the traces where the hoof-marks ran
And heard at last she was with Stordilan.

7

Beware, O Charles! such fury threatens you
And draws so nigh that no escape I see;
Not these two only, but Gradasso too
And Sacripant approach in enmity.
And now, as if to prove you through and through,
Fate robs you of both beacons: potency
In martial strife and acumen of mind,
Whence you are left to grope in darkness, blind.

8

Orlando and Rinaldo I here mean:
One in his furious and frenzied state,
In heat and cold, in sunshine and in rain,
Runs naked like a torrent in full spate.
And now the other, scarcely less insane,
Abandons you just when your need is great.
His love is not in Paris, he now knows,
And so in search of her at once he goes.

9

A fraudulent magician, as I said,
Made him believe by a fantastic spell
(By such illusion many he misled)
Angelica approached the citadel
With Count Orlando; to his heart there sped
A pang of jealousy more terrible
Than any lover knew; to Court he went
And straight away to Britain he was sent.

10

After the battle, when renown he earned
And glory by immuring Agramant,
To Paris then Rinaldo had returned.
To every fortress, every house he went,
And every cloister; every stone he turned,
All paths explored and followed every scent.
Seeing at last his lady was not there,
Nor yet the Count, he left to seek the pair.

11

Then, picturing Orlando's lustful joy
At Brava and Anglante, where he thought
That in those sweet delights which never cloy
The lovers were now dallying, he sought
Them both, in vain; then, hoping to employ
A ruse whereby Orlando might be caught,
To Paris he returns, to lie in wait,
For surely soon the Count must pass the gate.

12

Rinaldo tarries there a day or two.
Orlando does not come, so he decides
To visit both his strongholds, and anew
Sets off, in hope of hearing where he hides.
From early morning until night, all through
The burning midday heat, Rinaldo rides,
And back and forth, whether by moon or sun;
Two hundred times he travels, not just one.

13

But the old Adversary who caused Eve
To lift her hand towards forbidden fruit
His envious eyes now raises to perceive
Rinaldo's absence on his vain pursuit.
Seeing the harassment he can now give
To the whole Christian army, by astute
Manoeuvring he brings upon the scene
The greatest knights of all the Saracen.

14

First, in Gradasso's heart, and Sacripant's
(Companions since they fled Atlante's spell),
An eagerness the Prince of Darkness plants
To help the armies of the Infidel,
To add their valour to King Agramant's,
And Charles's stubborn contumacy quell;
And as along an unknown route they went
A demon to escort them Satan sent.

15

And then another demon he despatched
To urge on Rodomont and Mandricard
Where Malagigi's evil sprite, well matched
With this, drove Doralice's horse so hard.
And even further mischief Satan hatched
By sending yet another to retard
Marfisa and Ruggiero; they with less,
The other pair with greater, speed progress.

16

And so these two, delayed by half an hour,
Arrived in Paris after the first pair,
For the black Angel, who desired to shower
Disasters on the Christians, was aware
How much it would reduce the pagans' power
If now the quarrel of the destrier
Should be renewed, as it was sure to be
If they reached Paris simultaneously.

17

The previous four now all together came
Where both encampments they could see with ease,
The victors and the vanquished, and could name
The banners as they fluttered in the breeze.
First they conferred a little and the same
Conclusion reached after their colloquies:
They would defy King Charles, and help their liege,
King Agramante, to resist the siege.

18

In close formation on they ride again,
Making for where the Christian forces are.
Shouting their slogans, 'Africa!' and 'Spain!',
They show in full how pagans can make war.
'To arms!' 'To arms!' re-echoes clear and plain,
But not before the weapons clash and jar;
And of the rear-guard many are now dead,
While in confusion many more are fled.

19

The Christian army, taken by surprise,
Is at a loss to understand the cause.
It is the Swiss or Gascons, some surmise,
Those fiery troops which such commotion cause;
But most of them the tumult mystifies.
With drum or clarion, the captains cause
The nations to assemble, and a din
And clamour as of battle now begin.

20

The mighty Emperor is fully-armed,
Save for his head; his paladins stand nigh.
What has occurred, he asks, what has alarmed
The retroguard, where have they fled, and why?
Most of the fugitives are sorely harmed.
Angrily halting some as they run by,
He sees blood pouring from a head or throat,
Or faces slashed, or hands from forearms cut.

21

And even now he has not seen the worst,
For farther on, in a vermilion lake,
He finds more soldiers gruesomely immersed
In their own blood; no sorcerer could wake,
No doctor cure, them now; the limbs dispersed,
The headless trunks, a scene of horror make,
As from the first encampments to the last
Among the many dead King Charles goes past.

22

Wherever the small company of four
Had gone, deserving of eternal fame,
In a long line a flood was seen to pour,
An unforgettable and gory stream.
The cruel slaughter filled the Emperor
With rage, astonishment and bitter shame;
Like one whose house a thunderbolt has struck,
Along the trail of death he goes to look.

23

The four have not yet reached King Agramant's
Entrenchments, when along another way
Ruggiero and Marfisa now advance
To help to raise the siege that very day.
The splendid pair, first casting round their glance
At the terrain, select without delay
The quickest route by which to reach their lord,
Behind stockades defended and immured.

24

As when the slow-match of a fuse is lit,
So that the flame, like a lascivious tongue,
So fast the eye can scarcely follow it,
Runs licking the black powder all along
The trench, when roar on roar the hills emit,
As rocks or broken walls on high are flung,
So, when Ruggiero and Marfisa came,
Their fiery speed and impact were the same.

25

The heads of Christians, lengthwise and across,
They now begin to split; shoulders are cleft
And arms are lopped, while wholly at a loss
The troops attempt to scatter, right and left.
If you have seen a tempest tear and toss
Through hill or vale, leaving one side bereft
Of trees, you can imagine how these two
Cut down the ranks and hacked a passage through.

26

Many who had escaped in the first race
Were thanking God Who gave them legs and feet
Which let them scurry off at such a pace;
But being so unlucky as to meet
Ruggiero and Marfisa face to face
They saw that they must now concede defeat
And that a man, whether he stay or flee,
Cannot evade his hour of destiny:

27

Escaping from one danger, he is caught
By yet another and in flesh and bones
He finds that he must pay the final scot.
Just so a vixen with her little ones
Falls victim to the wily huntsman's plot
When, driven from her den by sticks and stones,
And fire and smoke, she creeps forth above ground,
And there is pounced on by the waiting hound.

28

Marfisa and Ruggiero now bring aid
To the encampment of the Saracen;
With eyes upturned to Heaven, thanks are made
To God in fervent prayers by grateful men.
No longer of the paladins afraid,
The meanest now would challenge ten times ten.
It is concluded that without delay
The field once more shall flow with blood that day.

29

Trumpets and Moorish drums and clarions
Fill heaven with their formidable sound
And, in the breeze, banners and gonfalons
Flutter and flap as armies rally round.
Meanwhile each of King Charles's captains dons
His helmet and prepares to stand his ground,
As with the French their allies mustered are
In close formation for a deadly war.

30

The strength of Rodomont the terrible,
The strength of Mandricard the furious,
Of King Gradasso, famed in chronicle,
Of good Ruggiero, bold and valorous,
Of Sacripant whom few can parallel,
And of Marfisa, brave and marvellous,
So menace Charles that on the saints he calls,
Withdrawing soon within the city walls.

31

The daring of these knights and of the maid,
Their skill and prowess, were of such a kind
That their description cannot be essayed
Nor yet imagined be by any mind;
And so, my lord, it scarcely need be said
How many deaths to them could be assigned
That day; beside them battled too
A Moorish squadron, led by Ferraù.

32

Many who fled had perished in the Seine:
The bridge was narrow, they too many were.
(The wings of Icarus were needed then.)
The paladins were taken prisoner.
Uggiero and the marquess of Vienne
Alone evaded capture: Oliver
Returned to Paris, his right shoulder hit;
Uggiero too went back, his head near split.

33

If like Rinaldo, like Orlando too,
Sweet Fiordiligi's love had stayed away,
Charles would have left the citadel, if through
The fire he had escaped alive that day;
But Brandimarte did what he could do,
Then let the pagan frenzy have its way.
So Fortune smiled on Saracen and Moor,
Who once again besieged the Emperor.

34

The cries of widows, of the old and blind,
Of orphaned children who their loss lament,
Rise from the murky regions of mankind
To the clear air beyond the firmament
Where Michael, turning his angelic mind
To earth once more, sees the predicament
Of the Believers and the fate of those
Who scattered lie, a prey to wolves and crows.

35

The blessèd Angel blushed bright red, ashamed
To have so ill Almighty God obeyed.
Dame Discord, the perfidious, he blamed.
By her he had been tricked, by her betrayed.
For sowing seeds of conflict she was famed.
This was the reason why he sought her aid
To split the pagans, but the contrary
Had been achieved, as anyone could see.

36

As when a loyal servant, with more love
Than sense endowed, commits some oversight
In an affair he should hold dear above
His life and soul, guarding it day and night,
And, ere his lord see what he's guilty of,
Attempts in haste to put the matter right,
So Michael would not rise to God until
This obligation he should first fulfil.

37

But to the monastery, where he has seen
Dame Discord often, Michael now takes wing,
And in the chapter-house, where she has been,
He comes on an election in full swing.
There she sits smiling gaily on the scene,
As at each other's heads the friars fling
Their breviaries; the Angel grasps her hair
And without mercy kicks and punches her.

38

Then on her head, her arms, her back, he breaks
The handle of a cross. Dame Discord calls
For mercy, and a piteous clamour makes,
As to embrace his knees she humbly crawls.
Michael does not release her yet but takes
Her to the pagan camp and there installs
Her, saying: 'Worse than this you may expect
If once again your duties you neglect.'

39

Though broken-backed and buffeted with pain,
Fearing another battering as cruel
(For well she knows, if she's remiss again,
Of Michael's wrath she'll suffer a renewal),
She runs to fetch her bellows, not in vain:
To flames already kindled adding fuel,
And lighting others, soon Dame Discord starts
A fire of rage rising from many hearts.

40

The flame in three opponents burns so hot –
Ruggiero, Mandricard and Rodomont –
They go before their king, since they are not
Now pressed by Charlemagne on any front
(For pagans the advantage have now got);
They tell their quarrels, making known the fount
From which they sprang, and ask their king to say
Which two of them shall duel first that day.

41

The brave Marfisa also puts her case:
She must conclude the fight begun by her
When Mandricard provoked her to her face,
Not knowing what her skill and prowess were;
And to no other pair will she yield place,
Not by one day, one hour, will she defer,
But vehemently pleads to be the first
To challenge Mandricard to do his worst.

42

But Rodomonte on his claim no less
Insists: he must conclude the fight
Which, while the Africans were in distress,
He has deferred till now, as he thought right.
Ruggiero, with an equal readiness,
Declares he can no longer bear the sight
Of Rodomonte mounted on his steed,
Nor can he wait to punish his misdeed.

43

The Tartar even further tangles things,
Saying Ruggiero has no right to bear
The Trojan eagle with the silver wings.
In him the flames of wrath so fiercely flare
And for revenge so keen a zest he brings
That all three quarrels in one fight he'd dare
To settle, if the other knights agreed,
And they no less, if thus their king decreed.

44

As best he can King Agramant essays
A reconciliation to induce;
But when he finds that, deaf to all he says,
They will consider neither peace nor truce,
How best to fix the order, he now weighs,
In this, at least, agreement to produce;
And he decides that to untie this knot
They must establish precedence by lot.

45

Taking four slips of paper, the king wrote
First 'Mandricardo–Rodomont' on one;
'Ruggiero–Mandricardo', he next put;
'Ruggiero–Rodomonte', he went on;
'Marfisa–Mandricard' was the fourth note,
And to the goddess Chance, when this was done,
He left the choice; and she that day decreed
That Rodomont and Mandricard should lead.

46

The Tartar with Ruggiero next is cast,
Who then with Rodomont must battle third.
The Tartar and Marfisa will fight last.
By this to discontent Marfisa's stirred.
Ruggiero's spirits are no less downcast.
He knows the first will fight on undeterred
Till nothing more of either one remain
To fight with him, or her, for both are slain.

47

Not far from Paris was an open space,
About a mile, or somewhat less, all round.
A lofty stone embankment ringed the place,
As in an ancient theatre is found.
Here once a castle stood, of which no trace
Remained, razed by besiegers to the ground.
One similar along the road between
Borgo and Parma may today be seen.

48

In this enclosure they prepare the lists,
First marking out a rectangle with stakes,
Such as is needed for the coming tests,
While at each end a spacious portal makes
The scene complete, as chivalry insists.
King Agramante his decision takes,
Choosing the day the jousting shall commence.
Pavilions are now set beyond the fence.

49

In the pavilion on the western side
Stands Rodomonte; on his giant frame
His ancient armour, made of dragon's hide,
Is fastened by two warriors of fame,
King Sacripant and Ferraù; with pride
Gradasso and Falsirone do the same
For Mandricardo, fixing on his limbs
The venerable arms which Homer hymns.

50

Sitting upon a wide and lofty seat
Are the two kings of Africa and Spain,
Also King Stordilan with the élite
Of pagandom; lucky are those who gain,
From tops of trees or from some high retreat,
An unimpeded view of the terrain.
Great was the press, and great the crowd which swayed,
Packed close together, round the vast stockade.

51

Attendant on the queen of all Castile
Were many a princess and many a queen,
From Aragon, Granada and Seville,
From where the marks of Hercules are seen.
There Doralice too gazes her fill,
Dressed in rich garments coloured red and green.
The latter hue was vivid, fresh and bright,
The red was pale and faded, almost white.

52

Marfisa, in a warrior's jerkin clad,
As well became her, seemed an Amazon,
Like Queen Hippolyta and those she led
In regions watered by the Thermodon.
The herald of King Agramante had
By now arrived; the coat which he had on
Displayed his monarch's arms, and he decreed
No favour must be shown by word or deed.

53

Impatiently the tight-packed throng awaits
The fight; it finds these preparations slow
And for delay the warriors berates.
A clamour rises suddenly and seems to grow
Where Mandricard, by one of the two gates,
Has his pavilion; this noise, you must know,
My lord, is a contention which breaks out
Between two disputants who rail and shout.

54

Gradasso, having armed the Tartar king
With his own hand, save only for his sword,
This splendid weapon was about to bring,
When on the pommel he perceived a word –
DURINDANA – likewise the quartering
Which once Almonte bore: as you have heard,
Both trophies were surrendered to the Count
Orlando, then a boy in Aspromont.

55

Seeing the sword, Gradasso had no doubt
This was the weapon which Orlando won.
To claim it back Gradasso had set out
With a great fleet; and no more splendid one
Had ever left the East; he put to rout
The kingdom of Castile; he had then gone
To France and was victorious; and now
The Tartar has it and he knows not how.

56

He asked if by accord or by onslaught
He took it from the Count, and where and when;
And Mandricard replied that he had fought
A mighty battle for the sword and then
Orlando had feigned madness. 'Thus he sought
To hide his apprehension, for, to gain
His weapon Durindana, he well knew
The combat I would ceaselessly pursue.'

57

Just as the beaver, he went on to say,
Which sees the hunter drawing near, and knows
The reason, rips its genitals away,
A similar resource Orlando chose,
And left his sword. Gradasso did not stay
To hear the story out. 'I don't propose',
He said, 'to yield to you or anyone
What I by such expense have rightly won.

58

'Another weapon let your squires provide.
Orlando's I here claim. I give my word,
Wherever he may wander, far and wide,
Sane or demented, this is now my sword.
Since no one to your claim has testified,
This weapon you illicitly procured.
I move a suit against you, and my blade
The prosecution's argument will aid.

59

'If you would wield this weapon in your fight
With Rodomonte, win it first from me.
This is a custom, known to every knight,
Long honoured in the code of chivalry.'
'There is no sweeter sound, no sweeter sight',
Proudly replied the king of Tartary,
'Than the defiance of a challenger,
So ask if Rodomonte will defer.

60

'I'll fight you first, if he will give consent.
His fight with me can move to second place;
And have no doubt concerning my intent:
All who defy me I will turn and face.'
Ruggiero shouted: 'I am not content:
The order fixed by lot you now erase.
Either the Sarzan monarch first must be,
Or his allotted place must yield to me.

61

'For, if Gradasso's argument prevails
(That arms, ere they are used, must first be won),
The white-winged bird you bear, this rule assails:
First prove your right to it, as I have done.
But if this rule a further change entails,
I'll not revoke what was agreed upon:
In battle-order I am number two,
If Rodomonte duels first with you.

62

'If you in part disturb the plan agreed,
I will disturb it totally, I vow.
The eagle you display I'll not concede
Unless you fight me for it here and now.'
'If both of you were Mars himself, indeed,'
The Tartar said, with fury on his brow,
'You could not either of you make me yield
Either my Durindana or my shield.'

63

He leapt, enraged, to where Gradasso stood.
The blow he struck him was so terrible
Gradasso's hand was numbed, as though of wood,
And from its lifeless grasp the weapon fell.
He little dreamt that such mad frenzy would
To such an act the Tartar king impel.
Taken thus unawares and off his guard,
He saw, dismayed, that he had lost his sword.

64

Vexed and discountenanced, with wrath and shame,
The colour mounts like fire to his face,
So violent he seems to shoot forth flame,
The more so that in such a public place
Dishonour should occur to harm his name.
Thirsting for vengeance, he steps back a pace
And draws his scimitar, but, nothing loath,
The Tartar is prepared to fight them both:

65

'Come forth together, both of you combined.
Let Rodomonte come and make a third.
All Africa, all Spain and all mankind
To battle I will challenge, undeterred.'
The Tartar, with a daring unconfined,
Assumed the shield which bore the Trojan bird,
And Durindana wielded without fear,
Defying both Gradasso and Ruggier.

66

'Leave me to settle him,' Gradasso said;
'For madness such as his I know a cure.'
'By God! I mean to deal with him instead,'
Ruggiero cried, 'for I will not endure
To lose my place and let you get ahead.'
'You must draw back!' Gradasso said; 'No, *you're*
The one who must withdraw!' Ruggiero cried,
While Mandricardo both of them defied.

67

To put an end to the three-cornered fray,
Many unwisely rushed upon the scene,
Who quickly learned the price they had to pay:
Their interference cost them their own skin.
Nor had the world entire sufficed that day,
Had not King Agramante entered in,
With King Marsilio, at sight of whom
The combatants respectfully made room.

68

Troiano's son enquired the reason why
So fierce and strange a fight had broken out;
And when he heard, he set himself to try
With all his tact to bring a truce about,
Asking Gradasso if he would comply
With his request, and the conventions flout:
Might not the Tartar king in his affray
With Rodomonte use the sword that day?

69

And while King Agramante reasoned first
With one and then the other litigant,
In the tent opposite, a quarrel burst
Involving Rodomont and Sacripant;
The latter, with the son of the accurst
Lanfusa, attended to the combatant,
On whom they fastened, as I said before,
The arms of Nimrod, his progenitor.

70

They had now moved to where the tethered horse
Stood lathering its costly bit with foam.
I speak of good Frontino here, of course,
For loss of which Ruggiero had become
So furious, no fury has been worse.
The monarch of Circassia, on whom
The Sarzan king, as on a squire, relied,
The steed's accoutrements now verified.

71

Looking more closely at the destrier,
Noting its markings and its agile frame,
He knew beyond a doubt, he was quite clear,
This was his charger, once known by the name
Of Frontalatte, which he held so dear,
And had defended against all who came;
When it was stolen he would only go
On foot, the loss of it had grieved him so.

72

Brunello stole it from him in Cathay
When from Angelica he stole as well
The magic ring; he also took away
Orlando's horse and horn, as you heard tell,
Likewise Marfisa's sword; and then one day
In Africa, where he returned to dwell,
He gave Ruggiero both the steeds, and one
Was ever after as Frontino known.

73

When he was sure there could be no mistake,
To Rodomonte Sacripant declared,
'Sir, what I say, as gospel you must take:
This is my destrier which someone dared
To steal, and to this witnesses could speak.
Since they are far away, I am prepared,
If anyone should challenge me today,
To prove by arms the truth of what I say.

74

'In token of the friendship you have shown
In our few days together, I'm content
To let you have this charger now on loan,
Which I can see you need for this event,
But on the understanding', he went on,
'That he is mine, else I will not consent.
If you maintain this horse is yours by right,
You must first win him from me in fair fight.'

75

No prouder warrior this era knows
Than Rodomonte; I would even say
That of the ancient heroes few were those
Who could be matched with him in every way.
He answers: 'You are wrong if you suppose
That I another knight would not repay
In the same coin, since anyone but you
I'd gladly give a well-earned lesson to.

76

'But for the sake of our companionship,
Newly sprung up between us, as you said,
I'll be content with giving you this tip:
Do not rush in where angels fear to tread.
Let me first smite the Tartar on the hip.
You will then say, if I am not misled,
"Such an unparalleled display of force
I cannot hope to rival: keep the horse."'

77

'Discourtesy to you is courtesy,'
Said Sacripante, filled with wrath and rage,
'But loud and clear and unmistakably
I'll tell you once again: if you engage
To claim this charger which belongs to me,
As long as I can wield this sword, I'll wage
Unceasing combat, or with tooth and nail
I will defend it if naught else avail.'

78

From this to formal challenges they passed,
To shouts and menaces, until they moved
To combat, than which never straw so fast
Was kindled nor so quick in burning proved.
The difference between the two was vast,
For Rodomont was armed as it behoved,
But Sacripant had neither plate nor mail;
Yet with his weapon he seemed covered well.

79

The Sarzan's prowess and ferocity
(Although no mightier warrior was born)
Are matched by Sacripant's agility.
No water-wheel was ever seen to turn
With greater or with like rapidity
The upper millstone when it grinds the corn,
As Sacripante whirls and spins with speed
Now here, now there, wherever he sees need.

80

But Ferraù and Serpentino, both
Courageous, drew their swords and rushed between,
Followed by King Grandonio, nothing loath,
And Isolier; and other Moors were seen
Who tried to stem the current of such wrath.
This was the noise and clamour which had been
The origin of such astonishment
To those who heard it in the other tent.

81

Someone conveyed the news to Agramant,
Assuring him that what was said was true:
That bitter combat between Sacripant
And Rodomont had broken out, these two
In claiming the same horse being adamant;
The king, dismayed at so much discord, to
Marsilio said: 'See that no worse occurs
While I resolve this matter of the horse.'

82

When Rodomonte sees his lord appear,
He instantly withdraws and checks his pride;
With equal homage, seeing him draw near,
From battle Sacripante turns aside.
King Agramante first demands to hear,
In awesome majesty and tones which chide,
The meaning of their wrath; when all is plain
He tries to reconcile them, but in vain.

83

King Sacripant refuses to allow
The king of Sarza to retain the steed,
Unless he comes with many a humble bow
To beg the loan of it to meet his need;
But Rodomont, who never bends his brow,
His right to ride the horse will not concede,
And he replies: 'Not you, nor Heaven above
My steadfast will in this regard could move.'

84

What right has Sacripante to the horse:
How did he come to lose it, where and why?
The truth, as it comes out, grows worse and worse
And Sacripante blushes to reply.
By guile the steed was taken, not by force;
As he sat lost in thought, a thief came by
Who propped the saddle on four blocks of wood
And stole the steed beneath him where it stood.

85

Hearing the shouts, Marfisa also came.
As soon as she had heard the story through,
Her countenance concerned and grave became.
Recalling how she lost her sword, she knew
This destrier must be the very same
Which seemed equipped with wings, so fast it flew;
Who Sacripant must be, she realized,
Whom hitherto she had not recognized.

86

Those who stood by had heard Brunello boast
Of his manoeuvre more than once; they turned
To point him out among the assembled host,
Where by all present he could be discerned.
Marfisa, her suspicions roused, now lost
No time: by asking bystanders she learned
Beyond all doubt, by general accord,
Brunello was the thief who stole her sword.

87

And for this deed the thieving miscreant,
Who well deserved a noose around his neck,
King of Tangier was crowned by Agramant.
Marfisa, in whose view for such a trick
A kingdom was a strange reward to grant,
Determined there and then revenge to seek,
For at his hands not only had she borne
Deceit and theft, but mockery and scorn.

88

Her squire now fixed her helmet on her head,
For she was fully-armed except for that,
As was her custom, for she had been bred
For war, and seldom could be seen in what
Young women like to wear; thus helmeted,
She strode at once to where Brunello sat
To watch the jousting on a lofty seat
Among the foremost ranks of the élite.

89

Clutching him by the breast, without a pause
She lifted up the villain there and then,
As sometimes in its sharp, rapacious claws
An eagle carries off a farmyard hen;
And where the king enquires into the cause
Of discord which divides the Saracen,
She carries him; Brunello knows that he
Can only weep and beg for clemency.

90

Above the pandemonium with which
The jousting-ground was filled from side to side,
Was heard Brunello's penetrating screech
As now for mercy, now for help he cried.
His alternating shrieks the welkin reach
And crowds come running up from far and wide.
Marfisa stands before Troiano's son
And proudly claims that justice shall be done:

91

'This thief, your vassal, let me now repay
As he deserves: I'll hang him by the throat
With my own hands, for on the very day
He stole that horse (and I went in pursuit),
He also stole my trusty sword away.
If anyone my story should refute,
Let him come forward: I will demonstrate
That he is lying and the truth I state.

92

'But since by someone it may be alleged
That until now this challenge I put off
When the most famous warriors, engaged
In other quarrels, can make no rebuff,
My word on this account is hereby pledged
To wait three days, if that is long enough;
If no one then prevents me in fair fight,
I'll hang this villain for the birds' delight.

93

'Three leagues away, beside a little wood,
A lofty tower rises, plain to see.
There I propose to make my promise good.
One serving-woman I will take with me,
And one young page to squire me as he should.
Whoever dares to set this villain free
Will find me there'; thus having said her say,
Awaiting no reply, she went her way.

94

First on her charger's neck she drapes the thief,
Holding him by his grizzled locks the while.
Brunello weeps and bellows in his grief.
His shouts for help are heard for many a mile.
To Agramant it seems beyond belief
That he should be thus flouted in such style.
He's much put out, but knows not what to say,
Seeing Marfisa take Brunel away.

95

Not that King Agramante now esteems
Or loves Brunello; there are days indeed
When fit for nothing but the noose he seems,
As when he stole the ring; but by her deed
She now commits *lèse-majesté*, he deems.
He's tempted to pursue her at full speed
And seek revenge in person for the slight
He thinks he has received, with all his might.

96

But King Sobrino, who was standing near,
Dissuaded him from such an enterprise.
Not only was Marfisa not his peer,
And hence to challenge her would compromise
His royal status (though there was no fear
As to the outcome); it would be unwise
To risk the censure which he would invite
If she should press him long in a hard fight.

97

The honour would be small, the danger great,
In combat with this woman warrior;
Better to let Brunello share the fate
Which for such felons is the end in store;
And if to save him, he went on to state,
To flick one eyebrow would suffice, no more,
Far better to let justice take its course
And keep a steadfast gaze without remorse.

98

'Send someone to Marfisa to request
That you shall be the judge in this,' he said,
'And promise that the hangman's rope will twist
About Brunello's neck till he is dead.
If in her obstinacy she persist,
Then let Marfisa deal with him instead.
Above all, do not lose her as a friend,
But let all villains meet with such an end.'

99

King Agramante readily paid heed
To King Sobrino's wise and shrewd advice.
He let Marfisa gallop off at speed.
To follow her would cost too high a price;
No challenger should go, no one should plead.
And so (God knows at what a sacrifice!),
To deal with urgent matters he now planned,
By quelling bitter quarrels close at hand.

100

At this Dame Discord laughs with frenzied glee.
Little has she to fear of peace and truce.
Now here, now there, diffusing enmity
She runs until no more can she produce.
Pride also skips and leaps for joy as she
Adds kindling to the fury, letting loose
So loud a shriek, it can be heard on high
And Michael takes it for a victor's cry.

101

All Paris trembled and the river Seine
Was swollen, as the fearful shouting spread
And, echoing and echoing again,
Drove woodland creatures from their dens in dread.
The Alps and the Cévennes had heard it plain.
From Blaye to Arles, to Rouen it soon sped.
To Rhône, Saône, Rhine, Garonne it caused unrest,
While mothers clasped their offspring to their breast.

102

There are five cavaliers whose minds are set
On fighting first, although the battle-list
Presents a tangled skein more intricate
Than all Apollo's wisdom could untwist.
King Agramante, to untie the net,
Begins with two who, as you know, persist
As claimants to fair Doralice's hand,
One from the East, and one from his own land.

103

In an attempt to terminate this pother,
King Agramante now resolves to go
First to the one and, second, to the other,
And, more than once returning to and fro,
Not only as their king, but like a brother,
Tries to remind them both of all they owe;
But both are deaf and both refuse to budge,
For both the lady each to each begrudge.

104

To this decision finally he came:
To ask if the two rivals were content
That Doralice one of them should name
To whom she would prefer to give consent;
And ever afterwards to play the game,
Accept her choice, whichever way it went,
And let the matter rest; this compromise
Pleases them both, for both expect the prize.

105

The king of Sarza loved her long before
The Tartar king appeared upon the scene
And many favours she bestowed of yore,
Though *comme il faut* the maid had always been;
And thus it was that Rodomont was sure
That he the fair princess was bound to win.
In this opinion he was not alone,
For all the Moors believed it, every one.

106

They knew what Rodomonte had achieved
For her, in jousts and tournaments and war,
And Mandricard was foolish, they believed,
In odds as long as these to trust so far;
But he knew what was given and received
From set of sun until the morning star.
He knew for certain how he stood with her
And laughed to think how wrong the others were.

107

So the two aspirants to married bliss,
To seal the pact, join loyal palm to palm,
And, kneeling, place them, as the custom is,
Between the monarch's hands; without a qualm
They go to hear their lady's verdict; this
She gives, with downcast eyes, but with a calm
Assurance: Mandricardo is her choice.
No cause has Rodomonte to rejoice.

108

Astonishment is seen on every face.
When Rodomonte raises his bowed head,
Anger and scorn his blush of shame replace.
The sentence was unjust and false, he said.
Seizing his sword, 'With this let me erase,'
He cried for all to hear, 'alive or dead,
The wayward judgement of a woman's mind,
Ever to do what she should not, inclined.'

109

'Let it be as you wish; you'll come off worst!'
The Tartar monarch answered, filled with scorn;
But many miles of sea must be traversed
Before that vessel into port is borne.
King Agramante will not be coerced,
Nor from his fixed refusal will he turn.
No challenge is permitted, that is certain.
On the dispute he firmly drops the curtain.

110

And when the king of Sarza with dismay
Sees he is doubly scorned, both by his king
And by his lady, in one single day,
He has no further arguments to bring,
He has no longer any wish to stay;
And for his simple needs commissioning
Two servants only, of his many men,
He leaves the purlieus of the Saracen.

111

As when a bull, defeated by a young
Victorious male, the heifer must now yield,
And, wounded, he departs to roam among
The woods or streams or sands, away from field
And pasture, and unceasingly gives tongue,
With amorous bellows filling down and weald,
So Rodomonte, stricken by the grief
Of his dismissal, could find no relief.

112

Ruggiero, to regain his destrier
(And for this aim he'd put his armour on)
Set out to follow Rodomonte where
He rode away, but not far had he gone
When he remembered he must now defer
This combat and begin instead the one
Which Mandricard and he were due to fight,
Before Gradasso could usurp his right.

113

To see the Sarzan take his horse away
Before his eyes and yet to be thus tied,
On his proud spirit cannot fail to weigh;
But Sacripante, not disqualified
By obligation in some other fray
Such as now makes Ruggiero turn aside,
In this imbroglio an opponent lacks
And gallops after Rodomonte's tracks.

114

He would have caught him too, had it not been
That on the way a strange event occurred:
A woman who had fallen in the Seine,
Whose cries for help as he rode by he heard,
Kept him for long so busy on the scene,
When he was free to go the trail was blurred.
For her survival she had him to thank,
Since he jumped in and dragged her to the bank.

115

And when he wanted to remount his steed
He found the animal had wandered off,
Not waiting for him to complete his deed.
He sought him over smooth and over rough
Terrain, for he was difficult indeed
To catch, though Sacripant ran fast enough.
At last he caught him, but had lost the trail
And rode at random over hill and dale.

116

Where, how, he found the horse and at what cost,
How Sacripant was taken prisoner,
And how Frontino once again was lost,
I will not tell you now, for I prefer
To say how Rodomonte shook the dust
From off his heels, leaving his king and her
Whom once he loved, but now for whom he burned
With anger for devotion unreturned.

117

The air is incandescent with his sighs
Wherever the afflicted lover goes,
And Echo in compassion for his cries
In hollow caverns more responsive grows.
'Ah! Woman, wayward, wanton, full of lies,
Full of pretences, changes and vain shows,
The opposite of faith and truth and trust!
He who believes in her, his hopes are dust.

118

'Neither long service, nor my constant love,
Which had been proved a thousand times and more,
Sufficed to hold your heart which ceased to prove
As fond towards me as it was before.
The Tartar king I was the rival of –
You could not think me his inferior.
No cause I find, though I search near and far,
Save only this: that you a woman are.

119

'Ah, female sex, which God and Nature made
To be a curse and burden to mankind,
Man, who a heavy penalty has paid,
Without you joy and happiness could find!
As snakes and wolves and bears his peace invade,
As flies and wasps and hornets are designed
To sting, as tares and darnel choke the grain,
So women are created for his pain.

120

'Why did kind Nature not provide for man
To multiply without your help, as we
By grafting pear with sorb or apple can
Cross-fertilize by careful husbandry?
But moderation is not Nature's plan,
And if I think about it well, I see
That Nature nothing perfectly can do,
For Nature, that blind force, is female too.

121

'You have no reason to be puffed with pride
That we, your sons, are born of women's wombs:
The thorn-bush by the rose is beautified
And from a fetid plant a lily blooms.
All spite, all cruelty in you reside.
Your lack of faith, of love, of mercy, dooms
All men to sorrow, victims of your scorn;
As an unending torment you were born.'

122

Ranting and railing Rodomonte rode.
His diatribes against the sex, now low,
Now audible for miles, unceasing flowed.
Too far from reason he would sometimes go,
As from his soul he shed the heavy load
Of disillusionment; for well I know,
For every two or three who prove unkind,
A hundred women true and good you'll find.

123

Although of all the women I have loved
Not one was faithful, yet I do not say
On this account that all are faithless proved.
The blame upon my cruel fate I lay.
Many there are who cannot be reproved
And no rebuke deserve in any way.
But if, among a hundred, one there be
Who is unkind, her prey I'm sure to be.

124

And yet I hope to find before I die,
Or ere my greying hairs grow whiter still,
One who is true, on whom I can rely
To keep all promises, all vows fulfil.
If this should ever come to pass (and I,
In spite of all, am hopeful that it will),
Her name I will extol to heights sublime
And praise untiringly in prose and rhyme.

125

Against his king the Sarzan raged no less
Than against Doralice and, beyond
All reason blaming him for his distress,
In violation of his loyal bond,
He longed to see his realm a wilderness,
Struck by a cataclysm so profound
That every Moorish house in twain were cleft
And not one stone upon a stone were left;

126

And, driven penniless to beg his bread,
A ragged monarch he'd go wandering,
Having no place to lay his royal head;
But Rodomonte timely help would bring
And to the throne which he'd inherited,
And to his wealth, restore the rightful king,
To show him what a loyal friend he slurred
When he let Mandricardo be preferred.

127

And thus he tried to soothe his troubled breast,
This way and that distributing the blame;
Long days and nights he journeyed without rest,
Making the good Frontino almost lame.
One day he found himself, sad and depressed,
Beside the Saône, for it had been his aim
To travel towards a harbour in Provence
And there take ship for Africa at once.

128

The river was alive from shore to shore
With lighters and with heavy craft which plied,
Stacked high with victualling and many a store
Which to the army was to be supplied.
This area had fallen to the Moor;
From Paris to the pleasant countryside
Of Aiguesmortes, then west as far as Spain,
The Infidel had no more lands to gain.

129

The stores, when disembarked, were piled in stacks
On carts for transport where no ships could go,
Or else were slung across the patient backs
Of mules, whose footing was secure but slow.
Fat cattle, destined for the butcher's axe,
Explore the banks for pasture, to and fro,
And all along the Saône, from left to right,
Are inns which offer shelter for the night.

130

The night was coming on, the air was dank,
So Rodomonte thought he would put up
For shelter at an inn along the bank
Where a kind host invited him to sup.
His horse being stabled, he then ate and drank,
But not as Moslems should: for in his cup
Were poured choice wines from Greece and Corsica,
Which by Mahomet's law forbidden are.

131

The landlord with good food and beaming face
Did everything he could to please the knight.
His presence there did honour to the place.
He recognized his valour at first sight,
And yet it seemed to him there was a trace
Of sadness, as of one who was not quite
Himself, for not a single word he spoke
And never once his mournful silence broke.

132

Despite himself, his thoughts were once again
With Doralice; the kind host, among
The best in all of France (although from Spain
And Africa the enemy now throng
His homeland, he decided to remain
And serve his clients), sensing something wrong,
Called his relations, but not one would dare
To rouse the Saracen who brooded there.

133

The pagan cavalier was lost in thought
And where he was he scarcely realized.
His head was bowed and, if he raised it, naught
He saw and no one else's glance surprised.
After long silence, all his will he brought
To bear, it seemed, and like a man disguised
Who throws aside a mask, his brow he raised
And at the company intently gazed.

134

He broke the silence and with milder mien,
In gentle accents, as one mollified,
He asked the host and others on the scene
If they had wives, and when they had replied
That all of them were husbands, or had been,
He questioned each of them about his bride:
How far could she be trusted? Was she true?
Were faithful wives the rule, or were they few?

135

And everyone replied, except the host,
That they believed their wives were pure and chaste.
The landlord said: 'There's nothing to be lost
By speaking as you find: to each his taste,
I often say; but think what it will cost
If on such foolery your breath you waste:
Greenhorns you'll be considered by this knight,
Unless you show him proof in black and white.

136

'Because, just as the phoenix is unique,
And never more than one of them is found,
So of a faithful wife let no one speak,
For thin indeed they are upon the ground;
Yet every husband thinks he is that freak
Whose marriage by fidelity is crowned.
How is it possible that all can be
What in the whole world is a rarity?

137

'Once I was guilty of the same mistake,
For I believed most womenfolk were true.
A gentleman from Venice chanced to make
A journey hither; after one or two
Of his ripe stories I was wide awake
And ever afterwards the truth I knew.
Valerio, Francesco was his name
Which graven on my memory became.

138

'The tricks of mistresses or of sedate
Young wives, he had them at his finger-tips.
On top of that, the tales he could relate!
Ancient and new, they tumbled from his lips.
He quoted his own case to demonstrate
The truth of what he said; from all these tips
I learned that women are not chaste and pure,
Although the clever ones may seem demure.

139

'Among the many stories which he told
(And not a third of them could I recall)
The one I shall remember till I'm old
Is this, the most amazing of them all.
This is the one which I will now unfold;
And if, as I relate it, I should call
A spade a spade, I'm but a simple man.
I'll tell the tale as plainly as I can.'

140

The pagan answered, 'What could please me more
At present than to hear an anecdote
Which will confirm the view I held before
And chime with my opinion, note for note?
Sit facing me, that I may keep the score.
Your best attention to the tale devote.'
The story which he told to Rodomont
In my next canto I will now recount.

CANTO XXVIII

1

Ladies, and all who the fair sex esteem,
For God's sake do not listen to this tale
By which the landlord now prepares to shame
And slander you! Yet his intent will fail:
Of no importance is the praise or blame
Of vulgar folk, whose custom is to rail
Against their betters and to talk the most
On what they know the least of, like mine host.

2

Omit this canto for without it you
Will find the story will be no less clear.
Turpin includes it and so I do too,
But not for spite or rancour, have no fear.
I love you and have shown that this is true
A thousand times; witness to this can bear
The praise of you which in my verse occurs,
For I am, nor could other be than, yours.

3

Turn a few pages, three or four maybe,
And do not read a single verse or word;
But if you do, no more credulity
Than to a fairy-tale to this accord.
But, to return you to the company
Which sat attentive, anything but bored,
The host, complying with the knight's request,
Began the story he remembered best.

4

'Astolfo, of the Lombard kingdom heir,
After the monk, his elder brother, died,
Was in his youth so handsome and so fair
That few with him in beauty could have vied;
Not Zeuxis nor Apelles could compare
With all their art, however hard they tried.
Handsome he was and so by all was deemed,
But he more highly yet himself esteemed.

5

'His rank to him was of less consequence
In setting him apart from other men.
His armed supporters and his affluence
Which made him, among monarchs, sovereign,
Were less important than the difference
In face and form which put a gulf between
Himself and other mortals; praise for this
To him was happiness, to him was bliss.

6

'And at his court was one whom he loved well,
Fausto Latini, a Roman cavalier.
With him the vain young king would often dwell
Upon his looks, his shapely hand, his hair.
He asked his friend if ever he heard tell
Of any man who could be judged his peer.
The answer which he gave the king one day
Was not what he expected him to say:

7

'"From what I've heard and seen," Fausto replied,
"Your beauty has few equals here below.
Few, do I say? If I searched far and wide,
One only would there be, as I well know:
My brother, named Giocondo. Though beside
You, other men have nothing they can show,
His only can stand up to equal you,
Not only equal, but surpass you too."

8

'This seemed to the young king beyond belief.
Till then his victor's palm was uncontested.
He longed to see this splendid youth; in brief,
He thought his rival should be fully tested.
Lest his uncertainty should cause him grief,
A visit from Giocondo he requested.
Fausto agreed and said that he would try,
But doubted if he could and told him why:

9

'In truth, in all his life (his brother said)
Giocondo had not ventured outside Rome,
But a serene existence always led,
A peaceful and contented stay-at-home.
The property which he inherited
Had not increased, nor had it less become.
Pavia would have seemed as far to him
As someone else the river Don might deem.

10

'Even more difficult the task would be
To separate him from his wife, because
Giocondo loved her so devotedly
Her wishes and desires for him were laws.
But Fausto, to obey His Majesty,
Said he would go to Rome and plead his cause.
The eager king had overwhelmed him by
So many gifts he could not but comply.

11

'So he departs and after a few days
Arrives in Rome and, at his father's house,
The king's request before Giocondo lays.
To his persuasiveness his brother bows.
Even his wife can no objection raise.
Indeed she sits as quiet as a mouse
While Fausto shows what benefits might come
If she will let her husband go from Rome.

12

'Giocondo fixed the day they should depart
And servitors and horses chose meanwhile.
Garments were made for him, adorned with art,
For beauty is enhanced by clothes of style.
His wife and he are never seen apart.
Her eyes are wet with tears, she cannot smile.
She does not know, she says, how she can bear
To go on living if he is not near.

13

'To think of it, she feels on her left side
As if her heart were torn up by the root.
"My life," Giocondo said, and he too cried,
"Do not distress yourself; I will be but
Two months away, then home you'll see me ride.
If Fortune favours me upon my route,
I'll not prolong my absence by one day.
Not for one half his kingdom would I stay."

14

'Giocondo's wife will not be comforted.
He will be too long absent, she knows well.
If on return he does not find her dead,
It will be nothing but a miracle.
She weeps all day, she weeps all night in bed.
She cannot eat; unable to dispel
Her grief, Giocondo, by compassion stirred,
Begins to wish he had not pledged his word.

15

'His wife was wont to wear about her neck
A little cross which hung upon a chain,
Adorned with relics and with gems set thick.
A pilgrim left it to her father when,
Arriving at his gate infirm and sick,
He was received and tended in his pain;
And, dying, he bequeathed the precious gem
Which he had carried from Jerusalem.

16

'She gave this gem to him and begged that he
Would wear it now in memory of her.
This pleased him and he promised readily.
Not that he needed a remembrancer;
No absence, length of time, or destiny,
No matter what befell, could ever blur
Her image and as long as he drew breath
He would remember her, and after death.

17

'On the last night before he goes, they lie
So close together, in so sweet a swoon,
In her Giocondo's arms she thought she'd die,
Knowing that she must do without him soon.
She did not sleep, she scarcely winked an eye.
Her husband, just an hour before the sun,
Came to his last embrace and off he sped.
His wife, who saw him off, went back to bed.

18

'He had not gone above a mile or two
When he remembered he had left the chain
Beneath his pillow. What was he to do?
"Alas!" he pondered, "How can I explain?"
For no excuses could he find, he knew.
His wife would think, and this would give her pain,
That little value on her gift he set,
Since he so soon his promise could forget.

19

'When he rehearses an excuse, he knows
It will not seem acceptable or good,
No matter whom he sends, unless he goes
Himself in person, as he clearly should.
So, reining in his horse, its pace he slows.
"Ride on," he says, "and in the neighbourhood
Around Baccano wait a while for me.
I will return and join you speedily.

20

'"I must go back; there is no other way
To do what I must do; I promise I
Will catch you up again without delay."
He turned his horse around and said goodbye.
Taking no servitor, he rode away.
The sunlight had begun to gild the sky
When he arrived and, entering his house,
He went upstairs to find his sleeping spouse.

21

'He drew the curtains of the bed aside
And saw what he could never have believed:
His chaste and faithful wife, his loving bride,
Clasped in a young man's arms, no longer grieved.
And who he was the covers could not hide.
He knew at once by whom he was deceived:
A lad of humble stock who had been taught
To serve the household and was raised from naught.

22

'Giocondo's sorrow and astonishment
Are better understood at second hand
Than known by personal experiment
Such as this husband's destiny had planned.
By rage and fury stung, he fully meant
To draw his sword and slay them but, unmanned
By pity for her (for he loved her still
Despite himself) his wife he could not kill.

23

'And Love the tyrant (judge to what degree
Giocondo was his victim) would not let
Him even waken her for fear lest she,
On catching sight of him, might be upset
That he should find her in adultery.
Tiptoeing out, he left them sleeping yet.
Pricked to the quick by Love, he pricked his steed
And reached the inn just as his brother did.

24

'Giocondo's countenance seemed changed to all.
They saw his heart was heavy now, not gay;
But what had happened in the interval
When he rode back to Rome no one could say.
His journey was in truth equivocal,
For to Corneto he had gone that day.
Everyone guessed that love must be the cause,
Though far from knowing what his secret was.

25

'His brother thinks Giocondo must be sad
Because of having left his wife alone,
Whereas the contrary is true: she had
Too much companionship when he was gone.
With furrowed brow and pouting lip, to add
To their perplexity, he gazed upon
The ground; all Fausto's efforts are in vain.
The cause unknown, he cannot soothe his pain.

26

'Without intending to, he treats the sore
With the wrong ointment; as though with a knife,
Where he would heal, he opens it the more,
By talking to Giocondo of his wife.
Small wonder is it this will not restore
His brother to his former joy in life.
His face, once beautiful, is changed so much,
It cannot be regarded now as such.

27

'His lovely eyes are sunken in his head.
His nose looks longer in his wasted face.
As for the beauty contest, the less said
The better, since of his there is no trace.
Stricken with fever, he remains in bed
In Florence and Siena; any grace
Which can be seen to linger withers soon,
Like severed roses wilting in the sun.

28

'Though Fausto, filled with sorrow and regret,
Was grieved to see his brother so distressed,
He was more vexed and troubled even yet
To think how he had praised him as the best
Of all the handsome men he'd ever met,
And now he would appear the ugliest;
But on towards Pavia all the same
They made their way and to the city came.

29

'Unwilling to surprise the king, he wrote
Despatches to prepare him in advance
(Lest he should take him for an idiot),
Saying his brother by a sad mischance
To such a state of illness had been brought,
And so transfigured were his lineaments
(Affliction of the heart had been the cause)
That he no longer seemed the man he was.

30

'Giocondo's coming pleased the king no less
Than if he were a loved and long-lost friend,
For great indeed had been his eagerness.
Now all uncertainty is at an end.
He is relieved to find, he must confess,
His rival's looks cannot with his contend,
Although but for Giocondo's malady
He might superior or equal be.

31

'Astolfo bids his servitors prepare
For him a set of rooms, and every day
He visits him; and every hour elsewhere
He asks about his health; in every way
He tries to honour him and show his care,
But still Giocondo languishes, a prey
To sadness which no music and no sport
Can cure, nor spectacle of any sort.

32

'His rooms were at the top, beneath the roof,
And often to an attic he withdrew,
For he desired to keep himself aloof
And all delight and company eschew;
And there he brooded on the dismal proof
That she whom he so loved had proved untrue.
There he discovered (who would credit it?)
The remedy which made him well and fit.

33

'The shutters at one end were always shut.
Giocondo sees that at a certain height
A space divides the plaster from a strut
And through a gap there shines a ray of light.
Giocondo is surprised and, having put
His eye to it, is startled by a sight
So unexpected he can scarce believe
The truth of what his very eyes perceive.

34

'He sees a charming little chamber where
The queen invited only those whom she
Regarded the most intimate and dear
Of all her friends, and in strict secrecy.
Amazed, Giocondo sees a writhing pair:
A dwarf entangled with Her Majesty;
And so adroit the little man has been
That he has placed himself above the queen.

35

'Giocondo by this sight is stupefied.
Thinking he must be dreaming, he looks on;
And when he sees his senses have not lied,
As earlier he thought they must have done,
"This hunchback, ugliness personified,"
He says, "a royal paramour has won,
Whose husband is the greatest king and quite
The handsomest; what a base appetite!"

36

'His wife, whom he has so condemned because
She took a youthful lover to her bed,
Now seems to him to have transgressed no laws
Of Nature, for the blame should not be laid
On her, but on the female sex which was
Insatiable; if it could be said
That all of them with the same brush were tarred,
At least his wife a hunchbacked monster barred.

37

'On the next day, at the same time, he went
To the same place once more and squinnied through.
He saw the queen and dwarf again intent
On cuckolding the king; the next day too,
And the next after that, their time was spent
In toiling at this sportive task anew.
Strangest of all, the queen (at this he paled)
The monster's lack of love for her bewailed.

38

'One day he noticed she was much distressed.
The dwarf being absent, she had sent her maid
Not once, but twice, to call him to their nest.
He did not come, the queen grew more dismayed
And for his presence for a third time pressed.
"Ma'am, he is playing cards," the damsel said;
"Just at the moment he is down one *sou*.
Till he breaks even he'll not come to you."

39

'Giocondo's face at this strange sight became
What formerly it was, smooth-browed, serene,
Bright-eyed, plump-cheeked, and jocund like his name;
His tears had ceased, once more his smiles were seen.
A radiance enveloped all his frame.
A cherub from on high he might have been.
The king, his brother, all astonished seem
To see the change that has come over him.

40

'If the king longed to hear Giocondo say
What remedy had brought about this cure,
Giocondo for his part desired straightway
To tell the king, but wanted to be sure
The queen would have no penalty to pay,
Nor any retribution would endure.
No matter what he heard, he made him swear
Upon the host that he his wife would spare.

41

'He made him swear that nothing which he heard,
That nothing untoward which he might see,
However painfully he might be stirred,
However flagrant the lese majesty,
Would make him take revenge, and by no word
The evil-doer should suspect that he,
The king, has fully understood the case
And knows precisely what has taken place.

42

'Astolfo gave his word without delay.
All else, except the truth, he could believe.
Giocondo then at last began to say
What had occurred to make him pine and grieve
(Not he alone has cause to feel dismay,
For women do not scruple to deceive):
To find his wife in bed with a young lad
Giocondo's very life endangered had.

43

'But in this palace a strange sight he'd seen
And now his deep despondency was gone.
Though he had fallen in the eyes of men,
In such dishonour he was not alone.
He leads Astolfo to the gap between
The plaster and the strut; the dwarf is shown
Astride the stolen mare, which by his spurs,
And by *manège*, to high curvets he stirs.

44

'You will believe, I have no need to swear it,
This despicable sight the king appals.
If he does not go mad, then he comes near it.
He almost bangs his head against the walls.
His anger is so fierce he cannot bear it,
He almost shouts, but this the pact forestalls.
He stops his mouth, as well he knows he must,
For he has sworn upon the sacred host.

45

'"Brother, advise me; what am I to do?"
Astolfo asked, "for since I am denied
All vengeance by the vow I swore to you,
What satisfaction is there for my pride?"
"Let's leave our two ungrateful wives to stew
In their own juice," Giocondo then replied;
"Let's see how many are adulterous
And do to husbands what was done to us.

46

'"We are both young, our looks exceptional.
What woman could resist us or refuse?
If to such brutes so easily they fall,
We shall possess as many as we choose.
If youth and beauty are of no avail,
With money in our purse we cannot lose.
Do not return till you have claimed as booty
A thousand wives; regard this as your duty.

47

'"Absence from home, travel in foreign parts,
The company of women in strange lands,
Are said to be a cure for broken hearts."
The king approves the plan and he commands
Two squires to bear them company; he starts
In a few hours and into Fortune's hands
The Lombard monarch and the knight of Rome
Their future both commit as forth they roam.

48

'They travelled through all Italy and France,
In Flanders and in England, in disguise.
Wherever pretty faces drew their glance,
They met with none but courteous replies,
And were invited soon to join the dance.
They gave and they received; to their surprise
The money which they offered was returned;
By some they were invited, by none spurned.

49

'And staying one month here and two months there,
Not once but many times they verified
Their wives no worse than other women were.
However far they travelled, far and wide,
They found none chaste and faithful anywhere.
After a time the two of them decide
To call a halt; in every neighbourhood
Husbands are waiting, thirsting for their blood.

50

'Better to choose one girl who by her face
And form would please them both and who
Would satisfy them equally; no trace
Of jealousy need come between the two.
Astolfo asked, "If I must yield my place
Not to a stranger but, instead, to you,
Why should I mind? In all the female clan
There is not one contented with one man.

51

'"One woman, without overdoing it,
But guided by our natural desires,
Let us enjoy in common, as is fit.
There is no need to quarrel: as one tires,
The other can take over for a bit.
She will be pleased; a wife perhaps requires
Two husbands, and if this could be arranged
The present state of marriage might be changed."

52

'The king's suggestion greatly pleased the knight,
Who liked to hear him talking in this vein.
The project he accepted with delight.
So, searching every hill and every plain,
They found at last a girl who seemed just right,
The daughter of an innkeeper in Spain.
His inn was in Valencia, near the bay,
And she was fair and sweet in every way.

53

'She was a damsel in the bloom of spring,
Of tender age and scarcely yet mature.
The poverty which broods of children bring
Such trials caused her father to endure
That to persuade him proved an easy thing.
His daughter he is willing to procure
And even for a modest sum to sell,
Provided they will always treat her well.

54

'They took the girl and had their pleasure of her.
In amity alternately they came.
First one and then the other played the lover,
As bellows in succession fan the flame.
Now when this trio's tour of Spain is over,
To visit Africa is their next aim.
They leave Valencia and that same day,
Arriving at Jativa, there they stay.

55

'The partners go to see the palaces,
The monuments, the churches and the squares,
For visiting the sights their custom is
On all their travels, in between affairs.
Back at the inn, the girl of service is:
Horses are stabled, beds are made upstairs;
She helps the kitchen boys set out a meal
To meet requirements of the clientele.

56

'There was a lad in service at the inn
Who at her father's house was once employed;
And from his earliest years this boy had been
The girl's admirer and her love enjoyed.
They eyed each other furtively, unseen
By those around them; careful to avoid
The knowing looks of the inquisitive,
When anyone is there, no sign they give.

57

'But when an opportunity arose,
He asked the damsel where she went and why,
And which her lord and master was of those
Two travellers she was escorted by.
Fiammetta (that's her name) tells all she knows.
(The young man's name is Greco, by the by.)
"Alas," he said, "when once again I find you,
You must depart and leave me far behind you!

58

'"All my sweet plans to bitterness are turned,
For you belong to others, not to me.
From tips and meagre wages which I earned,
I skimped and hoarded with economy.
In all this time for you alone I yearned
And in Valencia I longed to be,
Where, when I'd settled down, as I had planned,
I'd go and ask your father for your hand."

59

'The damsel shrugged her shoulders and replied
That it was now a little late, she thought.
Greco shed tears (some in pretence) and sighed.
"Ah! do not thus torment me," he besought.
"You will regret your scorn when I have died.
Let my desire have rein, ere I am brought
To my last hour; each hour with you I spend
Will help to reconcile me to my end."

60

'Fiammetta said, moved to compassion now,
"Believe me, I desire it too, no less;
But when can we achieve it, where and how,
Surrounded as we are by witnesses?"
Greco replied, "Were but the love you vow
A third of that which I for you confess,
You would contrive to find this very night
Some hideaway where we could share delight."

61

'"How can I," said the girl, "when all night through
I lie between two men and either one
Is taking pleasure of me, as is due,
And when one stops, the other has begun?"
Greco replied, "This need not trouble you,
For I will show you how it can be done,
And, if you wish, I'll even set you free.
Surely you wish it, if you care for me?"

62

'Fiammetta thinks a moment and then says,
When everyone appears to be asleep
That night, if her instructions he obeys,
He'll find it will be possible to creep
Unnoticed up and down the passage-ways.
When all is quiet, Greco, step by step,
Reaches her bedroom door, as she has said,
And softly tiptoes in towards the bed.

63

'And from the moment when his footsteps pass
The threshold of the room, as if on eggs,
Or like a man afraid of breaking glass,
He shifts his weight on to alternate legs,
Which in long strides thus gingerly progress;
And, like a blind man groping as he begs,
He finds the bed, and where the sleepers' feet
Are, Greco goes head first beneath the sheet.

64

'And, sliding up between Fiammetta's thighs,
Who on her back in expectation lay,
He reached so high, he could no further rise.
Thus they remain embraced till break of day;
And all that night no other mount he tries,
But on this filly gallops all the way.
She goes so well he needs no other horse,
And she is quite content to stay the course.

65

'Giocondo and the king were well aware
Of the vibration in the bed that night,
But each of them fell victim to the snare,
Thinking the other was the favoured knight.
When Greco knew he could no further fare,
He slipped away as he had come; the light
Of day on the horizon could be seen
When the girl rose and let the servants in.

66

'The king said to Giocondo, jokingly,
"Brother, you must have ridden quite a way.
You'd better rest a while, it seems to me.
You were on horseback till the break of day."
Giocondo answered him as smilingly,
"You have just said what I was going to say.
You are the one who needs a good long rest.
All night you galloped and your quarry chased."

67

'Astolfo said, "I also, I admit,
Should have been glad to give my dog a run
If you had let me ride the horse a bit.
For my need, a brief canter would have done."
Giocondo answered, "Do as you think fit.
I am your vassal, be there pact or none.
Such innuendoes wasted are on me.
You could have said, «Now let the damsel be.»"

68

'And soon at one another's head they fling
Annoyed retorts and, moving on from jests,
They come to bitter taunts, and jibes which sting.
Such mockery their patience sorely tests.
They call Fiammetta, who alone can bring
Some light upon the truth which each contests
And each continues to reiterate.
She is not far; they have not long to wait.

69

'"Come here," Astolfo said, with a fierce look,
"We will not hurt you, neither he nor I:
Who was it who such lusty pleasure took
Of you, that no one else all night could try?"
Each thought the other would be brought to book
And proved a liar by the girl's reply.
Fiammetta throws herself upon her knees,
Imploring pardon; all is lost, she sees.

70

'She pleaded that her love for a young man
And her compassion for his tortured heart
Had led her, wrongly, to devise a plan
Which they had carried out with skill and art.
A true account of it she then began,
Telling no lies concerning any part.
She said how Greco hoped to trick them both
In such a way they'd never know the truth.

71

'Exchanging glances of astonishment,
Giocondo and Astolfo at once knew,
From their expressions it was evident,
No men were made such fools of as they two.
Then, bursting into equal merriment,
They throw their heads back, open-mouthed, and screw
Their eyes up; scarce a breath can either fetch
As on the bed both fall and helpless stretch.

72

'When they have laughed so much they can no more,
With streaming eyes, holding their sides for mirth,
They ask each other, "How can we make sure
Our wives are faithful, when no power on earth
Our rights in this one woman can secure?
We lay so close to her: what was the worth?
If husbands had as many eyes as hairs,
Their wives would still betray them unawares.

73

'"A thousand women we have had in bed,
And all were beautiful and to our taste,
And no resistance any of them made.
To sample any more would be a waste.
We have now proved the wives whom we have wed
Are no more lecherous and no less chaste:
Così fan tutte! let us now go home,
Enjoy our wives ourselves and cease to roam."

74

'Having said this, they sent Fiammetta first
To fetch her lover, and they blessed the pair
With many witnesses; they then disbursed
A dowry to her, generous and fair.
Then, mounting on their horses, they reversed
Their route, from west to east; quite soon they were
United with their wives, and from that day
No fault they found with them in any way.'

75

The landlord brought his story to a close,
And keen attention everyone had paid.
No word did Rodomonte interpose,
But sat in silence till an end was made.
'I well believe the tricks a woman knows
Are almost infinite,' at last he said,
'And not a thousandth part of female guile
Could all the scribes in all the world compile.'

76

One man, mature in years, endowed with sense
And better judgement, and with courage too,
Such slander of the female sex resents,
Which should be more respected, in his view.
'Mine host,' he says, 'in my experience
I have heard many things which are not true,
And many tales which no assent have won.
Of these your anecdote is surely one.

77

'And I put no reliance on the man
Who first related it, not if he is
St John Evangelist himself. I can
Assure you that his harsh remonstrances
Are based on hasty judgement, rather than
True knowledge; two or three adulteries,
And he condemns all women! When his mood
Has passed, he'll praise them all as chaste and good.

78

'And if he wants to utter praise instead,
The scope is wider than it is for blame.
A hundred women could be garlanded
For every one who puts the sex to shame.
Opprobrium should not on all be spread,
When countless others worthy are of fame.
If otherwise you heard Valerio speak,
You may be sure he did so out of pique.

79

'Tell me: is there one man among you all
Who has not been unfaithful to his wife,
Who would refuse an extra-marital
Adventure as a change from married life?
A man must be a liar or a fool
Who would deny such episodes are rife.
Temptation is the test of constancy
(I'm not referring here to harlotry).

80

'Do you know any man who would not leave
His wife, however lovely, to pursue
Another woman, hoping to receive
Her favours easily? What would he do
If some invited him, or were to give
Him presents, to make love to them? Both you
And I would do our best, I think, to please
Not only those whom we pursue, but these.

81

'Those wives who are unfaithful (there are some)
Have had good reason for it, I dare say:
Their husbands, tired of what there is at home,
After new joys and new adventures stray.
They should give love, if they expect love from
Their wives, and in the same degree and way.
If it were in my hands I would impose
A law which no man rightly could oppose.

82

'According to this law, no woman known
To be adulterous would punished be
By death unless in court it could be shown
Her spouse had never in adultery
Been found; if with another he had gone
(Once would suffice) his wife should be set free.
Did not Christ say: "Unto others do not do
What you would not they should do unto you"?

83

'Incontinence is the besetting sin
Of women, but not all of them succumb;
And in this contest easily we win,
For not one man in all the world you'll come
Upon who's continent; when we begin
To list our other failings, then by whom,
I ask, are worse deeds done, than blasphemy,
Murder or theft, arson or usury?'

84

The earnest, just old man examples brought,
In reinforcement of his arguments,
Of women who by neither deed nor thought
Allowed a stain upon their innocence.
But truth was not what Rodomonte sought.
By threatening him with cruel truculence
He cut the old man short – but could not alter
The views he held; in these he did not falter.

85

When he had vented all his scorn and spleen,
The pagan king withdrew and went to bed.
He tried in vain to sleep, outstretched between
The sheets until the dark of night was sped.
When the first ray of morning light was seen,
Still weary from the tears which he had shed,
He rose and took his leave; he planned that day
To take a river-boat and sail away.

86

For he respected, as a cavalier
Should always do, the splendid horse he rode,
Of which both Sacripante and Ruggier
Had been deprived; two days upon the road
Without a pause, exceeded what a destrier
Should do; and so upon a ship he stowed
The steed, to let him take a well-earned rest,
This means of transport being the speediest.

87

He bids the boatman launch the boat straightway
And ply the oars; the vessel, light and trim,
With little cargo, soon gets under way
And floats along the river Saône, down-stream.
The pagan's sorrow haunts him all that day.
On water and on land it follows him.
It lies in wait for him on prow and poop;
It sits behind his saddle on the croup.

88

It takes possession of his head and heart
And to all consolation bars access.
Like one besieged, he knows not where to start
To look for help; there can be no redress,
For now the citadel in every part,
By those who should be guarding it, no less!
Is overrun; and he whose duty is
To help, betrays him to his enemies.

89

He voyages all day and the next night,
And heavy is his heart with grief and woe.
He cannot banish from his mind the slight
He suffered from his lady or the blow
Inflicted by his king; and no respite,
No matter how he travels, does he know:
No water anywhere will quench the flame.
He changes place: his state remains the same.

90

And as a sick man on a fevered bed,
Who turns and tosses in his weariness,
Hoping to be relieved or comforted
By lying first on that side, now on this,
And by his hopes is every time misled,
And nothing gains from all his restlessness,
So Rodomonte, fleeing from his pain
On land, on water, finds he flees in vain.

91

Impatient now with life on board he grows.
Stepping ashore, he mounts his steed, and soon,
Passing Lyons, Vienne, Valence he goes
To see the famous bridge at Avignon.
This territory now obedience owes,
With that between Subalda and the Rhône,
To Agramante and the king of Spain
Who in possession unassailed remain.

92

Near Aiguesmortes a right-hand route he takes,
Meaning to reach Algiers without delay,
But near a stream he finds a town which makes
Him change his mind and there decide to stay.
Of wine and corn this region nothing lacks,
But all the occupants have fled away.
It lies between the sea and sunlit vales
Where corn in golden waves the eye regales.

93

He finds a little church upon a brow.
It has been newly built, he notices,
But stands neglected and abandoned now,
For to escape the recent ravages
The priests have fled; he sees it will allow
Retreat and quietude, advantages
He values; so his journey to Algiers
In favour of this dwelling he defers.

94

All thoughts of Africa being thus postponed,
He lodged his servants and his destrier
And stowed his baggage in the same compound.
Near by the city of Montpellier
And other cities, too, the hill-tops crowned.
The village, which is situated near
A teeming river, every means provides
Of food for anyone who there resides.

95

One day as he was brooding on his pain
(As for long hours his habit was to sit)
He saw approaching on a grassy plain
Along a little path bisecting it
A damsel with a bearded monk in train;
And on her face the woes of love were writ.
Behind them walked a charger on whose back
Was borne a heavy burden, draped in black.

96

Who the monk is and who the doleful maid
And who it is they bring, is surely clear:
The grieving Isabella, as I said,
Zerbino's body, which she held so dear,
Upon his horse devoutly thus conveyed.
When I last spoke of her I left her near
Provence; the venerable monk had just
Persuaded her in God to put her trust.

97

Although her face bewildered is and wan
And all her locks dishevelled, and her sighs
Follow unceasing on each other, one
By one, and tears as from two fountains rise,
And other signs of sorrow undergone
Are evident to a beholder's eyes,
So much of beauty can be seen as well,
That Love and the three Graces there might dwell.

98

As soon as Rodomonte saw the fair
Young damsel, all his blame and hatred of
The female sex had vanished in thin air
As nearer into view he saw her move.
Worthy she seems to him beyond compare
To be the object of his second love.
His former love no longer now survives,
As from a plank one nail another drives.

99

He went to meet her, and with gentle speech
And in his most ingratiating style
He asked her what her trouble was; to which
The maiden answered frankly, without guile,
That with God's help she had resolved to reach
Some holy convent, to escape the vile
And foolish world, and to perform good works.
At this the unbelieving pagan smirks.

100

He calls her aim mistaken and perverse;
Her resolution is, he knows, unsound.
No better than a miser, perhaps worse,
It is to hide such riches underground.
The miser makes no use of his own purse,
And by no other men can it be found.
Lions and bears and snakes must be confined,
Not lovely creatures, innocent and kind.

101

The monk had overheard the Saracen
And so, to guide the maid in the right way,
He took the helm for her a while and then
A lavish feast proceeded to display
Of spiritual food such as the souls of men
Require to fit them for the Judgement Day.
Of this repast the pagan will not eat,
Having no inclination for such meat.

102

He tried to interrupt the monk in vain.
The flow of eloquence he could not quell;
And finally his patience broke the rein.
Enraged, upon the holy man he fell.
But now my flow of words I must restrain
Lest I exceed what is acceptable.
I end this canto lest I too incur
The anger which loquacity can stir.

CANTO XXIX

1

How vacillating is the mind of man!
How rapid are the changes which it makes!
How quickly jettisoned is every plan!
How soon new love in angry hearts awakes!
Through Rodomonte's veins such fire there ran,
Such burning hatred of the female sex,
I wondered whether there were any ways
Of quenching, or of cooling, such a blaze.

2

Sweet ladies, for the evil which he spoke
Concerning you, I have been so irate
That I'll not pardon him till I invoke
All my best skill and fully demonstrate
In pen and ink to all who read my book
How wrong and how unfounded was his hate;
Far better were it to have bitten through
His tongue, or held it, than speak ill of you.

3

That he was ignorant will now be shown,
And stupid too for, venting his tirade,
He aimed it at all women, every one,
Without reserve, and no exception made.
And now by Isabella he's undone.
A glance from her: all his convictions fade.
Straightway he puts her in the other's place –
Her name unknown, and scarcely glimpsed her face.

4

And so, by this new passion pricked and stung,
He urges further reasoning, in vain,
For Isabella, though she is so young,
In serving God salvation hopes to gain.
The hermit, like a shield robust and strong,
Her firm resolve continues to sustain;
With many sound and valid arguments
He valorously comes to her defence.

5

And when the cruel pagan has endured
For long enough the hermit's bold defence,
When he has many times in vain assured
Him he can get him to his desert hence,
When even then he finds he is not cured
Of persevering in his insolence,
Enraged, the holy hermit's beard he snatches
And where he pulls, it comes away in batches.

6

His wrath and fury grew till, like a vice,
His hand had gripped the hermit's neck and throat;
Then round his head he whirled him once or twice
And flung him towards the sea; whether or not
The holy man then paid the final price,
Varies according to the anecdote:
In one, his body struck against a stone
And there, unrecognized, his parts were strewn.

7

Some have suggested in the interim
He fell into the sea, three miles away,
And that he died because he could not swim:
All he could do was clasp his hands and pray;
Still others that a saint assisted him:
A hand came out of Heaven to convey
The drowning man ashore; howe'er it be,
No more about him now you'll hear from me.

8

The cruel Rodomonte, having thus
Removed the importuning holy man,
Now with a countenance less mutinous
Turned to the grieving damsel and began
In words much favoured by the amorous:
She was his heart, his life and dearer than
Whatever he held dear, his fondest hope,
And other terms which gave his passion scope.

9

His manner was so gentle and controlled,
No vestige of coercion it betrayed;
His pride, so fierce and furious of old,
Was humbled by the beauty of the maid.
He knew he had the fruit within his hold,
Yet not one move to pluck it he essayed.
It seemed to him it might not taste so sweet
If as a gift she did not offer it.

10

And by such gentle means, by slow degrees
He hopes to bend the damsel to his will;
And, helpless in that lonely place, she sees
The cat will pounce upon the mouse, and kill.
Rather than suffer such indignities,
A death by burning seems less terrible.
She tries to think of some device or act
By which she can escape from him intact.

11

She is resolved by her own hand to die
Rather than yield to Rodomonte's lust,
And his barbaric cruelty defy
Rather than violate her sacred trust.
Though unkind Fate had chosen to deny
Fulfilment of her love, she knew she must
Fulfil the vow of chastity she made
When in her arms her cavalier lay dead.

12

She saw the pagan king's blind appetite
Grow stronger still, and wondered what to do,
For when such frenzy rose to its full height
Resistance would be useless then, she knew.
But as she meditated on her plight
She found at last the course she must pursue
To save her chastity and her good name,
For which she well deserves undying fame.

13

The ugly Saracen, who moved towards
His victim with a resolute intent,
Was using less conciliatory words.
His evil purpose was now evident.
Then Isabella said, 'If the rewards
Of virtue will not lead you to relent,
I offer you a recompense to spare
My honour: you have only to forbear.

14

'So small a pleasure and so brief as this,
Of which there is a plentiful supply,
Is not to be preferred to that which is
A lasting boon; women with whom to lie,
Lovely in face and form, are numberless,
But no one else could give you, only I
(Or very few in all the world I'd say),
The gift which I can offer you today.

15

'I know a herb – along my way it grew –
And I can find it easily again;
It must be boiled with ivy and with rue
Over a fire of cypress-wood; to strain
The liquid, let it be pressed between two
Sinless hands; take the fluid next and stain
Your body with it thrice; you will grow hard
And can be harmed by neither fire nor sword.

16

'He who anoints himself with it, I say –
But not just once, three times, in every part –
Invulnerable for a month will stay;
The virtue of the juice will then depart
And more of it must be distilled; today,
I'll make you some, for I have learnt the art.
This day you'll see such liquid is worth more
Than if you now were Europe's conqueror.

17

'I ask you in return for this to swear
Upon your faith that by no word or deed
You will again molest me or come near,
And that my vow of chastity you'll heed.'
This offer made the Saracen forbear,
And to the stipulation he agreed.
He promised all she asked him and beyond,
Eager to be a knight whom none can wound.

18

And he will keep his word until he tries
The liquid for its marvellous effects.
All sign of violence he will disguise.
His menacing behaviour he corrects.
And yet he later means to have the prize,
For neither God nor Prophet he respects.
Of all the liars Africa can boast,
He is the one who breaks his word the most.

19

A thousand times and more the pagan king
Now promised her that she was safe with him,
If she procured the liquid which could bring
Immunity from wounds in every limb.
So, over cliffs the maid went clambering
And down into the valleys deep and dim.
She gathered many herbs; the Saracen
Followed her everywhere, alert and keen.

20

They picked as many herbs as she thought right.
Some had their roots and others rootless were.
When they regained their dwelling, late at night,
She, of a chastity beyond compare,
Boiled the concoction till the morning light
With full attention and the utmost care:
And Rodomonte watched her as she stirred
And, as it simmered, in the potion peered.

21

As he beguiles the time with cards and dice
With the few servitors who are awake,
The heat becomes oppressive; in a trice
A raging thirst they are obliged to slake.
Filling their flagons more than once or twice,
Refreshment more than once or twice they take.
Two barrels of Greek wine are soon left dry
Which they had pillaged from some passers-by.

22

Now, Rodomonte is not used to wine,
For alcohol the Muslim law proscribes;
And tasting it, he finds it more divine
Than nectar or the manna of the tribes
Of Israel; he curses as malign
The Saracen observance, and imbibes.
The wine was excellent and freely flowed.
That it was strong, their spinning heads soon showed.

23

And in the meantime Isabella took
The cauldron from the fire; the herbs were done.
No longer need she leave them there to cook.
'No empty words upon the wind I've sown,'
She said, 'as I shall prove if you will look.
Experiment, the means by which is shown
The truth which is distinguished from a lie,
On my own body I shall shortly try.'

24

And she went on, 'I want to be the first
To test the potent virtue of this juice,
For you might otherwise suspect the worst
And poisonous ingredients deduce.
When head and neck and breast I have immersed,
Then put your sword with all your strength to use.
See if this potion has the power to check
Your weapon's edge, or if it cuts my neck.'

25

She smoothed the mixture on, as she had said;
With joy her neck to the imprudent king
She bared – imprudent, and by wine misled,
Against whose fumes no helm or shield can bring
Defence; and like a stupid dunderhead,
His cruel weapon wildly brandishing,
Her breast and torso he divested of
Her lovely head, the dwelling once of Love.

26

It bounced three times, and from it a clear voice
Was heard to call Zerbino, for whose sake
Unflinchingly she made so rare a choice
And bravely this escape preferred to make.
Heroic soul, who paid so high a price,
Who, with your very life, so young, at stake,
Fulfilled your sacred vow of chastity
(A term unheard-of in our century),

27

Depart in peace, blest soul, so sweet and fair!
Would that I had the skill and eloquence,
And that my verse with art embellished were,
So that a thousand, thousand years from hence
Your celebrated name the world might hear
And learn the story of your innocence!
Depart in peace to the supernal throne,
Of all your sex the perfect paragon.

28

On such heroic courage God confers
Encomium: 'More highly I commend
This deed which thou hast done than hers
Who brought the rule of Tarquin to an end.
Among My laws, which time shall not reverse,
Lo! a new edict henceforth I intend
Which by the inviolable seas I swear
No man shall change nor future age impair.'

29

And the Creator uttered His decree:
'Whoever in the future bears thy name,
Wise, beautiful and courteous shall be,
And virtue cherish as her constant aim.
Renowned in rhyme, honoured in history,
It will be chronicled, and with its fame
Parnassus, Pindus, Helicon will ring,
"Isabella, Isabella" echoing.'

30

God spoke; the sea and the surrounding air
More tranquil then became and more serene.
Her soul, so chaste, ascends to the third sphere,
To be embraced anew by her Zerbin.
The pagan brute was left to stand and stare,
More cruel than Bréhus had ever been.
Then rage and shame his fuddled mind possess.
Blaming the wine, he curses his excess.

31

And to placate or partly satisfy
The soul of Isabella, now in bliss,
Since by his action she had come to die,
He thought he would attempt amends for this:
Her life, so brief, should be remembered by
The church: for all that he had done amiss
He would convert it to a sepulchre
And dedicate the monument to her.

32

From villages around he summons there
Stone-masons and six thousand men at least.
Some answer willingly, others in fear.
The height of the surrounding hills decreased
As heavy blocks were cut and trundled near.
From tip to base the stone they raised and dressed
Was ninety yards; his aim was to enclose
The church wherein the lovers now repose.

33

It emulates the mighty edifice
Beside the Tiber, built by Hadrian.
A tower is raised, near the necropolis;
To dwell therein is Rodomonte's plan,
And he gives orders that a bridge which is
Sufficient length the foaming stream shall span.
Though it is long, it has the width at best
For two good horsemen there to ride abreast.

34

Two horsemen riding level or who met
Half-way across its length-finding thereon
No guard-rail or defence or parapet,
Would fall into the stream from either one
Side or the other; thus a toll was set
For pagans and for Christians; very soon
The spoils of warriors adorn the shrine,
Where trophies in their thousands gleam and shine.

35

In ten days or in less the bridge was made.
At a high price the river could be crossed.
The tomb was not completed at such speed;
Nor had the tower reached its uppermost
And crowning summit, but a look-out stayed
On the top storey, watching from his post,
And every time a cavalier drew near
The watchman's horn was sounded, loud and clear.

36

Then Rodomonte armed himself and went
To challenge the intruder; now from one,
Now from the other, bank he would prevent
His progress; if the cavalier came on,
He had to battle in a strange event
Fought in a narrow list, its like unknown;
The destrier would fall at one false step
Into the river full and fast and deep.

37

By fighting in such peril on the brink,
Taking so many risks of falling in,
The pagan hoped that if obliged to drink
The water it would wash away his sin,
Which had been caused by wine; he seemed to think
That such a plunge would leave him purged and clean:
Water, which quenches thirst for wine, he says,
The errors which wine causes must erase.

38

Not long does Rodomonte wait in vain.
By many soon the bridge attempted is.
By those who made for Italy or Spain
No other route more travelled was than this.
Others who dare at any cost to gain
True glory such a challenge will not miss.
All of them hope to win a victor's crown.
All of them lose their arms, and many drown.

39

Those whom the pagan vanquished in the fight,
If they were Saracens, he was content
To strip, and on their weapons clearly write
Their names and hang them on the monument.
For Christians he devised a different plight:
To keep them prisoners was his intent
And send them to Algiers; and then one day
The mad, deranged Orlando passed that way.

40

The frenzied Count had turned his steps by chance
Towards the river, deep and swift and wide,
Where many masons laboured to advance
The tower and the tomb; for all they tried,
The work was not yet done; with sword and lance,
Without a helmet, Rodomont defied
All comers as Orlando then appeared
And river-bank and bridgehead quickly neared.

41

And with a madman's strength he leaps the gate
And runs across the bridge at frantic speed;
But Rodomonte, puzzled and irate,
Beneath the tower, on foot, not on his steed,
Bellows an order for him to retreat.
(To challenge such as him he sees no need.)
'Go back, you boor; this is no place for you;
Elsewhere your rash and headlong course pursue.

42

'This bridge was made for lords and cavaliers,
Not for such coarse and bestial passers-by.'
Orlando, being distracted, nothing hears,
But comes ahead despite the pagan's cry.
'I see I'll have to box this madman's ears,'
Says Rodomonte, his resentment high.
Meaning to push him off the bridge, he goes,
For who it is who comes he little knows.

43

A fair young damsel came in sight just then.
As she approached the bridge, her lovely face
And beautiful adornments could be seen.
She picked her way with care, at prudent pace.
My lord, this is the damsel who has been
In search of Brandimarte, but no trace
Of him has found, for she looks everywhere
But Paris, where he is, as you're aware.

44

When Fiordiligi (that's the damsel's name)
Arrived upon the bridge, the pagan king
Was wrestling with Orlando, for his aim
Had been to catch and in the water fling
The frenzied trespasser who onward came.
She knew Orlando's wits were wandering;
She realized at once this must be he,
And marvelled greatly at such malady.

45

She stops to watch the outcome of the fight
Between this pair of combatants, one nude,
The other armed, who strove with all their might
To throw each other down into the flood.
'This madman has the valour of a knight,'
The pagan muttered and, as best he could,
He turned and whirled and veered from side to side,
Swelling the while with scorn and wrath and pride.

46

With one and then the other hand he tries
To get a better hold; he waits his chance,
Trying to trip him, now between the thighs
And now between the feet; Orlando's stance
Is shaken by no force, nor by surprise.
The pagan, like a stolid bear which wants
To devastate the tree from which it fell,
His rage and fury spends on him pell-mell.

47

Orlando's mind is sunk, I know not where.
He uses in this battle force alone,
That mighty force, exceptional and rare,
In all the universe a paragon.
Locked swaying in a fierce embrace, the pair
Pitch headlong from the bridge they wrestle on
And plunge together to the utmost deeps.
The margins tremble as the water leaps.

48

The river makes them separate in haste.
Orlando, naked, agile as a fish,
Strikes out with arms and legs, and swimming fast
Soon lands upon the shore; he has no wish
To look behind or further time to waste,
But straightway rushes off; his heathenish
Opponent, whom his armour held beneath,
Emerged more slowly and with laboured breath.

49

Meanwhile the damsel was now seen to ride
Across the bridge and, venturing with care,
She searched the monument from side to side
To see if Brandimarte's shield was there.
No sign of her dear love was to be spied,
So she had hopes of finding him elsewhere.
But let us now the Count Orlando find,
Who river, bridge and tower leaves behind.

50

It would be mad if all his madnesses
One after one I tried to chronicle.
There were so many, what their number is
And where to finish them, I could not tell;
I will select whatever instances
For my heroic song are suitable,
Such as his deeds (which I must not refuse)
High in the Pyrenees above Toulouse.

51

Since madness took possession of the knight,
For many miles his fury drove him on,
Till finally he clambered to the height
Which has divided Frank from Tarragon.
He'd followed the direction of the light,
Ever pursuing the declining sun.
A narrow mountain-path he went along
Which on one side a valley overhung.

52

And face to face along this pass he met
Two woodcutters, both young, who goaded home
An ass which bore the wood they went to get;
And when they see this raving madman come,
They utter many a shout and many a threat,
And coarsely order him to give them room.
'Go back,' they call, or 'Stand aside,' they cry,
'And clear the way for us as we go by.'

53

Orlando makes no answer to their shouts,
Save that with fury he lets fly a kick
Which takes the donkey squarely in the guts.
Joined with the frenzy of a lunatic,
His strength is now extreme beyond all doubts.
The donkey soon becomes the merest speck
As through the sky it travels like a bird
And to a hill a mile off is transferred.

54

Next, he advanced upon the youths, and one,
Who had more luck than judgement, leapt below,
A jump of sixty yards, but not for fun –
Because there was no other place to go.
However, half-way down he landed on
A patch of grass and bramble, and although
He scratched his face a little, luckily
In other ways the lad escaped scot-free.

55

The other clambered up a jagged spur
And tried to gain the summit of the rock,
Hoping some hiding-places yonder were,
Where he might yet escape by hook or crook.
But this Orlando does not let occur:
He reaches up and seizes either hock.
Parting his arms as wide as they will go,
He tears his victim's body into two,

56

Just as we sometimes see a heron split
Apart, or see a chicken opened wide,
So that a falcon or a hawk can eat
The smoking entrails and be satisfied.
Lucky the lad who fell upon his feet,
Although to break his neck, it seemed, he tried!
And he it was who told the miracle,
And Turpin heard it and told us as well.

57

Such acts and many more astounding deeds
Are done as he continues to explore.
At last, towards noon, he takes a path which leads
Downhill to Spain, and there along the shore,
Where the salt wave advances and recedes,
In Tarragon he journeys as before.
The fury which possesses him has planned
That he shall make a shelter in the sand.

58

And so, to seek protection from the sun,
He ran for cover where the sand was dry
And there he lay, unseen by anyone,
When with her spouse Angelica passed by,
For to the coast of Spain they too had gone,
First having gazed along it from on high.
A yard away, Angelica the fair
Was passing, of his presence unaware.

59

Beholding him, she would not think this man
Could be Orlando, he was so much changed,
For ever since his malady began,
Quite naked in all weathers he had ranged.
He was as burnt and black as if Aswan
Or where the Garamanths their gods avenged
Had been his birthplace, or the mountains where
The sources of the river Nile appear.

60

His eyes were almost sunken in his head;
His face was thin and fleshless as a bone.
His tangled, bristling hair, inspiring dread,
And shaggy beard were wild to look upon.
Angelica in trembling terror fled;
In trembling terror, from this monster flown,
Filling the heavens with her piercing shrieks,
Help and protection from her guide she seeks.

61

And when Orlando, wild and witless, sees
That delicate and lovely countenance
And that sweet form which so delight and please,
He is consumed with greed for them at once
And, leaping up, he makes a rush to seize
Her whom he'd cherished with such reverence.
Devotion long forgotten, he gives chase
Just as a dog after its prey would race.

62

And young Medoro, seeing him pursue
His wife, against the madman spurred his mount.
He tried to run him down, and struck him too,
Meaning to cut his head off; but the Count
(That it was he in person no one knew)
Had skin so hard it made the sword seem blunt,
For his enchanted body was like steel,
Impenetrable, suffering no ill.

63

Feeling the blows descending from behind
He turned, and as he turned he clenched his fist.
With force beyond the measurement of mind,
He struck a blow which nothing could resist.
He struck the horse which galloped like the wind,
Like glass its head was splintered by that wrist,
And the same instant he had turned again
And after her who fled, once more he ran.

64

With whip and spur she urges on her mare.
In her predicament it would seem slow
If speeding like an arrow through the air.
Faster and faster yet she makes it go.
The magic ring, of which you are aware,
She puts at last into her mouth, and so
(The ring had kept its virtue, there's no doubt)
She vanished like a light which is blown out.

65

If capture by the madman she so feared,
Or if the mare stopped dead, I cannot tell,
But at the moment when she had transferred
The ring and thus became invisible,
High in the air her legs were upwards reared.
Leaving the saddle, on the sand she fell.
Behind her came Orlando in pursuit,
Gaining upon her though he ran on foot.

66

And she was lucky that she did not land
An inch or two behind; colliding then,
He would have left her dead upon the sand,
But Fortune favoured her and stepped between.
Once more to stealing she must put her hand
(And good at this she has already been):
For now she needs another destrier.
No further use will that one be to her.

67

But she will find another, have no fear.
We will pursue the madman's vestiges.
His rage and fury do not disappear
Simply because the lady vanishes.
Closer and closer he pursues the mare,
And level with her now he almost is.
He touches her, he has her by the mane,
And finally he grasps and pulls the rein.

68

Orlando takes her with the same delight
As when a lover takes a fair young maid.
Her bridle and her rein he first puts right,
Then, leaping in the saddle, rides the jade
For miles and miles; not resting day or night,
Unmercifully on her back he stayed,
Not once removing saddle, rein or bit;
And neither grass, nor hay, he let her eat.

69

Wanting to pass a ditch that bars his way
He tries to leap across it on her back.
She falls; he feels no shock and no dismay.
She puts her shoulder out, the poor old hack.
She cannot move, so to avoid delay
He hoists her on *his* shoulder like a sack.
He clambers up and carries her as far
Ahead as three lengths of a bowshot are.

70

And then, becoming weary of his load,
He set her down and pulled her by the rein
And, slowly limping, after him she trod.
'Gee up!' the Count commanded, but in vain,
And had she galloped like the wind, she would
Have been too leisurely for his insane
Desire; at last he took her bridle off
And tied it to her right and hinder hoof.

71

Tugging and dragging, he encouraged her,
As though she could have followed him with ease.
The rocks along the coast, which jagged were,
Stripped hair and hide from her until she is
At last the tattered remnant of a mare,
Sped to her death by senseless cruelties;
But to her state Orlando pays no heed
As on his madman's way he runs with speed.

72

Although the mare is dead, he drags her still,
Proceeding on his course towards the West;
Continuing to plunder, sack and kill,
He takes whatever suits his purpose best,
Fruit, meat or bread, provided he can fill
His paunch; a gruesome and unwelcome guest,
At every house he left some dead, some lame,
Then onward passed as quickly as he came.

73

He would have dealt likewise (and thought it right)
With his fair lady, had she not been hid;
For he could not distinguish black from white,
Believing good the evil which he did.
Curst be the ring and curst be, too, the knight
Who gave it to her! Else had we been rid
Of her, and by Orlando, at one stroke:
Just vengeance for the many hearts she broke.

74

And would not only *she* were in his hands,
But all the women in the world today!
Unkind to all their lovers in all lands,
There is no scrap of good in them, I'd say.
But now my grief my slackened strings expands
So that discordant melodies I play.
My song till later on I will defer,
When less displeasing it may be to hear.

CANTO XXX

1

When passions too much freedom are allowed,
When reason, overcome by rage, submits,
When our best judgement angry feelings cloud,
When tongue insults, or hand strikes out and hits
Our dearest friends, if then our head is bowed
In penitence, no tearful sigh acquits
Us of the wrong which we have done; in vain
I grieve to think my words have given pain.

2

But I am like a sick and ailing man
Who, after suffering for many years
In patience ever since his ill began,
No longer can endure the pain he bears:
He yields to rage, and curses all he can.
The pain subsides: his anger disappears.
Aghast, he lies repentant on his bed,
But what was said cannot be now unsaid.

3

I hope, sweet ladies, you will pardon me.
I trust that you will favour me this much,
For in the anguish of my malady
My wits went wandering, and I lost touch.
So pardon me and blame my enemy
On whose account my suffering is such
My state could not be worse, and God above
Knows how she wrongs me; *she* knows how I love.

4

I am deranged, just as Orlando was,
And I deserve to be excused no less.
Up hill, down dale, he rushes without pause.
Marsilio's kingdom sees him onward press.
The battered carcass of the mare he draws
For days behind him in his stubbornness.
Arriving where a river ends its course,
He is obliged at last to leave the horse.

5

And, swimming like an otter through the flood,
He soon emerged upon the other side,
And to the water's edge a shepherd rode
That there his horse might drink; and when he spied
Orlando coming, all alone and nude,
He had no fear of him and did not hide.
'I want that nag of yours,' the madman said,
'And in exchange I'll give you mine; she's dead.

6

'She's lying there upon the other bank.
Look, you can see her easily from here.
I don't know why it is, but down she sank,
But you can put her right again, it's clear.
She has no other blemish, so I'll thank
You for your nag, and something else to square
The bargain; pray dismount.' With no reply
Except a laugh, the shepherd passes by.

7

'Did you not hear? I want that nag of yours,'
Orlando shouted, running after him.
The shepherd, who proceeded on his horse
To where the river dwindled to a stream,
Struck out with a stout cudgel to endorse
His scorn and laid his heavy blows with vim.
Orlando, roused to rage, drove his fist full
Upon the shepherd's head and broke his skull.

8

He leaps into the saddle and is gone.
He robs, he sacks, he plunders and he slays.
He gives the nag no rest, but drives it on.
Deprived of nourishment, in a few days
It too expires and joins the other one.
But not for this the Count on foot delays,
For every mount he happens on he uses,
First killing any rider who refuses.

9

At Malaga the damage which he does
Is worse than all his ravages elsewhere.
Sacking and plundering without a pause,
He brings the population to despair.
The havoc which his devastations cause
Will not be remedied for many a year.
He burns or ruins, throughout Malaga,
One third of all the habitations there.

10

Rampaging on, at length Orlando came
To Algeciras, situated close
Beside the strait which some Gibraltar name,
But others, other appellations use.
A boat the madman spied (whom none could tame),
Laden with trippers who this moment chose
Upon the tranquil sea to take their ease,
Refreshed and solaced by the morning breeze.

11

Orlando in his madness shouted 'Wait!',
Desiring suddenly to go on board.
Not for such cargo would the boat abate
Its speed, for all he bellowed, yelled and roared,
But skimmed across the sea at such a rate
No swallow swooped more rapidly or soared.
Orlando beats and urges on his horse
And to the water kicks it on its course.

12

And willy-nilly the poor steed at last
Must yield, despite its preference for land.
The water, reaching to its knees, then passed
Its belly, next its rump, then soon had gained
The level of its head, which vanished fast.
Prevented from returning to the strand,
It had to swim to Africa, or sink –
Quite a dilemma for the beast, I think.

13

Orlando can no longer see the boat
Which prompted him to leave the Spanish shore;
Too far away the merry-makers float
Beyond the water's rim; yet all the more
He urges on the steed, though it is not
A sea-horse, as he might have seen before.
Not breath but water fills its lungs, and so
It finishes its swim, and life, below.

14

It sank below and almost took as well
The madman on its back, but just in time
He lifted both his arms; breasting the swell,
He struck out vigorously with each limb,
And puffed the water from his face; to tell
The truth, the gentle air assisted him,
For if the elements that day had frowned,
The paladin Orlando would have drowned.

15

But Fortune, who takes care of the insane,
Deposited the Count on Ceuta's coast.
For some time near the city he had lain
(A distance of two arrow-shots almost),
When eastwards he began to run again,
For many days, until a dark-skinned host
He found, in tents, encamped beside the sea,
Vast and unending as infinity.

16

Now let us leave the paladin to roam.
There will be time to speak of him anon;
And as to what, my lord, will now become
Of fair Angelica, so timely flown,
And how she will at last regain her home,
Finding a well-found ship to travel on,
And how she'll make Medoro India's king,
A lyre more resonant than mine may sing.

17

I have so many other things to say
That I no longer wish to follow her,
But to the Tartar king will make my way,
Whose rival could no longer interfere
When with his love in sweet content he lay.
In all of Europe none her equals were,
Now that the fair Angelica was gone
And Isabella's soul to Heaven had flown.

18

But Mandricardo, though he could rejoice,
Could not experience in full as yet
The benefit of Doralice's choice.
His pride had other challenges to meet.
One has been uttered by Ruggiero's voice,
Claiming the eagle on his banneret.
Gradasso too, the king of Sericana,
Will not renounce his claim to Durindana.

19

King Agramante does the best he can
And King Marsilio assists as well,
But neither of them hits upon a plan
Such enmity and rivalry to quell;
Ruggiero and the Sericanian
Continue to be adamant as steel.
The sacred bird once borne on Hector's shield,
Orlando's sword, these heroes will not yield.

20

Ruggiero will not let the Tartar wear
The Trojan eagle in another fight;
Against Gradasso only may he bear
The sword once borne by such a famous knight.
'Let us let Fortune settle the affair,'
Said Agramant, 'and no more words recite.
What she proposes for us, let us see,
And let us then abide by her decree.

21

'And if you wish to set my mind at rest
And earn my gratitude, I ask one thing:
Decide by lot which of you two shall test
His strength and will against the Tartar king,
And he whose name is drawn, I now suggest,
Shall fight for both of you and, triumphing,
Shall triumph twice, and if the combat goes
The other way, both shall be deemed to lose.

22

'If I compare the valour of these two
I see but little or no difference:
And either, if selected, in my view,
In combat will exhibit excellence.
The victory, predestined, as is due,
According to the will of Providence,
Will bring no stain to either knight's repute,
For such results to Fortune men impute.'

23

While he thus tries to solve this private war,
Ruggiero and Gradasso silent stand.
It is agreed, the terms accepted are,
That in one combat two disputes shall end.
So on two slips of paper, similar
In size and shape, two names are duly penned.
Then in an urn, on which a lid is fixed,
The papers are well mingled, tossed and mixed.

24

An innocent young boy his hand then put
Into the urn; of the two names, as Chance
Decreed, one slip of paper he drew out:
Ruggiero's, not the Sericanian's.
Ruggiero could not be more joyful, but
Gradasso wears a mournful, downcast glance.
However, he must take what Fate has sent
And reconcile himself to the event.

25

And he devotes his efforts to assist
Ruggiero to come off victorious,
Advising him on every turn and twist,
Being for both their sakes solicitous.
When to advance, withdraw or to resist,
Which thrusts are certain, which are perilous,
He counselled him, as to his mind returned
The repertoire of skills which he had learned.

26

Likewise, for the remainder of the day,
Friends gather to exhort the combatants,
Reminding them in the accustomed way
How best to handle sword and shield and lance.
The populace, impatient of delay,
Hurry to take their places in advance
And, not content to come before the light
Of morning, some keep vigil there all night.

27

The stupid crowd is waiting eagerly
For the two valiant heroes to contend.
No farther than their noses can they see;
A spectacle is all they comprehend.
Sobrino and Marsilio agree
That in disaster the dispute will end.
The more enlightened Saracens deplore
This fight between the Tartar and the Moor.

28

They tried to reason with King Agramant:
The danger to the Saracens was great,
For it was plain, whichever combatant
Was destined then to die by cruel Fate,
Of his assistance they would feel the want
Against those who defeated them of late;
Among ten thousand, hard it was to find
One who such prowess and such skill combined.

29

King Agramante knows that this is true,
But what he pledged he cannot now deny.
His only course is to entreat the two:
Will they consent to put their quarrel by
(Although they have no obligation to)?
Is theirs a worthy cause for which to die?
And if they are reluctant to obey,
Will they defer until another day?

30

Would they defer their duel for about
Six months, till Charlemagne, King Pepin's son,
From his French kingdom should be driven out,
With loss of sceptre, crown and robe and throne?
Both warriors desire, there is no doubt,
To obey their king, but neither will postpone
The combat; each opprobrious would deem
Whichever first consented to the scheme.

31

More than all those who argue thus in vain
With Mandricardo to defer the fight,
Fair Doralice, the princess from Spain,
Laments, entreats and pleads with all her might.
She begs him to consent and it is plain
She trembles for the safety of her knight.
She grieves that she must always suffer thus,
Filled with anxiety and timorous.

32

'Alas!' she said, 'is there a remedy
Which I can find to bring relief and rest?
By this, by that, will you for ever be
Drawn into battle, in full armour dressed?
What consolation has it been to me,
What joy can I now cherish in my breast,
That for my sake one combat you postpone,
If now another duel is begun?

33

'Ah, me!' she said, 'flown now is all the pride
I used to take that such a noble king,
That such a cavalier, would both have died
In battle for my sake; now for a thing
So trivial, devotion set aside,
You risk your life; and, this considering,
I know that natural ferocity
It was which made you fight, not love for me.

34

'If it is true your love is such indeed
As constantly you seek to demonstrate,
Then for the sake of such a love, I plead,
And for the fear I suffer for your fate:
Such flaunting of the eagle do not heed.
Do not resent Ruggiero's banneret.
It has but small importance, in my view,
Whether Ruggiero bears this bird, or you.

35

'The combat you propose to undertake
Small profit but great loss can only yield.
Suppose you are successful and can make
Ruggiero say he will renounce the shield?
If Fortune's forelock you should fail to take,
And if she turns her back and you are killed,
That is a consequence which even if
I think of it, pierces my heart with grief.

36

'And if your precious life you hold so cheap
That you esteem a painted eagle more,
Then for my life at least some pity keep,
For if you die, my life I too abjure.
Yet if I died *with* you I would not weep:
To follow you in life and death I swore;
But let me not depart this life alone,
Dying in wretchedness when you are gone.'

37

Thus Doralice reasons with her knight,
Mingling her many words with tears and sighs.
Unceasingly she pleads with him all night
And to dissuade him from his purpose tries.
And Mandricard responded to her plight;
First kissing the sweet moisture from her eyes
And the sweet sorrow from her lips more red
Than any rose, weeping himself, he said:

38

'Do not distress yourself, my love, my wife.
Than this, far greater perils I have seen.
Should all the forces marshalled here for strife
Advance against me, French and Saracen,
Harbour no apprehension for my life.
This grave concern you feel can only mean
That you have little confidence in me,
Since in this combat but one foe there'll be.

39

'Have you forgotten when without a sword
Or scimitar, with broken lance, alone
I entered into combat with a horde
Of cavaliers (they were all armed), and won?
Gradasso will admit, though it afford
Him grief and shame, if asked by anyone,
In Syria I took him prisoner:
Yet in renown he far exceeds Ruggier.

40

'And King Gradasso too does not deny,
Nor Isolier, your fellow-countryman,
Nor Oliver's two sons (who do not lie),
Nor Sacripante, the Circassian,
Nor yet a hundred more, that it was I
Who freed them from the castle, every man,
Baptized or infidel; none will gainsay
They owed their liberty to me that day.

41

'They marvelled then and they have never ceased
To marvel at the wonder of that deed,
More glorious than if I fought at least
Both the assembled hosts and made them bleed.
And this young falcon with its yellow breast,
What can it do alone? Why should I heed
Ruggiero when Orlando's sword I bear
And Hector's shield? What danger do you fear?

42

'Alas, would I had won you earlier
By force of arms! You would have truly known
My valour and predicted for Ruggier
The fate which waits for him when I have done.
So, dry your eyes, my love, and let us hear
No more such forecasts in this gloomy tone.
It is my honour drives me to the field,
And not a painted eagle on a shield.'

43

But Doralice reasoned with him still.
She spoke so movingly, so sadly sighed,
He could not long remain inflexible
(She could have made a column move aside).
A woman, she thus bent him to her will,
And he, a mighty warrior, complied:
If Agramante made his plea once more
He would postpone the combat with the Moor.

44

And this he truly meant, but when the morn,
Led by Aurora, the fair harbinger,
The sky with gold had started to adorn,
Resolved to vindicate his rights, Ruggier,
Who held all further dallying in scorn,
That the dispute might end the earlier,
To the enclosure, which the crowd surrounded,
Rode in full armour and his challenge sounded.

45

Hearing Ruggiero's horn, the Tartar king
No further words of peace would listen to.
Leaping from bed, he bade his servants bring
His arms; his face so formidable grew,
His attitude became so menacing,
That Doralice did not dare renew
Her efforts to persuade him to refrain;
The battle must proceed – this now is plain.

46

He arms himself and he can scarcely wait
Until the squires perform their services;
Then mounts the destrier, which once the great
Defender bore, that champion who is
Reduced by love to such a sorry state.
He gallops to the chosen square and sees
The king and court arriving for the fray
Which now will soon begin without delay.

47

Their shining helmets fastened on their heads,
They take the lances which the squires present.
The trumpet shrills, a signal which precedes
The long-awaited start of the event.
The crowd grows pale, the riders prick their steeds.
With lances couched, their backs and shoulders bent,
So fast they ride and with such impact hit,
The heavens seem to fall, the earth to split.

48

On either side is seen the silver bird
Which carried Jove aloft and through the air,
And which in Thessaly, as you have heard,
Was wont (with other feathers) to appear.
How each by daring and by wrath is stirred
Is manifested by the way they bear
Their weapons and resist as firm as rocks,
Erect as towers and unmoved by shocks.

49

The shattered lances rose into the sky
(So Turpin says and he speaks truly here);
Indeed one or two pieces flew so high,
They came down singed, burned in the fiery sphere.
The combatants now seize their swords and try
Once more, like men who have no sense of fear,
To bring the battle to an end; both knights
Aim with their sword-points at the helmets' sights.

50

Each tries to pierce the visor at first thrust,
But no intention either has to kill
The other's horse, an action which all must
Condemn, since it is not the horses' will
That battle should be waged; a special trust
(Though not a formal pact, yet it is still
Respected by all knights) makes them refrain:
To aim to kill a horse was shameful then.

51

Though reinforced, the visors almost broke
Beneath those blows, delivered with such might,
Which followed one another, stroke on stroke,
Thicker than any stones of hail which blight
The grain and fruit for which the farmers look.
No other swords than these more sharply bite,
And in such hands you can imagine how
Both Durindan and Balisard cut now.

52

Not yet the swords' full cutting power they show:
Waiting for the right moment, they refrain.
Then Mandricardo deals a deadly blow
By which the valiant Moor is nearly slain.
A stroke such as these weapons can bestow
Slices Ruggiero's Trojan shield in twain.
It splits apart the skirts of his cuirass
And to his flesh the blade is seen to pass.

53

The hearts of the spectators froze in fear
To see this harsh and terrible attack
Upon their well-loved favourite, Ruggier,
Who on that day supporters does not lack.
The Tartar would be taken prisoner
Or lying dead already on his back
If Fortune brought about what they desire:
His cruel stroke has roused them all to ire.

54

An Angel must have intervened at speed
To save Ruggiero from the full effect
Of such a blow; his vigour was not fled,
His fury, scorn and strength were still unchecked.
He crashed his sword on Mandricardo's head
So fast (I do not count it a defect),
The blade descended flat, not edgeways on,
Else had the Tartar monarch been undone.

55

If Balisarda's cutting edge had hit
The helm of Hector, no enchantment then
Would have protected or defended it.
The Tartar at this blow let go the rein.
Three times he toppled forward; with the bit
Between its teeth, the destrier was seen
To gallop round the field, disconsolate
That it no longer bore Orlando's weight.

56

No trodden snake, no wounded lioness
Such fury, such disdain had ever shown
As Mandricardo, roused to consciousness,
Which at Ruggiero's recent blow had flown;
His strength and valour, once again, no less
Than pride and anger, rapidly rewon,
He turned and spurred Orlando's destrier,
Raising his weapon high above Ruggier.

57

First rising in his stirrups, Mandricard
Had aimed Orlando's sword, as he judged best,
At his opponent's helmet, and prepared
To split him, as he thought, down to his breast.
But the young Moor, alert and on his guard,
Now proves himself well equal to the test:
His sword, ere Mandricardo's arm descends,
Straight underneath the armpit he now sends.

58

And from that gash, by Balisarda slit,
Hot blood came streaming forth, vermilion red.
With lessened impact Durindana hit
The Moor, failing therefore to leave him dead.
But even so, Ruggiero could not sit
Upright, such was the crash upon his head,
And if his helmet had been less well made,
The final penalty he would have paid.

59

Spurring his horse, Ruggiero does not cease,
And from the right he lunges at the king.
No metal can protect him now from this,
However fine the steel or tempering,
For Balisarda cannot strike amiss:
The sword, enchanted in its fashioning
By Falerina, pierces without fail
Enchanted armour and enchanted mail.

60

So, piercing all defence, the magic blade
Wounded the Tartar monarch in the side.
The ocean, tempest-tossed, inspires less dread
Than he whose blasphemies the gods defied.
Calling his uttermost resolve to aid,
First the disputed shield he cast aside
As though in scorn and furious distaste,
And both his hands on Durindana placed.

61

'Ah!' said Ruggiero, 'now you cast away
The sign which you despoiled; there is no need
To prove your claim is void in every way.
All further right to it you must concede.'
These words he spoke, but then no more could say,
For Durindana fell at such a speed
That if a mountain crashed upon the knight,
Its weight would in comparison be light.

62

It struck his visor with a central blow,
But luckily for him it missed his eyes,
Descending to the armoured saddle-bow.
The double plates on which the knight relies
Could not protect him as it passed below,
Slicing the steel like wax, and reached his thighs.
So grave an injury it gave the Moor,
That long his illness was and long the cure.

63

Now with each other's blood both swords are red,
For both had shrewdly wielded them that day;
And many, by the double stream misled,
Were undecided who had won the fray.
But now the sword which leaves so many dead
Soon sweeps all their remaining doubts away.
Its thrusting point a cruel blow inflicts
Where now no shield the Tartar's side protects.

64

It pierces from the left through the cuirass
And unimpeded reaches to the heart.
When Mandricardo feels that weapon pass
He knows he has received a mortal smart.
All claims for ever he now yields, alas!
With eagle, sword and life he has to part.
As from his failing grasp these treasures fall,
His life he deems most precious of them all.

65

Not unavenged, however, did he die,
For at the moment of that deadly thrust
His blade (now still less his) he raised on high,
Bringing it down at such a speed, it must
Have split Ruggiero's face, had *he* not, by
An intercepting stroke, its vigour just
In time diminished, when he ran his sword
Under the Tartar's arm, behind his guard.

66

But at the moment when Ruggiero slew
The king, this blow descended on his head.
His helm could offer no resistance to
The celebrated Durindana's blade.
Both casque and arming-cap it sliced; right through
The scalp and bone, two fingers deep, it sped.
Ruggiero fell, unconscious from the blow,
And there a crimson stream began to flow.

67

Ruggiero was the first to fall; the king
Remained so long upright, the crowd believed
Almost he was the victor, triumphing,
And the death-blow Ruggiero had received.
And she whose heart that day kept wavering
'Twixt joy and grief was equally deceived.
Raising her hands she offered thanks on high
That God had not let Mandricardo die.

68

But when from signs that no one can mistake
They see that from the lifeless, life has flown,
And life the living man does not forsake,
Those who rejoiced begin to weep and groan,
While through the barrier the others break –
Kings, nobles, cavaliers and everyone
Who longed to see Ruggiero win the fight,
And joyfully pay honour to the knight.

69

And they rejoice with all sincerity,
For every tongue with every heart concurs.
Only Gradasso stoops to flattery.
With joyful countenance, he too confers
Loud praises on the knight, but secretly
A pang of envy in his bosom stirs.
He might have won such glory and such fame,
But Fate, or Chance, preferred Ruggiero's name.

70

But how can I describe the many true
Congratulations and endearments of
King Agramante, on this triumph, to
The knight without whose help he could not move
His many troops from Africa to sue
For vengeance and their mighty prowess prove?
Now that King Agricane's son was dead,
Ruggiero in his eyes all others led.

71

Nor did such praise come only from the men,
But women gathered round him eagerly
Who with the troops of Africa and Spain
Had come to France to keep them company,
And Doralice, who with grief and pain
Was mourning her dead lover, even she
Perhaps, who knows?, but for a sense of shame,
Might likewise have paid homage to his fame.

72

I say 'perhaps', I do not say for sure,
And yet I think it highly probable,
Such are the fascination and allure
Of glory and of handsome looks as well;
And she, from what we knew of her before,
Is quick to change her mind, and, truth to tell,
Rather than see herself deprived of love,
Her heart she'd make him now a present of.

73

While Mandricardo lived, then, well and good:
But of what use is he, now he is dead?
She needs a man whose strength and hardihood
Both night and day will stand her in good stead.
A doctor after a brief interlude
Examined all Ruggiero's wounds and said
His life was in no danger; this submission
Was offered by the foremost court physician.

74

King Agramante ordered that the knight
Be carried gently to his royal tent.
He did not want to lose him from his sight.
His love for him was now so great, he meant
To give him every care both day and night.
The trophies he had won in this event
Were hung about his bed, except the sword,
Which to Gradasso goes as an award.

75

The other arms are given to Ruggier,
As is the case in combats of this kind,
And Brigliadoro too, the destrier
Orlando in his frenzy left behind.
He gave it to the king, as you shall hear.
But now no more of him, as I must find
The Maid who for Ruggiero sighs in vain,
And take in hand her story once again.

76

What were the pains of love with which she burned
While waiting for Ruggiero, I'll now say.
Ippalca to her mistress had returned
And told her all that had occurred that day.
First what had happened when the Sarzan spurned
Ruggiero's name and took his horse away;
How she had met Ruggiero at the fount
And of the others too she gave account.

77

How she rode off with him (she told her too),
Hoping to find the thieving Saracen,
And punish him severely, as was due,
For his unchivalry; and how this plan
Did not succeed, for, as they later knew,
He took another route; she told her then
The reason why Ruggiero had delayed:
All this and more Ippalca told the Maid.

78

Ruggiero's words she next began to quote,
Giving them all, exactly as they were,
For she had conned them carefully by rote.
The letter which Ruggiero gave to her
She handed to the Maid, who took the note
With troubled countenance, for happier
That day she would have felt, and more serene,
If only her dear love she could have seen.

79

Long had she waited for her love and now
She saw that she must be content instead
With ink and paper; thus her lovely brow
Was lined with fear and sorrow as she read.
She kissed the page ten times and more, I vow;
To him who wrote, her loving thoughts were sped.
Her tears protect the paper from her sighs,
Which, burning, might consume it otherwise.

80

Four times and six she read the letter through
And just as many times she also made
Her messenger repeat the tale anew,
Saying again all that her love had said;
And still she wept. I will confess to you
That she would never have been comforted
(And on such matters I am seldom wrong),
Save that she hoped to see her love ere long.

81

For, at the most, fifteen or twenty days
He'll be detained, he said, and he has vowed
That after this there will be no delays;
But, voicing all her fears for him out loud,
In tones of anguish Bradamante says:
'Misfortune, which impedes so many proud
And valiant knights, and most of all in war,
May rob me of my love for evermore.

82

'Alas, Ruggiero! ah, who would suppose,
When I love you more than myself, that you
Love, not another woman, but your foes?
The very people whom you should subdue
It is your purpose to assist, and those
Whom you should help, you now continue to
Oppress; between rewards and punishments
For good and ill, you see no difference?

83

'Do you not know it was Troiano's hand
Which killed your father? Why, the very stones
Have heard of it; and yet you now have planned
Without demur to rally to his son's
Assistance, to protect his honour and
His life; an action such as this condones
Your father's death. Thus you reward your friends?
And thus you cause me grief which my life ends?'

84

Such were the words Ruggiero's love addressed
To him (though he was absent) through her tears;
Not once, but many times, she thus expressed
Her apprehensions for him and her fears.
Meanwhile the kind Ippalca does her best
To comfort her: this promise of Ruggier's
Can be relied upon; beyond the day
Which he has mentioned, he will not delay.

85

Ippalca, by her words inspiring hope
(And hope the constant friend of lovers is),
Brings Bradamante's weeping to a stop
And her worst fears at last diminishes.
In Montalbano on the mountain-top
She waits, believing in his promises;
But when the day arrives for his return,
It seems as if Ruggiero is forsworn.

86

But if her love has failed to keep his word,
Not he at least is to be blamed for that.
If his return has been so long deferred,
It is that for a month he has lain flat
Upon his back; when Mandricardo's sword
(Though he himself will never more combat)
Had struck Ruggiero, it inflicted pain
So deadly that the knight was almost slain.

87

So all that day Ruggiero's loving Maid
Had waited for his coming, fruitlessly,
And nothing knew but what Ippalca said.
Later, her brother came and told how he
Was rescued by Ruggier, and how they sped
To set Vivian and Malagigi free.
To hear of these brave deeds the Maid was glad,
Yet something in the tale had left her sad.

88

For Ricciardetto told his sister then
How brave and beautiful Marfisa was.
He told her how Ruggiero followed when
She galloped off to aid the pagan cause,
Where Agramante and the Saracen
Had the most need of help. With no applause
She heard this news, although such company
Would for Ruggiero's valour fitting be.

89

Suspicion in her heart begins to grow,
For if Marfisa is in truth as fair
As her repute, if side by side they go,
And every danger, all adventures share,
Has she not won his heart? It must be so,
And Bradamante, verging on despair,
But ever hopeful she will see her love,
At Montalbano stays and does not move.

90

And as she waited there, the prince, the lord
Of that fair castle (not the eldest son,
For two preceded him at birth), whose sword
Such glory for the family had won,
Rinaldo, who, wherever he had warred,
In splendour like the sun in heaven shone,
Reached Montalbano at the hour of three,
A single page his only company.

91

When he was riding to and fro, from Blaye
To Paris, in pursuit, as I have said,
Of fair Angelica, he heard one day
How his two cousins, bartered by the dread
Lanfusa, were in peril, and straightway
To Agrismont for further news he sped,
To hear if Bertolagi had received
His victims and his evil aim achieved.

92

And when he heard that all their enemies
Were killed or scattered, and that both were free,
And that it was Ruggiero and Marfise
Who helped to rescue them from jeopardy,
And that his brother had returned with his
Two cousins, that they had been saved, all three –
Young Richard, Malagigi, Vivian –
He'd hastened eagerly to Montalban.

93

And so he came to Montalbano, where
His mother, wife and children he embraced,
His brothers and his cousins too, who were
The captives of Lanfusa, now released.
And when they saw their kinsman thus appear
They were like fledgling swallows when at last
The mother bird returns with nourishment.
After some days, away with him there went:

94

Richard, Alardo, Ricciardetto and
The eldest son, Guicciardo, with the two
Young cousins; six of them, a warlike band,
Clad in full armour, muster for review,
Then ride behind Rinaldo, as he planned.
But Bradamante, since the time was due
(She hoped) when Fate her longing would fulfil,
Did not go with them, saying she was ill.

95

Indeed, she spoke the truth, for she was sick,
But not of bodily disease or pain.
Ardent desire had left her spirit weak,
For all her hopes and longings were in vain.
Rinaldo rode away with all the pick
Of knights and men-at-arms of Montalban;
And how he came to Paris and brought aid
To Charles, in the next canto will be said.

CANTO XXXI

1

What sweeter bliss and what more blessèd state
Can be imagined than a loving heart,
With happiness and joy inebriate,
Possessed, in thrall to Love in every part,
But for the torment which Man suffers, that
Suspicion, sinister and deep, that smart,
That aching wretchedness, that malady,
That frenzied rage, which we call jealousy?

2

All other bitterness which may arise
To temper the excess of so much sweet,
The joys of love augments and multiplies,
Refining them and making them complete.
Water more exquisitely satisfies
When we are thirsty; hunger what we eat
Improves; Man cannot relish peace before
He has experienced a state of war.

3

If eyes do not behold what the heart keeps
For ever visible, this can be borne.
Absence, however long a lover weeps,
Heightens but more the joy of the return.
Service, unwavering and true, which reaps
No recompense, provided hope still burn,
This too can be endured, though it is hard:
A lover in the end has his reward.

4

Rejection, scorn and all the pains of love,
The sufferings which last for many a year,
Can, when recalled, increase the pleasure of
More joyful times when Fate is less severe.
But that dread poison nothing can remove
From a sick mind, for none is deadlier.
No happiness, no merriment avails
To cure a jealous lover of his ills.

5

This is that poisoned wound for which there are
No potions, unguents, salves or antidotes;
No secret charm, no magic formula
Such as the book of Zoroaster quotes,
No vigil for a favourable star,
No cabbalistic sign which power denotes,
Not all the magic arts, could heal that sore
For which, alas! death is the only cure.

6

Implacable and life-destroying wound,
How soon you fester in a lover's breast!
Suspicion, indiscriminate, beyond
All reasoning, of ills the cruellest,
The intellect you darken and confound
Till true is false, and false, truth manifest!
Ah, Jealousy, more cruel than the grave,
What pain in store for Bradamant you have!

7

First, what her brother and Ippalca said
Had pierced her tender heart with bitter woe.
Next, tidings still more terrible and dread,
Which after a few days she came to know,
Caused her more sorrow, and more tears she shed;
But this was nothing to a further blow
Which fell, as I'll explain; but now I must
To Paris, with Rinaldo and his host.

8

Late on the second day they met a knight
Who had a lady at his side; his shield
And surcoat were of black, save that a white
Bend sinister traversed the sable field.
He challenged Ricciardetto to a fight,
Who, riding fearlessly ahead, revealed
A readiness to take him at his word
(And he was never one to have demurred).

9

So, from the distance which the rules demand,
They ride to the encounter at top speed
(Asking no names), while all the others stand
To see which valiant horseman will succeed.
'I'll soon unseat him', Ricciardetto planned
(So saying, he was confident indeed),
'If I can strike him in my usual way.'
But the reverse result occurred that day.

10

For *he* was struck beneath the visor hard
By the black cavalier, of name unknown,
And, lifted from the saddle, off his guard,
Two lance-lengths from his charger he was thrown;
And to avenge his brother, next Alard
At once took up the challenge; he was soon
Unseated, and so potent was the shock
Of the encounter that his shield it broke.

11

Straightway Guicciardo put his lance in rest,
Observing his two brothers on the ground.
Although Rinaldo shouted, 'Wait! Desist!
I am the third. Let *me* fight the third round,'
Guicciardo paid no heed to his request.
Spurring his horse, he rode full tilt, but found
(Before Rinaldo had his helmet on)
That like his brothers he was also thrown.

12

Ricciardo, Malagigi, Vivian
All clamoured to avenge the fallen three.
Rinaldo quelled the quarrel which began.
Already armed, he said, 'Leave this to me.
Our duty is in Paris with Charlemagne.
There is no time to wait for you to be'
(But these last words he did not say outright)
'Defeated one by one by this strange knight.'

13

(If he had made these last remarks out loud
He would have given serious offence.)
The two opponents took the space allowed
According to the rules of such events
And, turning, to the harsh encounter rode.
Rinaldo now displays his excellence:
He does not fall; like glass both lances break,
Both cavaliers the impact fails to shake.

14

Quite other is the case with the two steeds
As to the ground their cruppers are brought low.
Rising at once, Baiardo onward speeds,
His course uninterrupted by the blow.
The stranger's horse, unequal to such deeds,
Its spine and shoulder smashed, no more will go
To war; the knight, perceiving it is dead,
Leaps free, prepared to fight on foot instead.

15

And to Count Aymon's son who, turning now,
Approached him empty-handed, he thus spoke:
'So fine a charger I cannot allow
To lie there unavenged, and you who broke
His back shall pay the penalty, I vow,
For having robbed me of him by this stroke.
So now advance and do your worst, I pray,
For you and I must settle this today.'

16

Rinaldo answered, 'If a destrier
Is all there is between us, then take one
Of mine instead; you'll find it, I declare,
Of no less use and value than your own.'
'You must be dense', replied the cavalier,
'If you believe that you can thus atone.
But if you do not see why I must fight,
I'll set it down for you in black and white.

17

'It would be counter to the code if I
Did not contend with sword as well as lance.
My honour is impugned unless we try
Our prowess also in this second dance.
So, as you please, dismount or stay on high;
I am prepared to give you every chance,
And whatsoever benefit you will,
So eager am I for this test of skill.'

18

Rinaldo did not keep him in suspense.
'I promise you this test,' he said, 'and so
That you may feel no doubt, I will dispense
With all my men-at-arms and bid them go
Ahead until I come'; he sent them hence
(Save for a page to hold his horse), to show
Good faith; for, in all matters chivalrous,
No cavalier was more punctilious.

19

This courtesy of the brave paladin
Commends him greatly to the unknown knight.
On foot, Rinaldo gives Baiardo's rein
To the young page, who leads him out of sight;
And when the standard can no more be seen,
Rinaldo, ready for this second fight,
Takes shield and sword, an eager challenger,
And shouts defiance at the cavalier.

20

The battle which between them then began
Appeared unequalled in ferocity.
Neither opponent thinks the other can
Resist so long, but each is proved to be
As good a warrior, as brave a man.
Neither rejoices yet in victory,
But neither combatant surrender will:
To gain advantage both use all their skill.

21

The blows, so merciless and obdurate,
Breaking the corners of the heavy shields,
Now slashing mail, now smashing armour plate,
While both no progress make, and neither yields,
With horrifying sounds reverberate.
Both in attack and in defence each wields
His sword, and grimly each resolves to make
(For this might well be fatal) no mistake.

22

The combat lasted for one hour and more
Than half the next; the sun had sunk below
The western waters, to the farthest shore
The shadows spread, but in the afterglow,
Taking no moment's respite to restore
Their strength, giving and taking blow on blow,
The warriors continue; not for rage
Or rancour, but for honour they engage.

23

Rinaldo wonders who this unknown youth
Can be, so bold, so stalwart and so strong.
Not only does he stand his ground, in truth
He presses his opponent hard and long.
By now the paladin would not be loath
(If honour could defended be from wrong),
Such the exertion is and such the heat,
To end the fight, or call a halt to it.

24

And, for his part, the unknown cavalier –
Who, likewise, did not know the other's name,
Who did not know this paladin and peer,
Rinaldo Montalbano, of great fame,
Whom opposite he saw and very near
With sword in hand – to the conclusion came
That this was someone of great excellence,
Unparalleled in his experience.

25

And of that pledge he'd gladly now be free
Which he had taken to avenge his horse.
If without fear of blame or calumny
He could withdraw, he would prefer that course.
Too desperate he deems the jeopardy.
The shadows his misgivings now endorse,
For almost all the blows exchanged miscarry
And scarcely can they see to thrust or parry.

26

Rinaldo was the first to speak the word
Which called a halt; but, he went on to say,
Let them regard the combat as deferred
Till slow Arcturus paled at break of day;
And, in the meantime, until this occurred,
The unknown knight should with Rinaldo stay,
Where he would be an honoured, welcome guest,
Well served, well squired, where he could safely rest.

27

To these proposals which Rinaldo made
The courteous cavalier at once agreed;
And now together through the darkling glade
To where the troops have halted they proceed.
All honour to the unknown knight is paid.
Rinaldo picks for him a handsome steed,
With splendid trappings, tested, tried and trained,
Which much experience in war has gained.

28

The warrior, who was unknown, now knows
It is Rinaldo who escorted him,
For on the way he happened to disclose
His name; since from one origin they stem
(For they are brothers), each affection shows
At this discovery; their eyes now brim
With tears of joy and tenderness and love,
As overwhelming these new feelings prove.

29

Guidon Selvaggio is this warrior's name
And you have heard me speak of him before,
When Sansonetto and Marfisa came
With Oliver's two sons and, making war
On Orontea's realm, saved him from shame.
Since then, that felon Pinabello more
Humiliation had imposed on him,
Making him implement his lady's whim.

30

And when Guidone understood at last
That this Rinaldo was, that famous knight
Who in his fame all other knights surpassed,
Whom, as the blind desire to see the light,
He'd longed to see, 'What fortune has thus cast
My lot,' he said, 'that I was led to fight
With you whom I so ardently admire,
Whom but to serve and honour I aspire?

31

'Costanza gave me birth, on the far shore
Of the Black Sea, the seed, as you were too,
Of that illustrious progenitor,
Aymon of Montalbano; when I knew
I was your kin, such was my longing for
My brothers' company, I sought for you.
I am Guidon; my only purpose was
To honour you, but pain to you I cause.

32

'Yet for my error, my excuse shall be:
I did not recognize my kith and kin.
If I can make amends for this, tell me
What I must do; I'm eager to begin.'
And when they had embraced repeatedly
And of each other's love assured had been,
Rinaldo answered, 'Seek no more, I pray,
To ask my pardon for our fight today:

33

'Nothing could better testify to us
You are a true branch of our ancient stock,
Nothing convince us like your valorous
Resistance in the battle's clash and shock;
But you would not have found us credulous
If quiet and pacific were your look:
Hinds are not offspring of the king of beasts,
No doves were ever hatched in eagles' nests.'

34

Proceeding, they continue to converse;
Conversing, they proceed upon their way.
Soon as Rinaldo has re-joined his peers,
He tells them who Guidone is, and they,
Who long have hoped to welcome him as theirs,
Rejoice to learn he has arrived that day;
And as around Guidone they assembled,
They said how much his father he resembled.

35

How welcome by his kinsfolk he was made,
How brothers, cousins, clasped him by the hand,
What joyful homage all the others paid,
How gladly they received him in their band,
What he to them and what to him they said,
I shall not tell you, but you understand,
In spite of all these things I do not say,
That he *persona grata* was that day.

36

Welcome Guidone would have been indeed
At any time, of this I am quite sure;
But since he had arrived in time of need,
His coming gladdened all their hearts the more.
When shadows at the break of day recede,
And the new sun, rising from Ocean's floor,
Is circled with an aureole of light,
Guidone and his kin go forth to fight.

37

Two days they travel on, at such a pace
That soon they find themselves beside the Seine,
Ten miles or so from Paris; in that place
Gismonda's sons Guidone sees again,
Accoutred each in his strong carapace,
Which weapons seek to penetrate in vain:
Grifon the White and Aquilant the Black,
Who nothing of the knightly virtues lack.

38

A damsel earnestly conversed with them;
Of no mean rank she seemed, for she was clad
In a white samite robe, which round the hem
A gold-embroidered decoration had.
Although her beauty sparkled like a gem,
Her tearful eyes proclaimed that she was sad.
Her gestures, bearing, aspect, all conveyed
A grave significance in what she said.

39

Guidone and the sons of Oliver
Have recognized each other straight away;
Not long ago all three together were.
Guidone to Rinaldo turns to say,
'Here are two knights for you; we cannot err
If they will side with Charlemagne today.
We'll put to flight all pagans with those two.'
Rinaldo says that what he says is true.

40

He too has recognized them at first sight,
For he remembers how they used to ride,
One surcoat black, the other surcoat white,
With blazoning ornate and beautified.
They, for their part, with manifest delight,
To greet Guidone with each other vied,
His brothers, cousins, eagerly embraced,
Rinaldo too, laying all hate to rest.

41

They had been enemies, but why and how
(The fault was Truffaldino's) would take long
To say; embracing one another now,
And setting memories of wrath among
Forgotten things, to lend their aid they vow.
To Sansonetto, who next joins the throng,
Rinaldo gladly all due honour pays,
For of his valour he has heard great praise.

42

The damsel, knowing every paladin,
Had recognized Rinaldo drawing near.
As soon as she was able to begin,
She told him tidings he was sad to hear.
'My lord,' she said, 'your cousin I have seen,
Of Church and Empire, champion and peer:
Orlando, once a man for every season,
So wise and so renowned, has lost his reason.

43

'How this has come about I cannot say,
Nor why he wanders witless all around.
I saw his sword and other arms, which lay
Thrown here and there, neglected, on the ground.
I saw a cavalier who passed that way,
Who in compassion gathered all he found,
Who hung them one by one upon a tree,
As a memorial, in piety.

44

'That very day Orlando's sword was gone,
Taken – consider what a grievous loss –
By Mandricardo, Agricane's son.
It is a serious affront to us
That Durindana, of all swords the one
We prize the most, should to the infamous
Return; and Brigliadoro, wandering,
Was also taken by the pagan king.

45

'I saw Orlando a few days ago
Running quite naked, witless, without shame,
Uttering terrifying shrieks; and so
To this conclusion with regret I came:
Orlando has gone mad; and this I know
(Though I should never have believed the same)
For I have seen him.' She went on to tell
How from the bridge Orlando wrestling fell.

46

'To everyone I judge to be his friend
And not his enemy, I speak of this,'
She added, 'for I hope that in the end,
By pity moved for what has gone amiss,
Someone the Count may rescue, and defend,
Till he is cured, from all hostilities.
I know if Brandimarte hears the news,
All speed and every effort he will use.'

47

For this was Fiordiligi, the sweet wife
Of Brandimarte, whom she long had sought;
And he loved her more dearly than his life.
She added that Orlando's sword had brought
Ferocious rivalry and bitter strife
Among the pagans; how the Tartar fought
And died, and how the weapon had then passed
Into Gradasso's eager hands at last.

48

On hearing of this strange calamity,
Rinaldo weeps and cannot be consoled.
As ice is melted to fluidity
By the hot sun, his heart, so brave and bold,
Is liquefied by grief; the memory
Of what Orlando was and did of old
Makes him resolve to bring his cousin home
And cure his ills, wherever he may roam.

49

But first, since Heaven or the hand of Chance
Has here assembled all this mighty host,
Rinaldo is determined to advance
Upon the Moors, who have surrounded most
Of Paris, but he does not move at once.
To make the pagans pay a higher cost,
He waited till the dark of night was deep
And Lethe's water sprinkled was by Sleep.

50

He placed his men-at-arms about the glade
And at their stations ordered them to stay
Until Apollo his departure made
And to his ancient nurse moved on his way;
When bears and goats and serpents were displayed,
No longer hidden by the lamp of day,
Rinaldo moved his silent forces on,
As pagans slumbered in oblivion.

51

And with him came Grifone, Aquilant,
Guidone, Viviano and Alard,
And Sansonet, a mile or so in front,
With quiet steps and speaking not a word.
Finding the sentinels of Agramant
Asleep, they did not spare a single guard;
Not one was taken prisoner; unseen,
Unheard, they crept among the Saracen.

52

Rinaldo takes the vanguard by surprise
And his destruction of it is complete,
For not a man is there but falls and dies.
Having no time to rally or retreat,
The pagans do not smile; since in their eyes
The future will not joyful be or sweet;
For half asleep, unarmed and ill-prepared,
Badly against such warriors they fared.

53

To terrify the Saracens still more,
Rinaldo gave the signal for a blast
Of clarions and trumpets; with a roar
Of 'Montalbano!' his supporters passed.
Over the barricades Baiardo bore
His master with one leap; then forward fast,
Trampling the fallen bodies, on they went,
Till no pavilion stood and scarce one tent.

54

Not one among the pagans was so brave
But that his hair stood upright on his head;
Soon as they heard the shout the Christians gave –
That formidable name, inspiring dread –
Spaniards and Africans alike, to save
Their precious skins, from their encampments sped.
On loading packs no precious time is wasted,
When once the fury of the foe is tasted.

55

Guidone follows him and does no less;
No less achieve the sons of Oliver;
Alardo, Ricciardetto, onward press,
And horror the two other brothers stir;
Vivian and Aldigiero spread distress
With Sansonetto as a harbinger.
And every knight who rallies to the sign
Brings yet more glory to the Clairmont line.

56

Of Montalbano's farmers and their sons
Rinaldo gathered seven hundred men.
Ferocious as Achilles' Myrmidons,
In winter's cold, in summer's heat they train;
No man among them but his armour dons
As soon as danger to their lord is seen.
One hundred would against a thousand stand –
A loyal, valorous and gallant band.

57

Rinaldo is not rich, in property
Or money, but his frank and open ways,
His readiness to share whatever he
Possesses, mean that every soldier stays
With him, unshaken in his loyalty,
Although a higher wage another pays.
Rinaldo never moves these troops unless
An urgent need arises somewhere else.

58

But since King Charlemagne has need of aid,
Rinaldo now denudes his citadel,
Taking his soldiers with him, as I said.
Against the Africans they fight so well,
No cruel wolf more fierce an onslaught made
When on the woolly-coated sheep it fell
By the Galaesus, no lion among the goats
Beside the Cinyphus e'er ripped more throats.

59

King Charles, to whom Rinaldo had sent word,
Knew that assistance would be soon at hand;
When of the night attack he also heard,
He armed in readiness to help the band.
When need arose, his paladins he stirred
To action (two were still in Paris) and
The son of Monodante, whom the fair
Young Fiordiligi loved, as he loved her,

60

Whom she for many days had sought in vain,
Wandering here and there throughout all France.
As soon as she beheld his emblem plain,
She recognized him from afar at once.
When Brandimarte saw his love again,
Setting aside all thoughts of spear and lance,
He hastened to embrace her, and above
A thousand kisses showered on his love.

61

In olden days they seemed to place great trust
In women, whether middle-aged or young;
Permitted to indulge their wander-lust,
They travelled unaccompanied along
Strange roads, up hill, down dale, from coast to coast,
But those at home suspected nothing wrong.
Fair Fiordiligi started to relate
What she had witnessed of Orlando's state.

62

Such tidings he would scarcely credit if
He heard them from another messenger;
But he believes his beautiful young wife
(Far more than this he had believed of her).
Not only did she hear, but large as life
She saw with her own eyes, as she can swear,
Orlando mad, the Count whom she knows well;
And where and when she now proceeds to tell.

63

She tells him of the bridge which Rodomont
Has built and holds as a pass perilous,
And of the tomb she also gives account,
With surcoats and with arms made sumptuous;
And she describes how she has seen the Count
Commit the wildest and most furious
Of follies, how he wrestled with the Moor,
And fell into the river, and much more.

64

And he who loved Orlando as a friend,
As ever brothers or a father loved,
As soon as Fiordiligi reached an end,
Resolved to search for him, as it behoved.
No hardship and no jeopardy should bend
His will from finding him, where'er he roved,
And to seek help for him from a physician,
Or else, if that should fail, from a magician.

65

Armed as he is and mounted on his horse,
He leaves with Fiordiligi as his guide.
Day after day they journey on their course
Until they reach the bridge where many tried
To cross and, failing, lost their arms, or worse,
Their lives. Alerted by the guard inside
The tower, Rodomonte takes his stand
As soon as Brandimarte nears the strand.

66

As soon as Rodomonte saw him come,
He matched his fury with a direful voice:
'Whoever you may be, who to your doom
Are here misled by Fate, whence I rejoice,
Dismount! Disarm! Here to this sacred tomb
Pay tribute; do not thank me, for no choice
I give you: I will slay you in a trice
And offer you as the next sacrifice.'

67

No other answer Brandimarte gave
Than with his lance; and spurring on his steed,
Batoldo, loyal, spirited and brave,
He rode against the pagan at such speed
And with such courage, he was seen to have
That valour which the knightly virtues breed.
And Rodomonte, as his foe approached,
Thundered across the bridge, his weapon couched.

68

So many times had Rodomonte's horse
Traversed the narrow bridge, from which now one
And now another knight was flung by force,
Secure, unfaltering he galloped on.
Batoldo, unaccustomed to the course,
Trembled in every sinew, nerve and bone.
The bridge was trembling too as on they rode,
And seemed about to fall beneath their load.

69

Both cavaliers are masters of the joust.
As thick as tree-trunks both their lances are.
The heavy blows they strike, to their great cost,
Are heavier than they have struck so far.
Though strong and skilled, the horses cannot trust
Their mighty frames to save them from the jar.
Their balance being unsettled, down they slip,
Both riders falling with them in a heap.

70

Both horses struggle to rise up again,
Urged by the spurs which both the knights apply.
So narrow is the bridge, they strive in vain
To find a foothold; neither can defy
The force of gravity, howe'er they strain.
They fall with such a splash, the sound on high
Re-echoes, as when in our river Po
Apollo's son, Phaëthon, fell below.

71

The horses carry with them on their backs
The weight of the two knights, who sit erect.
Total immersion neither of them lacks.
The bottom of the river they inspect
As though they followed in a naiad's tracks.
The pagan found it easy to direct
His underwater steed, for more than once
They have descended to these crystal haunts.

72

He knows where all the mud-banks are, and where
The water's deep or shallow; head and breast
And thighs at last emerge into the air.
But Brandimarte does not pass this test.
The river's current whirls him here and there.
Batoldo, sinking in the sand, sinks fast.
He tries to extricate himself, but down
He sinks again, till both, it seems, must drown.

73

The tumbling water turns them downside-up
And thus they float (as Turpin tells the tale),
The rider underneath, the horse on top;
And from the bridge, the damsel, deathly pale,
With sighs and sobs and tears, which never stop,
To Rodomonte utters this appeal:
'For her whose memory you so revere,
Be not so cruel! Save my cavalier!

74

'Ah! courteous knight, if love you ever knew,
On me have pity, who so love this knight.
Make him your prisoner, as is your due.
Adorn this sepulchre, as is your right,
With this fair banner, fairer far than you
Have ever conquered here in any fight.'
So well she pleads, the cruel pagan king
Is moved to pity by her suffering.

75

And to the aid of Brandimart, immersed,
He ran, and not too soon; the knight by then
Had fully quenched his (non-existent) thirst,
And wondered if he'd ever see again
The light of day; but Rodomonte, first
Relieving him of helm and sword, by main
Force dragged him, almost lifeless, to the shore
And locked him, among many, in the tower.

76

All joy had died in Fiordiligi's breast,
To see her lover led away and bound,
Though she consoled herself to think at least
In spite of everything he had not drowned.
The blame was hers, she inwardly confessed
(And this her grief with sharper sorrow crowned),
For she had told her love, and only she,
About Orlando's grievous malady.

77

The damsel rode away, for she had planned
To fetch Rinaldo, Sansonetto, or
Guidone, or another of their band,
Well-versed in every skill and art of war,
As nimble in the water as on land,
Who, if he was to overcome the Moor,
If not of greater strength, must be possessed
Of better fortune than her love at least.

78

She journeys on her quest for a long way
Before she meets with any cavaliers
Who in her view those qualities display
Which are essential for this task of hers.
She searches here and there until one day
She sees a knight approaching her who wears
A surcoat broidered with a fair design
Of cypress-trees, ornate and rich and fine.

79

But I will tell you later who this was,
For now my purpose is to take you back
To Paris, where the pagans have good cause
To flee before Rinaldo's fierce attack.
I cannot count them all, nor number those
Who are despatched for ever to the black
Infernal shores of Styx; though Turpin tried,
Such inky darkness his attempt defied.

80

King Agramante, sleeping in his tent,
Is wakened from his slumber by a knight.
His capture, he declares, is imminent.
He must as soon as possible take flight.
The king looks round him in bewilderment.
He sees his men and he observes their plight:
Naked and helpless, running here and there,
Having no time to arm or to prepare.

81

The king, confused, uncertain what to do,
Allows his squire to fasten his cuirass,
When Balugant, with others of that crew,
Arrive to tell him what has come to pass.
Grandonio and Falsirone, who
Accompanies his son, all round him press,
And on him urge the danger he is in:
He will be fortunate to save his skin.

82

So does Marsilio; good Sobrino's voice
Is mingled with the others there, to say
That Agramant must flee; he has no choice,
For ruin stares him in the face that day:
Rinaldo comes, his followers rejoice.
If Agramante now decides to stay,
His fate, his allies' fate, he will ensure:
Death or imprisonment they must endure.

83

Let him withdraw to Arles or to Narbonne,
Together with such troops as still remain.
Both fortresses are strong and either one
A siege, if necessary, could sustain.
When he is safe inside the garrison,
He can regroup his forces once again,
And every stratagem and means employ
To take revenge and Charlemagne destroy.

84

King Agramante heeded their advice,
Though harsh and bitter the decision was.
So, to avoid a greater sacrifice,
Along the road to Arles, without a pause,
He went; wings seemed to waft him in a trice,
Though, leaving in the dark, he had no cause
To fear pursuit; thus from the net that day
The wild-fowl (twenty thousand) got away.

85

But those Rinaldo and his brothers slew,
And those the sons of Oliver laid low,
And those who fell before the gallant few –
The seven hundred – who allegiance owe
To Montalbano, those whose death is due
To Sansonetto, *their* sum who can know?
One might as well attempt to count the flowers
Which star the meadow after April showers.

86

Some think that Malagigi had a share
In that night's triumph; so much butchery,
So many bodies scattered everywhere,
And broken heads, the work of sorcery
Must be; from Tartarean regions drear
He conjured up the Devil's cavalry,
Of which the banners, destriers and lances
The forces would outnumber of two Frances.

87

The crash of metal clashing, clattering,
The rolling thunder of so many drums,
So many thudding hoofs, the whinnying,
The roar which from so many voices comes,
O'er hill and plain and valley echoing,
A tumult which all pandemoniums
Exceeds must come from Hell, so it was said,
And that was why the pagans turned and fled.

88

Ruggiero, whose condition was still grave,
Was not forgotten by King Agramant,
Who to his squires precise instructions gave
To lay him on a steed which smoothly went
Along the safest path; and next, to save
Him pain or any untoward incident,
They were to find a ship and thence on board
Bring him to Arles to join the pagan horde.

89

Those who from Charles and from Rinaldo fled
Numbered a hundred thousand, I believe,
Or little less; o'er hill and dale they sped,
And over wood and plain, in haste to leave
The soil of France; and many stained it red
Where it was clad with green; but I deceive
You if I here omit Gradasso's name,
Who from the farthermost pavilion came.

90

For when he knows that Montalban is there,
That it is he who marshals the assault,
His joy is such he leaps into the air,
For at this news he cannot but exult.
He thanks his Maker that a chance so rare
Has come his way; and he will not default.
The longed-for moment has arrived at last
To win Baiard, that charger unsurpassed.

91

Gradasso longed with all his royal pride
(And this I think you have already heard)
To flaunt Orlando's weapon at his side,
And by the mad ambition too was stirred
Upon that flawless destrier to ride.
And so, this horse to mount, this weapon gird,
He'd brought a hundred thousand men to France
And had defied Rinaldo more than once.

92

And to the shore one day, where they agreed
To see which of the two would come off best,
Gradasso went, but did not then succeed
In putting Montalbano to the test,
For Malagigi made his cousin speed
On board a ship (lured by illusion) lest
He came to harm; and from that day to this
The king suspected him of cowardice.

93

Thus when he knows that it is Montalban
Who leads the assault, Gradasso feels delight.
He dons his arms as quickly as he can
And in pursuit rides off into the night;
And indiscriminately every man
Whom he encounters, be he Christian knight
Or Saracen, of Libya, or France,
Is laid low by the impact of his lance.

94

He sought Rinaldo here, he sought him there,
Louder each time he challenged him by name,
And to the centre of the turmoil, where
The dead lay thickest on the field, he came.
At last they meet, a formidable pair.
Swords are their weapons, for each lance the same
Fate overtakes: a thousand splinters rise
To join the starry wagon of the skies.

95

And when he sees the valiant paladin
He knows him straight away, beyond all doubt,
Not by his banner (which he has not seen),
But by the impact of his blows, without
Compare, and by the destrier between
His thighs; and he begins at once to shout
Abuse, reproaching him because he fled
And failed to keep the tryst they had agreed.

96

'You thought perhaps that if you hid that day',
He said, 'you'd never meet me face to face;
But, as you see, although you ran away,
I have now caught you, and whatever place
You chose, the furthest shores of Styx or, say,
The highest sphere of Heaven, I would trace
You (even if you rode your destrier),
In darkness or in light, no matter where.

97

'But if your courage fails you once again,
If, as before, you fear to fight with me,
And if your honour you would rather stain
Than risk your life, here is a remedy:
Give me your charger, and alive remain,
But go on foot; you don't deserve to be
The owner of that horse if you refuse
My challenge and a coward's part you choose.'

98

Two others near Rinaldo hear these words –
Guidon and Ricciardetto – who at once,
At the same moment, both unsheathe their swords
In answer to the Sericanian's
Abuse; but Montalbano turns towards
Them and, to check their resolute advance,
He says, 'Do you consider that without
Your help the outcome is in any doubt?'

99

Then to the pagan monarch he replied,
'Listen, Gradasso, I will make it clear
That to the shore I came; I did not hide
But kept my promise as a cavalier;
Then I will prove by arms that you have lied,
That what I tell you is the truth you hear.
You will commit an act of calumny
If you accuse me of unchivalry.

100

'But first, before we fight, attend, I pray,
And you shall hear my true and just excuse,
The reason why we did not meet that day,
And how unjustified is your abuse.
As for Baiard, it shall be as you say:
Your challenge for him I will not refuse,
But we must fight on foot and face to face,
As you decreed, and in some lonely place.'

101

The king of Sericana, courteous
As it behoves all cavaliers to be,
Whose heart, courageous and magnanimous,
Rejoices ever in true chivalry,
Follows Rinaldo without animus
Along a path beside the Seine, where he
With candour from the truth removes the veil,
All heaven being witness to his tale.

102

In further proof he calls for Buovo's son,
Who from his repertoire of magic charms
Recites in full again the very one
By which he drew his cousin from the harms
And perils of that day. 'Let us move on',
Rinaldo added then, 'to proof by arms.
What I have shown to be the truth by words,
I'll prove the more convincingly by swords.'

103

Gradasso, who desired at least to save
The first of the two reasons for dispute,
Accepted the excuse Rinaldo gave
(And any doubts he had he firmly put
Aside). This time, not where the waters lave
The shores of Barcelona is their route;
They choose a near-by fountain as their site,
Where they will meet next morning for their fight.

104

The terms are these: the destrier, Baiard,
Shall tethered be as trophy while they fight.
If he defeats his foe, the king's reward
Shall be to take the charger as his right;
But if Rinaldo presses him so hard
He has to choose between eternal night
And ignominy, then let him surrender
And to Rinaldo Durindana tender.

105

With great astonishment and greater grief
(As I have said) Rinaldo had heard tell
Of the disaster which (though past belief)
The greatest of the paladins befell.
The quarrel which broke out among the chief
Opponents of the Faith he also knew,
And thus he learned Gradasso had that blade
So famous by Orlando's prowess made.

106

When they had come to terms, Gradasso, though
Invited by Rinaldo to his tent,
Declined with thanks, for he preferred to go
To his own quarters, and away he went.
When in the East new light began to glow,
Both combatants were armed for the event
And to the fountain came, where they agreed
To fight for Durindana and the steed.

107

This duel which Rinaldo is to fight
With Sericana's monarch, hand to hand,
Is causing deep alarm in every knight
And fear in every soldier of his band.
Great is Gradasso's skill and great his might –
This they all know, and when they understand
He carries Durindana at his side,
Rinaldo's friends grow pale and terrified.

108

Viviano's brother, more than all the rest,
Feared for his cousin's safety in this fray.
He longed to put his magic to the test
And every blow against Rinaldo stay;
But though he was prepared to do his best,
He did not want to vex the knight that day.
He had incurred his anger once before
When to the ship he lured him from the shore.

109

However much the others doubt and fear,
Rinaldo goes off happy and secure.
His reputation he now hopes to clear.
Reproach, he finds, is bitter to endure.
His foes of Altafoglia and Pontier
Of arrogant pretensions he will cure.
So, bold and confident, he goes his way,
To win the triumph he expects that day.

110

From two directions the two combatants
Arrive beside the fount near the same hour.
First they embrace with friendly countenance,
As if the king were a relation or
At least a life-long friend of Montalban's.
Their brows are so serene, none could be more.
But what occurred when they began their fight
I will defer until another night.

CANTO XXXII

1

I now remember (it had slipped my mind)
I promised to enlarge upon that pang
Of jealousy, and why the Maid repined.
One cause of her uneasiness I sang.
Then a new doubt, more subtle and refined,
Torments her with a sharper, poisoned fang:
The words of Ricciardetto so infest
Her heart, it is consumed within her breast.

2

I meant to sing to you of her distress,
When suddenly Rinaldo came between.
Guidone next distracted me no less,
Holding Rinaldo long, as you have seen.
What with these two, and others, I confess
Of Bradamant forgetful I have been.
But I remember now, and will defer
The duel I began, and sing of her.

3

And yet, before I tell you of her plight,
I have to speak of Agramant again
Who, after all the terrors of the night,
Near Arles conducts such troops as still remain,
For this, he thinks, is a convenient site
To victual and regroup his forces; Spain
Is near at hand and, opposite, the coast
Of Africa he faces, with his host.

4

Through all his realm Marsilio recruits
Fresh men-at-arms and horsemen, good and bad.
In Barcelona every captain puts
His ship in fighting order; some are glad
To do so, for their purposes it suits.
Each day the generals confer; to add
To all these efforts, heavy taxes are
Imposed on every town in Africa.

5

To Rodomont an offer has been sent:
For bride he'll have a cousin of the king,
Almonte's daughter, if he will consent
To leave the bridge, and reinforcements bring
To help the Moors in their predicament.
With Rodomont there is no reasoning:
Even Oran as dowry he refuses.
To guard the lovers' sepulchre he chooses.

6

Marfisa does not copy him in this.
When word of what has happened reaches her –
The king defeated by his enemies,
So many dead, or taken prisoner –
She does not wait, but hastens where he is
Encamped beside the river Rhône; and there
She offers him her skill, her strength, her all,
And on her loyal service bids him call.

7

She led Brunello captive in her train
And gave him over to the king, unharmed.
Marfisa had done nothing but detain
Him for ten days; despondent and alarmed,
He waited to be hanged by her or slain;
But she, when no one challenged her in armed
Dispute, unwilling now to soil her hands,
Decided to release him from his bonds.

8

Instead of punishing his trickery,
She brings him to King Agramant at Arles.
You may imagine *his* delight that she
Has come to fight for him against King Charles.
In recognition of her loyalty,
He has the thief Brunello seized, who snarls,
And what she once desired the king to do
By Agramante is attended to.

9

The hangman left him in a lonely place
As food for vultures, as a meal for crows.
Ruggiero, who once saved the villain's face
And from his evil neck untied the noose,
Is lying at this moment, by the grace
Of God, upon his pallet; when he knows
About Brunello's miserable fate,
He cannot help the wretch, it is too late.

10

Meanwhile, fair Bradamante had bemoaned
The long, slow passing of those twenty days
Before Ruggiero was to keep his bond
To her and to the Faith; but he delays,
And, like a prisoner who long has groaned
For liberty, her toll of tears she pays,
Or like a patriot who long is banned
From his belovèd, smiling fatherland.

11

So slowly now the sun-god seemed to drive,
She thought one of his horses must be lame.
So slowly did the light of dawn arrive,
A broken wheel must surely be to blame.
No day so long did Joshua contrive,
Who stopped the sun, as then her days became.
The threefold night when Hercules was born
Did not so long delay the languid morn.

12

How often did she envy as she wept
The dormouse and the badger and the bear!
For gladly all that time would she have slept,
And nothing hear or see, and never stir
Until Ruggiero to her chamber stepped
And with his voice and kiss awakened her;
But to achieve that was beyond her power
Who could not even sleep one single hour.

13

She turns and tosses on her bed all night,
The downy feathers granting no repose,
Or window-gazes, eager for the sight
Of fair Aurora, old Tithonus' spouse,
Who scatters in the path of morning light
Her tribute of the lily and the rose;
And when day rises she no less desires
To see the sky ablaze with starry fires.

14

When four or five days only must go by
Before the ending of the time agreed,
Hour after hour she waited for the cry
'Here comes Ruggiero on his mighty steed!'
Often she climbed a tower and from on high
She scanned the woods and fields, as if to read
The longed-for message there, or glimpse perchance
A cavalcade along the road from France.

15

If from afar the gleam of arms is seen,
Or rider who might be a cavalier,
Her eyes, her brow, once more become serene,
For this at last, she thinks, must be Ruggier;
Or if some figure trudges on the scene,
Unarmed, she takes him for his messenger.
Though many times she is deceived by hope,
She does not cease to be illusion's dupe.

16

Sometimes she puts on armour and sets out,
Descending from the castle to the plain;
Failing to meet him, by some other route
She thinks he must have come; and once again,
With undiminished hope, she turns about
And enters Montalbano, but in vain.
She seeks him here, she seeks him there; at last
The day when he had pledged to come has passed.

17

One day, then two, then three, then six, then eight,
Elapsed; at last they mounted to a score.
She, knowing nothing of her bridegroom's fate,
Was troubled by his absence more and more.
Her bitter cries would make compassionate
The snake-haired Furies on the Stygian shore.
The beauty of her eyes she does not spare,
Nor yet her snowy breast, her golden hair.

18

'Can it be true, alas!' she cried, 'that he
For whom I search, from me attempts to fly?
He whom I hold so dear, despises me?
And he whom I entreat, will not reply?
To one who hates, my heart in bond must be?
Does he esteem his qualities so high
That an immortal goddess is required
Before his unresponsive heart is fired?

19

'Knowing how much I love him, in his pride
He spurns me both as lover and as slave.
Knowing my sufferings, he stands aside
And in his cruelty will feign to save
Me after I am dead; as serpents hide,
Blocking their ears from music, so this brave
Heroic warrior keeps out of range,
Lest by my grief his evil heart I change.

20

'Ah, stay him, Love!, who speeds from me so fast,
Whom I pursue with laggard steps and slow;
Or let me once again, as in the past,
About the world, a heart-free damsel go!
How foolish and fallacious was the trust
I had in you! Mercy you never show,
For it is your delight, your joy, your bliss,
To see your victims all reduced to this!

21

'But, in the end, of what do I complain
Except of my irrational desire,
Which lifts me far above the azure plain,
Until at last its pinions have caught fire?
My weight no longer able to sustain,
It drops me to the earth; then even higher
It raises me; its wings are singed anew;
To such repeated falls no end I view.

22

'And yet, my fault was greater, I must own;
For it was I who welcomed to my breast
A love which banished reason from its throne.
My powers are unequal to the test.
From bad to worse the charger bears me on;
I have no rein, I cannot check the beast.
It makes me realize my death is near,
To render life more difficult to bear.

23

'But why should I thus take myself to task?
My only error was in loving you.
What marvel was it that I could not mask
My feelings, or my female heart subdue?
Why should I shield myself, when I might bask
In manly beauty, grace, and wisdom too?
Such radiance as yours, how could I shun?
As well refuse to greet the rising sun!

24

'I was impelled, not only by my fate,
But by a sacred pledge that I would be
By a felicitous and blessèd state
Rewarded for my love and constancy.
If now, I realize, alas!, too late,
That I was duped by a false prophecy,
Then Merlin I revile, him I reprove,
But never will I cease to love my love.

25

'Both Merlin and Melissa I will blame
Until the end of time, for by a spell
They showed me my descendants, to their shame,
As spirits conjured from the depths of Hell;
And of this trickery their only aim
Was to delude me – why, I cannot tell.
Perhaps they envied me my peace of mind.
No other reason for it can I find.'

26

Grief so possesses her, there is no place
In her whole body which is comforted.
Yet hope within her bosom still finds space.
Though she is sure that she has been misled,
The recollection of Ruggiero's face
And, when they parted, of the words he said,
Although no evidence can she discern,
Persuades her to believe he will return.

27

This hope sustains her after twenty days
Have passed, and for a month her grief is less
Acute; her expectation helps to raise
The heavy burdens which her soul oppress.
She wonders why Ruggiero still delays
But ever at the reason fails to guess;
Then, as she searches for him here and there,
Some tidings come which throw her in despair.

28

She met one day by chance a Gascon knight
Who from the Africans had lately fled.
He had been taken prisoner that night
When the surprise attack Rinaldo led.
She closely questioned him about the fight
And listened eagerly to all he said.
Then she enquired if he had seen her love
And from that subject would not let him move.

29

He was acquainted with the pagan court
And of the duel he was well aware.
He gladly gave the Maid a full report:
How Mandricard was killed and how Ruggier
Had almost died, so badly was he hurt.
And if his message had but stopped just there,
This would have been a perfect alibi.
Her eyes already she began to dry.

30

But he went on to say that a young maid,
As fair as she was brave, Marfisa named,
Had come to the encampment, bringing aid.
For skill in battle she was justly famed.
She and Ruggiero were in love, he said.
They were together always, unashamed.
They were betrothed, so everyone believed,
And each the other's promise had received.

31

And when Ruggiero is quite well once more,
The wedding will be published far and wide,
And every leader, Saracen and Moor,
By this announcement will be gratified.
Nothing could please the pagans better, for
They know the prowess of the pair; with pride
And confidence a race of supermen
They prophesy, such as were never seen.

32

The Gascon thought that what he said was true,
And with good reason; every Saracen
And every Moor believed the rumour too.
The many indications that were seen,
The mutual affection of the two,
The origin of this belief had been.
From mouth to mouth the story quickly spread
That soon the loving couple would be wed.

33

That she had come to help King Agramant
And reached the camp just when Ruggiero did,
Confirmed the rumour; and although she went
Away, taking Brunello, to be rid
(And well rid) of the thieving miscreant,
She had returned (as I have said) amid
The Saracens, without being summoned there,
Solely that she might see and tend Ruggier.

34

To visit him appeared her only aim,
As he lay gravely wounded on his bed.
Not only once but many times she came.
All day beside him in his tent she stayed,
And left, when evening fell, for her good name;
And what was even stranger, people said,
Though for her pride Marfisa was well known,
To him a humble sweetness she had shown.

35

All this and more the Gascon verified.
When Bradamante heard this terrible
Account, the pain and grief which pierced her side
Caused her such torment that she all but fell.
Sadly she turned upon her homeward ride.
Her rising jealousy she could not quell.
All hope by rage was driven from her breast
As to her room she hastened, to seek rest.

36

She does not stop to take her armour off,
But flings herself upon her bed, face down.
The bed-clothes in her mouth she tries to stuff,
Hoping by this her anguished cries to drown.
Ruggiero's absence caused her grief enough,
And now this Gascon has arrived to crown
Her misery; unable then to bear
Her grief, she thus gave vent to her despair:

37

'Alas! whom shall I ever trust again?
If you, my love, are cruel and untrue,
Untrue and cruel are all other men;
With all my heart and soul I trusted you.
What cruelty has ever caused such pain?
And in what ancient tragedy, or new,
Was such betrayal ever heard or shown?
What fate so undeserved was ever known?

38

'How does it come to pass that you, Ruggier,
In courage, beauty, valour, chivalry,
The paragon, the perfect cavalier,
Have not the virtue of fidelity?
In courtesy and grace you have no peer;
Your only blemish is inconstancy.
How is it that, of all the virtues this,
The greatest of them, you do not possess?

39

'Without this saving grace (did you not know?)
All other virtues of a noble knight
Remain unnoticed; for, how can one show
A thing of beauty where there is no light?
How easy to deceive a maid who so
Adored you as her idol, in whose sight
You were a god, and whom you could have told
(She trusting) that the sun was dark and cold!

40

'Ah, cruel one! Of what do you repent
If killing her who loves you will not cause
Remorse? If broken faith an incident
Of no account you hold, are there no laws
Which you respect? And if you so torment
A loving friend, how do you treat your foes?
There is no justice in this world, I know,
Nor yet in Heaven, if my revenge is slow.

41

'If more than any other sin Man hates
Ingratitude, knowing no keener smart,
And if for this, exiled from Heaven's gates,
The Light-bearer in darkness dwells apart,
And if grave punishment grave sin awaits,
When due repentance does not cleanse the heart,
Beware! On you harsh punishment descends
Who for ingratitude make no amends.

42

'Of theft, that crime most evil and most foul,
I also have good reason to complain.
I hold you guilty, not because you stole
My heart, for that will ever yours remain;
I mean the gift you made me of your soul,
Which now, ah cruel! you take back again.
Restore yourself to me, ignoble thief,
And be absolved of guilt and of my grief.

43

'You have abandoned me, but I from you,
Not even if I would, could never part.
But there remains one thing which I can do,
And will, to cure this pain within my heart:
My days I will now end, though they are few.
Would that the gods had not seen fit to thwart
Me in my last desire: to die while yet
Ruggiero loved me! Then had death been sweet.'

44

So saying, ready and disposed to die,
She leaps up from her bed and draws her sword.
Rage and despair within her bosom vie.
She turns her weapon's deadly point toward
Her breast upon the left-hand side, up high –
But armour finds; her better self a word
Now whispers in her heart: 'You, nobly born,
Will thus incur eternal shame and scorn?

45

'Would it at least not be more suitable
To die in battle, honoured on the field?
If in the presence of Ruggier you fell,
Your death might move his heart; if you were killed
By him, could any woman die so well?
– For by his deed your wish would be fulfilled;
And right it were, if you by him were slain,
Since he it is who fills your life with pain.

46

'Before you die, it may be you will wreak
Revenge upon Marfisa, whose deceit
And female wiles have caused your heart to break
And from you your Ruggiero alienate.'
These whisperings a good impression make
Upon the Maid, who an elaborate
Device invents, by which to signify
Her desperation and resolve to die.

47

Her surcoat is the colour of the leaf
Which fades when it is parted from the tree,
Or sap no longer rises; and the chief
Design consists of cypress-stumps, which she
Selects as fit to represent her grief;
For never they regain vitality,
Once they are severed by the woodman's axe,
Just as the Maid her source of life now lacks.

48

She takes the steed Astolfo used to ride.
She takes his golden lance, which at a touch
Unseats all combatants and flings them wide.
The reason why Astolfo gave her such
A horse and lance, on which he so relied,
And how he first obtained them, would take much
Too long to tell again. The Maid by chance
Has chosen, unaware, the magic lance.

49

Taking no shield-bearer or company,
She rode downhill and started on her way
To Paris, for she thought the enemy
Was still encamped outside and there would stay.
No news had reached her of the strategy
By which the siege was raised, nor of the fray
In which Rinaldo slew the pagan horde,
By Malagigi helped, and Charles's sword.

50

All Quercy and its capital, Cahors,
She left; the mountain she had lost from view
Where the Dordogne (her river) has its source,
And close to Montferrand and Clermont drew,
When all at once a lady on a horse,
Serene of brow, benign and gracious too,
Passed on ahead of her upon the road.
Three knights, escorting her, beside her rode.

51

A train of squires and ladies came with her.
Some rode in front and others rode behind.
The Maid enquired of one who passed quite near,
'Pray tell me, sir, if you will be so kind,
Who is this lady?' 'As a messenger
She has been sent from the Far North, to find
The king of all the Franks,' the squire replied;
'The Arctic seas to reach him she defied.

52

'Our region, the "Lost Isle" some people call.
By others, Iceland it is also named.
Our queen by far the loveliest of all
Whom Heaven blessed with beauty is acclaimed.
She sends this shield to Charlemagne, who shall
Award it to that knight, of all those famed
For chivalry, whom he declares the best
In the whole world, by every proof and test.

53

'Since she esteems herself, and rightly so,
The loveliest of women, she will have
Only that cavalier whom she can know
To be above all others strong and brave;
And nothing her resolve can overthrow:
No man will she accept as husband save
That knight who in the lists is proved supreme.
It is for him she waits and only him.

54

'She hopes that at the famous court of France,
Where Charlemagne is ruler, such a knight
Is to be found, who with both sword and lance
Has proved a thousand times his skill and might.
The three who by the lady proudly prance
Are kings; their kingdoms I will now recite:
In Sweden, Gothland, Norway, they were crowned.
In skills of combat few are so renowned.

55

'These three, whose countries are less far-away
Than others from the Isle men call the Lost
(Because, according to what people say,
There are few mariners who know that coast),
Have been enamoured of our queen since they
First saw her, and desire at any cost
To marry her; for her, such things they've done
As shall for all eternity be known.

56

'But she the hand of no man will accept,
Unless above all others he excel.
"That in these regions you are proved adept",
She says to them, "is a poor test of skill.
Whoever wins, I grant is not inept:
A sun among the stars, he shines quite well.
But that does not entitle him to claim
A champion's renown, a hero's fame.

57

'"To Charlemagne, whom I esteem and hold
In all the world to be the wisest lord,
I plan to send a costly shield of gold,
Which I expressly ask him to award
To the most valorous, to the most bold,
Of all who fight for him with lance or sword.
And be he knight or vassal, any man
I will accept if chosen by Charlemagne.

58

'"When Charlemagne shall have received the shield
And given it to that courageous knight
Who is the champion of all who wield
Their sacred weapons in a holy fight;
Or if to one of you all others yield,
To whomsoever brings it back by right,
My hand and heart I offer in reward.
He will my husband be, my love, my lord."

59

'These words of hers induced the kings to come
To France, so distant from the Arctic main.
Each plans to take the golden trophy home,
Or by the winner vanquished be and slain.'
The Maid has listened silently and from
The tale she gathers all there is to glean.
Her courteous informant spurs his steed
And catches his companions up with speed.

60

She gladly lets him gallop on ahead,
Content to wend more slowly on her route.
Turning the contest over in her head,
Mischief, she sees, will be its only fruit.
Such rivalry as this is bound to lead
To enmity and discord and dispute
Among the paladins and others, if
King Charles agrees to countenance such strife.

61

This weighs upon her heart, but even more
She is cast down, oppressed and troubled by
The thought which weighed so heavily before
That in her grief she has resolved to die:
The love which once for her Ruggiero bore
Is now Marfisa's; she can scarce descry
The path, nor does she seek a night's abode,
So sunk is she beneath her sorrow's load.

62

And as a vessel, which an off-shore wind,
Or some mishap, has loosened from her berth,
The river's quiet reaches leaves behind,
Whirling unpiloted towards the firth,
So Bradamante wandered, with her mind
Fixed on Ruggiero, whom no power on earth
Made her forget; her thoughts were miles away
While Rabicano chose the course that day.

63

Raising her eyes at last, she sees the sun
Has turned his back on Mauretania's shore
And, diving like a goosander, has gone
To seek his ancient mother's lap once more.
And if she thinks that she will sleep upon
The ground beneath the trees, there is in store
The prospect of a night of rain or snow,
For cold and menacing the winds now blow.

64

She urges on her charger to a trot
And soon observes a shepherd with his flock,
Leaving the pastures for his simple cot.
Then, of her situation taking stock,
She asks the shepherd if he knows a spot
Where she may find some shelter; any nook
Will do, for no one is ill-lodged if warm
And dry he keeps, protected from a storm.

65

The shepherd said, 'The only place I know,
Unless I send you several miles from here,
Is Tristan's fortress, where not many go.
The doors are shut to every cavalier
Who does not first in single combat show
A winner's claim to a night's lodging there,
And, having won it with his lance, will fight
Against all comers to defend his right.

66

'For when a knight one foe has overcome
He is admitted by the castellan
(Always supposing there's a vacant room);
But he must arm himself and fight again
If any other claimants chance to come.
If not, he may in peace all night remain.
In this new combat, he who wins may stay,
The other sleeps outside till break of day.

67

'If two or three or more arrive at once,
They run but little risk of being turned out,
For if a single knight comes next by chance,
He has to fight them turn and turn about.
Just so, one cavalier in residence
To such a test of prowess may be put;
If two or three or more come after him,
The combat will be strenuous and grim.

68

'Likewise, if any lady should approach
The fortress-gate, escorted or alone,
She is obliged to yield her downy couch,
And sleep beneath the starry sky, if one
Arrives whose grace and loveliness are such
As to surpass and to eclipse her own.'
And, not content with words, the shepherd showed
The Maid with gestures where the fortress stood.

69

And Bradamante, eager to complete
The journey (of about six miles, or five,
The shepherd said) urges with hands and feet
Her willing horse, who does his best to strive
Against the muddy paths which spell defeat.
It is already dark when they arrive.
The fortress is shut fast, the gate is barred.
The Maid requests a lodging of the guard.

70

He told her all the rooms were occupied.
A group of knights and ladies had reserved
Them, who now waited in the hall inside
Around a fire for supper to be served.
'That meal is not for them,' the Maid replied.
'I know the custom; let it be observed.
Go in and tell them that a knight has come
To prove his right to occupy a room.'

71

The sentinel departs as he is told
And gives the message to the cavaliers.
Though they are valorous and brave and bold,
The challenge falls unwelcome on their ears.
The prospect of the dark and rain and cold
With present ease and comfort ill compares.
Reluctantly they arm and go outside
To meet the knight by whom they are defied.

72

They are those three whose valour is so great
By few in all the world they are surpassed.
They are those three whom we have seen of late
Beside the messenger whose troop went past.
They are those three who, hazarding their fate,
Resolve to win the golden shield; so fast
They spurred, they galloped on ahead of her
Who, now arriving, is their challenger.

73

Those who surpassed these cavaliers were few,
But Bradamante of those few was one.
Her night would not be spent outside, she knew,
In rain and darkness, hungry and alone.
The others who remained inside could view
The combat through the windows, for the moon,
Though veiled by clouds, yet shed a fitful light
Through drenching rain, illumining the fight.

74

As when a lover, burning with desire
To enter and enjoy that sweetest fruit
For which his senses long have been on fire,
Has heard the bolt which held the portal shut
Slide softly open and with love conspire,
So Bradamante, eager now to put
Her prowess to the test, rejoiced to hear
The drawbridge lowered as her foes drew near.

75

As soon as she has seen the three emerge
And cross the bridge, abreast or riding close,
She turns to take her distance and to urge
Her splendid destrier towards her foes.
The lance her cousin gave her on the verge
Of his departure is in rest; it throws
All enemies it touches, without fail;
Against it Mars himself could not prevail.

76

The king of Sweden, who rode forth ahead,
Turned first and came towards her on the plain.
The magic weapon smote him on the head,
That lance which never lowered was in vain.
The king of Gothland was the next who sped:
His horse went wandering with dangled rein,
Its rider far away and upside-down,
Who, like the third, in mud seemed like to drown.

77

With these three blows the score the Maid has notched
Is three heads down and six legs in the air.
So, none of these encounters having botched,
She gallops back towards the castle where
She claims a bed; the castellan (who watched
The combat) first obliges her to swear
That if her claim is challenged she will fight,
And then he grants her lodging for the night.

78

He pays her all due honour and respect,
Having observed her prowess and her skill.
So does the lady who, you recollect,
Has come to do the queen of Iceland's will.
The Maid approaches, formal and correct;
The lady, rising with an affable,
Serene and gracious smile, extends her hand
And leads her to the fire where others stand.

79

And Bradamante, taking off her shield,
Had next removed her helmet from her head.
In doing so, the golden coif, which held
Her tresses coiled and flat, she likewise shed.
They fell about her shoulders and revealed
Her unmistakably as a young maid,
Who was as beautiful in countenance
As she was skilled with horse and sword and lance.

80

As when the curtain falls to show a scene
Illumined by a thousand brilliant lights,
Where archways, statues, monuments are seen,
Where paint and gilding add to the delights,
Or when the sun emerges from between
The clouds and with his radiant face invites
Us to rejoice, so now before their eyes
The helm, removed, discloses Paradise.

81

Her tresses which the holy hermit cut
Have grown again; though shorter than they were,
They can be coiled again to form a knot
Behind her neck, and thus she binds her hair.
The castellan now knows, beyond all doubt,
That this is Bradamante, brave and fair,
For he has seen her many times before,
And now he pays her homage even more.

82

They sit beside the fire, and pleasant food
Is offered to their ears by what they say,
While for their bodies nourishment as good
Will be provided in another way;
And Bradamante, in this interlude,
Asked why all travellers this fee must pay
For lodging; was the custom new or old?
This story in reply the host then told.

83

'Once in the days of good King Pharamont,
Prince Clodione loved a fair young maid.
Her beauty, grace, and manners elegant
Put many other damsels in the shade.
Such was his love for her that he was wont
To keep his gaze on her as, it is said,
Argus watched Io at the will of Jove,
For jealousy in him was strong as love.

84

'On him the king this fortress had bestowed.
He kept the lady here and seldom went
Beyond the gates; and in this same abode
Ten of the bravest knights were resident.
One day by chance there passed along the road
The noble Tristan on adventure bent.
He had just saved a damsel in distress
From a fierce giant's undesired caress.

85

'Tristan arrived just as the setting sun
Had turned its shoulders to the Spanish shore.
He asked here for a bed (elsewhere not one
Could he have found, not for ten miles or more):
But entry was refused by Clodion.
Such were his love and jealousy, he swore
That to no stranger lodging would he give,
Long as his lovely lady here should live.

86

'When Tristan knew that prayers were in vain,
That Clodione never would agree,
"What I by gentle words could not obtain,
I hope to take from you by force," said he.
And so the prince he challenged and the ten
Who waited on him; and then instantly,
His sword unsheathed, his mighty lance in rest,
With a loud shout he called them to the test.

87

'These are the terms of combat he proposed:
If he unseated them and stayed upright,
The portals of the fortress would be closed
To *them* and *he* inside would spend the night.
Since such a challenge could not be refused,
Prince Clodione risks his life to fight.
He falls; and Tristan, turn and turn about,
Unseats the other ten and locks them out.

88

'And, entering the fortress, Tristan sees
The lady so beloved of Clodion.
Nature to women seldom lavish is
And yet of her she made a paragon.
Tristan exchanges a few courtesies.
Meanwhile outside the lover hammers on
The door, sparing no effort and no pain
To get his lovely lady back again.

89

'Tristan, although he does not highly prize
The lady (nor for any save Iseult
Whom he so greatly loves, could he have eyes –
The potion which he drank has this result),
To take revenge on Clodion replies:
"It would be a great wrong and a great fault
To turn such beauty out into the cold.
To do so is unchivalrous, I hold.

90

'"But if the prince declines to sleep alone
Beneath the sky and asks for company,
I have a damsel here; her charms, I own,
Are less outstanding; but, despite that, she
Is young and fair; to pleasure she seems prone,
So let her do his will; it seems to me
That it is only right and only just
The fairest should reward the most robust."

91

'These haughty words of Tristan do not please
The prince, who snorts with rage, and all night through,
As if for those who slept inside at ease
He were on guard, he paces to and fro;
And much more than the cold and rain which freeze
His bones, his lady's absence does he rue.
Tristan, who had compassion on his grief,
Next morning gave her back, to his relief.

92

'He grieved no more, for Tristan told him plain
The lady was restored to him intact;
And though for his ill manners and disdain
The prince deserved worse punishment in fact,
The night which he had passed in wind and rain
Tristan accepted, and dissolved the pact.
But he would not accept as an excuse
That Love thus drove the prince to such abuse.

93

'For Love refines a rough and churlish heart;
The opposite result should be unknown.
When Tristan and his company depart,
It is not long before Prince Clodion
For a new domicile prepares to start;
But first the fortress he entrusts to one
Whom he has long held dear, who will impose
The rule which Tristan made; and then he goes.

94

'And thus the cavalier of greatest might,
The lady who is seen to be most fair,
Shall turn the others out into the night,
To sleep upon the grass or anywhere
They can; and, as you saw, this custom, right
Until today, is honoured by us here.'
The castellan thus finishes his tale;
Meanwhile the steward has prepared the meal.

95

It is laid ready in the dining-hall.
No finer room in all the world was seen.
With lighted torches, pages come to call
The ladies, who are ushered to the scene.
When Bradamante enters, every wall
Attracts her gaze; the other damsel in
Astonishment likewise admires the sight
Of paintings which extend from left to right.

96

In ecstasy before such loveliness,
Each guest the noble paintings contemplates,
Though need for food they have, as you may guess,
After a tiring day; the steward waits
Impatiently: it causes him distress
To see the supper cooling on the plates.
The cook calls out, 'First fill your stomachs, pray;
Then feast your eyes on what the walls display.'

97

When they were seated, ready to commence,
The castellan remembered there were two
Fair ladies present; this was an offence.
The fairer one must stay, the other go
And brave the fury of the elements.
And there was nothing else which they could do,
For Bradamante and the messenger
That night had not arrived together there.

98

He calls two servitors and several maids,
Whose judgement and discernment he can trust.
They scrutinize the ladies from their heads
Down to their toes, and finally they must
Admit that Bradamante's beauty leads,
And everyone agrees this view is just.
In loveliness she is victorious
As she in combat proved more valorous.

99

The host the other lady then addressed
(Who had with apprehension waited for
The verdict): 'I regret, since in this test
You are the loser, you must yield before
Your rival; she, not you, must be our guest,
And I, alas! must show you to the door,
For she, though unadorned, surpasses you,
And this the law obliges me to do.'

100

As suddenly an inky cloud is spied
Which from a marshy vale on high ascends,
That pure and shining countenance to hide
Which radiance to all creation lends,
So, when she hears the sentence which outside
Will banish her, her head the lady bends,
And all her face is clouded with despair
Which only now so joyful was and fair.

101

Her countenance has altered and turned pale,
This verdict is so terrible to hear.
But Bradamante's wisdom does not fail;
She reassures the lady in her fear.
She says, 'No judgement rightly can prevail
Unless the arguments well-weighed appear,
And the accused must also testify,
To affirm the evidence, or to deny.

102

'Now as the counsel for defence, I say:
Whether or not I am more fair than she,
Not as a woman I came here today,
Nor do I want a woman's victory.
Unless I strip quite naked, who can say
If what she is I can be shown to be?
What is not proved should not be used in court,
And even less, if someone it may hurt.

103

'Consider all the knights who have long hair:
Not all of them are women, you'll allow.
I won my lodging as a cavalier.
That fact was obvious to all. Why now
The name of woman do you make me bear,
If masculine my every deed is? How
Can you be said to keep the law, if men
With women fight? What is your verdict then?

104

'Let us suppose that, as it seems to you,
I am a woman (which I don't concede)
And that my beauty is unequal to
This lady's beauty: would you have agreed
To take away from me what is my due?
It would be scarcely justice if you did:
To take away from me for lesser charms
What I've already won by force of arms.

105

'Even supposing such your custom was
And she must leave whose beauty is surpassed,
I should remain in any case, because,
Whatever the result, I should stand fast.
The test between us two defies your laws;
The die against her is already cast,
For if she wins in beauty, I contend
In arms, and must defeat her in the end.

106

'There must be perfect parity between
Competitors; if not, it should be clear
The judgement is invalid; it is seen
That as of right or as a gift to her
A lodging must be granted, and herein
She must remain; if any challenger
His verdict against mine would like to test,
I am prepared to show that mine is best.'

107

So deeply was Count Aymon's daughter stirred
By the sad prospect of the lady's plight,
And so regretted all that had occurred
To put her at the mercy of the night,
Without a roof, the castellan who heard
Her arguments now judged that she was right.
Her final words convinced him above all:
Agreement with them seemed most logical.

108

As when beneath the burning summer sun
A need of moisture in the grass is plain,
And when a flower in which almost none
Of its life-giving fluids now remain
Delights to feel in all its vessels run
The sweet refreshment of the friendly rain,
So the queen's messenger became once more
As joyful and as lovely as before.

109

The supper which before them had been spread,
Which had remained in all this time untasted,
They now enjoyed; no claimants for a bed,
No passing cavaliers their peace molested.
By all, the food was relished, save the Maid.
On her alone such *haute cuisine* was wasted:
Her fears, her doubts, her jealousy, which quite
Unfounded were, had spoiled her appetite.

110

She leaves the table soon to feast her eyes
Upon the beauty of the painted walls.
The queen of Iceland's lady does likewise.
The castellan at once a servant calls
Who, lighting countless candles of great size,
Sheds splendour everywhere a shadow falls,
Till the whole chamber is as bright as day.
And what next happened in my next I'll say.

CANTO XXXIII

1

Such ancient painters as Parrhasius,
Zeuxis, Timàgoras, Protògenes,
Apollodorus and Polygnotus,
Timanthes, Alexander's Àpelles,
Whose names for ever will be known to us
(In spite of Clotho and her cruelties)
As long as men shall write and men shall read
What artists' hands in former ages did,

2

And those of recent times, or living still,
Leonardo and Mantegna and the two
Named Dossi, Gian Bellino, he whose skill
In paint and marble may be likened to
The Angel Michael's, Bastian, Raphael,
And Titian to whose mastery is due
Such glory that Urbino shares no more,
And Venice shines no brighter, than Cador;

3

And many others, in whose works is seen
The selfsame genius of the past, have all
Depicted with their brushes what has been,
Some upon board and some upon a wall;
But you have never known or heard, not in
The art of ancient times, nor those we call
The new, of artists who have painted things
To come – such works as now my poem sings.

4

But of this talent let no artist boast,
Whether he be of olden times or new;
To sorcery, which sets the infernal host
A-tremble, all such works of art are due.
That painted dining-hall which I discussed
The book of Merlin (whether sacred to
Avernus or Nursia) brought to sight
By demons' labour in a single night.

5

The magic art by which our ancestors
Did many wondrous things is dead today.
But now the guests have waited many hours
To see the painted room, so let me say
Again how rapidly the light devours
The dark when servants hasten to obey
Their lord's command and flaming torches bring,
And the room's splendours into vision spring.

6

The castellan addressed the company:
'I want you all to understand', he said,
'That of the wars which painted here you see
Few have been fought, so do not be misled.
This is not only art but prophecy.
What victories, what failures, lie ahead
For us in Italy, these walls make plain
And will illumine many a campaign.

7

'The battles which the Franks predestined are
To wage beyond the Alps, for good or ill,
The prophet Merlin with spectacular
Effect depicted, from his time until
A thousand years from thence; this theme of war
The sorcerer set forth with all his skill.
The British king had sent him on this task:
"What purpose did he have?" I hear you ask.

8

'King Pharamond had been the first to lead
An army of the Franks across the Rhine
To Gaul, and there as sovereign he stayed.
To seize proud Italy was his design,
Seeing the Empire day by day decline;
So with King Arthur Pharamond had made
A pact, to join the British strength with his
(For these two monarchs were contemporaries).

9

'No act of war King Arthur entered on
Without consulting Merlin (him I mean
Who was conceived and born a demon's son,
By whom events to come were clearly seen);
And from him Arthur learned, and he made known
To Pharamond, the danger which had been
Foretold if he invaded Italy,
The land girt by the Alps and by the sea.

10

'Merlin revealed that almost all the kings
Who in the future were to govern France
Would meet destruction in their plunderings
By steel, by famine and by pestilence.
Joys will be brief, and long their sufferings,
And losses rather than inheritance
They'll find in Italy, for in that plot
God wills the fleur-de-lis shall ne'er take root.

11

'King Pharamond believed the sorcerer
Who saw the future clearly as the past,
And planned instead to send his troops elsewhere;
And Merlin, it is said, at his request,
Depicted all the scenes which you see here,
And by a magic spell made manifest
The future deeds of Frankish kings, as though
They had already happened long ago.

12

'Thus all successive kings might understand
That victory and honour would reward
Whoe'er stood forth as champion of that land
Against the onslaughts of a savage horde.
Contrariwise, if any should descend
To subjugate her or become her lord,
Him from his own undoing none should save:
Beyond the Alps he'd dig his certain grave.'

13

With this preamble, the kind castellan
Led the two ladies to the painted wall
And showed them where the histories began.
To Sigibert he pointed first of all:
'From the Mons Iovis to the Lombard plain
See him descend, lured by imperial
Mauricius and his promises of gold;
Here his defeat by Authari behold.

14

'See Clovis who a hundred thousand leads,
And more, across the Alps; and see the duke
Of Benevento who by guile succeeds,
Although outnumbered; see, he has forsook
The camp and lies in ambush, which misleads
The Franks, who like a fish upon a hook
Are caught: they rush with glee upon the casks
Of Lombard wine – no better the duke asks.

15

'And see how large a host King Childebert
Has brought to Italy, yet he, no more
Than Clovis, can supremacy assert,
Nor claim that he has waged successful war.
In Lombardy he meets his just desert:
A blazing sword which Heaven has in store
For him, descends; in droves his troops succumb
To dysentery; not one in ten gets home.'

16

He points to Pepin and to Charlemagne,
Showing how each to Italy descends,
How each of them succeeds in his campaign,
For neither harm to that fair land intends;
But one against Aistulf the sovereign
Pope Stephen aids; the other first defends
Pope Adrian against the Lombard might,
And next to Leo he restores his right.

17

Pepin the Younger he moves on to show,
Who with his army seems to cover all
The region from the outlet of the Po
As far as Pellestrina's littoral;
Who builds a pontoon bridge at Malmocco;
Whose troops attack Rialto, but to fall
Into the depths of the lagoon and drown
When wind and water wash the structure down.

18

'Look, here is Ludwig, King of Burgundy,
And here is one who takes him prisoner,
And here he makes him promise solemnly
That he will never more return; but here
The monarch breaks his promise, as you see,
And falls into the trap his foes prepare.
They rob him of his eyes, and like a mole
He is borne home to France to count the toll.

19

'See Hugh of Arles who from the Lombard plains
Has put two Berengarii to flight:
One helped by Huns, one by Bavarians,
Each fails in turn to reassert his right.
But Hugh at last is forced to yield his gains
And soon he dies; so does his offspring, quite
Soon after him (the cause was dubious).
The realm then passed to Berengarius.

20

'See there another Charles, the Angevin,
Who sets the land of Italy ablaze
To aid the Pope; Manfred and Conradin
In two relentless battles he now slays,
And here his cruel army may be seen
Oppressing the new realm in countless ways.
Now see it scattered through the citadel,
Killed at the signal of a vesper bell.'

21

And next he shows, after an interval
Of many lustres, let alone of years,
A captain who descends the Alps from Gaul
With a vast host of foot and cavaliers
Against the great Visconti, which the wall
Of Alessandria to gird appears.
But Galeazzo has things well in hand:
Defence within, ambush without, are planned.

22

And where the cunning net with skill is spread,
By the imprudent Count of Armagnac
The unsuspecting men of France are led.
Visconti's army strikes them from the back.
The countryside is littered with the dead;
Of captives too it seems there is no lack.
With blood no less than water, they see flow
The river Tanar, reddening the Po.

23

The castellan, proceeding as before,
Names others to the ladies one by one:
'La Marca and three Angevins are four
Who, each in turn unleashing havoc on
The south, in waves through all its regions pour.
But, spite of aid from Franks and Latians, none
Remains; however many times they come,
Alfonso or Ferrante sends them home.

24

'See Charles the Eighth who with the flower of France
Descends the Alps and Liri's flood has crossed.
No sword is drawn and lowered is no lance.
The realm of Naples none the less is lost,
Save for that rock which to Typhoeus grants
No respite, there spread-eagled to his cost.
Inigo Vasto by his brave defence
The Frenchman's further progress here prevents.'

25

And here the castellan, who showed the Maid
How to interpret future history,
Pointed to Ischia; and then he said,
'There are so many paintings yet to see,
But first let me relate what as a lad
My grandfather was wont to tell to me,
What he had often heard his father say,
Repeating what *he* heard in his young day,

26

'When in his turn his father would relate
What he had heard his grandsire recollect
What he had heard his father's father state,
Back to the one who heard the tale direct
From him who undertook to decorate
These walls without a brush, with the effect
Of brilliant colours which you here behold:
This is the story I will now unfold.

27

'It was foreseen that from this cavalier
Who bravely holds the threatened citadel,
And scorns the raging fury far and near,
Another would arise invincible
(And Merlin told the very month and year)
Who in his deeds all others would excel,
Who would surpass in might and chivalry
All other heroes known to history.

28

'Nereus was less beautiful, less strong
Achilles was, Ulysses was less bold,
Less fleet was Ladas, Nestor who among
The wisest men was held, less wise I hold;
Less liberal was Caesar, famed in song,
To pleas for mercy deaf, to justice cold:
Beside him who in Ischia is born,
Such heroes seem of all their virtues shorn.

29

'If ancient Crete was jubilant because
The grandson of Uranus was born there,
As Thebes for Hercules and Bacchus was,
If Delos boasted of the heavenly pair,
The isle of Ischia will have no cause
Not to exult and triumph in her share
Of glory when the marquess in that place
Is born, endowed with all celestial grace.

30

'Merlin the prophet many times foretold
That Providence would long delay his birth
Until the Empire toppled; by his bold
Exploits (of which you'll see there is no dearth)
He'll render her illustrious as of old;
But let me not anticipate his worth.'
And with these words, the kindly castellan
Moved on along the painted walls again.

31

'His folly Ludovico here repents',
He said, 'in bringing Charles to Italy.
His plan was not to drive his rival hence,
But harass him; stirred now to enmity,
He joins with Venice and to Charles presents
These serried ranks of hostile soldiery.
The king with resolution puts his lance
In rest and opens up a path to France.

32

'But all his troops who in the south remain
Will undergo a very different fate.
Ferrante, aided by the Mantuan,
Returns so strong that not a single pate
Is left unbroken: all the French are slain
In a few months; and vengeance comes too late
When he who with a Moor a pact has made
By that same traitor is himself betrayed.'

33

And that unhappy marquess he now shows,
Alfonso of Pescara, and he says,
'More brightly than the fiery garnet glows
His glory; countless are the foes he slays.
But see the traitor's net around him close,
Spread by an evil Ethiop, who plays
A double game; see now an arrow strike
His throat; the world will never know his like.

34

'With an Italian escort, Louis is
The next to cross the Alps; the mulberry
He first uproots, then plants the fleur-de-lis
In rich Visconti soil of Lombardy.
Where Charles's army went he now sends his.
By means of pontoon bridges rapidly
They cross the Garigliano, but soon all
His troops are slain or in the river fall.

35

'See in Apulia no fewer dead
Where the French troops are likewise put to rout.
Consalvo is that general', he said,
'Who tricks them twice; then Fortune turned about.
She frowned on Louis here, but on him shed
Her smile in the rich northern lowlands, cut
Between the Alps and Apennines, right to
The Adriatic, by the river Po.'

36

Then he rebukes himself, remembering
Another episode which he omitted;
And, going back, he shows one bartering
A castle which his lord to him committed.
And next the Swiss falsely imprisoning
A master whom to serve it more befitted.
These two betrayals give the king of France
The victory, who couches not one lance.

37

And Caesar Borgia he next indicates,
By Louis raised on high in Italy,
By whom all barons in the Roman States
And every subject lord deposed will be.
Then in Bologna the same king enstates
(Removing first the Saw from sovereignty)
The papal Acorns; Genoa rebels,
And Louis straight away the tumult quells.

38

'Behold how Ghiaradadda's countryside
Is littered with the many thousands slain.
All city-gates to Louis open wide.
Venice her freedom scarcely can maintain.
See how beyond Romagna passage is denied
To Julius who seeks, but seeks in vain,
To rob Ferrara's duke of Modena;
Here Acorns from Bologna banished are.

39

'For Louis now restores the rightful lords:
The Bentivoglio family returns.
And next his army marches on towards
The walls of Brescia, which it sacks and burns,
Then to Bologna instant help affords
Against the Pope, and double glory earns.
Here, as you see, both armies meet again
Beside Ravenna, upon Classe's plain.

40

'Here are the French and there the troops of Spain.
The battle now is merciless and dire.
On both sides bodies fall and scarlet stain
The soil; in every ditch the mud and mire
Are mingled with the life-blood of the slain.
Mars stands uncertain, but Alfonso's fire
At last secures the victory for France;
Of no avail to Spain are sword and lance.

41

'Ravenna will be sacked, as you can see.
Biting his lips with frenzied grief, the Pope
Summons the German hordes to Italy,
Who pour in raging torrents down the slope.
They chase the Frenchmen forth relentlessly,
Granting no quarter, leaving them no hope;
And of the Mulberry they plant a shoot
Where the fair Fleur-de-lis they first uproot.

42

'The French return and are destroyed again
By the disloyal Swiss, employed to aid,
To his great risk, young Maximilian,
Whose father they had captured and betrayed.
But see how, under a new sovereign,
The army is reformed and plans are made
That Frenchmen may obliterate the shame
Inflicted at Novara on their name.

43

'Observe with what high hopes they now set out.
Observe the king of France who rides ahead,
Who by his prowess puts the Swiss to rout.
Many are slain, the others all are fled.
Their motto is usurped, there is no doubt.
No longer on their banners will be read:
"Tamers of Princes", "Of the Church of Rome
Defenders"; vain have all their boasts become.

44

'See how despite the League he takes Milan
And with young Sforza reaches an accord;
And see how Bourbon Charles does all he can
To fend the Germans off with lance and sword.
The monarch, busy elsewhere with a plan
To stem the Emperor's advance, the abhorred
Excesses of his regents cannot check,
And so Milan from him the allies take.

45

'Behold the young Francesco Sforza who
In prowess as in name his ancestor
Resembles; to his heritage anew
He comes, assisted by the Church; once more
The French return, but are unable to
Proceed unchallenged as they did before.
The duke of Mantua, who blocks the way,
On the Ticino glory wins that day.

46

'See Federigo, on whose youthful cheeks
No down has blossomed yet: Mantua's duke.
Eternal glory with his lance he seeks
And with his diligence and cunning. Look!
He saves Pavia from the French and checks
The Lion's plan. Two marquesses, who brook
No opposition, both will prove to be
Our terror and the boast of Italy,

47

'Both of one blood, both born in the same nest.
Alfonso of Pescara's son is he
(You saw his sire shot in the throat, who least
Expected such an act of treachery).
The French from Italy will oft be chased
By his advice; the other whom you see,
Benign and glad of countenance, is named
Alfonso, for his rule of Vasto famed.

48

'He is that gallant knight of whom I said,
When Ischia I pointed out to you,
That Merlin many centuries ahead
Had prophesied the deeds that he would do,
Foretelling that his birth, long heralded,
Should be deferred until the time was due
When stricken Italy his help would need,
And from their wounds both Church and Empire bleed.

49

'With his Pescara cousin (in their rear,
Prosper Colonna) how he makes the Swiss
Pay dearly for Bicocca! And more dear
The French will pay, as you may tell from this.
Look how the French, led by their king, prepare
To make their losses good; one army is
Descending to the fertile Lombard plain;
The other, Naples tries to take again.

50

'But Fortune, who does with us what she will,
As the wind whirls the particles of sand,
Tossing them in a cloud on high until
It dies away and drops them on the land
From which it lifted them, her utmost skill
Now uses to persuade the king a band,
One hundred thousand strong, Pavia rings.
Heedless, he gives his mind to other things.

51

'But, owing to the greed of ministers,
And to the king's indulgent trust in them,
He has but few, not many, followers;
And when, at night, "To arms!" the trumpets scream,
The king, to his surprise, meets a reverse:
The Spaniards cunningly leap out at him.
By the Avalos cousins they are led
And Heaven or Hell itself they would invade.

52

'See how the finest noblemen of France
Lie dead, their bodies scattered on the ground.
See how the Spanish troops with sword and lance
The gallant monarch on all sides surround.
See how his horse in full accoutrements
Has fallen, but the king is not yet downed.
He does not cry, "Enough!", he does not yield:
Alone, unaided, he confronts the field.

53

'The valiant king defends himself on foot,
Drenched by the blood of foes as if by rain.
Numbers at last prevail; here, you will note,
The king is captured, here he is in Spain.
The marquess of Pescara shares the fruit
Of victory with Vasto's lord: the twain
Are never seen apart, and both receive
The glory for the deeds which both achieve.

54

'This army now destroyed, the other one,
En route for Naples, which it hoped to take,
Is like a lamp from which the oil is gone,
Or like a taper, flickering and weak,
For lack of wax. The king returns alone,
Leaving his sons in prison; see him make
New war on Italy, while on his soil
Invading armies enter and despoil.

55

'Here sacrilegious murderers you see,
And Rome in all her regions desolate.
With rapine, rape and arson equally
The sacred and profane they violate.
The army of the League, which ought to be
The Pope's defender, leaves him to his fate;
Hearing the Roman people shriek and wail
And witnessing their sorrows, it turns tail.

56

'The king with reinforcements sends Lautrec,
Not to wage war on Lombardy again,
But from those impious, thieving hands to take
The Church's head and to its limbs re-join.
Too long is the delay which he will make.
Ere he arrives the Pontiff will regain
His freedom; so to Naples he next turns
His hostile forces, and the city sacks and burns.

57

'Behold the imperial fleet set sail to aid
The stricken city of Parthènope.
Behold them now by Doria waylaid,
Who burns their ships and drowns them in the sea.
Behold how fickle Fortune has betrayed
The French, so favoured by her recently:
To fever they succumb, not to the lance.
Of many thousands, few return to France.'

58

Such were the tales depicted in the hall
In many different colours, bright and fair.
Long it would take me to describe them all.
The meaning of the paintings now is clear.
Repeatedly the ladies scan them all
And fascinated at the future stare.
Repeatedly they read the words of gold
Which name the heroes and their deeds unfold.

59

The two fair ladies mingled with the rest,
Discoursing on the paintings for a while.
The castellan then led them to their rest
(His visitors were honoured in this style),
But Bradamante, troubled and distressed,
The long, slow hours unable to beguile,
Tossing and turning on her bed all night,
Now on her left lies wakeful, now her right.

60

Soon after dawn she shuts her eyes at last
And sees her dear Ruggiero in a dream,
Who says to her, 'Why are you so downcast?
What you believe is false. Sooner a stream
Would flow uphill than I could ever wrest
My thoughts from you; my very eyes I'd deem
Less dear, my very heart I would abhor,
If than myself I did not love you more.'

61

And then he seems to add, 'I come today
To be baptized and to fulfil my vow.
Wounds, other than of love, caused my delay
And kept me lying helpless until now.'
Ruggiero and the dream then melt away.
No further words from him the Fates allow.
Fair Bradamante wakes, and weeps anew,
Convinced that the sweet vision is untrue.

62

And with herself communing in this wise,
'The pleasurable dream is false, alas!
My waking torment is the truth,' she cries;
'Too soon the lovely vision vanished has,
And harsh reality now greets my eyes.
Ah! Why do I not hear and see him as
Just now I heard him clearly in my thought
And saw him plainly while my eyes were shut?

63

'Sweet sleep has brought me promises of peace,
But bitter waking brings me back to war.
Sweet sleep, I know, but an illusion is,
But bitter waking does not, cannot, err.
If truth brings sorrow and illusions please,
Then of the truth, ah! leave me unaware.
If sleep brings happiness and waking pain,
Then may I sleep and never wake again!

64

'Happy the creatures that for half the year
Sleep undisturbed and waken not at all!
And though with death such slumber we compare,
My hours of waking, life I will not call,
For I alone a strange misfortune bear:
Waking I die, but when to sleep I fall
I live; and if such sleep is a demise,
Ah, Death, I pray, make haste to close my eyes!'

65

Far in the East, the early morning sun
Had crimsoned the horizon with its ray.
The clouds of the preceding night were gone
And fair the promise seemed of the new day.
The Maid arose and put her armour on,
Desiring to be soon upon her way,
But first she sought the kindly castellan
And thanked him for his courtesy again.

66

She found the queen of Iceland's messenger
Had left the castle with her retinue.
Outside, three warriors awaited her,
Whom Bradamante vanquished, owing to
The golden lance; each from his destrier
Had been unseated, and the whole night through
Exposure to the elements endured,
In howling winds and in the rain which poured.

67

They and their steeds, to add to their mishaps,
Were left with empty bellies all that night
To champ and stamp; and, worst of all, perhaps
(No, beyond any doubt, this crowned their plight),
Their queen would surely hear of their collapse.
The messenger the tidings would recite,
How each had failed, laid low by the first lance
Which they had met to run against in France.

68

And they were ready now to do or die;
Their one desire was to avenge their shame.
That the report to be delivered by
The messenger (Ullania is her name)
Might be more favourable, they would try
Their strength once more. When Bradamante came
Across the drawbridge, straight away they called
A challenge to her, resolute and bold.

69

They had no inkling she was not a man,
For not one gesture gave the truth away.
At first she scorned their challenge and began
To gallop off, unwilling to delay;
But after her insistently they ran.
For honour's sake she had to turn and stay.
Couching her lance, three monarchs with three blows
She floored, and brought the conflict to a close.

70

For, riding off, she did not turn again,
But from their sight she disappeared at speed.
The kings, who came so far in hope to gain
The golden shield by some heroic deed,
Rose to their feet in silence; it was plain,
Despite their resolution to succeed,
All three of them had failed. In their disgrace
They dared not look Ullania in the face.

71

Too many times with her along the road
They'd boasted of their prowess and had claimed
No paladin or knight who ever rode
To arms, of the most brave or skilled or famed,
Could stand against them; and such pride they showed,
Ullania, to make them more ashamed,
Told them, in punishment for arrogance,
They were unseated by a woman's lance.

72

'So, if a female knight can thus defeat
All three of you, what do you think', she says,
'Will be the outcome if by chance you meet
Orlando or Rinaldo, whom men praise,
And not without good cause, for many a feat?
I put it to you, if a woman lays
You flat, will you fare better against them?
I do not think so, nor do you, I deem.

73

'Let this suffice, you need no further proof:
You understand now what your valour is.
If one of you has not yet had enough
And wants to make another test of his,
He'll to the warp of shame add but the woof
Of mortifying wounds and injuries,
Unless he's eager to be vanquished by
Such warriors and at their hand to die.'

74

And when the messenger had proved to each
That by a woman they had been unseated;
That their bright fame was blacker now than pitch;
That what she said could well have been repeated
By ten more witnesses at least, the breach
Thus opened in their self-esteem defeated
Them anew; on their breasts they all but turned
Their weapons, with such grief and rage they burned.

75

By wrath and fury stung, each king in haste
Undoes his armour, tearing off his coat
Of mail, his sword unclasps from round his waist
And throws it deep into the castle moat.
That by a woman they have been outfaced,
That twice, so soundly, each of them she smote,
Is such a lapse from valour, they all swear
They will not put on armour for a year.

76

And everywhere on foot they meant to go,
Whether the path be smooth or rough or steep.
And when a year had passed, then even so
Their vow they would continue yet to keep
Until a horse and armour from a foe
They won; thus of their fall all three would reap
The consequence by this self-punishment:
On horse the others rode, on foot they went.

77

Fair Bradamante, riding onward, came
That evening to a castle, on the way
To Paris. Here she heard her brother's name
And Charlemagne's, and learned about the fray
Which to King Agramante had brought shame;
And here good victuals on the tables lay,
Here were good beds: to her of little use,
Who little eats and little can repose.

78

But I must not delay so long with her
That I forget to tell you what took place
When those two knights I mentioned earlier
Prepared to fight each other face to face.
Each by the fount had tied his destrier.
The winner of the battle would possess
Orlando's sword and on Baiardo ride:
The time had come these matters to decide.

79

And so, unheralded, untrumpeted,
Hearing no formal signal to commence,
Unwatched, unaided and unseconded,
With none to warn, or shout encouragements,
They move towards each other, as agreed,
As agile in attack as in defence;
And the repeated crash of heavy blows
Reverberates around as anger grows.

80

Not two such swords I know, however tested,
However solid, firm and hard they are,
That of these blades three strokes could have resisted,
For they beat all comparison, by far.
No others of such temper e'er existed,
No others proved so trustworthy in war,
For they a thousand times and more might clash
Together blow on blow, and never smash.

81

This way and that, Rinaldo, with great skill,
First on the one and then the other foot,
Evaded Durindana, knowing well
That through unyielding iron she could cut.
Gradasso flashed the celebrated steel
And wielded her with all his vigour, but
Either his strokes were wasted on the air
Or smote Rinaldo where they harmless were.

82

Rinaldo plies his sword with greater care
And many times he numbs the pagan's arm.
Now in his side he thrusts the blade, now where
The corslet joins the helmet, but no harm
Can he inflict, nor of his mail-coat tear
A single mesh, for it was woven by a charm.
His breastplate had been forged by magic too
And was impenetrable through and through.

83

They took no rest, so fixed was their intent,
Although a great part of the day was gone.
Both were incensed and neither would relent
But, gazing straight ahead, they battled on,
When suddenly another clamour rent
The air; their combat they suspend, with one
Accord they turn to find the reason why,
And see Baiardo menaced from on high.

84

They saw a monster harass and attack
The steed; it was a bird of giant size,
And yet some bird-like features seemed to lack.
Its beak was three yards long, but otherwise
Its head was like a bat's; its plumes were black
As ink, its talons merciless, its eyes,
Darting their cruel glances, were as red
As flame, its wings as wide as sails full-spread.

85

Perhaps the monster truly was a bird,
Yet I know none in any century
Like this, nor any land, nor have I heard
Of one, except in Turpin's history,
Wherein to such a creature he referred.
I am inclined to think that it may be
A devil Malagigi conjured up
From Hell to bring the combat to a stop.

86

Rinaldo thought so too, and angry words
Will be exchanged by the indignant knight
With Malagigi not long afterwards;
But he does not confess, and by the Light
Which lights the sun he swears that neither birds
Nor demons he despatched to stop the fight.
The monster, whether bird or bat it was,
Swooped on the steed and seized him with its claws.

87

Baiardo, who is strong, soon snaps the rein.
Enraged, he plunges, rears and bites and kicks.
The monster rises in the air again
And, downwards swooping, with its talons pricks
The destrier and maddens him with pain.
No reason to allow the bird to vex
Him further the outraged Baiardo sees,
Who from the scene of battle quickly flees.

88

So to the near-by wood Baiardo fled,
Seeking the thickest boughs to hide among.
The feathered beast pursued him overhead,
And watched which path its quarry went along;
But soon that wingèd monster was outsped.
The wonder-horse, alert and swift and strong,
Had found a cave to hide in, and away
The creature flew, in search of other prey.

89

Rinaldo and Gradasso, who thus see
One bone of their contention take its leave,
To cease their combat readily agree
Until the monster's quarry they retrieve,
Which gallops through the darkling wood; and he
(Their solemn promise each to each they give)
Who first succeeds in capturing the mount
Shall bring him back and tie him by the fount.

90

So they depart and, following the clue
Of grasses freshly trampled to the ground,
The hoof-marks of Baiardo they pursue,
Who will not easily by now be found.
Gradasso mounts his Spanish mare and through
The forest gallops, leaving with one bound
The paladin behind, disconsolate
And deeply discontented with his fate.

91

He quickly lost the hoof-prints of his horse.
By river-banks, by boulders and by trees,
Baiardo chose so strange and wild a course,
The thorniest thickets and the roughest screes,
To escape the monster plummeting with force
Upon his back, inflicting agonies.
So, when he saw his efforts were in vain,
Rinaldo waited by the fount again,

92

To see if King Gradasso brought him there,
As they agreed; when this had borne no fruit,
Rinaldo left the fountain, in despair,
And sadly he went back to camp on foot.
Now let us leave him and return to where
Gradasso gallops off in hot pursuit.
His journey ends in quite another way
When near at hand he hears Baiardo neigh.

93

He found him hiding in a hollow cave
Where he had taken refuge in his fright.
He was so terrified, he would not brave
The open, so Gradasso caught him quite
Without resistance; though he knows they have
Agreed to bring him back, now, uncontrite,
Gradasso has resolved to overlook
His promise, and within himself thus spoke:

94

'Let those who will, obtain this steed by force,
But I prefer in peace to make my claim.
From the Far East I travelled a long course,
To call Baiardo mine being my sole aim;
And now that finally I have the horse,
I will not give him up; and as I came
To France, so let Rinaldo travel east,
If he desires so much to have the beast.

95

'No less secure will Sericana be
For him, if he should venture in those parts,
Than France has twice already proved for me.'
Choosing a level pathway, he departs.
To Arles he comes and, making for the sea,
He finds the fleet, and on a galley starts
For home, with sword and charger making off;
But on this matter I have said enough.

96

I want to find the English knight once more,
Who rode the hippogriff just like a steed.
So fast above the clouds he made him soar,
Eagles and falcons travel at less speed.
Over all France the paladin it bore,
From sea to sea, from west to east it sped,
Then turned towards the mighty mountain-chain
Which separates the land of France from Spain.

97

Over Navarre and thence to Aragon
They pass, causing amazement down below.
Biscay is on his right and Tarragon
Is on his left; Castile is next in view,
Galicia, Portugal he gazes on,
Then changes course to Còrdova and to
Seville; and not one city in all Spain
Does he omit, on coast or hill or plain.

98

Astolfo hovers next above Cadiz
And the two signs set up in early days
By the indomitable Hercules.
The coast of Africa now meets his gaze;
The Balearic Islands too he sees,
Which for their rich fertility men praise.
Then, changing course again, towards Tangier
He flies, and soon Arzilla he draws near.

99

Fez in Morocco he observes, Oran,
Algiers, Bougie and Bone, proud cities all,
Centres of commerce and far richer than
The other cities on that littoral.
Then on he spurs to the Tunisian
Biserta and the thriving capital,
Gabes and Djerba and, next, Tripoli,
Benghazi and the shores of the Red Sea.

100

Thus every town and region he surveyed
Between the sea and Atlas' tree-clad spine.
To the Carena mountains then he bade
Farewell, flying directly in a line
To Cyrenaica, thence to Baiad
In Nubia, not far from the confine.
The tomb of Battus now behind him lay
And Ammon's temple, derelict today.

101

Another Tremesin Astolfo passed
(As in Algeria, here too the style
Of worship is Mahommedan); then fast
To Ethiopia, across the Nile
He flew, from Dobada until at last
He came to Coalle after many a mile.
Here these are Christians, while those pagans are,
And at their confines is unending war.

102

The Emperor Senapo (Prester John)
Rules Ethiopia, and in his hand
He wields no sceptre but the Cross alone.
The Red Sea is the border of his land,
Where cities teem and golden bullion
Abounds; if I mistake not, here they brand
The neophyte upon his brow, as well
As using water – or so travellers tell.

103

Senapo's faith, like ours in some respects,
Exempted him from banishment to Hell.
Astolfo has dismounted and inspects
The castle where the king, he thinks, must dwell.
Its costly style more wealth than strength reflects.
The drawbridge and portcullis chains, as well
As hinges on the doors, and bolts which hold
Them shut, are not of iron but of gold.

104

Though gold is here abundant, it is true,
The use of it is held in high esteem.
Columns of crystal lend enchantment to
The spacious loggias; brilliant colours gleam –
Yellow and red and green and white and blue –
In patterned friezes which adorn the rim
Of royal monuments and palaces –
Emeralds, sapphires, rubies, topazes.

105

Inlaid on walls, on roof-tops and on floors,
Are rarest pearls and other precious gems.
Here balsam is produced, in richer stores
Than any portion of Jerusalem's.
Amber from here arrives at many shores,
And here the hunter by his stratagems
Deprives the musk-deer of his sweet perfume:
From here so many things of value come.

106

And the Egyptian Sultan, it is said,
Pays tribute and is subject to the king,
Who could divert into another bed
The river Nile, and thus disaster bring
On Cairo, and on all that region spread
The blight of famine and great suffering.
Senapo by his subjects he is named;
As Prester John among us he is famed.

107

Of all the many kings of this domain
None could compare with him in wealth and might;
But all his wealth and power were in vain
For he had lost that greatest treasure – sight.
This was the very least of all the pain
To which Senapo was condemned: despite
His wealth (if wealthy such a man can be)
He suffered cruel hunger endlessly.

108

If the unhappy man, driven by thirst
Or a desire for food, drew near the board,
Avenging harpies, monstrous and accurst,
Swooped down in an abominable horde.
With beak and claws they did their hellish worst.
Viands were snatched away or spilled and poured,
And when their greedy bellies had been glutted,
Whatever was left over they polluted.

109

The reason was, the king in his young days,
Having achieved such honour and such fame,
Finding himself the subject of much praise,
And being bolder far than most, became
As proud as Lucifer; daring to raise
His eyes against his Maker, and on Him
Make war, he marched his army many a mile
Towards the secret sources of the Nile.

110

A mountain stretches far into the skies;
It soars beyond the clouds, it is so tall.
And there was the Terrestrial Paradise
Where Adam dwelt with Eve before the Fall,
Or so Senapo has been told, who tries
With camels and with elephants to haul
His troops up to the summit where some new
Terrain he hopes to conquer and subdue.

111

But God, beholding such ambition, quells
The troops' foolhardiness; as they advance,
He sends an Angel in their midst, who kills
A hundred thousand; for his arrogance,
Senapo's eyes are dimmed, and of all Hell's
Horrendous and accurst inhabitants,
God sends the harpies, that rapacious brood,
To steal or to contaminate his food.

112

His torment was increased unendingly
By a far-seeing sage who prophesied
Senapo's victuals would no longer be
Defiled and stolen when a knight astride
A wingèd horse should come, when all should see
This marvel through the air serenely ride.
Such an event appeared impossible
And so the king was inconsolable.

113

Now, climbing up on every tower and wall,
The people in amazement see that knight
Arrive; some of them hurry off to tell
Senapo of this unexpected sight.
Their words the fateful prophecy recall.
Leaving his staff behind in his delight,
Senapo, with his hands held out before him,
Goes forth to greet the marvel and adore him.

114

Before the castle gate Astolfo lands,
First swooping low with many a graceful gyre.
And when the blind Senapo understands
He has been brought before the wondrous flyer,
He kneels and, clasping his imploring hands,
He cries, 'Angel of God! O new Messiah!
Though I have sinned, thy heart to me incline.
To err is human, to forgive divine.

115

'Conscious of all my sins, I do not dare
To ask if thou wilt give me back my sight,
Although thou couldst, for thou, I am aware,
Art of that host in whom God takes delight.
Let it suffice that I am blind, and spare
Me now this hunger, added to my plight.
Chase back to Hell at least this fetid brood
Which mercilessly robs me of my food.

116

'And I will build for thee a marble shrine
And set it high upon my citadel.
The portals and the roof with gold will shine,
The walls will glow with gems, inside as well
As out; to honour thee is my design,
And to commemorate thy miracle.'
Thus spoke the king, who could not see one jot
And tried in vain to kiss Astolfo's foot.

117

'I am no Angel from on high, no new
Messiah,' said Astolfo modestly,
'I am a mortal and a sinner too,
Unworthy of the grace vouchsafed to me;
But what you ask I will attempt to do,
And if your kingdom of this plague I free,
You must thank God for it, and Him alone,
For hither by His guidance I have flown.

118

'To Him belong all honour and all praise,
To Him', Astolfo said, continuing,
'Your churches dedicate, your altars raise.'
He moves towards the castle with the king
And barons, who pay heed to all he says.
Senapo orders servitors to bring
The finest viands, hoping that at least
For once the harpies will not spoil the feast.

119

At his command a banquet was prepared.
The hall was fair, the décor richly wrought.
Only the duke the place of honour shared
With King Senapo; when the food was brought
A frightful clamour in the air was heard
As, beating their vile wings, the harpies sought
Once more their filthy bodies to obtrude,
Attracted by the odour of the food.

120

These monsters, who a band of seven formed,
Had women's faces, lean, as if their jaws
Had long known hunger; ravenous they swarmed.
More horrible than death their aspect was.
Each had wide wings, repulsive and deformed,
Rapacious hands, with twisted, curving claws,
A foul distended belly, a long tail
As convoluted as a serpent's trail.

121

No sooner are they heard than they are seen
And all together, swooping on the board,
They overturn the goblets and between
Their claws snatch up the food; the filthy horde,
Fouling the tables, leave them so unclean
The stench which rises cannot be endured.
Holding his nose, Astolfo seized his blade
And frequent lunges at the monsters made.

122

One on the neck and one upon the back
He strikes, one on the wing, one on the breast.
It has no more effect than on a sack
Of tow: they are not wounded in the least.
The strokes fall dead, failing in their attack.
No dish is left unspoilt of all that feast,
No cup is left upright, and not till all
The food is sullied do they leave the hall.

123

The king (who hoped that now his luck would turn,
And that the duke would drive the fiends away),
Groaning, bemoans the hour that he was born.
All hope is gone, extinguished the last ray.
Astolfo then bethinks him of his horn –
His help in peril – this will be the way
To rid Senapo of these pests, and so
A terrifying blast he means to blow.

124

But first he makes Senapo block his ears
With molten wax (as all the barons do),
Lest when that shrill and piercing sound he hears
He may be driven from his kingdom too.
Bidding Senapo set aside his fears,
He leaps upon the hippogriff anew
And to the steward plainly indicates
That he should bring more victuals, cups and plates.

125

Accordingly a meal is laid once more,
On other tables, in another hall.
The harpies swoop in as they did before
And greedily upon the viands fall.
Astolfo sounds his horn; its loud uproar
The birds cannot endure, and one and all,
Their ears being unprotected, terrified,
Heedless of victuals now, they swarm outside.

126

And after them at once Astolfo flies.
He leaves the citadel of Prester John
And to the hippogriff his spurs applies.
The harpies flee: Astolfo follows on,
Still blasting with the horn which terrifies.
The harpies make towards the torrid zone
Where a tall mountain lifts its lofty head
And where the Nile begins (so it is said).

127

Here almost at the mountain's very root
There is a passage leading underground.
Here it is certain if a man sets foot
The way down into Hell is to be found.
And here that horde take refuge from pursuit
And, to escape the horn's tormenting sound,
All seven hurry to the further shore
Of the Cocytus, where it's heard no more.

128

And at this murky aperture, which leads
For ever downwards those who lose the Light,
Astolfo's horn is silent; ere he speeds
His destrier on yet another flight,
Let me defer the story of his deeds,
As is my custom, till another night.
My pages now are full, and it is best
That I should cease my song a while and rest.

CANTO XXXIV

1

O cruel harpies, ever ravenous,
Which on blind, erring Italy descend
To ravage every meal prepared for us,
A punishment perhaps the Powers send
In judgement for our past iniquitous
And vile wrong-doing! Who will now defend
The starving mothers and the innocent,
Robbed by these monsters of their nourishment?

2

He greatly erred who opened wide the cave
Which for so many years was sealed and blocked,
From which these vile and stinking poisons have
Emerged and spread, and Italy have choked.
All peace, all quiet now are in the grave,
All fair, sweet arts of civil life are mocked.
War and its horrors, poverty and tears,
Have reigned since then and will for many years,

3

Until one day, when Italy will shake
Her heedless, hapless children by the hair
And from their long, Lethean slumber wake,
Shouting, 'Is there not one who can compare
With Calais and with Zetes? None to make
Our tables clean again as once they were,
Freed from these stinking monsters' greedy claws,
As Phineus was and as Senapo was?'

4

The paladin the harpies had pursued
And with his horn had scattered them in fright,
And now inside a mountain cave the brood
Had entered and had disappeared from sight.
Astolfo to the aperture had glued
His ear, and, hearing sounds of souls in plight,
Shrieks, wails and lamentations, he could tell –
The evidence was plain – this must be Hell.

5

Astolfo thought that he would enter in
To see those who have lost the light of day,
And search the circles of the realm of sin
Till to Earth's centre he had made his way.
'What should deter me?' said the paladin,
'I have my horn which I can always play.
Pluto and Satan from my path will flee,
And Cerberus, that dog whose heads are three.'

6

And so, dismounting from the hippogriff,
He left it tethered to a little bush,
And entered in, clasping his horn as if
His life depended on it. In a rush
The foul air overwhelmed him like a whiff
Of sulphur or of pitch. Trying to brush
The vapour from his nose and eyes, the duke
On his descent yet further footsteps took.

7

And now the lower down Astolfo goes,
The darker, thicker, murkier the fume,
And stronger steadily his feeling grows
He must return the way that he has come.
But something suddenly (Astolfo knows
Not what) he sees above him in the gloom.
Much like a corpse which in the rain perhaps,
Or wind or sun, has dangled long, it flaps.

8

It was so dark, the duke could scarcely see
Along the smoky thoroughfare of Hell,
And what this object in the air might be,
In his bewilderment, he could not tell.
In an attempt to solve the mystery,
He drew his sword to strike it; the blows fell
Without effect, as though he slashed through mist.
A spirit it must be, Astolfo guessed.

9

He heard a plaintive voice, which these words spoke:
'Do not molest us, pray, as you descend,
Tormented as we are by the black smoke
Which the infernal fires upward send.'
Astolfo, stupefied, arrests his stroke
And to the shade replies, 'As God may end
The rising of these fumes from deepest Hell,
Be not displeased about your state to tell.

10

'And if you wish me to take news of you
Into the world above, I am your knight.'
The spirit answered, 'To return anew
By fame into the sweet, life-giving light
So pleases me that my deep longing to
Receive this boon urges me to recite
And pulls my story from me by the roots,
Though ill such speech my inclination suits.'

11

And she began, 'Sir, I am Lydia,
Born of the Lydian king to high estate.
By God's will, to this smoky area
Eternal condemnation is my fate,
For, while I lived above in the sweet air,
For faithful love I gave not love, but hate.
These regions an infinity contain,
For a like fault condemned to a like pain.

12

'Harsh Anaxàrete dwells farther on,
Suffering more torment in a denser fume.
Her body in the world was turned to stone,
Her soul to suffer in this realm has come,
For she could see, unmoved, her lover wan
Hanged at her door, so desperate become;
And, near by, Daphne knows how much at last
She erred to make Apollo run so fast.

13

'If one by one these souls I were to name
Of the ungrateful women here below,
It would be long ere to the end I came,
For to infinity their numbers grow;
And longer still, if it should be my aim
To tell you all the men who deeper go
To a worse place; for their indifference,
Where flames are hotter, smoke is yet more dense.

14

'Since women are more easily deceived,
Justice demands that their betrayers should
Be lower down; he who Medea grieved,
He who left Ariadne by the flood,
He who abandoned Dido, have received
Worse pains, with him who drove to deeds of blood
Prince Absalom, by raping of Tamar.
Here erring wives, there erring husbands, are.

15

'But now, to tell you more about the sin
Which for my punishment has brought me here:
I was so beautiful and proud that in
My life on earth I was beyond compare.
Yet of these two, I know not which would win:
Beauty and pride, which rivals in me were;
Since pride, it seemed, continued to arise
From beauty which was pleasing to all eyes.

16

'There was a cavalier who lived in Thrace,
Esteemed in all the world the best in arms.
So many praised the beauty of my face,
My loveliness of person and my charms,
My image henceforth he could not erase.
A champion, undeterred by war's alarms,
He thought that if he offered me his love,
His valour and brave deeds my heart would move.

17

'He came to Lydia; by a stronger noose,
Soon as he saw my beauty, he was caught,
And, from these bonds unable to get loose,
He served my father, and so well he fought,
So varied were his valiant deeds, the news
Of them on the swift wings of Fame was brought.
Long would it take to say all he deserved,
If but a grateful monarch he had served!

18

'Pamphilia, Caria, Cilicia
Were conquered for my father by the knight,
For never was the army sent to war
Unless he judged that they would win the fight.
So, having now a cornucopia
Bestowed, he asked my father, as of right,
If in reward for so much toil and strife
He would consent that I should be his wife.

19

'He was rejected by the king, who aimed
To marry me to one of high degree,
Not to a knight-at-arms, however famed,
Possessed of nothing but his gallantry.
By avarice, that sin which is acclaimed
The school of vice, the king is ruled, and he
Appreciates good deeds about as much
As tunes upon a lyre a donkey touch.

20

'But when Alcestes, he of whom I speak,
Received this snub, his anger was intense.
He felt that he was injured to the quick
By such ingratitude and insolence;
And, not disposed to turn the other cheek,
Vowed he would bring his lord to penitence,
And to Armenia's king, our enemy,
He went, and stirred up his hostility.

21

'And to such enmity he roused the king
That on my father he made war; Alcest,
So celebrated for his soldiering,
As captain of those troops was judged the best;
And all the spoils he promised he would bring
To the Armenian monarch, but, his breast
Still burning to enjoy my fair young limbs,
Those for himself as a reward he claims.

22

'He caused the king, my father, in that war
More injury than I could ever tell.
Four armies in one year defeated are:
He leaves him not a town or citadel,
Except for one which perpendicular
And lofty walls render impregnable.
Therein the king, with those whom he loves best,
Flees with what treasure can be snatched in haste.

23

'Our adversary then besieged us there.
By dint of his assault and battery
He soon reduced my father to despair,
Who willingly would then have bartered me
As wife, and servant too, and named him heir
To half his kingdom, if he might go free:
Seeing how low the stores of victuals were,
He knew that he would die a prisoner.

24

'Before this happens, he resolves to try
Whatever remedy seems possible.
As his first hope, he chooses me, and I,
Whose beauty was the cause of so much ill,
To parley with Alcestes go; and my
Intention is to do my father's will:
To plead with him to take me as his wife,
And half our kingdom, for an end to strife.

25

'Alcestes, having heard of my intent,
Proceeds towards me, pale and tremulous,
More like a captive in whom hope is spent
Than a commander so victorious.
The words which I now use are different
From those I planned before I saw him thus,
And when the situation I discern
I change my tactics as I see him burn.

26

'So I begin to curse his love for me
And to lament what it has brought us to:
My father victim of his cruelty,
Myself a hostage: this (I said) was due
To his decision to use force; if he
Had been content, I added, to pursue
His former ways, so pleasing to us all,
I had been his after an interval.

27

'For, though my father had at first refused
The honourable wish he had expressed
(Of stubbornness the king might be accused
And never would he grant a first request),
He did not thus deserve to be abused
With such ferocious anger; for the rest,
I said, still braver deeds he should have tried
To win the boon my father had denied.

28

'And had my father still ungrateful proved,
I should have prayed and urged him in my turn
To let me wed the cavalier I loved;
And if he had continued still to spurn
All our entreaties, and remained unmoved,
We should have wed in secret; but the stern,
Unyielding course that he had chosen then
Had changed my mind, nor could it change again.

29

'Although I had come forth to speak with him,
Moved to compassion by my father's plight,
No fruit would ever grow on such a stem,
For never now his love would I requite;
And sooner would I let him tear me limb
From limb than in my person take delight
And on my body satisfy his lust.
By force first overpower me he must.

30

'These words I used and others similar,
Knowing what power over him I had.
Repentant he became and humbler far
Than any saint or hermit; then he made
Obeisance, and, like a prisoner,
Kneeling he drew and handed me a blade.
I was to take revenge with it, he said,
For all his evil deeds and strike him dead.

31

'Finding him in this state, I formed a plan
To follow through my triumph to the end.
I let him hope that, if as he began
He now continues, I will be his friend
And grant those joys desired by every man,
If he agrees his errors to amend:
My father's kingdom he must first restore,
Then win my love by loyalty, not war.

32

'He gave his word and to our citadel
He sent me back, untouched, as I set out.
He did not dare to kiss me, such the spell
By which I bound him, for beyond all doubt
Cupid, as you can see, was aiming well
And still more arrows was prepared to shoot.
He then departed to negotiate
With the Armenian king he'd served of late.

33

'And with the utmost courtesy he speaks,
Entreating him to leave my father his
Now ravaged kingdom and, no more to vex
Him, to withdraw behind the boundaries
Of old Armenia; scarlet in both cheeks,
The angry king is deaf to all such pleas:
He will not end the war which has been planned
The while my father has one inch of land.

34

'And if some whining woman's wily ways
Have made Alcestes alter his design,
So much the worse for him, the monarch says.
He for his part refuses to resign
Their hard-won gains. Once more the other prays:
His words, he sees, are useless (unlike mine).
First he laments, then vows the king will rue it,
For willy-nilly he will force him to it.

35

'His anger grew, and soon from threats he passed
To actions even worse and angrier.
He drew his sword against the king at last,
Though countless of his nobles present were,
And ran him through as they looked on aghast,
Helpless to aid him or to interfere.
And he defeated the Armenian troops
With Thracians whom he paid, and other groups.

36

'After one month and at his own expense
(And not one penny did my father pay),
Our kingdom he restores; in recompense
For widespread ruin under which it lay,
Not only costly booty he presents,
But makes Armenia heavy tribute pay,
With Cappadocia which borders it,
While to his raids Hyrcanians submit.

37

'No triumph for Alcestes had we planned,
But plotted how to kill him, though at first,
Since he had many friends, we held our hand,
Knowing a chance would come to do our worst.
Day after day I said I loved him and
With female guile his fondest hopes I nursed;
But other foes, I say, he must bring low
Ere the sweet joys he longed for he could know.

38

'I send him here, I send him there, alone
Or with few troops, on many a strange task
Or perilous adventure, from which none
But he would e'er return, but all I ask
He does, killing the monsters, every one,
And earning glory in which heroes bask.
By cannibals and giants he is tested
With which my father's kingdom is infested.

39

'Not Hercules such labours had to face
For King Eurystheus or for Juno, in
Nemea, Erymanthus, Lerna, Thrace,
Aetolian valleys and Numidian,
By Tiber, Ebro – whatsoe'er the place.
The tasks which he performed could not begin
To rival those on which my swain I sent
With winsome words and murderous intent.

40

'And when my plan has failed in its effect,
I choose another, which is better still.
The minds of those who love him I infect
With poison, and such hatred I instil,
His reputation in their eyes is wrecked.
His greatest joy is to obey my will.
I raise my finger: at my side he stands
And blindly he performs my least commands.

41

'When by these means I see that I have rid
My father of all enemies, and not
One friend, because of everything I did,
Stands by Alcestes, then I tell him what
(Until this moment came) from him I hid:
That he has been the victim of a plot,
That ineradicable is my hate
And his demise with joy I contemplate.

42

'I thought the matter over carefully:
If my intention was too plainly shown
I might incur a name for cruelty
(Too many knew the deeds which he had done).
And so I banished him from sight of me
(I judged this deprivation would alone
Suffice); no letter would I read of his,
And turned a deaf ear to all messages.

43

'And my ingratitude such bitter pain
Inflicted on him that his spirit broke.
When he had pleaded many times in vain,
Illness confined him to his bed; he spoke
No more, and soon he died, by sorrow slain.
And now I weep and on my face the smoke
Has left a tinge that is indelible,
For no redemption can be found in Hell.'

44

Thus the unhappy Lydia ends her tale.
The duke moves onward to seek other souls,
But the avenging fog, like a thick veil,
As he advances, still more thickly rolls.
Soon not a handbreadth farther down the vale
Can he proceed; the smoke his senses dulls.
Not only must his footsteps be retraced,
But if he wants to live he must make haste.

45

And, striding rapidly, he seems to run,
Not walk, as he completes his upward climb
To where his journey to Inferno was begun.
He sees the aperture in a short time
Where the dark air is tempered by the sun.
Escaping breathless from the choking grime,
From the vile depths where he has been confined
He clambers forth, leaving the smoke behind.

46

And that those greedy pests may never more
Return, Astolfo gathers stones and rocks,
From pepper- and amomum-trees a store
Of branches cuts, and with these sticks and stocks
He makes a wall and hedge to bar the door;
So well this aperture Astolfo blocks,
The harpies will not find it possible
To make their exit thence again from Hell.

47

While he had visited that murky place,
The black smoke rising from the burning pitch
Not only stained Astolfo's hands and face
But worse, it left an inner blemish which
Was hidden by his clothes; searching apace,
He found a spring at last in a small niche.
In this, to cleanse away the grime and soot,
Astolfo washed himself from head to foot.

48

Seated upon the hippogriff again,
Away into the air Astolfo flies.
The mountain's summit he intends to gain,
Which almost to the moon is said to rise.
Now for the solid earth he feels disdain,
Ascending ever higher in the skies.
He does not once look down, nor does he stop
Until he lands upon the very top.

49

Sapphires and rubies, pearls and topazes,
Diamond, jacinth, chrysolite and gold
Might be compared with flowers which the breeze
Has painted there; and could we here behold
Those grassy slopes which now Astolfo sees,
The green would brighter seem than emerald.
The branches of the trees are no less fair,
Bright with the blossoms or the fruit they bear.

50

The little song-birds a sweet concert make
And gay their multi-coloured feathers gleam.
Clearer than crystal shines a quiet lake,
Translucent flows an ever-murmuring stream.
The foliage the breezes softly shake.
So constant, so unfaltering they seem,
The air so tremulous at their caress,
That nowhere can the heat of day oppress.

51

From flowers, fruit and grass the breezes stole
The varied perfumes, wafting to and fro;
And on this mingled sweetness fed the soul
Which only this delight desired to know.
Midway along a plain, upon a knoll,
A palace stood; with flame it seemed to glow.
Such light and splendour by its walls were cast,
All mortal buildings by it are surpassed.

52

Astolfo slowly rides towards the pile
And gazes on the wondrous monument.
It stretches, he observes, for many a mile,
For more than thirty is circumferent.
The beauty of the landscape and the style
Of the fair palace (so he argued) meant
Our fetid world by Heaven abhorred must be,
So sweet and fair that other is to see.

53

And when he next observes how luminous
The palace is, what can he do but stare?
A single gem, carved by a Daedalus,
Brighter and ruddier than rubies are!
Stupendous fabric! Nothing built by us
With structure such as this could we compare.
Let everyone be silent who would try
The seven wonders here to glorify.

54

And on the threshold of that house of bliss
An elder stands to greet the duke; his gown
Is white as milk, redder his mantle is
Than minium, silver his hair, and down
His breast extends a snowy beard, which his
Ethereal aspect heightens, while a crown
Of light irradiates him in such wise
He seems of the elect of Paradise.

55

The duke approached on foot, in reverence,
And with a joyful face the elder said:
'A will divine, O paladin, consents
That on the earthly paradise you tread.
Why you have come, nor where you go from hence,
You have not heard, but do not be misled:
For long predestined was your journey here
From the far distant northern hemisphere.

56

'To rescue Christendom and Charlemagne
From present peril of the Infidel
You have been brought on high to this terrain.
Be now advised by what I have to tell:
Courage and knowledge would have been in vain,
My son – your horn, your wingèd horse as well;
Nothing could help you to attain this height
If God did not so will it in His might.

57

'We shall discuss it later at our ease,
When I shall tell you what you have to do.
First take refreshment with us, if you please.
So long a fast is wearisome for you.'
And he proceeded, with such words as these,
The duke's surprise and wonder to renew;
And in the end the greatest marvel came
When the old man revealed his saintly name.

58

For he was the Evangelist, that John
Whom Christ so loved that the belief was spread
That when his span of years was past and gone
He would not die, because these words were said
To Peter the Apostle by God's Son:
'If he await me, why art thou dismayed?'
Although He did not say: 'He will not die',
Yet we see plainly what His words imply.

59

For he ascended to this mountain where
Enoch the patriarch had come to dwell.
Elijah, the great prophet, too was there
Who has not perished but is living still.
And far beyond our pestilential air
They will enjoy eternal Spring until
The trumpets from on high shall sound aloud
And Christ shall come again on a white cloud.

60

With gracious hospitality the knight
Was welcomed to a chamber by the saints.
The hippogriff was stabled for the night.
With corn in plenty, it had no complaints.
And when Astolfo tasted the delight
Of fruits of paradise, of the constraints
On our first parents he revised his views:
Their disobedience he could excuse.

61

When the adventurous duke had satisfied
His natural needs for food and for repose
(With every comfort he had been supplied),
Aurora from her husband's bed arose
(Despite his age her love has never died,
But as he older, she the fonder, grows).
Astolfo, rising too, saw standing near
The loved disciple Jesus held so dear.

62

Clasping Astolfo's hand, of things he spoke
Which I in silence deem it best to pass;
And then he said, 'My son, the Christian folk
In France (more than you know) are in distress,
For you must learn that your Orlando took
The wrong direction and is now, alas!,
Enduring retribution, for God sends
Dire punishment when one He loves offends.

63

'On your Orlando God bestowed at birth
The greatest strength and courage, and beyond
The usage of all combatants on earth,
His body cannot suffer any wound.
Our holy Faith's Defender, he stands forth,
And so appointed by God's mighty bond,
Like Samson, champion of the Hebrew lines
Against their enemies, the Philistines.

64

'But your Orlando for his gifts has made
To his Creator but a poor return.
The more it was his duty to lend aid,
The more the Faithful have been left forlorn.
His blinding passion for a pagan maid
This Christian knight of judgement has so shorn
That cruelly his cousin twice he fought
And with impiety his death has sought.

65

'And God for this has caused him to run mad,
With sides and chest and belly stripped and bare
(So that his foes have reason to be glad),
Of others and himself quite unaware;
And a like retribution, I will add,
Nebuchadnezzar was obliged to bear
For seven years, when, as the Bible says,
On pasture, like an ox, God made him graze.

66

'Since the wrong-doings of the paladin
Are less to be condemned, so they incurred
Less retribution than the monarch's sin;
And, for the ways in which Orlando erred,
A sentence of three months was passed, and in
This period his intellect was blurred.
And now God wills that you from us shall learn
How you can make Orlando's wits return.

67

'Another journey I must take you on,
Leaving the earth beneath us far below,
Until we reach the circle of the moon –
The nearest of the planets, as you know.
The only means to cure Orlando soon
Is hidden there and that is why we go.
And when the moon is riding high tonight
We shall set out together on our flight.'

68

Of this and other matters with the duke
St John Evangelist discoursed that day;
But when the sun the western world forsook,
The moon her horn had started to display.
Then that same chariot which in God's Book
From the Judaean mountains bore away
Elijah out of sight of mortal eyes
Is now made ready for the enterprise.

69

Four chestnut steeds, shining and ruddier
Than flame, the saint first harnessed to the coach
And, seated now beside his passenger,
He takes the reins and at his skilful touch
The horses rise; first, like a hoverer,
The chariot rotates, then they approach
The sphere of fire, and by a miracle
They are not burned or singed, and all is well.

70

When they have left the ring of fire behind,
They reach the kingdom of the moon, which bright
As spotless steel, for the most part, they find,
Equal (though somewhat smaller) in their sight
To our own globe, the last of those confined
Within the circling spheres, although not quite
Identical, for if that were to be
The moon would be encompassed by the sea.

71

Astolfo had two reasons for surprise:
First, that the kingdom of the lunar sphere
Should be so large, when such a tiny size
Its circle seems to us when glimpsed from here;
Next, that he had to screw up both his eyes
To see the globe we live on plain and clear.
Since earth and ocean have no proper light,
Their image does not rise to a great height.

72

There, other lakes and rivers, other rills
From ours down here on earth are to be found,
And other plains and valleys, other hills.
Cities and castles on the moon abound;
The size of houses with amazement fills
The paladin; extending all around
Are deep and solitary forests where
Diana's huntress-nymphs pursue the deer.

73

The duke did not delay to view each sight,
For that was not the aim of his ascent.
Between two mountains of prodigious height
The travellers to a deep valley went.
What by our fault, or Time's relentless flight,
Or Fortune's chances, or by accident
(Whatever be the cause) we lose down here,
Miraculously is assembled there.

74

Not only wealth and kingdoms, which the wheel
Of Fortune whirls at random among men,
But what she has no power to give or steal,
Such as the following, I also mean:
Tatters of fame are there, on which a meal
Is made (the tooth of Time is sharp and keen);
Prayers to God and penitential vows
Which sinners make with humbled knees and brows,

75

The tears of lovers and their endless sighs,
The moments lost in empty games of chance,
Vain projects none could ever realize,
The fruitless idleness of ignorance,
And unfulfilled desire – which occupies
More room than all the rest and more expanse:
In short, whatever has been lost on earth
Is found upon the moon, for what it's worth.

76

Between the garnered heaps Astolfo passed,
Asking to be enlightened by his guide.
He heard the whistling shriek and gusty blast
Of swollen bladders; these, St John replied,
Had once been crowns, by monarchs worn, long past,
Who once were celebrated far and wide,
Whose very names now scarce remembered are,
Of Persia, Greece, Lydia, Assyria.

77

Fish-hooks of gold and silver, a vast hoard
Of treasure, were the futile offerings,
Made in the hope of mercy or reward,
To patrons, avaricious princes, kings.
Garlands with hidden snares were praises poured
In adulation, like the chirrupings
Of cicadas which, empty now and spent,
The homage sung by poets represent.

78

Fetters of gold and bonds with gems encrusted
Were fruitless love-affairs pursued in vain.
Talons of eagles were the powers entrusted
To eager toadies by their sovereign.
The princely favours for which minions lusted
And granted favours willingly to gain
(No longer prized when youth had lost its bloom),
Were bellows filled with empty air and fume.

79

Ruins of cities and of fortresses
Lay scattered all about, with precious stores,
Plots ill-contrived, broken alliances,
Feuds and vendettas and abortive wars,
Serpents whose faces had the semblances
Of thieves and coiners and seductive whores.
Phials lay broken – he saw many sorts –
The futile service of ungrateful courts.

80

And pools of soup from many basins spilled
(Such was the explanation of St John)
Were all bequests which dying persons willed
For charitable ends; then, moving on,
They passed a heap of flowers which once filled
The air with perfume but turned putrid soon.
This was the gift (if such it can be said)
Which Constantine to Pope Sylvester made.

81

Traps, snares and lures, he saw, besmeared with lime.
These, ladies, your sweet charms and graces were.
But if I weave a pattern in my rhyme
Of all the things shown to Astolfo there,
Unending it will be and long the time.
Every event in life, every affair
Is found, with one exception, on the moon:
Never will madness from the earth be gone.

82

Some days the duke had lost next caught his eye;
Some of his deeds which he performed in vain,
St John interpreted as they walked by;
And what we think we never lose, I mean
Our wits (for *them* we raise no prayers on high),
Towering like a mountain on the plain,
Exceeded all the other smaller mounds
In which the kingdom of the moon abounds.

83

A liquid, thin and clear, Astolfo sees,
Distilled in many vases, large and small,
Which must (so volatile the fluid is)
Be tightly corked; the largest of them all
Contains the greatest of those essences:
The mind of mad Anglante, of whose fall
You are aware and of his frenzied fits.
And on it the duke read: 'Orlando's wits'.

84

On other bottles too the names are shown
To whom the wits belong. To his surprise,
Astolfo finds a great part of his own;
And, more astonished still, before his eyes
He sees the wits of those he thought had none.
But this his first impression verifies:
That little wit they must retain down here
If such a quantity is found up there.

85

Some lose their wits for love, some for reward
Of fame, still others scour the seas for gain;
Another hopes for favours from his lord;
Others in futile magic trust in vain;
Some paintings treasure, others jewels hoard;
All for their hearts' desire have gone insane:
Astrologers and sophists by the score
Have lost their reason, poets too, still more.

86

Astolfo takes his wits (for this St John
Allows); putting the bottle to his nose,
He sniffs, and to their former place they run;
And Turpin says (and I believe he knows)
Astolfo lived more wisely from then on,
Save for one error, as I will disclose,
Which later made him lose his wits again
And all his friends' remonstrances were vain.

87

The largest, fullest bottle, which contained
Orlando's wits, Astolfo also took.
He found these were less easily attained
(Since they were higher up); before the duke
Descended from the moon, and earth regained,
The author of the apocalyptic book
Led him to where a river ran beside
A palace, and invited him inside.

88

Fleeces and bales were stacked in every room,
Of flax, of silk, of cotton and of wool,
Bright-hued, or sombre with the tones of doom.
A white-haired woman wound a spindleful
Of skeins from all these fibres, as when some
Young country lass the moistened spoils will pull
From the cocoons in summer-time anew,
When the silk-harvest of the year is due.

89

When all the fibre from one fleece is gone,
The next is brought; the worst and the best thread
Are separated by another crone
(For she who winds it pays no heed to grade).
'What work is this?' Astolfo asked St John.
'The two old women are the Fates,' he said,
'They the divinities immortal are
Who spin your mortal lives from stamina.

90

'Long as a skein endures, so long will last
A human life, and not one moment more.
Death takes away the fibres of the past,
And Nature's watchful task is to restore.
And by the second Fate the threads are classed.
Some will adorn the robes of souls before
The heavenly throne, but the defective will
Be fashioned as harsh bonds for those in Hell.'

91

The spindles, full of fibres to be spun,
And for their several uses set aside,
Were tagged with little disks; on every one,
Iron, silver, gold, a name could be descried.
And as the progress of the work went on,
Untiring to and fro an old man plied,
Taking away the spindles from the store
And always coming back again for more.

So swift and nimble was that ancient man,
You would have thought he had been born to race;
And to reduce that heap appeared his plan,
Decreasing it as he increased his pace.
The reason why he did and where he ran
I'll tell you at some other time and place,
If I receive a welcome sign from you
That I should take my story up anew.

CANTO XXXV

1

Who will ascend for me into the skies
And bring me back the wits which I have lost?
The dart you aimed, my lady, with your eyes
Transfixed my heart, to my increasing cost.
Yet I will utter no complaining cries
Unless more triumph over me you boast;
But if my wits continue to diminish,
I know that like Orlando I will finish.

2

But to regain my sanity, I know
I have no need to journey to the moon
Or to the realms of Paradise to go,
For not so high my scattered wits have flown.
Your eyes, your brow, your breasts as white as snow,
Your limbs detain them here, and I will soon
Retrace them with my lips, where'er they went,
And gather them once more, with your consent.

3

Through spacious, lofty halls the paladin
Strode on, gazing at lives that were to be,
When on the fateful distaff he had seen
Those other lives complete their destiny.
Among them he perceived a golden skein.
The brightest gems, fashioned as filigree,
Not by one thousandth would with this compare,
However exquisite and fine they were.

4

The wondrous lustre of this life outshone
All other skeins; though they were numberless,
This golden marvel had no paragon.
Whose life it was Astolfo longed to guess,
And when it would begin on earth. St John
Revealed that twenty years (no more, no less)
Before that designated M and D
This life would enter on its infancy.

5

And as that lovely skein no equal had,
So the blest age that would arise with it
Would put all former ages in the shade,
By such unprecedented splendour lit!
To bounteous Nature's gifts, Fortune would add
Her kindly share and Man his part remit
These rare endowments to perpetuate
And a fair paradise of grace create.

6

'The king of rivers holds in his embrace
A humble little town. The waters flow
In proud twin branches where it turns its face;
Behind, to a deep, misty marsh they slow.
And as the centuries roll on apace,
In splendour and in fame I see it grow.
Through all the length of the peninsula
Its buildings and its arts unrivalled are.

7

'And not by chance, for it is Heaven's plan
This city shall so quickly gain repute
To be a birthplace worthy of this man,
Just as the branches which will bear the fruit
Are grafted by the skilful husbandman,
Who watchfully thereafter tends the shoot,
Or as a jeweller refines the gold
Which in its circle a fair gem will hold.

8

'Never a lovelier vesture has been worn
By any spirit in the realms below;
And rarely has been, rarely will be, born
A soul as noble as Ippolito,
Who at the will of Heaven will adorn
The Este lineage; for you must know
Ippolito d'Este is the name by which
He will be called whom God will so enrich.

9

'Those ornaments of soul, of which a few
Suffice to honour many men, will be
Combined in him of whom I speak to you,
Whose merits, gifts and talents I foresee.
Virtue he will protect, and learning too.
But if I list in their entirety
The noble deeds he will perform, it's plain
Orlando for his wits will wait in vain.'

10

These were the words which Christ's disciple said
In converse with the duke. When they had been
In all the rooms where lives were stored, he led
Astolfo to the stream which he had seen
On entering; sand, rising from the bed,
Rendered the water clouded and unclean.
There on the bank they found that ancient man
Who to and fro perpetually ran.

11

I do not know if you remember him
From the last lines of Canto Thirty-four?
Old in the face, but lean and lithe of limb,
As fast as any deer he runs, and more.
He fills his lap with labels to the brim
In vain endeavour to deplete the store,
And in the stream, named Lethe, which takes all
His precious load of plaques, he lets them fall.

12

When he arrived upon the river-bank
That prodigal old man his garment shook,
And all those names, no matter what their rank,
The turbid stream engulfed; and as the duke
Observed, by far the greater number sank
Beyond the reach of fishing-line and hook;
Out of a hundred thousand thus obscured
Beneath the silt, scarce one, he saw, endured.

13

A flock of vultures wheeled about the flood
With jackdaws, crows and other birds of prey,
Hovering greedily as if for food
And cawing in a raucous roundelay.
They swooped upon the waters like one brood
Soon as they saw the treasures cast away.
These shining tokens of renown they seek
And bear them off (not far) in claws or beak.

14

But when such birds attempt to soar on high
They lack the stamina to bear the weight,
And of the names they choose, howe'er they try,
Oblivion in Lethe is the fate.
Two birds there are, and only two, which I
Believe can sing the praises of the great:
Two silver swans, as white, my lord, as your
Proud eagle; in their mouths fame is secure.

15

So, counter to the impious design
Of the old man who each and every name
To the Lethean waters would consign,
These kindly swans a few preserved for fame.
Now moving, mirrored, in a stately line,
Now by their beating pinions borne, they came
Beyond the stream, but not yet out of sight,
To where a noble temple crowned a height.

16

Sacred it is to immortality.
Thence a fair nymph to Lethe's shore descends.
From the swans' beaks the precious tokens she
Removes and near a sculptured form appends,
Reared on a column to eternity.
These plaques the nymph so consecrates and tends
That their renown will shine for evermore
In poetry and legendary lore.

17

Who this old man can be, the reason why
He casts the shining names into the stream,
The birds of prey which fail to reach the sky,
The swans, the temple and the nymph, which seem
Recondite mysteries to signify,
Astolfo begs to have explained to him.
St John with his request at once complies
And in the words which follow he replies:

18

'You must believe, my son, no frond is stirred
On earth that is not mirrored in this sphere.
Every result of every act and word
Its corresponding counterpart has here.
That ancient man, by speed so swiftly spurred
That nothing with his pace can interfere,
The selfsame work performs, the same effects,
As Time performs on earth, in all respects.

19

'When all the fibre of a reel is spun,
A human life completed is and past.
Its fame on earth is here inscribed upon
A plaque, such as you saw the old man cast
Into the turbid stream; and either one
(But for its foe) eternally would last:
The bearded man who runs and never waits,
And Time who men's renown obliterates.

20

'And, as up here the vultures and the crows,
The jackdaws and the other birds of prey
Swoop for the labels which the old man throws,
And the most shining try to bear away;
So ruffians, sycophants, buffoons, all those
Who bear false witness, ganymedes who play
The loyal friends of rulers (all these are
More welcome than the virtuous by far),

21

'Who are called courtiers and thought well-bred
Because the ass and hog they imitate –
These, when that white-haired crone has spun the thread
Of their lord's life (who dies inebriate
As like as not, or of excess in bed),
These hangers-on, whose aim is but to sate
Their bellies, take his name upon their lips,
Then let it sink for ever in eclipse.

22

'But, as the silver swans with joyful song
Convey these medals safely to the shrine,
Poets on earth renown and fame prolong
Which Time would to oblivion consign.
Wise and far-sighted princes (few among
So many!) who the steps of the benign
Augustus follow and hold writers dear,
Of Lethe's waters *you* need have no fear.

23

'Poets (like swans up here) are rare on earth;
I mean true poets, who deserve the name.
The will of God, perhaps, ordained this dearth;
Or princely avarice may be to blame,
Which beggars makes of those whom at their birth
The Muses have endowed with sacred flame,
And Good suppresses but on Evil smiles,
And every true and noble art exiles.

24

'But God deprives such ignoramuses
Of intellect and so bedims their sight
That art to them abomination is;
And so the sepulchre consumes them quite.
Yet, notwithstanding all iniquities,
Their reputation would be lily-white,
More fragrant it would smell than nard or myrrh,
If they in life the friends of poets were.

25

'Aeneas not so pious, nor so strong
Achilles was, as they are famed to be;
Hector was less ferocious; and a throng
Of heroes could surpass them, but we see
Their valour and their deeds enhanced in song,
For their descendants had so lavishly
Rewarded poets for their eulogies
With gifts of villas, farm-lands, palaces.

26

'Not so beneficent Augustus was
As Virgil's epic clarion proclaimed.
His taste in poetry must be the cause
Why his proscriptions were left uncondemned.
No one would know of Nero's unjust laws,
Nor would he for his cruelties be famed
(Though he had been by Heaven and earth reviled)
If writers he had wooed and reconciled.

27

'Homer makes Agamemnon win the war;
The Trojans cowardly and weak he shows.
Although the suitors so persistent are,
Penelope is faithful to her spouse.
But if for truth you are particular,
Like this, quite in reverse, the story goes:
The Greeks defeated, Troy victorious,
And chaste Penelope notorious.

28

'Consider Dido; she, whose heart was pure,
Was faithful to Sichaeus to the end;
But she is thought by all to be a whore,
Because Vergilius was not her friend.
And do not be amazed that I deplore
The fate of writers and on them expend
So many words: I love them, and I do
But pay my debt: I was a writer too.

29

'Reward above all others I have won,
Which neither Time nor Death can take from me,
Which I was justly granted by the Son
Whom I so praised, as was my destiny.
And now I grieve for those whose course is run
In times ungenerous, when Courtesy
Has shut the door, and writers, lean and pale,
Beat on it night and day, to no avail.

30

'And so there is no cause to be amazed
If poets and if scholars now are few;
For where there is no pasture to be grazed,
Nor shelter, such a terrain beasts eschew.'
As the Disciple spoke, his eyes so blazed,
That like two fires of righteous wrath they grew.
Then with a smile he turned towards the duke.
Serene, no longer troubled, was his look.

31

But for the present let Astolfo keep
In converse with the Gospel-writer. I
The distance from the moon to earth must leap;
My wings are tired with bearing me so high.
I will return to Bradamante, whom a deep
And painful wound torments, inflicted by
The lance of jealousy. I left her just
As she had made three monarchs bite the dust.

32

When evening fell she came to a redoubt
Along the road to Paris, where she heard
That Agramante had been put to rout
And all his camp to Arles had been transferred.
There her Ruggiero is, she has no doubt.
No sooner had the light of day appeared
Than towards Provence where Charlemagne, she knew,
Pursued the pagans, she set out anew.

33

Towards Provence, along a route direct
She rode, and met a damsel in distress.
Though she was sad, the observer could detect
The beauty of her face and of her dress,
Her gentle manner which inspired respect.
She is that stricken sweetheart, you can guess,
Of Monodante's son, a captive now
Of Rodomonte who fulfils a vow.

34

She had been looking for a cavalier
To fight as well in water as on land
(As though an otter, not a knight, he were),
And fierce enough to take a valiant stand.
She who so sadly yearned for her Ruggier
This sadly-yearning damsel greeted, and,
After exchange of courtesies, she next
Enquired by what affliction she was vexed.

35

Gazing upon her, Fiordiligi sees
(She thinks) a cavalier who meets the case.
She tells her, therefore, what the trouble is:
How at the bridge the king all comers stays,
And how her lover he had come to seize;
Not by his greater strength, but by his base
Manoeuvring, that monarch, fierce and grim,
Gained an advantage from the bridge and stream.

36

'If you', she said, 'as valiant are and brave
As by your aspect you appear to be,
Avenge me, for God's sake, upon the knave
Who, to my sorrow, took my love from me;
Or, if some other mission you now have,
Is there a knight of equal gallantry,
Who in so many wars so well has fought,
The pagan's vantage he can bring to naught?

37

'Not only will you thus fulfil the part
Of a knight-errant and a courteous man;
You will bring succour to a faithful heart
With whose fidelity no lover can
Compete; his virtues (but I must not start
To speak of them) exceed the normal span
Of goodness; and if anyone you find
Who knows not this, he must be deaf and blind.'

38

The noble-hearted Maid, to whom such feats
Are always welcome for the fame they bring,
Who every worthy challenge gladly meets,
No time desires to waste in dallying.
And the more readily this risk she greets:
Death, if it comes, will end her suffering.
Despairing now of being Ruggiero's wife,
The unhappy Maid has no desire for life.

39

'For what I'm worth, love-smitten lass,' she said,
'I'll undertake this exploit as you ask.
The reasons why I offer you my blade
Are chiefly such as I prefer to mask;
Yet one there is which I will not evade,
Which above all inclines me to the task:
Your lover's faithfulness; I swear to you
That I believed all men to be untrue.'

40

These final words were uttered on a sigh,
A sigh which came from deep within her breast.
Then, 'Let us go,' she said. And when the sky
Is gold with dawn, they reach that narrowest
Pass perilous which boldly they defy.
By his guard's trumpet summoned to the test,
The pagan arms himself and by the bridge
Takes his position at the water's edge.

41

And when he sees that warrior draw near,
He threatens her with death unless she makes
Oblation of her arms and destrier.
But Bradamante's courage he mistakes;
She knows the story of the sepulchre,
And Isabella's fate her wrath awakes
(The damsel told her of it as they came),
And thus she answers the proud pagan's claim:

42

'You brute! You make the innocent atone
In reparation for your evil deed?
You killed the maiden, as by all is known.
The sin, the guilt, are yours, and you should bleed.
And better than the victims you have thrown,
Robbing them of their weapons and their steed,
A sacrifice I'll offer that is due:
Her death I will avenge by killing you.

43

'My gift will be more pleasing for the fact
That I too am a woman as she was,
And I have come here to perform this act
To avenge her death, and for no other cause.
But let us first between us fix a pact
In true conformity with knighthood's laws:
If I by you am vanquished, I agree
To join the others in captivity.

44

'If I beat *you* (as I believe and hope)
I take your weapons and your destrier.
These and these only I will offer up
And of all others strip the sepulchre,
And you must free the captives from their coop.'
'What you propose', the pagan answered her,
'Seems just; but you must know that I could not
Release the vanquished captives on the spot.

45

'I sent them to my African domain;
But rest assured, for solemnly I vow
That if (by chance) on horseback you remain
And I on foot to you defeated bow,
I will set all the captives free again,
If you the interval of time allow
Which is required to send a messenger,
To do as you command, from here to there.

46

'But if instead it is your fate to fall,
As I am sure is bound to be the case,
I'll not suspend your trophy on the wall,
Nor any evidence of your disgrace.
My triumph over you in arms I shall
Donate to your sweet eyes, your hair, your face.
Such loveliness I cannot but adore,
If you will love, not hate me as before.

47

'My valour and my prowess are so great,
No scorn you'll suffer if I lay you low.'
He gave a smile, a smile of bitter hate
And wrath; no other feeling did it show.
The Maid did not reply, nor did she wait,
But to the bridge-head turned at once to go.
She spurred her horse and with the golden lance
Against the Moor made ready to advance.

48

And Rodomonte for the joust prepares.
He rides so fast, he makes the bridge resound
With echoes which must deafen many ears,
I think perhaps, for many miles around.
The golden lance which Bradamante bears
Performs as usual, and to the ground
It throws the Moor, a champion of the joust.
Poised in mid-air, he drops, and bites the dust.

49

And as she passed him on that narrow strip,
The valiant Maid could scarce find room enough.
It almost seemed as if her horse would slip
And she was on the verge of falling off.
But Rabicano never missed a step.
This charger was not made of equine stuff,
But fire and wind; along the bridge he pranced,
And on a sword's edge too he could have danced.

50

She turns and to the pagan whom she tossed
She gallops back and utters this *bon mot*:
'Now you can see', she said, 'which one has lost
And which of us has now to lie below.'
The pagan king, astonished and nonplussed
To think a woman dealt him such a blow,
Cannot, or it may be will not, reply,
But as one stupefied can only lie.

51

Speechless and crestfallen, he rose at last
And doffed his helm, his armour and his shield.
These with his arms against the rocks he cast.
Alone, on foot, with bitter hatred filled,
From the Maid's vision Rodomonte passed;
But not before his vow he had fulfilled,
Giving a message to a squire to free
The vanquished champions in captivity.

52

He went; and nothing more of him was heard,
Except that he took refuge in a cave.
Meanwhile the Maid the pagan's arms transferred
To the great sepulchre; those of the brave
True paladins, by Charlemagne preferred,
She bade the squire take down; the rest to leave
Untouched upon the walls the Maid saw fit,
And their removal she would not permit.

53

As well as those of Monodante's son
Were those of Sansonet and Oliver.
When looking for Orlando they had gone,
The route they took (the straightest) led them here,
Where they were vanquished by the pagan on
The narrow bridge and taken prisoner.
The Maid commanded that their arms be stripped
From where they hung, and in the tower kept.

54

She left the other trophies on the wall,
For pagans' weapons such was her disdain:
Even the armour of a king, who all
Those many steps had taken, but in vain,
Searching for Frontalatte – you recall
The king I speak of – the Circassian,
Who at this bridge his other charger left
And thence departed, of his arms bereft.

55

Disarmed, the king departed, and on foot,
Leaving the bridge of peril far behind.
Others of his religion followed suit,
For Rodomonte then was of no mind
To call them back or to attempt pursuit.
Yet Sacripante did not feel inclined
To make his way to camp: he'd suffer scorn,
After his boasting, should he thus return.

56

New longing urged him to pursue his quest
Of her his heart enshrined (and her alone).
I know not if he heard, or if he guessed,
But Fate ordained that he should learn quite soon
That she had left for home, towards the East.
And as Love goaded him and spurred him on,
He left straightway to follow in her track.
But I to Bradamante must turn back.

57

She placed a new inscription first, to show
That by her deed this pass was rendered free.
To Fiordiligi then, whose face, held low,
Was bathed in tears, she turned, and tenderly
Enquired of her where she now wished to go.
The damsel said, 'The only road for me
Is that which leads to Arles, that I may gain
The territory of the Saracen.

58

'I hope to find a vessel and a crew
To take me safely to the other shore.
I will not rest, all efforts I'll renew
Until I reach my lord whom I adore,
My husband Brandimarte, fond and true.
I will try every means, that evermore
He will be free; should Rodomonte fail
To keep his word, my help must then avail.'

59

'I will escort you,' Bradamante said,
'At least along a portion of your course,
Until you come where Arles lies close ahead.
There, for my sake, employ all your resource
To find Ruggiero (no more valiant aid
Has Agramante). Give him back this horse,
Which I from the proud Saracen have won,
Since by my weapon he was overthrown,

60

'And say to him, exactly as I say:
"A cavalier who has good reason to
Believe that he can demonstrate today
That you have broken faith, and proved untrue,
That you may be equipped in every way,
Gave me this destrier to give to you,
Bidding you put your armour on at once
And meet him where he waits with sword and lance."

61

'Say this and nothing else; if he should ask
You who I am, tell him you do not know.'
The damsel, ever courteous, the task
Accepts; she says, 'I'd never weary grow
Of serving you' (her thanks she does not mask);
'My life I'd pay, not words, for all I owe.'
The Maid, well pleased, gives her Frontino's rein
And thus together they set out again.

62

Along the river the fair travellers
Ride resolutely on their route until
They catch a glimpse of Arles and in their ears
The booming of the surf is audible.
Here at the boundary the Maid prefers
To wait, some distance from the citadel,
And of the time required allowance makes
For her who to her love his charger takes.

63

The damsel enters by the outer gate
And, with a faithful squire for company,
Crosses the drawbridge at a spanking rate.
Finding the lodging of Ruggiero, she
Dismounts, her message ready to dictate.
She trusts a servant with her embassy.
Expecting no reply, she gallops on
And to *her* love's assistance soon is gone.

64

Ruggiero is bewildered and perplexed:
Who it can be he cannot tell, who thus
Reproaches him one moment, and the next,
Sending Frontino, is so courteous.
What man is there so bold as to have vexed
Him by an insult so gratuitous?
No answer to the problem can he find;
All names, save Bradamante's, come to mind.

65

It may be Rodomonte is the one;
But still there is a mystery to solve.
Why should he challenge him in such a tone?
This problem he continues to revolve.
Except for him, in all the world, there's none
With whom he has a quarrel to resolve.
Meanwhile the Maid, with martial pride and scorn,
Beyond the walls, in challenge, sounds her horn.

66

Soon Agramante and Marsilio
Have heard the news; and present there, by chance,
Is Serpentino, who asks leave to show
The knight what he can do with sword and lance.
He promises that he will bring him low
In retribution for his arrogance.
Already on the walls spectators throng,
Every inhabitant, both old and young.

67

Clad in a surcoat costly and enriched,
With fair accoutrements, Galicia's king
Rode forth to joust – and at first blow lay stretched
Upon the ground; his horse, it seemed, took wing.
The gallant Maid rode after it and fetched
It by the rein; she waited, menacing,
And said, 'Remount, and tell your lord from me
To send a knight of more ability.'

68

King Agramante from a near-by wall
Has watched the joust with a large retinue.
He is amazed by Serpentino's fall
And by the gesture of the unknown foe.
The Saracens, on hearing of it, call:
'He is his prisoner, he lets him go.'
Then Serpentino comes and, as the Maid
Commands, asks for an abler knight instead.

69

Grandonio of Volterna, wild with rage,
The proudest cavalier throughout all Spain,
Desired to be the second to engage
In combat with the stranger on the plain.
'Your courtesy,' he threatened, 'I'll presage,
Will be of no avail; if you remain
Alive, I'll lead you captive to my lord;
But you will die, if deeds with might accord.'

70

The Maid replied, 'Your vile discourtesy
Will not provoke me to an equal spite.
Before you learn how hard the ground can be,
Go back; I give you warning, as is right.
Go back, and tell your lord and king from me
That not with such as you I come to fight,
But with a warrior of such esteem
That it is fitting I should joust with him.'

71

This biting, bitter answer which she made
The bosom of the Saracen inflames.
He says no word but turns his horse instead
And combat with the challenger thus claims.
Turning her horse likewise, at him the Maid
Both golden lance and Rabicano aims.
The magic weapon barely strikes the shield:
Heels in the air, he's stretched out on the field.

72

Holding the bridle of his destrier,
The Maid then says: 'I told you in advance
You would be wise to be my messenger,
Rather than be so ready with your lance.
Now tell your king to choose a cavalier
Who equals me in skill and valiance.
I have no wish to waste my time in fights
With inexperienced and untrained knights.'

73

The watchers on the wall are at a loss:
Who is the warrior who sits upright
While one by one the others take a toss?
They name those names which chill their blood with
Many say Brandimarte, others guess   [fright:
Rinaldo (the majority), the knight
Whom they most fear; and many would have said
Orlando, save that news of him has spread.

74

Lanfusa's son, requesting the third joust,
All hope of being victorious disclaimed.
'But if I too', he said, 'shall bite the dust,
Less reason these will have to feel ashamed.'
All the accoutrements a warrior must
In jousting wear, this combatant (named
Ferraù) put on; he chose one steed
(Out of a hundred), skilled and of great speed.

75

Thus he rode forth to tilt against the Maid;
But first, as was correct, he greeted her,
And she returned his greeting; then she said,
'In courtesy, pray tell me who you are.'
Rarely, if ever, did the knight evade
Such a request; the valiant challenger
He satisfied: 'though I'd prefer to fight',
She said, 'instead of you, another knight.'

76

'Who?' asked the Saracen; and she replied
'Ruggiero', stammering upon the name,
Suffused with blushes which she could not hide,
Till like a rose her lovely face became.
Then she went on, 'His praises far and wide
Are sung and I, attracted by his fame,
Am here with one desire: to prove and test
His prowess, and with him alone contest.'

77

She said these words in all simplicity
(Though some may take them in another sense),
And Ferraù replied, 'First let us see
Who is the better-trained for tournaments.
If, as before, you also vanquish me,
I shall be comforted in my laments
By that brave cavalier with whom you say
The joys of jousting you would now essay.'

78

While they discourse the Maid does not replace
Her visor, thus revealing to the eyes
Of Ferraù the beauty of her face.
He, as though conquered, gazes in surprise,
And to himself, but not aloud, he says:
'Can this an Angel be from Paradise?
Though by no lance I'm wounded or unseated,
By those fair eyes already I'm defeated.'

79

They turned their horses round and, as before,
This combatant was toppled and thrown clear.
The Maid secured the destrier once more
And said, 'Now keep your word.' The Saracen,
Ashamed, rose to his feet and, bruised and sore,
Returned to tell Ruggiero, who was in
Attendance on his king, that the strange knight
Desired with him, and only him, to fight.

80

Not knowing he is challenged by the Maid,
Ruggiero, at these words of Ferraù,
Accepts with joy, for he is unafraid.
The deadly blows which from their saddles threw
The other knights have left him undismayed.
His coat of mail, his helm and hauberk too
He dons, and forth he rides; but what occurred
Must now to my next canto be deferred.

CANTO XXXVI

1

A noble heart (no matter whose it is)
Will always gracious, kind and just remain.
Nature and habit formed it in this guise;
It is beyond its power to alter then.
A base, ignoble heart not otherwise
(No matter whose) its villainy makes plain.
Nature has given it an evil trend
Which habit then finds difficult to mend.

2

Many a noble deed of courtesy
By warriors in former days was done,
And few in modern times; but treachery
And sacrilegious acts to you were known,
My lord, when trophies of the enemy
Adorned your churches and when you alone
Led their proud vessels, captured in that war,
Loaded with booty to your native shore.

3

All the inhuman acts and cruelties
Which Tartar, Turk or Moor had ever wrought
(But Venice truly not the culprit is:
With chivalry unstained the Lion fought)
Were perpetrated by the mercenaries
Whose evil hands such woe and havoc brought.
Of homesteads set on fire I will not speak,
Of farms destroyed and blazing every rick.

4

Though a vile act of vengeance against *you*
That was; for at the siege of Padua
(Where Maximilian was present too)
It was by your command that in that war
Fires were put out, as the Venetians knew,
And villages and churches, near and far,
Were spared, such the nobility and worth
Which graced your nature ever since your birth.

5

That deed I will omit, and other ones
As cruel and unchivalrous, and turn
Instead to this event which tears from stones
Should cause to flow and marble move to mourn
Whenever woe the tragic tale intones:
That day when those who honour held in scorn
Abandoned ship and to a fort withdrew,
Followed by loyal troops despatched by you.

6

Like Hector and Aeneas who defied
The deep to burn the Grecian fleet they went.
An Alexander, Hercules, I spied
Who, spurring neck and neck, on havoc bent,
Reached the redoubt and passed so far inside
(To goad the enemy being their intent),
The former almost failed to get away,
The latter captured was and held that day.

7

Ferruffino escaped: Cantelmo stayed.
O duke of Sora, what were your thoughts then,
Your feelings when your valiant son was led
On board a ship, amid a thousand men,
And helmetless, across a gunwale laid,
Was there beheaded? Execrable scene!
I marvel that the spectacle alone
Did not despatch you, as the sword your son.

8

Cruel Slavonians! Where did you learn
Such soldiering? In what barbaric lands
Are rules of war so merciless and stern
That he who has surrendered and who hands
His weapons to his captors shall thus earn
His death? Its light the sun unjustly lends
To this our age which the vile deeds renews
Of Tantalus, Thyestes and Atreus.

9

Cruel barbarians, thus to behead
The bravest youth this century has known!
From pole to pole, or from the Ganges' bed
To the Far West, he had no paragon.
E'en Anthropophagus, of brutal breed,
And Polyphemus, mercy would have shown
To such fair limbs, but you are worse than all
The Cyclopès or any cannibal.

10

No such example of barbarity
Among the cavaliers of old you'd find.
To honour, noble deeds and chivalry
They pledged themselves with heart and soul and mind;
Nor were they cruel after victory.
The Maid, as you recall, was not unkind
To those whom she unhorsed; holding the rein,
She bade them mount upon their steeds again.

11

I told you how this valorous, fair Maid
First Serpentino Stella had unseated;
Grandonio Volterna next I said,
Then Ferraù, to a like shame were fated.
They climbed back to their saddles with her aid
And none of them for further combat waited.
The third imparts her challenge to Ruggier,
Who does not doubt she is a cavalier.

12

The challenge was accepted joyfully,
And while Ruggiero armed, the others turned
To the discussion of the mystery.
King Agramante and his nobles burned
To know the cavalier's identity,
And Ferraù was asked if he discerned,
From converse, who it was who with his lance
Gave in all ways such proof of excellence.

13

'You can be certain', Ferraù replied,
'He is not one of those whom you have guessed.
Seeing him with his visor lifted, I'd
Have sworn he was (and this seemed likeliest)
Rinaldo's brother; but now, having tried
His valour, Ricciardetto by this test
I must exclude; his sister it may be:
I hear there is great similarity.

14

'Renowned for prowess and for fortitude,
The equal of Rinaldo she is deemed
And of her cousin; and today she showed
Such skill that their superior she seemed.'
And when Ruggiero heard these words, a flood
Of crimson all his face suffused and brimmed,
As when the morning paints the sky anew.
His heart distraught, he knows not what to do.

15

A shaft of love so pricks him at this news,
His passion is rekindled in a trice;
And at that very moment too there flows
Through all his bones a chill of fear like ice –
Fear that a love so ardent he may lose,
That of delay disdain may be the price.
Perplexed, Ruggiero cannot now decide
Whether to go to meet her, or to bide.

16

It happened that Marfisa too was there
And longed to try her skill against the knight;
And she was fully-armed, for it was rare
To find her otherwise, by day or night.
She thought that if she waited for Ruggier
He would deprive her of the chance to fight.
Thus she resolved that she would get there first,
So great for glory was Marfisa's thirst.

17

She mounts her horse, impatient to depart
To where the daughter of the Montalbans
Awaits Ruggiero with a beating heart.
Longing to take him prisoner, she plans
And carefully considers in which part
It will least harmful be to aim her lance.
Marfisa through the gateway now appears.
A phoenix on her helm as crest she wears,

18

Either in pride, to signify that she
In all the world in prowess is unique,
Or as a symbol of her chastity,
Since never for a consort would she seek.
The Maid observes her; when she does not see
Those features she so loved, she bids her speak:
What is her name? 'Marfisa,' she replies –
And there her rival is, before her eyes.

19

Or rather, not her rival, but the one
With whom she thinks Ruggiero has betrayed
Her trust, who (so she thinks) his love has won.
Resolved that retribution shall be paid,
She turns her destrier and spurs him on
In hate, in wrath, the purpose of the Maid
Not being to unhorse but through the breast
To pierce her and from jealousy find rest.

20

Marfisa by this stroke was flung below
And if that day the ground was soft or hard
A good position she was in to know.
So seldom is she taken off her guard,
She is infuriated by the blow
And to avenge herself she draws her sword.
But Aymon's daughter proudly calls to her:
'What are you doing? You're my prisoner.

21

'Though courteous with others I may be,
I will not show such courtesy to you,
Who are endowed with every villainy,
And insolent and overweening too.'
As in a rocky cavern by the sea
A piercing wind is heard to shriek, just so
Marfisa's rage is uttered not in speech
(She cannot find the words) but in a screech.

22

She wields her weapon, aiming it as much
At her opponent's steed in paunch and breast
As at the rider. At a skilful touch
Upon the rein, it rises to the test
And leaps aside; at the same moment, such
Is Bradamante's rage, that, lance in rest,
She strikes her adversary down again,
Sending her sprawling backwards on the plain.

23

No sooner is she down than to her feet
She springs, and lays about her with her sword.
The Maid, her lance in rest, the selfsame feat
Renews and sends her rolling on the sward.
Though Bradamante's skill and strength are great,
She could not thus at every blow have floored
Marfisa, had it not been for the lance
Which magic virtue adds to excellence.

24

Some cavaliers arrived upon the scene
And stayed as witnesses of the event –
Some of the Christian cavaliers, I mean,
Who to the area of jousting went,
Which lay about a mile or two between
The camps; they saw the prowess which had sent
Marfisa to the ground; the Maid they deemed
A Christian cavalier – and so she seemed.

25

They see the late Troiano's gallant son,
Alert and vigilant, approach the walls.
He lays his plans and nothing leaves undone:
All danger and reverses he forestalls.
He bids his captains put their armour on
And muster for whatever now befalls.
Among them is Ruggiero, whom in haste
And eagerness Marfisa had replaced.

26

Such was his apprehension for his bride
He could not quell the tumult in his breast,
For well he knew that she whom she defied
In many a deadly combat came off best.
This was at first, when they began to ride
In wrath towards each other, lance in rest;
But when he saw how the encounter went,
Ruggiero was amazed at the event.

27

And when from combat they did not withdraw,
As was the case with the preceding three,
With deep foreboding stricken, he foresaw
Both warriors would be in jeopardy.
Although remaining faithful to Love's law,
He loves them both in all sincerity:
His love for one all ardour is and flame;
His other love affection I would name.

28

Gladly Ruggiero would have stopped the fight,
Save that his honour he would thus impugn;
But his companions deem it just and right
To snatch the palm from Charles's champion
(Who seems to them superior in might)
By bursting forth upon the field; and soon
The Christians also, from the other side,
To the encounter in a body ride.

29

Now here, now there, the trumpets sound 'To arms!'
As was the custom almost every day.
'All cavaliers on foot, to horse! Take arms,
All those unarmed!', their piercing voices say,
And 'He who would defend his lord from harms,
Around his banner rally straight away!'
And while the trumpets rouse the cavalry,
Tabors and drums arouse the infantry.

30

A fierce and bloody skirmish was engaged,
And terrible the slaughter was indeed.
The Maid in wrath and disappointment raged
That in her purpose she did not succeed –
To kill Marfisa; while the others waged
A deadly war, she turned her mighty steed
And, twisting here and there, on every side
For her Ruggiero searched, for whom she sighed.

31

She knows him by the eagle on his shield
Which the young Moorish hero always bears.
(Argent it was, upon an azure field.)
She stops and at his handsome aspect stares.
Her eyes, remembering, caress his build,
His girth, his shoulders, all his graceful airs.
Another woman now this form enjoys
And she exclaims, with fury in her voice:

32

'Can I allow another's lips to kiss
Those sweet and lovely lips, if mine may not?
No other woman shall enjoy that bliss,
Fate to no other woman shall allot
The boon which I no longer may possess,
Since all your vows of love are now forgot.
Die with me here! Inferno will restore
You to me, to be mine for evermore.

33

'On your account I die, so it is right
That by revenge I shall be comforted:
Justice demands, whoever kills in spite,
By his own death, the forfeit shall be paid.
And yet your death will not my own requite:
Yours is deserved and mine unmerited.
I slay a man who longs for me to die,
You slay the one whom you are worshipped by.

34

'My hand, why should you now reluctant be
To pierce with steel the bosom of my foe
Who under pledge of love has wounded me,
Who safely dealt me many a mortal blow,
Who now would slay me, not unwillingly,
Having no scruple for my bitter woe?
Be bold, my heart, against this ruthless one:
Avenge my thousand deaths by his alone.'

35

She spurs against him now, but first 'Beware!',
She shouts. 'As long as I can summon force,
You shall not flaunt, perfidious Ruggier,
The trophy of a maiden's heart.' Her horse,
Which she then urges onwards, brings her near.
Ruggiero thinks (and it is true, of course)
This is his bride; her voice, which he would know
Among a thousand others, tells him so.

36

And from her words he clearly understands
That something more she wishes to imply:
That with a breach of promise she intends
To charge him; signalling, he hopes to try
To parley with her and to make amends;
But she, her visor closed, is driven by
Her grief and rage; her purpose is to loft
Him, where the ground is hard perhaps, not soft.

37

And as he watched the angry Maid advance,
Ruggiero for her fierce attack sat braced.
In readiness the lover couched his lance,
But, that it might not harm his bride, he placed
It to one side; and she, although she wants
To slay him and all mercy has effaced,
Discovers with surprise, as she draws near,
She cannot bring herself to use her spear.

38

So on the empty air the lances bore,
And neither in this combat came off best.
This was as well, for Love the warrior
A lance of passion drove into each breast.
The Maid, no longer wishing, as before,
To harm Ruggiero, still by anger pressed,
Vents it upon the Infidel near by,
Performing deeds whose fame will never die.

39

In a short space of time she had unseated
Three hundred with her magic lance of gold.
The Maid alone that day the Moors defeated;
The victory was hers. Ruggiero called
Her name, and as he searched for her, entreated:
'Pray let me talk with you; do not withhold
This favour, or I die. What have I done?
Ah! why is it my presence you now shun?'

40

As when mild winds which blow across the sea,
Wafting the warm breath of a southern clime,
Dissolve the snows and set the torrents free,
In rigid ice enclosed all winter-time,
So at Ruggiero's voice and at his plea,
From Bradamante's heart the frosty rime
Is melted; from her anger, which to stone
Was turning her, to pity she is won.

41

Unwilling or perhaps unable yet
To answer him in words, she rides athwart
His path, and signals where her course is set.
Leaving the battlefield, she draws apart
From all the multitude and fevered fret
Towards a valley; at its very heart
Are cypress-trees outlined against the sky –
Each printed, so it seems, from the same die.

42

Within the glade there was a marble tomb,
Newly erected, large, and gleaming white.
To anyone who cared to know for whom
The sepulchre was built, verses invite
Perusal; but I doubt the Maid had come
To read what monumental masons write.
Ruggiero gallops after her; the grove
Of cypresses he reaches, and his love.

43

But let us find Marfisa once again.
Remounted on her mighty destrier,
She had been searching for the Maid in vain,
Who with her well-aimed weapon did not err.
She saw her leave the field on Rabican,
She saw Ruggiero turn and follow her.
She little thought that love thus spurred him on:
She judged there was a combat to be won.

44

Pricking her steed, she followed without pause
And caught the others up just by the grove;
And how unwelcome her arrival was
I need not say to those who are in love.
The Maid, moreover, saw her as the cause
Of all her sorrow; who could now remove
The firm conviction that what brings her there
So fast is her devotion to Ruggier?

45

Again she charges him with perfidy:
'So you were not content, perfidious one,
That rumour of your infidelity
Should reach my ears; but now', so she went on,
'You bring that woman face to face with me?
I know you scarce can wait till I am gone,
So with your wish I'm willing to comply,
But I will make him come who makes me die.'

46

No viper's fury can with hers compare
As, having spoken thus, she swivels round
And at Marfisa's shield so drives her spear,
She topples her, head foremost, to the ground;
And half her helmet seems to disappear,
So deep a dent she makes; nor can this round
Be said to take Marfisa by surprise:
Yet head first, down she goes, for all she tries.

47

Count Aymon's daughter, who intends to kill
Marfisa (or to die herself instead),
Being incensed with rage, no longer will
Employ her golden lance, which she has shed.
Her purpose now – more dire and terrible –
Is to divide the torso from the head,
Which from afar seems buried in the sand.
Dismounted, she approaches, sword in hand.

48

But she arrives too late; Marfisa stands
To face her, furious that once again
So easily upon the ground she lands.
Her longing for revenge she does not feign.
Ruggiero pleads and shouts, 'Put up your brands!'
But all his well-meant efforts are in vain.
He sees that, blinded by their wrath and hate,
Both women warriors are desperate.

49

They clash their weapons without more ado,
Burning with inextinguishable pride.
Their blades are crossed; all that remains to do
In this impasse is cast their swords aside.
Seizing their daggers, they begin anew.
His deep concern Ruggiero does not hide.
He begs and pleads, but might as well be mute,
The words he utters bear so little fruit.

50

Seeing that words are so much empty air,
He tries by force to separate the twain,
And takes their daggers from their hands; to spare
Them (and himself) all further risk or pain,
He lays them by a cypress-tree with care.
He threatens and cajoles, but all in vain:
For neither of the warriors desists,
And, *faute de mieux*, they fight with feet and fists.

51

Ruggiero perseveres: first one he takes
And then the other by the hand or arm.
Against himself Marfisa's wrath he wakes.
She who would gladly the whole world disarm
And who in battle many a buckler breaks
Is now prepared to do Ruggiero harm,
And, snatching up her sword from where it lies,
From Bradamante turns and *him* defies.

52

'You are discourteous, you are uncouth,
Ruggiero, to presume to intervene;
And by this hand I promise you, in truth,
I'll cause you to repent; it will be seen
One hand suffices to defeat you both.'
Ruggiero tries to calm her with serene
And civil words, which are inadequate
Marfisa's scorn and fury to abate.

53

Her anger finally provoked the knight.
He too with rage was scarlet in the face.
No spectacle, I think, no epic fight
In Athens, Rome, or any other place
Afforded onlookers so much delight
As Bradamante felt; for now all trace
Of jealousy had vanished and all doubt;
All anguish from her heart was blotted out.

54

She now retrieved her sword and passively
Withdrew, though vigilantly keeping guard.
The god of war himself she seemed to see
When she beheld Ruggiero turn toward
His foe, prepared for combat; whereas *she*
With an Erinys might have been compared,
Unleashed but recently from Hell; in truth,
The sight of her unnerved the valiant youth.

55

But, knowing well the virtue of his blade,
Which he had tested many times before,
That, by enchantment, every stroke he made
(Unless the weapon lost its magic power)
Would be unerring, to himself he said
That use of point and edge he would abjure.
This for a time Ruggiero tried to do,
But suddenly his anger flared anew –

56

Because Marfisa, with a mighty stroke,
Lifted her sword as though to split his head.
Ruggiero raised his shield and on it took
The impact of the savage blow instead.
The eagle was unharmed; but by the shock
His arm was rendered senseless, as if dead,
And, but for Hector's armour, which he wore,
Would have been lost to him for evermore.

57

The blow would then Ruggiero's skull have cleft,
As pitiless Marfisa had intended.
Ruggiero can scarce move his arm (his left),
Nor bear the shield by which he is defended.
So now at last, of all restraint bereft,
With blazing eyes, his wrath with frenzy blended,
He drives his weapon's point straight at his foe.
Had it struck home, Marfisa, alas for you!

58

I cannot tell you how it came to pass:
The weapon struck against a cypress-tree
And by a handbreadth entered it, no less.
(The grove was thickly planted.) Suddenly
The plain and near-by hills were shaken as
By a vast tremor of the earth; all three
At the same moment from the sepulchre
A voice, louder than any mortal's, hear.

59

The voice, in tones inspiring terror, said:
'Cease from this conflict! You commit grave sin.
Let not a brother strike a sister dead:
Let not a sister kill her kith and kin.
You, my Ruggiero, you, my warrior-maid,
Marfisa, hear the truth from me: within
One womb and from one seed you came to birth;
Together you emerged to life on earth.

60

'Ruggiero, called the Second, was your sire,
And Galaciella was your mother's name.
Her brothers slew your father and with dire
Unbrotherly indifference, to their shame,
Though she was pregnant, left her to expire
(Though from their origin you also came),
Placing her helpless in their cruelty
In a frail vessel on the open sea.

61

'But Fortune, who had chosen you, unborn,
For glorious achievements here on earth,
Guided the vessel, which was safely borne
To empty Libyan shores, where, giving birth,
Your mother perished, leaving you forlorn.
(Of joy her soul in Heaven has no dearth.)
And I, as God and as your fate decreed,
Was near at hand to help you in your need.

62

'I gave your mother decent burial,
As best I could on that deserted strand.
I wrapped you, tender nurselings, in my stole
And bore you to the mountains, where I planned
To rear you; from the forest, at my call,
A lioness came forth; at my command,
She left her cubs and tame and docile grew;
For twenty months I made her suckle you.

63

'As it befell, I was obliged one day
To take a journey and by chance there passed
A band of Arabs, who stole you away,
Marfisa; but Ruggiero was too fast
For them; do you remember? My dismay
When I returned was infinite; downcast
At losing you, a solemn oath I swore
That I would guard Ruggiero all the more.

64

'Ruggiero, if Atlante guarded you,
If he was zealous, you can testify.
A prophet who could read the stars, I knew
A victim of betrayal you would die
Among the Christians. I endeavoured to
Conceal you from them, but, defeated by
The destiny to which your soul aspired,
I pined away in sorrow and expired.

65

'Before I died, here, where I had foreseen
That pre-ordained you were one day to come
And would engage in combat with your twin,
I gathered heavy stones to form this tomb
(With Hell's assistance) and to Charon in
Loud tones I thus decreed: "When I succumb,
My soul must tarry in this cypress-glade
Until my wards to battle here are led."

66

'And so my spirit in this pleasant grove
Has waited for you long and eagerly,
That you, fair Bradamante, who so love
Our dear Ruggiero, pangs of jealousy
Shall cease to suffer; now I must resolve
To go where darkness will encompass me.'
He ceased. Wide-eyed, Marfisa and Ruggier
And Bradamante in amazement stare.

67

Ruggiero claims his sister with great joy;
Marfisa also recognizes him,
And they embrace; but this does not annoy
The Maid, although her ardour is no whim.
They recollect when they were girl and boy
And, though at first the memories are dim,
As each and every detail they renew,
They find that what the spirit said is true.

68

Ruggiero from his sister did not hide
How Bradamante had transfixed his heart,
And he described in words of loving pride
How much he owed to her; with subtle art
The former enemies he pacified.
No disagreement kept them now apart,
So, as a sign that hatred was erased,
As he desired, they lovingly embraced.

69

Marfisa then desired to know still more
About their father, who his forebears were,
And how he died: in a closed combat or
In battle? And their mother, what of her?
Why did she die upon an alien shore?
Who set her thus adrift? Did none demur?
In years gone by she may have heard it all,
But none, or little, could she now recall.

70

Ruggiero told her then of their descent
By Hector's line from Trojan ancestry;
How Astyanax escaped the dire intent
Of cunning Ûlysses, who cruelly
Despatched a substituted innocent.
The princeling, after many months at sea,
Found refuge on Sicilian shores, and there
He was Messina's king for many a year.

71

His heirs, leaving Messina's straits behind,
Ruled over regions in Calabria;
And later generations had a mind
To seek the city of the god of war.
Many a king and emperor, she'll find,
From this same Roman branch descended are,
Beginning with Constantius and then
To Constantine and up to Charlemagne.

72

'Ruggiero, called the First, and Giambaron
Were of this stock, Buovo, Rambaldo and
Ruggiero, called the Second, who upon
Our mother sired us, as you understand.
The deeds of our descendants will be known
In history and famed in many a land.'
And he described to her King Agolant's
Arrival, with his sons, to menace France.

73

A daughter too the king accompaniéd.
Such was her valour, many a paladin
She had unhorsed from many a brave steed;
And she, who came to love Ruggiero, in
Defiance of the king, the Christian creed
Accepting, was baptized; not long she'd been
Ruggiero's wife before Beltramo burned
With an incestuous love and traitor turned.

74

His country, father, brothers he betrayed,
Hoping thereby to gain Ruggiero's bride.
He opened Reggio to the foe, who made
A cruel havoc once they were inside.
Then Agolante, whom no mercy stayed,
And his two sons, who kinship's laws defied,
Placed Galaciella, six months gone with child,
Adrift in winter, tossed by tempests wild.

75

Marfisa listened with a brow serene,
Absorbed at first in all her brother said,
Rejoicing that their fount and origin
Two rivers of such sparkling lustre fed.
She knew Monglane and Clairmont both had been
Descended from the Trojan fountain-head
And that for many years both lines had won
Renown and splendour, paralleled by none.

76

Yet when she hears her new-found brother say
Not only Agramante's father, but
His grandfather and uncle made away
With their brave sire Ruggiero and then put
His wife, their mother, in such jeopardy,
The sister scarce can hear the story out.
She interrupts him, 'Brother, with respect,
Our father's honour how can you neglect?

77

'For if Almonte's or Troiano's blood
You cannot shed, since they did not survive,
Why do you not exterminate their brood?
Why, if you live, is Agramant alive?
After so many injuries, how could
You hold your hand? Nay, how could you contrive
To serve him at his court and in the field?
This blemish to no bleach will ever yield.

78

'I swear to God that I will worship now
Christ the true God to whom my father prayed;
And I will not put off these arms, I vow,
Till vengeance for my parents has been paid.
And you will cause my head with grief to bow
If from today I see you use your blade
In Agramante's ranks, or any Moor's,
Unless their swift undoing it ensures.'

79

Fair Bradamante lifts her face anew,
Alight with happiness, soon as she hears
The course his sister tells him to pursue;
And to her admonition she adds hers,
Bidding him come and kneel in homage to
King Charles, who honours, praises and reveres
Ruggiero's father yet for his renown,
Than whom no greater warrior was known.

80

Ruggiero wisely said that both were right,
That he should thus have acted from the start,
But since he had misjudged the matter quite,
It was too late to play another part;
For Agramant it was who dubbed him knight.
If he now drove a dagger through his heart,
It would be treachery, for he had sworn
To guard him as his lord from harm and scorn.

81

As he had promised Bradamante, so
He gave his promise to Marfisa that
All avenues would be explored and no
Occasion overlooked whereby his fate
Might make it possible for him to go
With honour to serve Charles; and if of late
He seemed inactive, he was not to blame,
But Mandricard, who left him sore and lame.

82

And she who every day sat by his bed,
That he was gravely wounded testified.
Much by each woman warrior was said
On the affair, and each in full replied.
At last to this conclusion they were led:
Ruggiero should return to fight beside
King Agramante till a circumstance
Arose to let him serve the king of France.

83

'Let him depart,' Marfisa said at last
To Bradamante, 'put aside your fears.
I promise that ere many days have passed
I'll find a way to set him free.' She swears,
But at that moment she could not have guessed
What she had promised by that oath of hers.
They say farewell and with no loitering
Ruggiero mounts his steed to join his king.

84

But all at once they heard a piteous wail
Which stopped the comrades in their tracks, all three.
It seemed to echo from a near-by vale;
The timbre of the tones was womanly.
But now I wish to interrupt this tale
And in this wish of mine please bear with me,
For better things I promise you next time,
If you will hear what follows in my rhyme.

CANTO XXXVII

1

As to perfect some precious gift or bent
Which Nature without toil cannot bestow,
Women have laboured, day and night intent,
And well-earned recognition sometimes know,
Would that they chose to be as diligent
And a like dedicated care would show
In studies more esteemed and highly prized,
Whence mortal virtues are immortalized.

2

And would they might their powers then devote
To women's own commemorative praise,
Rather than look to men to sound this note,
Whose envious spite their judgement overlays,
For Woman's merits many a man will not
Proclaim, though gladly ill of her he says.
By women, women's fame could reach the skies,
Higher perhaps than men's renown could rise.

3

And often men are not content to sing
In praise of each the other's world renown,
But all their efforts they apply to bring
To light why purists should on women frown.
Unwilling they should rise in anything,
They do the best they can to keep them down
(I speak here of the past), as if the fame
Of women would dissolve or dim *their* name.

4

And yet no powers of the hand or tongue,
Transformed to voice or words upon the page
(Though ill-repute be magnified among
All men, and virtue by an envious gauge
Be minished), could contrive to leave unsung
All women's merits, for despite the rage
Of male detractors, some are known about,
Although the greater part are blotted out.

5

Harpàlyce, Tomyris and the maid
Who fought by Turnus, Hector's Amazon,
She whom the men of Tyre and Sidon made
Their leader and to Libya sailed on,
Zenobia and she who, unafraid,
Assyria, Persia, India warred upon,
These women warriors are but a few
Whose fame the chronicles of war renew.

6

And women, wise and strong and true and chaste,
In other regions than in Greece and Rome,
Wherever the sun shines, from the Far East
To the Hesperides, have had their home,
Whose virtues and whose merits are unguessed.
Concerning them historians are dumb:
Contemporary authors, filled with spite,
The truth about such women would not write.

7

But, ladies, do not cease on this account
To persevere in works which you do well.
Let not discouragement ambition daunt,
Nor fear that recognition never will
Be yours. Good no immunity can vaunt
From change, Evil is not immutable,
And if in history your page was blurred,
In modern times your merits will be heard.

8

Marullo and Pontano championed you;
Both Strozzi: first the father, then the son;
Now Bembo and Cappello pay their due,
And he who formed the courtier's paragon,
And Luigi Alamanni and the two
Beloved of Mars and of the Muses, one
And the other equally, both of the blood
Which rules the town which stems the Mincio's flood.

9

One of these two, whose natural desire
Is to pay honour to your excellence,
Up to Parnassus, Cynthus, even higher,
His praises of you offers, like incense;
But more: the love, the faith, in spite of dire
Afflictions and of menacing events,
His Isabella's courage which abjures
Defeat, have made him, not his own, but yours.

10

And so he never wearies of the theme
Of lauding you in his enduring songs.
If some speak ill, you can depend on him
To take up arms at once and right your wrongs.
He holds his life but little in esteem
Compared with giving praise where praise belongs.
He is himself a theme of eloquence,
For he gives fame to others' excellence.

11

And it is fit that one so well endowed
With virtue that she seems to comprehend
All goodness that on women is bestowed,
From wifely constancy should never bend,
But like a column has unswerving stood,
Whatever shocks or ill the Fates might send.
He deserves her, and she deserves him too;
No pair was better coupled than these two.

12

New trophies he has brought to Oglio's shore,
Composing many a·well-turned line of verse
Amid the clamour and the clash of war,
Which envy on the near-by Mincio stirs.
Ercole Bentivoglio's praises soar
In celebration of you to the spheres.
Trivulzio and Guidetto cannot fault you,
Nor Molza, named by Phoebus to exalt you.

13

And Ercole, the duke of Chartres, the son
Of my Alfonso, spreads his mighty wings
And, not unlike the legendary swan,
Flying, your praises to the heavens sings.
My lord of Vasto, whose exploits alone
Would furnish Rome's and Athens' chronicling
A thousand times, shows it is now his will
To render you immortal with his quill.

14

Besides all these who champion you today
And many more who praise you lavishly,
You to yourselves could equal homage pay;
For many women leave embroidery
To seek the Muses and their thirst allay
At Aganippe's fount; and then we see
That greater is our need of words of yours
Than you have need of any words of ours.

15

And if a good account I were to give,
And fully to such women's worth attest,
I'd fill so many pages, I believe,
This canto would be nothing but a list.
And if I were to choose, say, six, or five,
I might offend and anger all the rest.
How shall I solve the problem? Speak of none?
Or choose among so many only one?

16

I will choose one and she whom I will name
No envious disdain or scorn will stir.
No other women will be put to shame
If I omit them all and praise but her.
Not only has she won immortal fame
With her sweet style – no sweeter do I hear;
To him of whom she speaks or writes, she gives
New life: awakened from the tomb, he lives.

17

As Phoebus his fair sister, pure and white,
Gazing upon her, renders fairer still
Than Venus, Mercury or other light
Which circles with the heavens, or at will:
So into her I speak of, more insight
And sweeter eloquence he breathes to fill
Her lofty-sounding words with such *élan*
That in our heavens shines a second sun.

18

She is Vittoria and justly crowned,
As one to victory and triumph born.
Where'er she walks, the laurel-leaves abound
And diadems of fame her brow adorn.
Like Artemìsia, lauded and renowned,
Who her Mausòlus never ceased to mourn,
She is a yet more pious, loving wife:
She gives her spouse not burial, but life.

19

If Laodamìa and if Brutus' spouse,
Evadne, Arrìa, Argìa and many more
Were praised, and praised deservedly, because
Each wished to share her husband's sepulchre,
What greater marvel does that wife arouse
Who draws from Lethe and the ninefold shore
Of Styx her consort back to life and breath
Despite the Fates and in despite of Death!

20

If fierce Achilles envy in the breast
Of Alexander stirred for deeds proclaimed
By the Maeonean poet's epic blast,
Then all the more would you, by all acclaimed,
Francesco di Pescara, by your chaste
And loving wife, rightly for ever famed!
By her your glory echoes ever higher.
No more resounding peal could you desire.

21

If everything that might be said of her,
And all I wish to say, I'd here unfold,
I'd cover many pages, I aver,
Yet much would even so remain untold.
And of Marfisa who is waiting there
With her two comrades, resolute and bold,
The story which I promised to pursue
Would have to be deferred today anew.

22

So now, since you have come to hear my tale,
And not to break the promise I have made,
At greater leisure I'll myself regale
With all the praise of her I would have said;
Not that I think my lines are of avail
To her whose vein such richness has displayed,
But for the need I feel to honour her
Whose genius I acknowledge and revere.

23

So, ladies, I conclude: in every age
There have been women worthy of renown;
But envious writers have left blank the page
Which after death should make your glory known.
This will no longer be: you must engage
To make yourselves immortal from now on.
Had the two sisters been aware of this,
They had been sooner friends than enemies.

24

I speak of Bradamante and the twin
Of her Ruggiero; their brave deeds I strive
To bring to light, though nine times out of ten
The facts are missing; yet I will revive
The memory of such as still remain.
For noble acts which men to hide contrive
Should be revealed; also in token of
My wish to please you, ladies, whom I love.

25

Ruggiero, as I said, was just about
To leave and had already bid goodbye
And from the tree had pulled his weapon out
(And no one now opposed him), when a cry
Arrested him and held them all in doubt.
Not far away it sounded but near by;
And, with Marfisa and his bride, he made
Towards the sound, if need be to lend aid.

26

Forward they rode and louder grew the sound,
Until at last the words were audible.
Reaching the vale, three women there they found
Whose plight indeed was strange and terrible.
Shrill cries they uttered, seated on the ground,
For cut short up to the umbilical
Their skirts had been; to hide herself each tries
As best she can and, sitting, dares not rise.

27

And like the son of Vulcan who from dust
Came forth to life, not from a mother's womb,
By Pallas to Aglauros as a trust
Committed (and he his serpent feet from
Her keen eyes concealed, sitting with legs crossed
Beneath him on the quadriga which some
Have said he first constructed), even so
These three their secret parts tried not to show.

28

This monstrous and dishonourable sight
To two brave warriors' cheeks is seen to bring
An altered hue, as vivid and as bright
As a red rose in Paestum in the Spring;
And Bradamante recognizes, quite
Beyond all doubt (but greatly wondering),
Ullania, whom she had met by chance,
The queen of Iceland's messenger to France.

29

She recognized no less the other two,
For at Ullania's side they always were;
But she addresses her enquiry to
The one whom she most honours, asking her
Who was the miscreant who had been so
Devoid of decency as to lay bare
Those secrets, by all casual passers eyed,
Which Nature, it would seem, prefers to hide.

30

Ullania has recognized the Maid,
By her insignia and by her speech
For she recalls her as the one who had
Some little time ago unseated each
Of the three kings; now in reply she said
That at a castle, within easy reach,
The evil folk not only cut her skirt,
But beat her too, and did her other hurt.

31

What happened to the shield she cannot say,
Nor how the kings had fared who by her side
Had travelled many a land for many a day.
They might be prisoners, they might have died.
Although on foot, she chose to come this way,
Hoping to be avenged if she applied
For help to Charlemagne to right the wrong;
She judged he would not suffer it for long.

32

From the three faces of the cavaliers,
Whose bosoms no less tender are than brave,
Serenity has vanished: wrath appears.
When they have seen and heard how vile and grave
An injury her ladies' was and hers,
Their other obligations they now waive;
She has no further need to plead her case:
They gallop off at once towards the place.

33

With one accord they drew their surcoats off,
Stirred by the deep compassion in their hearts.
These garments, as it proved, were long enough
To cover the poor women's shameful parts.
The Maid, to spare Ullania the rough
Uneven path and further pain and smarts,
Takes her up pillion on her destrier.
Marfisa follows suit, so does Ruggier.

34

Ullania, on Bradamante's horse,
Points out the shortest routes along the way,
While Bradamante, for her part, assures
Her charge that she will be avenged that day.
They leave the valley for a winding course
Which to a hill-top climbs, first now this way
And then the other; long before they stopped
For rest, the sun behind the sea had dropped.

35

They find a little hamlet perched on high.
The path to it is steep and bleak and bare.
Here they take lodging and are glad to try
The supper, which is good but humble fare.
They look about them and where'er they spy
They see the inhabitants all women are,
Some young, some old; no matter where they turn,
In that vast crowd, no man do they discern.

36

Jason, I think, no greater marvel knew,
When on the isle of Lemnos he set foot
(Nor did the Argonauts, his faithful crew),
And no one there but women saw, who put
Their sons and brothers all to death, who slew
Their husbands and their fathers, so that but
One virile face was seen, than did Ruggier
And his companions on arriving there.

37

The women warriors give orders soon
That the three ladies should be brought attire.
Three dresses are supplied, which they put on.
If they lack style, they are at least entire.
The good Ruggiero beckons to him one
Among the women, wishing to enquire
Where all the men are: not one can he spy;
And she obliges, eager to reply.

38

'This, which to you is strange and marvellous,
That all these women live here without men,
Is an intolerable grief to us.
Here we are banished to this wretched den.
To make our exile more monotonous,
Our fathers, husbands, sons, we know not when
We'll see, whom we so love; and this divorce
A tyrant has imposed on us by force.

39

'And from his kingdom, which not distant is
Two leagues from us, the land where we were born,
He drove us forth with many cruelties,
First bitterly reviling us with scorn.
Our men and us (alas!) he menaces
With death by torture if to him are borne
Reports that they have visited us here,
Or we with love receive them, should they dare.

40

'Of women he is such a bitter foe,
He cannot bear us near him, nor consent
That any man should come near us, as though
They might be poisoned by the female scent.
We've seen the branches shed and twice regrow
Their crowning glory since we here were sent,
And still the tyrant rages in his wrath
And no one curbs him on his frenzied path.

41

'His subjects feel for him the greatest fear
That death itself could ever inculcate,
For Nature to his spite beyond compare
Has joined a giant size and strength so great,
All others he surpasses in this sphere;
Nor to his female *subjects* is this threat
Confined; for to all women visitors
This tyrant's hostile acts are even worse.

42

'So, if your honour and the honour of
These ladies you escort are dear to you,
It is to your advantage not to move
Another step along the pathway to
The castle of this tyrant who no love
For women has, whose plan is to subdue
By scorn and shame all those who there ascend
Both men and women – to his evil end.

43

'This villain, Marganorre (thus is named
The lord by whom we women are coerced),
More Nero-like than Nero, or others famed
For cruelty, more evil, more accurst,
The blood of humans, like a beast untamed,
Desires; for female blood a greater thirst
He has; no wolf a lamb more relishes,
Than he who every woman banishes.'

44

What drove the tyrant to this frenzied state
The women and Ruggiero long to know.
The tale in full they beg her to relate
Or, rather, back to the beginning go.
'This lord', said she, 'was always filled with hate
And always cruel, but he did not show
These vile propensities at first; the role
He played concealed the evil in his soul.

45

'While his two sons were yet alive, whose ways
To Marganorre's no resemblance bore
(They were as different as chalk and cheese),
For they were kind, enjoying nothing more
Than visitors and friends from overseas,
Good manners, courtly deeds were seen to flower,
And, though the king was parsimonious,
His sons could, if they wished, be generous.

46

'Ladies and cavaliers were formerly
So well received that each and every one
Rode off delighted with such courtesy
And by the two young men all hearts were won.
Both took the solemn vows of chivalry;
They kept their vigil side by side. The one
Cilandro was, the other youth was called
Tanacro; both were regal, gallant, bold.

47

'And they might always have been worthy of
Such praise and honour, but they both fell prey
To that desire we dignify as love;
And from the straight path wandering astray,
Through labyrinths of error now they move,
And all the good they did is straight away
Perverted to become its opposite,
As though some sickness had infected it.

48

'A cavalier arrived, as it befell,
From the Byzantine court, and in his train
There rode a lady who, as I heard tell,
Drew the admiring glances of all men.
So deep in love with her Cilandro fell,
So grievously he languished in his pain,
He thought that he would die if she departed
Leaving him unfulfilled and broken-hearted.

49

'Because entreaties would have borne no fruit,
His purpose was to capture her by force.
He armed and hid himself along the route
The two had chosen for their homeward course.
The frenzied passion which had taken root
Left him no time to think, and when the horse
Of the Greek cavalier he saw advance
He galloped to attack, lance against lance.

50

'He thought he would succeed at the first blow,
Winning both lady and the victory,
But the Greek knight, who knew a thing or two
About the art and skill of chivalry,
Shattered like glass the hauberk of his foe.
The tidings reached the father instantly,
Who, seeing he was dead, beside their great
And ancient forebears buried him in state.

51

'The welcome all received was not decreased,
The hospitality remained the same;
For no less affable to every guest
Tanacro was, who shared Cilandro's fame
For courtesy; but not a year had passed
When from afar a lord and lady came.
He was a gallant, handsome man, and she
Most beautiful and lovely was to see.

52

'And no less virtuous she was than fair
And truly worthy of all men's esteem.
Courage was in his blood, and bold and rare
Those rivals must have been who equalled him;
And it is just that those who greatly dare
Should win a coveted reward. His name
Olindro was, Baron of Lungavilla,
And she, the baroness, was called Drusilla.

53

'No less for her the young Tanacro burned
Than did Cilandro for the lovely Greek
When all his life to dust and ashes turned;
No less now than his brother did he seek
(So little from that precedent he learned)
The laws of hospitality to break
Rather than to this strange and new desire
Acknowledge his surrender, and expire.

54

'Having his brother's death before his eyes
And wary of Olindro's wrath, he planned
To take the lady from him in such guise
He'd have no fear of his avenging hand.
That virtue soon diminishes and dies
On which Tanacro stands, as on dry land,
Above the floods of vice which round him sweep,
In which his father flounders fathoms deep.

55

'So in the depths of night, without a sound,
Some miles away, he stationed twenty men
In grottoes which along the route are found,
Or where the cross-roads intersect; and then
Olindro's passage was cut off all round.
He could not forward move, nor back again.
That day the baron was deprived of wife
And, after a courageous stand, of life.

56

'Her husband slain, Tanacro captive led
The lovely baroness; she, bowed with grief,
Would not by any means be comforted,
But at his hands she begged for the relief
Of death; her one desire was to be dead.
She flung herself at last from a high cliff.
She did not die, but with a broken skull
She lingered, frail and bruised and sorrowful.

57

'Tanacro had no other way to bear
Her home than on a stretcher; and the best
Of medical attention, every care
He lavished on her, fearing death might wrest
This precious booty from him; they prepare
Meanwhile to celebrate the wedding feast:
The name of wife, Tanacro judged, was more
Acceptable to her than paramour.

58

'Tanacro had no other waking thought,
No other wish, no other care, no dream
But of possessing her; all else was naught.
He begged her to forgive, he took the blame,
But all in vain; the longer he besought,
The more he tried, the more she hated him
And stronger grew, with each and every breath,
Her fixed desire to bring about his death.

59

'Her hatred of him did not so erase
Her wits that she no longer understood
That cunning was essential in the case,
That her true feelings she must mask and hood.
While plotting secretly, she must efface
All outward tokens of her inward mood
And (though all she desired was to destroy him)
Show every sign of longing to enjoy him.

60

'"Peace", her face pretends; "vengeance", her heart
And will no other purpose contemplate.   [cries,
The ways and means that pass before her eyes
Seem good or bad or indeterminate;
At last it seems to her that if she dies
She will succeed, and eagerly this fate
She welcomes; how or for what better cause
Can she now die than to avenge her spouse?

61

'She seems all joy and happiness, and feigns
The utmost longing for the wedding-day;
And it appears from all the evidence
That she is eager to avoid delay.
Before her looking-glass she prinks and preens.
Thoughts of Olindro now seem far away,
But she has one request: the marriage vows,
As in her land, must honour her dead spouse.

62

'It was untrue, however, that the rite
Was in her land conducted as she said;
But since no other answer to her plight
She could devise, she told this lie instead,
Hoping by such a method to requite
The miscreant who struck her husband dead;
She wants the wedding to be held, she says,
According to her native country's ways.

63

'"A widow who remarries," she pretends,
"Ere she becomes the wife of someone new,
Must first placate the soul whom she offends
By masses, which are celebrated to
Remit past scores; thus she must make amends
Before the dead man's tomb; then, as is due,
At the conclusion of this offering,
The bridegroom on the bride bestows the ring.

64

'"And meantime the officiating priest
Over a flask of wine will offer up
A holy prayer; when the wine is blessed,
He pours it from the flask into a cup
And hands it to the bride and groom to taste;
The bride must first receive the holy stoup
And be the first to lift it to her lips,
Before the bridegroom from it also sips."

65

'Tanacro does not see what this implies,
And if the rite does not involve delays
He offers no objection, he replies.
The wretch does not perceive that by such ways
She leads him to his death, nor realize
That for Olindro's murder he thus pays;
And so intently he is fixed on one
Thing only, for all else his wits have flown.

66

'Drusilla had with her an agèd maid
Who, having come to serve her, stayed to serve.
She called her to her and discreetly said,
Where none could overhear them or observe,
"Mix me a poison of the kind you've made
Before, such as all traitors well deserve,
And I will punish Marganorre's son
For the foul villainy which he has done.

67

'"I know a way to save myself and you:
I'll tell you later; now do as I ask."
The old and faithful serving-maid withdrew
And secretly performed her fearful task.
With a sweet wine from Candia the brew
Was stirred and mingled in a crystal flask
Which would do duty on the wedding-day;
And now there was no reason for delay.

68

'At the appointed hour, adorned with gems
The bride arrived, dressed in a lovely gown.
Olindro in the place of honour seems,
His tomb raised on two columns; they intone
The office of the mass with solemn hymns.
The people flock to hear from court and town,
And Marganorre, joyful just this once,
Comes with his son and his companions.

69

'The rites were said for him who lay in state,
The flask containing poisoned wine was blessed.
The priest continued to officiate,
Filling a golden cup, at her request.
She drank as much as was appropriate
And for her promised husband left the rest.
With joyful face she handed him the cup:
Tanacro drank it down to the last drop.

70

'Handing the chalice to the priest, he turns
With joy to clasp his bride in his embrace.
Her docile tenderness has gone: there burns
Instead a wrathful passion in its place.
Pushing him back, his fond advance she spurns
With fury blazing in her eyes and face;
And in an awesome voice and chilling tone
She shouts: "Traitor, keep back, from me be gone!

71

'"You think to take your joy of me, while I
From you have tears and suffering and woe?
These hands have done their work: you will now die.
That wine was poisoned (what? you did not know?).
Your execution is too mild and by
A death too kind, alas!, you are brought low.
What hangman's hands, what savage penalty
In all the world could match your treachery?

72

'"It grieves me that your death does not perfect
My sacrifice; if I had managed it
As I desired, there would be no defect;
My act of vengeance would have been complete.
May my belovèd husband not reject
My offering, but may he find it sweet.
Unable to despatch you as I would,
I've done for you the only way I could.

73

'"The punishment I long to give you here
I hope your soul will suffer, as is due,
Among the dead and damned down yonder; there
I'll take my fill of joy in watching you."
Such were her words; with eyes no longer clear
She looked above; then she began anew,
Her face aglow with love: "Olindro, take
This wifely offering for vengeance' sake;

74

'"And pray that by the grace of our dear Lord
I may ascend to you in Heaven today.
If only souls who merit such reward
May be admitted to His kingdom, say
Against an evil monster I have warred
And bring the spoils of battle to array
His shrine; is there a more deserving deed
Than to exterminate so vile a breed?"

75

'Together life and words came to a close.
Her face in death was joyful and content
That such a traitor she had punished thus,
He who the life-blood of her spouse had spent.
Whether he died before her, no one knows.
I rather think he was the first who went.
The poison sooner worked in him because
His portion of the wine the greater was.

76

'When Marganorre sees his only son
Collapse, when in his arms he lifeless lies,
He, unprotected, through the breast is run
By grief so sharp that he too almost dies.
Two sons he had and now he is alone.
Two women are to blame for their demise:
One was the cause of death of the first brother,
And one with her own hands destroyed the other.

77

'Love, pity, anger, grief and frenzied rage,
Desire for death and for revenge as well
In the bereaved and anguished father wage
A conflict, as when wild winds lash and swell
The sea; his pain unable to assuage,
Drusilla's body, now insensible,
Goaded and stung by burning spite he tries
To desecrate and ravage where it lies.

78

'Just as a snake in vain the spike will bite
Which, piercing it, has pinned it to the ground,
Just as a mastiff vents its futile spite
Upon a pebble with a snarling sound,
Maddened by bestial rage or appetite,
So Marganorre – worse than any hound
Or snake – continues his assault upon
That helpless body from which life has gone.

79

'Nothing induces him to hold his hand;
Nothing his thirst for vengeance will allay.
The church is tightly packed with women, and
Not one of us he spares, but tries to slay
Us all, slicing us with his cruel brand
Just as a peasant scythes a field of hay.
He slaughters thirty, then a hundred more
He wounds, and leaves them lying in their gore.

80

'So feared is he by troops and servitors,
No man dare raise a finger to his wrath.
The women flee the church in headlong course.
No villager but takes the homeward path.
At last his impetus has spent its force.
He quits the scene, leaving an aftermath
Of death and lamentation down below,
And to his fortress he consents to go.

81

'He yielded then (though still his rage was hot)
To those who begged him not to kill us all;
Perpetual exile was to be our lot.
And that same day (there was no interval)
He published a decree: all women out!
Here was the boundary, and woe befall
Whatever woman dared to show her face
Nearer the castle than this dismal place.

82

'And thus it was that husbands from their wives
Were separated, sons from mothers too.
If any man to visit us contrives
And Marganor gets wind of it, then woe
To him! it will be strange if he survives.
Such culprits die a cruel death and slow.
And at the castle he has passed a law
More dire than anyone e'er heard or saw.

83

'A woman who is captured in the dale
(And some do venture there, I must confess)
Is to be whipped and sent beyond the pale;
But first, according to this law, her dress
Is cut so high and short that none can fail
To see what Nature hides and seemliness.
If any on an armed escort relies,
The law is even more severe: she dies.

84

'If any is escorted by a band
Of cavaliers, before the dead sons' tombs
She's dragged and sacrificed by his own hand.
To ignominious restraint he dooms
The knights, relieving them of horses and
Their weapons, armour, retinue and grooms.
This is within his power, for all around
More than a thousand men-at-arms are found.

85

'And further, any knight whom he may spare
(If it shall ever please him) lifelong hate
For all the female sex is made to swear
And on the holy wafer consecrate
His vow; so if, in spite of all, you are
Resolved to lose your lives, ride to the gate
Where you will find this fiend at home, and see
Which is the worse – his strength, or cruelty.'

86

Her words the women warriors incite
First to such pity, then to so much ire,
That if it had been day instead of night
They would have left at once; but all retire
To take their rest; and when Aurora's light
Signals the stars to yield before their sire,
The cavaliers rearm and on their steeds
Remount, resolved to punish such vile deeds.

87

When they are ready to set off, the sound
Of many hoofs is heard not far away
Behind their backs; at this they all turn round
And gaze into the valley; I should say
About a stone's throw from the higher ground
A company along a narrow way
Progressed, twenty armed men, or thereabout;
Some were on horseback, others were on foot.

88

And with them, mounted on a horse, they brought
A woman; from her wrinkles you could guess
That she was old; her aspect, you'd have thought,
Suggests a felon taken to the place
Of execution; though she was distraught,
Though so much time has passed, her dress and face
The village women recognize at once:
It is Drusilla's servant, they pronounce:

89

That serving-wench who with her mistress stayed
(When she was captured by the second son),
To whom was then entrusted, as I said,
The task of mixing poison; she'd not gone
To church that day to see Drusilla wed:
She feared the consequence of what she'd done;
But from the village she escaped to where
She hoped to live in safety, free from fear.

90

But Marganorre traced her through his spies
And found that she had fled to Austria.
Unceasingly he thought how to devise
A plan to capture and to punish her:
The gallows and the stake were in his eyes
Too mild a penance for a poisoner.
A baron who her safety had ensured
Betrayed her, by rich spoils and offers lured.

91

He sent her all the way to Constance, bound
Like merchandise upon a donkey's back.
Since she was gagged, she could not make a sound,
And none could see her hidden in a sack.
Thence Marganorre's troops, who now surround
Her, had received commands to bring her back
By him in whom all mercy now is fled,
Whose rage will not be spent till she is dead.

92

As the great river which from Viso flows,
The nearer it descends towards the sea,
And more and more to the Ticino owes,
To Lambra, Adda and many a tributary,
In swelling pride and spate of water grows,
So does Ruggiero's anger rise when he
Has heard the crimes of Marganor, and thus
The women warriors wax furious.

93

Their hearts were so inflamed with wrath and hate
Against the tyrant for his cruelties,
Such crimes they were resolved to castigate,
Despite the number of his troops; to seize
And slay him quickly seemed too kind a fate,
Unworthy of offences such as his.
It will be better to prolong the throes
So that no single pang unnoticed goes.

94

Their duty first is to the serving-maid,
To save her from the fearful death she faces.
With slackened reins and ready heels they aid
Their eager steeds to show their fastest paces.
No sharper onslaught has that cavalcade
Experienced; each man for safety races.
Lucky are those who leave behind their gear,
Their shields, their armour and the prisoner.

95

As when a wolf, returning to his lair,
Clenching between his jaws his helpless prey
And confident no enemies are near,
Sees all at once a hunter cross his way
With all the pack, his booty drops in fear,
And where the bush is thickest lopes away,
So did those troops as speedily make off,
Escaping from attack into the rough.

96

Arms and the woman thus abandoning,
And of their horses a fair quantity
(So as to speed their flight), themselves they fling
From cliffs and grottoes, unrestrainedly.
This to the others was a welcome thing.
Of the unwanted horses they took three,
For the three women who the day before
Had made three other horses' cruppers sore.

97

Then with all haste their journey they pursue
Towards that infamous and cruel peak.
They want the servant to come with them too,
As witness of the vengeance they will wreak.
This the old creature is afraid to do,
But finds it all in vain to shout and shriek;
Ruggiero lifts her to Frontino's croup
And with her thus behind him gallops up.

98

They reached the summit whence they saw below
A large and thriving town; on every side
It could be entered without hindrance; no
Enclosing bastion or moat they spied.
A crag rose in the midst, with lofty brow,
And on its back a castle seemed to ride.
Towards this eagerly the warriors rode,
For this they knew was Marganor's abode.

99

When they have entered, men-at-arms who guard
The entrance shut the outer fortress-gate.
The exit too the warriors see is barred;
And Marganorre, issuing in state,
Surrounded by his chosen bodyguard
Of horse and foot, for parley does not wait.
Briefly and arrogantly he disclosed
The cruel customs which he had imposed.

100

Marfisa had already formed a plan
With which Ruggiero and the Maid of France
Were in agreement: for reply she ran
Against him, but not lowering her lance,
Nor brandishing her famous sword; with an
Astounding force upon his helm she plants
Her fist; he scarcely can remain astraddle,
But droops insensible across his saddle.

101

At the same moment Bradamante spurs,
Nor does Ruggiero long inactive stay,
But with an impetus to equal hers
He runs his lance through six without delay,
Yet from its rest his weapon never stirs.
One paunch, two breasts, one neck, one head display
Its deadly thrusts; and in the sixth it snaps,
Piercing the coward's spine through to his paps.

102

As many as are touched but lightly by
Count Aymon's daughter's golden lance, she floors.
It seems a bolt, hurled from the burning sky,
As when the Thunderer against us wars.
The people scatter, some of them on high,
Some to the plain; some lock themselves indoors;
Some to the churches, others home are fled,
And in the square all who remain are dead.

103

Marfisa in the interval had bound
The tyrant with his hands behind his back.
Drusilla's maid had charge of him and found
That pleasure in this work she did not lack.
They plan to raze the city to the ground
And all the dwellings they will burn and sack
Unless the tyrant's laws are changed in haste
And by Marfisa's legal code replaced.

104

The people will accept without demur
Marfisa's rule; not only do they dread
That further penalties they may incur,
That she may go beyond what she has said,
But they fear Marganorre even more
And all the cruel laws which he has made;
But, like most subject peoples, those whom most
They hate they most obey, to their great cost:

105

So no man trusts his neighbour or his brother,
No man his thoughts of vengeance dare confide.
They let him exile one, and kill another,
One dispossess, rob one of rightful pride.
Though here the heart its anguish has to smother,
In Heaven its sufferings aloud are cried.
God's vengeance comes at last in recompense,
And punishment, though tardy, is immense.

106

And now that mob, seething with rage and hate,
Desired to be revenged on tyranny.
No man, the proverb says, will hesitate
To gather firewood from a fallen tree.
So let all rulers mark this tyrant's fate:
The fruit of evil deeds will evil be.
To see him punished for his sins gave joy
To great and small, to every man and boy.

107

Many whose sisters, daughters, mothers, wives
By Marganorre have been put to death,
No longer now in terror of their lives,
Run, hands uplifted, eager for his death.
A wonder it will be if he survives.
The trio save him for a different death:
They plan that he shall die by slow degrees,
As though by torture, rack and little-ease.

108

Into the hands of that old serving-wench
As naked as the day when he was born
They gave him, bound so tight that by no wrench
Could he break free; with all a woman's scorn
And hate she made him tingle in revenge
For all the suffering which she had borne,
Poking him mercilessly with a goad
Which someone handed to her from the road.

109

Ullania and both the damsels, who
Their shameful treatment never will forget,
Are actively engaged in vengeance too.
They, like the servant, have to square a debt.
Their strength gives out, but they begin anew
(For they are far from finished with him yet):
They stone and scratch and bite him for his sins,
Or prick and stick and needle him with pins.

110

As when a torrent, proud and swollen made
By heavy rain betimes or melting snows,
Uproots in a precipitous cascade
The rocks, the trees, the corn that riper grows;
But when its force is spent, a child can wade,
A woman step across it with dry shoes,
No longer now the raging flood which poured,
Shrunk to the trickle of a narrow ford:

111

So Marganorre, at whose very name
His subjects trembled, of his antlers shorn,
From being so proud has now become so tame
That even children hold him up to scorn
And tweak his beard and pull his hair in game.
So, leaving him on all sides pricked and torn,
Ruggiero, Bradamante and Marfise
Approach the summit where the castle is.

112

The garrison did not resist the three.
The castle with its costly furnishings
Was yielded up; a part relentlessly
They sacked and burned; but for her sufferings
They gave Ullania some finery.
They found the golden shield and the three kings
Imprisoned there; I think I told you how
They'd gone unarmed, on foot, to keep their vow.

113

Unseated by the Maid, that very day
All armour, arms and horses they forswore,
And with Ullania went on their way,
Whom they'd escorted from so far a shore.
And whether it was worse I cannot say,
That they in her defence no weapons bore:
She was thus unprotected, but the cost
Would have been heavy if the kings had lost.

114

She would have shared the other women's doom
Who with an escort came, and in a trice
Have been conducted to the brothers' tomb
And by their father slain in sacrifice.
Less terrible than dying, I presume,
It is to show those parts that are not nice;
And every shame is lessened and excused
If we can say that on us force was used.

115

Before the women warriors depart
All the inhabitants are called to swear
That wives henceforth shall take the leading part
In government; if anyone shall dare
To flout this law, he shall be made to smart.
To sum the matter up, just as elsewhere
Husbands are masters, here the wives shall be
By right invested with authority.

116

As well as this they had to promise more:
Whoever here on foot or horseback came
Must not admitted be by any door,
No matter who they were or what their fame,
Unless by God and all His Saints they swore
(Or any god which has a better claim)
To help all women in adversity
And of their foes for ever foes to be.

117

And if they married late or married soon,
Or if they stayed unmarried all their lives,
The law would be the same for everyone:
Subjection and obedience to wives.
Marfisa would return before the sun
Moved south, before the trees had shed their leaves,
And if the law neglected then she found,
She'd sack and burn the city to the ground.

118

Drusilla's corpse from the unhallowed pit
Wherein it lay they lifted reverently,
And with her husband's body buried it
In a rich sepulchre, most fair to see.
The serving-maid continued still to hit
The back of Marganorre lustily.
She longed to have the strength to use the spike
Without a pause for rest, as she would like.

119

The sisters see a column in the square
Which Marganorre's vile and infamous
Decrees and legislation used to bear.
But now these two, who are victorious,
Append his helmet as a trophy there
With his cuirass and shield (and hazardous
It were to take them down). And under those,
New laws are then inscribed, which they impose.

120

Marfisa waited till this work was done.
The law the mason cut was the reverse
Of what was once inscribed upon the stone,
To women's ignominy, death or worse.
Ullania remained when they had gone.
She did not think that makeshift gown of hers
Was suitable for court, and she desired
To be once more appropriately attired.

121

She, left with Marganorre in her power,
Fearing he might revert to his old ways
If he escaped in an unguarded hour,
No longer his deserved despatch delays,
But makes him leap below from a high tower.
No greater leap he'd made in all his days.
But now I'll leave her and her *demoiselles*
And of the ones who go towards Arles I'll tell.

122

All through that day, and on the next they race,
Till after the third hour; at last they reach
A branching of the path; this is the place
Where they must say farewell; clasped each to each,
Repeatedly the lovers re-embrace.
They verify at length which path is which.
The women ride towards the camp, Ruggier
To Arles; and I will end my canto here.

CANTO XXXVIII

1

Sweet ladies, who such kind attention give
To these my verses, from your looks I'd say
News of Ruggiero's going you receive
With deep displeasure and as much dismay
As Bradamante; that a knight could leave
His promised bride again and ride away
Suggests to you (from what I say above)
In him but faintly burns the flame of love.

2

But if, against the wishes of his bride,
He had departed on some other quest,
If hopes of wealth had lured him on his ride –
A vaster sum than in his treasure-chest
Croesus or Crassus e'er amassed – then I'd
Agree with you: Love's arrow to his breast
Had failed to penetrate: such joy, such bliss,
No purse of gold or silver purchases.

3

Since to protect his honour he has gone,
Not only pardoned, lauded he should be;
For to do otherwise than he has done
Discredit would incur and obloquy.
And if his lady had insisted on
His still remaining in her company,
One of two things would have been clear to him:
She loved but little, or her wits were dim.

4

As she who is in love should value more
Than her own life her lover's life (I speak
Of love that strikes a lover to the core),
So pleasure second place must always take
To honour, since of all the joys in store
Which life can offer or that Man can seek,
Honour above all others is revered
And sometimes is to life itself preferred.

5

Ruggiero, in continuing to serve
His lord, fulfils his duty as a knight,
And from this path he is not free to swerve
Without good reason; for it is not right
To think that Agramante should deserve
To suffer for Almonte's act of spite,
Since for Ruggiero many things he's done
Which for his forebears' evil deeds atone.

6

Ruggiero honourably kept his bond
And Bradamante did her duty too,
Not clinging to him with repeated fond
Entreaties; at another time, she knew,
Though now to satisfy her was beyond
His power, this he would return to do.
But honour may be injured in a trice:
To satisfy it then no years suffice.

7

Ruggiero goes to Arles, where Agramant
Deploys such troops as still remain to him.
The warrior-maids, Marfise and Bradamant,
Joined now in fond and sisterly esteem,
Set off to where King Charles attempts to daunt
The foe by mustering his force; his scheme
Is by a battle or by siege to free
The land of France from her long agony.

8

When Bradamante's presence there was known,
The camp was in a ferment of delight.
Welcomed, saluted, hailed by everyone,
She bows her head in answer, left and right.
Rinaldo, hearing news of her, had gone
To meet his sister; nor must I omit
Ricciardo, Ricciardetto, all her kin,
Who rise and joyfully escort her in.

9

And when the word went round and it was plain
That her companion was Marfisa, she
Who from Cathay as far as western Spain
Was crowned with laurel-wreaths of victory,
Not one of all the soldiers would remain
In the pavilions; out they poured to see,
Jostling and elbowing, from here, from there,
That splendid, martial and heroic pair.

10

They came before King Charles with reverence.
This was the only time (so Turpin says)
Marfisa knelt to make obeisance.
To Pepin's son this homage she now pays.
That majesty he only represents
Which she has never seen in all her days
In Christian or in pagan kings renowned
For glory or by virtue's halo crowned.

11

The Emperor received her graciously,
And forth from his pavilion towards her came;
And at his side desired that she should be,
In precedence of princes of great fame.
And some who did not leave, but lingered, he
Dismissed, for an élite was now his aim,
Of paladins and foremost lords; the crowd
Beyond the palisade was not allowed.

12

Marfisa in a pleasing tone thus speaks:
'Illustrious Caesar, famed in many lands,
From India's sea to Hercules' twin peaks,
From Scythian snows to Ethiopian sands,
Before your silver cross the proudest necks
Have bowed; most wise and just are your commands.
Led by your fame, which knows no boundary,
I journeyed far to see Your Majesty.

13

'To tell the truth, envy my motive was.
My only aim was to make war on you.
No king so mighty but must keep the laws
I kept; the battlefields a scarlet hue
With Christian blood I stained; and for this cause
I would have shown you other tokens too
Of my hostility; but in the end,
As it befell, I changed from foe to friend.

14

'When most intent on spilling Christian blood,
I learned I was the daughter (at some other
Time I'll tell you more) of the famed and good
Ruggiero of Reggio by his evil brother
Slain; I, as yet unborn, so it ensued,
To Africa was carried by my mother.
She died in childbirth; in my seventh year
Some Arabs stole me from a sorcerer.

15

'In Persia then they sold me as a slave.
The king who purchased me I later slew.
He tried to take my maidenhood and have
His way with me; I killed his courtiers too
And chase to his degenerate sons I gave.
I seized the realm and such good fortune knew,
No less than seven kingdoms I possessed,
When scarce my eighteenth birthday I had passed.

16

'As I have told you, envious of your fame,
I had determined in my heart to bring
Disaster down on you, defeat and shame.
Who knows if I'd have failed in such a thing?
But now extinguished is my fury's flame
And such ambition droops upon the wing
Since I have heard (and blood, my lord, less thin
Than water is) that we are kith and kin.

17

'My sire, your kinsman, served you as his lord,
And I, your kinswoman, will serve you too.
The jealousy, the hate, I felt toward
Your Majesty, I now forget, or to
A better purpose it's reserved and stored:
Against Troiano's son and any who
Are kinsfolk of my father's murderers,
For in me now desire for vengeance stirs.'

18

She wished to be a Christian, she next said,
And when King Agramante had been killed
The subjects of her kingdom would be made
To undergo conversion, if Charles willed;
And, next, wherever in the world men prayed
To Termagant, or by Mahomet held,
She would take arms against them in the name
Of Holy Church and for the Empire claim.

19

The Emperor was no less eloquent
Than he was valorous and wise; he praised
The damsel for her deeds; then her descent,
Her father's virtues too, on high he raised.
His heart's nobility was evident
From his reply, so courteously phrased.
He thanked her for the motive which had brought her,
Accepting her as kinswoman and daughter.

20

He then arose, embracing her once more,
And like a father kissed her on the brow.
The paladins who were her foes of yore,
The Monglanes and the Clairmonts, claimed her now
With joyful faces as their friend; before
Her too, Rinaldo came to make his bow.
Long it would take me to record his praise
Of all her deeds of their Albracca days.

21

Long it would take me to describe the joy
Of Aquilant, Guidone, Sansonet
And of Grifone (that imprudent boy),
As they recall the city where they met.
Repeatedly the other three destroy –
Viviano, Malagigi, Ricciardet –
Lanfusa's traffickers, Maganza's men,
Recalling how Marfisa helped them then.

22

Her baptism is fixed for the next day;
And Charles himself makes it his special care
That everyone his orders shall obey.
A place of rich adornment they prepare.
Bishops from near at hand and far away,
And learned clerics, searched for everywhere,
Well-versed in doctrine, hither are conducted,
That in the Faith Marfisa be instructed.

23

In sumptuous pontificals arrayed,
Archbishop Turpin came to christen her.
Charles with due ceremony raised the maid
From the health-giving, saving lavacer.
But it is time now to apply the aid
So needed by the frenzied cavalier,
Which Duke Astolfo carried from the moon,
Returning in the chariot with St John.

24

Astolfo had returned from the bright sphere
And landed on the highest point on earth,
Bringing that precious phial with him here,
To give Orlando's witless mind rebirth.
St John then shows the English cavalier
A herb, whose virtue is of wondrous worth,
And with it, when to Nubia he flies,
He is to touch the king and heal his eyes.

25

For this and former benefits the king
Will give him troops for an attack upon
Biserta; inexpert in soldiering,
They must be trained and armed; when this is done,
He must instruct them in manoeuvring
Across the dazzling sand in blinding sun.
And point by point, all that Astolfo ought
To do, the venerable Elder taught.

26

The duke remounted the winged quadruped
Which first Atlante, then Ruggiero, rode
And, parting from St John, away he sped,
Leaving behind our parents' first abode.
Next by the Nile's divarications led,
Which now to one side, now the other, flowed,
To Nubia he came and in the town
Which is the capital he fluttered down.

27

Great was the joy and great was the delight
He caused the king by his return, who well
Recalled how he had freed them from the blight
Of harpies, monstrous, hideous and fell.
And when that thickness which obscured the light
The potent juices of the herb unseal
And he can see as clearly as before,
He worships his deliverer still more.

28

Not only does he give him all the men
He asks, to take Biserta by surprise,
But adds a hundred thousand more, and then
His service offers in the enterprise.
So large a host is mustered that the plain,
It seems, the vast array can scarce comprise.
All are on foot – no horses there are found,
Though elephants, and camels too, abound.

29

And on the eve of the appointed day
When King Senapo's army shall march forth,
Astolfo in the darkness flees away,
Urging the hippogriff for all it's worth.
He reaches Auster's hill without delay,
That frenzied wind which blows from south to north,
And finds the narrow slit through which it streaks
Whenever from its slumber it awakes.

30

And, as St John instructed, he had brought
An empty wineskin with him on his ride
And, moving quietly, as he was taught,
Not to disturb the sleeping wind inside,
Which, weary from its work, suspected naught,
The wineskin to the narrow crack applied.
The wind next morning, bursting from the crag,
Was caught and held securely in the bag.

31

The paladin, delighted with his prize,
Returns to Nubia, and that same morn
With his black army of so vast a size
Sets out; provisions after them are borne.
The desert sand (a peril otherwise)
Astolfo does not fear but holds in scorn
(The wind being prisoner), and all his host
As far as Atlas' foothills safely crossed.

32

And once beyond the range, he led them where
The land is broadened to a coastal plain,
And, choosing his best squadrons, those who were,
He judged, the best and easiest to train,
He spaced them out, some here, and others there.
Like one who has momentous plans in train,
He left them at the bottom of a hill
And set off to the summit with a will.

33

And when he reached the top, he knelt and prayed
(His mentor-saint would answer him, he knew).
Next, down the hill, rock after rock he sped.
How much a firm belief in Christ can do!
The rolling stones no natural laws obeyed,
For, as they tumbled down the slope, they grew
A rounded belly, legs, a neck, a muzzle
(And how they did it still remains a puzzle).

34

And with shrill neighs and whinnyings they speed,
Bounding and leaping down the craggy way,
Then shake their cruppers, every one a steed,
Some dapple and some roan and others bay.
To their arrival paying careful heed,
The waiting squadrons seized them straight away.
Soon every man was mounted on a horse.
(Saddled and bridled they were born, of course.)

35

Ten times eight thousand, ten times ten, plus two
That day from infantry to cavaliers
He changed; then Africa they scoured all through,
Burning and sacking, taking prisoners.
King Agramante had entrusted to
The king of Fers, the king of Algaziers
And King Branzardo all the safety of
His realm: these now against Astolfo strove.

36

But first they have despatched a slender dhow
Which speeds by oar and sail as if on wings,
And messages to Agramant of how
The Nubians invade his kingdom brings.
By day, by night, the pilot will allow
No rest, but urges on his underlings
Until they reach Provence; and there in Arles
Is Agramante, threatened by King Charles.

37

When Agramante heard this and saw plain
What danger to his kingdom he had brought
By his invasion of the Franks' domain,
The counsel of his leaders he first sought;
He knew he would not look to them in vain.
Sobrino's and Marsilio's eye he caught
(They were the most experienced and wise)
And he addressed the meeting in this wise:

38

'It ill becomes a commandant, I know,
To tell his men, "I did not think of this",
But such is my predicament, I owe;
And yet, if from remote contingencies
Disaster strikes (and this indeed was so),
Less blameworthy perhaps the error is.
In leaving Africa unarmed, I erred,
If Nubia's attack was to be feared.

39

'But who could have foreseen, save God alone,
To Whom (whatever is concealed from us)
No aspect of the future is unknown,
So vast an army from so far would cross
Those shifting sands, by winds for ever blown,
And prove so menacing and dangerous?
Yet it has come: Biserta is attacked
And a great part of Africa is sacked.

40

'In this dilemma your advice I need:
Should I depart, my task unfinished here,
Or should I battle on till I succeed
And Charlemagne is taken prisoner?
How can I both these claims together heed:
Our kingdom save, this Empire rend and tear?
If any of you know, speak out, I pray;
So let us find and follow the best way.'

41

Thus Agramante speaks, then turns his glance
On King Marsilio who sits near by,
As if to indicate that he first wants
His second-in-command to make reply.
He kneels and bows his head in reverence,
Then on his throne of honour, placed on high,
Once more reseats himself, and thus gives voice
Concerning Agramante's fateful choice:

42

'Rumour her tidings, whether bad or good,
Has always tended to exaggerate.
My courage sinks no lower than it should,
Nor rises higher than the facts dictate,
For, whatsoever the vicissitude,
My hopes and fears I always moderate.
And so, my liege, I lend but half an ear
To all the many voices which I hear.

43

'And all the less acceptance do I give
The more such tales defy my common sense.
Now, it is plain that no one can believe
That, contrary to all experience,
A king a region so remote would leave
With such a vast array of regiments,
To cross those sands unwisely hazarded
By troops too rashly by Cambyses sped.

44

'I can believe that Arabs have descended
And sacked and killed and pillaged and laid waste
Wherever citadels were ill-defended,
And that Branzardo, whom you there had placed
As viceroy and lieutenant, has amended
The numbers of the foe and has made haste
To add two noughts to every ten of them,
That his excuse acceptable may seem.

45

'Let us concede that they are Nubians,
Rained down miraculously from the sky;
Or it may be the clouds hid their advance,
Since nobody could see them passing by:
What could they do against your Africans,
Unaided by a powerful ally?
Your garrison poor stuff must be indeed
If frightened by so unwarlike a breed.

46

'Send over a few ships, just to display
Your standards, scarce will ropes be cast off here
Than to their borders they'll have fled straightway –
These Nubians, or Arabs, or whate'er.
Because they know that you are far away
From your domain across the sea, they dare
(What in your presence they would fear to do)
To take advantage and make war on you.

47

'This is the moment of revenge to take
Against King Charles, for in the absence of
Orlando no one else a stand will make;
But if to seize this palm you do not move,
Or from your hesitation do not wake,
The wisdom of this saying you will prove:
"Time has a forelock, but is bald behind",
As to our shame and injury we'll find.'

48

With these and other cunning words he sought
To bring the Council to his point of view:
That till King Charles was driven forth, they ought
To stay and finish what they came to do.
But King Sobrino, who could read the thought
Behind the urgings of the Spaniard (who
Promoted his own interest rather than
The common good) his answer thus began:

49

'When my advice was "Stay at peace", my king,
Ah, how I wish my prophecy had erred!
But since events its truth to light now bring,
Would you had trusted your Sobrino's word!
But Rodomonte's bold adventuring,
Alzirdo, Martasino you preferred,
And Marbalusto: would I might confront
Them with their boasts, above all Rodomont!

50

'How I'd reproach him for his arrogance!
For it was he, as I remember well,
Who promised you that he would shatter France
Like glass, and that in Heaven or in Hell
He'd follow, nay, he'd leave behind, your lance.
And now his paunch he scratches, in a fell
Stupor; I, who for telling truth was set
Down for a coward, I am with you yet!

51

'So I will always be until I end
This life, which, burdened now with many years,
For you each day to risk of death I lend
Against the bravest champions and peers
Of France, and whatsoever Fate may send.
No man is there in all the world who dares
To call me coward; I as much have done,
Nay more, than many a boastful champion.

52

'Thus you can see that what I said before
And what I am again about to say,
From no faintheartedness or fear of war
Arises, but from love and loyalty:
Go back, I urge, to your paternal shore
As fast as possible, perhaps today.
Unwise is he who loses what is his
To try to gain what someone else's is.

53

'You know the gain: thirty-two vassal kings
Set out with you from port, their sails full-spread;
And now, according to my reckonings,
Barely a third are left, the rest are dead.
Pray God will spare us further sufferings,
But if you persevere, our fate I dread:
For scarce a fifth or quarter will remain
And all your hapless army will be slain.

54

'Orlando's absence is a help to us;
We are but few, we might have been wiped out.
But our position is still perilous,
Our agony is but the more drawn-out.
Rinaldo is still there, as dangerous
As was the Count (of this there is no doubt).
There are his kinsmen, all the paladins,
Eternal terror of our Saracens.

55

'They also have that second god of war
Named Brandimarte; though to praise the foe
Gives me no joy, he and Orlando are,
As I and others have good cause to know,
Well-matched as paladins and similar
In martial skill; and then, as you must owe,
For many days Orlando has been gone,
Yet we have lost far more than we have won.

56

'If in the past our losses have been grave,
They will be yet more numerous, I fear;
For Mandricard is dead and in his grave,
Gradasso has withdrawn, no one knows where,
Marfisa has deserted us, to save
Her soul; if only Rodomonte were
As true as he is valorous, no need
There'd be of captains of an Eastern breed.

57

'While we of their assistance are deprived,
And many thousands of our troops lie slain
(And all who were to come have now arrived –
For further shiploads now we look in vain),
Four valiant cavaliers Charles has contrived –
As though to match our fourfold loss – to gain,
Who with his nephews are compared, with reason;
Knights such as these are few at any season.

58

'I do not know if you know who Guidon
Selvaggio is, or Sansonetto, or
The twin-born sons of Oliver? I own
That I respect and fear each of them more
Than any other Christian champion
Who comes to help the Empire in this war,
Of German or whate'er outlandish tongue
Of northern lands barbaric and far-flung.

59

'Whenever you go forth to take the field
You will be routed and disgraced, I know.
If Africa and Spain were forced to yield
When they were twice as many as the foe,
Now that the whole of Europe forms a shield
Around King Charles, what does our future show?
When twice our number we shall have to face,
What else have we to hope for but disgrace?

60

'Your army you will lose and your domain,
If in this venture you are obstinate;
But if you change your plan, you will retain
The remnants of your forces and the State.
But you would be regarded with disdain
If you should leave your ally to his fate.
There is a remedy – with Charles make peace.
If you, then he, would like the war to cease.

61

'But if you think your honour jeopardized
That, disadvantaged, you for peace should sue,
If martial triumphs are more highly prized,
At least make sure the victor will be you!
And this ambition can be realized,
Despite our lack of fortune hitherto:
Entrust your quarrel to one cavalier
And as that delegate select Ruggier.

62

'I know and you know too Ruggiero is
A formidable foe in single fight.
Neither Orlando nor Rinaldo his
Resource can match, nor any Christian knight.
If you insist on full hostilities,
Though superhuman is Ruggiero's might,
He against many will be only one
And by a greater strength must be undone.

63

'The right course seems to me, if you agree,
To send this message to their sovereign:
To halt this bloodshed which both you and he
Are still inflicting on each other's men
(And Charlemagne on yours especially),
Two knights, one Christian and one Saracen,
Be chosen from the bravest on each side,
And let their duel the whole war decide.

64

'The pact to be: the loser's king must face
Defeat, and tribute to the other pay.
Charles will accept this offer with good grace,
Though the advantage now has gone his way.
And in Ruggiero so much trust I place,
I know that his strong arm will win the day.
So evident it is that right is ours
That he would win if he encountered Mars.'

65

With these and still more telling arguments
Sobrino overrules the king of Spain.
Interpreters that very day ride hence
With the ambassadors to Charlemagne.
In all his peers he has such confidence
The outcome of the fight to him is plain.
He chose Rinaldo for the Christian side,
On whom, after Orlando, he relied.

66

Both armies are delighted with the pact
And equally on both sides they rejoice.
By weariness of mind and body wracked,
All long for rest; and every soldier's choice
Will be a life of ease henceforth – in fact
All bitterly regret and with one voice
They curse the wrath, the frenzy and the rage
Which made them in such martial strife engage.

67

Rinaldo sees that Charles to a great height
Has raised him, for in such an enterprise
He trusts him more than any other knight,
And gladly to the task himself applies.
Ruggiero he disdains, for all his might:
A poor opponent in Rinaldo's eyes,
No match for such as him, although he slew.
King Mandricard in combat, as he knew

68

Ruggiero, on the other hand, although
Much honoured to be chosen by his king
Among so many valiant knights, for so
Important and responsible a thing,
Cannot disguise his sorrow and his woe.
Not that his heart with fear is fluttering:
He'd take on both the cousins, let alone
Rinaldo Montalbano on his own.

69

He is aware Rinaldo's sister is
His dearest and most faithful bride to be,
Who showers him with countless messages,
Urging her grievance and anxiety.
Now if he adds to former injuries
The will to wound her brother mortally,
Her love for him will turn to bitter hate,
Beyond Ruggiero's powers to placate.

70

If silently Ruggiero mourns and grieves,
Regretting the sad task he undertakes,
His future wife, when she the news receives,
Into a fit of tears and sobbing breaks
And her despair and anguish next relieves
By beating her fair breast; her tender cheeks
She ravages, her golden locks abuses,
Her love ungrateful calls, her fate accuses.

71

Whichever way the duel was to end,
For her the only consequence was grief.
That death to claim Ruggiero might descend,
She dare not let herself imagine; if
For past offences Christ on high should send
A judgement down on France, beyond relief
Her sorrows then would be: her brother dead,
And she in a dilemma dire and dread.

72

For censure she would then incur, and scorn,
And all her kindred's deep hostility,
If to Ruggiero she should then return
And claim him as a husband openly,
A thing she dreamed of doing night and morn,
Planning the manner of it frequently.
Such is the promise which unites these two,
No second thoughts will now their bonds undo.

73

But she who is accustomed to lend aid
And does not fail her loved ones in distress
Could not endure to hear the doleful Maid
(I mean Melissa, the kind sorceress).
She came at once to comfort her, and said
At the right moment she would bring redress
By the disruption of the coming fight
Which was the cause of Bradamante's plight.

74

Rinaldo and illustrious Ruggier
Put on their arms for the ensuing test.
The choice lay with the Christian cavalier,
Defender of the Empire of the West.
He, ever since he lost his destrier,
Has fought on foot, and so he held it best
To fight with battle-axe and dagger, clad
In mail and armour; and this choice he made.

75

Whether by chance, or whether by advice
Of Malagigi, provident and shrewd,
Who knows how Balisarda loves to slice
Through plated armour, it is understood
(Perhaps I do not need to tell you twice)
The warriors the use of swords exclude.
The site they choose is a broad plain, outside
The ramparts by which Arles was fortified.

76

As soon as vigilant Aurora from
Tithonus's abode had raised her head,
In signal that the day and hour had come
When preparations now might go ahead,
Those delegated now emerge, by whom
Pavilions are erected at the head
Of the stockades, and altars then are raised
Where God by both the monarchs will be praised.

77

Soon afterwards the pagan troops parade,
Rank after rank, in martial discipline.
In sumptuous, barbaric pomp arrayed,
King Agramante in their midst is seen.
Ruggiero on a charger is conveyed:
A bay, black-maned, white-blazed, it steps between
Two kings, and level keeps; and he of Spain
To be Ruggiero's squire does not disdain.

78

The helmet which he won some time before
In pain and travail from another king,
The helmet which the Trojan Hector wore,
As you have heard a greater poet sing,
Marsilio beside him humbly bore;
And other princes, other barons, bring
His other arms, his other weapons hold,
With gems encrusted and adorned with gold.

79

And from the other side King Charles appears.
He sallies forth with all his men-at-arms,
With all the panoply, as bold and fierce,
As if in answer to a call to arms.
He is surrounded by his famous peers.
Rinaldo comes on foot in all his arms –
Except his helmet, won from King Mambrin,
Borne by Ugier, the Danish paladin.

80

One axe is carried in Duke Namo's hand
And one by him of Brittany's domain.
Charles to one side assembles all his band,
Facing the host of Africa and Spain;
And in between is a large tract of land
Where nobody may step, because, on pain
Of death, that was reserved, as they all knew,
By edict, for the combat of the two.

81

The ritual of second choice began
(Ruggiero had this right); when this was done,
Two priests, one Christian, one Mohammedan,
Came forward, bearing volumes, of which one
Was our Lord's life, the other the Koran;
But neither of the priests came forth alone:
The Emperor was at his chaplain's side,
The king his holy man accompanied.

82

Before the altar which his men had made,
Charles in petition raised his palms on high:
'O God, Who suffered for our sakes,' he prayed,
'O Lady, who so pleased the Almighty by
Thy virtue that to bring us timely aid
He took from thee our form in which to die
And dwelt for nine months in thy sacred womb
(Yet still unsullied was thy virgin bloom),

83

'Bear witness to the promise which I swear
For me and all successors who hold sway,
To Agramante and to every heir
Who shall succeed him in his realm, to pay
A score of asses'-loads of gold each year,
If overthrown my champion is today.
I promise that the truce shall now commence
And that I guarantee its permanence.

84

'May thy just anger blaze, if I should fail,
And in swift retribution upon me
And mine send down a formidable flail,
Though sparing all these in my company,
That they may know what vows to thee entail,
How great the cost of broken faith can be.'
His hand lay on the Bible as he spoke
And heavenward enraptured was his look.

85

The others then approached and stood before
The altar which the pagans had arrayed
With costly ornament; their monarch swore
His troops across the sea would be conveyed
And the same tribute to the Emperor –
Of twenty golden ass-loads – would be paid,
If on this day Ruggiero vanquished fell.
A lasting truce he guaranteed as well.

86

And he likewise, in accents clear and loud,
On his great Prophet could be heard to call;
And by the book his Imam held he vowed
That what he said he would observe in full.
Then from the field the monarchs quickly strode,
Each to his waiting troops. No interval
Elapsed before the moment came when both
The champions stepped forth to take their oath.

87

Ruggiero promises, if in this fight
His king (or deputy) should intervene,
He will no longer serve him as his knight;
The Emperor shall be his sovereign.
Rinaldo promises the opposite:
If Charlemagne removes him from the scene
Before he is defeated or Ruggier,
Allegiance to the African he'll swear.

88

The ceremony being now complete,
Each combatant returns to his own side;
And soon, by shrilling trumpetings which greet
The day, the hour of Mars is signified.
The champions step forth; on cautious feet,
With skill and wariness, they choose each stride.
See now the fateful strokes which they begin
And hear the axe-heads' formidable din.

89

Now with the blade, now with the haft, at first,
They simulate attack on foot or head;
In all such nimble moves they are so versed,
A true account would not be credited.
Ruggiero, sadly pledged to do his worst
On him whose sister he so longed to wed,
Delivered blows so cautious and so few
He seemed the less courageous of the two.

90

His moves aim less to strike than to defend,
But what he hopes he knows no more than I.
He would be saddened by Rinaldo's end,
Yet he himself has no desire to die.
But now I reach a point where I will end,
And it is good to put the story by.
The rest in the next canto you will hear,
If next time you desire to join me there.

CANTO XXXIX

1

Indeed the anguish of Ruggiero is
Relentless, bitter, harsh, beyond all grief.
Faced by two deaths, to one of them he sees
He must succumb, he can find no relief:
Death from Rinaldo if his expertise
Prevails, or from his promised bride; for if
He kills her brother, he'll incur a fate
More terrible than death – her bitter hate.

2

Rinaldo meanwhile harboured no such thought,
But aimed at victory with every blow.
With frenzy and ferocity he fought,
Swinging his battle-axe now high, now low.
Swerving this way and that, Ruggiero sought
To parry with his haft and, if his foe
He sometimes struck, he seemed to do his best
To choose a spot where it would hurt him least.

3

This does not please the pagan chiefs one bit.
Unequal, they consider, is the fray:
Ruggiero is too hesitant to hit,
Rinaldo has it too much his own way.
King Agramante, looking on at it,
Fretted and fumed, revealing his dismay.
He blamed Sobrino for his bad advice,
Of which this blunder was the bitter price.

4

Melissa in the meantime, living fount
Of every magic art and sorcery,
Put off the female shape which she was wont
To wear, and took the form convincingly,
In gestures and in face, of Rodomont.
Her armour, dragon's hide appeared to be;
Just such a shield, just such a blade she bore,
His own they could not have resembled more.

5

Spurring her conjured demon-thoroughbred
Before the late Troiano's doleful son,
With furrowed brow, in a deep voice, she said:
'My liege, I must protest, this is ill-done,
To expose a callow youth to risk so dread
Against this famous Gallic champion,
And in an enterprise of such a sort,
To African renown of vast import.

6

'Forbid this combat; it must not proceed.
Too great will be the detriment to us.
On Rodomonte be it! Pay no need
To broken oaths: this pact is dangerous.
Let each man show his mettle and his breed.
You are a hundred times more numerous
Now I am here.' These words on him so wrought,
The king rushed on the field without a thought.

7

Belief that Rodomont was with him there
Made Agramante disregard the pact.
If he had seen a thousand knights appear,
He would have felt less reassured, in fact.
Horses were spurred, and couched was every spear,
As each the other army reattacked.
Melissa, who the battle had ignited
By means of phantoms, disappeared, delighted.

8

Seeing their combat interrupted thus,
In violation of a sacred oath,
The two heroic and illustrious
Opponents ceased exchanging blows, and both
Agreed, pledging their faith in chivalrous
Accord, not to resume until the truth
As to which king was guilty could be told:
Young Agramant, or Charlemagne the old.

9

And their avowed intent they swear anew,
To be the enemy of him who broke
The truce. The ranks are seen to run in two
Directions: faces back or forwards look,
And feet a corresponding course pursue.
A single move reveals two kinds of folk,
For while they run at the same speed, the cowards
Are running backwards, and the brave men forwards.

10

Imagine if you will an eager hound
Which sees the other dogs pursue the hare
As it eludes them, running round and round.
The hunter holds it back and in despair
It tugs the leash, its howls and yelps resound
In vain, it struggles, leaping here and there:
Just so, until that moment held at bay,
Marfisa and her sister were that day.

11

That day until this moment they had seen
Rich booty on the spacious battlefield,
And bitter the regret of both had been
That by the pact they were restrained and held.
Their sighs were deep and their impatience keen
To chase the prey and harvest such a yield.
Now that the pact was merely empty words,
Joyful they leapt upon the pagan hordes.

12

Marfisa's lance emerged two yards behind
The breast of her first foe; then with her blade
She split four helmets (my words lag behind
Her speed) as if of glass they had been made.
And Bradamante with a different kind
Of lance, with like success, about her laid.
All those it touched, the weapon overthrew
(And they were twice as many), but none slew.

13

In all this derring-do, they were so close,
Each was the other's witness at first hand.
Then, separating, where wrath leads, each goes
To strike at random in the Moorish band.
Who the full tally of the fallen knows,
Thrown by the lance in Bradamante's hand?
Or of the heads split open or truncated
By that dread sword no blood has ever sated?

14

As, in the season when the winds blow mild
And on the Apennines green shoulders peep,
Two torrents rise, impetuous and wild,
Which at the outset close together keep,
Then plunge their separate ways, by speed beguiled,
And boulders loosen, trees from summits rip,
And cornfields wash into the vale below,
Like rivals in the havoc they would show,

15

Thus these two sisters, valiant warriors,
Redoubtable Marfisa and the Maid,
Divided now to devastate the Moors,
One with her spear, the other with her blade.
With difficulty from a headlong course
King Agramant his fleeing army stayed.
In vain he asked, and looked behind, in front:
Nowhere was there a trace of Rodomont.

16

Yet at his instigation (he declared)
The pact which Agramante swore that day,
Calling the gods to witness, he had dared
To break, but now he'd vanished clean away,
And King Sobrino too had disappeared.
(*He* was in Arles and there he meant to stay;
For such a breach of faith dire punishment
Would fall that day, he thought, on Agramant.)

17

Marsilio had likewise fled to Arles,
Aghast at such a sacrilegious deed:
So Agramant was left to face King Charles,
Who all his allied troops against him led,
His Marios, his Henrys and his Karls,
All of them valiant, of heroic breed.
His paladins among them stand out bold
Like jewels on embroidery of gold.

18

Among them also were some paragons
Of perfect chivalry, of the world's best:
For instance, Oliver's two famous sons,
Guidon Selvaggio, of intrepid breast;
I have already spoken more than once
Of the two damsels and their martial zest.
So many Saracens by these were slain,
To try to count them all would be in vain.

19

But I will leave this battle for a time
And go without a ship across the sea.
I've said enough about the French and I'm
Returning to Astolfo. Let me see:
I have already told you in my rhyme
All that St John had done; it seems to me
You also know the Algazieran king
And Branzard all their troops against him fling.

20

This army had been marshalled at top speed
With remnants from the whole of Africa;
The old, the sick were taken, such the need;
This was no time to be particular.
For Agramante twice his kingdom bled,
So obstinately he pursued the war;
Those now remaining were not numerous –
A band of raw recruits and timorous,

21

As they now prove by scampering for their lives
As soon as from afar they glimpse the foe.
Astolfo, with more hardened warriors, drives
Them on like sheep; across the fields they go
And there they stay; some band perhaps contrives
(Those few who greater skill at running show)
To reach Biserta, where Branzardo flees,
But Bucifar Astolfo's prisoner is.

22

Branzardo feels the loss of Bucifar
To be more serious than all the rest.
He wonders what the terms of ransom are.
He knows unaided he will fail the test
Of siege: Biserta is too big by far.
And while he ponders, moody and depressed,
His prisoner, Dudone, comes to mind,
Whom he has held for several months confined.

23

The king of Sarza in a coastal raid,
When first he reached the walls of Monaco,
This Danish paladin his captive made.
(He was the son of Ugier, as you know.)
A message from Branzardo is conveyed
To the commander of the Nubian foe
(His true identity from spies he hears),
Suggesting an exchange of prisoners.

24

He knows Astolfo as a paladin
Another paladin will gladly free.
The noble duke, when he informed has been,
Straightway concurs; once more at liberty,
Dudone thanks the duke and joins him in
The conduct of the war; wherever he
Can best assist, he lends a helping hand,
For he is expert both on sea and land.

25

The army of Astolfo was so vast,
It would have daunted seven Africas.
Recalling now the converse which had passed
Between him and St John, and how he was
To free Provence and Aiguesmortes at last
From Agramant, who held those areas,
The duke selected a large company,
The least inept, he judged, to put to sea.

26

Then, filling both his hands, he quickly tore
Innumerable leaves from many plants –
Palms, laurels, olives, cedars; to the shore
He carried them without a backward glance
And on the water threw his precious store.
O grace which God to men so rarely grants!
O wondrous miracle which from the leaves
Arose, soon as they floated on the waves!

27

They grew in number beyond estimate,
Becoming heavy, curved and thick and long.
The slender veins traversing them of late
Changed into ribs and planking, firm and strong.
The pointed tips in which they terminate
Remain the same, and every leaf ere long
Becomes a ship, and the varieties
Reflect the different fronds of different trees.

28

O miracle! They were transmogrified
To form tall galleons, galleys, caravels.
O miracle! They were as well supplied
With oars and sails and rigging and all else
As other ships. For mariners well-tried
Astolfo does not lack (nor miracles):
Near-by Sardinia and Corsica
Both good recruiting grounds for seamen are.

29

Twenty-six thousand soldiers put to sea;
Of every sort they were, of every skill.
Dudone was their commandant and he
Was ever shrewd, in fortune good or ill,
By land or sea; and while the company
For a fair wind in port was waiting still,
A ship put in upon that very shore,
A ship which many captive warriors bore.

30

They were the cavaliers who on the strait
And narrow bridge were taken prisoner
By Rodomonte, as you heard me state.
There was Orlando's brother (Oliver),
And faithful Brandimart and Sansonet
And others whom I need not name; they were
Italians, Gascons, Germans, brave and bold,
All now inactive in the vessel's hold.

31

And here the pilot confidently steers
Into the bosom of the enemy,
Leaving astern the harbour of Algiers
(For this his destination was to be,
But a strong wind had blown him on). No fears
He has, no further risks can he foresee.
He comes, he thinks, to a home port to rest,
Like Procne winging towards her twittering nest.

32

But when the pilot the Imperial Bird,
The Golden Lilies and the Pards has seen,
He blanches like a man whose foot has stirred
A deadly serpent hidden, sleeping, in
The grass, who when he sees how he has erred,
Recoils in pallid terror from the scene,
Running as fast and far as legs will take
Him from the venom of the angry snake.

33

The pilot is unable to draw back,
Nor can he hide the prisoners down below.
The only future facing him is black,
And with the paladins he's forced to go
Before Dudone and the duke; no lack
Of joy on seeing friends again they show.
The pilot's passengers ask that he be
Chained to the galley-benches as his fee.

34

As I was saying, by King Otto's son
The Christian cavaliers were welcome made.
A banquet in their honour in his own
Pavilion was prepared and tables laid.
Arms were supplied to each and every one.
To speak with them a while, Dudone stayed.
Their company is no less gain, he's sure,
Than setting out a day or two before.

35

They briefed him on the state of things in France
And Charlemagne's position – where he could
Most safely land and have the greatest chance
Of making his proposed offensive good;
And while they gave him this intelligence,
A hurly-burly in the neighbourhood
Gives rise to frantic calls: 'To arms! To arms!',
And startles everybody and alarms.

36

Astolfo and his noble company
Who dined and talked together in his tent
Put on their arms and mounted instantly
And to the source of the commotion went,
Hoping along the way some signs to see
Of what the nature was of the event.
They come to where they see a man so savage
That, naked, the whole army he could ravage.

37

He whirled a heavy cudgel round and round,
Of solid wood, and in so firm a grasp,
Each time it fell, a man dropped to the ground.
More than a hundred lay at their last gasp,
Whom Death at this unguarded moment found
And carried off inert in a chill clasp.
Arrows were shot at him from far away,
But nobody for his approach would stay.

38

Dudone, Brandimarte and the duke,
With Oliver, towards the tumult sped.
The strength and spirit of the savage struck
Them with a sense of marvel mixed with dread;
And, while on that stupendous force they look,
Attired in black as if she mourned the dead
A damsel gallops up – and to her heart
With both her arms embraces Brandimart.

39

This was fair Fiordiligi, who so burned
With love that Rodomonte's penalty,
Which robbed her of the one for whom she yearned,
Brought her with grief near to insanity.
Then from his cunning captor she had learned
That he had sent her love across the sea,
In company with many cavaliers
To languish in a prison in Algiers.

40

At Marseilles, on the point of setting sail,
She saw a ship arrive from the Levant.
On board was a retainer, old and frail,
Once of the household of King Monodant.
He had sought Brandimart, to no avail,
By land, by sea, a questing immigrant;
Then news of him in France he heard at last
And so just now to Europe he had passed.

41

She recognized him as Bardino, who
Had stolen Brandimart when he was small.
(To manhood in Silvana he then grew,
Having no knowledge of his home at all.)
So when Bardino's aim the damsel knew,
She asked his help; and in the interval
She told him what the circumstances were
And how her love was taken prisoner.

42

When they had landed on the Afric shore,
News reached them of Astolfo's victory.
Of Brandimarte's fate they were not sure,
But rumour had it he had been set free.
Fair Fiordiligi, seeing him before
Her very eyes, with spontaneity
Rushed to reveal how all her former sadness
Served to intensify her present gladness.

43

No less delight the noble cavalier
Experienced on seeing his dear wife.
She was more precious to him and more dear
Than any thing or person in his life.
He clasps and tenderly embraces her
And would have never ceased from kissing if
He had not seen, on lifting up his eyes,
Bardino standing there, to his surprise.

44

With open arms to welcome him he strode,
Intending to enquire why he had come;
But he was interrupted ere he could,
By the aforesaid pandemonium.
The bludgeon brandished by the savage nude
In a wide ring created ample room.
Then Fiordiligi, turning to confront
The naked man, called out, 'It is the Count!'

45

At the same moment too the English duke
By certain signs the Count could recognize,
For which the holy ancients bade him look
Up yonder in the Terrestrial Paradise.
His former noble aspect so forsook
Him now, they'd ne'er have known him otherwise.
And for so long his body he disdains,
His face is like a beast's, more than a man's.

46

Astolfo, pierced by pity through his breast,
Turned, weeping, to Dudone who was near,
And then to Oliver and all the rest
And, pointing, cried, 'That is Orlando there!'
To recognize him they all did their best,
Eyeing him with a fixed, unblinking stare.
To find him in this terrible condition
Fills all of them with stupor and contrition.

47

They wept to see the state the Count was in,
So grievous, they could not imagine worse.
'Now is the time to give him medicine,'
Astolfo says, 'not tears,' and from his horse
He leaps. And soon no less than five are seen
Converging in a group with headlong force
To seize King Charles's nephew, hoping to
Control his madness and his rage subdue.

48

Orlando, seeing them round him in a ring,
Wielded his cudgel like a maniac.
Dudone, with his buckler covering
His head, moved closer, and a heavy whack
Taught him the foolishness of such a thing.
But for the blade of Oliver, the crack,
Though devastating, would have been still more so,
And would have split shield, helmet, head and torso.

49

It only broke his shield, but such a thump
It landed on his helmet that he fell.
The sword of Sansonetto to a stump
Reduced the club, chopping it by an ell.
Then Brandimarte seized him by the rump
With both his arms, as tight as possible;
And while he pinions thus Orlando's flanks
Astolfo holds him firmly by the shanks.

50

Orlando gave a jerk: the Englishman
Ten paces off upon his beam-end landed;
But Brandimart he does not find he can
Dislodge; his body-grip is iron-handed.
When Oliver too close unheeding ran,
Orlando gave him just what he demanded,
And knocked him senseless; ashy pale he lies,
The life-blood gushing from his nose and eyes.

51

And if his helmet had not been robust
That would have been the end of Oliver;
Even as it was, he lay unconscious, just
As if his soul had joined the heavenly sphere.
Dudone and the duke rise from the dust
(A swollen face the son of Ugier
Presents), and on the Count, with Sansonet
Who neatly chopped the club, once more they set.

52

Dudone gripped Orlando from behind,
Attempting with one foot to trip him up.
Astolfo and the other three combined
To hold his arms, but he defied the group.
If you will call a baited bull to mind,
Beset with fangs about its ears and crop
As bellowing it drags the dogs along
Which still hang on, although it is so strong,

53

You can imagine how Orlando tugged
Those warriors along with him that day.
Then Oliver who, sprawling like one drugged,
Beneath the impact of that cudgel lay,
Rose up and from himself the stupor shrugged.
He looked and saw that this was not the way
To bring Orlando down; and he bethought
Him of a plan which to success he brought.

54

He calls for ropes and quickly on the ends
He fastens running knots; first he lassoes
Orlando's limbs; then, as each rope descends,
Curling, about the madman's trunk, he throws
The warp to one or other of his friends
And, pulling hard, they tighten every noose.
Just as a farrier will fell a horse,
So was Orlando tumbled in mid-course.

55

Once he is down, they fling themselves on top
And tighter yet by hand and foot secure him.
Orlando jerks and twists to make them stop:
In vain, for every time they overpower him.
The duke commands that he be lifted up
And carried to the shore, where he can cure him.
Dudone, of a size to bear the brunt,
Upon his sturdy back conveys the Count.

56

Astolfo bids them wash him seven times
And seven times immerse him in the waves
So that the filthy coating that begrimes
His brutish face and limbs the water laves.
Then certain herbs which he has picked betimes
He stuffs into that mouth which puffs and raves,
For he desires the orifice to close
So that he cannot breathe save through his nose.

57

Astolfo had prepared the precious phial
In which Orlando's wits preserved had been,
And placed it to his nose in such a style
That with one breath he drew the contents in
And straightway emptied it. O miracle!
His intellect returned to its pristine
Lucidity as brilliant as before,
As his fair discourse later witness bore.

58

As one who wakes from a distressful dream
Of gruesome monsters which could never be,
However grim and menacing they seem,
Or of committing some enormity,
And though his senses have returned to him,
From his amazement cannot yet shake free,
So now Orlando, wakened from illusion,
Remained in stupefaction and confusion.

59

In silence first he stared at Oliver,
At Brandimarte, at the English duke.
Then next he gazed all round, now here, now there,
With an astonished and bewildered look,
Wondering how and why and when and where
All this had happened, but to no one spoke.
That he is naked, further puzzles him,
And tied with ropes all round and on each limb.

60

Then, like Silenus when he was secured
By captors in a cave, '*Solvite me*',
Orlando said; and they, being reassured
By his expression of serenity,
Released him, and some clothes for him procured.
And when he was attired in decency,
They all consoled him, for the bitter grief
Which overwhelmed him then was past belief.

61

Orlando, now a man again and wise
(Still manlier and wiser than before),
Discovered he was cured of love likewise.
The one whom he was wont so to adore,
Who was so fair and queenly in his eyes,
He now dismisses and esteems no more.
All his desire and all his zeal he'll use
To reacquire what Love has made him lose.

62

Meanwhile Bardino spoke with Brandimart
And told him of the death of Monodant,
And that he came to call him, on the part
Not only of his brother, Ziliant,
But of the islands many miles apart,
To take the throne, and rule in the Levant;
In all the world there was no kingdom which
So joyful was, so populous and rich.

63

Among the many reasons which he gave
Was the sweet love of fatherland and home,
That if he once would taste its joys, he'd have
No inclination ever more to roam.
The prince replied that he must try to save
The realm of Charlemagne and Christendom.
If he could see the conflict to its end,
To his own plans he could then best attend.

64

On the next day, while to Provence is sped
The great armada of Dudon the Dane,
Orlando with the duke is closeted
And hears from him the state of the campaign.
Next, all Biserta under siege is laid.
Orlando credit gives for every gain
To Duke Astolfo, though he but conducts
The operation as the Count instructs.

65

Where they deploy their troops and when and how,
And from what side they take the citadel,
To whom the bravest deeds I must allow,
Why at the first assault Biserta fell –
If I do not pursue these matters now,
Be not dismayed, all this you'll hear me tell.
But in the meantime let me go to Arles,
To see the Pagan harassed by King Charles.

66

King Agramant is left almost alone
In this, the greatest peril of the war.
Sobrino and Marsilio have gone
To Arles, which seems the safest place by far,
While many more discretion still have shown
And to the ships which close by anchored are
Have fled; and many a Moorish soldier took
A leaf from many a Moorish leader's book.

67

But Agramante stays and holds his ground;
Not easily does he give up the fight.
When he can do no more, he swivels round
And gallops to the near-by gates in fright.
The hoofs of Rabican behind him pound,
Whose mettle Bradamante's spurs excite.
She yearns to kill him for depriving her
So many times so long of her Ruggier.

68

Marfisa also harboured in her breast
An urge to avenge her father (better late
Than never); she too gave her steed no rest;
But neither damsel reached the city gate
In time; despite their eagerness and haste,
They failed to cut off Agramant's retreat.
Beneath the battlements he disappeared
And thence for safety to his fleet repaired.

69

As when a brace of handsome hunting pards
At the same moment from the leash set free,
Dash in pursuit of deer or goats, which yards
Ahead of them have tantalizingly
Escaped, lope back, as if ashamed, towards
The waiting huntsman, almost guiltily,
So the two warrior-damsels, sighing, turned
When they the king's escape at last discerned.

70

Despite their setback, they do not draw rein.
To left, to right, among the fugitives
Such merciless, such deadly, blows they rain
And each so well her thwarted wrath relieves,
That many fall and do not rise again.
The routed army no respite receives.
For his protection Agramant has shut
The city gate, which keeps all comers out.

71

All bridges too across the Rhône are down.
Unhappy plebs! Tyrants to their own good
(Or what may seem the interest of the Crown)
Will sacrifice you like a helpless brood
Of sheep or goats; some in the river drown,
And some enrich the pastures with their blood.
Many are killed, few taken prisoner
(Since few of value for a ransom were).

72

Of the great multitude which on each side
Was slain in this engagement of the war
(The figures do not equally divide,
For heavier the pagan losses are,
Above all where the warrior-maidens ride),
The evidence can still be seen: not far
From Arles, along the delta of the Rhône,
Tomb after tomb bears witness in mute stone.

73

But to resume, at Agramant's command
The heavy ships set sail for the deep sea,
Leaving some lighter vessels near the strand,
To wait for others hoping yet to flee.
They rode at anchor for two days, as planned
(The winds, moreover, had been contrary).
On the third day the sails were spread once more
To take the king to his paternal shore.

74

Marsilio was filled with deepest dread
Lest Spain the penalty should have to pay
And lest the tempest lowering overhead
Should burst in fury on his fields one day.
He landed at Valencia and sped
To strengthen his defences; in this way
He brought about his ruin, and the cause
Of the undoing of his allies was.

75

King Agramante sails for Africa
With ships ill-fitted, almost void of men
(Though fully laden with complaints they are).
Three quarters of his troops are lost or slain.
Some call the king too arrogant by far,
Some call him cruel or foolish, others vain.
All bear him rancour in their secret hearts
But none of them, for fear, his thoughts imparts,

76

Save two or three who each to each unseal
Their lips; trusting as friends to loyalty,
Their anger and resentment they reveal.
Unhappy Agramante thinks that he
Can surely count on their devotion still;
And this he thinks for he can only see
False faces, and the only words that greet
His ears are adulation, lies, deceit.

77

He thought it would be inadvisable
To put in at Biserta; certain news
That Nubians held all that littoral
Had reached him, so elsewhere he had to choose,
And his intention was to make shore well
Beyond, where none his landing would oppose,
And then return to bring his people aid
In their affliction: thus his plans he laid.

78

But cruel Destiny, at variance
With this design so provident and wise,
Decrees that the armada which from plants
Was seen miraculously to arise,
Now furrowing the waters towards France,
The ships of Agramante shall surprise
By night, when it is stormy and so black,
That there can be no warning of attack.

79

No spy had told King Agramante yet
Of the vast navy which Astolfo sent
(If any had, he wouldn't credit it,
So unbelievable was the event –
That plants turned into ships); and so he set
No look-outs but, serenely confident
That no one dared attack him, on he sailed,
And from aloft no warning voices hailed.

80

So the armada which Dudon the Dane
Commanded for the duke, in the half-light
Of evening saw the other vessels plain
And turned in their direction to give fight.
With grappling-irons their ships the Christians chain.
All unprepared, the Moors a fearful plight
Now face. The Christians quickly get to know
That these are Moors: their speech reveals the foe.

81

And as the fleet for the attack moves in
(Seconded by the wind which blows their way),
At such a speed they ram the Saracen
That many Moorish ships are sunk that day.
With hands (and wits) the Christians then begin
To add their rain of missiles to the fray:
Fire-brands and boulders which no targets miss.
No storm at sea has ever equalled this.

82

Dudone's men, on whom the Powers on high
Unwonted strength and daring now bestowed
(The time for punishment at last was nigh
Which to the Saracens had long been owed),
Such deadly blows, from far off or near by,
Inflicted, to the king himself they showed
No quarter; clouds of arrows clatter round him,
On all sides grapnels, axes, pikes confound him.

83

He hears the sound of heavy boulders crashing,
Hurled by ballistas and by catapults,
The prow and stern of many a vessel smashing,
Opening a passage for the waves' assaults;
And of Greek fire he sees the dreaded flashing,
Igniting eager flames which nothing halts.
The hapless rabble scrambling to escape
Is caught between the Devil and the deep.

84

Some whom the enemy pursues with swords
Dive overboard and drown; one who can swim
With long and rapid strokes makes off towards
An overladen boat; the crew repulses him
(And its own safety thereby thinks it guards).
His hand – too eager – clutching at the rim
Is left, the bleeding stump is seen to slip
Below where it incarnadines the deep.

85

Some to preserve their life trust to the sea
(Or hope at least to lose it with less pain);
But when their breath deserts them and they see
For all their efforts no respite they gain,
To the voracious flames which they would flee
The fear of drowning brings them back again.
They clutch a burning hulk and seek to shun
Two deaths – and are by both at once undone.

86

Others in terror of an axe or pike
Which comes too near, try what the sea can do;
But from behind them stones or arrows strike
And so the strokes which they can make are few.
Perhaps it is now best, while you still like
My song, to end it, rather than pursue,
Lest by excessive length I put you off,
Failing to see when you have had enough.

CANTO XL

1

If all the details of this naval joust
I were to tell, I should not soon be done.
Reciting them to you would seem almost,
Unconquered, noble, Herculean son,
Like owls to Athens, so much labour lost;
Or pots to Samos; or, I might go on,
Like crocodiles to Egypt; you, my lord,
Have demonstrated what I but record.

2

Your subjects a long spectacle beheld
When you provided day and night a show
As in a theatre, that time you held
The hostile vessels on the river Po
Trapped between fire and sword. Ah, how they yelled
As the waves crimsoned with a gory flow!
You saw and showed to many in that war
How many different ways to die there are.

3

But, as you know, I did not witness it,
For I had gone six days before post-haste
(With frequent change of horses) to entreat
The Holy Shepherd to lend aid – a waste
Of time – it was not needed; such defeat
The Golden Lion was obliged to taste,
I have not feared those teeth or claws of his,
Thanks to your action, from that day to this.

4

But Trotto and Afranio were there,
Alberto, Bagno, Zerbinatto too;
Three of my kinsmen who my surname share,
Annìbale, and Piero Moro knew.
They told me, and the banners made it clear,
And all the trophies, in the church on view,
And fifteen galleys, if I needed more,
And other captive vessels on our shore.

5

All those who of that scene were witnesses,
Who saw that carnage and that holocaust –
Vengeance for pillage of our palaces,
Pursued till every ship was sunk or lost –
Can see the horror which now menaces
The stricken and defenceless Moorish host,
At sea with Agramante that dark night,
Predestined victims of Dudone's might.

6

When battle was first joined, the night was black
And not a gleam could anywhere be seen;
But once the foe began the harsh attack
By pouring sulphur, pitch and bitumen
On prow and stern, which all defences lack,
The greedy flames illuminate the scene
With such a pyrotechnical display,
It seems as if the night has turned to day.

7

King Agramante in the darkness thought
The foe was of but little consequence,
And whatsoe'er the strength with which they fought,
His forces could resist and drive them hence;
But when the shadows lifted, he was taught
That twice as many (a great difference)
As he had judged the hostile vessels were,
And so he changed those plans made earlier.

8

With only a few men he boards a ship
(With Brigliadoro and such things as he
Holds dear); in silence furtively they creep
Between the vessels to a safer sea;
Thus the king gives his harassed fleet the slip,
Leaving it to the Dane's ferocity,
To fire and flood, to death in every shape,
While he, the cause of it, makes his escape.

9

Thus Agramante fled and with him took
Sobrino, whose advice he disobeyed.
By ills foreseen now sadly brought to book,
In self-reproach he humbly bowed his head.
But let us to Orlando, who the duke
Advised, before Biserta could get aid,
To raze it to the ground, so that no chance
It had henceforth of making war on France.

10

Astolfo gave the order for attack
Within three days; he had already planned
For this by holding many vessels back
When the armada sailed; and the command
Of these he gave to Sansonet – no lack
Of skill he had on sea as on dry land.
His fleet was anchored now a mile away
Outside the harbour, ready for the fray.

11

True to their Christian faith, the paladins,
Who, facing peril, never fail to pray,
Give orders that before the siege begins
All troops shall fast and their devotions say,
Then, armed with spears (or native javelins),
The signal shall await; on the third day
Biserta's time will come to be attacked
And, being captured, to be burned and sacked.

12

Then, after prayers had been devoutly said
And fasting was religiously observed,
Friends, relatives, acquaintances broke bread
Once more together and refreshment served
To weary bodies needing to be fed.
Then, weeping, they embraced, as if unnerved,
Their words and gestures such as people use
When they their dearest are about to lose.

13

Inside Biserta too the holy men
Are weeping with their people in their grief.
They beat their breasts as they entreat again,
Calling on their Mahomet, who is deaf.
What offerings are made in secret then!
What vigils kept! It passes all belief
What temples, altars, statues are erected,
Eternal monuments to woes inflicted!

14

The Imam blessed the people; after this
They took their arms and to the walls went back.
While fair Aurora lingered yet in bliss
With her Tithonus and the sky was black,
The duke his forces, Sansonetto his,
On land and out to sea were holding back;
But when they heard Orlando's whistle-blast,
The terrible assault began at last.

15

Biserta, bounded on two sides by sea,
Upon the other two stood on dry land.
Her walls, of unexampled masonry,
Had been constructed by a master hand.
These almost were her sole security;
No other reinforcement could be planned.
When King Branzardo there for refuge fled,
Masons were scarce and time was limited.

16

Astolfo gives the task to Prester John
Of shooting at the line of battlements
With sling-stones, fire-brands, arrows, till not one
Of those inside his face outside presents.
So to the walls, the soldiers, one by one,
Of infantry and mounted regiments,
Pass unmolested, bearing boulders, beams
And planks, and anything that useful seems.

17

Rubble and refuse of all kinds were cast
Into the moat (the water was cut off
The day before). From hand to hand it passed;
The muddy bottom disappeared and soon enough
The cavity was filled, for they worked fast.
Then to the walls they levelled out the rough.
The duke, the Count and Oliver now call
Upon the infantry to scale the wall.

18

The Nubians, impatient of delay,
Lured by the hope of booty, disregard
The heavy price which they might have to pay.
In 'tortoises' and 'cats' themselves they guard.
Equipped with battering-rams (a vast array),
They move towards the citadel, prepared
To break down towers and gates, to breach the walls –
And find the Moors on watch for what befalls.

19

Fire, metal missiles, roofs and merlons pour
In molten rain and like a tempest burst,
Shattering planks and beams assembled for
The catapults and siege-machines; at first
During the darkest of the hours before
The dawn, the baptized heads came off the worst;
But when the sun had left his rich abode,
Fortune turned hostile to the pagan brood.

20

Orlando gives the order to increase
The strength of the attack by sea and land.
The fleet which a mile off at anchor is
Now enters port and opens fire as planned.
Arrows and sling-stones fly without surcease,
And engines operate on every hand.
Ladders and spears meanwhile assembled are
With the full arsenal of naval war.

21

Orlando, Oliver and Brandimart
And he who flew so boldly through the skies
A fierce attack now launch upon that part
Which from the sea the farthest inland lies.
Each paladin commands a quarter part
Of the remaining troops, and with them hies
To beat down walls or gates; no matter where
They go, their valour shines beyond compare,

22

Which can be better seen than if they fought
Pell-mell; all those deserving of esteem,
All those by whom the bravest deeds are wrought,
Are obvious to many watching them.
On wheeled contraptions wooden towers are brought,
And elephants, trained for such stratagem,
Bring others on their backs, which reach so high,
The battlements far down below them lie.

23

The valiant Brandimarte came; he put
A ladder to the wall and up he went,
Encouraging his men to follow suit;
And many did so, bold and confident,
Thronging the rungs with many an eager foot;
And no one heeded if the ladder bent
Beneath the weight; the foe his sole concern,
Their leader clambers up and does not turn.

24

No skill in climbing Brandimarte lacks.
Now on the ramparts, brandishing his blade,
He slashes, slices, pierces, thrusts and hacks,
And amply shows the stuff of which he's made;
But all at once the burdened ladder cracks
(Too much the unforeseeing climbers weighed)
And, save for Brandimarte, one and all
Head over heels into the gulley fall.

25

But Brandimarte's courage does not fail.
He has no thought of making a retreat.
An easy target now, he does not quail,
Nor listen to the voices which entreat
Him to return (and how could they prevail?);
And though the ramparts measure ninety feet
From top to bottom (as I have heard tell),
He jumps below into the citadel.

26

As if he landed upon down or straw,
He hit the ground without the slightest jolt.
He cut, he ripped, he slashed all those he saw,
Just as one slashes, rips and cuts a bolt
Of cloth; the others hastily withdraw
And if he makes to follow them, they bolt;
While those outside who saw him leap within
Think nothing now can save the paladin.

27

Through all the camp a buzz of rumour flies.
From voice to voice the murmur swells and grows.
Rumour, once vague, repeated, gathers size,
Increasing danger everywhere it goes.
To Oliver, to Otto's son, it hies,
And to Orlando, eager to disclose
The message of ill-fortune which it brings,
No rest affording to its rapid wings.

28

These warriors (Orlando most of all)
Love and hold Brandimarte in esteem.
They know that they must leave no interval
In rescuing a comrade such as him.
So, placing ladders up against the wall,
They climb and show themselves; so fierce and grim,
Of those three heads so angry is the glare,
The enemy, to see them, quake with fear.

29

As when at sea the stormy waters lash
A ship which too adventurous has been:
Against the prow, against the poop they dash,
Seething with fury, seeking a way in;
The pilot, pale, can only groan and gnash,
His wits adrift, his courage turned to spleen;
One wave engulfs his vessel with a roar
And where that enters, all the others pour;

30

So, when these three had stormed the bastion,
The breach they opened was so large and wide,
The others could then safely follow on.
A thousand ladders were affixed outside.
Meanwhile, the battering-rams now more than one
Way in, with a loud, rumbling crash, provide.
Thus many entrances at once are made
Through which to bring bold Brandimarte aid.

31

With the same rage as when the stately king
Of rivers banks and margins overtops
And, on the fields of Ocnus trespassing,
Rich plough-lands sweeps along and fruitful crops,
A flock complete with winter quartering,
The dogs, the shepherd, while in elm-tree tops
Fishes are seen to dart where formerly
Birds flying to and fro we used to see,

32

With that same rage the impetuous soldiery
Rushed through the spaces in the broken wall
With blazing torches, gleaming weaponry,
To kill those ill-led pagans once for all.
Violent hands were laid on property
And persons, bringing to a rapid fall
The city, rich with many spoils of war,
Which once was queen of all of Africa.

33

The dead lie everywhere; from countless wounds
A swamp has formed which more repellent is,
And darker, than the quagmire which surrounds
The Fury-ridden battlements of Dis.
From house to house a trail of fire compounds
Destruction, burning mosques and palaces.
From houses plundered of possessions, cries
And shrieks and thuds of beaten breasts arise.

34

Laden with booty, victors are seen leaving
Ill-omened doorways, silver figurines
Of household gods or vases in their thieving
Hands, or rich garments; pitiable scenes
Occur as children are dragged forth or grieving
Mothers raped; for here no mercy intervenes.
That day a thousand unjust deeds are done.
The Count, the duke, are powerless to stop one.

35

King Bucifar of Algaziers was slain
By one of valiant Oliver's shrewd blows.
Seeing all hope and courage were in vain,
Release by his own hand Branzardo chose.
Astolfo struck three times: in triple pain
The life of Folvo flickered to its close.
King Agramante left these three behind
To guard Biserta and its treasures mind.

36

Meanwhile the king, who with Sobrino fled,
Had seen the conflagration on the shore.
Mourning Biserta, bitter tears he shed,
Then, drawing closer, he wept even more
To learn the truth: his city, people said,
Would never now be what it was before.
He even contemplated suicide
But, for Sobrino, put this thought aside.

37

Sobrino said, 'What happier victory,
My liege, than the report of your demise
Could be imagined by your enemy,
Who would, unchallenged, then enjoy the prize
Of Africa in all security?
But your existence all such hope denies.
He knows he cannot long hold Africa
Unless departed from this life you are.

38

'Your subjects by your death would be deprived
Of hope – the only asset left to them.
I trust that if you live, those who survived
You may yet from imprisonment redeem,
From misery withdrawn, their strength revived.
I know that if you die, you will condemn
Our land to servitude; live then to spare
Us that, if for your life you cease to care.

39

'Your neighbour, Egypt's Sultan, will not fail
To send you troops and money; he'll not let
King Pepin's son in Africa prevail.
And Norandino is your kinsman yet:
He'll drive your enemies beyond the pale
And on your throne again you will be set.
Armenians, Turks and Persians, Arabs, Medes,
If you but ask them, will supply your needs.'

40

With similar advice the shrewd old man
Tries to restore his liege's confidence
That all may not be lost, that soon he can
Recover Africa; and yet events
Such hope (it may be) from his bosom ban.
He knows how bitterly a king repents
Who, having lost his realm, must turn for aid
To foreigners; this error many made.

41

Good witnesses to that were Hannibal,
Jugurtha and many a king of old
And Ludovico il Moro, to the Gaul
(Another Ludovic!) by allies sold.
Your brother, Duke Alfonso, learnt from all
Such cases; he, my lord, is known to hold
That anyone who trusts in others more
Than in himself is mad beyond all cure.

42

Thus, when the Pope, enraged, made war on him,
Although the duke's resources were but weak,
And slight were the defences he could scheme,
And though his would-be champion, to check
Invasion of *his* land (as it would seem)
Had fled from Italy, he would not seek
For aid, and for no promise, for no threat,
Would he his realm to alien hands commit.

43

Meanwhile King Agramante eastwards sailed,
Making far out into the open sea,
When from the land an angry storm assailed
The ship, lashing her side with savagery.
The pilot, sitting at the helm, bewailed
(As he looked up) the signs which he could see:
'So violent a tempest looms,' he said,
'I fear the vessel now will make no head.

44

'If you will follow my advice, my lords,
Until the fury of the storm is spent,
There is an island we should run towards,
Close by, to port.' The king gave his consent,
And to the shelter which the beach affords
To many a hard-pressed seaman, they now went.
It lies between the shore of Africa
And where the furnaces of Vulcan are.

45

The little isle, of habitation bare,
With humble tamarisk and myrtle clad,
Offered the stag, the roebuck and the hare
A solitude remote, secure and glad,
Unknown except to fishermen; and there
They hung their nets on branches which they had
For this same purpose of their foliage stripped,
While fishes in the tranquil waters slept.

46

The fugitives discovered soon that Fate
Had forced another vessel to the isle,
Bearing Gradasso, whom we saw of late
At Arles (Baiardo he'd procured meanwhile).
Once on dry land, the warrior-kings with great
And mutual respect in regal style
Embraced, for they were friends, and comrades too:
Shared combat beneath Paris' walls they knew.

47

With deep dismay the Sericanian heard
The Moor's account of the catastrophe,
And to its depths his loyal soul was stirred.
He promised his support, in chivalry;
But to seek aid from Egypt, he averred,
Would be too dangerous. 'The memory
Of Pompey should suffice', he said, 'to warn
All fugitives who to that quarter turn.

48

'But since you say Astolfo, with the aid
Of Ethiops, the folk of Prester John,
This onslaught against Africa has made,
Burning your capital, and that the son
Of Milo, who till recently was mad,
Is with him too, I have now hit upon
The very plan, I think, whereby you may
Recoup your losses and your grief allay.

49

'I will engage Orlando, for your sake,
In single combat; you need have no fear,
For no defence against me could he make
If solid iron or bronze his body were.
When he is dead, the Christian force will quake
Like lambs before a hungry wolf, I swear.
I know too how to drive the Nubians out.
I'll do that in an instant – have no doubt.

50

'I will command the other Nubians
This side the Nile, who other laws obey,
Arabs (both men and steeds), Macrobians,
A wealthy race, who'll make a fine array,
Chaldeans also and Iranians,
And many more I hold beneath my sway,
To wage such war on Nubia that soon
From Africa – your land – they will be gone.'

51

King Agramante thought this second scheme
Of King Gradasso's opportune and sound,
And he blessed Fortune, who had driven him
On this deserted island thus aground;
But his first proposition did not seem
Acceptable on any terms; he found
(Even to save Biserta) such a plan
His honour would irrevocably stain.

52

'If Count Orlando challenged is to be,'
The king replied, 'that combat is my due,
And I am ready; let God deal with me
As He thinks fit.' 'My plan let us pursue,'
Gradasso said, 'and in conformity
With what you deem appropriate to you.
I have just thought of this: let us both fight
The Count, and let him bring another knight.'

53

'If I am not left out, I'll not complain,
And whether first or second, I don't mind,'
The other said; 'a comrade in such vein
As you in all the world I could not find.'
Sobrino cried, 'And where do I remain?
If I seem old to you, let me remind
You that I have the more experience.
In danger, strength has need of common sense.'

54

Sobrino, though not young, is still robust,
And famous for his feats of arms; he says
That to his vigour they can safely trust –
He feels as strong as in his salad days.
Sobrino's claim is recognized as just.
A messenger is sent with no delays
To Africa: the challenge of the three
Delivered to the Count by him shall be.

55

If he accepts, he and two knights shall make
For Lampedusa (a small island, this,
Set in the self-same sea); and they shall take
Their armour and all such necessities
For the encounter; the envoy does not slack
The speed of oars and sail until he sees
Biserta; there he finds the paladin
Awarding spoils and captives to his men.

56

The messenger the challenge of the three
Made known, causing Orlando such delight
That gifts with ample generosity
He showered on the envoy, left and right;
For in the meantime from his comrades he
Had learned that King Gradasso (by no right)
Was girt with Durindana, for which blade
A journey to the East he would have made;

57

For he believed Gradasso to be there,
Since he had heard the king had gone from France.
Now, in a place not far away, but near,
Fate offered him this unexpected chance.
Almonte's horn, so resonant and clear,
And Brigliadoro, too, no less, he wants.
And both of these, Orlando has long known,
Are in the hands of King Troiano's son.

58

He chose as comrades in this triple test
His brother Oliver and Brandimart.
He knew their expertise was of the best
And that they truly loved him from the heart.
Then of good destriers he went in quest,
Good weapons, armour good in every part,
Not for himself alone, but for all three.
(You will recall why this was necessary.)

59

Orlando (as I many times have said)
Scattered his arms in madness all around.
The other two their armour had to shed
When captives of the Sarzan they were bound.
Of the best weapons Agramante bled
His kingdom for the war; thus few are found
And even those few lack the qualities
Which worthy are of heroes such as these.

60

Such armour as there is, inferior,
Rusty and tarnished, Count Orlando takes
And with his comrades goes towards the shore
And plans for the ensuing combat makes.
When they have gone about three miles or more
The sea's horizon with his gaze he rakes,
And spies a vessel with her sails full-spread
Which for the coast of Africa is sped.

61

No seamen are on board, no pilot steers;
Impelled by wind and Destiny alone,
Her canvas billowing, the vessel nears
The coast and to a beach is carried on.
But now the love I bear Ruggiero veers
Towards his story and I must be gone
To Arles, where with the valiant Clairmont knight
Unwillingly he fought a bitter fight.

62

The warriors their combat had suspended,
For, as I said, the truce, which had been sworn
By both the king and Emperor, was ended
And bitter conflict once again was born;
And which of the two monarchs had offended,
Holding his solemn pledges thus in scorn,
Ruggiero and Rinaldo strive to know
From those who pass before them to and fro.

63

Meanwhile a squire who served Ruggiero well,
A faithful lad, quick-witted and astute,
Who in the tumult, fierce and terrible,
Which now arose, his lord (who was on foot)
Had never lost from sight, but marked him still,
Brought him his horse and sword; but the pursuit
Of battle for Ruggiero holds no charms,
Though he remounts and with his blade rearms.

64

Then he departs, but first he promises
To keep the vow which earlier he swore,
That if he finds his Agramante is
The culprit he will never serve him more,
But leave him and his vile accomplices;
And he performs no further feats of war,
Seeking that day only to ascertain
Who broke the pact: his king, or Charlemagne?

65

He hears the same report on every hand:
King Agramante broke his promise first.
Ruggiero loves him (you must understand);
He sees the pagans broken and dispersed,
And to deny the help of his good brand
When Fortune's wheel their fate has thus reversed
Would be a grievous error, he thinks now,
And he is less inclined to keep his vow.

66

Conflicting thoughts within his mind discourse:
Should he remain or follow Agramant?
Love of his lady rides him like a horse:
To Africa? The bit is adamant.
His head is twisted to another course.
By spurs and menaces of punishment,
He is reminded of the pledge he made
With Montalbano, which must be obeyed.

67

And from the other side he's whipped and spurred
No less by the disquieting concern
That if he now deserts his stricken lord
A coward's reputation he will earn.
Many will say that he should keep his word,
But many others that excuse will spurn,
And many more will say that he should break,
Not keep, an oath which it was wrong to make.

68

He meditated all that day and night.
The next day too he pondered, quite alone.
Which of these two decisions would be right:
To stay, or follow where his lord had flown
And bring assistance to him in his plight?
At last the cause of Agramante won.
Love of his bride was strong, and of her beauty,
But stronger still his honour and his duty.

69

He rides to Arles, in hope that he will find
The fleet to take him back to Africa,
But not one vessel has been left behind,
The only Saracens all dead men are;
And Agramante to the flames consigned
The ships he did not salvage from the war.
Ruggiero, since his first decision fails,
Proceeds along the coast towards Marseilles.

70

He'll seize some vessel (such is now his plan)
And make the pilot carry him across.
But there was the armada of the Dane,
With captured ships (in all a grievous loss
To the barbarians); and not one grain
Of millet in the water could you toss,
So crowded were the ships at anchor there,
Which crammed with conquerors and captives were.

71

Such pagan ships as were not burned that night,
Or sunk, save for those two or three which fled,
Dudone added to his fleet, by right,
And to Marseilles in convoy safely led.
And seven kings, acknowledging their plight,
To the inevitable bowed their head,
Their seven ships surrendered to the foe,
And silent stood, cast down and full of woe.

72

The Dane had disembarked some time before:
His aim had been to visit Charles that day.
Long lines of captives and a splendid store
Of spoils formed a spectacular array.
The prisoners were marshalled on the shore.
Around them, jubilant, as is the way
Of victors, Nubians on high proclaim,
And Echo's voice resounds, Dudone's name.

73

Ruggiero hoped, while riding from afar,
And to confirm this hope he pricked his steed,
This was the missing fleet of Africa;
But drawing near, he recognized instead
The king of Nasamona, prisoner,
With Baliverzo, Agricalte, led
In chains with Manilard and Farurant,
Who with Clarindo wept and Rimedont.

74

Ruggiero's love was such, he grieved to see
How much they suffered in their wretchedness.
He knows it will be sheer futility
To plead with empty hands; to gain redress
He must use force. Couching his weapon, he
Attacks the guard: a hundred men, no less,
Are lying on the ground and not by chance,
Struck either by his sword or by his lance.

75

Dudone hears the uproar and looks round:
The spectacle of fleeing men he sees,
The havoc and the slaughter on the ground,
But has no notion who Ruggiero is.
Calling for shield and helmet, with one bound
He leaps upon the destrier with ease
(Though wearing armour), as befits a peer
And paladin who means to use his spear.

76

He shouts commands for all to clear the way
And of his spurs he makes his steed aware.
In prisoners who saw Ruggiero slay
A hundred more, the signs of hope appear.
Seeing Dudone come with no delay
Alone on horseback (all the others were
On foot), he judged him leader of that host:
To fight with him was what he wanted most.

77

Though in mid-course, the Dane, when he discerned
That his opponent was without a lance,
His own flung far away; for he'd have spurned
To benefit from such a circumstance.
Ruggiero by this courteous gesture learned
This was a noble paladin of France,
And to himself he said, 'I know him by
Such chivalry; this he cannot deny.

78

'I will entreat him to reveal his name,
If he is willing, ere we come to blows.'
And so he did, and he achieved his aim
And learned that he the son of Ugier was.
Dudone asks Ruggier to do the same
And in return he pays the debt he owes.
Each having told his name, each next proceeds
To challenges and then from words to deeds.

79

Dudone had that iron club which brought
Him lasting honour in a thousand fights,
And with it demonstrated as he fought
He was the scion of brave Danish knights.
The sword (no better sword was ever wrought),
Which opens every breastplate that it smites
And every helm, allowed the Dane to test
Ruggiero's skill and valour at their best.

80

But in his deep concern to spare his bride
Whatever pain and suffering he could
(As out of love for her he always tried),
And, knowing if he shed Dudone's blood,
This would offend her – on her mother's side
(His knowledge of the House of France was good)
She was his cousin in the first degree,
Both of two sisters being the progeny –

81

He never used the point against his foe
And rarely used the edge; where the club fell
He stepped aside or warded off the blow.
Turpin believes (and I believe as well)
Ruggiero could have laid Dudone low
With a few strokes; but, he goes on to tell,
Although the Dane was many times exposed,
Only the flat of Balisard was used;

82

For he could use the flat of it just like
The edge, so sturdy was its tempering.
Repeatedly the blade descends to strike
The Dane in a strange game of ring-a-ding,
Producing stars Dudone does not like,
For he can scarcely to his saddle cling.
But you will all the more enjoy my chime
If I defer it to another time.

CANTO XLI

1

A perfume clinging to the lustrous hair
Or silky beard or dainty raiment of
A youth or maiden, exquisite and fair,
Which often wakens tearful thoughts of love,
Releasing a new sweetness on the air
Which lasts for many days, will clearly prove
By manifest, convincing evidence
Its pristine and unchanging excellence.

2

That heavenly liquid which Icarius
Rashly induced his harvesters to taste
(Which lured, they say, the Celtic tribes to cross
The Alps, heedless of hardships to be faced),
At the year's end retains, matured, for us
The sweetness of the grapes when they were pressed.
Leaves on a tree in winter show how green
The foliage in spring-time must have been.

3

That famous House, whose glory long has shone,
Illustrious in deeds of chivalry,
Whose splendour, still increasing, yields to none,
Clearly proclaims this truth with certainty:
The line of the Estensi springs from one
Who in all ways by which a man can be
Uplifted rose to a celestial height
And like the sun irradiated light.

4

Ruggiero, who in every worthy deed
The honour of a valiant cavalier
And signs of magnanimity displayed
Which lately ever more apparent were,
Dissembled with Dudone, as I said.
Mercy it was which caused him to forbear;
How strong in truth he was he would not show,
Lest he should deal the Dane a mortal blow.

5

Dudone knew for certain how things stood.
Ruggiero had no wish to take his life:
He left so many chances unpursued,
As when Dudone wearied in the strife
Or failed to keep his guard; he understood
That this was an affair of honour. If
Ruggiero in the combat came off best,
He would not yield in chivalry at least.

6

'In God's name, sir,' he said, 'let us make peace,
For I have lost all hope of victory.
I have no hope of winning, I confess,
And I surrender to your courtesy.'
Ruggiero answered, 'I desire no less
To call a halt, but this the pact shall be:
You must consign to me these seven kings,
Freed from their bonds and from their sufferings.'

7

Ruggiero pointed to the seven, who
In fetters stood dejected, as I said.
With them to Africa he means to go,
And nothing their departure shall impede.
The paladin makes no objection to
Ruggiero's terms: the seven kings are freed.
He lets them choose the vessel which seems best
And so for Africa they sail in haste.

8

The ship's mast bears its canvas spreading white,
Each bellying to the treacherous wind in turn.
At first this fills the pilot with delight
As straight upon her course the ship is borne.
The shore recedes and soon is lost to sight,
As though the sea were bounded by no bourne.
The wind, as darkness fell, its treachery
Made clear as day for all on board to see.

9

From blowing dead astern, it veers to cross
Their bows, then gusts head-on; and shifts again
To whirl the vessel round; at hopeless loss
The seamen try to sail her, but in vain.
From all four quarters towering breakers toss;
No curb the foaming seas can now restrain.
The travellers look on in awe and dread,
And with each threatening wave they think they're dead.

10

Now from the poop, now from the prow, a blast
Impelled the vessel on, then in reverse;
Over her bulwarks yet another passed.
The threat of shipwreck at each gust grew worse.
The helmsman, sicklied with the pallid cast
Of terror, sighed, or shouted himself hoarse,
Or signalled with his hand, time and again,
To swing or drop the yard, but all in vain.

11

His shouts, his signals are of no avail:
The rain, the dark have blotted him from sight
And noises louder than his words assail
The air as voices of the crew unite
To mourn their fate in a concerted wail,
While crashing waves together join their might.
To port, to starboard, at the stem or stern,
Not one command could any man discern.

12

The wind in fury screeches through the spars.
Flash after flash of lightning streaks the sky.
Clap after clap of thunder rolls and roars.
All their accustomed skills the sailors try:
Some hurry to the helm, some to the oars;
While some the rigging loosen, others tie;
Some bail the water out, repeatedly
The sea repouring back into the sea.

13

Boreas in a frenzy castigates
The raging storm which, shrieking louder still,
The sails against the mainmast flagellates.
The water rises up almost until
It laps the sky; the rowers at their seats
Grasp broken oars and at the tempest's will
The vessel, unresisting, veers her prow,
Her bulwarks to the waves exposing now.

14

The starboard gunwale dips beneath the flood,
Threatening to turn the vessel upside-down,
And all on board commend their souls to God,
Now more than ever sure that they will drown.
The blows of Fortune with no interlude
Disaster with yet more disaster crown.
The ship in many parts is gaping wide,
And hostile water rushes through inside.

15

From every quarter now the tempest wreaks
An onslaught yet more dire and terrible.
Sometimes the sea mounts up as though it seeks
The highest circle where the Angels dwell;
Sometimes it lifts them to such lofty peaks
That looking down they see the depths of Hell.
They have no comfort now in hope or faith.
Before them looms, inevitable, Death.

16

All night across a turgid sea they speed,
Now here, now there, as drives the changing wind.
It should have dropped by day-break, but instead
It blows again, more dangerously inclined.
And now they see a naked rock ahead.
Towards it willy-nilly, howling blind,
The tempest, still reluctant to relent,
Carries them angrily, malevolent.

17

The helmsman, pale with terror, tries to force
The tiller round in a vain hope to steer
The ship along another, safer course;
But far away the mocking waters bear
The broken rudder, while with no remorse
The wind so fills the sails, no time is there
To lower them, or orders seek afresh;
At any moment now the ship will crash.

18

When it is seen that nothing can be done
To save the ship from her impending fate,
Then every man looks after number one.
Concerned for their own lives, they do not wait,
But scramble down into the boat; and soon
So burdened it becomes beneath their weight,
It threatens to surrender to the wave
And drown all those whom it was meant to save.

19

Seeing the captain, bos'n and all hands
Desert the vessel without more ado,
Ruggiero, in his tunic as he stands,
Unarmed, decides at once to join them too;
But when he does he quickly understands
The boat will sink beneath the overflow.
As still more people clamber for a place,
It plummets to the depths without a trace.

20

The little lifeboat disappears from sight
With all who left the vessel to her fate.
The piteous shrieks they utter in their plight,
As help from highest Heaven they entreat,
Are not for long continued, for with spite
The angry sea pours over them in spate,
Choking the larynges from whence emerge
The plaintive cries, soon silenced by the surge.

21

Some sink below, never to reappear,
Some break the surface, bobbing on the waves.
A head, an arm, a leg shoeless and bare,
Are glimpsed as hopefully some swimmer braves
The flood. Ruggiero will not yield to fear;
His body from the sea's embrace he heaves.
He sees the naked rock not far away,
Where all assumed the ship must crash that day.

22

With arms and legs Ruggiero means to strive
Towards that dry, though rocky, piece of land.
Blowing the waters back, which would deprive
Him of his breath, he battles for the strand.
Meanwhile the raging wind and tempest drive
The empty vessel, left with not a hand
On board, of all whose evil destiny
Led them to seek salvation in the sea.

23

How fallible are the beliefs of men!
The vessel did not perish but sailed on.
Her captain and her crew no hope had seen.
They let her drift, abandoned and alone.
The wind, it seems, its tactics altered then.
Seeing the exodus of everyone,
It steered the ship towards a clear fairway,
Well out to sea where safer waters lay.

24

Though unresponsive to the pilot's hand,
Once she was free of him she sailed a route
Direct to Africa and came to land
Beyond Biserta, two or three miles out,
On the Egyptian side, and in the sand
She grounded; there Orlando, who set out
With his companions, as I said before,
Was walking and conversing on the shore.

25

He wonders what can be the state of her:
Has she a crew? a cargo? He must know.
With Brandimarte then and Oliver
He takes a skiff and to the ship they go.
She's empty of all hands; only the destrier
Frontino they discover down below
(He is the only living thing on board),
And find Ruggiero's armour and his sword.

26

Ruggiero had departed at such speed,
To buckle on his sword there was no time.
The Count knew Balisarda well – indeed
This weapon had belonged to him one time.
I know that the whole story you have read:
How Falerina lost it at the time
Orlando laid her lovely garden waste,
And how Brunello stole it from him next,

27

And to Ruggiero's keeping gave it then
Near the Carena mountains; just how good
Its tempering, how sharp its edge, had been
From previous experience he could
Well testify on oath (the Count, I mean);
And fervently he offered thanks to God,
For he believed (and later often said)
This was God's gift for the great task ahead.

28

And a great task it was, for he would fight
With Sericana's ruler, who he knew
Was a ferociously courageous knight,
Who had Baiard and Durindana too.
He did not prize Ruggiero's armour quite
As much as those who had good reason to;
He judged it good, but most of all because
So finely-wrought and beautiful it was.

29

Since armour he had little need to wear
(For he could not be wounded, being enchanted),
He gave Ruggiero's arms to Oliver.
The sword he girded on, for this he wanted.
To Brandimart he gave the destrier.
And so to the companions there was granted
(As he desired, and was his bounden duty)
An equal share and portion of the booty.

30

Each for the day of battle sumptuously
In a new surcoat strove to be attired.
The tower of Babel in embroidery,
Struck by a thunderbolt, the Count required.
A hound his brother's emblem was to be,
Argent, couchant, unleashed, and he desired
The motto, 'Till he come'; surcoat all gold
He ordered, as became a knight so bold.

31

By Brandimarte, on that battle morn,
Both for his honour and his father's sake,
No brightly-coloured garment would be worn;
But a dark surcoat he resolved to take,
Which skilful Fiordiligi would adorn
With bordering as fair as she could make.
When she had done, with many a costly gem
The sombre surcoat glittered at the hem.

32

So fine a surcoat and caparison
His lady makes, in beauty they exceed
The less distinguished armour he has on,
Nobly adorning both the knight and steed;
But from the day this labour was begun
Until it was completed, and indeed
Long afterwards, on Fiordiligi's face
Of joy, of happiness, there was no trace.

33

A constant dread and torment fill her heart
Lest she may widowed be of her dear knight.
In countless battles he has taken part,
And countless perils faced, yet no such fright,
No terror such as this, nor piercing smart,
So froze her blood, nor turned her deathly white.
Such apprehension, being new to her,
Makes her heart tremble with a double fear.

34

As soon as their equipment they prepare,
The cavaliers hoist sail and put to sea.
Astolfo and Sansonetto, who now share
Command, stay with the army faithfully.
Sweet Fiordiligi's heart is rent with fear;
Filling high Heaven with many a vow and plea,
She strains her eyes to gaze with all her might
Till out at sea the sails are lost to sight.

35

The duke and Sansonetto were constrained
(Since to cajoling words she paid no heed)
To carry her, resisting, from the strand.
They left her in the palace on her bed,
Distraught and trembling; meanwhile the brave band
Of three by a propitious wind are sped
Directly to the island where a test
Of prowess will conclude the war at last.

36

Orlando stepped ashore, with Oliver
And Brandimart, and on the eastern side
They placed their tent, arriving earlier
Than Agramant, who later occupied
The other end (in this the Christians were
More skilled in strategy). The six decide,
Since it is late and night is drawing on,
Their combat till the morning to postpone.

37

On either side, until the early light,
Armed guards are posted who stand vigilant.
At evening Brandimarte, the black knight,
With the permission of his commandant
(Which he had first requested, as was right),
Approached the foe, to speak with Agramant:
Once they were friends, for with the pagan host
Under their flag from Africa he crossed.

38

When greetings were exchanged and hand clasped hand,
The Christian knight enjoined the pagan king
With many a cogent reason, as a friend,
To take the necessary steps to bring
The combat without bloodshed to an end:
His former cities (to this parleying
Orlando had agreed) he would yet own,
If he would but believe in Mary's Son.

39

'Because I loved you deeply and still do,
I give you this advice, my lord,' said he;
'I followed it myself, which proves to you
How prudent I consider it to be.
That Christ is God I recognized was true.
A dupe henceforth Mahomet seemed to me.
Salvation's path I long for you to tread,
And to this truth may all I love be led!

40

'Your good consists in this, in this alone.
No other counsel is of any use,
And least of all to fight with Milo's son.
Greater will be the peril if you lose
Than any benefit which might be won
By victory, or spoil which you might choose.
For if you win, what do you hope to gain?
Whereas defeat will bring you loss and pain.

41

'What if you kill Orlando here, what then?
Or us, who come resolved to win or die?
Your lost dominions you will not regain;
The state of things will not be changed thereby.
You cannot hope that if we three are slain
Charles will lack men on whom he can rely
To guard the frontiers and to garrison
The outposts and the towers, every one.'

42

Thus the knight spoke, and would have added more,
But he was interrupted by the king,
Whose countenance a proud expression wore,
Whose angry voice was harsh and menacing:
'For such temerity there is no cure.
None to the madness remedy can bring
Of meddling busybodies who (like you),
Without being asked, tell others what to do.

43

'That the advice you give me springs from love
Which once you felt for me and still profess,
Now that I find you the companion of
Orlando, seems unlikely, I confess.
Rather, that dragon which is wont to rove
In search of souls now holds you in duress
And you desire, as far as I can tell,
To pull the whole world down with you to Hell.

44

'Whether I lose or win, whether I can
Regain my kingdom, or shall banished be,
The mind of God has settled, which no man,
Not I, not you, not Milo's son, can see.
Whatever is the outcome of His plan,
No craven cowardice will coerce me
To an unkingly act. If death were sure,
I'd die ere I my faith and blood forswore.

45

'And now you may return. If you display
No better prowess in tomorrow's fight
Than as an orator you showed today,
The help the Count will find in you is slight.'
Fury impels King Agramant to say
These final words, inspired by spleen and spite.
Then each returned and rested till the sun
Rose from the sea and morning had begun.

46

The dawn was silvering the sky when all
The combatants had armed and quickly leapt
Upon their steeds. There was no interval
And no delay. Few words were said. Adept,
They couched their lances. But, my lord, I shall
Be much at fault if I too long have kept
Ruggiero in the sea and he should drown
While of these others talking I go on.

47

Ruggiero strikes out boldly with each limb
And battles with the overwhelming waves.
The wind and tempest, menacing and grim
(But not his troubled conscience), the youth braves.
He fears that Christ is now baptizing him,
Not in that water, clean and pure, which saves,
Which he was slow to seek (by his own fault),
But in this flood so bitter and so salt.

48

And all the many promises he made
To Bradamante now come flooding back,
The pact sworn with Rinaldo and betrayed –
Of all such memories there was no lack.
Four times, ten times, in penitence he said,
If God would overlook these sins so black,
If ever he set foot on land again,
He would become a Christian there and then.

49

Never again would he use sword or lance
Against the Faithful to support the Moor,
But he would straight away return to France
And render service to the Emperor.
No longer would he lead his love a dance
But as a husband honour her, he swore.
O miracle! When he has promised this
His strength and his agility increase.

50

His strength redoubled, and with heart undaunted,
Ruggiero struck the waves and pulled them past
As hard upon each other's trail they flaunted.
One flung him up, another downward cast.
Now he descended, now again he mounted,
With great distress and labour, till at last
He landed; where the hill most gently verged
Towards the water, dripping he emerged.

51

And all the others who abandoned ship
Are left behind, unequal to the wave.
Alone upon the solitary steep,
Ruggiero, whom it pleases God to save,
Has clambered forth. Though rescued from the deep,
He has another danger now to brave:
Marooned upon this barren rock, he'll die
Of hunger and privation by and by.

52

Yet with indomitable spirit, ready
To endure what fate the heavens had in store,
Among harsh stones, his progress bold and steady,
He climbed towards the summit; but before
A hundred steps he'd numbered by his tread, he
Saw a man bowed down in years, who bore
The signs of abstinence; his dress, his air,
A hermit worthy of respect declare.

53

When he was close at hand he cried 'Saul! Saul!
Why do you persecute me?', in the words
Our Saviour used when he appeared to Paul
Who lay beneath the blow which heavenwards
Would raise him; 'you have come on a long haul,
Cheating the boatman of his just rewards;
But God has a long arm and reaches you
Just when you think He is least likely to.'

54

The holy hermit had a dream that night
Which God had sent to show how by His aid
Ruggiero would be rescued from his plight
And reach the rock; a vision he then had
Of the past life and future of the knight,
And of his death, how he would be betrayed.
His progeny, his grandsons, God revealed:
All the descendants which his line would yield.

55

The hermit first continued to rebuke
Ruggiero (but consoled him in the end)
For not submitting to the gentle yoke
When Christ had called him to Him as a friend;
That what he spurned in freedom, he now took
With little grace, only prepared to bend
His neck, when he was threatened with a lash
Which, as he feared, upon his back would crash.

56

Then he consoled him: Heaven is not denied
By Christ to any soul who soon or late
In true repentance on His name has cried.
The story he proceeded to relate
About the vineyard labourers who plied
Unequally but equal payment met.
With zeal and love, his steps sedate and slow,
He schools the knight as to his cell they go.

57

Above the hermit's cell, carved in the stone,
There is a little church which faces east,
Convenient and fair to look upon.
Below, down to the sea, the gaze may rest
On evergreens, a refuge from the sun,
And date-palms offering a fruitful feast.
They are kept verdant by a limpid rill
Which murmurs as it trickles down the hill.

58

And close on forty years it now must be
Since Christ had sent the hermit here to dwell
Where nothing would distract the solitary
From holy contemplation in his cell.
Pure water, fruit or berries from a tree
Sustained his life and kept him strong and well;
Few men were healthier or happier.
He had now entered on his eightieth year.

59

Inside the cell the old man lit a fire
And heaped the table with a choice of fruit;
And when Ruggiero's clothes and hair were drier
He helped himself and started to recruit.
The hermit led him higher yet and higher
In knowledge of our Faith and in pursuit
Of truth; in the pure water of the spring
Next day the knight received his christening.

60

As to the place, Ruggiero was content
To stay, the more so as the man of God
Had told him formerly of his intent
To send him back in a few days where God
Intended he should be; meanwhile, anent
Such matters as the Kingdom-come of God
They spoke, or of Ruggiero's own affairs,
Of his posterity and of his heirs.

61

For God, Who knows and sees all things, had shown
The hermit what the future held in store:
That when he was baptized, from that day on
Ruggiero would live seven years, not more;
For Pinabello's death (the deed, though done
By Bradamante, at Ruggiero's door
Was laid), for Bertolagi's too, he'd meet
His death in ambush, by Maganzans set.

62

So secret will the treachery remain,
No news of it will spread, nor ever could,
For in the very spot where he is slain
He will be buried by the evil brood.
His wife and sister, that heroic twain,
Will therefore late avenge that turpitude.
His faithful wife, his offspring in her womb,
Will seek him out at last and find his tomb.

63

Between the Brenta and the Àdige,
Below the mountains which so greatly pleased
The Trojan Antenor that willingly
Those sulphur springs by which the sick are eased,
Those fertile fields and smiling meadows, he
Exchanged for Ida, and for the Xanthus ceased
To sigh, for Lake Ascania – her heir
Near Phrygian Este in the woods she'll bear.

64

In beauty and in valour he will grow,
This new Ruggiero, Bradamante's joy.
His Trojan origins these Trojans know
Who choose him as the founder of new Troy.
To the defence of Charlemagne he'll go
Against the Longobards while yet a boy,
And Charles will justly in reward donate
This lovely region as a marquisate.

65

The Emperor will say in Latin: '*Este*
Hic domini'; the gift being thus bestowed,
The name of the fair city will be Este
(Auspicious omen!) and thenceforth exclude
The first two letters of the form *Ateste*.
And to the anchorite God also showed
The future vengeance, terrible and dire,
Which would be taken for Ruggiero's sire;

66

For in a vision to his faithful wife
He'd show himself a little before day.
Telling her who it was who took his life,
He'd show the place in which his body lay.
Then with her sister, born and bred for strife,
With fire and flame Pontiero she'd destroy.
And the Maganzans no less cause for tears
Would have when young Ruggiero came of years.

67

Many an Azzo and Obizzo passed
Before Ruggiero's vision as they spoke,
And many an Albert, till they came at last
To the sublime descendants of these folk,
To Ercole, Alfonso, unsurpassed,
And him to whom I dedicate my book,
And Isabel. Not everything was told:
Silence, the hermit sometimes judged, was gold.

68

Orlando, Brandimart and Oliver
Meanwhile with lowered lances ride to meet
That Mars of Saracens (thus I prefer
To call Gradasso and the name is fit)
And the two other combatants, who spur
Their destriers, so spirited and fleet.
At more than walking pace they cover ground:
The shore, the sea re-echoes to the sound.

69

At the encounter of three versus three,
In fragments to the sky flew every lance.
The mighty crash was seen to swell the sea,
The mighty crash was even heard in France.
Orlando and Gradasso seem to be
Well-matched, save that Gradasso (not by chance)
Rode on Baiard, which an advantage gave
And made him seem more valorous and brave.

70

Baiardo jolts against the lesser horse,
Taking Orlando also by surprise,
And sends it reeling with the sudden force
From port to starboard, till at last it lies
Full length upon the ground; with hand and spurs
Three or four times in vain Orlando tries
To make it stand; then, grasping sword and shield,
He hastens back on foot to face the field.

71

The king of Africa and Oliver
Had clashed in an equality of blows.
Sobrin was lifted from his destrier
By Brandimarte's lance, yet no one knows
Which is to blame, the horse or cavalier.
He rarely falls, but this time down he goes
And finds himself – a horseman so renowned –
To his discomfiture, upon the ground.

72

But Brandimarte leaves him where he lies
And turns against the Sericanian;
Seeing Orlando is unhorsed likewise,
He speeds to bring him all the aid he can.
The king and Oliver in the same guise
Proceed, in parity as they began.
Their lances broken on each other's shields,
A naked blade each brandishes and wields.

73

Seeing Gradasso also disinclined
To press home his advantage (the black knight
Was giving him no chance to change his mind,
But pressed and harried him with all his might),
Orlando turned, and was surprised to find
Sobrino too on foot, with none to fight;
The Count advanced, so menacing and grim,
The heavens trembled at the sight of him.

74

Against the onslaught of so great a man
Sobrino braced himself, alert and tense.
Just as a helmsman in a hurricane
Straight to the raging flood the prow presents,
Holding his course as steady as he can
(Though as the waves mount up his preference
Would be dry land), Sobrino tries to guard
Against the crash of Falerina's sword.

75

So finely tempered Balisarda is
That plates of armour poor protection are;
And in the hands of such a knight as this,
A knight in all the world unique or rare,
It cuts the shield; nor can it fail or miss,
Despite the rim of steel beyond compare.
It cuts the shield from crown to base all through,
It cuts the shoulder underneath it too.

76

It cut Sobrino's shoulder; no avail
Against the blade was anything he wore,
No double armour plate, no coat of mail.
The gaping wound was deep and wide and sore.
All his attempts to strike Orlando fail.
The Mover of the heavens granted sure
Defence to Milo's son from injury:
His body cannot penetrated be.

77

Orlando now redoubles his attack,
Resolved to sever his opponent's head.
Sobrino knows that valour and draws back
(His shield being useless now, as I have said),
But not in time, for with a mighty crack
The weapon strikes him on the brow. The blade
Descended flat, but smashed the helmet in,
Dazing the wits and senses of Sobrin.

78

He fell beneath the impact of the blow.
For a long time he did not rise again.
The paladin, who sees him thus brought low,
Thinks he is dead and lets him there remain.
His purpose now is with all speed to go
To Brandimarte's help, lest he be slain.
In steed, arms, sword, perhaps in prowess too,
Gradasso is the stronger of the two.

79

But Brandimarte on Ruggiero's horse
Acquits himself so well and is so brave,
The other knight, despite his greater force,
Not much of an advantage seems to have.
If, like Gradasso, he had had recourse
To a fine hauberk, strong enough to save
Him from all thrusts, he would have had no need
To step from side to side, as now he did.

80

No horse is more responsive to commands.
When Durindana falls, Frontino leaps
Now here, now there, so well he understands,
And every time a well-judged distance keeps.
The other duel inconclusive stands.
Here neither warrior advantage reaps.
Locked in a parity of strength and skill,
They fight a battle dire and terrible.

81

The son of Milo, who had left his foe
Sobrino on the ground, resolved (I said)
To Brandimarte's help at once to go.
As he advanced on foot with hurried tread
And was about to strike the king a blow,
He noticed wandering at large the steed
Sobrino had vacated; by the Count
No time was lost in capturing the mount.

82

He seized the horse and, leaping unopposed
Into the saddle, in one hand he held
His sword on high; the other hand was closed
Upon the ornamented reins; he yelled
Gradasso's name, who, unconcerned, proposed
For all three Christians, when all three were felled,
To make the darkness of the night descend
Before the light of day was at an end.

83

Turning towards the Count from Brandimart,
He aims his weapon straight at the camail.
It pierces everything, the flesh apart:
All efforts to pierce *that* are doomed to fail.
Then down comes Balisard: no magic art
Against *her* strokes can anywhere avail.
From helm to shield, from hauberk down to cuish,
She slices all she touches in one swish.

84

In face, in breast, in thigh Gradasso bore
The marks of Balisarda's swift descent.
His blood has not been shed since first he wore
Those arms, yet by this weapon they are rent,
And not by Durindana (all the more
He's irked and puzzled by this strange event).
From closer to, or had the length been such,
It would have split him down from head to crutch.

85

The proof is plain: he can no longer trust
His magic arms as he was wont to do.
More thought and greater wariness he must
Employ, and parry more than hitherto.
Since now the Count relieves him of that joust,
Bold Brandimarte stands between the two
Encounters, watching how they both proceed
And ready to assist if there is need.

86

And when the combat to this stage had passed,
Sobrino, who for long had prostrate lain,
Rose to his feet, come to himself at last.
His face and arm were causing him much pain.
He raised his eyes and round about him cast.
He saw his lord fighting with might and main.
With rapid strides, to help him he drew near him,
Moving so quietly that none could hear him.

87

Approaching Oliver, who nothing sees
But Agramant, intent upon the fight,
Sobrino strikes his horse behind the knees,
Which straight away collapses with the knight.
So unforeseen this evil action is
That Oliver, who fails to stay upright,
His left foot from the stirrup cannot free
And lies beneath the horse in jeopardy.

88

A sideways stroke Sobrino tries to deal
To cut his head off – this does not occur:
He is prevented by the shining steel
Which Vulcan tempered and which Hector wore.
Then Brandimarte rushes to reveal
How great a love for Oliver he bore.
He strikes Sobrino down; not long he lies.
The fierce old warrior is quick to rise.

89

He turns to Oliver again, to send
His spirit speeding to the world above;
Or, at the least, the king does not intend
That from beneath that burden he shall move.
But Oliver, despite it, could defend
Himself with his right arm; so well he strove,
Striking and lunging at him with such strength,
He kept Sobrino distant at sword's length.

90

By warding off Sobrino in this style,
Though still beneath the horse, he hoped and planned
Soon to be extricated from its pile.
The king's life-blood was crimsoning the sand;
He must accept defeat in a short while.
He was so weak that he could scarcely stand.
Though Oliver had tried repeatedly
To rise, inert the charger seemed to be.

91

The black knight, having turned to Agramant,
Tempestuous assault had now begun,
First at the side of him, and next in front,
His charger whirling as a lathe is spun.
Well-mounted is the son of Monodant,
No less well-mounted is Troiano's son.
Ruggiero gave him Brigliador to ride
When he had humbled Mandricardo's pride.

92

The armour which he wears, well-tried and sound,
Confers advantage on the king indeed,
For Brandimart had seized what arms he found
And put them on in haste to meet his need;
But he'll be donning armour more renowned
(His courage reassures him) with all speed,
Although the king has dealt him such a blow,
From his right shoulder blood begins to flow;

93

And though Gradasso gave him when they fought
A wound upon the thigh which is no joke.
Watching his moment, Brandimarte caught
King Agramante off his guard and broke
His buckler, wounding his left arm, then sought
And slashed his sword-hand with a glancing stroke.
But this is child's-play in comparison
With what between the other two went on.

94

Gradasso has disarmed the Count almost.
His helmet at the crown and sides is split.
His shield upon the meadow has been tossed.
His hauberk and his coat of mail are slit
(Though every thrust upon his flesh is lost).
And yet Gradasso had the worst of it:
On face and throat and breast he bears still more
Of Balisarda's markings than before.

95

Gradasso in his desperation sees,
Though he is drenched in his own blood, that by
So many blows unharmed Orlando is
And that from head to foot he stays quite dry.
His mighty weapon now behold him seize
In both his hands and lift it up on high.
Meaning to split Orlando's trunk in two,
He brings it down just where he aimed to do.

96

But such a blow is wasted on the Count.
No blood had stained the shining virgin blade,
As if it came down flat or had been blunt.
Yet by its impact stunned, Orlando swayed,
And stars below on earth began to count,
And long it was before he saw them fade.
He dropped the reins – he would have dropped his brand,
But it was chained securely to his hand.

97

The heavy crash had terrified the steed
Which on its back the Count Orlando bore.
Giving a demonstration of its speed,
It raised a cloud of dust along the shore.
The Count, who by the blow seemed atrophied,
Could not control the charger as before.
Gradasso followed hard upon his track:
Of speed Baiardo likewise had no lack.

98

But looking round, he saw King Agramant
Facing the last extremity of man.
In his left hand the son of Monodant
Has grasped the helmet of the African.
He has undone the leather straps in front;
The dagger which he holds reveals his plan.
To Agramante no defence is left
Since even of his sword he is bereft.

99

Gradasso turns; he lets Orlando go;
He rides to bring King Agramante aid.
Incautious Brandimarte does not know;
His eyes, his thoughts, have not an instant strayed
From his intent to give the final blow
And in the pagan's throat to plunge the blade.
Gradasso has arrived: with all his might,
Both hands upon his sword, he strikes the knight.

100

Father of Heaven, to a martyr's throne
With Thy Elect, admit this soul, I pray,
Who through life's stormy voyages has gone
And in the harbour furls his sails today!
Ah Durindana, what a deed was done!
Your cruelty, could no compassion stay?
The truest friend he ever had, or will,
Before Orlando's very eyes you kill?

101

His helmet, circled by an iron rim
Two fingers thick, the coif beneath, of steel,
No longer offered a defence to him
Against the blow Gradasso's sword could deal.
It split them both apart; the world grew dim,
And from his charger Brandimarte fell,
And with the blood which from his head now drained
In widening crimson streaks the sand was veined.

102

Orlando, coming to himself again,
Looks back; and there his Brandimarte lies.
Gradasso's air of triumph makes it plain
That he is dead; and in him now arise
(I know not which is stronger) rage and pain.
Having no time for weeping, he denies
His grief, and thus his rage the faster flows;
But now at last this canto I must close.

CANTO XLII

1

What curb is there so harsh, what iron bond,
What chain of adamant (if such there be)
To which the force of anger will respond
By keeping to a lawful boundary,
If one to whom your heart by love is joined,
And firmly riveted by constancy,
Is seen to be dishonoured, or to meet
With harm by violence or by deceit?

2

If to a cruel or inhuman deed
Such impetus may drive it on, the soul,
Thus overmastered, an excuse can plead,
Since reason has surrendered its control.
Achilles, when he saw Patroclus bleed,
Dragged Hector's body round the Trojan wall.
The killing of the killer did not sate him:
He had thus to destroy and desecrate him.

3

Invincible Alfonso, by such fire
Your troops were kindled when the heavy stone
Fell on your brow with injury so dire
That all believed your soul on high had flown.
Then no defences from such blazing ire
Could save your foes, who perished, every one.
No rampart, wall or ditch was of avail,
And not a man was left to tell the tale.

4

The grief it caused your men to see you fall
Moved them to frenzy and to cruelties.
Had you been on your feet, perhaps the toll
Would have been less, and they content to seize
And to restore to you the citadel
Of Bastia in fewer hours than days
Which needed were to take it, earlier,
By men of Còrdova and Grànada.

5

Perhaps the avenging Deity permitted
That you should be laid low in that event,
That an excess of cruelty committed
Should meet, as it deserved, with punishment:
When Vestidello in good faith submitted,
Weary and wounded, all his spirit spent,
Unarmed, among the men-at-arms of Spain
(Who mostly served Mahomet) he was slain.

6

But now, to bring this matter to an end,
I tell you that no other wrath is like
The wrath you feel when you see one offend
Your liege lord, kinsman, comrade, or the like;
So it was right that for so dear a friend
A sudden wrath Orlando's heart should strike
When dead upon the ground he saw him lie,
Felled by the blow Gradasso slew him by.

7

As a Numidian shepherd, who has seen
A hateful snake slide off across the sand
When it has left its deadly poison in
His child, will grasp his cudgel in his hand
With rage, so now that sword, more sharp and keen
Than any other, Falerina's brand,
Orlando grasps and turns to do his worst:
His angry gaze meets Agramante first.

8

Bleeding, with half a shield, his helm unstrapped,
Swordless and with more wounds than could be said,
From Brandimarte's clutch he had escaped,
As from the talons of a hawk, half dead,
A falcon frees itself, for spite uncapped,
Or for some foolish whim unwisely sped.
Orlando reached him: and exactly where
The head and body join, he struck him, there.

9

The neck, being undefended, like a reed
Was severed cleanly with a single slash.
That regal torso, following the head,
Ended its Libyan kingship with a crash,
And to the Acheron its spirit fled,
Where Charon hoisted it aboard. A flash –
And Balisarda, active once again,
Has sought, and found, the Sericanian.

10

When King Gradasso on that fateful shore
Has seen the headless torso fall – dread sight -
A thing occurred, unknown to him before:
His heart within him quailed, his face grew white.
Now, when Orlando down upon him bore,
He seemed to know and almost to invite
His doom, for no defence he made, and no
Attempt to intercept the mortal blow.

11

Gradasso on the right-hand side was cleft
Beneath the lowest rib; the blade went through
His belly and emerged upon the left,
Where it protruded by a palm or two,
Empurpled with his blood from tip to haft.
Thus the best warrior the world e'er knew
Brought to his death a mighty lord than whom
None was more powerful in Pagandom.

12

Small joy Orlando feels at his success
As, leaping with impatience from his steed,
His countenance distorted with distress,
His eyes suffused with tears, he makes all speed
Towards his Brandimart, for whom redress
Has come too late; he sees how he has bled.
He sees the helm, as by an axe, split wide:
Frail bark as much protection would provide.

13

Orlando took the helmet from his face
And found that from his forehead to his nose
Gradasso's sword had left its deadly trace;
Yet breath enough remained in his last throes
To ask for God's forgiveness and for grace
Before his life descended to its close,
And to exhort the Count to find relief
In patient resignation for his grief.

14

These words he uttered just before the end:
'Remember me, Orlando, when you pray';
And he continued, 'To you I commend
My Fiordi . . .' but the 'ligi' could not say.
On high, angelic voices sweetly blend
With the celestial instruments which play,
As from the mortal veil his soul, set free,
Is wafted heavenwards in melody.

15

Orlando should feel naught but happiness
At so devout an end; he can believe,
He knows, that Brandimart is now in bliss;
He saw the heavens open to receive
His soul; but human will is weak in this.
At such a loss he cannot help but grieve,
At such a loss the tears pour down his face,
A loss no brother even could replace.

16

Sobrino's face and side were drenched with gore.
Some time ago he'd fallen helplessly
Upon his back; continuing to pour,
His veins by now must almost empty be.
And Oliver is lying as before,
Pinned by his charger; and whatever he
Contrives, his foot, half-crushed beneath the weight,
And out of joint, he cannot extricate.

17

And if Orlando had not rescued him
(His countenance still sorrowful and wet
With tears), he never could have freed his limb.
The pain is such, he cannot stand, or set
One foot before the other; in this grim
Predicament, while numb and lifeless yet
His whole leg seemed, without Orlando's aid
No single step could Oliver have made.

18

Small joy Orlando took in victory.
The death of Brandimarte was too high
A price to pay, too harsh a penalty;
And Oliver's condition made him sigh.
Sobrino's senses intermittently
Revived and sank, for Erebus was nigh.
So copiously from his wounds he bled,
His life was hanging by the merest thread.

19

Orlando had him carried to a tent
To have his bleeding gashes stitched with care
And spoke some words of kind encouragement,
As if two relatives, not foes, they were.
He felt no rancour after the event,
Humane his actions and benign his air.
Claiming the arms and horses of the dead,
The servants might take all the rest, he said.

20

Here Frederick Fulgoso casts some doubt
Upon my tale and wonders if it's true.
When with his fleet he journeyed round about
The coast of Barbary, this isle he knew:
He landed and explored it all throughout.
He found it mountainous and, in his view,
On all that rough and rocky piece of land
No-one, no single foot, could level stand.

21

And on that crag (he says) six cavaliers,
The flower of the world though they might be,
Could not have run and jousted with their spears.
To this objection which he puts to me
I answer: at that time (so it appears)
There was a space for tilting, near the sea;
But it was covered when a pinnacle
Of massive rock, dislodged by earthquake, fell.

22

So, bright Fulgosan splendour, brilliant gleam,
Serene refulgence which for ever glows,
If in the presence, it may be, of him
To whom your land its peace and safety owes,
You have declared that I untruthful seem,
Let us our difference in friendship close:
Do not be slow in telling him that I
Perhaps as elsewhere in this do not lie.

23

Orlando, gazing out to sea meanwhile,
Noticed a little craft, its sails full-spread,
Making, it seemed to him, straight for the isle
As with all haste before the wind it sped.
But who it was approaching in this style
I will not tell you now; let us, instead,
Return to France, where they have chased away
The Moors, and see if they are sad or gay.

24

And let us see how fares that constant Maid
Who sees her only joy depart again.
I speak of Bradamant, who is dismayed
When she discovers that the vow is vain
Which a few days ago Ruggiero made
In earshot of the troops of Charlemagne
And Agramant; and if in this he fails,
Her heart, bereft of hope, within her quails.

25

Then, newly giving vent to her distress,
Repeating her by now familiar wails,
Calling Ruggiero cruel, pitiless,
To the full blast of woe she spreads her sails
And in an anguished voice with bitterness
Against high Heaven itself she rants and rails,
Calling it weak, unjust and impotent,
Since perjury receives no punishment.

26

She turned against Melissa in her grief,
The grotto and the oracle she cursed,
To which she has accorded such belief,
She'll perish in the sea of love immersed.
She turned next to Marfisa for relief;
Her mounting frenzy rising to its worst,
She cried and shrieked and endless clamour made
And on her kindness threw herself for aid.

27

Marfisa shrugs; what little she can say
To comfort her, she says; she has no doubt
Ruggiero will return to her straightway
And claim her as his bride; if he does not,
Marfisa will not let him get away
(She gives her solemn word) with such a blot
On his escutcheon (which is hers as well):
Fulfilment of his vows she will compel.

28

And thus she helps the Maid to check her grief
Which, being vented, is less bitter now.
So, having seen and heard her gain relief,
Her love reviling for his broken vow,
Let's find her brother and discover if
He better fares, although I don't see how:
In every nerve he is aflame with love –
It is Rinaldo I am speaking of,

29

Rinaldo who so loved, as you recall,
Angelica the beautiful; and yet,
Although her beauty held him now in thrall,
He had been drawn by magic in Love's net.
The other knights a peaceful interval
Enjoy, after the Saracens' defeat.
Of all the victors, he alone remains
A captive, bound in sorrow by Love's chains.

30

A hundred men for news of her he sent.
He too had searched; when no one could succeed,
To Malagigi in the end he went,
Who many times had helped him in his need;
And he confessed to his enamourment,
Standing with downcast brow and blushing red.
He begged him finally to tell him where
He'd find his love, Angelica the fair.

31

Amazement at such love, so strange and new,
Went spinning round in Malagigi's head.
Rinaldo could have had the girl, he knew,
Had he so wished, a hundred times in bed;
And he himself did all that he could do,
And all that he could find to say, he said.
He threatened and cajoled but nothing moved him.
He did not want her then, although she loved him.

32

And what is more, if he had yielded then
She'd promised to set Malagigi free.
But now what has the sorcerer to gain?
Why should he listen to Rinaldo's plea?
What of the suffering, what of the pain
Which he endured while in captivity?
In that dark dungeon he might well have died
Because Rinaldo his request denied.

33

But as Rinaldo's pleas for aid still more
Insistent and importunate appear,
His cousin Malagigi they assure
The love which they betoken is no mere
Caprice; and all the injuries of yore
As in the ocean sink and disappear.
He does not let Rinaldo plead in vain
But now resolves to help him in his pain.

34

Setting a certain time for his return,
He gave Rinaldo hope, and went his way
The fate of fair Angelica to learn:
Was she in France, or was she far away?
Such matters conjured demons could discern.
He reached his secret cave without delay
(To no one else was it accessible)
And summoned droves of spirits by a spell.

35

He chooses one who in affairs of love
Is well informed; he asks, 'How can it be
Rinaldo's heart, once hard, which naught could move,
Is now so soft?' He learns the mystery
Of the two fountains, how the water of
The one enkindles passion; contrary
Effect the other has; no cure is known,
But each is cancelled by the other one.

36

The waters which the heart from loving bar
Rinaldo drank, and harsh and cold became.
No pleadings of the fair Angelica
Availed; but then at last the moment came
When he was led by an unlucky star
To drink the waters which the heart inflame.
His passion now for her is desperate
Whom beyond measure he was wont to hate.

37

An evil star, a cruel fate indeed!
The fever from the icy stream he sips
Just when the fair Angelica is led
To touch the loveless water with her lips.
All soft emotion from her heart is shed;
Henceforth her flesh for him with horror creeps
As for a snake; and he as much loves her
As he abhorred and scorned her earlier.

38

The demon tells him everything he can
About Rinaldo's strange vicissitude;
About Angelica's young African
He tells him too, how he possessed her nude,
And how the damsel's love for him began,
How they left European soil for good,
How they took passage on a ship from Spain
And sailed for India across the main.

39

And when Rinaldo came for his reply,
His cousin Malagigi told him all:
Angelica had left him high and dry
And at a lowly Berber's beck and call
No joy did she withhold, no whim deny.
He must stop loving her for good and all.
Now she was half-way home and far from France,
Of tracing her he had but little chance.

40

The damsel's flight itself would not have been
A blow the eager lover could not bear;
Thoughts of returning to the East to win
Her back would not have made him turn a hair;
But when Rinaldo hears a Saracen
Has plucked the first fruits of a love so rare,
Such anguish and such torment rend his heart,
He never in his life has known such smart.

41

And not a word in answer can he say.
Tongue-tied, he cannot form one syllable;
His trembling lips his trembling heart betray,
He twists his mouth, as if he tasted gall.
Not one more instant can he bear to stay
But lets his fury drive him where it will.
And after many tears, and bitter woe,
Eastwards once more he knew that he must go.

42

He asks the son of Pepin for consent,
Making his horse Baiardo an excuse:
Gradasso took it with him when he went,
Committing thus a serious abuse
Of chivalry; to make him now repent,
Rinaldo, honour-bound, this course must choose:
Gradasso else would boast how with his lance
He won the charger of a peer of France.

43

Charles granted leave of absence with regret
And all in France were sad to see him go;
But since the quest on which his heart seemed set
Was honourable, he could not say no.
Rinaldo would on no account permit
Dudone or Guidone to come too,
But, leaving Paris, he rode forth alone,
With many a lover's sigh and many a groan.

44

And ever by this memory he's haunted:
A thousand times he could have known delight,
But he rejected what she would have granted,
And foolishly such beauty chose to slight.
Of that sweet pleasure which he had not wanted
What years were lost! Ah! now if one short night
Of love's fulfilment she would not deny,
How gladly he would come, how gladly die!

45

And ever in his mind and in his heart
He asks himself: how could a lowly Moor
Drive every recollection from her heart
Of her devoted aspirants of yore?
This is the thought which lacerates his heart
As on he journeys eastwards heading for
The Rhine and Basle; still brooding on his pain,
He enters the great forest of Ardennes.

46

Mile after mile the paladin rode on,
Where the dense wood grew more mysterious,
Where hamlets and where castles were unknown,
Where tangled paths were rough and dangerous;
And all at once a shadow veiled the sun:
Over the sky a gloom spread, ominous,
While from a cavern, dark and dank and deep,
He saw a monstrous female figure creep.

47

A thousand lidless eyes which cannot blink,
A thousand ears the creature has; it takes
No rest; it cannot ever sleep, I think.
In place of hair – a writhing mass of snakes,
A sight from which the bravest heart would shrink.
A larger and more cruel serpent tweaks
Its coils about the torso like a tail.
This form had issued from the shades of Hell.

48

And what in all Rinaldo's deeds of war
Had never happened to him, happened then.
As the dread monster down upon him bore
And all its hostile panoply was seen,
Fear such as none perhaps e'er felt before
Flooded him through and through in every vein;
Yet with a show of courage a brave stand
He made, his sword grasped in a trembling hand.

49

The monster crouches for a deadly spring,
In all the arts of war a champion.
Its tail (the venom reptile) brandishing,
It rushes at Rinaldo, now upon
This side and now another menacing.
Of all his strokes, transverse or straight, not one
The monster's head or any part can find;
His sword each time on empty air falls blind.

50

The monster pierces through his coat of mail
And with its icy poison numbs his heart.
Next, through the visor's sights it flicks its tail,
Stinging his face and neck in a quick dart.
Nothing Rinaldo does is of avail;
He has no other course than to depart.
The monster is not lame, and with one jump
It sits behind him on the charger's rump.

51

And whether left or right or straight ahead
He goes, the cursèd beast is with him still.
He tries all means: the plague he cannot shed.
The charger bucks: it sits immovable.
Rinaldo's heart is trembling, not with dread
That it may further seek to do him ill,
But with disgust and horror, and he groans,
Reviling life with his laments and moans.

52

Through the most intricate and tangled trails
Rinaldo spurs, up the most hazardous
Of cliffs, and down the thorniest of vales,
Deep in the darkest and most ominous
Of shadows; but in spite of all he fails
To loosen from his back that venomous
And hateful beast; his end indeed seemed nigh,
But to the rescue came one riding by.

53

A cavalier in shining armour came.
A yoke, fragmented, as his crest he bore.
The emblem on his buckler was a flame
Of crimson blazing on a field of or.
His surcoat was embroidered with the same,
Like the caparison his charger wore.
His sword was sheathed, his lance in readiness,
And coruscations sparkled from his mace.

54

With an eternal flame this weapon burns,
Yet it is not consumed; and every shield,
Cuirass and helm, however strong, it scorns.
Before its blaze a cavalier must yield;
Whichever way the fiery weapon turns,
It clears all opposition from the field.
No less was needed to relieve our knight
Who found himself in such a cruel plight.

55

And, like a brave bold-hearted cavalier,
He makes for where the sound of combat is
And at a gallop speedily draws near.
The monster on Rinaldo's back he sees,
Wrapping its tail around him, till in fear
It makes the paladin both burn and freeze.
The rescuer attacks and at one blow
The monster tumbles to the left below.

56

But scarcely has it fallen than anew
It springs erect and brandishes its tail.
The cavalier next tries what fire can do
(The lance, he thinks, will be of less avail).
He grasps the mace, the snake twists to and fro,
The blows descend as fast and thick as hail,
And not an instant can the creature find
To get a single stroke in, true or blind.

57

Forcing it back or holding it at bay,
Avenging many a shame with every blow,
He lets Rinaldo make a getaway
And up towards the mountain bids him go.
The paladin is willing to obey:
The path and the advice he is not slow
To take, but quickly vanishes from sight,
Though harsh is the ascent towards the height.

58

The cavalier fights on; through the black hole
He drives the monster down to the Abyss.
There it devours itself; there tears from all
Its thousand eyes will trickle limitless
And through eternity unchecked will fall.
The rescuer, having accomplished this,
Up to the mountain-top proceeds to ride
To be Rinaldo's counsellor and guide.

59

Rinaldo's gratitude was infinite;
He was in debt to him for evermore,
And with his life he'd willingly remit
His obligation and redress the score.
He asked his rescuer (as he thought fit)
If he'd divulge to him the name he bore,
That he might make his deed of valour known
To Charles and sing his praise to everyone.

60

The cavalier replied, 'If I conceal
My name a while, be not displeased, I pray,
For my identity I will reveal
Before the shadows lengthen.' A short way
They rode until they came upon a rill
As clear and sparkling as the light of day.
All passers-by who, by its murmur lured,
Drink from this water, of love's pains are cured.

61

This was the very selfsame stream, my lord,
Of which the icy water quenches love.
Angelica who drank from it abhorred
Rinaldo from then on; but when she strove
To win his heart (for once she had adored
The paladin, as I have said above),
He hated her; of this the reason was
That from this fount he sipped – no other cause.

62

The knight who travelled at Rinaldo's side
Drew rein as they approached the crystal spring,
Being heated with the combat and the ride.
He said, 'To rest here will be no bad thing.'
'Nothing but good will come of it,' replied
Rinaldo; 'the noon sun is menacing
And the foul monster has so harried me,
Welcome and timely some repose will be.'

63

So each dismounted and allowed his steed
To roam the forest, grazing at its will;
And each then drew his helmet from his head,
Prepared to take his rest and look his fill
Upon the flower-spangled verdant mead.
Rinaldo ran towards the sparkling rill
And quenched, with but one sip of the cold stream,
Both thirst and love which so tormented him.

64

The other knight, who watched him as he raised
His mouth all dripping from the icy spring,
His every thought of mad desire erased,
Then rose to his full stature, challenging,
As sternly on the paladin he gazed.
Then he divulged what I to light now bring:
'Rinaldo, you must know my name is Scorn:
I free you from a yoke ignobly borne.'

65

And with these words he vanished instantly
And with him vanished too his destrier.
Rinaldo, marvelling, cried, 'Where is he?'
All he could do was turn about and stare.
He wondered what the knight and horse could be:
Enchanted phantoms conjured in mid-air
By Malagigi, sent to break the chain
Which for so long had fettered him in pain?

66

Or else despatched from the Celestial Host
By God, Whose goodness is ineffable,
Who sent an Angel once in times long past,
Blind Tobit's vision to restore and heal?
Rejoicing to be free again at last,
Whether the spirit be from Heaven or Hell,
Rinaldo offers thanks and praise; he knows
To it alone release from love he owes.

67

Angelica he hated once again.
For half a league he would not now pursue
One whom he'd sought so far and long in vain;
But none the less he is determined to
Ride on to Sericana to regain
His destrier Baiardo, as is due:
In the first place, his honour is involved,
And he had told his lord what he resolved.

68

Rinaldo reaches Basle on the next day,
Where rumour has it that the Count Anglant
Has pledged in a three-cornered final fray
To fight Gradasso and King Agramant.
This, nobody had heard Orlando say,
No message of the kind by him was sent,
But he who brought the news arrived hotfoot
From Sicily, and he was in no doubt.

69

Rinaldo longs to reach Orlando's side.
The journey he must undertake is vast.
Every ten miles he changes mount and guide.
Not sparing whip or spur, he gallops fast,
Crosses the Rhine at Constance, in his stride
Surmounts the Alps, to Italy at last
Descends; Verona, Mantua recede,
Then to the Po's south bank he makes all speed.

70

The sun, already low, towards evening sank,
Already the first star was visible,
As he stood pensive on the river-bank:
Should he change horses here, or rest until,
Once more discountenanced, the darkness shrank
Before the light Aurora would unveil?
Just then he saw a cavalier approach,
In aspect courteous and *sans reproche*.

71

First greeting him with every compliment,
He asked the paladin if he were wed.
Rinaldo heard him with astonishment:
'The wedded yoke does couple me,' he said.
The other then replied, 'I am content.'
Next, on his words some clarity he shed:
'If you this night near by desire to rest,
I beg you will accept to be my guest,

72

'For I will show you what all married men
(I do not doubt) would dearly love to see.'
Rinaldo's curiosity being then
Aroused (for he was drawn to mystery
And to adventure) and since he had been
So long upon the road, he willingly
Accepted the kind offer of the knight
And took the unknown path into the night.

73

Veering a bowshot from the main highway,
They came upon a palace, great and tall.
Pages with burning torches, bright as day,
Escorted them inside the spacious hall.
Rinaldo gazed about him every way,
At every entrance and at every wall.
Here was a dwelling rarely to be seen,
Too costly, surely, for one citizen.

74

The portal has a priceless pediment
Of hardest serpentine and porphyry.
The doors are bronze; figures which ornament
Them seem to breathe and turn their eyes to see.
Beneath an arch through which Rinaldo went
Lovely mosaics gleam deludingly.
Beyond, a courtyard, where on every side
Loggias extend, a hundred cubits wide.

75

Each loggia has its entrance, separate,
Preceded by an arch, each width the same,
But in relief distinctively ornate
(A lavish plenty was the sculptor's aim).
A ramp goes up at such a gentle rate
A burdened ass would find it a mere game.
Another archway crowns the topmost stair
And leads to an apartment, rich and fair.

76

The upper-storey arches were so wide,
They straddled the majestic entrances,
Supported by two columns, one each side,
Of bronze or marble, or like substances;
But it would be excessive if I tried
To sketch all the ornate appurtenances,
Not only the delights above, which show,
But those the architect designed below.

77

High pillars with their gilded capitals,
Bearing the gem-encrusted porticoes,
Marble, imported to adorn the halls,
Fashioned in many a skilful form and pose,
Paintings and metal castings, and much else,
Though all their beauty night does not disclose,
Show clearly that for such an edifice
The riches of two kings would not suffice.

78

Supreme among the many ornaments,
So rich and fair, which gladdened the abode,
In copious rivulets and affluents
A fountain with refreshing water flowed.
From the four doors in equal evidence,
And with a central view of them, it stood.
The servants who the evening meal prepare
Are busy setting out the tables there.

79

The fountain, by a master craftsman made
With many a subtle touch of artistry,
Was shaped like a pavilion, giving shade;
Each of eight sides was fashioned differently,
Crowned with a golden cupola, inlaid
Beneath with blue enamel, fair to see.
Eight statues of fine marble, gleaming white,
Their left arms held aloft, supported it.

80

And sculpted with the master's cunning skill
In their right hand a horn of plenty was,
Whence water with a pleasing murmur fell
And flowed into an alabaster vase.
These female figures were majestical
(Of artistry sublime which had no flaws),
Diverse in raiment and diverse in face,
But equal in their beauty and their grace.

81

And firmly fixed were every statue's feet
Upon two other figures placed below.
That these found song and harmony a sweet
Delight, their mouths, wide open, seemed to show.
Their pose suggested they would dedicate
Their lives in praise of the fair ladies who
Were standing on their shoulders, were but they
In truth those whom these semblances portray.

82

Each pair of the supporters has a scroll
Which in their arms unfolded is and spread.
Incised on it are writings which extol
The more exalted statues overhead.
Their own names are not absent from the roll
And, like the women's, can be plainly read.
Rinaldo scrutinized them, one by one,
While in the dark the light of torches shone.

83

A first inscription meets Rinaldo's eyes:
Lucrezia Borgia with all honour named,
Whose loveliness and virtue Rome should prize
Above her ancient namesake's, likewise famed.
The two who raise her statue to the skies,
Strozzi and Tebaldeo, gladly claimed
The glorious burden and will serve her long,
A Linus and an Orpheus in song.

84

The statue by her side is no less fair:
'Isabella, daughter of Ercole,
Behold!' (so runs the script); 'Ferrara, where
She will be born, greater felicity
Will owe to this, more thankfulness declare,
Than for the heaping of prosperity
Which Fortune has in store and will reveal
As through the turning years she turns her wheel.'

85

The pair which loving eagerness displays
That her renown for ever shall resound
Are both Gian Iacopi, the writing says,
But one to Bardelone will respond,
One to Calandra; in the next two bays,
Whence water trickles with a pleasing sound,
Two women stand, alike in blood and race,
Alike in honour, loveliness and grace.

86

Elisabetta one of them is named,
The other Leonora; they will bring
To Mantua, as Virgil's birthplace famed,
No less renown (the marble lettering
Predicts); the first for whom this legend claimed
Such glory is upheld by two who sing
Her praise: Iacopo Sadoleto and
Pietro Bembo. Beneath the other stand

87

A courtly Castiglione, and, beside,
The learnèd Muzio Arelio;
These names, upon the marble scroll descried,
Were at that time unknown, but now are so
Deservedly renowned. Rinaldo's guide
Next points to her on whom the heavens bestow
The virtue to sustain whatever ill
Or good shall come to her by Fortune's wheel.

88

She is proclaimed in gold calligraphy
Lucrezia Bentivoglio; she in whom
Ferrara's duke rejoices, proud to be
Her father; chanting her encomium
In a sweet voice with limpid melody,
Camillo stands; Bologna, overcome,
The Reno, rapt in wonder, will pay heed
As to its shepherd once Amphrysus did.

89

With him is one on whose account the town
Where the Isauro, growing brackish, flows
Into the sea, will gain a world renown,
From Auster's region to the northern snows,
From East to West; on him a double crown
Together Phoebus and Athene pose.
The Roman origin of Pèsaro
Will be outweighed by Guido Postumo.

90

Next is Diana and of her they read:
'She is as kind of heart as she is fair
Of face; to her proud bearing pay no heed.
Her glory Celio Calcagnin will bear;
Combining poetry', so runs the screed,
'With erudition, from the kingdom where
Monaeses ruled, to Juba's Africa,
His trump is heard from Spain to India.'

91

Marco Cavallo's words her praise endorse
And in Ancona will arise a fount
As when on Helicon the wingèd horse
(Some say it happened on Parnassus' mount)
Struck with its hoof the enchanted watercourse.
Of Beatrice they next read this account:
'Her spouse she blesses long as she draws breath;
Disconsolate she leaves him on her death.

92

'All Italy is stricken by her loss,
Triumphant once, now plunged in slavery,'
A poet of Correggio, Nicholas,
With high-flown eloquence appears to be
Intoning as he writes. Mellifluous,
The Bendedei's glory, Timothy,
Joins in her praise. Where tears of amber flow,
A river at their plangent tones will slow.

93

Between this, and that statue which portrays
The Borgia I have mentioned in my rhyme,
On a tall figure now they fix their gaze,
In alabaster carved, and so sublime,
No other form is worthier of praise.
Veiled and in black, adorned with neither gem
Nor gold, yet no less lovely she appears
Than Venus does among the other stars.

94

One cannot tell by looking at her face
Which of these qualities prevail in it,
Such are her beauty, majesty and grace,
The upright virtues of her mind, her wit.
This message on the marble scroll they trace:
'Who speaks of her as fully as is fit,
His gifts to a most worthy task will lend,
Yet such that he will never reach the end.'

95

Though to her image all these virtues clung,
And though so sweet and gracious was her air,
She seemed disdainful that with humble song
One so uncouth should seek to honour her
As he who stood below, unique among
The rest (I know not why), with none to share
His burden. All the others were revealed;
These names alone the sculptor had concealed.

96

The statues on the fountain form a ring.
The coral floor is dry and rendered cool
By the clear water, sweetly murmuring,
Which pours unending in a crystal pool,
And thence in conduits channelled is to bring
Refreshment to the meadows, beautiful
With green and blue and white and yellow flowers,
To tender grasses and to shady bowers.

97

Sitting at table with the courteous knight,
Rinaldo urged him many times to say
What he had promised to reveal that night.
He longed to hear it now without delay;
But glancing at him when he deemed it right,
He saw that on his heart some burden lay,
He heard with every moment that went by
His breast give vent to an impassioned sigh.

98

So, many times Rinaldo held his peace.
Questions, impelled by curiosity,
Rose to his lips but did not gain release,
By tact restrained and modest courtesy.
The meal at last had come to a surcease
When a young page, whose task it seemed to be,
Placed on the board a goblet, gold and fine,
Inlaid with gems, filled to the brim with wine.

99

The lord and master smiled a little then,
Looking Rinaldo in the face, but one
Who closely scrutinized him could have seen
That in his eyes tears, not of laughter, shone.
He said, 'I know how eager you have been
To hear the end of what I have begun.
Now is the time, I think, to bring you proof
For which no husband could give thanks enough.

100

'In my opinion, every married man
Should keep a prudent watch upon his spouse,
And learn if she deceives him, if he can,
Or if she guards the honour of his house.
Nothing is easier than to obtain
A pair of horns, for all the shame they cause.
To almost everyone they're obvious,
Except the husband, who's oblivious.

101

'If you are certain that your wife is pure,
You'll love her more, and have good reason to,
Than he who knows his has a paramour,
Or he who suffers doubt and anguish too;
And many unjust jealousy could cure,
Whose wives are chaste and innocent and true,
While many more, though feeling no concern,
Are wearing horns which others can discern.

102

'Thinking your wife is chaste, as I believe
That you believe and as believe you must
(Though to believe is hard, till you receive
Clear evidence of what it is you trust),
If you desire to have proof positive,
Drink from this goblet; it is placed here just
For this, that I may demonstrate to you
The test I spoke of, as I promised to.

103

'Drink from this goblet; if you wear the crest
Of Cornwall (let us say), you'll find it tips
The total of its contents down your breast
And not a drop of wine will pass your lips.
If on the other hand your wife is chaste,
Between you and the cup there'll be no slips.'
And with these words he fixed his gaze upon
Rinaldo's bosom where the wine would run.

104

Almost convinced and half at least inclined
To make the test, Rinaldo reaches out
And takes the golden cup, wherewith to find
What it were best perhaps to leave in doubt.
Then, pausing, he considers in his mind
The risk he faces if he tries it; but
Let me now rest a while, my lord, and I
Will let you know the paladin's reply.

CANTO XLIII

1

O execrable avarice! O greed!
I do not marvel that a low-born soul,
Tainted with other sins, thou dost succeed
In grasping and in holding as thy thrall;
But that thou shouldst as helpless captive lead,
And with those selfsame talons strike and maul,
One who for nobleness of intellect,
If he avoided thee, would earn respect!

2

Some men can measure earth and sea and sky,
The origins of Nature's works retrace,
Her every how disclose, her every why,
And, scaling Heaven, look God in the face;
Yet, if their souls should be infected by
The fatal poison of thy fangs, a base
Desire for wealth becomes their chief concern:
For this alone they hope, for this they yearn.

3

Others can vanquish armies and with zest
Will breach the portals of a garrison,
The first to offer their undaunted breast,
The last from scenes of battle to have flown;
Yet in thy dungeon thou imprisonest
Their souls, and no defences have they, none.
Others who other arts and skills pursue
Remain obscure, for them thou dost undo.

4

And what of women, lovely and high-born,
Who no reward for faithful service grant,
Who handsome looks and manly virtue scorn?
I see them hard and cold and adamant.
Lo! Avarice draws near: at once they burn
(Such power has the monster to enchant)
And not for love, but for their pockets' sake,
The old, the ugly, the deformed they take.

5

Not without reason do I thus deplore
The ill effects of avarice and greed.
I know what I am doing; I assure
My listeners I have not lost the thread.
My words apply to the above no more
Than to what later on must yet be said.
Let us now seek the paladin who was
About to test the powers of the vase.

6

I told you that he wished to think a while
Before he raised the goblet to his lips.
He thought, and then he argued in this style:
'Foolish it is to rouse a dog which sleeps.
Women are women, easy to beguile.
My wife's a woman: I will take no steps
(In what way would it make me happier?)
To test the confidence I have in her.

7

'What good will come of it? Perhaps much ill,
For God is vexed by those who probe and pry.
Whether I am a foolish man, or sensible,
I know not, but this wine I will not try.
So let it be removed, I pray; I feel
No thirst for it and no such thirst do I
Desire, for God denies such certainty,
More than to Adam He denied the tree.

8

'When Adam ate the apple long ago
Which the Lord God with His own lips forbade,
He fell from joy and happiness to woe
And ever afterwards his life was sad.
Likewise a husband who desires to know
All that his wife has ever done or said
Will from contentment fall to pain and grief
And never henceforth will he find relief.'

9

Rinaldo with these words pushed back the vase
Which he had come to hate; to his surprise,
On looking at his host, he saw there was
A stream of sorrow pouring from his eyes;
And as he wondered what could be the cause,
The sobbing man, grown calmer, in this wise
Began to speak: 'Ah! bitter is the cost
I paid, for by this test my wife I lost.

10

'A curse upon my evil counsellor!
Would that ten years ago I had known you!
Would I had taken your advice before
Such sorrow and such blinding tears I knew!
But let the curtain hide the scene no more.
Let the whole story be displayed to view.
I'll tell you the beginning and the cause
Of my long torment, which no equal has.

11

'You passed a city to the north of here:
A river, issuing from Garda, slows
Its pace, spreading around it like a mere,
Then swiftly downward to the Po it flows.
When Thebes collapsed, whose snake-born founders
By Cadmus harvested, this city rose.   [were
There I was born, of noble family,
Though raised in lowliness and poverty.

12

'If Fortune did not take sufficient care
Of me to give me riches at my birth,
Nature, to compensate, an extra share
Of beauty gave me (of far greater worth).
None of my fellows could with me compare,
And in my younger days I had no dearth
Of women who desired me, and I knew
How to respond and how to please them too,

13

'(Though it is not for me to boast of this).
And in our city dwelt a learnèd sage,
Well versed in all the arts and sciences;
And when he closed his eyes in death, his age
One hundred eight-and-twenty was, no less.
And when he had approached the final stage,
Though up till then he'd lived a hermit's life,
By Love induced he bought himself a wife.

14

'By her he had a daughter secretly;
And that she might disdain her mother's ways,
Who for a price sold her virginity
(Than which no treasure higher value has),
He hid her from the world's society,
And in this lonely place resolved to raise,
First calling demon masons to his aid,
This spacious palace, sumptuously arrayed.

15

'And here by chaste old dames the girl was reared,
Who grew, as time went by, in grace and charm.
So greatly for her innocence he feared,
Such was his dread that she might come to harm,
No man (apart from him) she saw or heard;
And by examples her resolve to arm,
Of every woman who resisted lust
He placed a portrait, statue or a bust.

16

'Not only women who as Virtue's friends
Adorned the world when it was young, whose fame
By ancient chronicles to us descends,
Whom everlastingly we shall acclaim:
To future ages the design extends,
And women who will glorify the name
Of Italy are pictured here in stone
Or paint, such as these eight whom I have shown.

17

'And when he judged the fruit was ripe to pluck,
In his opinion I was worthier
(Whether by my misfortune or good luck)
Than any other man to marry her.
The corn-fields, fed by many a stream and brook,
Replete with every kind of provender,
Which stretch for twenty miles around outside,
He gave me as a dowry for the bride.

18

'So gently reared, so beautiful was she,
In all respects a very paragon!
Her drawn-thread work and her embroidery
Equalled the best Athene might have done.
No mortal being – a divinity
In walk, in voice, she seemed to everyone.
In art and letters she was almost as
Accomplished as her learnèd father was.

19

'Endowed with intellect and loveliness
(Which would have made the very stones relent),
She had so fond a heart that I confess
To think of it, with grief my heart is rent.
Her greatest joy, her keenest happiness,
Was to be near me whereso'er I went.
No quarrel had we in the years which passed –
But we fell out, and by my fault, at last.

20

'Five years went by in conjugal delight
And then the sage, her father, passed away.
At once began the woes that to this plight
Reduced me which you find me in today.
While I yet sheltered 'neath Love's wings that quite
Enfolded me, content in every way,
For me a lady of the neighbourhood
With ardour burned, as fierce as any could.

21

'In every magic charm and spell as versed
As any sorceress, she plied her skill:
The night to day, or day to night reversed,
Halted the sun or moved the earth at will;
And yet, for all she tried to do her worst,
She could not make me cure her of her ill:
For I abhorred the only remedy,
Which would have done my spouse an injury.

22

'Her charm and beauty were of no avail,
Her love for me (though it was deep, I knew),
Her gifts, her promises were doomed to fail,
Though many times repeated and not few.
My resolution she could not assail.
No spark from my first love to fire the new
Would I transfer; and what restrained my lust
Was knowing that my consort I could trust.

23

'Such hope, such faith, such certainty I had
That she was true, I could have looked with cold
Disdain on Helen, and the offer made
To Paris, of great wisdom and much gold,
When he a shepherd on Mount Ida played,
And judged the goddesses in days of old,
I would have scorned; yet, spite of all I did,
Of my enchantress I could not be rid.

24

'She found me wandering alone one day
Outside these walls (Melissa was her name)
And spoke at greater length in such a way
My peace was turned to strife; her cruel aim
Was to use jealousy to drive away
My trust and set my heart with wrath aflame.
First she commends me for my constancy
To one who I believe is true to me:

25

'"You cannot say your wife is true until
You have proof positive; she may not sin
And yet of sin she may be capable:
How do you know, if she has never been
Allowed away from you? How can you tell
How she would act if she saw other men?
Tell me on what your confidence is based
When you assure me that your wife is chaste.

26

'"Absent yourself a while, leave your domains,
And let the villages and cities hear
That you have gone away and she remains,
And let all gallants know the coast is clear;
Then if she proves, in spite of all their pains
(And thinking you could not discover her),
Unwilling to betray the marriage-bed,
Then true to you and chaste she may be said."

27

'With words like these Melissa urges me
To verify the faith I had expressed,
Until at last I yield and I agree
To put my consort's virtue to the test;
But first I say, "Let us suppose that she
Is not the wife by whom I think I'm blest,
How can I tell for certain this is so?
If I am far away, how can I know?"

28

'Melissa said, "I will present to you
A goblet with a power strange and rare.
Morgana made it for King Arthur who
Discovered by its help that Guinevere
Had sinned; a husband, if his wife is true,
Can drink from it, but can be proved to wear
The horns if when he puts it to his lips
All down his chest the content spills and drips;

29

'"But test the goblet first before you leave.
It's my belief your chest you will not stain:
So far your wife is spotless, I believe.
But if on your return you try again
No guarantee from then on can I give.
If when you quaff your wine your chest is clean,
Of all the husbands in the world you'll be
Most blest in conjugal fidelity."

30

'I followed her advice; I took the vase
And, testing it, as I expected to,
I found my dear wife true and constant was
And virtuous, just as I always knew.
"Now leave her for a while," Melissa says,
"Absent yourself from her a month or two
And then return and once more make the test:
See if you drink your wine or drench your chest."

31

'I found it difficult to go away;
Not that I doubted her fidelity –
I could not bear to leave her for a day,
An absence of an hour seemed hard to me.
Melissa said, "Along another way
I'll take you, where the truth you'll plainly see.
To change your face, your speech, your dress, I plan,
And send you back to her another man."

32

'Close by there is a city, you must know,
My lord, which stands as guardian between
The menacing, proud antlers of the Po.
To where the tidal waves sweep out and in
Upon the shore, its rule extends; although
Less ancient, among neighbours she's a queen:
By Trojan settlers founded, it is said,
When from the scourge of Attila they fled.

33

'The reins of power are held, now slack, now tight,
By a young lord, wealthy and fair to see,
Who, following one day his falcon's flight,
Entered my home and saw my wife; and she
So pleased him by her beauty at first sight,
Her imprint marked his heart indelibly.
From then, in his attempts he never tired
To make her yield to him as he desired.

34

'But she repulsed him time and time again,
Until he ceased to pester her at last,
But from his memory he tried in vain
To pluck her beauty, whence Love holds him fast.
Melissa, who cajoled me in the strain
I have described, a spell upon me cast,
Changing to his my face, my voice, my hair,
Though how she did it I am unaware.

35

'But first I bade my loving wife farewell,
Pretending to depart for the Levant.
Then I returned, but this no one could tell,
I so resembled her young aspirant.
Melissa had transformed herself as well:
A page attentive to my every want
She seemed, and had of gems a costlier store
Than ever Ethiop or Indian wore.

36

'Knowing my way, since my domain it is,
I walk straight in; Melissa enters too.
I find my lady sitting at her ease.
There is no footman and no woman who
Attends on her; my chance at once I seize.
I plead with her; before her eyes I strew
Emeralds, rubies, diamonds, amethysts,
A stimulus to evil none resists.

37

'I tell her that such offering is small
Compared with what she may expect from me.
I urge her to enjoy this interval
In which her husband absent plans to be.
My long devotion to her I recall.
She knew she could not fault my constancy:
Her faithful lover who so long had served
(I argued) surely some reward deserved.

38

'At first she frowned and blushed and shook her head,
And she refused to hear another word;
But when she saw those lovely jewels shed
Their fiery radiance, her heart was stirred.
Vanquished, in a low voice she briefly said
(It kills me to remember what I heard)
That she will grant the boon which I entreat
If nobody will ever hear of it.

39

'For me her answer was a poisoned dart
Which through my bones and veins an icy chill
Diffused as soon as it transfixed my heart.
My voice stuck in my throat, inaudible.
Melissa at this moment by her art
From my true form removed the magic veil.
Just think how pale my consort then became,
Perceiving I had caught her in such shame.

40

'We both turned pale as death, both silent stood
And both for very shame cast down our eyes.
My tongue does not obey me as it should,
The faltering tones I muster scarce suffice:
"And so, my consort, this is how you would
Betray your husband's honour for a price?"
She cannot answer me save by the tears
Which drench her cheeks, so stricken she appears.

41

'Great was her shame, but greater still her scorn
That I should play so base a trick on her;
And on a mounting tide of anger borne,
No sooner had the sun-god charioteer
Dismounted than, not waiting for the morn,
She acted on her plan and fled from here.
She hurried to the river and, despite
The dark, took ship and sailed all through the night.

42

'And she presents herself next day before
The cavalier who'd loved her for so long,
Under whose guise, in clothes such as he wore,
I tempted her to do me grievous wrong.
In him who loved her still and even more,
The surge of joy (you may be sure) was strong;
And later she sent word to me to say
That she would never love me from that day.

43

'Alas! she lives with him in great delight
And mocks at me and at my foolishness.
By my own fault I languish in this plight,
For which I find no cure and no redress.
My sufferings increase and it is right
That I should die soon of unhappiness.
In the first year I think I would have died
But for one thing which comfort has supplied.

44

'My comfort is that in the past decade,
Of all the men who underneath my roof
Have been received and as my guests have stayed
(And I induced them all to try this proof),
There was not one who had not been betrayed.
You are the only husband wise enough
Not to risk ruining your married life
By measuring the virtue of your wife.

45

'My eagerness beyond due bounds to see
Has meant that I shall never know again
In all my life, if long or short it be,
An hour of quietness, unracked by pain.
Melissa, overjoyed initially,
Soon saw that all her arts had been in vain.
The cause of my distress, I hated her;
To look upon her now I could not bear.

46

'Restive at being hated by the one
Whom she declared she loved more than her life
(She hoped, once she had seen her rival gone,
She would become my mistress or my wife),
From these environs she departed soon;
My coldness to her cut her like a knife.
She left this land and city far behind.
No trace of her thereafter did I find.'

47

This was the tale which the sad knight related
And when at last he brought it to an end,
Rinaldo mused; then, filled with pity, stated:
'Melissa, it is certain, was no friend;
With caution nests of hornets should be treated,
So your behaviour I do not commend.
Too little prudence then by you was shown:
You looked for what was better left unknown.

48

'If by cupidity your wife was won
And thus persuaded to break faith with you,
Be not surprised; by no means the first one
Is she, of all the married women who
Have vanquished been, or who worse things have done
For less reward, whose wills were stronger too.
And of how many men must it be said
That they their lords and friends for gold betrayed?

49

'Weapons too fierce you used against your wife,
If her resistance you desired to see.
Gold, marble, if submitted to such strife,
Even the hardest steel, will vanquished be.
You of the two were more at fault, for if
She had thus tempted you, it seems to me,
You would yourself have shown no greater strength,
But as she did, would have succumbed at length.'

50

Rinaldo ends and, rising from the board,
He asks permission to retire; he plans
To rest a while, and when he is restored,
An hour or two before the dawn's advance
He will set out, for he can now afford
But little time, and what he has he wants
To allocate with care; his host's reply
Is to point out a room where he may lie.

51

The chamber was prepared, likewise the bed,
But he put this proposal to the knight:
He could, if he desired, be swiftly sped
For several miles in somnolent delight.
'A little ship I'll fit you out,' he said,
'Which will convey you safely through the night,
And you will gain a journey of a day,
Which will advance you nicely on your way.'

52

Rinaldo found this offer to his taste
And fervently he thanked his kindly host;
Then straightway, since he had no time to waste,
He went on board, and there with the utmost
Enjoyment he lay down at ease to rest.
The sailors, who expected him, then loosed
The ropes; the little ship, sped by six oars,
Skimmed like a bird along the river's course.

53

No sooner did the cavalier of France
Lay down his head than he was sleeping fast;
He'd said he wanted to be roused at once
When they approached Ferrara. First they passed
Melara on the port side; then a glance
To starboard upon Sermide they cast.
By Figarola and Stellata next they slipped
Where Po its threatening horns in anger dipped.

54

Of the two horns the pilot chose the right,
Letting the left-hand course towards Venice flow.
He passed Bondeno, and the blue of night
In the east sky now pale began to show,
As all the flowers in her basket, white
And red, Dawn scattered in a single throw.
When from afar the turrets of Tealdo
Came into view, a noise awoke Rinaldo.

55

'Most fortunate of cities!' he exclaimed,
'Of thee my cousin Malagigi read
In stars and planets, and a demon tamed
To tell him of the years that lie ahead
And of the glories which for thee are framed
By Destiny; all this to me he said,
Foretelling thy supremacy and sway
When we were travelling along this way.'

56

Such were his words; the boat sped on meanwhile
As if the sailors plied not oars but wings.
Along the king of rivers to the isle
Which near the city lies, the knight it brings.
Bare it was then, and of its future style
There was no sign, yet in his heart there springs
Great joy; he hails it as they pass, for he
Knows well how lovely it will one day be.

57

When he had passed this way before, he learned
From Malagigi, when the solar sphere
Had seven hundred times with Aries turned
This little island would be lovelier
Than any other which renown had earned.
Its beauty being held beyond compare,
No one who saw it would thereafter praise
Nausicaa's island, as in olden days.

58

And for fine buildings it would be preferred
To the fair isle loved by Tiberius;
And the Hesperides would yield, he heard,
As to exotic plants; so plenteous
The breeds of animal that Circe's herd,
In sty and stable, was less numerous;
The Graces, Venus, Cupid there would dwell,
Cyprus and Cnidus leaving, strange to tell.

59

And all these future wonders would be due
To the devoted zeal and care of one
Whose power and knowledge would be added to
His wish to make the city so immune
By dykes and walls that she need fear no foe,
Nor ever call for aid from anyone.
The father and the son of Hercules
Would be the lord who would accomplish this.

60

In such a way Rinaldo called to mind
All that his cousin in the stars had read
When things which were to come he had divined
(They often spoke about what lay ahead).
Before they left the lowly town behind,
He gazed in awe and to himself he said:
'How can it be that from this marsh will rise
Such arts and learning, liberal and wise?

61

'How from so small a village can so wide
A city grow – and one so beautiful?
And what is swamp and bog on every side
Be changed to fields, smiling and plentiful?
City, I greet thee, and with joy and pride
Rise to revere thy lords who here will rule,
Their love, their deeds of fame and courtesy,
The knights' and citizens' nobility.

62

'May the Redeemer in His boundless good,
May justice in thy princes, kind and wise,
Keep thee in happiness and plenitude
With lasting peace and love which never dies.
On thy defences may no foes intrude:
Let all their wiles be known and all their lies.
May all thy neighbours rage at thy success,
Rather than thou of them be envious.'

63

While he thus speaks, the little vessel speeds
Along the waters of the river Po
So fast no peregrine its pace exceeds
When, summoned to the lure, it drops below.
The right-hand branch once more the pilot heeds.
The walls and roofs of San Gregorio
They leave behind; behind them too, afar,
Gaibana's and La Fossa's towers are.

64

Rinaldo, as it happens when one thought
Leads to another, which leads on again,
To a remembrance of the knight was brought
Who had invited him to his domain
To dine; this was the city not for naught
His host had cause to recollect with pain,
And he reflected on the drinking-cup
Which shows a woman's misdemeanours up.

65

And he recalled the story of the test
Which the knight told him he had carried out,
How every man who tried it drenched his chest,
How of their wives' misdeeds there was no doubt.
Now he repents, now says, 'No, it was best
For me that I decided not to put
My consort to the proof. What could I gain?
A confirmation of my trust, or pain.

66

'My faith is just as strong as if I knew
For certain, so not much is there to add.
If in the test my wife had been proved true,
Small benefit from that I would have had;
From the reverse no small ill would accrue.
To spy upon my Clarice I'd be mad:
Better a thousand-to-one chance than try it,
And lose so much or gain so little by it.'

67

And while the cavalier sat musing thus,
His face held low, a steersman opposite
Fixed him with eyes intent and curious.
He thought he knew what had induced this fit
Of pensiveness, and judged it courteous
To draw him out and make him speak of it;
And like a man articulate and bold
The topic he resolves now to unfold.

68

And the conclusion of their argument
Was that the husband ill-advised had been
To test his wife by an experiment
Such as no woman ever could sustain;
She who can stand against an armament
Of gold and silver and still pure remain,
Would find a thousand swords' attack less dire
A peril, or survive in raging fire.

69

The boatman added, 'You were right to say
That he was wrong to offer her such riches.
Not every breast presented to the fray
Stands fast in combat, as experience teaches.
I wonder if you know the tale (you may,
If rumour of it to your country reaches)
Of the young wife condemned to die for sin –
The same as she then caught her husband in?

70

'My master ought to have remembered what
A glittering prize can do to bend the will,
Yet at the crucial moment he forgot
And all his fortune changed from good to ill.
Both he and I hail from the very spot
Where the events occurred which I now tell,
The city which a marsh and lake enclose,
Where at a sluggish pace the Mincio flows.

71

'I mean the story of Adonio
Who gave the judge's wife a dog – a rare
And costly gift.' 'This tale we do not know,'
Rinaldo said, 'in France or anywhere
North of the Alps where I have been, and so
Tell on, if you don't mind, while I prepare
Most willingly to listen to the tale
With which my mind you promise to regale.'

72

The boatman thus began: 'Once in our town
There lived a man, well born, who lacked for naught,
Who spent his youth clad in the flowing gown
Of those who study what Ulpianus taught.
Anselmo was his name, of high renown.
A noble and a virtuous wife he sought,
And one near by, most beautiful he found,
Who to his fame and honour would redound.

73

'Her ways so winning and so gracious were,
She seemed all love and loveliness combined.
She was perhaps more amorous, I fear,
Than was conducive to his peace of mind.
As soon as he had won and married her,
No husband more suspicious could you find:
And yet he had no reason save this cause:
That she too lovely and too loving was.

74

'In the same city lived a noble knight
Whose ancient lineage was held in awe,
For he descended from that race of might
Which sprang from teeth sown from a serpent's jaw,
Whence Manto too descended, and some write
That its beginnings thence my city saw.
Adonio the knight was named; and he
This lovely lady loved most ardently.

75

'And to achieve fulfilment of this love
The knight began without restraint to spend
On clothing and on feasts, his worth to prove,
And lustre to his reputation lend.
Such squandering would soon the treasure of
Tiberius the Emperor expend.
I do not think two winters had gone by
Before his patrimony had run dry.

76

'The house, which formerly from morn to eve
Was thronged with all his friends, deserted is,
For they depart as soon as they perceive
There will be no more quails and partridges.
The leader of the junketing they leave;
Almost a beggar's portion now is his,
And he resolves, since all his wealth is flown,
To seek asylum where he is unknown.

77

'Without a word to anyone at all,
One morning he departs; with tears and sighs
He walks along the lake outside the wall.
His lady (nay, his queen) is in no wise
Forgotten for she holds him still in thrall,
And as he wanders in this woeful guise
Lo! Fortune turns her wheel to lift him high
From grief to joy supernal by and by.

78

'A peasant with a cudgel, thick and stout,
He sees belabouring a bush, and so
He stops and asks him what he is about.
The peasant's answer to Adonio
Is that he saw a snake, he has no doubt:
There in the undergrowth he saw it go,
The longest, thickest which had ever been,
The oldest too that ever could be seen.

79

'He was determined not to go away
Till he had found and killed the snake; the knight
Was angered by the things he heard him say.
Since he liked snakes, his patience was but slight.
It was his forebears' custom to display
A serpent as their emblem, and of right,
In pious memory of how they sprang
From a snake's teeth, as many poets sang.

80

'With words and deeds he makes the peasant drop
The task in hand and soon, though grumblingly,
He is persuaded he had better stop.
The serpent is not killed, nor yet will be
Pursued or hurt; the sport being given up,
The knight resumes his way and finally
A region reaches where *incognito*
He lives for seven years in grief and woe.

81

'Distance and straitened means (which do not give
The thoughts much freedom to go wandering)
Love's ruthless hold on him do not relieve.
His heart is burning yet, his wounds still sting.
At last he knows he can no longer live
Without the solace she alone can bring;
So, bearded, bowed with sorrow and ill-clad,
He travelled back where he departed had.

82

'It happened that my city had to send
A legate to the papal court at Rome,
Who with His Holiness would have to spend
A time unspecified ere he came home.
The lots are drawn, the judge gets the short end.
Ill-omened day! What sorrow was to come!
He made excuses, promised, bribed and pleaded,
But *force majeure* he finally conceded.

83

'The pain and grief seem no less hard to bear
Than if he saw his bosom torn apart
And if a cruel hand should then appear
And mercilessly snatch away his heart.
His face is ashy pale with jealous fear:
What will his wife do when they are apart?
He tries all means to make his wife obey him;
He begs and pleads that she will not betray him.

84

'He says not beauty, not nobility,
Not fortune will suffice to raise a wife
To highest honour and esteem if she
Neglects to lead a chaste and seemly life;
He says most valued is that chastity
Which, tested, does not yield, whate'er the strife.
Now his departure will provide a chance
For her to practise wifely abstinence.

85

'With words like these and many others too
He tried to coax his consort to be chaste.
She wept and promised that she would be true.
Her tears along her cheeks each other chased.
She could not bear to think he had to go.
She swore the sun in heaven would be effaced
Ere she so cruel to her love would be;
She'd rather die than think of it, said she.

86

'Though he believed her promises and vows
And by her tears was somewhat reassured,
His mind was not at rest about his spouse
Till further information he procured
(And further grief, which this was bound to cause).
He had a friend (whom would he had abjured!):
Of every sorcery and magic art
He knew the whole, or else the greater part.

87

'He begged this sorcerer and wheedled him
His wife Argìa's constancy to test:
Would she be faithful in the interim,
Or would she in temptation prove unchaste?
The fortune-teller yielded to his whim.
Choosing the moment which he judged was best,
He charted out the aspect of the sky.
The judge returned next day for the reply.

88

'The lips of the astrologer were sealed.
He did not wish to cause the lawyer pain.
Making excuses, he tried not to yield,
But when he saw his efforts were in vain,
That she would be unfaithful, he revealed,
As soon as he stepped forth from his domain.
Not beauty, not entreaties would induce her,
The bribery of riches would seduce her.

89

'How such a warning from the spheres above,
Combined with doubts which had assailed him first,
Weighed on Anselmo's heart, if you know love,
You can imagine for yourself; the worst
Affliction, so the lawyer judges, of
All those with which his soul is now accurst,
Is knowing that his consort's chastity
By avarice thus overcome will be.

90

'He took all the precautions he could take
To stop her falling into such a pit.
(Want is a master which can sometimes make
A man the gravest sacrilege commit.)
Jewels and gold (of which he has no lack)
He gives to her to use as she sees fit;
Income and benefits from all his lands,
All that he has, he places in her hands.

91

' "Feel free", he said, "to spend it as you will,
Not only for your pleasures and your needs:
Squander it, lavish, throw away or sell,
Do as you wish, whatever Fancy bids.
I hold you for one thing accountable:
When Fate at last my footsteps homeward leads,
If you restore yourself intact to me,
Do as you like with all my property."

92

'He begs her, till she hears of his return,
To leave the thronging city far away
And to their villa prudently adjourn,
In rustic sweet contentment there to stay.
The humble folk who work from early morn
Till eve, tending the sheep or making hay,
Unlikely are, he thinks, to tempt his wife,
Who chastely longs to live an unstained life.

93

'Argìa held her lovely arms embraced
About her apprehensive husband's neck,
Wetting his countenance with tears which raced
Like a small river that she could not check.
It saddened her to think, as if unchaste
She were, he sought to keep her thus in check,
For such suspicion must arise, i' faith,
Because her husband lacks in *her* faith, faith.

94

'Long it would be if I were to repeat
What at their parting by them both was said.
"Be careful of my honour, I entreat,"
He says at last and mounts upon his steed.
He turns: his heart no longer seems to beat;
It is as if it left his breast indeed.
He rides away: to follow him she seeks
With eyes which overflow and drench her cheeks.

95

'Meanwhile Adonio, forlorn and sad
And bearded, as I said before, and wan,
Some progress on his homeward journey made.
Not recognized, he hoped, by anyone,
He reached the lake where he had given aid
To an old serpent which a countryman
Was busy searching for amid the scrub,
Wanting to kill it with his heavy club.

96

'He had arrived just at the break of day
When a few stars still twinkled in the sky.
A damsel came towards him on the way,
Attired for travel; though escorted by
No page or maid, in every other way
She seemed to be of noble birth and high.
She gave him greeting with a friendly smile
And afterwards addressed him in this style:

97

'"Although you do not know me, cavalier,
I am your kinswoman and in your debt.
First, how we are related you must hear:
We both descend from Cadmus. I who set
The first stone of a village yonder there
Am Manto: and my name is living yet
In Mantua, for as perhaps you know
'Twas thus I named the city long ago.

98

'"I am a sorceress; let me explain
Just what this fateful status signifies.
We are so born that all ills we sustain,
Save only death; but you must realize
Our immortality is tinged with pain
As sharp as death and all that it implies.
For, every seventh day we have to take
Another shape, the dread form of a snake.

99

'"We see our bodies slither on the ground.
We see them clad in ugly reptile scales.
In all the world no equal grief is found;
Each sorceress her cursèd state bewails.
The debt I owe to you I will expound
As well as what a serpent's life entails,
For when we change our forms, as you must see,
We are exposed to endless jeopardy.

100

'"No creature is so hated as a snake
And we who its appearance must put on
Suffer relentless outrage and attack,
For we are chased and hit by everyone.
If refuge underground we do not take
We feel the weight of missiles plied or thrown.
Better it were to die than to remain
Lamed and disabled by the blows which rain.

101

'"My obligation to you thus is great,
For, once when you were passing through this grove,
You rescued me from an unhappy fate.
Beating around a bush, a peasant strove
To kill me; but for you, the sorry state
I'd have been in does not bear thinking of,
With fractured skull, crippled and broken-backed
(Though power to demolish me he lacked);

102

'"For on the days when slithering we trail
Our bodies in a snake's involucre,
At other times submissive to our will,
Heaven our incantations does not hear.
At other times, we speak: the sun stands still,
Its light is minished, darkness clouds its sphere,
The earth, no longer stable, spins and wheels,
Ice kindles, and fire freezes and congeals.

103

'"I am here now to give you a reward
For the great favour which you did me then.
No boon that you can ask me is too hard,
Now I no longer wear my viper's skin.
Your father left you rich, but as my ward
You will be thrice as rich: never again
Will you be poor; henceforth the more you spend
The more your wealth will grow, and never end.

104

'"By that same knot you are still bound, I know,
Which Love in former years about·you tied.
The manner and the method I will show
Whereby your longings may be satisfied.
I hear her husband is abroad; with no
Delay, I want this venture to be tried:
Seek out your lady at her country seat.
I will come with you, if you will permit."

105

'And she proceeded to explain what guise
He must adopt, how he must dress, how speak,
How he must plead his suit, and how entice.
Meanwhile she plans the form which she will take,
For she is able to assume disguise
(Save on the days when she becomes a snake)
As any creature she desires to be
Of all of Nature's vast variety.

106

'She dressed him in a pilgrim's garb, like one
Who begs for alms for God from door to door.
She changed into a dog, so tiny none
So small was seen in Nature's world before.
Its long-haired coat whiter than ermine shone.
Of pleasing little tricks it had a store.
Disguised like this, together they draw near
The country-dwelling of Argìa the fair.

107

'At first outside the gates the young man stopped
And on some pipes at once began to play.
The little dog reared up and danced and hopped.
The sound was heard both near and far away.
His lady to the window went and propped
Her elbows; then to Adonio sent to say
That he was welcome in her court below
(The judge's destiny had willed it so).

108

'Adonio accepted and began
To put the little dog through all its paces.
In dances, foreign and Italian,
With entrechats its steps it interlaces.
Obeying orders like a little man,
It bows and pirouettes and about-faces,
And so amazed are all who watch it that
They scarcely breathe and not an eyelid bat.

109

'Argìa, by amazement overcome,
Longed to possess the charming animal
And offered, through her nurse, a goodly sum.
The wily pilgrim had no wish to sell
And he returned an answer with aplomb
(Instructed by the sorceress): "Not all
The wealth which female greed would satisfy
One single paw of this my dog could buy."

110

'To show the nurse the truth of what he said
He drew her confidentially aside.
He told the dog, which did as it was bade,
A bright new golden ducat to provide.
It shook itself: a coin was promptly shed.
He gave it to the nurse and added, "I'd
Be glad to hear if you can name a price
Which for a dog so useful could suffice.

111

'"Whatever treasure I request of it,
I never come away with empty hands.
Pearls, rings and bracelets tumble at my feet,
Sometimes a fine brocaded garment lands.
But tell your lady, though no gold could meet
The price (and this make sure she understands),
If she will let me lie with her one night,
I'll let her have this dog for her delight."

112

'The little dog shook out a gem, unmatched,
Intended by Adonio for his love.
The nurse all these proceedings closely watched;
She rated the dog's value high above
The ten or twenty marks she was despatched
To offer; and her lady she then strove
To influence to buy the dog; the cost
Was such that what she paid would not be lost.

113

'At first the fair Argìa hesitates;
Partly, she does not wish to break her word;
Partly, the miracles her nurse relates
Appear impossible, if not absurd.
The nurse keeps on at her and nags and prates:
Rarely has fortune good as this occurred.
Argìa yields, and sets a day to see
The dog when fewer witnesses there'll be.

114

'And when Adonio appeared once more
The judge's honour was as good as dead.
For as doubloons were scattered by the score
And strings of pearls and countless gems were shed,
Argìa's heart was melted to the core.
Learning he was no pilgrim but instead
The knight who long ago for love of her
Had left, she lowered the last barrier.

115

'The urgings of her nurse (no prude was she!),
Her lover's pleas, his presence in her room,
The gain he spreads before her temptingly,
The prolonged absence of the judge in Rome,
The hope that she would not discovered be,
Argìa's chaste resolve soon overcome.
She takes the little dog; prepared to pay
The price, she yields, as lover and as prey.

116

'Adonio long enjoyed the fruit he plucked.
His lady by the spell was set alight
With love and greed, and only with reluct-
ance let the little dog out of her sight.
The sun through all his signs a year had clocked
Before the judge was granted a respite.
He left at last – but with misgivings filled,
By the astrologer's forecast instilled.

117

'When he arrived he went at once to call
On the astrologer: was his wife chaste,
Or did she, as he had predicted, fall?
A chart was plotted by the seer in haste
Which figured the position of the pole,
And every planet in its mansion placed.
Then he replied that just as he had feared,
And had foretold, the judge's wife had erred.

118

'His wife by precious gifts seduced had been
And fallen prey to a skilled predator.
The judge's heart received a blow so keen,
It pierced him deeper than a dagger or
A lance; but first, the truth to ascertain
(Although of the diviner he was sure),
He went to find the nurse, and all his skill
In questioning he used, to make her tell.

119

'Approaching in wide circles, round and round
He went, trying his best to scent the trace.
At first no vestige anywhere he found,
Despite the care he lavished on the case.
The nurse, who was no novice, held her ground.
She just said "No" with an impassive face.
More than a month she fenced so skilfully
He dangled between doubt and certainty.

120

'How sweet his doubt would seem if he but knew
The grief and pain which certainty would bring!
His soft speech and his presents nothing drew;
The nurse could not persuaded be to sing.
None of the keys he played upon rang true,
So, wisely, he deferred his questioning
Until she had a quarrel with his wife:
Where women are, are arguments and strife.

121

'As he expected, so it came about:
A tiff between the women soon occurred.
The nurse at once returned to him, without
Being asked, and every detail, every word,
Reported to him, leaving nothing out.
The pain he suffered when the truth he heard,
His consternation, would be long to tell;
A prey to madness soon the husband fell.

122

'And he resolved in an access of rage
To end it all, but first to kill his spouse:
By the same blade his sorrow to assuage
And her misdeeds to punish; back he goes
To town a trusty henchman to engage,
And, driven by the frenzy of his woes,
He sends him to the villa straight away,
Giving strict orders which he must obey.

123

'The henchman is to seek the judge's wife
And in his name inform her that he lies
Stricken with fever so severe his life
Hangs by the merest thread; not otherwise
Escorted she must come to see him, if
She loves him – and on this the judge relies;
He bids the trusty henchman also note
That on the way he is to cut her throat.

124

'The servant went to do his master's will.
The lady seized her dog, and on her steed
Set out; the dog had cautioned her, but still
Advised her on her journey to proceed;
She could rely upon its canine skill
To give her what assistance she might need.
It had already planned what it would do
When finally too close the danger drew.

125

'The henchman left the highway far behind;
Along strange, solitary paths he rode,
Then to a stream he came, as he designed,
Which to this river from the mountains flowed.
Here a dark wood its branches intertwined;
No city was near by and no abode.
This seemed a quiet, likely spot to him
To execute his master's cruel scheme.

126

'The henchman bared his deadly weapon now;
But first he told her of the gruesome task
He must perform (he did this to allow
Her to confess her sins, and pardon ask).
She disappeared – I cannot tell you how –
Behind what must have been a magic mask,
Just as the blow descended; everywhere
He sought her, then could only stand and stare.

127

'And to the judge returning, much dismayed,
His face expressing deep astonishment,
He told him everything that passed, and said
He still could not account for the event.
The husband did not know Argìa had
The help of Manto – whether by intent
Or oversight, the nurse omitted it,
Though she had told him every other bit.

128

'He wonders what to do; the grave affront
Is unavenged, his woes remain the same;
His anguished heart has still to bear the brunt;
What was a mote has now become a beam;
The case was secret, but a full account
Will soon be known to many, thanks to him.
Argìa's sin could have remained concealed,
But his to all the world will be revealed.

129

'Now that his consort knows his evil plan
(The wretched husband sees this very well),
She'll never to his rule submit again;
And his dishonour will be visible
If she takes shelter with another man;
The mockery will be unbearable.
Perhaps she'll even fall a victim to
A lewd seducer who's a pander too.

130

'Hoping the worst disasters to prevent,
Throughout all Lombardy, in every town,
Letters and messengers in haste he sent
To ask her whereabouts and track her down,
Then in pursuit of her in person went;
No path was unexplored, unturned no stone,
Yet not a single clue could he uncover,
Nor any news of where she was discover.

131

'At last he called the henchman whom he bade
Perform the cruel deed which came to naught,
And went with him to where Argìa had
Concealed herself; by day, the husband thought,
She might have hidden in the bush and made,
When darkness fell, for shelter in a hut.
The henchman led the way towards the wood
(As he believed), but there a palace stood.

132

'Argìa's sorceress (at her request)
Had conjured up with instantaneous
Effect an alabaster palace, dressed
With gold inside and out, more beauteous
Than heart has ever dreamed or tongue expressed,
In all its contents rich and sumptuous.
My master's, which your admiration won,
Would seem a hovel by comparison.

133

'Woven with costliest materials,
Curtains and arrases and tapestry
Adorned the cellars, outhouses and stalls,
As well as rooms prepared for company.
The tables glitter in the dining-halls
With gold and silver vessels; gems they see
Carved into goblets, cups and many a plate,
Red, blue and green, and silken cloth ornate.

134

'The judge (as I was saying) came upon
This palace suddenly where nothing but
A forest should have been; and like a stone
He stood, so great were his surprise and doubt.
Amazed, he wondered if his wits had flown,
Or if he was asleep or drunk; a hut
He might have credited perhaps, but this
Beyond belief in his opinion is.

135

'Before the gate he sees an Ethiop,
Broad-nosed, thick-lipped; the judge would roundly
This of all ugly faces is the top.   [swear
Comparison with Aesop he would bear.
The music of the spheres would surely stop
If this monstrosity in heaven were.
Greasy and dirty, like a beggar dressed –
Still only half his squalor is expressed.

136

'Anselmo (who no other person spies),
Longing to know who owns this fine abode,
Questions the Ethiop, and he replies,
"This house is mine." Anselmo, in no mood
For foolery, is certain that he lies.
And yet in spite of threats, the Negro stood
His ground and reaffirmed repeatedly
That the sole owner of the house was he.

137

'And he invites Anselmo on a tour:
Would he not like to see inside? If there
Is anything which takes his fancy for
Himself or for his friends, as if it were
His own he is to take it; without more
Ado the judge dismounts (his squire is near)
And, through the sumptuous apartments led,
The house from top to bottom visited.

138

'To the design, the site, the taste, the skill,
The opulence, the judge attention pays.
"Not all the gold on earth would meet the bill
For such a noble edifice," he says.
The Moor replies, "There's one thing which I will
Accept for it and which the price defrays:
Not gold or silver, but a payment which
Costs you so little that it leaves you rich."

139

'And to the judge he put the same request
Which to his wife Adonio had made.
Anselmo thinks, so deep is his disgust,
The Ethiop is bestial and mad.
Rejected thrice, four times, the Moor still pressed,
In many ways attempting to persuade.
The palace won the day and, as he hoped,
To his vile wish at last Anselmo stooped.

140

'Argìa, hiding all this time quite close,
Seeing her husband fall, at once leapt out
And cried, "Ah! What a venerable pose
For one so learned and of such repute!"
Discovered in a deed so vile and gross,
Anselmo blushed bright scarlet and was mute.
O earth! why did you not split open wide
That he might plunge into your depths and hide?

141

'Excusing what she did, she poured reproach
Upon Anselmo till his eardrums split:
"What punishment in justice could approach
The sin which with this monster you commit?
To Nature's urge I yielded and with such
A lover – handsome, noble, as was fit!
For this you tried to kill me, though as naught
This palace is to the rare gift he brought.

142

'"And if you think that I deserved to die,
You ought to die a hundred times; but though
Here in this place I have such strength that I
Could do with you just as I liked, yet no
More vengeance I desire; let us then try
To give and take on equal terms, and so
Now, husband, on this bargain let's agree:
I'll pardon you if you will pardon me.

143

'"Let us make peace; in mutual accord
Let our past sins to Limbo be consigned,
And let us ne'er again in deed or word
Each other of each other's lapse remind."
These terms the husband thought he could afford
And to forgive he was not disinclined.
Thus joined once more in peace and harmony,
For ever after they lived happily.'

144

This was the story which the pilot told.
Rinaldo laughed a little at the end,
Though he blushed red on hearing how the old
And learnèd judge to such disgrace could lend
Himself; he praised Argìa for her bold
And clever plan: she made the bird descend
And with the very net she caught him, in
Which she too fell, but for a lesser sin.

145

As the sun journeyed higher up the sky
A meal before the paladin was laid.
(The host had not neglected to supply
A plentiful provision for his need.)
To port, the lovely countryside slipped by;
A vast and stagnant marsh to starboard spread.
Where the Santerno noses to the shore,
Argenta's walls are passed, then seen no more.

146

Bastia, I think, scarcely existed then,
Of which the Spaniards have small cause to boast,
Despite their flaunted flag; Romagna's men
Will there bewail a still more bitter cost.
The boat speeds on as if it flies again:
The reach to Filo is direct almost.
Then through a sluggish ditch they make their way,
Which brings them to Ravenna at midday.

147

Though many times the paladin was low
In funds, this time he was so flush he tipped
The rowers lavishly; he was not slow
To take his leave; a steady pace he kept,
With frequent change of horse and groom, and so
Passed Rimini; that night he never slept
But, leaving Montefiore, galloped on,
Reaching Urbino with the morning sun.

148

There was no Federigo in those days;
Elisabetta, Guidobaldo brave,
Francesco, Leonora beyond praise,
Were not yet born, else they would surely have
Insisted firmly (but in courteous ways)
That such a knight who proofs of valour gave
Should be their guest, a custom they for years
Have kept with passing dames and cavaliers.

149

Since no one ran to hold his bridle there,
Rinaldo rode straight down to Cagli; then
He crossed the Apennines precisely where
The Gauno and Metauro cleave them, when
No longer on his right the mountains were.
Tuscany, Umbria, Rome, and west again
To Ostia, and thence across the sea
To where Anchises lies at Tràpani.

150

Here he changed ships, and for the island made
Which had been chosen for the final test
Whereon the six their confrontation had.
Rinaldo bids the boatmen make all haste,
Urging the oarsmen to lend timely aid.
The winds, being contrary, do not assist:
They cause the paladin, to his disgust,
To reach the isle too late, but only just.

151

He landed at the moment when Anglante
His glorious and useful deed had done,
Gradasso having slain, and Agramante,
But with a bloody victory, hard won,
Costing the life of the heir of Monodante;
And Oliver, his ankle broken, on
The sand lay pinned beneath a heavy weight,
In pain and suffering obliged to wait.

152

The Count wept bitterly, for all he tried,
Then he embraced Rinaldo and related
How his dear faithful Brandimart had died;
And when Rinaldo saw him mutilated,
His head split through, he could not stay dry-eyed.
Not long to mourn for him he hesitated,
But ran to comfort Oliver who lay,
His foot beneath his charger, as I say.

153

Rinaldo comforted, as best he could,
His two companions, but himself remained
Disconsolate; for him there was no food,
This feast of glory was now at an end.
Attendants bore their monarch, as they should,
And bore Gradasso too, their monarch's friend,
Back to the ruins of Biserta, where
They hid them and made known the tidings there.

154

Orlando's victory rejoiced the heart
Of Sansonetto and the English duke,
But less so when they heard that Brandimart
No longer on the light of day would look.
Their joy was much diminished by the smart,
And gladness now their countenance forsook.
How could they let fair Fiordiligi know
The tidings of such grievous loss and woe?

155

The night before, sweet Fiordiligi dreamed:
The coat which covered Brandimarte's mail,
Which she with skill for him had stitched and hemmed
To send him suitably adorned to sail
To Lampedusa, in her vision seemed
With crimson spots all spattered, as by hail.
She thought that she had thus embroidered it
And in her dream was filled with vain regret.

156

She seemed to say, 'My lord instructed me
To make for him a surcoat all of black.
Why did I do this strange embroidery
And for his wish consideration lack?'
This dream, she thought, was a bad augury.
The news, announced that evening, was held back
Until the duke and Sansonetto went
To tell her of the tragical event.

157

When in their eyes she saw no triumph shine
At such a victory in such a war,
She knew without a word, without a sign,
Her Brandimarte was alive no more;
And at a premonition so malign
Her heart is overwhelmed, her eyes abhor
The light, and all her senses lifeless grow
As like a corpse her body falls below.

158

When she revives, she lacerates her cheeks,
Calling in vain upon her husband's name.
A savage vengeance on herself she wreaks,
Tearing her tresses in her frenzied aim.
Like one possessed by demons, loud she shrieks,
Or as (we hear) the Maenads wild became
And rushed together at the shrill horn's sound,
She writhes and twists and whirls herself around.

159

Now one and now the other she beseeches
To let her plunge a dagger in her breast;
Now she would run to where the vessel beaches,
Bringing the pagan monarchs to their rest,
And when their lifeless bodies there she reaches,
Wreak bitter vengeance on them like a beast;
Now to the island sail across and try
To find her love and near his body die.

160

'Ah, Brandimarte!' she exclaimed, 'alas!
Why did I let you go without me to
So great a contest, to so dire a pass?
Your Fiordiligi always followed you;
No journey, combat, trial came to pass
But I was present, vigilant and true.
I could have helped you: if Gradasso tried
To come behind, a warning I'd have cried;

161

'Or else I might have intervened at speed
And taken on myself the mortal blow,
Making a buckler for you of my head.
If I had died, the cost would have been low,
For soon in any case I shall be dead,
And profitless will be my death by woe.
If I had died defending you, a wife
Could in no better way have lost her life.

162

'But if harsh Fate and if the whole of Heaven
My efforts to assist you had denied,
A last embrace at least I could have given,
Drenching your visage with the tears I cried;
And ere your spirit, from your body riven,
Rose to the choirs of the beatified,
"Go now in peace," I'd say, "wait there for me,
For I will join you wheresoe'er you be."

163

'Is this, O Brandimart, is this your reign?
Like this you claim your sceptre for your own?
Is this the way I enter the domain
Of Dammogir, like this ascend your throne?
Ah, cruel Fortune, with what harsh disdain
You thwart my plans! Ah, what sweet hopes are flown!
Since I have lost the loveliest and best
Of life, why do I wait to lose the rest?'

164

With these and other words, she fell once more
To tearing out her lovely locks as though
For this calamity the blame they bore.
Her frenzy and her rage possessed her so,
She bit her hands, her lips and bosom tore
With merciless and savage nails; but to
The Count Orlando and his comrades I
Return and leave her to lament and cry.

165

The Count with Oliver (who had great need
Of medical attention for his foot),
To order worthy burial for their dead
Companion, for that mountain now set out
Whose fires light up the dark, and darkness spread
Across the face of day; ere long the boat,
Propelled by a fair wind, drew near the shore
Which to the right located was, not far.

166

When evening had descended, off they cast,
The wind being favourable at close of day.
Amid the dark the silent goddess passed
And with her horn of silver lit the way.
On the next morning they arrived at last
Where Agrigento's pleasant coastline lay.
Orlando here the ceremonial
Arranged for Brandimarte's burial.

167

When his instructions were completed quite
And all the splendour of the day was spent,
Nobles whom he deemed proper to invite
Came flocking from near by to the event.
As flaming torches to the shore give light,
Amid a wailing chorus of lament
The Count returns to where his comrade lies,
Loved in his life and loved in his demise.

168

Bardino wept beside the funeral bier,
Bowed down beneath the burden of his age.
So much he'd wept on board on the way there
He scarce had eyes to weep with; to assuage
His pain, he cùrsed the stars in his despair
And like a fevered lion roared in rage,
While on his agèd locks and face assault
His frenzied hands committed in revolt.

169

There rose, upon the paladin's return,
A louder wailing, a redoubled cry.
The Count Orlando, silent and forlorn,
To Brandimarte's càdaver drew nigh;
A lily in the evening plucked at morn
Is not more pallid; drawing a deep sigh,
Keeping his eyes fixed on that countenance
Orlando voiced this woeful utterance:

170

'O my belovèd comrade, strong and true!
Here dead to us, in Heaven you now live;
A life no heat or·cold can take from you
Is the reward which you have gained. Forgive
My tears; I weep that I am left below.
This is the only reason why I grieve:
That with you in your joy I cannot be,
But not that you are not on earth with me.

171

'Without you I'm alone, and nothing more
On earth which I possess will give me pleasure.
Ever in tempest with you and in war:
Ah, why not now in fair winds and in leisure?
This clay imprisons me, I cannot soar
And follow you; ah, failure beyond measure!
If I companioned you in strife and pain,
Why am I not beside you in your gain?

172

'For you have gained and I have lost; alone
You stand, but in my sorrow many share:
France, Italy and Germany bemoan
Your death; my lord and uncle, every peer,
How bitterly they'll grieve now you are gone!
How will the Church, how will the Empire fare?
The greatest champion of all, the most
Secure defence, the bravest now is lost.

173

'Ah, how the terror of the enemy
Will lessen at the news of your demise!
Ah, how much stronger Pagandom will be!
What courage now will sparkle in their eyes!
Ah, how your consort suffers! Bitterly
I see her weep, I hear her anguished cries.
Me she accuses, perhaps hates me too,
Since all her hopes by me are slain with you.

174

'But Fiordiligi, let this comfort us
Who of our Brandimarte are bereft:
He's envied for a death so glorious
By all the warriors who alive are left.
For not the Decii, not Curtius
Who leapt into the Roman Forum's cleft,
Not Codros, so esteemed by the Argives,
Achieved more honour when they gave their lives.'

175

These words Orlando said, and others too.
Meanwhile the friars, black and grey and white,
With other clergy, walking two by two,
Formed a long line; observing every rite,
They prayed that God would grant admittance to
This soul to rest in the supernal height.
Candles before, behind, along the way,
The sombre evening seemed to change to day.

176

The bier was lifted, and the bearers, placed
Alternately, were counts and cavaliers;
Purple the silken pall, on which was traced
A rich design in gold, with pearls for tears;
And no less splendid work the pillows graced,
Adorned with gems by skilled embroiderers.
In purple robed likewise, there lay the knight,
With jewels glittering, a regal sight.

177

A column of three hundred men precedes,
Chosen among the poorest in the land,
All dressed alike in long, black mourning weeds
Which sweep the ground; they're followed by a band
Of squires, a hundred on as many steeds,
Strong, sturdy thoroughbreds, for battle trained.
Both squires and horses being draped *en deuil*,
Their garb as they passed onward brushed the soil.

178

Banners before the hearse, banners behind,
In proud heraldic colourful display
Fluttered their diverse emblems in the wind,
Trophies of many a victorious fray
Fought against foes in Africa and Ind
For Christendom, by him who lifeless lay;
And many shields of vanquished warriors
Were borne along, the spoils of many wars.

179

Hundreds of others followed who fulfilled
Yet other roles in the procession; these,
Like all the others, lighted torches held.
They too were clad in sombre draperies,
Or truer it would be to say, concealed.
The Count comes next; his weeping copious is;
Rinaldo, no more joyful, follows him;
Not Oliver, by reason of his limb.

180

Long it would take to tell you in my verse
Of all the ceremonies, all the lines
Of mourners clad in mantles black or perse,
Of torches flaring till their light declines.
To the cathedral they escort the hearse.
The knight such valour, beauty, youth combines,
In all that concourse not an eye is dry;
The young, the old, the men, the women cry.

181

They laid him in the church; when useless tears
Were wept by women, when eleisons
Were chanted over him and holy prayers,
Such as for funerals a priest intones,
They set the precious casket on two piers,
Draped temporarily (this the Count condones)
With cloth of gold, until a sepulchre
More seemly could be made and costlier.

182

From Sicily the Count did not depart
Till he had sent for marbles, alabasters,
And ordered at high price a work of art,
Designed and sculpted by the finest masters;
When Fiordiligi came, she played her part,
Supplying panels and superb pilasters,
Which, when the Count had gone, she ordered from
North African deposits, for the tomb.

183

Her tears continued inexhaustible,
Her sighs unceasing issued from her breast.
The masses she recited, prayers as well,
Procured for her no respite in the least;
So she conceived a longing there to dwell
Till the time came when she should be deceased;
And in the tomb a cubicle was made;
She shut herself inside and there she stayed.

184

Envoys Orlando sends and messages,
He goes in person to the sepulchre,
A handsome pension and appointment as
Companion to the Empress offers her.
If to re-join her father her wish is,
He will escort her home; should she prefer
To dedicate her life to God, he'd build
A convent for her wheresoe'er she willed.

185

Within the tomb she stayed; and there, worn out
By penance, praying day and night, not long
She lingered; by the Fate the thread was cut
On which her life precariously hung.
By then the mariners had rigged the boat
And from the island of the Cyclops, sung
In ancient times, the three French knights departed,
At their companion's absence broken-hearted.

186

To find a doctor was their first intent
For Oliver, whose foot had need of care.
The danger of delay was evident;
Too many hours already wasted were.
They heard him moan and grumble and lament
And for his state they all began to fear.
As they discussed his case, a pilot who
A sudden thought had near Orlando drew:

187

Not far from Sicily, the pilot said,
A hermit dwelt upon a lonely reef.
Recourse to him in vain was never made
For counsel, or assistance, or relief.
He gave sight to the blind, and raised the dead,
And miracles he wrought beyond belief.
He signed the Cross: the wind was hushed, the sea
Was calmed, however stormy, instantly.

188

The pilot added, they need have no doubt:
A man so dear to God would cure the knight;
Let them not hesitate to seek him out;
The clearest signs he'd given of his might.
They turned the prow towards the holy spot
(The scheme had filled Orlando with delight),
And never veering from their chosen way,
They saw the hermit's rock at break of day.

189

The sailors are old sea-dogs, every one
Knows how to bring the vessel to with skill.
All hands stand by and when the course is run
They lower Oliver for good or ill
Into a little skiff which lands upon
The rugged rock; thence to the sacred cell
They scramble up and to the holy seer
Whose hands had recently baptized Ruggier.

190

The servant of the Lord of Paradise
Welcomed Orlando and his comrades too.
He blessed them, smiling and with joyful eyes,
Then asked to what their visit here was due
(Though to the elder it was no surprise,
For owing to the Powers above, he knew).
The Count replied the journey had been made
Because of Oliver, who needed aid;

191

While fighting for the Faith and Christendom,
He had been wounded and to death brought near.
The holy man relieved him of all gloom
And promised he would heal the cavalier.
Provided with no ointment or nostrum
Or skill in human medicine, the seer
Entered the little chapel, where he prayed;
Then he stepped forth, in confidence arrayed.

192

And in the name of the Eternal Three,
Father and Son and Holy Ghost, he gives
His blessing. Lo, a miracle they see!
What power is granted when a man believes
In Christ! The cavalier is instantly
Restored, the suffering departs and leaves
His foot more firm than it had ever been.
Sobrino too was present at the scene.

193

Sobrino was reduced to such a state,
His wounds were growing worse from hour to hour,
And, witnessing so evident and great
A marvel, he decided to abjure
Mahomet; scarcely could he bear to wait
Christ to confess in all His living power.
Thus, filled with faith and with a heart contrite,
He begged admittance to our sacred rite.

194

The holy man, delighted by his choice,
Baptizes him and heals him too by prayer.
Orlando and the other knights rejoice,
No less than at the cure of Oliver,
And one and all their jubilation voice.
No one was more delighted than Ruggier –
Indeed his joy exceeded all the rest,
So much his faith and piety increased.

195

Ruggiero, ever since he reached that spot
By swimming, had remained there to this day.
The holy elder, gentle and devout,
Continued with the warriors to pray
That they might be defiled and stained by naught
As through this vale of death they made their way
Which is called life, so dear to the unwise,
And on the path to Heaven fix their eyes.

196

Orlando sends a servant to the boat
To bring them bread, good wine and ham and cheese.
The holy elder, used to eating fruit,
Had long forgot the taste of foods like these;
But they prevailed on him to follow suit
And he partakes of meat and wine to please.
When they are all restored, they start to chat
Of many different things, of this and that.

197

As one thing to another tends to lead,
Orlando, Montalbano, Oliver
Look at Ruggiero and at last succeed
In recognizing the great warrior,
Renowned for many an heroic deed,
In praise of whom all cavaliers concur.
Rinaldo had not known him as the knight
With whom he once had entered on a fight.

198

Sobrino his identity had guessed
As soon as he had seen him in the cell,
But to keep silent he had judged it best,
In case he was mistaken after all;
And when it is reported to the rest
That this Ruggiero is, whose deeds men tell
Throughout the world, whose courage, courtesy
And valour seldom paralleled can be,

199

Knowing he is a Christian, they approach,
A smile of joyfulness on every face.
Some, to congratulate him, his hand touch,
Some kiss him, some enfold him and embrace;
But not one of them honours him as much
As does Rinaldo; in another place,
If you desire, and on another day
The reason for this I'll go on to say.

CANTO XLIV

1

In poor and humble homes, in cottages,
In hardship and disaster, hearts are joined
More lastingly and truly than where ease
And opulence with envy are combined,
In regal courts and splendid palaces,
Where cunning and conspiracy you find,
Where fellow-feeling long extinct has been,
Where there's no friendship that is genuine.

2

Thus pacts and treaties of great potentates
Crumble and fall at the first wind that blows.
Popes, emperors and kings and heads of states,
Allied today, tomorrow will be foes.
No way their inner mind or heart relates
To what their simulated aspect shows.
Heedless of right and wrong, of false and true,
Their own advantage only they pursue.

3

However little talent they possess
For friendship, which is withered by deceit,
Though none their thoughts will honestly profess
On topics grave or gay or bitter-sweet,
If a misfortune, harsh and merciless,
Should cast them down together in a pit,
In a short time, in shared calamities,
They learn, as ne'er before, what friendship is.

4

The holy elder in his humble cell
Joined his companions in a knot so tight,
True lovers never bonded were so well;
Not thus do hearts in royal courts unite.
In later years it proved so durable,
Only death loosened it; the anchorite
Found their hearts loving, candid and sincere,
And whiter inwardly than swans appear.

5

He found them amiable and courteous,
Not like those hypocrites of whom I spoke,
Whose inner motives are iniquitous
And ever hidden by their outward look.
The blows they had exchanged were numerous,
But recollection of them they forsook.
If sprung from the same womb and the same seed,
No greater love they'd feel than now they did.

6

More than the others, Montalbano's lord
Showed honour and affection to Ruggier:
First, he had tested him with lance and sword,
He knew his martial skills for what they were;
And, secondly, because in deed and word
He knew him for a perfect cavalier;
But, most of all, because in many ways
So many debts to him Rinaldo has.

7

His brother Ricciardetto, as I said,
Seized by the orders of the king of Spain
(When he and the princess were found in bed),
Was rescued by Ruggiero; I made plain
That both the sons of Buovo too he freed
When they were captives of the Saracen,
Who planned to barter them for gold and silk
With evil Bertolagi and his ilk.

8

These debts appeared to him of such a kind
That honour, homage and great love he owed,
And grievously it weighed upon his mind
That he had never shown his gratitude;
Since in opposing camps they were aligned,
To do so would have been against the code.
Now that he found him there, and of our creed,
What earlier he could not do, he did.

9

The courteous paladin, to make amends,
Pledges and promises was quick to give.
The prudent hermit, seeing them now friends,
Approaching them, took the initiative:
'All that remains is but to tie the ends.
Without demur I hope you will receive
And heed my counsel: friends you are, I see,
So now between you kinship let there be.

10

'From your two families, which in our age
Remain unequalled for nobility,
There shall arise a splendid lineage,
Brighter by far than the sun's panoply,
Which, as events unfold, page after page,
More fair and more illustrious will be
(As God decrees I shall reveal to you),
Long as the heavens circle as they do.'

11

And he pursues the matter with such zest
That he persuades the son of Aymon (though
No call was there to plead or to insist)
His sister on Ruggiero to bestow.
The Count and Oliver (you will have guessed)
Delight at this proposed arrangement show,
Hoping the Emperor and all of France,
As well as Aymon, will approve their plans.

12

They did not know that Aymon had agreed
(And Charlemagne had given his consent)
His daughter Bradamante should be wed
To Leon, the young prince of the Levant;
His father Constantine he would succeed,
Who on his son's behalf to France had sent.
The youth the warrior-maid had never seen,
But with her valour long in love had been.

13

Duke Aymon had replied that he alone
The marriage contract would not sign before
He had discussed the matter with his son
Rinaldo, now by reason of the war
Away from court and Montalbano gone.
He would be glad (of this, the Duke felt sure)
To have so great a brother, but he meant
To wait (out of respect) for his consent.

14

But now, of these arrangements unaware
And from his father many miles away,
Rinaldo gives his sister to Ruggier
On his own word and on Orlando's say,
Supported by the others present there.
(The hermit's words exert the strongest sway.)
He truly thinks in all sincerity
His father Aymon will delighted be.

15

They tarried there that day and the next night
And the next day, conversing with the saint,
As if their voyage was forgotten quite.
Many a message by the crew was sent:
The wind for France, they said, now stood just right.
At last, agreeing it was time they went,
They took their leave with sorrow and regret
Of the wise hermit, by good fortune met.

16

Ruggiero, who had been so long exiled,
And from the island not a foot had stirred,
Then said farewell to him who had beguiled
The time by lessons in God's holy Word;
And with his weapon (Balisarda styled)
Orlando girt him, Hector's arms restored,
And gave him back Frontino – all of these
For love, acknowledging that they were his.

17

Although Orlando had a better claim
To the enchanted weapon, which he won
With pain and travail on the day he came
To Falerina's garden (whereas none
Ruggiero had – as to the steed the same
Is true – they were both stolen, as is known),
Yet he restored it gladly with the rest
Of the knight's arms, at once, at his request.

18

The hermit blesses them as they at last
Depart; eager once more to spread their sails
To the south wind, they ply their oars so fast,
And so serene and clear a sky prevails,
No prayers, no vows are needed; soon they cast
Their anchor in the harbour of Marseilles.
There let them stay, and I meanwhile will look
For the renowned and valiant English duke.

19

When he had heard the news of victory
(So dearly won, it muted his delight),
No longer fretted with anxiety
Concerning France, he thought it would be right
To set the Nubian, Senapo, free
With what remained of his assembled might.
He planned to send them home along the route
They took when for Biserta they set out.

20

The son of Ugier had dismissed the fleet
Which smote the vessels of the Infidel.
Soon as the Negroes disembarked from it,
They witnessed yet another miracle.
The poops, the prows, the rigging, every sheet
Were changed to leaves again (incredible!).
Then came the wind; the leaves uplifted were
And swiftly whirled away like gossamer.

21

The Nubians, some mounted, some on foot,
Leave Barbary for Ethiopia;
The duke, before they take their homeward route,
Conveys to Prester John, who came so far
And all his troops at his disposal put,
His thanks which infinite and lasting are,
And gives him back the sturdy bladder-skin
With raging Auster tightly sealed within.

22

He had enclosed that wind in skins, I say,
Which in such rage emerges from the South
The desert sand is whirled aloft like spray;
But borne like this along their homeward path,
It could not hinder them in any way,
For they were well protected from its wrath;
Once they were back in Ethiopia
They would release the angry prisoner.

23

Soon as they crossed the lofty Atlas chain,
Their destriers (so Turpin says) all turned
To rocks; attempts to ride were now in vain;
As they had sallied forth, so they returned.
Now I must send Astolfo back again
To France; a respite having truly earned
By seeing to the Moors' provisionings,
He mounts the hippogriff, which spreads its wings.

24

A wing-beat, and Sardinia appears;
Another, and he's over Corsica.
Crossing the sea, towards the left he veers
And comes at last to where the lowlands are
Of rich Provence; now to the end he nears
Of riding high and travelling so far;
On landing here, the hippogriff he freed,
Just as St John Evangelist decreed.

25

St John had said that when he reached Provence
He must no longer ride the wingèd horse,
But lighten it of all accoutrements
And set it free upon its chosen course.
The magic horn had lost its resonance;
Its voice was mute as if it had grown hoarse,
For in the moon, where all we lose is found,
The horn was minished instantly of sound.

26

Astolfo reached Marseilles the very day
Orlando had arrived with Oliver,
Rinaldo also, famed in many a fray,
With good Sobrino, and reformed Ruggier.
The thought of their belovèd friend who lay
Bereft of life in a dark sepulchre
Lessened their joy; although the war was won,
Small triumph do they feel in what was done.

27

The news had reached King Charles from Sicily:
Two kings were slain, a prisoner the third;
He knew that Brandimart had ceased to be
And with a hero's rites had been interred;
This weighed upon his heart most heavily.
About Ruggiero he had also heard
And he rejoiced, though in the midst of grief:
It will be long before he knows relief.

28

To honour those who were the chief support,
The prop and stay of his imperial throne,
Charles sent the highest nobles of his court
To ride ahead to greet them at the Saône.
Then he came forth with a select escort
Of kings and dukes; beside him rode his own
Fair lady; all around him thronged and pressed
Noble and lovely damsels, richly dressed.

29

King Charles, with a serene and smiling face,
A welcome to the victors now extends.
Nobles and commoners and populace
And paladins and relatives and friends
Hasten to show their love with an embrace.
'Monglane!' they cry; 'Clairmont!' the shout ascends.
Rinaldo and the Count and Oliver
Then duly to their lord present Ruggier.

30

He is the son, they tell the Emperor,
Of the renowned Ruggier of Reggio,
Equal in prowess to his sire of yore.
His courage and his strength our squadrons know.
Marfisa and the Maid step to the fore
(Together everywhere these damsels go).
Marfisa runs at once to clasp her brother;
Respect and modesty restrain the other.

31

Charles bids Ruggiero mount his steed again
(He had dismounted to show reverence),
And neck and neck with his own charger rein.
His every word and gesture represents
The utmost courtesy a sovereign
Can pay; a full account of the events
Which brought Ruggiero back into the fold
The warriors when they landed soon had told.

32

Triumphal pomp, joyful festivity
Mark the procession's entry in Marseilles.
The city is bedecked with greenery;
Bright-coloured bunting all the streets regales;
A cloud of petals, scattered copiously
All round, the victors from above assails,
As from each balcony and window-ledge
Matrons and damsels grateful tributes pledge.

33

Now round a corner the procession turns
And through an archway passes, built that day:
In painted scenes Biserta, ruined, burns;
Now here a stage is set as for a play,
Now there, now everywhere, the gaze discerns
A spectacle, a mime or a display.
Inscriptions on all sides are to be read:
'Hail to the heroes who the Empire freed!'

34

Amid the shrill of pipes, the trumpets' blare,
The harmony of divers instruments,
Applause and joy which greets them everywhere
From thronging crowds, the Emperor dismounts
Before the portals of his palace; there
For many days with masks and tournaments,
Dances and plays and feasts, the company
Rejoices in conviviality.

35

One day Rinaldo to his father said
It was his dearest wish that Bradamant
To their new friend Ruggiero should be wed,
That he had promised him this boon to grant,
And that the Count and Oliver agreed
(They being present); nobody would want
A finer match for valour or for blood:
Nay, where could one be found that was as good?

36

The duke with anger listens to his son;
Without consulting him his daughter's hand
He dared to pledge, whereas another one
As Bradamante's husband Aymon planned:
The heir of Constantine, young Prince Leon.
Not only does Ruggiero rule no land,
No territory can he claim as his.
(Not virtue, wealth the first requirement is.)

37

And Beatrice the duchess even more
Rebukes her son and calls him arrogant;
His wish she never ceases to deplore
In private and in public; Bradamant
(On this her mother sets the greatest store)
Must now become the Empress of Levant.
Rinaldo is unmoved, budge he will not,
Nor from the pledge he gave withdraw one jot.

38

The duchess, who but little understood
Her daughter's mind, exhorted her to say
Rather than be a poor man's wife she would
Prefer to die; if she did not obey,
She'd be disowned, her mother said, for good
(She could not fail, she thought, to get her way).
How could her brother force her in her choice
If she said 'No' in a bold tone of voice?

39

The lovely Maid stands mute; her mother's words
She would not ever dare to contradict,
Such is the reverence she feels towards
The one who gave her birth, such the respect.
Yet with her honour it but ill accords
To trifle with the truth – a grave defect.
She cannot now unwill her will, which Love,
In small things and in great, has robbed her of.

40

She did not dare say 'No', nor give consent;
Only one answer could she give – a sigh.
Where nobody could overhear she went
And floods of bitter tears began to cry.
She made her bosom share the punishment
And tore her golden tresses all awry.
Her grief and her despair were piteous
As, weeping, to herself she murmured thus:

41

'Alas! shall I oppose my mother's will
When she, not I, should have command of mine?
What she desires shall I esteem so ill
That to my wishes I instead incline?
No daughter could commit more terrible
A sin, or a more heinous fault combine
Than this, if I obedience forsake
And contrary to her wish a husband take.

42

'Shall duty to my mother then prevail?
Must you and I, O my Ruggiero, part?
Alas! what pain and grief my breast assail!
And must I now admit into my heart
New love, new hope and new desire? Or shall
I rather from that reverence depart
Which children owe good parents, and consult
My wishes, in my joy alone exult?

43

'I know what I should do, I know, alas!
I know how a good daughter should behave.
What use is that if Reason's powerless,
Compared with the command the senses have,
If Love reduces me to this impasse
And deals with me as if I were his slave,
Forbidding me to think or speak or act
Except as his express demands exact?

44

'If I displease my parents, I can look
For pardon as their daughter in the end,
Though I deserve their anger and rebuke;
But if my master, Love, I should offend,
Who no rebellion from his slave will brook,
No-one protection from his wrath could lend.
There is not one excuse which he would heed
Before he raised his hand to strike me dead.

45

'What arduous endeavour did I use
Before Ruggiero the true Faith embraced!
If now the fruit to someone else I lose,
For me all I have gained is laid to waste.
Just so the bee, not for herself, renews
The honey every year which others taste.
But I would rather die, and this I swear,
Than take another husband than Ruggier.

46

'If I am disobedient to my mother
And if my father's wishes I gainsay,
I shall be dutiful towards my brother:
No dotard he, and shrewder far than they;
His wish has the approval of no other
Than Orlando; what more is there to say?
My cause is championed by this famous pair
Whom all men honour and whom all men fear.

47

'If they are seen by all to be the flower,
The glory and the splendour of our line;
If, like the brow above the foot, they tower;
If every cavalier they far outshine,
Must I surrender to Duke Aymon's power,
Rather than to these paladins incline,
And if, when to Ruggiero I was pledged,
With Leon no agreement had been reached?'

48

While Bradamante thus laments and wails,
Ruggiero's mind is likewise not serene.
The news, though not yet current in Marseilles,
To him no secret for some time has been.
Against his fortune bitterly he rails:
So niggardly his portion is, and lean,
His cup of gladness from his grasp is twitched,
While thousands, undeserving, are enriched.

49

But of all other boons which granted are
By Nature, or by toil and effort won,
He knows he has as plentiful a share
As anybody he has ever known;
His manly beauty is beyond compare,
In prowess rarely can he be outdone.
For courage and for magnanimity
No one could better claim the prize than he.

50

But honours by the vulgar are conferred;
They give or take away, as they think fit;
And note that no one from the common herd,
Except a prudent man, would I omit.
To popes and emperors and kings the word
Applies, no crown, no mitre cancels it,
But only prudence and good sense, which Heaven
To but a few of us on earth has given.

51

The herd has no respect except for gold;
This is of all things what they most admire.
Where it is not, in no esteem they hold
The noblest deeds to which the brave aspire.
For beauty, courage, their regard is cold,
Prowess and martial skill, heroic ire,
Wisdom and goodness are of no account,
Still less in such a case as I recount.

52

Ruggiero said, 'If Aymon is disposed
To make his daughter Empress of Levant,
Would she were not so soon to be espoused!
A year at least I would that he might grant.
Leon and Constantine will be deposed
By then; when their imperial crown I vaunt
(As I intend and hope), Aymon will see
A not unworthy son-in-law I'll be.

53

'But if without delay, as he has said,
Daughter-in-law to Emperor Constantine
His daughter he donates, to Leon wed,
Despite the promise that she would be mine,
By Montalban and by his cousin made,
The hermit, Oliver and King Sobrin
Being present, what then shall I do? Shall I
Endure a wrong so grave or, rather, die?

54

'What shall I do? Shall I avenge the wrong
Upon her sire? I will ignore the fact
That such an enterprise would take me long,
I will not ask myself if such an act
Is wise; I will suppose that I have sprung
Upon this evil dotard and attacked
And slain his lineage: am I content?
Will this not, rather, thwart my whole intent?

55

'For my desire was always and is yet
To fill the lovely Maid with love for me,
Not give her cause for vengeance, scorn and hate;
But if I slay her father cunningly,
If I an ambush for her brother set,
Will she not justly call me enemy?
Will she not cease to want to be my wife?
Sooner than that, I would renounce my life.

56

'Why should I die? Rather let Leon bear
The punishment, he and his sire to boot.
Revenged I'll be on this imperial pair.
Of their iniquity, death be the fruit!
Helen her Trojan lover cost less dear,
Pirithous in times still more remote
For love of Proserpina suffered less,
Than I will make them pay for my distress.

57

'Or can it be you are not sad, my life,
To leave me, your Ruggiero, for this Greek?
Could Aymon force you to become his wife
When both Rinaldo and Orlando seek
To make you mine? My heart is fraught with strife,
Thinking that you perhaps prefer to take
An Emperor for husband, rather than
(A lesser match indeed!) a private man.

58

'Ah! could the pomp, the crown imperial,
The fame, the splendour of a royal court,
Corrupt my noble Bradamante's soul,
Her valour and her virtue so distort
That to this lure of splendour she would fall,
Holding her pledge to me of less import?
And rather than her sire antagonize,
Make all her words to me so many lies?'

59

Long with himself Ruggiero thus communed
And many other things he also said.
Those who were near him often heard the sound
Of his laments and knew how his heart bled,
So more than once to her for whom his wound
Grew worse, the tidings of his woe were sped.
She grieved to hear that he too grieved, no less
Distraught by his than by her own distress.

60

But, more than all those sorrows which she hears
Torment Ruggiero, this torments her most:
The anguish he endures because he fears
The Greek his image from her heart will oust.
That on this issue he may dry his tears,
She sends him, by a maid whom she can trust,
A letter which Ruggiero's doubts allays
And in these words her true desires conveys:

61

'As I have always been, so will I be
Till death, Ruggiero, and till far beyond.
If Love is harsh or is benign to me,
If Fortune whirls me high, or to the ground,
I am a rock of true fidelity,
Battered by wind and water all around,
Unchanging in fair weather and in foul,
Long as the heavens in their circles roll.

62

'Sooner a chisel or a file of lead
Will carve a diamond, than any blow
Which Love in wrath calls down upon my head,
Or Fortune has in store to bring me low,
Will change my heart, to you for ever wed;
Uphill returning, streams will sooner flow
Than new events for better or for worse
Will turn my thoughts along a different course.

63

'I gave to you, Ruggiero, full command
Of me (this some, perhaps, do not believe).
I know that no new ruler of a land
An oath more true or loyal could receive,
And in your princedom more secure you stand
Than any kings or emperors who live.
No need have you of rampart or of tower;
To take me from you, no one has the power.

64

'Of mercenary troops you have no need,
For all assailants will be driven out.
To conquer me no riches will succeed
(By a vile price no noble heart is bought).
No rank, no crown my judgement will mislead,
So dazzling to the crowd, to me as naught.
No beauty, which a shallow lover lures,
Will please me more than I delight in yours.

65

'You need not be afraid that on my heart
Another image will be cut; your own
Is carved so deeply, with consummate art,
It cannot be removed; a precious stone,
Not wax it is, and sound in every part.
Love struck it first a hundred times, not one,
Ere he could flake the first rough chippings hence
Or the fair image of your face commence.

66

'Ivory, stone or any gem that makes
A firm resistance to the engraver's skill,
If to great violence subjected, breaks,
But no new image bears, nor ever will.
My heart of marble's character partakes,
Or any stone which fights against the steel:
For Love will crumble it or pulverize
Ere other beauty on it he incise.'

67

She added many other words to these,
All full of love, of comfort and of faith.
The reassurance which she thus conveys
Would bring him back a thousand times from death.
But when the lovers think their vessel is
Approaching port, safe from the tempest's wrath,
Another storm, impetuous and black,
All their sweet hopes assails and forces back.

68

For Bradamante, wishing to achieve
Much more than she has yet aspired to do,
Resolves their threatened fortunes to retrieve;
And, with less reverence than is his due,
She goes to Charles and says, 'Sire, by your leave,
If anything I did seemed good to you,
If I have served you well by any deed,
The boon which I shall ask, I pray concede.

69

'Before my wish is openly expressed,
Give me your royal word', the Maid went on,
'That you will grant me what I shall request;
I'll show you then the justice of the boon.'
'Your valour, put so often to the test,'
King Charles replied, 'the deeds which you have done,
Have earned, dear Maid, whatever you may want;
Part even of my kingdom I would grant.'

70

'The gift I ask of you, Your Majesty,'
The Maid resumed, 'is that you will permit
No man (whate'er his rank) to marry me
Unless in arms he proves that he is fit.
Whoever woos me must first show that he
With lance or sword can bring me to submit.
Who conquers me shall win my hand besides,
And those who lose must marry other brides.'

71

The Emperor answers with a joyful face
That the request most worthy is of her,
So all disquiet let her now erase:
He'll do as she has asked, without demur.
This parley does not secretly take place;
Its purport other people plainly hear.
Of it that day her agèd parents learn
And with fierce wrath and indignation burn.

72

Aymon and Beatrice against the Maid
Are both incensed and with an equal ire.
From all that to the Emperor she said,
They know full well that she does not aspire
To Leon, but Ruggiero wants to wed.
As an impediment to her desire,
They take her, by a ruse, to Rochefort
And keep her there with them, away from court.

73

This was a fortress which the Emperor
Had recently bestowed on Duke Aymon.
A castle of importance, by the shore
It stood, 'twixt Perpignan and Carcassonne.
Therein her parents Bradamant immure
And they intend one day to send her on
To the Levant; they mean her to forsake
Ruggier and willy-nilly Leon take.

74

The gallant damsel was obedient
As well as valorous and spirited.
Though she might come and go without restraint
(No guard was posted at her door), she stayed
And to her father's wishes meekly bent.
But she would sooner captive be, or dead,
And any martyrdom or pain endure
(So she resolved), than her dear love abjure.

75

Rinaldo saw his sister led away
By Aymon's guile and henceforth it was plain
As to her husband he would have no say;
His promise to Ruggiero was in vain.
Forgetting the respect which he should pay,
He dares to chide his father and complain.
Duke Aymon takes but little heed of it
And with his daughter deals as he thinks fit.

76

Ruggiero heard of this and was afraid
Without his lady he'd be left to pine;
By hook or crook, Leon would have the Maid
Unless some strategy he could combine.
Without a word, this counter-plan he made:
To raise him from Augustus to Divine,
Depriving both the father and the son
(Or so he hopes) of life as well as throne.

77

He dons those arms which Trojan Hector's were
And later Mandricard's, and bids his squire
Saddle Frontino, his good destrier.
His silver eagle he does not desire,
His usual crest and surcoat he'll not wear
(The enterprise demands disguised attire);
A unicorn he chooses for his shield,
White as a lily, on a crimson field.

78

He takes, of all his squires, the one most true
And wants, apart from him, no company.
He gives him strictest orders never to
Reveal the truth of his identity.
The Moselle and Rhine they cross, and, passing through
The Austrian region, enter Hungary.
Next, southwards on they gallop at great speed
Along the Danube till they reach Belgrade.

79

Then, where the Sava joins the Danube's flood
And, thus commingled, towards the Black Sea turns,
A vast array of tents, a multitude
Of men-at-arms assembled he discerns;
For Constantine has judged the moment good
To take Belgrade (the Bulgars, whom he scorns,
Had seized it); near the imperial gonfalon
Wait, resolute, both Emperor and son.

80

Within Belgrade, and outside on the hill,
As far as to the river at its foot,
The Bulgars are encamped; to drink their fill
Both sides draw near; the Greeks intend to put
A bridge across, the Bulgar army will
With might and main all such attempts rebut.
Just as Ruggiero comes upon the scene
And looks about, hostilities begin.

81

The Bulgars are outnumbered, one to four;
The Greeks, in aspect fierce and merciless,
Resolved by force to reach the other shore,
Hold their pontoons and boats in readiness.
Meanwhile Leon, inactive heretofore,
By an astute manoeuvre leaves the press,
And circling from the river far and wide,
Returns, and crosses to the other side.

82

With a great host, some mounted, some on foot,
No less than twenty thousand, Leon sped.
Arriving by this unexpected route,
A fierce attack on the foe's flank he made.
No sooner does the Emperor gladly note
His son across the water lending aid,
Than, bridge to bridge and boat to boat being tied,
He leads his army to the other side.

83

The Bulgar chief, King Vatran, skilled and brave,
A warrior of wide experience,
Laboured in vain his followers to save
From such ferocity and violence:
His steed, at the first blow which Leon gave,
Beneath him fell, all life departed hence.
Then, as the Bulgar chief refused to yield,
By myriad swords surrounded, he was killed.

84

The Bulgars had resisted until then;
Now that they saw their leader thus struck dead,
Where all their faces formerly had been
They turned their backs, and from the tempest fled.
Ruggiero, mingled with the Greeks, had seen
The rout; at once it came into his head
That he would be the Bulgars' champion,
For Constantine he hates, still more Leon.

85

Frontino rushes past the cavalry
Just like a gust of wind; the Bulgar troops
For safety up the hill in panic flee.
Ruggiero a good number of them stops
And makes them turn to face the enemy.
His lance in rest, for the attack he stoops.
His aspect as he spurs his destrier
Would frighten Mars himself, or Jupiter.

86

Of knights in the front rank he noticed one
Who on his crimson surcoat seemed to wear
A stalk of millet, golden as the sun,
Fashioned in silk by an embroiderer:
Nephew of Constantine (his sister's son)
Who like a loving father holds him dear.
His buckler and his breastplate break like glass
As through his frame the lance is seen to pass.

87

Ruggiero leaves him dead; clutching his sword,
He rides against the nearest band of Greeks.
First one and then another man is gored;
He pierces torsos, slits and slashes cheeks;
No armouring against his strokes can ward.
Breasts, flanks and thighs his Balisarda seeks.
On shoulders, arms and hands she rains her blows;
Blood like a river to the valley flows.

88

While he thus laid about him, no one durst
Remain to face him, such was the dismay.
The tide of battle was at once reversed;
The Bulgars turned about and won the day,
Though they had fled from certain death at first.
The Greeks are put to rout in disarray.
Breaking their ranks, they scatter in a trice,
Nor do the ensigns think about it twice.

89

Leon Augustus to a rise of ground
Withdrew, whence with a mind downcast and sad
He watched his army fleeing all around.
A perfect view of the terrain he had.
He saw the corpses littering the ground,
And to the score of slaughter he must add
The havoc of his camp; one knight alone,
Who wrought all this, his admiration won.

90

His shining arms, his gilded panoply,
The unicorn embroidered on his coat
Show that, for all he helps the enemy,
Yet plainly of their number he is not.
An Angel from the heavenly hierarchy
His superhuman deeds seem to denote,
In retribution on the Greeks descended
Who many times the Almighty have offended.

91

Leone, noble and magnanimous,
While many others would be filled with hate,
Of valour such as this enamoured was.
Although the losses of the Greeks are great,
Six times as many men he'd rather lose,
Than see him suffer at the hands of Fate;
He'd rather lose a part of his domain
Than see a cavalier so valiant slain.

92

As when a child, whose mother beats him well
And angrily excludes him from her sight,
His sorrows to his father does not tell,
Nor to his sister will confide his plight,
But hurries back, in spite of what befell,
And puts his arms around his mother tight,
So now Leon does not resent Ruggier:
For valour he must love him and revere.

93

But if Leone loves him and admires,
A poor return he gets, it seems to me.
Ruggiero hates Leone and aspires
To kill him there and then; most eagerly
He searches and of many he enquires
As to his whereabouts, but prudently
And by good luck Leon keeps out of sight,
Avoiding an encounter with the knight.

94

Leone, to prevent his total force
From being wiped out, gave orders for retreat.
He sent an envoy on the swiftest horse
The Emperor's withdrawal to entreat:
It was now urgent he should alter course
(Lucky he'd be if he could manage it);
Then with the remnants of his regiment,
To where he'd crossed the river, Leon went.

95

Many are left behind, by Bulgars slain,
And many more the hillside would have strewn
But for the river which divides the plain;
Many go back across it by pontoon;
Many are drowned and never seen again;
Many, not looking back, run farther on
To find a shallow ford where they can wade;
And many are led captive to Belgrade.

96

And so the battle ended on that day.
The Bulgars, who had seen their leader killed,
Dejection would have suffered and dismay,
But for the knight who on a crimson shield
Bore the white unicorn – a proud display –
Who intervened and forced the foe to yield;
They all drew near him, conscious that they owed
The victory to him, and gladness showed.

97

One man saluted him, another bowed,
Some kissed his hand, still others kissed his foot;
Whoever touched him, joyful was and proud,
For supernatural he seemed, if not
Divine; jostling around him in a crowd,
As close as possible the Bulgars got,
And clamoured for him raucously and cried
To be their king, their captain and their guide.

98

Ruggiero said that he would gladly be
Their captain and their king, as they desired;
But he would not assume authority,
To neither rod nor sceptre he aspired,
Nor to Belgrade would march in victory,
But he must leave before Leon retired
Still farther out of sight and crossed the stream;
To catch him and despatch him was his aim.

99

A thousand miles and more, for this alone
He came, for this intent with no delay
He leaves the Bulgar army and is gone.
He turns in the direction which they say
Was taken by the fugitive Leon.
Fearing perhaps to lose him on the way,
Or lest obstruction his design impede,
Without his squire he gallops off at speed.

100

So good a start has Leon in his flight
(For flight it must be called, not planned retreat),
He breaks the bridge and sets the boats alight.
Ruggier arrives just as the sun has set.
Alone, without a lodging for the night,
He looks around him; no one does he meet;
Beneath the moon he travels hopefully,
But not a house or castle does he see.

101

Not knowing where to go to lay his head,
He rides all night without dismounting once.
When the new sun has turned the East to red,
He sees a city on his left and plans
To spend the day there, for his horse has need
Of rest, and this will be a welcome chance
To let Frontino now at last be idle,
After so many miles, freed from the bridle.

102

Ungiardo ruler of this city is,
A vassal much beloved of Constantine
Who horse and foot for these hostilities
To muster for his liege did not decline.
Here visitors may enter as they please.
The welcome is so sumptuous and fine,
No need Ruggiero has to look elsewhere
For better lodging or for choicer fare.

103

At the same hostel there arrived that night
A cavalier who from Romania hailed,
Who had been present at the bitter fight
When for the foe Ruggiero took the field;
He had been lucky to escape; with fright
He trembled yet, his soul within him quailed:
After him galloped still (he could have sworn)
The cavalier of the white unicorn.

104

As soon as he observes the shield, he knows
This is the knight who bore the sign of dread,
Who on the Greeks inflicted many blows,
And by whose hand so many men lie dead.
To seek an audience the stranger goes,
And to Ungiardo's ante-room is led.
Admitted to his presence straight away,
He says at once what I will later say.

CANTO XLV

1

The higher up on Fortune's wheel you see
A wretch ascend, the sooner he will fall,
And where his head is now, his feet will be.
Polỳcrates, for instance, I recall,
Croesus and Dionysius equally,
And many more – I cannot name them all –
Were good examples of such change of fate,
Plunged from supreme renown to low estate.

2

And the reverse is true contrariwise:
The lower down a man is to be found,
The sooner he will come where he must rise,
Provided that the wheel keeps turning round.
One day, upon the block a victim lies,
The next, as ruler of the world he's crowned,
Like Servius, Marius, and Ventidius
In ancient times, King Louis among us:

3

The father-in-law of my duke's son, I mean,
King Louis who was taken prisoner,
And almost lost his head at Saint-Aubin,
But he survived; and, somewhat earlier,
Still greater peril faced Matthew Corvin.
He too escaped the executioner.
The lowest point was passed; one rose to be
The king of France, and one of Hungary.

4

From history's examples we conclude,
And modern instances teach us the same:
Good follows Evil, Evil follows Good,
Shame ends in glory, glory ends in shame.
Thus it is evident that no man should
Put trust in victories or wealth or fame,
Nor yet despair if Fortune is adverse:
She turns her wheel for better, as for worse.

5

Emboldened by the triumph he has won
Against his rival and the Emperor,
Ruggiero now so confident has grown
He trusts to luck and daring even more.
Without support or company, alone,
Facing a hundred squadrons, cavalry or
Infantry or both, against him banded,
He'll kill the son and father single-handed.

6

But she who does not wish that any man
Shall feel assured of her, in a few days
Shows him beyond all doubt how soon she can
Cast down her victims and how quickly raise,
From friend to foe revert and back again.
Her fickle nature Fortune now displays:
The knight who from Ruggiero fled, hard pressed,
Will render him dejected and distressed.

7

He told Ungiardo that the cavalier
Who put the troops of Constantine to flight,
Leaving them tame and cowed for many a year,
Was there that day and would remain that night;
And if he now seized Fortune by the hair,
He'd give his king, without another fight
(If prisoner this guest of his he took),
The chance to bend the Bulgars to the yoke.

8

From fugitives who from the battle fled
In batches to Ungiardo's safe retreat
(Not all could cross the river, as I said,
And countless hordes were still arriving yet),
Ungiardo knew that half the Greeks were dead,
He knew the full extent of the defeat,
He also heard a single champion
Had wrecked one camp and saved the other one.

9

And that this warrior has fallen now
Head first into the net without being chased,
Amazes him; by all his words, his brow,
His every move, his pleasure is expressed.
Gauging the time that's needed to allow
Ruggiero to retire and take his rest,
He sends the guards and bids them softly creep
And seize him while he lies in bed asleep.

10

Ruggiero is betrayed by his own shield
And as a prisoner in Novigrad
Is now by merciless Ungiardo held,
Who at this triumph joyful is and glad.
Ruggiero wakes: what can he do but yield,
Finding himself in fetters and unclad?
Ungiardo sends to Constantine post-haste
And not a moment does the courier waste.

11

The Emperor the day before was quick
To move his troops from Sava's banks and go
With them for safety on to Beletic
Ruled by his brother-in-law Androfilo,
Whose son was killed: his armour could not check
(It seemed like wax) the penetrating blow
Received at first encounter from the knight,
Who captive is of cruel Ungiard's might.

12

Here Constantine had had the gates repaired
And all the city's bulwarks fortified,
Lest a renewed attack the Bulgars dared.
With such a leader on the other side,
The Greeks would have good reason to be scared.
But of Ruggiero's capture notified,
Of Bulgars he no longer feels afraid,
Not if the whole world with them were arrayed.

13

Now Constantine swims in a sea of milk
And scarce knows what to do for very bliss.
'That is the end of Bulgars and their ilk!'
He cries; so confident is he of this,
His brow, unfurrowed, is as smooth as silk.
He is as sure that naught can go amiss
As if he'd lopped an enemy's two arms;
This is the end, he thinks, of all alarms.

14

His son has reason for rejoicing too.
He hopes not only to retake Belgrade,
But every Bulgar region to subdue;
And it is his intention to persuade
The warrior, by means of favours, to
Become his friend; if he enlists his aid,
No envy he will ever feel again,
For all his paladins, of Charlemagne.

15

Quite different from this is the design
Of Theodora, for it was her son
Whose breast Ruggiero's lance pierced to the spine,
Protruding by a handbreadth; she had thrown
Herself before the feet of Constantine.
She is his sister and his heart she soon
Contrives to touch with bitter floods of woe
Which copiously down her bosom flow.

16

'I will remain thus at your feet, my lord,'
She said, 'if on this prisoner who slew
My son, just vengeance you do not accord.
He was your nephew, but consider too
How much he loved you and with lance and sword
How many noble deeds he did for you.
If on this wretch you take no vengeance now,
A heinous wrong you will commit, I vow.

17

'God to our sorrow is compassionate.
See how He takes this felon from the war
And guides him like a bird straight to our net,
So that my son upon the Stygian shore
Not long for his revenge will have to wait.
Give me this wretch to punish, I implore,
And grant this boon to me, O Constantine,
That with his torment I may lessen mine!'

18

So well the mother weeps, so well she moans,
So well she speaks, so moving are her pleas,
That though her brother tries, and more than once,
Yet all in vain, to raise her from her knees,
The justice of her cause at last he owns;
And since no other remedy he sees,
He orders that the unnamed prisoner
Shall be straightway delivered up to her.

19

The warrior was brought without delay
(Known only from his sign, the unicorn),
And in the space of but a single day
Subjected was to Theodora's scorn.
She longs to kill him, but too mild a way
It seems to her to quarter him or burn,
And so she ponders, striving to invent
Some cruel or unusual punishment.

20

Meanwhile she has him in her fiendish power,
Chained by his neck and by his hands and feet,
Deep in the gloomy dungeon of a tower.
The light of Phoebus never reaches it.
A little mouldy bread of meanest flour
(Not every day) was all he had to eat.
The gaoler whom she chose to be his guard
Was merciless and pitiless and hard.

21

Oh! if the valorous and lovely Maid,
Oh! if the brave Marfisa were to hear
The news of how Ruggiero was betrayed,
How he now languished as a prisoner,
They would both risk their lives to bring him aid.
Though Bradamante holds her parents dear,
Without respect to what they now might say
She'd leave to help her love without delay.

22

King Charles meanwhile his promise bears in mind:
Fair Bradamante shall not wed until
A husband worthy of her she can find,
Who equals her in courage and in skill.
Trumpets announce the plan he has designed;
Not only do his courtiers learn his will,
To every city subject to his sway
The tidings of it reach without delay.

23

And these were the conditions, word for word:
Whoever Aymon's daughter would espouse
Must face her first, fighting with lance or sword
From morning until eve without a pause;
If he should last so long, as his reward
He'll win the Maid, and she will not refuse,
If he has not been vanquished in this strife,
To let him take her as his wedded wife.

24

The Maid the choice of weapons will concede
Without regard to who makes the request.
She could afford to offer this indeed,
Skilled as she was in every martial test.
Aymon could not oppose the Crown and he'd
No wish to; he was beaten, he confessed;
After much talk, from Rochefort where he brought her
They then returned to Court, he and his daughter.

25

Although her mother was still furious,
She ordered gowns for her, for honour's sake,
Of many colours, fair and sumptuous,
Of many styles; the Maid and Aymon make
Their way to Court: it is soon obvious
Ruggiero absent is and she can take
No pleasure in a court which once so fair
And radiant had seemed when he was there.

26

A garden seen in April or in May,
Resplendently adorned with bloom and leaf,
If visited anew when the sun's ray
Is slanted south and day-time here is brief,
Forlorn and squalid seems and bleak and grey;
So now the court, to Bradamante's grief,
Of her Ruggiero widowed and bereft,
No longer seemed to be the one she left.

27

She does not dare to ask where he has gone
In case still more suspicion is incurred.
She hangs upon the lips of everyone,
Hoping to hear the news in a chance word.
She knows he has departed, but upon
Which road or route no man has seen or heard;
For when he left he kept his secret close:
Only the squire who travels with him knows.

28

Oh, how she sighs! Oh, how distraught she is!
Oh, what misgivings aggravate her plight!
This is the worst of her anxieties:
That to forget her he has taken flight.
With Aymon's obduracy, he foresees
No hope of wedlock, and since out of sight
Is out of mind, he hopes perhaps to prove
If distance will release him from his love.

29

And she imagines further in her pain
That, to erase her sooner from his heart,
While wandering through many a domain
He'll seek another love to heal the smart.
(One nail drives out another, it is plain.)
Next, a new image in her mind will start:
Her dear Ruggiero constant is and true
And loves her always as he used to do.

30

Then she rebukes herself for lending ear
To such iniquitous and foolish doubt.
Alternately one thought defends Ruggier,
And one accuses him; she hears them out,
First this one and then that engages her.
Neither conclusion is convincing, but
She leans to the more comforting; the worse
(The contrary) she shrinks from and abhors.

31

And she remembers intermittently
The love her love has many times expressed.
Her error then seems of such gravity,
Her conscience is remorseful and distressed;
She bitterly regrets her jealousy.
Aloud she blames herself and beats her breast:
'I am at fault,' she cries, 'this I admit,
But more at fault is the true cause of it.

32

'Love is the cause; he printed on my soul
Your handsome form, your grace, your comeliness,
Your skill and daring which your peers extol,
Your valour which they emulate no less;
So that to me it seems impossible
That women do not long for your caress,
That, having seen you, any can abstain
From using all her skill your heart to gain.

33

'If only Love permitted me to read
Your thoughts as now he conjures up your face,
I know that plain would be what now is hid,
I know that different would be my case.
At last of Jealousy I would be rid,
No longer would I suffer her embrace;
While seldom now her onslaught I evade,
Not only would she be repulsed, but dead.

34

'I'm like a miser who so loves his gold,
His very heart lies buried with it too.
By fear of robbery his life is ruled;
He keeps the hiding-place in constant view.
Since now my treasure I may not behold,
The fear of loss does more than hope can do.
Although such fear is false, as I believe,
I let it thus mislead me and deceive.

35

'Yet when I see once more the radiance,
Now hidden from my eyes, I know not where,
Of your belovèd, smiling countenance,
True hope will instantly depose false fear,
Thrusting it down, for all its arrogance.
Return to me, return, O my Ruggier!
My hope restore and strengthen once again –
My hope which by my fear is almost slain.

36

'As, when at sunset shadows longer grow,
Of darkness vain and empty fears are born,
As, when the East with light is seen to glow,
Fears, like the shadows, vanish with the morn,
Without Ruggiero's presence, fear I know,
When he approaches, fear at once I scorn.
Come back to me, Ruggiero, come, ah, come,
Before my hopes to fear and doubt succumb.

37

'The stars like torches are ablaze at night,
By day no spark of all their splendour burns.
Thus, when my sun deprives me of his light,
To menace me fear lifts its evil horns;
When the horizon in the East is bright,
Fear vanishes at once and hope returns.
Return to me, return, belovèd sun:
Bid my devouring, evil fear be gone.

38

'The sun withdraws: earth will no longer show
Her former loveliness, the days are brief,
The bleak winds bluster, bringing ice and snow,
Song-birds are silent, withered flower and leaf.
You, my fair sun, withdraw from me, and lo!
My day is changed to night, my joy to grief,
And winter in my soul, induced by fear,
Occurs not once but many times a year.

39

'O my dear sun, return to me, restore
The sweet, the long-departed, longed-for Spring.
On ice, on snow your melting vigour pour,
And to my stormy skies fair weather bring.'
As Procne can be heard lamenting, or
As Philomel, returned from foraging
To find an empty nest, or as the dove
Will moan and mourn the absence of her love,

40

So Bradamante wailed and grieved, afraid
That her Ruggiero she had lost for good;
And tears not once but many times she shed
(Although in secret) which her face bedewed.
How much more stricken, how much more dismayed
She'd be if the true facts she understood:
That her betrothed a prisoner remains,
Condemned to death, which he awaits in chains!

41

The cruelty of the revengeful dame
Against the noble knight she held thus bound,
Her plan that he should die a death of shame
When some unheard of punishment she found,
By God's will to the ears of Leon came.
The Emperor's son, for chivalry renowned,
Was moved by this to think how he could save
A cavalier so valiant and so brave.

42

Leone loves Ruggiero (though men speak
Of him, he does not know that this is he).
Stirred by that valour which he calls unique
And which he thinks must superhuman be,
Henceforth his one intention is to seek
A way to rescue him, and finally
He finds a plan for which his cruel aunt
The blame on him, he knows, will never plant.

43

Leone spoke in secret to the guard
Who kept the dungeon key; to him he said
He wished to see the knight on whom so hard
A sentence had been passed; the man agreed.
When darkness fell, Leon approached the ward.
With him he brought a henchman, born and bred
For cutting throats; the gaoler swore to say
No word and let Leone in straightway.

44

Indeed he thought it best to come alone
In order to observe the secrecy
The prince so urgently insisted on.
Where those condemned to the last penalty
Were held, he led the henchman and Leon;
And, as he turned his back to turn the key,
The others threw a rope around his neck,
Then drew it tight and his despatch was quick.

45

They pulled a trap-door up and bent to look.
Seizing a torch which blazed as bright as day,
By a stout rope which dangled from a hook
Leon climbed down to where Ruggiero lay
Stretched out on a bare board; the sun forsook
So deep a place, and scarce a palm away
Beneath him water flowed; a month or less
And death, unaided, would have brought release.

46

With deep compassion Leon holds Ruggier
In his embrace a while and then he says:
'Your valour binds me to you, cavalier,
And indissolubly; for all my days
My willing vassalage to you I swear.
Your safety now above my own I place.
Friendship with you I hold more precious than
With my own father or with any man.

47

'That you may understand, I am Leon
Who come in person here to bring you aid.
Yes, it is true, I am the Emperor's son.
I am in danger, if I am betrayed,
If by my father this is ever known,
Of exile or disfavour; at Belgrade
You killed and routed such a multitude,
Not well-intentioned is his attitude.'

48

And other words with careful thought he chose
Which a return of vigour would permit,
While as he spoke he cut the fetters loose.
Ruggiero said, 'My thanks are infinite.
This life which now you give me, I propose,
When in the future you have need of it,
To offer up in recompense to you.
Regard it as your own and as your due.'

49

Ruggiero was removed from the dark cell;
The strangled gaoler in his place remained.
They leave unrecognized; till he is well
Leon persuades Ruggiero as a friend
In peace and safety for some days to dwell
With him; and in the meantime he will send
A page to fetch the arms and destrier
Which by Ungiardo taken from him were.

50

Next day when doors are opened, all is known:
The gaoler strangled and Ruggiero fled.
The question is discussed by everyone.
They wonder: who is guilty of this deed?
The last they would imagine is Leon.
It seems to many he has cause indeed
To kill the cavalier (but not to aid)
Who turned the tide of battle at Belgrade.

51

Such chivalry has so abashed Ruggier
And so astounded and confused his mind,
That the intention which had brought him here
Yields to another and is left behind.
And if the two intentions you compare
No vestige of resemblance you will find:
The first, derived from venom, hate and ire,
The second, love and comradeship inspire.

52

By night, by day, he thinks of nothing else;
No other cause, no other wish has he
Than to repay the indebtedness he feels
With equal or with greater courtesy.
However many dangers and ordeals
He suffers, whether short his life may be
Or long, if he devotes it to Leon
It will be less than all the prince has done.

53

Meanwhile throughout the land the tidings spread
Of the announcement by the king of France,
That anyone who wished to woo the Maid
Must prove himself with her by sword or lance.
When Leon hears of this he feels dismayed,
His cheek turns pale, he knows he has no chance,
For he has noted well her expertise;
No match for her in arms he knows he is.

54

He thinks a while and sees he can make good
His lack of vigour by the use of wit.
Bearing *his* sign (Leone's understood),
This warrior (whose name he knows not yet)
Shall fight for him; there is no Frank who could
Withstand his valour or his skill defeat.
The knight is sure to conquer, thinks Leon,
And thus the Maid will vanquished be and won.

55

Two things he has to do: first, to request
The knight to lend himself to this emprise;
Then, so arrange his entrance in the list
That nobody shall see through his disguise.
He calls Ruggiero to him; with his best,
With his most winning eloquence he tries
To induce him to agree to fight the Maid,
With a false emblem on his shield displayed.

56

The eloquence commanded by the Greek
Does much to win the cavalier's assent;
But, though the prince persuasively can speak,
Ruggiero's debt is still more eloquent.
This is a bond which he can never break.
However sad his heart, he must present
A smiling face; he is prepared, he says,
To serve his benefactor in all ways.

57

No sooner has he said these words than pain
Has pierced his heart, and all that day and night
It stabs and throbs and the next day again
It tortures him and gives him no respite.
His death will be the outcome, it is plain.
Yet he does not repent, for all his plight.
Sooner by far than not obey Leon,
A thousand deaths he'd die, and not just one.

58

His death is certain: for, if he must lose
His lady, both his life he'll lose and her.
Either his grief will bring it to a close,
Or he will strip off the involucre
Which girds his captive soul and set it loose;
For any suffering he'd rather bear
And any other sorrow sooner prove
Than live to see her someone else's love.

59

He is prepared to die; and yet what kind
Of death he would prefer he does not know.
Sometimes the notion comes into his mind
To feign less strength, exposing to his foe
His naked side; no sweeter death he'd find
Than to expire at his beloved's blow.
But if the Maid in combat is not won,
He will discharge no debt towards Leon.

60

For he has promised, against Bradamant
To fight in single combat in the lists
And over her a victory to vaunt,
Not yield by simulated thrusts and twists.
He stands by his decision, adamant.
Although a battle with his thoughts persists,
He routs them all save one which says he must
Abide by what he promised and keep trust.

61

By now Leon, with Constantine's consent,
Had ordered horses, arms and retinue
Such as became a prince, and off he went.
He had Ruggiero with him too and he
Was clad in his own arms for the event
And on Frontino mounted was anew.
They rode for days, and many countries passed,
Then came to France, and Paris reached at last.

62

Outside the city walls, Leon prefers
To set up his pavilion and at once
He gives instructions to his messengers
To ride to Court to tell the king of France
He has arrived; when Charles these tidings hears,
He visits him and courteous gifts presents.
Leon explains why he has come today
And begs that matters be arranged straightway.

63

He asked King Charles to summon forth the Maid
Who her avowed intention had declared
No man whose strength is less than hers to wed,
For he this challenge to accept now dared:
Either she marries him or strikes him dead.
The king consents; a stockade is prepared
That very night beneath the city walls.
Next day a herald Bradamante calls.

64

Ruggiero the preceding night had passed
As when a man condemned awaits the morn
In anguish, knowing it will be his last;
Who tosses sleepless, haggard and forlorn.
He judged it wise to wear full armour, lest
He should be recognized; he had forsworn
Both steed and lance; no weapon would he use
Except a sword (but not his own he chose).

65

He left his lance behind, but not because
He feared to face his lady's lance of gold,
Which Argalìa's, then Astolfo's was,
Which felled all combatants, however bold,
For no one knew that magic was the cause:
That it was made by Galafron of old
By magic, that he gave it to his son,
Who many battles subsequently won.

66

Astolfo and the Maid believe indeed
That in the jousting-field by their own skill
And strength, and not by magic, they succeed;
That any lance would serve them just as well,
One snatched at random would supply their need.
The only reason why Ruggiero will
Not joust is that he'd rather not display
Frontino, who would give the game away.

67

For if his lady saw the destrier
She'd know him for Frontino easily,
Since he was long at Montalban with her
And bore her as a rider frequently.
The sole concern and object of Ruggier
Is to prevent her knowing it is he.
He leaves Frontino and all else which might
Reveal him to her as her own true knight.

68

For this emprise he chose another sword.
He knew all breastplates were as soft as dough
Before the cut and thrust of Balisard.
No tempering her furious speed can slow.
He hammered this new weapon long and hard
To blunt the edge; at the first gleams which show
On the horizon, as his pledge insists,
Ruggiero makes his way towards the lists.

69

Hoping to be mistaken for Leon,
Ruggiero dons the coat which Leon wore.
A golden eagle with two heads upon
A scarlet field Ruggiero also bore,
And thanks to this disguise which he puts on
He is successful in his purpose, for
Ruggiero and Leon are the same size
And Leon is now hidden from all eyes.

70

The purpose of the Maid is different:
Whereas Ruggiero hammered on his sword,
Eager to blunt its edge and so prevent
Himself from causing pain to his adored,
She grimly sharpens hers for the event,
So that with every stroke he shall be gored,
And pierced by every thrust in every part,
Until at last she penetrates his heart.

71

As, eager for the signal to be off,
A fiery thoroughbred of Barbary
Paws at the ground with an impatient hoof,
Its nostrils flaring and ears pricked, so she,
For combat having waited long enough,
Not knowing that her foe her love will be,
Awaits the herald's trumpet with her veins
On fire, and her impatience scarce contains.

72

As when a thunder-clap is followed by
A cataclysmic gust of wind which churns
The troubled sea and tosses to the sky
A cloud of dust which light to darkness turns,
When the wild beasts and flocks and shepherds fly
From rain and hail, so now the Maid discerns
The signal to begin, her weapon takes,
And on Ruggiero a fierce onslaught makes.

73

No solid bastion, no ancient oak
Resists the battering of Boreas more,
No angry waves by an unyielding rock
Are more disdained as endlessly they pour,
Than, in those arms, secure from every shock,
By Vulcan made, which Trojan Hector wore,
Ruggiero spurns the fury and the hate
Which on his head and body rain in spate.

74

The Maid with cut and thrust her weapon wields,
Seeking a chink between the armour-joints;
No spot is there which to her anger yields,
But every stroke resists her sword and blunts;
So well that armouring his body shields,
That every lunge deludes and disappoints.
Now here, now there, she whirls about and spins,
Maddened by her vexations and chagrins.

75

As the besieger of a citadel
With solid walls and sturdy buttresses
Repeatedly attacks and probes it well –
A lofty tower now his target is,
A gate, a moat which he intends to fill,
Though many men are lost, no entrances
He finds – so Bradamante fumes and frets
And fails to pierce the solid armour-plates.

76

Now flying from his shield or helm she sends
A shower of sparks, as now from his cuirass,
As now a blow upon his arm descends,
Now on his head or chest; her strokes surpass
The fall of hail on roofs which never ends
When in the country stormy clouds amass.
Adroit and skilled, the movements of Ruggier
Serve to defend him without harm to her.

77

Now he stands firm, now pivots, now withdraws;
In concert with his hand his foot moves too.
When harm her hostile hand attempts to cause,
With shield or sword he fends her off anew.
He never aims at her; if he has cause,
He strikes her where the blow least harm will do.
The Maid is eager to conclude the fray
Before the light declines at close of day.

78

For she recalled the edict which decreed
If in one day she did not take or kill
The challenger (to this King Charles agreed),
She was his captive and must do his will.
Phoebus was soon to plunge his golden head
Into the western sea when of her skill
And strength the Maid at last began to doubt,
While her fatigue was putting hope to rout.

79

As hope diminished, so her anger grew
And she redoubled her ferocious blows
Against that armour which the whole day through
Intact remained, whichever spot she chose,
Like one who at the work which he must do
Has dawdled and, perceiving night is close,
Makes all the haste he can until at length
The daylight ends, together with his strength.

80

Ah, if you knew the truth, unhappy Maid!
The knight whom you would slay is not your foe.
He is Ruggiero; from him hangs the thread
Of your own life; you'd kill yourself, I know,
Sooner than be the one to strike him dead;
And when you learn that he whom you have so
Belaboured is Ruggiero, you will mourn
To think what strokes of yours your love has borne.

81

Charles and his courtiers were looking on.
Greatly they marvelled at the challenger
(They all believed, of course, it was Leon
Who duelled with the Maid, and not Ruggier);
And when they saw how the event had gone,
How well he parried without wounding her,
They were convinced and said: 'Well paired they seem;
He is the match for her and she for him.'

82

When Phoebus disappeared behind the sea,
The Emperor called finis to the fight.
He said the Maid must Leon's consort be
And she must not refuse; it is his right.
Ruggiero takes no rest but instantly,
Still helmeted, departs into the night.
Mounted astride a palfrey, off he sets
To the pavilions where Prince Leon waits.

83

Leone threw his arms in fond embrace
Three times and more about Ruggiero's neck,
Then gently drew the helmet from his face
And kissed him with a love he did not check.
'Myself at your disposal I now place,'
He said, 'I will be ever at your beck
And call; my love for you will never end:
Draw on it lavishly and freely spend.

84

'There is no recompense that I could make
Which would release me from the debt I owe,
Not if the crown itself I were to take
From my own head and on your head bestow.'
Ruggiero felt as if his heart would break.
Life was abhorrent to him; almost no
Reply he made; the shield which he had worn
He yielded, and resumed the unicorn.

85

With listless, weary step he took his leave
And to his own pavilion made his way.
He armed himself anew from helm to greave,
Saddled Frontino and without delay
Set out; no indication did he give
Of his intent, no farewell did he say.
At midnight, mounted on his destrier,
He left the route to him, and cared not where.

86

Frontino bears his master on all night
Through woods and fields, by winding paths and
Ruggiero's sorrow gives him no respite.   [straight.
His bitter tears unceasing flow in spate.
He calls on death to save him from his plight,
The only cure for grief so obstinate;
Grim death alone, severe and merciless,
Can end his unendurable distress.

87

'Whom shall I blame', he said, 'for my reverse,
The loss of all I cherish at one blow?
If I am not to suffer even worse –
Injury unavenged – against which foe
Should I resentment in my bosom nurse?
I am my own worst enemy, I know:
I brought myself to this unhappy state;
Against myself I must direct my hate.

88

'If I had injured but myself alone,
I might forgive myself, unwillingly,
For all the harm which I have undergone;
Yet I would not deserve such clemency.
So much the less should mercy then be shown
Since Bradamante shares the injury!
Even if I my score were to remit,
To leave her unavenged would not be fit.

89

'So to avenge her I deserve to die:
This is a duty I do not regret,
For in no other way can I defy
My bitter grief, no respite can I get.
Would I had died much earlier when I
Had not offended Bradamante yet!
Would I had died when I a captive lay,
Helpless in cruel Theodora's sway!

90

'If after she had done her cruel worst
She had despatched me, I could hope at least
That Bradamante for me would have nursed
Some pity and compassion in her breast;
But when she learns that I put Leon first,
That willingly I granted his request
And placed him as her husband in my stead,
She will be right to hate me, live or dead.'

91

These words and many more he says, by sighs
And sobs accompanied with every breath.
When the new light of day begins to rise,
He wanders from a wild and rugged heath
To gloomy woods which hide him from all eyes.
Since he is desperate and longs for death,
This seems the very place, remote from view
And suitable for what he means to do.

92

Deeper and deeper, of the secret wood
He penetrates the tangled mystery;
But first of all, unharnessing his good
Frontino, whom he loves, he sets him free,
Saying, 'O my Frontino, if I could
Reward you as rewarded you should be,
You would not envy Pegasus his glory,
Set among stars, immortalized in story.

93

'Neither Cyllarus nor yet Arion
Surpassed you or deserved more lasting praise,
Nor any other destrier made known
By Romans or by Greeks in ancient days;
But even if perhaps it could be shown
That they your equals were in other ways,
One honour and prestige they cannot claim
Which will for ever guarantee your fame.

94

'A lady, the most noble, the most fair
And the most valorous, so cherished you,
With her own hand she tended you with care,
Harnessed you, saddled you and fed you too,
As I have often heard. My lady held you dear:
I call her mine? That is no longer true!
The right to call her mine I forfeited.
Why do I wait? O sword! now strike me dead!'

95

While thus Ruggiero vents his sorrow here,
Moving to pity every bird and beast
(No other creatures his lament can hear,
Nor see the tears which inundate his breast),
You must not think the Maid is free from care
In Paris; she is bitterly distressed,
For she has neither reason nor excuse,
But must take Leon now to be her spouse.

96

Sooner than take another husband than
Ruggiero, she would rather break her word.
By this the odium of every man,
Of Charles, especially, would be incurred,
And of her family and friends; a plan
She also had by poison or her sword
To kill herself; for she would much prefer
To cease to live than live without Ruggier.

97

'O my Ruggiero!' Bradamante cried,
'Where can you be, my love? Where have you gone?
The proclamation published far and wide,
Has it remained unheard by you alone?
I know that you'd have rallied to my side
Faster, if you had heard, than anyone.
Alas! what explanation can there be
Except the worst of all? Ah, woe is me!

98

'How is it possible you did not hear
What everyone has heard? And if you did,
And still you have not hastened to be here,
How is it possible you are not dead?
Or, if you are alive, a prisoner
Of Leon's you must be; the traitor laid
A snare to catch you and to block your way,
That he, not you, should first arrive today.

99

'I begged of Charles this grace, which I received:
No man whose strength was less than mine could claim
Me as his bride; against you, I believed,
And only you, I could not stand; my aim –
To yield to you – is cruelly deceived.
My own audacity is much to blame.
God now chastises me, for I am won
By him who no courageous deeds has done.

100

'If I am won because I could not kill
Or capture him, this seems unjust to me;
And I do not abide, nor ever will,
By what in this King Charles has said shall be.
If thus my promise I do not fulfil
I shall seem guilty of inconstancy,
But I am not the first, nor yet the last,
To change her mind, in present times or past.

101

'If to my lover I am staunch and true
And, firmer than a rock, hold to my vow,
If I surpass in this all women who
Have ever loved in ancient times or now,
In other things, in other people's view,
Let me appear inconstant; if somehow
Our love is served thereby, let them declare
Me fickle as a leaf, I do not care.'

102

These plaintive words, expressive of her plight,
With sighs and copious weeping interspersed,
She ceaselessly repeated through the night
Which had succeeded to that day accurst;
But when Nocturnus with his shades took flight
And in Cimmerian grottoes was immersed,
The heavens which *ab eterno* chose the Maid
To be Ruggiero's bride came to her aid.

103

The morning brought Marfisa, proud and strong,
Before King Charles; her angry words rang clear:
Her twin, Ruggiero, suffered grievous wrong;
It was an outrage which she would not bear;
Without a word, his bride, to whom he long
Had been betrothed and whom he held so dear,
Was taken from him; she would prove by strife
That Bradamante was Ruggiero's wife.

104

First she would prove to Bradamant with swords,
If she should be so rash as to deny it,
That in her presence she pronounced the words
Which sanctify the marriage-knot and tie it;
And by the ceremony afterwards
Their union was confirmed, they must stand by it:
Neither was free to take another spouse,
For they had solemnized their marriage vows.

105

Whether Marfisa spoke the truth or not,
She spoke with the intention, wrong or right,
Of hindering Leone; beyond doubt,
To everything she said the Maid was quite
Agreeable, being party to the plot
Which, as she hopes, will quickly reunite
Her with Ruggiero; no more honest scheme,
Or speedier, suggests itself to them.

106

King Charles is much disturbed by what he hears.
He sends for Bradamante straight away.
At court her father Aymon, too, appears.
Charles tells him what Marfisa has to say.
The Maid looks down, confused, and close to tears;
She will not answer 'No', nor answer 'Yea'.
Her bearing lets it easily be seen
That what Marfisa said may true have been.

107

Rinaldo and the Count are overjoyed
To hear what has occurred, for this will cause
The pact with Leon to be null and void
Which he assumed already binding was.
No violence requires to be employed,
To thoughts of rescue now they call a pause.
Though Aymon still persists in stubbornness,
The Maid will be Ruggiero's none the less.

108

If they support Marfisa, all is well:
Ruggiero's case is now as good as won.
The promise which they made they can fulfil
With honour and without a sword's being drawn.
'This is a plot designed to thwart my will,
But I am not defeated,' said Aymon,
'Not even if this rigmarole were true,
Which has, I know, concocted been by you.

109

'Supposing, for the sake of argument
(Though I do not believe it or concede),
That Bradamante, as you represent,
To wed Ruggiero foolishly agreed
And *vice versa*: where did this event
Take place and when? I know that, if it did,
There is one fact which cannot be disguised:
It must have been before he was baptized.

110

'Such a betrothal is untenable.
This contract is of no concern to me.
She was a Christian, he an infidel:
Their union cannot have validity.
Did Leon put his life at risk for nil?
Has he then lost, despite his victory?
Our Emperor, for something so absurd,
Will not, I think, go back upon his word.

111

'What you now say should have been said before,
When Charles had not yet granted the request,
When he had not announced arrangements for
The combat which brought Leon to the West.'
These words from Bradamante's father pour;
The cousins' case they bitterly contest.
Charles listens to both sides in the affray
But not a word for either will he say.

112

As Auster and Boreas can be heard
Rustling the foliage of lofty trees,
Or as when Aeolus to wrath is stirred
And waves in tumult hiss among the screes,
So now a murmur through all France occurred.
Discussions rage; wherever converse is,
There is one matter only in dispute.
On every other topic tongues are mute.

113

Some for Ruggiero speak, some for Leon,
But many more are on Ruggiero's side,
By a majority of ten to one.
The Emperor, unwilling to decide,
Let the debate continue and upon
His parliament as arbiter relied.
Marfisa (as the wedding is deferred)
Steps to the fore and once again is heard:

114

'Since while Ruggiero lives', Marfisa said,
'No other man can marry Bradamant,
Let Leon fight my brother in her stead
And show his mettle as her aspirant.
Which of the two shall strike the other dead
Will have no rival and may rest content.'
Charles lets Leone hear about this test,
As earlier he told him all the rest.

115

Leon is confident that he can meet
This challenge, for the cavalier who bears
The unicorn can easily defeat
Ruggiero, as to this he has no fears.
He little knows that in a dark retreat
Deep in the wood the knight is shedding tears.
Thinking his champion will return ere long,
Leone makes his choice – and chooses wrong.

116

He soon regrets it, for the knight on whom
He placed undue reliance, all that day
Is nowhere to be seen, nor does he come
The next day or the next, and none can say
Why he has gone, nor where he chose to roam.
Leone has no stomach for the fray.
Fearing to suffer injury and scorn,
He seeks the warrior of the unicorn.

117

He sends his scouts to every citadel,
And far and near they search them, every one.
Then, not content with this, he goes as well
And does his best to find the champion.
No word of him could anybody tell,
No word of him would anyone have known,
But for Melissa's help; but as to her,
The tale to my next canto I defer.

CANTO XLVI

1

Now, if the bearings of my chart speak true,
Not far away the harbour will appear.
On shore I'll make my votive offering to
Whatever guardian Angel hovered near
When risks of shipwreck threatened, not a few,
Or of for ever being a wanderer.
But now I think I see, yes, I am sure,
I see the land, I see the welcoming shore.

2

A burst of joy which quivers on the air,
Rolling towards me, makes the waves resound.
I hear the peal of bells, the trumpets' blare,
Which the loud cheerings of a crowd confound;
And who these are I now become aware
Who the approaches to the port surround.
They all rejoice to see me home at last
After a voyage over seas so vast.

3

And oh! what lovely witty women wait,
What gallant knights do honour to the strand,
What friends to whom I'll always be in debt
For the glad welcome shown me as I land!
'La Mamma', and Genevieve, and others yet
Who from Correggio come I see who stand
At the quay's tip and, waiting with them there,
Veronica, held by the Muses dear.

4

Of the same blood, another Genevieve
I can make out and, with her, Julia too,
Ippolita the Sforza I perceive,
And la Trivulzia, the damsel who
Drinks at the holy spring and, as I live!
Emilia Pia; Margaret, with you
Are Angela and Grace; Ricciarda d'Este's
There, with Bianca, Diana and their sisters.

5

And lo! the fair, yet still more wise and just,
Barbara of the Turchi, and her friend
Laura: though you might search from East to West,
Two better women you would never find;
And Genevieve, she who the Malatest
Adorns and gilds with virtue of such kind
That never regal nor imperial palace
Had worthier adornment for its solace.

6

If long ago, this side the Rubicon,
To the proud conqueror of Gaul she'd come
When he was doubtful whether to press on
Across the stream dividing him from Rome,
No banners, I believe, would he have flown,
No heavy spoils would he have carried home;
But laws he would have made as she thought best,
And freedom he might never have oppressed.

7

My lord of Bòzolo, your womenfolk,
Your wife, your mother, sisters, cousins, aunts
Are here, with those of Bentivoglio stock.
Torellos and Viscontis meet my glance,
Pallavicino ladies too; and look!
There is the one whose lovely countenance
And grace deserve all fame that ever was.
All women, past and present, she outdoes.

8

Julia Gonzaga is this lady's name.
Where'er she walks, where'er she turns her eyes,
To beauty other women yield their claim.
As if she were a goddess from the skies,
They look at her amazed; and with her came
Her brother's wife who would not compromise
Her love, though long by Fortune put upon.
Lo! Vasto's light, Anna of Aragon:

9

O high-born Anna, wise and kind and fair,
A temple of true love and chastity!
Her sister's radiant beauty, I declare,
Puts other beauties in the shade; I see
Vittoria who from the murky air
Of Styx her consort drew by poetry.
He, by this feat unique, the Fates defies,
Among the stars resplendent in the skies.

10

My fair ones of Ferrara I behold,
Of Mantua and of Urbino's court,
Ladies of Lombardy, by all extolled,
And lovely Tuscan girls of good report.
My vision by their radiance is dulled,
Yet I can still distinguish in a sort
Someone they welcome in their midst – a knight,
Accolti, called Unique, Arezzo's light.

11

And Benedict his nephew there I see,
With purple hat and mantle, and as well –
Glory and splendour of the Consistory –
Campeggio, with Mantua's Cardinal.
And each I note (unless I raving be)
In face and gestures is so jovial
At my return that surely it will tease me
From such an obligation to release me.

12

With them Lattanzio and Claudio Tolomei,
Paolo Panza, Trìssino, Latino,
The Capilupi (Mantuan brothers, they),
Sasso and Molza, Florian Montino,
And he who guides us on the Muses' way
Along new paths (the speediest that *we* know),
Giulio Camillo; Marco I discern (he
Who's called Flaminio), Sanga and Berni.

13

See Alessandro di Farnese come,
A leader of a learnèd company:
'Phaedra', Capella, Porzio, Filippo whom
Bologna claims, Volterra's pride, Maffei,
The Pierian and Maddaleni of Rome,
Blosio and Vida (of Cremona he),
Lascaris and Musurro, Navagero,
Andrea Marone and the monk Severo.

14

Two other Alessandros in that band
I see: one Orologio, one Guarino,
Mario d'Olvito and, look! near at hand
That scourge of princes, divine Aretino.
And two Girolamos before me stand:
One Verità, the other Cittadino.
Mainardo I behold, Leoniceno,
With Pannizzato, Celio, Teocreno.

15

Capel I see, and Pietro Bembo who
Restored to us our pure, sweet native speech,
Purged of the dross of common use and to
Perfection brought, as his own verses teach.
Guasparro Obizzi comes behind him too,
Amazed that ink should yield a crop so rich.
Now Bevazzan and Fracastoro appear,
Trifon Gabriel, and Tasso in the rear.

16

Two Niccolos draw near (Amanio
And Tiepoli) who fix me with their eyes.
Anton Fulgoso see, who seems to show,
As I approach the shore, joy and surprise;
And there is my good friend Valerio,
Who from the ladies stands apart; he tries
Perhaps, seeking advice from Barignan,
Not to fall victim to their charms again.

17

I see, conjoined in friendship and in blood,
Pico and Pio, geniuses sublime.
The noblest spirits in that multitude
Revere one of the greatest of our time.
I never met him but long wished I could,
And gladly bid him welcome in my rhyme:
Iacopo Sannazaro, he who lures
The Muses from the mountains to the shores.

18

There is the learnèd, loyal, diligent
Pistòfilo, Alfonso's secretary:
His pleasure and relief are evident.
Angiar and the Acciaiuolo family
Their happiness and joy have come to vent.
No longer need they fear the sea for me.
My cousin Malaguzzo I discern,
And Adoardo: fame, I know, he'll earn.

19

Vittore Fausto, Tancred show delight
On seeing me, as do a hundred more;
And every woman, every man in sight
Rejoices at my safe return once more.
Enough of this delay: the wind is right
And of my course remains but little more.
Let us return to where Melissa comes
To aid Ruggiero who to grief succumbs.

20

Melissa, as I many times have said,
Desires with all her heart to see the day
When Bradamante and Ruggier will wed.
So heavily their fortunes on her weigh,
From hour to hour of tidings she takes heed
Which bands of spirit-messengers relay:
As one returns, another one departs;
As one his message ends, another starts.

21

She sees Ruggiero in the gloomy wood;
Gripped by inexorable grief he lies.
He has resolved that he will take no food
Of any sort, but fast until he dies,
So melancholy is his present mood;
But to his aid Melissa quickly hies.
She leaves the place where she abides and soon
Along her chosen route she meets Leon.

22

He sent first one and then another scout
To search now here, now there, from early morn
Till evening fell. Then he himself set out,
To find the warrior of the unicorn.
A clever sorceress, Melissa put
A saddle on a sprite, making it turn
Into a palfrey, and on this she rode
When she encountered Leon on the road.

23

'My lord,' she said, 'if your nobility
Of face is a reflection of your soul,
If inward goodness and true courtesy
Are shown by your appearance, may I call
On you for help? I pray you, come with me
And rescue the best cavalier in all
The world; if we delay to bring him aid,
I fear, ere we arrive, he may be dead.

24

'The noblest knight who ever swung a sword,
The handsomest who ever bore a shield,
And the most chivalrous who ever warred
In past or present times on any field,
Now, for a gallant act to which his word
Was pledged, to the last enemy will yield
If no one rouses him; come, sir, I pray;
See if advice his sorrow can allay.'

25

An explanation instantly occurs
To Leon's mind: the knight of whom she speaks
Must be the one his scouts and foragers
Are looking for and whom he also seeks.
Eager to bring him aid, Leone spurs
And follows her; she too her palfrey pricks;
And soon they came (after a little way)
Where almost at death's door Ruggiero lay.

26

Ruggiero had been fasting for three days.
He is so faint that if he tried to stand
He'd fall without being pushed, nor could he raise
Himself upon his feet, or lift a hand.
He lies stretched out, with an unwinking gaze,
His helmet on his head, girt with his brand;
And of his shield a pillow he has made
On which they see the unicorn displayed.

27

And he continued, lying there, to brood
Upon the injury he'd done his bride;
And as he thought of his ingratitude
He was enraged as well as mortified.
From time to time, his hands, his lips he chewed
And bitter tears, which drenched his breast, he cried;
Engrossed thus deeply in his self-reproach,
He did not hear his rescuers approach.

28

He does not call a halt to his lament,
Nor does he check his sighing or his tears.
Leon draws rein; he gazes down intent,
Then he dismounts and to the figure nears.
It is the pains of love which thus torment
The sufferer, he knows, from what he hears,
But who she is for whom he suffers pain,
Ruggiero's words of grief have not made plain.

29

Leone, step by step, on cautious feet
Approaches; when he sees him, face to face,
With brotherly concern he kneels to greet
The knight and takes him in a fond embrace.
I cannot quite be sure, I must admit,
If Leon's sudden presence in this place
Was pleasing to Ruggier, for he supposed
His plan to kill himself would be opposed.

30

Leone, with the sweetest words, essays
With all the love he feels to bring relief.
'Have no misgivings, speak your mind,' he says,
'Disclose to me the reason for your grief.
There is no sorrow in the world which weighs
So heavily it can't be lightened if
The cause is known; and no one should give up,
For it is true that while there's life there's hope.

31

'It grieves me that you hide yourself from me.
Have I not shown that I am your true friend,
Not only since your act of chivalry
For which my bond of debt will never end,
But even when I had good cause to be
Your mortal enemy? You can depend
On me for aid, in danger and in strife.
I give you all I have, my friends, my life.

32

'Confide in me, say what is grieving you.
Your scruples set aside and let me try
What force or skill or flattery can do,
What wiliness will win or gold will buy.
If I do not succeed, you can renew
The resolution you have made to die,
But do so only as a last resort,
First trying other means of every sort.'

33

And his entreaties so persuasive were,
So gently, so benignly Leon spoke,
He could not fail to influence Ruggier,
Whose heart is not of iron nor of rock.
He sees if he refuses to defer
His grim resolve, he will deserve rebuke
For churlishness; he tries in vain to speak,
For in his throat his words twice, three times, stick.

34

When he could speak at last, 'My lord,' he said,
'I'll tell you who I am, and when you know,
Not sorrow you will feel when I am dead,
But joy and satisfaction you will show;
For I am he you hate and hold in dread,
I am Ruggiero who abhorred you so,
Who, with the aim of killing you, set out
And gladly would have killed you, have no doubt.

35

'I could not bear to lose my Bradamant
To you, when Aymon had declared his will.
Humans propose and strive for what they want,
But God alone makes all things possible.
When Fortune showed herself so adamant,
Your gallant action in my prison-cell
Not only made me shed my hate for you,
I swore that all you wanted, I would do.

36

'Not knowing who I was, you uttered your
Request: to win my bride for you – a role
Which was equivalent to asking for
The heart out of my body or my soul;
But if I put your fond desire before
My own, you know, my lord, who know the whole.
The Maid is yours; to her in peace return.
Your good, more than my own, is my concern.

37

'Grant that, deprived of her, I be of life
Deprived as well, for I could live without
My soul as soon as live without my wife;
And while I live, of this there is no doubt,
She cannot be *your* lawful wedded wife.
Your claim to be her husband is as naught,
For we have plighted each to each our troth;
She cannot be the wife at once of both.'

38

Ruggiero so astonishes Leon,
When he has learned of his identity,
He neither speaks nor moves, and made of stone,
A votive offering, he seems to be.
Such chivalry as this he's never known,
Nor ever heard of in all history;
Nor will it equalled be in future times
In any regions or in any climes.

39

Now that the cavalier's true name he knows,
The love he felt for him becomes no less,
But deeper his devotion to him grows;
So that he suffers anguish and distress
At least as keenly as Ruggiero does.
An Emperor's son, he'll show his worthiness.
Ruggiero in all other things may be
Superior, but not in chivalry.

40

'Ruggiero,' Leon said, 'if on the day
You valiantly attacked and slew my men,
So great was my amazement in that fray
Although Ruggiero's name was hateful then,
If I had known what you reveal today,
Your staunch admirer I would still have been;
My hatred from my bosom would have fled,
With love, as now, remaining in its stead.

41

'Ruggiero's name I hated and maligned.
This I admit; that was before I knew;
So banish thoughts of hatred from your mind.
Do you remember how I rescued you
When in that prison-cell you lay confined?
If I had known – I swear that this is true –
That it was you, I would have done the same,
As now to help you further is my aim.

42

'If willingly this favour I'd have done
When I was not, as now, in debt to you,
How much the more so now, when you have shown
What chivalry and courtesy can do!
For you renounced to me a treasured boon,
Yourself depriving of your rightful due;
But I restore it to you, happier
Than if I the possessor of it were.

43

'You are much worthier of her than I.
It's true I love her for her martial fame,
But I do not intend, like you, to die,
If someone else can prove a better claim.
I do not want your death thus to untie
The bonds which link you in the sacred name
Of Hymen; do not sacrifice your life,
Not thus do I desire to win a wife.

44

'Not only would I sooner now forgo
The valiant Maid, but all that I possess,
My life itself, than be the cause of woe
To such a cavalier; I feel distress
That you so little confidence should show
In me, on whom you can rely no less
Than on yourself: you chose to die of grief
Rather than turn to me to gain relief.'

45

These words and many others Leon said,
But to repeat them all would take too long.
Objections which Ruggiero tried to plead
Were answered easily or else proved wrong;
And so Ruggiero finally agreed:
'If you insist, I will remain among
The living, but, pray, what am I to do
To pay this double debt of life to you?'

46

Now in a trice (Melissa waved her wand)
Delicious food and choicest wine were brought.
She urged him to partake, e'er he be found
(And he was near to it) reduced to naught.
Meanwhile Frontino, having heard the sound
Of horses, once again his master sought.
Leon bade his attendants seize the steed
And saddle him; and this straightway they did.

47

With difficulty hoisted on his horse
By Leon's help, Ruggiero takes the rein.
Quite vanished now is that majestic force
Which recently so many Greeks had slain,
That stalwart stamina which stayed the course
When victory was falsely won in vain.
They all set forth, and half a league beyond
Or less, an abbey for their refuge found.

48

And there they took their rest until the morn.
For two more days they wait until at last
The cavalier of the white unicorn
Regains his health and strength as in the past.
To the imperial city they return.
An embassy of Bulgars, having passed
The gate, makes formal application to
The Emperor; he hears them, as is due.

49

The people who elected as their king
That warrior who saved the day for them
Now send ambassadors to France to bring
Ruggiero back (for he is there, they deem).
They want to swear allegiance, honouring
Their monarch with a royal diadem.
Ruggiero's squire, who with the Bulgars stayed,
The tidings of Ruggiero had relayed.

50

The squire had seen the battle of Belgrade,
Won for the Bulgars by Ruggiero's skill,
When Leon and his father were dismayed
To see him rout so many Greeks, or kill.
For this, king of the Bulgars he was made:
No other man they want, nor ever will.
Ungiardo took him captive – none could save him –
And into Theodora's keeping gave him.

51

The news had been confirmed, the squire went on,
Of how the gaoler was discovered dead,
The cell-door open and the captive gone,
But where Ruggiero was, none knew, he said.
Ruggiero with his visor down, unknown,
Along a secret route to Paris sped.
He and Leon, when morning comes again,
Request an audience with Charlemagne.

52

Ruggiero's emblem is the golden bird
Twin-headed on a crimson field, just as
He and Leone had agreed when they conferred.
He wears the surcoat and those arms he has
By which his true identity was blurred
When Leon's representative he was.
Slashed, holed and battered, his appurtenance
Proclaims him as the duellist at once.

53

Attired in costly style and jewelled too,
Unarmed, Leone enters royally,
Escorted by an endless retinue,
An honoured and a fitting company.
He bows his head to Charles, who, as is due,
Rises and goes to greet him graciously.
Taking Ruggiero's hand, on whom all fix
Their eyes, before the court Leone speaks:

54

'This is the gallant cavalier who fought
From daybreak to the setting of the sun.
Since Bradamante's efforts came to naught –
She did not overpower him nor run
His body through, nor did she drive him out –
Acknowledged it must be that he has won.
If he has understood your edict, sir,
He comes to claim his bride and marry her.

55

'To his entitlement by virtue of
This feat, I add: who has so good a claim?
For if a suitor prowess has to prove,
What cavalier can equal him for fame?
Or if the test is the degree of love,
Who can approach the ardour of his flame?
He is prepared by force of arms to show
The justice of his case to any foe.'

56

King Charles and all the court are stupefied
When these extraordinary words they hear.
They thought Leone was the knight who vied
With Bradamante, not this stranger here.
Marfisa her impatience could not hide
(For while he spoke, she too was present there).
She scarcely waited till he reached an end
But leapt at once her brother to defend:

57

'Ruggiero is not here to claim his right.
He cannot settle this dispute by means
Of single combat with this unknown knight;
And by default, if no one intervenes,
He'll lose his lawful wife without a fight.
I am his sister, he and I are twins.
Ruggiero's rivals, whosoe'er they be,
Will have to reckon in his place with me.'

58

Marfisa was so fierce and vehement
That many feared she would begin straightway,
Not waiting for the Emperor's consent,
And bring the matter to an end that day.
Now to Leone it was evident
The time had come Ruggiero to display.
He drew his helmet off: 'Behold the knight',
He said, 'who the full story will recite.'

59

As when Aegeus, old and silver-haired,
About to offer at that vile repast
The poison, by his evil wife prepared,
To one whom he now recognized at last
As his own offspring, by the sword declared
In time, so now Marfisa stood aghast
When she discovered that the cavalier
Whom she so hated proved to be Ruggier.

60

She flung herself upon him and embraced him
And scarcely could she bear to let him go.
Rinaldo and Orlando too both kissed him,
But Charles had been the first his love to show.
Dudone, Oliver, Sobrin caressed him:
It seemed that weary they would never grow.
Of paladins and barons none held back;
Of gladness shared by all there was no lack.

61

When all was calm, Leon, with eloquence,
Began to give King Charles a full report,
Holding him spellbound by the strange events.
I need not say the members of the court
Were an attentive, eager audience.
Ruggiero's valour was of such a sort
When he defeated Leon at Belgrade,
It caused all sense of injury to fade.

62

So, when a prisoner Ruggiero lay
And mercilessly tortured would have been
By her who held him in her cruel sway,
He (Leon) had defied his kith and kin
And set him free; and, eager to repay,
Ruggiero did a deed so gallant then
That it surpassed all deeds of chivalry
Which ever were or ever yet would be.

63

Then he went on to tell them of that deed.
No detail of the story did he hide:
Of how it made Ruggiero's heart so bleed
With anguish to renounce his promised bride
That he preferred to die; and soon indeed,
If help had not arrived, he would have died.
Leone told the tale so movingly
That every eye was moist with sympathy.

64

And next, with all the eloquence he could
Command, he turned to speak with Duke Aymon.
Not only did he change his stubborn mood
And make him want Ruggiero as his son,
But now so altered is his attitude,
To Bradamante's consort he is won.
He asks his pardon for the long delay
And gladly now his daughter gives away.

65

To where she sat, her very life in doubt,
Weeping in secret at her bitter fate,
More than one joyful messenger set out
These happy tidings gladly to relate.
Her blood, which instantly her heart had sought
When sorrow made her so disconsolate,
Went pulsing through her veins at the surprise
And almost caused the joyful Maid's demise.

66

So drained is she of her vitality
That she can scarcely hold herself upright,
Though spirited and strong she's known to be.
A man condemned to hang or to the plight
Of block or wheel or other devilry,
Bandaged already from the dreadful sight,
At his reprieve no greater gladness voices
Than she who at these tidings now rejoices.

67

Monglane and Clairmont joyfully applaud
This new conjoining of two kindred strains;
But those past-masters of deceit and fraud,
Gano, Ginami, Gini, Anselmo – clans
For ever by a furtive envy flawed,
In whom the threat of treachery remains –
Vengefully bide their time with wily smirks,
As for the hare the fox in waiting lurks.

68

Not only had the Count and Montalban
Despatched a number of this evil brood
(Though Charles insisted wisely on the plan
Of hushing up the spilling of bad blood);
With Pinabel and Bertolagi gone,
Sombre indeed was the Maganzans' mood;
But they were careful to conceal their aim,
Pretending not to know who was to blame.

69

The Bulgars who had come (as I have said)
In search of the heroic cavalier
Who on his shield the unicorn displayed –
Their chosen king – on finding he is there,
Rejoice and thank their lucky stars which led
Them to King Charles's court; and they draw near
And fling themselves in reverence at his feet
And his return to his domain entreat.

70

In Adrianople crown and sceptre wait,
Ruggiero is expected eagerly,
His help is needed to defend the State;
New danger threatens their security,
For Constantine is arming, they relate,
And leader of his troops intends to be;
But if their king will come they hope to make
The Empire Bulgar and no longer Greek.

71

Ruggiero finds their offer and request
Acceptable; he vows he will return,
Fortune permitting, when three months have passed.
Leone hears the promise he has sworn
And warmly recommends him to stand fast,
For when the Bulgar crown by him is worn
There will be peace, he can be sure, between
The Bulgars and the Emperor Constantine.

72

Nor need he hurry to depart from France
To lead his squadrons forth in a campaign:
Leon will urge his father to renounce
Whatever land was once Bulgarian.
Of all the merits which Ruggiero vaunts,
None is so likely the consent to gain
Of Bradamante's mother as to hear
Her future son-in-law is *King* Ruggier.

73

A wedding, splendid and spectacular,
Is now arranged, and a right royal one.
Charles sees to the arrangements with such care,
It might have been a daughter of his own
Who was to wed; but such her merits are
And such the worth of every Montalban,
It would not seem excessive if he spent
Half of his kingdom's wealth for this event.

74

The heralds now proclaim an open court
Where all may come and safely take their ease,
And freedom of the lists, where every sort
Of quarrel may be settled, for nine days.
Pavilions rise, and bowers, for the sport,
Embellished by green boughs and flowering sprays,
With draperies of silk and cloth of gold –
A scene of joy and gladsome to behold.

75

Paris alone could not have housed so great
A crowd of visitors from foreign lands:
Poor, rich, of high degree, of low estate,
Greeks, Romans, lesser breeds in lawless bands,
Ambassadors and lords and heads of state,
Whom every country to the wedding sends,
Are each in a pavilion, booth or tent
In comfort lodged and catered for, content.

76

Melissa, the resourceful sorceress,
The night before prepares the bridal room,
Adorning it with magic loveliness.
Long has she waited for this time to come!
This marriage, dreamed of by the prophetess
For many years, abundantly will bloom.
She knows the virtue which the Fates will grant
In future times to issue from this plant.

77

Melissa set the fertile thalamus
In a pavilion costlier and more
Resplendent, wider and more sumptuous
Than ever was set up in peace or war
In regions far away, or known to us.
She had removed it from the Thracian shore
When it had sheltered Constantine, who lay
At ease beside the sea one sunny day.

78

Melissa, first obtaining the consent
Of Leon, to surprise him with her skill
(For she could put a bridle of restraint
Upon the neck of the great Worm of Hell
And on him and the whole malevolent
And God-defying crew could work her will),
Had given demons orders to transfer
The tent, and in obedience to her

79

From off the prostrate Emperor of all
The Greeks, the demons lifted at mid-day
The tent, the guy-ropes and the centre pole,
And fittings, both inside and out. Away
They flew, nor did they let their burden fall,
But set it down, a lodging fair and gay,
Where it would serve the noble bride and groom.
They then restored it to Byzantium.

80

Two thousand years before, the costly tent
Had been embroidered by a Trojan maid.
Prophetic powers to her the gods had lent
And many true and tragic things she said.
Both day and night long hours at work she spent
And with her needle a fair story made.
She was Cassandra, sister of the brave
And dauntless Hector; him the work she gave.

81

The noblest, the most gallant cavalier
Of all who from her brother's stock would spring
(Though many branches, she was well aware,
Would intervene to which much fruit would cling),
She had depicted with a skill so rare,
In gold and silk, of hues so ravishing,
That for its sake and hers, long as he lived,
Her brother prized the gift he had received.

82

When he had met his death by treachery,
And Troy fell victim to the wooden horse,
Deceived by cunning Sinon's strategy
(And what ensued was infinitely worse
Than ever was described in history),
By lot to Menelaus in due course
The gift was passed; and, next, to Proteus
Of Egypt, where the lovely Helen was.

83

The king of Egypt in exchange for her
From grateful Menelaus received the tent;
And in succession, next, from heir to heir,
From Ptolemy to Ptolemy, it went.
Then lost by Cleopatra in the affair
Of Actium and by Agrippa sent
To Augustus; with Tiberius in Rome
It stayed, and then to Constantine had come,

84

That Constantine whom Italy will rue
Long as the spheres revolve in harmony,
That same who of the Tiber weary grew
And eastwards bore the precious canopy.
It was not he from whom Melissa drew
The ropes of gold, the pole of ivory,
The stitches which Apelles' brush outshine
In beauty, but a later Constantine.

85

The Graces, in gay, festive garments clad,
Are in attendance as a queen gives birth.
So beautiful a child is there portrayed,
His equal has been never seen on earth.
Jove, Venus, Mars and Mercury, lending aid,
Ethereal flowers scatter, with no dearth
Of sweet ambrosia and every bloom
Whose petals breathe celestial perfume.

86

'Ippolito' in tiny lettering
Is written on the infant's swaddling-bands.
Next, Valour as their guide acknowledging,
Adventure and the growing boy join hands.
Long-haired ambassadors a message bring;
Long garments show they come from foreign lands.
They beg the father for consent to take
His son abroad for Matthew Corvin's sake.

87

Of Ercole he takes a reverent leave
And of his mother Leonora too.
Next, on the Danube, crowds the boy receive
And homage pay which to a god is due.
The king of Hungary (whom few deceive)
Admires and honours one so young who to
Such wisdom has attained; he raises him
Even above his barons in esteem.

88

He places in his nephew's childish hand
The sceptre of Strigonia, and close
To him he likes the noble youth to stand;
At court, abroad and everywhere he goes,
Ippolito is always near at hand.
When Turks or Germans are his uncle's foes
He witnesses the strategy of war
And understands what deeds of valour are.

89

Next he is shown employing his best years
In the pursuit of learning and of art.
Tommaso Fusco close to him appears
And teaches him what ancient works impart:
'Follow this precept, from that be averse,
If glory is the course which you would chart.'
He seems thus to be heard as well as seen,
So well depicted have his gestures been.

90

And next he is a Cardinal, still young,
In solemn conclave in the Vatican;
And as he speaks his lofty mind among
The Consistory, his elders scarcely can
Conceal their stupor and burst out ere long:
'What will he be when he becomes a man?
Oh, if St Peter's mantle falls on him,
How blest, how fortunate our age will seem!'

91

The pastimes of the noble boy, elsewhere
Depicted, show him climb the craggy peaks
And unperturbed confront the mountain bear;
Or else the boar in swampy vales he seeks,
Or hunts the roebuck or the veteran deer,
As swifter than the wind his jennet streaks
And, overtaken, by one sword-stroke hit,
His prey collapses and in half is slit.

92

And here with poets and philosophers
He's found among an honoured company.
With one about the heavens he confers,
With one discourses of geography;
One recites elegies, one joyful verse,
One epic poems or gay odes maybe.
Musicians sing and play and as he dances
His graceful steps attract admiring glances.

93

The first part of the canopy displayed
This godlike progeny's sublime *enfance*.
Cassandra on the other had portrayed
His prudence, justice, valour, temperance.
To these four virtues she saw fit to add
A fifth: the virtue of munificence,
Which ever with the other four combines.
With all these radiant attributes he shines.

94

Still in his youth, as counsellor he's shown
To the unhappy Sforza of Milan.
In times of peace, their two minds are as one.
In times of war, with him he leads the van.
His friendship is to be depended on,
Whatever Fortune in caprice may plan.
With him in his sad exile he resides;
In grief he comforts him, in danger guides.

95

Elsewhere he is depicted deep in thought:
The safety of his brother and the State
Is jeopardized, but he reveals the plot;
By a strange means he catches in his net
Alfonso's dearest relatives, who sought
With treacherous intent to seal his fate.
For this the Ferrarese on him bestow
The name the Romans gave to Cicero.

96

In haste to help the Church, behold him ride
In shining armour, with a motley band,
To face an army fully trained and tried.
The force by which the priests can make a stand
His presence is sufficient to provide.
The fire is doused before the flame is fanned.
To him those words can be applied of which we
Read in history: *veni, vidi, vici.*

97

Now from his native shore behold him seek
To drive the strongest navy ever sent
By the Venetians against Turk or Greek.
He scatters it and after the event
He leads the broken vessels up the creek,
Where to his brother he will then present
The spoils he brings as victor of the fray,
Save honour, which he cannot give away.

98

The cavaliers and ladies gathered round
And at the tent uncomprehending gazed,
For there was no one near who could expound
The meaning of the figures they appraised;
Yet pleasure in the craftsmanship they found
And pointed to the lettering, amazed.
Fair Bradamante was the only one
To whom the sense had fully been made known.

99

Ruggiero does not know the tale as well
As Bradamante, but he calls to mind
The stories which Atlante used to tell:
Ippolito, whose glory he divined,
He often praised. Alas! impossible
It is to sing in full all those refined
Delights, the varied games, the festive mood,
The tables plentifully spread with food.

100

They test the mettle of a cavalier,
They break a thousand lances in one day,
They fight on foot, astride a destrier,
They fight in single combat, or mêlée.
None else is so proficient as Ruggier:
He always wins in every kind of fray,
In dancing, wrestling; whatsoe'er the fight,
He keeps on top with honour, day and night.

101

For the ninth day (it was to be the last)
A solemn banquet Charlemagne had planned.
The hour had struck, they had begun the feast,
Charles had the bridal pair on either hand,
When suddenly they saw approach in haste
A knight in arms; against the festive band,
A towering bulk and hostile, he rode on.
Black were his surcoat and caparison.

102

The knight was Rodomonte of Algiers.
When Bradamante felled him on the pass,
To use no arms, to ride no destriers,
He swore, but in a hermit's cell to pass
His time in prayer and repentant tears
Until a year, a month, a day should pass,
For it was customary in those days
For knights to purge their errors in such ways.

103

He heard the news of Charles's victory,
He heard the news of Agramante's fate,
But he observed his vow religiously
And in his hermit-cell preferred to wait.
A year, a month, a day had finally
Gone by and then at last, though it was late,
With a new horse, new arms, new sword, new lance,
He started for the royal court of France.

104

Without an inclination of the head,
Without a single gesture of respect,
Without dismounting from his thoroughbred,
With scorn he faced that noble and select
Assembly; they sat open-mouthed indeed,
Their meal suspended and their converse checked;
Amazed at his contemptuous display,
They wondered what the warrior would say.

105

Advancing now to where he could confront
Charles and Ruggiero, angrily he roared:
'I am the king of Sarza, Rodomont.
I challenge you, Ruggiero; with my sword
E'er sunset I will settle our account,
I'll prove you are a traitor to your lord;
No honour you deserve among these knights;
Apostate, you have forfeited your rights!

106

'Your felony is obvious and clear,
Your change of faith is not to be denied,
But plainer still I'll make the truth appear.
If anyone declares that I have lied,
I'll prove him wrong and any challenger
By whom my charge of treason is defied;
Against not one, but five or six or ten,
I'll fight and what I've said I will maintain.'

107

Ruggiero at this challenge stood upright.
With Charles's leave, he uttered his retort:
Who called him traitor, lied, as he was quite
Prepared to prove in presence of the court
Against his false accuser in fair fight,
For he was innocent of any tort.
He'd always served his monarch as he should.
The truth of what he said he would make good.

108

Being well able to defend his cause,
He had no need of help from anyone.
He hoped to show that his opponent was
Unable to combat with more than one.
Rinaldo and Orlando did not pause:
The marquess, Aquilante and Grifon,
Marfisa and Dudon rushed to his side,
And one and all the infidel defied.

109

They were unwilling that, so newly wed,
Ruggiero should thus interrupted be.
'Do not disturb yourselves, my friends,' he said,
'Excuses such as these seem base to me.'
The arms of Mandricard (who is now dead)
Were brought. All spring to help him instantly:
Orlando fastens on his golden spurs,
The hands that gird him are the Emperor's.

110

Marfisa and his bride with loving care
The greaves and breastplate have secured in place.
Astolfo holds his famous destrier,
Ugier his stirrup, while, outside, a space
Rinaldo, Namo and the marquess clear;
All bystanders and onlookers they chase
From the stockade, which ever ready is
For battles and encounters such as this.

111

The matrons and the maidens, blanched with fright,
Flutter like doves which from the fields of grain
Are driven to their nests by the winds' spite
When lightning flashes and when hail and rain
Are threatened by a sky as black as night,
And farmers see their labour all in vain.
For Bradamante's husband are their fears,
Who than the pagan less robust appears.

112

The commoners and the majority
Of cavaliers and barons thought the same,
For they recall – ah, horrid memory! –
What Paris at the pagan's hands became,
When single-handed unremittingly
He laid the city low with sword and flame.
The signs of the destruction still remain,
And will for long, the worst in the domain.

113

More trembling than all others was the heart
Of Bradamante; not that she believed
The Saracen more courage could assert,
Or promise of success he had received
From knowing he could claim the greater part
Of right and justice; none the less she grieved,
For apprehension for the one we love
Is no unworthy consequence of love.

114

How gladly to herself she would transfer
The trial which as yet uncertain is,
Even if all the indications were
That the ordeal would end in her decease!
To die, and more than once, she would prefer
(If death can offer more than one release);
Sooner than see her consort risk his life,
She'd take his place in the ensuing strife.

115

All her entreaties are of no avail.
Ruggiero will not yield to her request.
She stands to watch the combat from the rail,
Tears in her eyes, a tremor in her breast.
And now Ruggiero and the infidel,
Their visors down and each of each in quest,
Are riding hard; their lances break like ice,
The hafts, like birds, fly upwards in a trice.

116

The pagan's lance which struck Ruggiero's shield
Full centre had the puniest effect.
The steel of Trojan Hector did not yield,
So well does Vulcan's tempering protect.
Likewise the weapon which Ruggiero held
Struck Rodomonte's shield, but passed unchecked
Despite the covering of steel and bone
And thickness of a palm, or more than one.

117

Splinters and larger fragments flew so high,
Each might have been a feathered shuttlecock,
Soaring beyond the gaze of every eye.
This for the pagan was a stroke of luck:
His breastplate would have been split open by
Ruggiero's lance, but on the shield it broke.
The battle might have ended save for that,
But now both chargers on their haunches sat.

118

No time is lost, for both the cavaliers
With spur and bridle urge their steeds to stand.
Their lances now being broken, each prefers
To test and prove the other with his brand.
Their blows, as they resume, are shrewd and fierce.
Their destriers are nimble and well trained.
Twisting now here, now there, for chinks they seek
Or thrust their sword-points where the steel is weak.

119

That day the breastplate which the pagan wore
Was not the dragon's hide, as hard as stone.
He did not wield the blade which Nimrod bore.
The helmet on his head was not his own.
His usual arms (did I not say before?),
When vanquished by the lady of Dordogne,
He placed as a memento in the shrine,
Where many other arms and weapons shine.

120

The other arms the Saracen possessed
Were excellent, though not so fine or hard;
But neither these nor Nimrod's could resist
The penetrating strokes of Balisard.
Not even magic armour stands the test,
The finest steel can no defence afford.
So well Ruggiero goes to work with her,
The pagan's arms soon look the worse for wear.

121

When Rodomonte sees so many gashes
And knows he is unable to elude
The greater part of Balisarda's slashes,
Which pierce him to the body and draw blood,
More furious than the winter sea which crashes
From full height to the shore in raging mood,
He casts away his shield and with both hands
A blow on his opponent's helmet lands.

122

Just as an engine on the river Po,
Steadied on two pontoons, is winched on high
And, then released, inflicts a mighty blow
Upon the pointed stakes beneath, now by
The Saracen, the better to bestow
A stroke by which his enemy shall die,
The sword is lifted in two hands: it drops.
Its force Ruggiero's magic helmet stops.

123

Ruggiero staggers twice and forward bends,
His arms and legs apart, for balance, flings.
The Saracen again his sword upends,
And down upon Ruggiero's helmet brings
A second blow, a third; but there it ends.
The sword cannot endure such hammerings.
It flies in pieces and the pagan's hand
Is left, to his surprise, without a brand.

124

The Saracen is not to be deterred:
He leaps upon his foe, who nothing feels;
His head is so concussed, his mind so blurred,
That everything revolves and spins and wheels;
But from his slumber he is quickly stirred.
The pagan wrenches him about the gills,
Uproots him from between his saddle-bows,
And on the ground with frenzied vigour throws.

125

No sooner is he down than to his feet
He springs, and anger moves him less than shame.
His eyes the eyes of Bradamante meet,
He sees her cheeks with grief and rage aflame.
When she had seen her gallant husband hit
The ground, aghast with terror she became.
But now, to make amends for his disgrace,
He grasps his sword and turns, his foe to face.

126

The pagan urged his horse against Ruggier.
He nimbly stepped aside and, as it passed,
He caught the bridle of the destrier.
His left hand turned it round and held it fast,
His right meanwhile attacked the cavalier
In thigh, in flank, in abdomen, in breast.
Twice he succeeded, twice inflicted pain,
First in the flank, then in the thigh again.

127

The sword had splintered in the pagan's hand,
But now he crashed upon Ruggiero's head
The pommel and the hilt which still remained.
At this, Ruggiero's senses might have fled,
But right was on his side and fate had planned
That he should be the victor; so instead,
Using both hands, he seized his arm and tugged him
Till from the saddle finally he lugged him.

128

The pagan's strength or skill had let him fall
On equal footing with his enemy.
I mean, he landed on his feet, that's all.
Ruggiero had a sword, so it was he
Who was advantaged; seeking to forestall
The Saracen's approach, which would not be
A welcome move, he kept him at arm's length,
For bulk like that would overcome his strength.

129

Meanwhile the Saracen was losing blood
From side and thigh and other wounds as well.
Ruggiero hoped that bit by bit he would
Become enfeebled and incapable
Of further strife, and yield at last for good.
The pagan held the hilt and pommel still.
With all his might he flung this broken arm
Against Ruggiero, causing grievous harm.

130

On cheek and shoulder he receives the blow.
The impact makes him reel from left to right.
He staggers, off his balance, to and fro,
And scarcely can he hold himself upright.
Now is the moment for the pagan to
Close in and take advantage of his plight.
He tries to do so, but too hastily:
His thigh-wound brings him down upon one knee.

131

And not a moment does Ruggiero lose.
He strikes him in the chest and in the face.
He hammers him so hard and keeps so close,
The ground appears the pagan's favourite place.
But up he rises and his arms he throws
Around Ruggiero in a tight embrace.
They strained and writhed and wrestled intertwined,
Their superhuman strength with skill combined.

132

The pagan's stamina was growing less,
His gaping wounds so copiously bled.
Ruggiero had great skill and nimbleness.
To bouts of wrestling he was born and bred.
Thus his advantage he knew how to press,
And where the most amount of blood was shed,
Where Rodomonte's injuries were worst,
His arms and chest and both his feet he thrust.

133

But Rodomonte, full of rage and scorn,
Seizes Ruggiero round the neck; he hugs
And presses, squeezes, pulls and twists; in turn,
Ruggiero pushes, Rodomonte tugs.
High off his feet the Christian knight is borne
Upon the pagan's chest; with shakes and shrugs
He tries to·throw him down with every move.
Ruggiero tries his best to stay above.

134

Ruggiero, changing holds this way and that,
The pagan round the middle tried to seize.
Pinning his left side down with all his weight,
He held him helpless in a rigid squeeze;
And while he had the pagan in this state,
He thrust his right leg over both his knees;
Then, with this purchase, hoisted him at last
And head first from his back his burden cast.

135

With head and shoulders Rodomonte struck
The earth and such a thump his body made,
Blood spurted from his wounds as from a rock
A fountain springs, and stained the earth bright red.
Ruggiero, who had Fortune by the lock,
Knelt on his belly, while one hand he laid
Upon his throat; lest he attempt to rise,
He held a dagger poised above his eyes.

136

As sometimes where the miners dig for gold
In Hungary or, it may be, in Spain,
If suddenly the roof caves in, to hold
As captives those who burrowed there for gain,
So heavy is the fall of earth which rolled
Upon their chests, they cannot breathe for pain,
So now the pagan, once he had been floored,
His conqueror's oppressive weight endured.

137

Ruggiero holds the dagger at the sights
Of Rodomonte's helm; he makes it clear
By threats that his surrender he invites,
And says that in exchange his life he'll spare.
The thought of death the pagan less affrights
Than of betraying the least sign of fear.
To heave Ruggiero off, he twists and shakes
With all his might and not a word he speaks.

138

A mastiff under a ferocious hound
Whose fangs are fast embedded in its throat
In vain will writhe and struggle on the ground,
Its eyes ablaze, and flecked with spume its coat;
It knows that in its enemy is found
A greater strength, a greater skill, though not
More rage; so now the pagan must despair
Of throwing off his conqueror, Ruggier.

139

And yet he twists and turns in such a way,
He manages to pull his right arm free.
He too had drawn his dagger in the fray
And now attempts to use it furtively.
Ruggiero sees the danger straight away:
Stabbed in the back he knows that he will be
If here and now he does not end the strife
By cutting short the evil pagan's life.

140

Raising his arm as high as would suffice,
He plunged his dagger in that awesome brow,
Retrieving it not once, but more than twice.
To Acheron's sad shores, that spirit now,
Freed from its body, colder far than ice,
Fled cursing from the world, to disavow
The right which all his life he had defied
With insolence and arrogance and pride.

FINIS

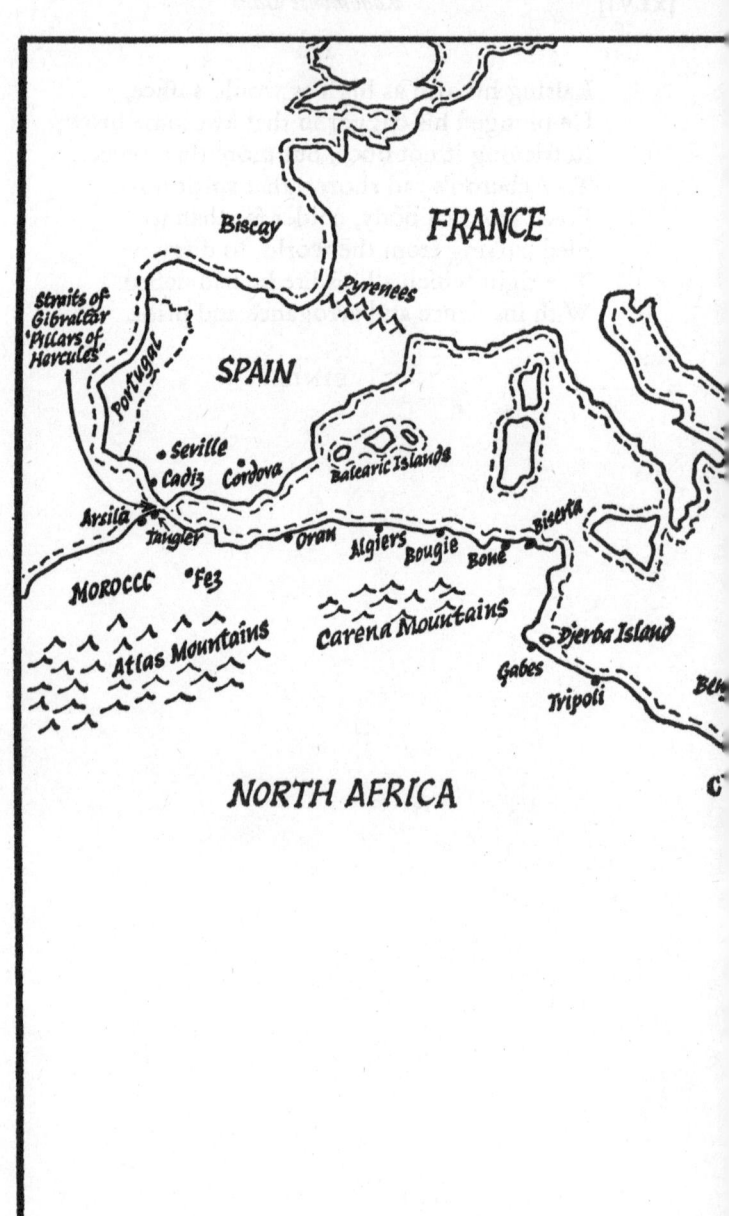

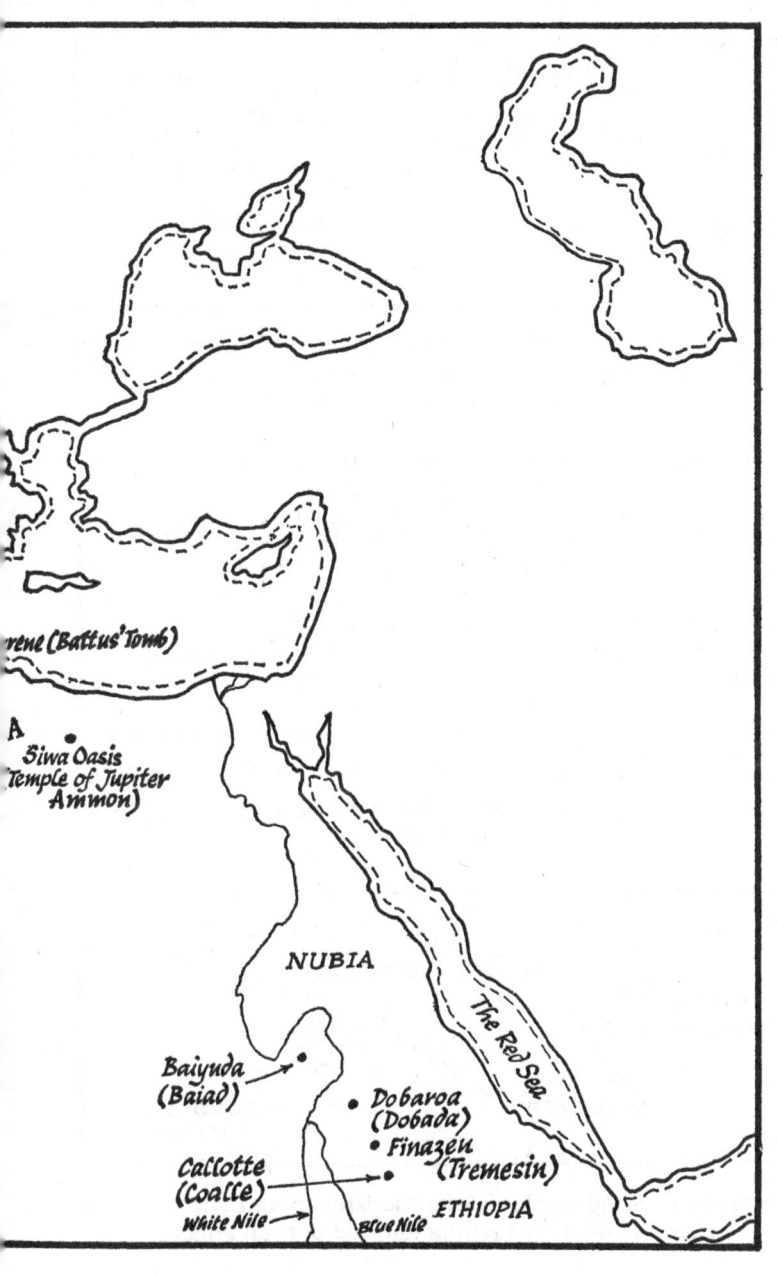

rene (Battus' Tomb)

A
Siwa Oasis
Temple of Jupiter
Ammon)

NUBIA

The Red Sea

Baiyuda
(Baiad)

Dobaroa
(Dobada)

Finazen
(Tremesin)

Callotte
(Coalle)

White Nile   Blue Nile

ETHIOPIA

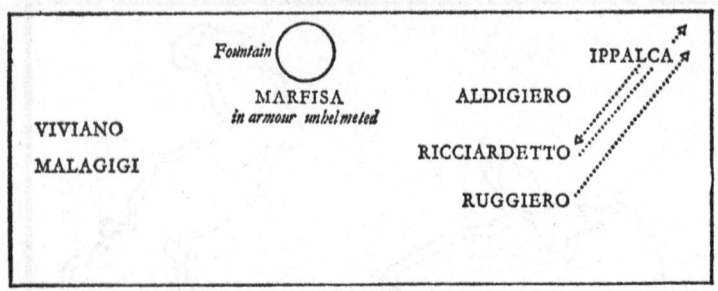

XXVI. 28–9; 54–61. Viviano and Malagigi, mounted, are on guard; the others are at ease. Ippalca arrives, tells Ricciardetto about Frontino; Ruggiero leaves with her.

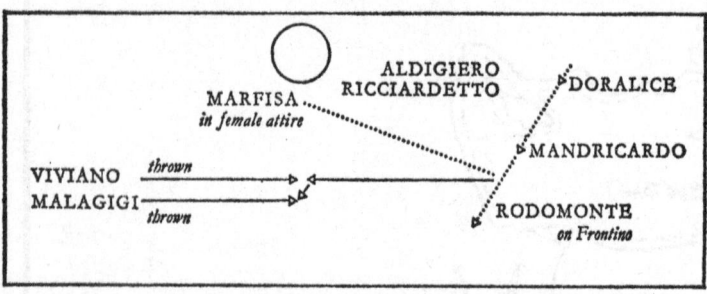

XXVI. 69–74. Mandricardo challenges the Christians for Marfisa. Rodomonte looks on as Viviano and Malagigi are unhorsed by Mandricardo.

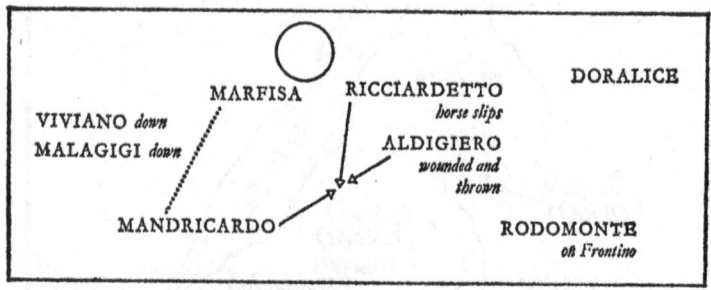

XXVI. 75–9. Mandricardo defeats Ricciardetto and Aldigiero and claims Marfisa. She refutes him and puts on armour.

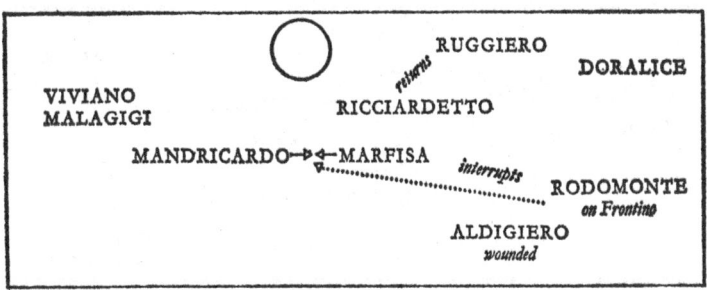

XXVI. 80–88. Rodomonte interrupts combat between Mandricardo and Marfisa. Ruggiero returns.

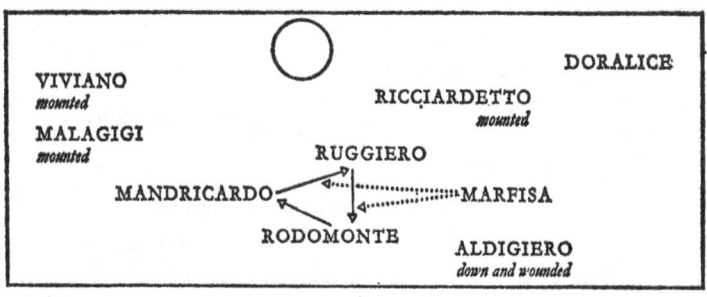

XXVI. 92–112. Ruggiero challenges Rodomonte, who at first refuses combat; Mandricardo challenges Ruggiero. Rodomonte challenges Mandricardo. Marfisa tries to interrupt the triple combat.

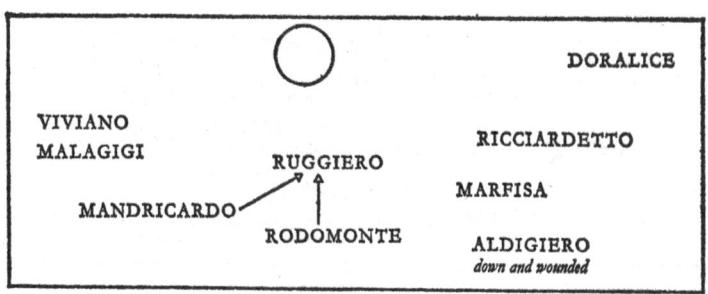

XXVI. 115–17. Rodomonte and Mandricardo both attack Ruggiero. He drops his sword, Balisarda, and loses his balance.

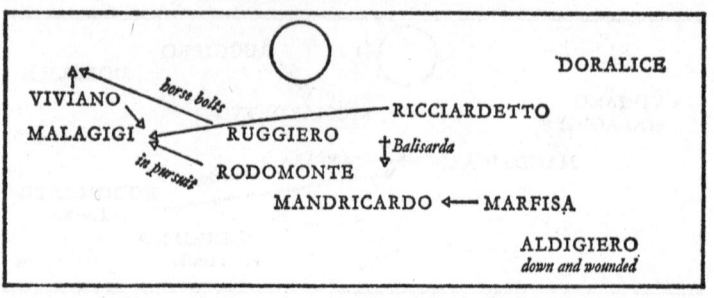

XXVI. 118–19. Ruggiero's horse bolts; Rodomonte, pursuing, is blocked by Viviano and Ricciardetto; Viviano gives Ruggiero another sword; Marfisa attacks Mandricardo.

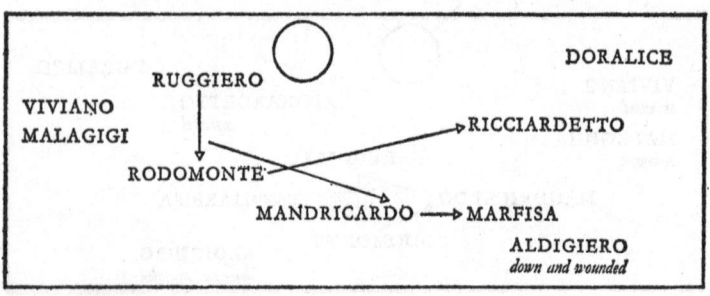

XXVI. 120–127. Rodomonte, struck by Ruggiero, dangles from his saddle. Marfisa's charger slips; Ruggiero goes to her rescue. Rodomonte recovers his balance and rides against Ricciardetto.

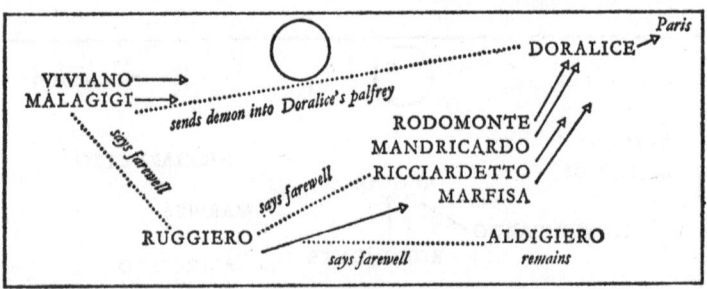

XXVI. 128–37. Malagigi bewitches Doralice's palfrey. She gallops off, followed by Rodomonte and Mandricardo. Marfisa pursues them. Ruggiero bids farewell. Only Aldigiero remains.

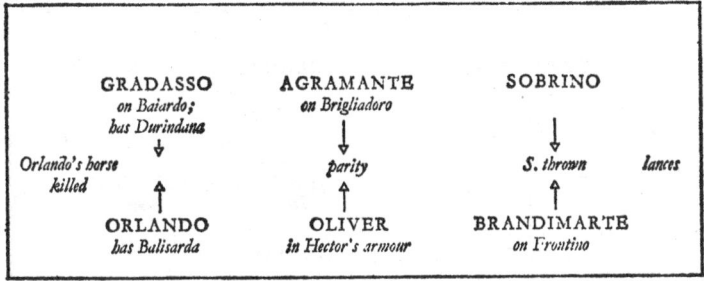

XLI. 69–71. At the first encounter Orlando is left without a horse.

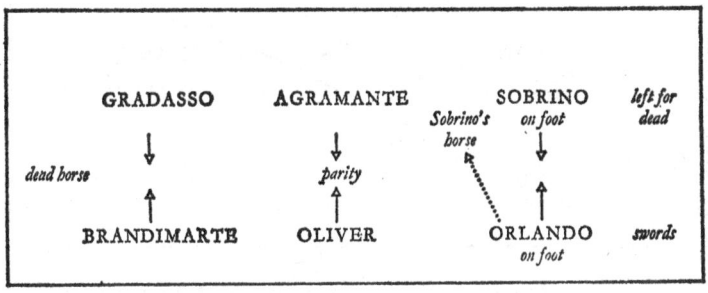

XLI. 72–6. Brandimarte and Orlando change places.

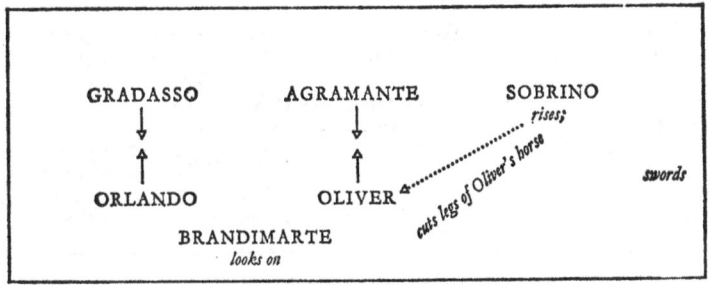

XLI. 77–87. Orlando, remounted, continues combat with Gradasso.

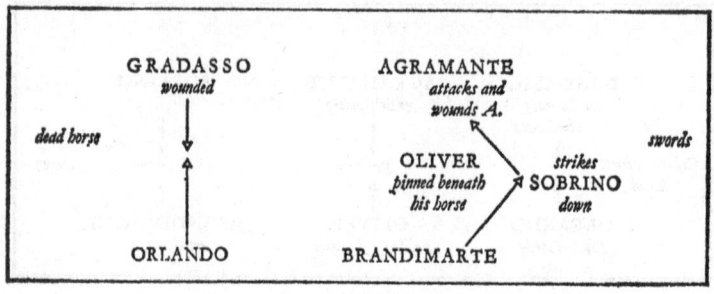

XLI. 87–93. Brandimarte takes action.

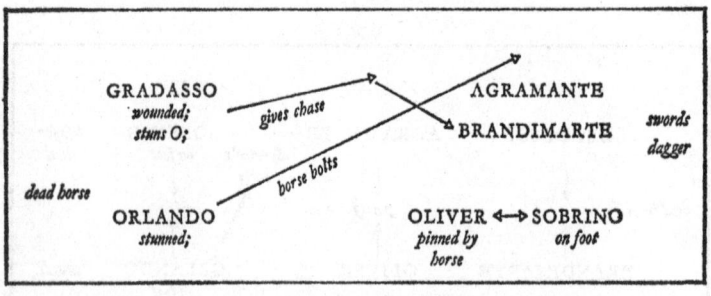

XLI. 94–101. Gradasso turns from pursuing Orlando to rescue Agramante; he mortally wounds Brandimarte.

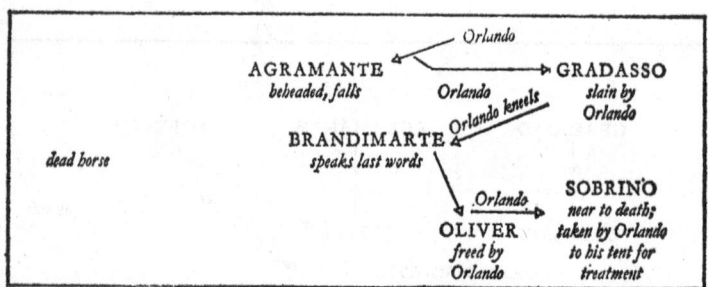

XLI. 102; XLII. 8–15. Orlando, looking back, sees Brandimarte wounded and avenges him.

NOTES

CANTO XXIV

4. cf. Vol. I, XXIII. 129–36.

10. l. 5. cf. XII. 49.

ll. 6–8. *God on high had planned . . .* cf. St John's words to Astolfo in the Terrestrial Paradise (XXXIV. 62–6).

11. l. 2. Ariosto avoids the issue of Orlando's death at Roncevaux. His invulnerability is not, however, inconsistent with the manner of his death; cf. *Chanson de Roland* (Laisse 134–5; 156; 168).

14. The bridge and tower mentioned here have been constructed by Rodomonte (XXIX. 33–5).

15. ll. 1–3. For Orlando's instructions to Zerbino, see XXIII. 98–9.
ll. 7–8. The knight is Odorico; the two cavaliers are Corebo and Almonio. For Odorico's betrayal of Isabella, see XIII. 20–29.

18. l. 5. *The markings on his shield.* For Zerbino's royal bearings, see X. 83–4 and Note.

19. l. 2. *where the humble clasp the great.* Round the knees.

26. l. 1. The king mentioned here is Alfonso, who occurs in Boiardo's *Orlando Innamorato* (II. xxiii. 6), where he is shown to be a Christian.
a free field. Where jousting is allowed without indemnity.

35. l. 7. *the hag.* Gabrina. For Mandricardo's unbridling of her horse, see XXIII. 92–5.

39. l. 8. cf. stanza 91, ll. 5–7.

44–5. For the story of Gabrina as custodian of Isabella, Ariosto is partly indebted to the *Metamorphoses* (*The Golden Ass*) of Apuleius. In Book IV there is a grotto inhabited by thieves who have kidnapped a princess and placed her in the keeping of an old crone. Like Gabrina, the old woman too is finally hanged.

46. l. 4. cf. X. 83–4.

47. l. 1. *the brave paladin.* Orlando.
l. 5. *the Tartar knight.* Mandricardo.
l. 8. cf. XXIII. 96–8.

49. cf. XXIII. 132–3; for the brass helmet, see XII. 67.

53. ll. 7–8. Ariosto here keeps the promise he made in VIII. 90.

55. Brandimarte was imprisoned in Atlante's palace and released by Astolfo (XII. 11 and XXII. 20).

57. ll. 3–4. This inscription on the bark recalls the inscriptions of the names of Angelica and Medoro (XXIII. 102 ff.).

60. l. 3. *The blade of Hector*. Durindana.

61. ll. 7–8. Virgil, *Aeneid* (VI. 440–44), places the souls of lovers in a myrtle-grove. In this he is followed by Petrarch in his *Trionfo dell' Amore* (I. 150).

66. l. 3. *that hand*. The hand of his lady, Alessandra Benucci. The comparison is perhaps an adaptation from the *Iliad* (IV. 141–5).

71. l. 7. Doralice is accompanying Mandricardo; cf. XXIII. 89–94.

74. l. 6. *as she crossed a river*. This is the river spanned by the bridge constructed by Rodomonte (XXIX. 33–5).

83. l. 4. *Your father's shores*. Galicia; cf. XIII. 4, 14.

84. cf. XII. 86–94; XIII. 15–29 and 32–43.

85. ll. 2–5. For this simile, cf. Petrarch, *Trionfo della Morte* (I. 163–4).

93. ll. 5–6. The knight is Rodomonte, who will meet Isabella later in the story (XXIX. 3 ff.). He comes now to meet Mandricardo.

95. ll. 7–8. Doralice, on her way to join Rodomonte, was kidnapped by Mandricardo (XIV. 40–64).

97. l. 4. *The monarch of Algiers*. Rodomonte.

l. 8. *the rash deed*. The kidnapping of Doralice.

102. ll. 5–6. *more than the stars that ring | The world*. The stars of the eighth heaven.

l. 8. *his lady*. Doralice (though she is no longer his).

104. l. 2. *the son of Agrican*. Mandricardo.

105. ll. 7–8. Mandricardo wears Hector's armour and helmet; cf. XIV. 31.

108. For the pagans' reverses, see XVIII. 156–62.

112. l. 4. *Troiano's son*. Agramante.

Ulieno's son. Rodomonte.

113. ll. 3–6. They do so; cf. XXX. 47 ff.

114. The plans of Discord and Pride to foment enmity between Rodomonte and Mandricardo have been only temporarily successful; cf. XVIII. 26–37.

115. l. 5. Brigliadoro has been left by Orlando to wander; cf. stanza 49.

CANTO XXV

3. ll. 5–8. The dwarf had been sent by Doralice to summon Rodomonte's help (xviii. 28–9, 32–5; xxiii. 33, 38).

4. ll. 1–4. The two knights wearing helmets are Viviano and Malagigi (cf. xxvi. 54); the two without helmets are Ricciardetto and Aldigiero; the damsel is Marfisa (cf. xxvi. 68–9 and 72).

ll. 7–8. cf. xxii. 90–93.

6. ll. 5–8. *The lady* . . . This is the unnamed lady who sought the help of Bradamante and Ruggiero for a youth condemned to be burned alive (xxii. 37–41 and 89).

8. l. 8. *the youth.* He is revealed as Ricciardetto (cf. stanza 24 ff.).

11. l. 2. *his last combat.* Ruggiero's combat with four knights at Pinabello's castle (xxii. 64 ff.).

13. l. 7. *metal caps.* Roughly-shaped protections for the head.

14. ll. 5–8. Earthquake and Great Devil were the names of two of Duke Alfonso's cannons. Two others were named Julia (a bronze statue by Michelangelo of Pope Julius II was melted down to make this one), and Queen. (The Italian names are: Terremoto, Gran Diavolo, Giulia and Regina.)

15. ll. 7–8 and 16. ll. 1–4. *The cruel sword.* Balisarda, made by Falerina (see Note to vii. 76).

22–3. See Table, Vol. I, p. 735.

24. ll. 1–2. Bradamante's injury is mentioned by Boiardo, *Orlando Innamorato* (iii. v. 45; viii. 54).

27. l. 8. The story of Fiordispina's love for Bradamante is begun by Boiardo, *Orlando Innamorato* (iii. viii. 63 ff., ix. 3 ff.). She is first mentioned, though not named, by Ariosto in xxii. 39–40.

32. ll. 3–5. Bradamante's early years in Arzilla have not been mentioned before. Arzilla is probably the modern Arsila, on the Atlantic coast of Morocco, south of Tangier.

35. Ariosto is here being disingenuous concerning Lesbianism.

36. l. 5. *The wife of Ninus.* Semiramis, the Assyrian queen, whose legendary love for her son Ninyas was the subject of a drama by Voltaire (*Sémiramis*, 1748). She is among the lustful in Dante's *Inferno* (v. 52–60).

l. 6. *Myrrha.* The mother of Adonis by her father Cinyras.

l. 7. *Pasiphae.* The wife of Minos, King of Crete, and mother of the Minotaur, the offspring of her union with a bull.

37. This stanza and the story of Fiordispina and Ricciardetto are inspired by Ovid's story of Iphis in *Metamorphoses* (IX. 705 ff.).
    ll. 4–7. Daedalus, the father of Icarus, was an inventor at the court of King Minos of Crete. He constructed the wooden cow in which Pasiphae concealed herself to achieve union with the bull. Imprisoned by Minos, he escaped with Pasiphae's help and fastened wings on himself and Icarus by means of wax. Fiordispina cites him as the supreme inventor; even his ingenuity would be defeated by her dilemma.

44. l. 2. *To her Mahomet*. Fiordispina, the daughter of Marsilio, is a Saracen.

52. l. 6. *their queen*. Fiordispina. Strictly, she is a princess.

63. Ariosto seems to be making fun of the lines which Dante gives to St Thomas Aquinas concerning Solomon's choice, in *Paradiso* XIII. 94–102.

64. There are witty echoes here of Ovid's *Metamorphoses*, III. 173–252, where Diana, seen bathing by Actaeon, splashes water in his face, causing horns to grow on his brow; turned into a stag, he is destroyed by his hounds. In the story Ricciardetto tells, the splash of water causes a horn of another kind to grow, and he is about to be pleasurably devoured by Fiordispina. This juxtaposition of the tragic and the comic is a feature of Ariosto's art.

68. The original of this stanza has been set as a madrigal by Vincenzo Ruffo (see *The Penguin Book of Italian Madrigals*, edited by Jerome Roche, pp. 81–7).

69. l. 5. *The sinuous acanthus*. The acanthus leaf is a decorative motif of the Corinthian column.

71. No more is heard of Fiordispina.
    l. 7. Agrismonte is a fortress owned by Buovo of Antona.

72. l. 1. For Aldigiero's connection with the Clairmont line, see Table, Vol. I, p. 735.
    ll. 3–5. Pulci says that Aldigiero is the *illegitimate* son of Gherardo (*Morgante*, XX. 105).

74. ll. 4–8. Bertolagi of Bayona is of the Maganzan line, the traditional enemies of the Clairmonts. Lanfusa is the mother of Ferraù. Her part in the bargain is derived from the epic *La Spagna*; cf. I. 30 and Note.

76. l. 7. This line is an adaptation of the words of St Matthew, 'The spirit indeed is willing, but the flesh is weak' (Matthew XXVI, 41).

77. l. 7. *This sword*. Balisarda.

81–3. cf. xxii. 34–7.

84. l. 8. cf. xxii. 74–5, 88, 97–8.

85. ll. 5–6. He does: Ippalca (cf. xxvi. 89–90).

88. l. 8. cf. Shakespeare, *The Phoenix and the Turtle*: 'So they loved as love in twaine, / Had the essence but in one, / Two distincts, Division none, / Number there in love was slaine'.

97. l. 3. *a knight*. Marfisa.

l. 6. *the phoenix*. In Boiardo's epic, Marfisa is said to have as a crest a green dragon which spurts fire (*Orlando Innamorato*, I. xviii. 4).

CANTO XXVI

3. ll. 5–8. *a cavalier . . . the bird*. See Notes to xxv. 97.

4. l. 1. *the three*. Aldigiero, Ricciardetto and Ruggiero.

8. ll. 6–8. cf. xx. 121–8.

10. ll. 5–6. *the two / Defenceless brothers*. Viviano and Malagigi.

13. l. 1. *Count Buovo's [son]*. Aldigiero.

Count Aymon's son. Ricciardetto.

20. ll. 7–8. In Ptolemaic astronomy, the heaven of Mars is fifth in order from the earth.

24. l. 3. *Bellona*. Roman goddess of war. Macbeth is called 'Bellona's bridegroom' (i, ii, 56).

26. l. 8. *many a willing hand*. Squires, pages, etc., are always in attendance on the knights, though seldom mentioned.

30. ll. 1–2. *one of four / In France*. In the epic *La Spagna*, Merlin is said to have constructed magic fountains in Spain. Boiardo mentions three in France, but does not make it clear if they were all made by Merlin.

31. l. 1. *a loathsome beast*. It symbolizes avarice and cupidity.

32. ll. 4–6. Ariosto is echoing Dante, *Inferno* (vii. 46–8; xix. 112–14); cf. vii. 4. of this poem.

33. ll. 5–8. Ariosto is alluding here to the simonists and to the sale of indulgences.

ll. 7–8. cf. *Inferno* (xxvii. 103–4).

34. l. 2. *A knight*. Francis I, King of France (1515–1547) is presented as the foremost opponent of avarice. His reign was characterized by lavish spending which left the treasury drained. The 'imperial laurel' (l. 1) symbolizes the victory of Francis I against the Swiss at the battle of Marignan (1515).

l. 5. *a banner similar*. Louis XI had given the Medici leave to add the golden fleur-de-lis to their arms.

34. l. 6. *A lion.* Pope Leo X (Giovanni dei Medici, Pontificate 1513–1521); cf. XVII. 79 and Note.
35. l. 4. *Maximilian.* The Emperor Maximilian I (1493–1519). He was so lavish with money that he came to be nicknamed 'Maximilian the Penniless'.

l. 5. *Charles the Fifth.* Holy Roman Emperor (1519–1556). This reference was inserted in the third edition.

l. 8. *Henry the Eighth* (1509–1549). His reputation for liberality and splendour was widespread at the beginning of his reign.

39. cf. *Macbeth* (IV, 1).
40. l. 1. *from the depths of Hell.* cf. Dante, *Inferno* (I. 110–11). In Ovid's *Metamorphoses*, the age of gold, when all was communally enjoyed, was followed at last by the age of iron which was dominated by the evil love of possession ('*amor sceleratus habendi*', I. 124–8).
41. ll. 1–4. In stanzas 36–7 the monster is shown to be destroyed. It seems that Malagigi gives warning of an ever-present and increasing danger of avarice and cupidity.

l. 5. *The famous python.* In Ovid's *Metamorphoses* (I. 438–44), after the flood, the earth brings forth monsters, among which is an enormous python, slain by Apollo's arrows.

44. ll. 1–2. *In the first year* ... Francis I came to the throne of France on 25 January 1515. The events referred to here occurred in August and September.

ll. 3–4. Francis I, advised by Giangiacomo Trivulzio, thwarted Prospero Colonna, who was holding the Col de Genèvre, by crossing the Alps by the Col de l'Argentière, a route no army had ever used before.

l. 6. *the disgrace.* The defeat of the French by the Swiss at Novara (1513).

l. 7. *frenzied herdsmen.* The Swiss, though among the best mercenaries in Europe, were contemptuously spoken of by the French troops as 'hares in armour'. In ll. 6–8, Ariosto uses words suggestive of primitive shepherds and herdsmen.

45. ll. 1–4. The scene of the battle was the northern outskirts of the village of Melegnano (Marignan) on the river Lambro, ten miles south-east of Milan. The Duke of Milan, Maximilian Sforza, was supported by the Emperor, Ferdinand of Spain, Pope Leo X, Florence and the Swiss cantons. The battle lasted 28 hours. Of the 25,000 Swiss who fought, only 3,000 escaped. Of the French, it has been estimated that 8,000 died.

l. 6. *A fortress.* The castle of the Sforza in Milan.

46. ll. 1–3. *The weapon*. Liberality, by which Francis bought over many former enemies.

47. ll. 3–4. Hannibal defeated the Romans at the battles of Trebbia and Lake Trasimene.

l. 5. Fortune favoured Francis at the beginning of his reign. His later misfortunes are acknowledged by Ariosto in the third edition of the poem; cf. XXXIII. 42–57.

48. ll. 6–8. Cardinal Bernardo Dovizi (1470–1520) of Bibbiena, a town in the Casentino region of Tuscany, was a generous patron of the arts and the author of a prose comedy, *Calandria*.

49. ll. 1–4. Three Cardinals are here mentioned: Sigismondo Gonzaga, Giovanni Salviati and Ludovico d'Aragona.

l. 5. *Francis of Mantua*. Francesco Gonzaga, Marquess of Mantua.
his son. Federigo II (the first Duke of Mantua), son of Francesco and Isabella d'Este.

ll. 7–8. *Two dukes*. The Duke of Ferrara was Alfonso I, brother-in-law of Francesco Gonzaga; Urbino's duke was Francesco Maria della Rovere, who married Francesco's daughter, Eleonora.

50. l. 1. *Guidobaldo*. This is Guidobaldo II, son of Francesco Maria della Rovere.

ll. 3–4. *Ottobono . . . Sinibaldo*. Ottobono and Sinibaldo Fieschi of Genoa were brothers.

l. 5. Luigi Gonzaga, Count of Sabbioneta and Gazolo, known for his strength and daring, was nicknamed 'Rodomonte'. Since he was a poet as well as a warrior, he is equipped with bow and arrows by Apollo, as well as with a sword by Mars; cf. XXXVII. 8–12.

51. l. 1. *Two Ercoles*. Ercole I and Ercole II, Dukes of Ferrara.
two Ippolitos. Cardinal Ippolito I, to whom the poem is dedicated, brother of Alfonso I; and Cardinal Ippolito II, son of Alfonso.

ll. 2–3. *another two*. Cardinals Ippolito dei Medici and Ercole Gonzaga.

l. 5. *Giuliano with his offspring*. Giuliano dei Medici, father of Cardinal Ippolito.

l. 6. *Ferrante with his brother*. Ferrante Gonzaga, brother of Cardinal Ercole.

l. 7. *Andrea Doria*. cf. XV. 30–35 and Note.

l. 8. Francesco Sforza, son of Ludovico il Moro, Duke of Milan.

52. l. 2. *Two of Avàlos*. The cousins, Francesco d'Avalos, Mar-

quess of Pescara, and Alfonso, Marquess of Vasto; cf. xv. 28–9 and Note.

52. ll. 3–4. *A mighty rock.* Mt Epomeo on the island of Ischia, which was a possession of the Avalos family. The giant Typhoeus is said by Ariosto to be buried beneath this mountain, not beneath Etna, where he places Enceladus (xii. 1). (Since there were two versions of the legend it is possible that the reference to Typhoeus in xvi. 23 implies Mt Etna.)

53. ll. 1–4. Consalvo of Cordova, the 'Great Captain' (1443–1515), who conquered the kingdom of Naples for Ferdinand the Catholic, and defeated the French on several occasions.

l. 6. *William of Monferrat.* Of the family of the Paleologhi; Marquess of Monferrato. He died in 1518.

54. l. 5. *the two brothers.* Viviano and Malagigi, who have their helmets on, as well as their armour; cf. xxv. 4.

55. ll. 1–6. cf. xxiii. 29–38.

56. ll. 7–8. The Montalbano family knows nothing of Bradamante's love for Ruggiero.

58. l. 6. *A region near Marseilles.* The shrine at Vallombrosa. (Ippalca is being discreet.)

59. l. 5. *an African.* Rodomonte.

60. l. 6. *a warrior.* Mandricardo; cf. xxiv. 95 ff.

67. l. 6. *the three.* Mandricardo, Doralice and the dwarf.

68. l. 2. *their king.* Agramante.

70. l. 3. *his lady.* Doralice.

l. 5. *The Sarzan monarch.* Rodomonte.

72. For the moves of this combat, see diagram on pp. 674–6.

81. l. 8. *the Troy-defending Amazon.* Penthesilea, the Amazon queen who defended the Trojans and was slain in an encounter with Achilles. This event occurs in the continuation of the *Iliad* (*Where Homer Ends*) by Quintus of Smyrna of the fourth century A.D.

83. l. 6. *magic armour.* Marfisa's armour is enchanted. Mandricardo wears the armour of Hector, which would seem to have acquired magic properties.

86. l. 4. *King Troiano's son.* Agramante.

87. ll. 1–5. cf. xviii. 99–100.

90. l. 1. *the letter.* cf. xxv. 85–92.

94. l. 1. *the Sarzan.* Rodomonte.

99. ll. 1–4. For Ruggiero's lineage, see Table, Vol. I, p. 734.

ll. 6–7. Mandricardo, who won the arms of Hector, claims exclusive right to bear the Trojan eagle; cf. xiv. 31.

100. l. 1. *the bird.* The eagle, into which Jupiter changed himself in order to seize Ganymede.

    ll. 3–8. This story is related by Boiardo, *Orlando Innamorato* (111. i. 2).

101. ll. 1–4. Ruggiero and Mandricardo have challenged each other's claim to the eagle on previous occasions; cf. stanza 104 and Note.

104. ll. 1–4. In Boiardo's *Orlando Innamorato* (111. vi), Ruggiero and Mandricardo are at odds over the Trojan emblem, when Ruggiero notices that Mandricardo has no sword. Mandricardo declares he will use no other sword than Durindana. Gradasso intervenes, saying that he also claims Durindana. He and Mandricardo then fight with branches and the duel with Ruggiero is deferred. Ariosto takes up the story at this point.

105. ll. 3–4. cf. xxiv. 57.

121. l. 2. *the sword.* Balisarda.

    l. 7. *king of Babel.* Nimrod.

122. cf. xxvii. 34–9.

    l. 4. *her sister.* Pride.

125. ll. 5–6. Mandricardo has taken possession of Brigliadoro (xxiv. 115).

128. In earlier romantic epics, Malagigi has studied magic in Toledo and he is qualified to practise it. He is for this reason called 'Mastro Malagigi'.

129. ll. 5–6. *Minos' black / Angels.* Demons in Hell, where Minos is a judge.

131. l. 1. *Ulieno's son.* Rodomonte.

136. ll. 1–4. Ruggiero has established friendly contact with the Christian knights by his rescue of Ricciardetto and by his help in rescuing Viviano and Malagigi. This is an important step in his progress towards conversion and acceptance by the Christian side.

137. l. 2. *stricken Aldigiero.* His wound is healed in time for him to rise to the next occasion; cf. xxxi. 55.

CANTO XXVII

2. l. 5. *two foes.* Rodomonte and Mandricardo.

3. l. 2. *his cousin.* Ricciardetto, who was threatened by Rodomonte; cf. xxvi. 127.

    l. 5. *the damsel.* Doralice, into whose horse Malagigi has sent a demon.

Notes

4. l. 5. *The demons*. The rebellious Angels who fell with Lucifer.

5. l. 5. *where the French and English troops were massed*. To the west of Paris, south of the Seine; cf. map of the Siege of Paris, Vol. I, pp. 474–5.

l. 8. *Granada's king*. Stordilano.

7. ll. 3–4. cf. XXII. 20. Sacripante was among the 'other warriors'.

9. cf. II. 15–27.

10. l. 1. *the battle*. i.e. the siege of Paris.

11. l. 2. *Brava . . . Anglante*. Two castles belonging to Orlando; Brava (also Blavia, Blaia) is thought to correspond to Blaye on the river Gironde; cf. stanza 101 and XXX. 91.

14. ll. 1–2. cf. XXII. 20.

15. l. 8. *The other pair*. Rodomonte and Mandricardo.

16. l. 3. *the black Angel*. Lucifer, now Satan.

l. 6. *the quarrel of the destrier*. Ruggiero's intention to regain Frontino from Rodomonte.

17. l. 1. *The previous four*. Rodomonte, Mandricardo, Gradasso and Sacripante.

19. l. 3. *the Swiss or Gascons*. The Swiss and Gascon mercenaries were reputed to be turbulent.

l. 7. *The nations*. The soldiers of each region are mustered under the banner of each leader. Each group is called a 'nation'.

20. l. 2. *Save for his head*. His helmet is carried, as was usual before battle, by his shield-bearer; cf. stanza 88. In all other respects he is armed. Since his head is visible, he is easily recognized by those whom he questions.

23. l. 3. *Ruggiero and Marfisa now advance*. They have been delayed half an hour behind Rodomonte, Mandricardo, Gradasso and Sacripante; cf. stanza 16.

ll. 7–8. See diagram of the Siege of Paris for position of pagan encampments (Vol. I, pp. 474–5).

32. l. 5. *the marquess of Vienne*. Oliver.

34. For the Archangel Michael's mission to Discord at the behest of God, see XIV. 75–90. Discord's efforts to kindle enmity between Rodomonte and Mandricardo have been thwarted by Love; cf. XXIV. 114. The combat by Merlin's fountain has made her over-confident and she has returned to the monastery, thinking that her work is done; cf. XXVI. 122.

41. For Marfisa's quarrel with Mandricardo, see XXVI. 78 ff.

47. ll. 7–8. *One similar . . .* This is Castel Guelfo, on the road from Parma to Borgo San Donnino.

49. l. 3. *His ancient armour*. It belonged to Rodomonte's ancestor, Nimrod; cf. XIV. 118–19.

l. 8. *The venerable arms*. These are the arms of Hector.

50. l. 2. *the two kings*. Agramante and Marsilio.

51. l. 1. *the queen of all Castile*. Marsilio's wife.

l. 4. *where the marks of Hercules are seen*. The Straits of Gibraltar.

ll. 7–8. The colours of Doralice's garments are said to be symbolic. The fresh green signifies her readiness to turn to a new love (Mandricardo); the pale red, her fading love for Rodomonte. This is a forecast of her choice; cf. stanza 107; also xxx. 71–3.

52. ll. 3–4. Hippolyta, Queen of the Amazons, was said to have her realm on the banks of the river Thermodon, which flows into the Black Sea.

54. l. 1. *the Tartar king*. Mandricardo.

ll. 5–8. cf. xii. 60 and xiv. 43. The story of Orlando's conquest of Almonte's helmet and sword is related in *Aspremont* (see Vol. I, Introduction, p. 57).

55. Gradasso's expedition to win Durindana is related by Boiardo, *Orlando Innamorato* (i. i. 23 ff.). Ariosto follows him in sending Gradasso by fleet round Africa; cf. xv. 20.

56. cf. xxiii. 70–87 and xxiv. 58–9.

57. This belief concerning the beaver was commonly held by the ancients. It is mentioned by Pliny (*Naturalis Historia*, 3) and by Juvenal (*Satires*, xii. 34–6). The genitals of the beaver were prized for their medicinal property.

60. l. 7. *the Sarzan monarch*. Rodomonte.

61. l. 3. *The white-winged bird*. The silver eagle.

68. l. 1. *Troiano's son*. Agramante.

69. ll. 5–6. *the son of the accurst / Lanfusa*. Ferraù.

70. l. 6. *The monarch of Circassia*. Sacripante.

l. 7. *The Sarzan king*. Rodomonte.

71. ll. 4–6. *once known by the name/Of Frontalatte*... This name means 'brow of milk', which indicates that the horse had a white blaze on its muzzle. Ruggiero, receiving it from Brunello, called it Frontino.

72. Boiardo relates the story of Brunello's many thefts in *Orlando Innamorato* (ii. v. 33–41; xl. 6; xvi. 56).

84. See Note to stanza 72, above.

85. l. 4. cf. xviii. 109.

86. l. 4. Brunello was spared by Bradamante, against Melissa's advice; cf. iii. 74 and iv. 13–15.

88. cf. Note to stanza 20, and xxvi. 69.

92. l. 4. *can make no rebuff*. Some of the pagans might wish to champion Brunello.

96. Sobrino, whose name means 'prudent, sober', always counsels caution and restraint. He originally advised Agramante not to undertake the expedition to France; cf. xxxviii. 49 ff.

102. l. 1. *five cavaliers*. Rodomonte, Mandricardo, Ruggiero, Gradasso and Sacripante.

116. ll. 1–2. cf. xxxv. 54.

117–21. Rodomonte's outburst against women is perhaps intended as a parody on sixteenth-century anti-feminist writings.

123–4. Ariosto may perhaps be contrasting Alessandra Benucci with women who proved unfaithful.

128. l. 7. *Aiguesmortes*. This city did not exist in Charlemagne's time. It was founded by Louis IX in the thirteenth century.

131. There is an echo here of the shepherd's concern at Orlando's depression; cf. xxiii. 118. He too resolves to cheer his guest with a story. There is a deliberate parallel between Orlando and Rodomonte in their respective situations as rejected lovers.

137. Francesco Valerio, a Venetian and a priest, was a friend of Ariosto, who includes him among the throng on the quay who welcome him on his return from his long voyage (xlvi. 16). He is believed to have written short stories, which remained unpublished. From the fact that Ariosto humorously gives his name to the originator of the tale of Fiammetta in Canto xxviii, some idea of the stories may perhaps be formed. Francesco Valerio was hanged in St Mark's Square in 1539 for conspiring with the enemies of Venice.

CANTO XXVIII

3. l. 8. *the story*. The tale which follows has many points of resemblance with the Prologue of *A Thousand and One Nights* (first European translation by Galland, 1701). Ariosto may have heard it from Francesco Valerio; but see Pio Rajna, *Le Fonti dell'Orlando Furioso*, 1900, pp. 435–55.

4. l. 1. *Astolfo*. He has been identified with Agilulf, King of the Lombards (591–615 A.D.), but this identification is rejected by some commentators, who refer to Rachis (the 'elder brother' of line 2) as the preceding king, who abdicated to become a monk in 749.

l. 5. *Zeuxis*. See Note to xi. 71.

Apelles. See Note to xxxiii. 1. 4.

18. ll. 6–8. cf. *The Merchant of Venice* (iii, ii, 171 ff.; v, i, 166 ff.).

19. l. 7. *Baccano*. A village near Rome.

24. l. 6. *Corneto*. An appropriate place, given the resemblance of the name to *cornuto* ('cuckolded'). The name was changed to Tarquinia in 1922.

54. ll. 7–8. Jativa is about thirty miles south of Valencia.

82. ll. 7–8. cf. Matthew VII, 12. Jesus states the Golden Rule positively; the negative form is derived from Hillel, *Babylonian Talmud, Tractate Shabbath*, 31a.

86. l. 2. *the splendid horse*. Frontino.

90. ll. 1–6. Ariosto is mocking Dante; cf. *Purgatorio*, VI. 149–51.

91. l. 4. *the famous bridge* ... The bridge at Avignon dates only from the twelfth century.

l. 7. *the king of Spain*. Marsilio.

92. l. 1. *Aiguesmortes*. See Note to XXVII. 128.

96. l. 6. *When I last spoke of her*. See XXIV. 93.

CANTO XXIX

1–2. cf. stanza 74.

3. l. 7. *the other's*. Doralice's.

4. l. 5. *The hermit*. cf. XXVIII. 95 ff.

6. This episode may have been suggested by Hercules' casting Lichas into the sea (Ovid, *Metamorphoses*, IX. 211 ff.).

7. Ariosto seems here to be gently mocking the conventions of hagiography.

11. ll. 5–8. cf. XXIV. 76–86.

13. The story of Isabella's sacrifice is derived from the fifteenth-century Venetian Francesco Barbaro's *De re uxoria* (II. 6), where Brasilla (or Drusilla) di Durazzo, a noble damsel, falls into the hands of enemies. In danger of being raped by Cerico, she persuades him to spare her in return for a magic unguent, which she invites him to test first on her own neck. Francesco Barbaro in his turn derived the story from eleventh- and twelfth-century accounts by Byzantine chroniclers of a similar self-immolation by a Christian martyr of the time of Diocletian or by an Egyptian nun of the eighth century (cf. P. Rajna, *Le Fonti dell'Orlando Furioso*, pp. 459–63). It is significant that Ariosto used the name Drusilla for another example of heroic chastity (XXXVII. 52–75).

15. l. 1. *a herb*. This recalls the herb (dittany) gathered by Angelica to heal Medoro's wounds (XIX. 21–4).

22. ll. 4–5. *manna*. The 'bread from heaven' granted to the Israelites in the wilderness (Exodus xvi, 35).

26. l. 1. *It bounced three times*. Ariosto has been considered wanting

in taste for these three bounces, as though they were an example of his humour. In fact they are entirely appropriate to Isabella's heroism, recalling as they do the martyrdom in Rome of St Paul, whose head was said to bounce three times on his decapitation. According to legend, three fountains gushed forth from the three spots touched by his head. A church named San Paolo alle Tre Fontane marks the place where the apostle is said to have been martyred. In the courtyard are three springs. By one there stands a column of white marble to which St Paul is said to have been bound at his execution. The church is near San Paolo Fuori le Mura. There are however some epic decapitations which seem to operate on the borders of comedy and horror: *Iliad*, x. 457, where the severed head falls to the ground, still speaking, and xiii. 203–5, where the head spins like a ball until it comes to rest at Hector's feet. (I am indebted to Dr Richard Webster and Professor Claude Rawson for these allusions.)

ll. 7–8. cf. xxii. 1–4.

28. ll. 2–4. Lucretia, raped by the son of the tyrant Tarquinius Superbus, took her own life. This incident led to a popular rising, led by Junius Brutus against the Tarquins, who were expelled from Rome (*c.* 509 B.C.).

29. l. 7. *Parnassus, Pindus, Helicon*. The mountains sacred to the Muses.

l. 8. Possibly a further tribute to Isabella d'Este; cf. xiii. 59–60.

30. l. 3. *the third sphere*. In Ptolemaic astronomy, the third heaven or sphere (from the earth) carries the planet Venus.

l. 6. *Bréhus*. In the romance *Palamedès*, a ferocious enemy of women. There is also a fourteenth-century romance entitled *Il Febusso e Breusso*. Breusso is mentioned by Pulci in *Morgante* (xiii. 54).

33. ll. 1–2. *the mighty edifice*. The Mausoleum built by the Emperor Hadrian on the bank of the Tiber, in which he was buried. It became Castel S. Angelo.

39. l. 8. cf. xxiv. 14.

43. cf. xxiv. 74 and xxvii. 33.

44. l. 6. cf. xxiv. 56.

45–6. The wrestling-match between Orlando and Rodomonte anticipates the wrestling of Ruggiero and Rodomonte (xlvi. 131–4).

49. l. 4. Rodomonte hangs the armour and weapons of defeated pagans in the shrine as trophies; but he imprisons defeated

Christians and sends them by ship to Algiers, as well as stripping them of their weapons and armour; cf. stanza 34, ll. 7–8 and stanza 39, ll. 1–8.

51. ll. 3–4. *the height*. Probably Mt Subalda, which divides France from the region formerly known as Tarragon; or perhaps the Pyrenees generally, which separate France from Spain.

58. ll. 4–8. Angelica and Medoro have descended from Gerona and are journeying towards Barcelona. Before they arrive there, they meet a madman (xix. 41–2). The encounter occurs therefore somewhere north of Barcelona, along a sandy shore.

59. l. 5. *Aswan*. City of Egypt on the border of Ethiopia.

l. 6. *the Garamanths*. A people of southern Libya. In the oasis of Ammonium (El-Siwah) stood the temple of Jupiter Ammon.

ll. 7–8. *the mountains where | The sources of the river Nile appear*. The ancients believed that the Nile rose in Ethiopia in the so-called 'Mountains of the Moon'.

61. l. 6. cf. i. 5 and 55; viii. 71–8.

62. l. 7. *his enchanted body*. cf. xii. 49 and Note.

64. l. 5. *The magic ring*. This was restored to her by Ruggiero to protect her from the ray of the magic shield when he rescued her from the sea monster (x. 107–9). Placed in her mouth, it renders her invisible (xi. 2–6; xii. 34–7).

66. ll. 5–8. Angelica has already stolen a mare in Brittany (xi. 10–12).

73. l. 5. *the knight*. Ruggiero; see Note to stanza 64.

74. Ariosto here belies the sentiments expressed in the first two stanzas of this canto. In stanzas 1–4 of Canto xxx, he apologizes for his irrationality, drawing a parallel between himself and Orlando, as he has done elsewhere (cf. ix. 1–2 and xxiv. 1–3). He may mean he is in danger of becoming like Rodomonte.

CANTO XXX

3. l. 5. *my enemy*. The stanza was composed before he met Alessandra Benucci in 1513. That he let it stand perhaps indicates that Alessandra, like her predecessors, made him suffer.

4. l. 4. *Marsilio's kingdom*. Spain.

l. 5. *The battered carcass of the mare*. cf. xxix. 63–71.

l. 7. *a river*. Probably the Almeria, which empties into the gulf of the same name.

8. l. 5. *the other one*. Angelica's mare.

15. l. 2. *Ceuta's coast*. The tip of north Africa nearest to Spain.

l. 6. *a dark-skinned host*. The army from Ethiopia, assembled outside Biserta, led by Senapo and Astolfo; cf. XXXVIII. 35.

16. l. 6. *Finding a well-found ship*. At Barcelona.

l. 7. Angelica's father and brother being both dead, she becomes Queen of Cathay and Medoro is made King.

l. 8. The story of Angelica was continued by Vincenzo Brusantini in a romantic epic entitled *Angelica Innamorata*; by L. Dolci in *Sacripante*; by P. Aretino in *Le Lagrime d'Angelica*; by L. Barahona de Soto in *Primera parte de l'Angelica*; and by Lope de Vega in *La Hermosura de Angelica*. See also Cervantes, *Don Quixote* II. I, pp. 479–80 of the translation by J. M. Cohen (Penguin Classics edn). The original of this line is quoted by Cervantes at the end of I (p. 461, ed. cit.).

17. l. 3. *the Tartar king*. Mandricardo; cf. XXVII. 107.

l. 4. *Whose rival*. Rodomonte.

l. 5. *his love*. Doralice.

18. ll. 4–8. cf. XXVII. 46 and 54–60.

l. 7. *Sericana*. See Note to X. 71.

32. l. 7. *one combat you postpone*. The combat with Rodomonte; cf. XXIV. III.

33. l. 2. *such a noble king*. Mandricardo, King of Tartary.

l. 3. *a cavalier*. Rodomonte.

ll. 4–5. *a thing / So trivial*. The silver eagle.

35. ll. 5–6. cf. the proverb 'Occasion has a forelock but is bald behind'; cf. also the saying 'to seize Time by the forelock'.

39. ll. 1–4. Mandricardo perhaps refers here to his victory over the armed knights who were guarding Doralice; cf. XIV. 39–48.

ll. 5–8. Boiardo relates a duel between Mandricardo and Gradasso in Syria (*Orlando Innamorato*, III. I. 39 ff.).

40–41. A sorceress in Syria granted Mandricardo Hector's arms on his victory and freed Gradasso, Isoliero, Aquilante, Grifone and Sacripante, who were prisoners in her castle.

40. l. 2. *your fellow-countryman*. Isoliero is a Spaniard; he is the brother of Ferraù.

46. ll. 3–4. *the destrier*. Brigliadoro.

the great / Defender . . . that Champion. Orlando.

48. ll. 1–4. The ancients represented Jove carried by an eagle or by a chariot drawn by an eagle. Ariosto may have had in mind a painting by Raphael which also thus represented him. As an emblem of might, the eagle was borne on the Roman battle-standards.

ll. 3–4. *in Thessaly . . . Was wont*. Ariosto alludes here to the battle of Pharsalus (48 B.C.) between Caesar and Pompey, and to the battle of Philippi (42 B.C., Octavian against Brutus and Cassius). Though Philippi is in Macedonia, Ariosto follows classical authors in placing it in Thessaly.

l. 4. *with other feathers.* Down to the time of Marius, the Roman eagle was silver; later, it was gold. Ariosto is perhaps thinking of the Imperial eagle of the Middle Ages which was black. In the *Cinque Canti*, III. 73, Ariosto says that Ruggiero had taken as his emblem the 'white bird and the black', that is, he had joined the Imperial with the Roman. Piero della Francesca in his Victory of Constantine, at Arezzo, shows the Roman standard as a black spread eagle on a gold banner.

49. ll. 1–5. *The shattered lances* . . . cf. *Coriolanus*, IV, v, 109–10, 'My grained ash an hundred times hath broke, / And scarr'd the moon with splinters.'

l. 4. *the fiery sphere.* The circle of fire which according to Ptolemaic astronomy encircled the earth.

50. In the fifteenth and sixteenth centuries, it was permissible by previous agreement for the knights to try to kill each other's horses. Ariosto here expresses disapproval of this custom.

52. l. 6. *Trojan shield.* The shield bearing the Trojan eagle.

59. ll. 6–7. cf. XXV. 15–16 and Note.

l. 8. *Enchanted armour.* The armour of Hector.

63. l. 5. *the sword.* Balisarda.

64. l. 6. *sword.* Durindana.

66. l. 5. *arming-cap.* A cap of steel net worn beneath the helmet.

69. l. 6. *A pang of envy.* cf. the envy felt by Aquilante and Grifone at Astolfo's defeat of Orrilo (XV. 88).

70. l. 7. *King Agricane's son.* Mandricardo.

72. l. 5. *from what we knew of her before.* Her inconstancy in kindling to a new love (Mandricardo) is symbolized by the colour of her garments; cf. XXVII. 51. ll. 7–8 and Note.

74. l. 7. *the sword.* Durindana.

75. ll. 3–4. cf. XXIV. 49.

l. 5. *as you shall hear.* cf. XLI. 68 ff.

l. 7. *The Maid.* Bradamante.

76. l. 5. *the Sarzan.* Rodomonte; cf. XXIII. 33–7.

l. 6. *his horse.* Frontino.

ll. 7–8. cf. XXVI. 54–60.

77. l. 2. *the thieving Saracen.* Rodomonte; cf. XXVI. 66–7.

78. cf. XXVI. 89–90.

83. Boiardo relates that Ruggiero II was killed by Troiano, the father of Agramante (*Orlando Innamorato*, II. I. 70 ff.). Else-

where (xxxviii. 5) Ariosto seems to attribute his death to Almonte.

87. l. 4. *her brother*. Ricciardetto; cf. xxv. 11–18.

l. 6. *To set Vivian and Malagigi free*. cf. xxvi. 13–26.

88. cf. xxv. 97; xxvi. 14–26 and 134–6.

90. ll. 2–3. Guicciardo and Alardo are senior to Rinaldo in age but not in status. The law of primogeniture did not then apply.

91. l. 1. *Blaye*. One of Orlando's castles was at Brava (Blavia, Blaia); cf. xxvii. 11.

ll. 4–8. *his two cousins*. Viviano and Malagigi; cf. xxv. 74–5.

93. l. 2. *His mother*. Beatrice of Bavaria, wife of Duke Aymon; *wife*. Clarice, sister of Ugo of Bordeaux; *children*. Their names are not known.

l. 3. *His brothers*. Alardo, Guicciardo, Ricciardo, Ricciardetto; *his cousins*. Viviano and Malagigi.

94. l. 1. *Richard*. Ricciardo is not mentioned in the Old French chanson de geste, *Les Quatre Fils Aymon*, in which there are four sons only.

CANTO XXXI

5. l. 4. *the book of Zoroaster*. The sum total of the wisdom of Zoroaster, believed in antiquity to be the inventor of the art of magic.

7. l. 1. *her brother*. Ricciardetto; cf. xxx. 88.

Ippalca. cf. xxx. 76–8.

ll. 3–5. See stanzas 27–9; 30–34.

8. l. 1. *a knight*. Guidone Selvaggio, last seen, unconscious, at Pinabello's castle (xxii. 85–6).

l. 2. *a lady*. Aleria, his wife, who helped in the escape from Alessandretta (xx. 74–5; 80–81; 95).

11. l. 4. *I am the third*. Rinaldo is third in order of age; cf. xxx. 90 and Note.

15. l. 1. *Count Aymon's son*. Rinaldo.

26. l. 4. *slow Arcturus*. Probably not Arcturus proper (a star in the constellation of Boötes), which is too far south, but a star in the tail of the Little Bear which describes a small circle round the North Pole and hence seems to move slowly.

28. l. 5. *For they are brothers*. Guidone, an illegitimate son of Aymon, is half-brother to Rinaldo; cf. xx. 6.

29. cf. xix. 78 ff.; xxii. 52 ff.

34. l. 8. *his father*. Duke Aymon of Montalbano.

37. l. 4. *Gismonda's sons.* cf. xv. 73.
38. l. 1. *A damsel.* Fiordiligi.
l. 3. *samite.* A rich silk fabric.
40. ll. 1–4. cf. xv. 67 and Note.
41. ll. 1–2. Boiardo relates that Truffaldino, King of Babylon, had caused enmity between Rinaldo and the sons of Oliver (*Orlando Innamorato*, 1. xxvi. 13 ff.).
42. cf. xxiv. 56 and 74; xxix. 43–9.
43. l. 5. *a cavalier.* Zerbino.
44. cf. xxiv. 58–9 and 115.
47. ll. 4–8. For Durindana, cf. xxvii. 62–4 ff. and xxx. 74; for Mandricardo's death, cf. xxx. 47 ff.
49. l. 8. *Lethe's water.* Oblivion.
50. ll. 3–4. The nurse of Apollo the sun-god was Tethys, the goddess of the sea.
56. l. 3. *Achilles' Myrmidons.* The Myrmidons were a people of southern Thessaly. Achilles, who was their king, led them to the Trojan war.
58. l. 7. *the Galaesus.* The river which flows near Taranto, a region famed for its flocks.
l. 8. *the Cinyphus.* A river in Africa, no longer identifiable, famed in antiquity for the herds of goats which grazed along its banks.
59. l. 6. *two were still in Paris.* Uggiero and Oliver; cf. xxvii. 32.
ll. 7–8. *The son of Monodante.* Brandimarte.
63. cf. xxiv. 74 and xxix. 43–8.
67. l. 3. *Batoldo.* In Boiardo's *Orlando Innamorato*, Batoldo was the horse of Barigaccio, whom Brandimarte killed (11. xxi. 24, 47, 48).
70. ll. 7–8. cf. iii. 34. ll. 2–7 and Note.
75. l. 8. Rodomonte intends to ship all his Christian prisoners to Algiers; cf. xxix. 39.
78. ll. 6–8. *a knight.* Bradamante; for the emblem on her surcoat, see xxxii. 47.
91–2. In Boiardo's *Orlando Innamorato* (1. i. 4; v. 7 ff.) Gradasso challenges Rinaldo for possession of Baiardo. Malagigi, wishing to take Rinaldo to Angelica, lures him on board ship before Gradasso reaches the place assigned for the combat.
96. ll. 5–6. The lowest depths on earth and the highest of the spheres (the Primum Mobile, according to Ptolemaic astronomy).
98. l. 4. *the Sericanian's.* Gradasso's.
102. l. 1. *Buovo's son.* Malagigi.

103. l. 6. *Barcelona*. Where their previous, interrupted combat took place.
108. l. 1. *Viviano's brother*. Malagigi.
 l. 2. *his cousin's*. Rinaldo's.
 ll. 7–8. See Note to stanzas 91–2.
 l. 8. *the shore*. At Barcelona.
109. l. 5. *Altafoglia and Pontier*. Two castles belonging to the Maganzans. Pontiero is perhaps to be identified with Ponthieu in Picardy. Altafoglia has not been identified. It may be a slip for Altaripa, the Maganzan stronghold in Ponthieu; cf. XXIII. 2–4.

CANTO XXXII

1–3. A good example of the delight which Ariosto takes in playing with the reader. This canto lacks a true prelude; cf. XXXIX, in which the action is continued without interruption.
 1. l. 3. *the Maid*. Bradamante.
 l. 4. *One cause . . .* Ruggiero's delay; cf. XXX. 79–83.
 l. 7. *The words of Ricciardetto*. See XXX. 88–9.
 2. l. 8. *The duel I began*. Between Rinaldo and Gradasso; cf. XXXI. 106–10.
 5. l. 3. *Almonte's daughter*. Her name is not given. Almonte, the brother of Troiano, was Agramante's uncle.
 l. 7. Oran, offered as a dowry, has been vacant since the death of the giant king, Marbalusto (XIV. 17; XVI. 47).
 l. 8. *the lovers' sepulchre*. The tomb of Isabella and Zerbino for which Rodomonte has built a mausoleum (XXIX. 31–2).
7–8. cf. XXVII. 85 ff.
9. Boiardo relates that Ruggiero saved Brunello from being hanged for killing Bardulasto, whom Ruggiero himself had killed (*Orlando Innamorato*, II. xxi. 42 et seq.).
 l. 6. *upon his pallet*. Ruggiero, gravely wounded in his combat with Mandricardo, has been transferred by Agramante to Arles (XXXI. 88).
10. ll. 3–4. *his bond / To her and to the Faith*. His promise to return and to be baptized; see his letter to Bradamante, XXV. 85–92.
11. l. 2. *one of his horses*. The chariot of the sun was drawn by four horses: Pyrois, Eous, Aethon and Phlegon. They are listed by Ovid (*Metamorphoses*, II. 153–4). In the original, Ariosto says Bradamante thinks either Aethon or Pyrois must be lame.
 ll. 5–6. For the stopping of the sun and moon, see Joshua x, 12–14.

l. 7. *The threefold night*. Juno prolonged the night when Hercules was born in order that Eurystheus should be born first. It is possible, however, that Ariosto is alluding to the night when Hercules was conceived, extended by Jove that he might prolong his pleasure with Alcmena.

12. l. 2. Pliny the Elder (*Naturalis Historia*, VIII. 36) says that bears hibernate.

13. l. 4. Aurora (Dawn), enamoured of Tithonus, the brother of Priam, asked the gods to grant him immortality. They did so, without also granting eternal youth. He thus grows older and older but Aurora remains for ever enamoured. She is represented by Ovid and other Latin poets as rising at the close of every night from the bed of her spouse and in a chariot drawn by swift horses ascending the heaven from the river Oceanus to announce the coming light of the sun.

14. l. 8. Montalbano is in Gascony. Bradamante thinks Ruggiero is near Paris; cf. stanza 49.

24. ll. 5–8. For Merlin's prophecy of Bradamante's future, see III. 16–19; and for Melissa's conjuration of demons representing Bradamante's descendants, III. 23–62.

28. l. 1. *a Gascon knight*. Gascons were reputed to be unreliable and garrulous.

l. 4. *surprise attack*. cf. XXXI. 50 ff.

33. l. 6. *as I have said*. See stanzas 6–8.

41. l. 4. *The Light-bearer*. Lucifer.

47. cf. XXXI. 78.

48. l. 1. *the steed Astolfo used to ride*. Rabicano; cf. XXIII. 9–11.

l. 2. *his golden lance*. Originally Argalia's, it unseats all opponents; cf. XXIII. 14.

49. ll. 4–8. cf. XXXI. 85–7.

50. This is the beginning of a passage inserted in the third edition (1532), extending to XXXIII. 76.

ll. 2–4. The river Dordogne rises on the Puy de Sancy, one of the three groups of the Mont-Dore in the Massif Central, and flows into the Garonne; together they form the Gironde estuary. Bradamante is the 'lady of Dordogne', and the Dordogne is 'her river' because of the vicinity of Montalbano.

l. 4. Montferrand and Clermont, two neighbouring towns, were joined to form Clermont–Ferrand in the seventeenth century.

l. 5. *a lady*. Ullania.

l. 8. *Three knights*. The kings of Sweden, Gothland and Norway who are never named; cf. stanza 54.

51. l. 7. *The king of all the Franks.* Charlemagne.
52. l. 1. *the Lost Isle.* See stanza 55.
    l. 3. *Our queen.* The queen of Iceland is not named.
57. l. 3. *a costly shield of gold.* From a surviving fragment of manu-
script (first printed in 1730), it appears that Ariosto originally
intended to describe Ullania's golden shield as the first (and
sole survivor) of a series of twelve, made in the fourth century
A.D. by the Cumaean Sibyl and hung up in the Lateran in an
attempt to dissuade Constantine I from removing the seat of
government to Byzantium. They were embossed with scenes
prophetic of the woes of Italy for 1,200 years to come, that is,
100 years' events to each shield. Ariosto evidently changed his
mind and substituted the paintings on the wall in Tristan's
castle; cf. XXXIII. 6 ff.
63. l. 2. *Mauretania's shore.* The western half of north Africa.
    l. 3. *like a goosander.* The bird *Mergus merganser* is a fish-eating
duck of great diving powers, with a long, narrow, serrated bill,
hooked at the tip.
    l. 4. *his ancient mother.* Tethys, goddess of the sea, mother or
nurse of Apollo. The sun has set below the horizon of the
western sea, beyond Morocco.
    ll. 5–8. The time of year is advanced.
65. l. 3. *Tristan's fortress.* The law imposed by Tristan and the story
of its origin, as related by the castellan, in stanzas 83–94, are
derived from two Arthurian texts, *Bret* and *Guiron.* In *Bret*,
Tristan is out riding one day with Dynadan. Meeting some
shepherds, they enquire of them where they may find a lodging
and are directed to a sumptuous palace. To gain admittance it is
necessary to defeat the owners in combat. Tristan and his
companion are successful and enter. Soon afterwards two other
knights arrive and challenge them. In *Guiron*, the knight of that
name and Danayn arrive in company with a damsel at a tower.
In order to gain admittance they defeat two knights who have
arrived earlier and enter. They are then told by the owner of
the tower the origin of the custom: Utherpendragon, the father
of Arthur, arriving there one day, found the tower occupied by
a knight. The owner refused admittance as there was not room
for two guests. Utherpendragon challenged the other knight
and was defeated. He entered the tower the next day, after the
victorious knight had departed, and he then established the
custom which is still in force. At the conclusion of the story,
Guiron and Danayn are given a meal and they retire to bed.
The next morning, they meet the two knights whom they

defeated and are challenged by them; but they make peace and travel on together.

To these elements, Ariosto has added the beauty contest between women who arrive at Tristan's castle.

72. l. 1. *those three*. The three kings; cf. stanza 50.

ll. 7–8. *her . . . challenger*. Bradamante.

75. ll. 5–6. cf. stanza 48, and XXIII. 15.

78. l. 3. *the lady*. Ullania.

80. l. 1–4. In Italian Renaissance theatres, the curtain was *lowered* to reveal the scene, not raised. The removal of Bradamante's helmet is therefore appropriately compared by Ariosto to the *fall* of a curtain on the stage.

81. ll. 1–2. cf. XXV. 26.

l. 7. *many times before*. The castle is situated in a region fairly near to Montalbano.

83. l. 1. *King Pharamont*. Long considered the first Merovingian king, but mentioned in no reliable chronicle, he was said to be the son of Marcomir. In Arthurian romances he appears as a cavalier, a contemporary of Arthur and Tristan. He was also said to be the first to lead the Franks south of the Rhine. (See Shakespeare's *Henry V*, I, ii, where the Archbishop of Canterbury quotes the Salic law which is attributed to Pharamond [Pharamont].)

l. 2. *Prince Clodione*. Clodio, son of Pharamond; cf. Gregory of Tours (*History of the Franks*, Penguin Classics edn, trans. Lewis Thorpe, p. 125).

83. ll. 6–7. Jove, enamoured of Io, transformed her to a heifer (to conceal her from the jealousy of Juno) and gave her into the custody of Argus of the hundred eyes; cf. Ovid (*Metamorphoses*, I. 601 ff.).

89. ll. 1–4. Tristan had drunk a love potion intended by Iseult's mother for Iseult's husband, King Mark of Cornwall. This inflamed him with an exclusive passion for Iseult.

108. l. 7. *the queen's messenger*. Ullania, sent to Charlemagne by the queen of Iceland.

CANTO XXXIII

1. ll. 1–8. Ariosto's knowledge of these eight painters was probably derived from Pliny's *Naturalis Historia*.

l. 1. *Parrhasius*. Greek painter (fifth century B.C.), mentioned by Pliny (*Naturalis Historia*, XXXV. 67). Among paintings attributed to him was 'The Feigned Madness of Odysseus'. He discusses painting with Socrates in the *Memorabilia* of Xenophon. He wrote on painting and was famed for expressive detail and subtlety of outline. His gods and heroes became types for later artists; his drawings on parchment and wood were used by craftsmen in Pliny's time.

l. 2. *Zeuxis*. He is said to have achieved such realistic effects that his painting of grapes deceived the birds. See also Note to XI. 71.

Timagoras. He has not been identified.

Protogenes. Greek painter and sculptor of Caunys of the late fourth century B.C. He wrote two books on painting. His works included 'Alexander and Pan' and a portrait of Aristotle's mother.

l. 3. *Apollodorus*. Athenian painter of the fifth century, said to have been surpassed by Zeuxis. He was famed for his illusionistic painting (plastic shading by a gradation of colour).

Polygnotus. Greek fifth-century painter; probably a friend of Sophocles. Pliny dates him before 420 B.C. Among his paintings were scenes illustrating the *Iliad* and the *Odyssey*. Theophrastus considered him the first great painter. Pliny speaks of his skill in painting transparent drapery.

l. 4. *Timanthes*. Greek painter of the late fifth century B.C., a contemporary of Zeuxis. His painting of the sacrifice of Iphigenia was famed for its expressive representation of grief.

Apelles. Greek painter of the fourth century B.C. and author of a book on painting. Pliny dates him 332 B.C. He painted portraits of Philip, Alexander, Ptolemy and Protogenes. It is said that the tone of his works was due to a secret varnish.

l. 6. *Clotho*. One of the three Fates (the other two being Lachesis and Atropos). She is the spinning Fate who cuts the thread when a human life is ended.

Of the contemporary artists chosen by Ariosto to rank with the painters of ancient Greece, only Lazzaro Sebastiani no longer justifies inclusion. Titian, who was a friend of Ariosto, painted at the courts of Ferrara, Mantua and Urbino, as well as for the Emperor Charles V and his son Philip II, King of Spain. Duke Alfonso I commissioned three mythological paintings from him, executed between 1517 and 1523: 'Worship of Venus', 'Bacchanal of the Andrians' (now in the Prado, Madrid), and 'Bacchus and Ariadne' (now in the National Gallery, London). Among his portraits is one of Alfonso d'Avalos, Marquess of Vasto.

l. 2. *Leonardo da Vinci* (1452–1519), Florentine.

    Andrea Mantegna (1431–1506), Paduan.

ll. 2–3. *the two/Named Dossi.* Dosso (1479–1542) and his brother Giambattista (d. 1545), of Ferrara.

    Gian Bellino. Giovanni Bellini (1426–1516), Venetian.

ll. 3–5. *he whose skill . . . The Angel Michael's.* Michelangelo Buonarotti (1475–1564), Florentine.

l. 5. *Bastian.* Lazzaro Sebastiani (*c.* 1430–1512), Venetian.

    Raphael. Raffaello Sanzio (1483–1520), of Urbino.

l. 6. *Titian.* Tiziano Vecelli (*c.* 1487(90)–1576), of Pieve di Cadore, in the Veneto.

4. ll. 3–4. Not even the demons in Hell can withstand the powers of sorcery.

    ll. 6–7. The grotto of the Cumaean Sibyl was near Lake Avernus at Puteoli, Italy. It was believed to lead to the underworld (cf. *Aeneid,* VI. 237 ff.). In the Middle Ages the Sibyl, transformed into a sorceress, was reputed to have her dwelling in Nursia on Mt San Vittore. It was believed that enchanters took their books of magic to be consecrated there.

7. This stanza ushers in a traditional theme in Italian literature, namely the invasion of Italy by foreigners from beyond the Alps; see Gustavo Costa, *Le antichità germaniche nella tradizione culturale italiana da Machiavelli a Vico* (Guido Editori, Naples), 1976; P. Amelung, *Das Bild der Deutschen in der Literatur der italienischen Renaissance (1400–1559),* Munich, 1964 (Münchner romanistische Arbeiten, XX).

    l. 7. *The British king.* Arthur. In Geoffrey of Monmouth's *History of the Kings of Britain* and in early Arthurian romances, King Arthur never met Merlin, who disappears from the story immediately after Arthur's miraculous conception.

8. See Note to XXXII. 83. 1.

9. ll. 2–3. Merlin was the son of a Welsh princess who had become a nun, and an incubus who visited her (see Geoffrey of Monmouth, VI. 18, ed. cit., pp. 167–8).

13. l. 4. *Sigibert.* Historically the fifth son of King Lothar I by Ingund (535–575 A.D.). He never invaded Italy. Ariosto attributes to him actions undertaken by Childebert, who was induced by the Emperor Maurice Tiberius (reigned 582–602) to fight against the Longobards; he was defeated by Authari; see stanza 15 and Note.

    l. 5. *Mons Iovis.* St Bernard.

14. l. 1. *Clovis.* King of the Franks, son of Childeric and of Basina, ex-Queen of Thuringia. Ariosto mistakenly attributes to him

the invasion of Italy by Clothair III (reigned 657–673 A.D.), who was urged by Bertaridus to attack Grimoaldus, formerly Duke of Benevento but then King of the Longobards. He marched through Provence and entered Asti, where he was tricked by Grimoaldus, who pretended flight, leaving abundant food and wine behind. During the night Grimoaldus returned and slaughtered the sleeping Franks.

15. Childebert II, King of the Franks (reigned 575–595) invaded Italy several times to attack the Longobards, urged on by the Emperor, Maurice Tiberius; cf. Note to stanza 13. Authari, King of the Longobards, allowed the Franks to dally in the regions of Modena and Parma, until the heat of summer brought on an epidemic of dysentery and Childebert retreated along the river Adige with what was left of his army.

16. King Pepin and his son Charlemagne both entered Italy in defence of the Pope against the Longobards, Pepin to aid Pope Stephen II against King Aistulf (754, 756), and Charlemagne to aid Pope Adrian I against King Desiderius (773–4), and Pope Leo III (800) to put down rebellious tumults in Rome.

17. Pepin, the son of Charlemagne, was believed to have invaded Italy in A.D. 810 to subdue Venice. According to tradition, he occupied the shore of the Adriatic from the mouth of the Po to the stretch of coastline, formerly called the Pellestrina littoral, which extends from Chioggia to Malamocco. By means of a pontoon bridge, Pepin then attacked Rialto, the largest of the Venetian islands, but the bridge was swept away in a storm.

18. Ludwig (Lewis) III of Burgundy invaded Italy and was taken prisoner by Berengarius I, who released him on the understanding that he would never return. He broke his word and was taken prisoner a second time. Berengarius had his eyes put out and sent him back to Burgundy (A.D. 905).

19. Hugh, Count of Provence (Arles) invaded Italy against Rudolph II of Burgundy (who was the enemy of Berengarius I). Crowned king in Pavia, Hugh was challenged by Berengarius II, who had the support of the Emperors Arnulphus and Otto. Hugh sent his son Lotharius to the Council held at Milan in A.D. 945, to claim the kingdom for himself, but was forced to withdraw two years later to Provence, where he died (947). Lotharius died soon afterwards, perhaps poisoned by Berengarius II.

20. Charles of Anjou, invited by Pope Clement IV, defeated Manfred at the battle of Benevento and Conradin at the battle of Tagliacozzo. He became king of Naples and Sicily (1266–

1282). At the signal of the sounding of the vesper bell, his subjects rose in rebellion and he was driven from Sicily (1282).

21–2. *A captain.* The Count of Armagnac, invited by the Florentines and the Bolognese, made war on Giangaleazzo Visconti (l. 5). He surrounded Alessandria but Giangaleazzo attacked his troops in the rear and took him prisoner (1391). The slaughter of the French was such as to redden the Tanaro, which flows into the Po.

23. l. 3. *La Marca.* Giacomo di Borbone, Count of La Marca.

three Angevins. Louis III, René and Jean; these in turn attempted to conquer the kingdom of Naples, wreaking havoc on Calabria, Apulia, Abruzzo and the region of Otranto. Despite the alliance of French and Italians, they were driven out by Alfonso and Ferdinand of Aragon. (The dates of these events are *c.* 1415–17.)

24. Charles VIII invaded France in 1494 and advanced almost without striking a blow as far as the river Liri. Ischia, however, resisted him, defended by Inigo d'Avalos, Marquess of Vasto.

l. 5. *Typhoeus.* See XXVI. 52 and Note.

25. l. 3. *Ischia.* See Note to stanza 24.

27. l. 1. *this cavalier.* Inigo d'Avalos, mentioned in stanza 24.

l. 2. *the threatened citadel.* Of Ischia.

l. 4. *Another.* Alfonso d'Avalos, Marquess of Vasto; cf. XV. 28–9 and Note.

28. l. 1. *Nereus.* The most beautiful of the Greek heroes, after Achilles.

l. 3. *Ladas.* The swift courier of Alexander the Great.

Nestor. King of Pylos, who lived to a great age.

l. 5. *Less liberal was Caesar.* There is an active contrary tradition that Julius Caesar was merciless and cruel, and that his reputation for clemency was undeserved. On this point (as on the opposite) he was traditionally linked with Alexander. An important early source for Caesar's merciless cruelty is Lucan, *Pharsalia, passim.* On Caesar and Alexander in declamation exercises, see M.P.O. Morford, *The Poet Lucan,* 1967, pp. 13–19. (I am indebted to Professor Claude Rawson for these and other Lucan references.)

l. 7. *him who in Ischia is born.* Alfonso d'Avalos (A.D. 1503–46).

29. l. 1–2. Jove, the son of Saturn and grandson of Uranus, was born in Crete.

l. 3. *Hercules and Bacchus.* Born in Thebes.

l. 4. *the heavenly pair.* Apollo and Diana, who were born on the island of Delos.

30. l. 3. *the Empire*. Of Charlemagne.

31. Ludovico Sforza, called 'il Moro' (see Note to stanza 34, line 2), encouraged Charles VIII to invade Italy. He then allied with Venice and the Pope to prevent Charles' re-entry into France when he returned north from Naples; but at the battle of Fornovo (1495), Charles cleft a passage for his troops and escaped.

32–3. Charles had left troops in the kingdom of Naples, which were then attacked by Ferdinand II with the help of Francesco Gonzaga, Marquess of Mantua. Alfonso d'Avalos (father of Francesco), Marquess of Pescara (cf. stanza 47), conspired with an Ethiopian slave of the French to allow the Aragonese entry into Castel Nuovo in Naples which was occupied by the French; but the slave, who had also been bribed by the French, shot Alfonso with an arrow through the throat.

34. Louis XII entered Italy in 1499 with an army under the command of Giangiacomo Trivulzio; cf. xiv. 9.

l. 2. *the mulberry* ('il moro'). This was the emblem in the armorial bearings of Ludovico Sforza.

l. 4. *Lombardy*. Under the rule of the Visconti family before the Sforzas came to power.

l. 5. *Where Charles's army went*. To Naples.

ll. 7–8. *the Garigliano*. The lower course of the river Liri in the extreme north of the kingdom of Naples. The Spanish troops under the command of Consalvo of Cordova defeated the French there in 1503.

35. l. 1. The defeat of the French in Apulia preceded that on the river Garigliano.

ll. 5–8. Louis was successful in the plain of Lombardy.

36. l. 3. *one bartering . . .* Bernardino da Corte, who was bribed to yield the castle at Milan to the French.

ll. 5–8. Ludovico Sforza returned from Germany with Swiss mercenaries and tried to regain the duchy of Milan; but his troops, refusing to fight against other Swiss mercenaries employed by the French, betrayed him and handed him over to the enemy (A.D. 1500).

37. ll. 1–4. Louis made Cesare Borgia a Duke and aided him against his Roman rivals.

ll. 5–6. Louis next aided Pope Julius II against the Bentivoglio family of Bologna, whose emblem was a saw (1506).

l. 7. *The papal Acorns*. An oak with golden acorns formed part of the armorial bearings of the Pope (Giuliano della Rovere: *rovere* means 'oak').

ll. 7–8. With the conquest of Milan, Genoa, previously subject to the Sforzas, passed to the control of the French, though retaining autonomy as a republic. A rebellion occurred and was put down by Louis (1507).

38. ll. 1–4. *Ghiaradadda*. A region between the river Adda and the river Oglio, where battle took place between the French and the Venetians in 1509.

ll. 5–8. Pope Julius II, hostile to Duke Alfonso I, had wrested Romagna and Modena from Ferrara (1510). The French helped the duke to regain his territories and reinstated the Bentivogli in Bologna.

l. 8. *Acorns*. See Note to stanza 37. l. 7.

39. l. 4. Brescia rebelled against the French and was sacked (1512).

ll. 7–8. The battle of Ravenna, fought on 11 April 1512 on the plain of Classe, which Melissa prophesies (III. 55); cf. Vol. I, Introduction, pp. 23–4; XIV. 1–9.

40. ll. 7–8. For Alfonso's decisive use of artillery at the battle of Ravenna, see Vol. I, Introduction, pp. 21–2.

41. l. 3. *German hordes*. Swiss mercenaries.

ll. 6–8. Maximilian, son of Ludovico Sforza, was instated in the duchy of Milan after the expulsion of the French.

42. ll. 1–4. The French returned but were defeated at Novara by Maximilian, who, at the risk of being betrayed, employed Swiss mercenaries (1513).

ll. 5–8. *a new sovereign* . . . Francis I, who invaded Italy to wipe out the humiliation of Novara (1515).

43. ll. 1–4. The battle of Marignano, at which Francis defeated the Swiss; cf. XXVI. 45.

ll. 5–8. On the banners of the Swiss were the mottoes: '*Domatores Principum*' ('Tamers of Princes), '*Defensores Sanctae Romanae Ecclesiae*' (Defenders of the Holy Roman Church); cf. XVII. 77 and XXVI. 45.

44. l. 1. *the League*. Maximilian of Austria, the king of Spain, the Republic of Florence and Pope Leo X.

l. 2. *young Sforza*. Maximilian, son of Ludovico Sforza; cf. XXVI. 46.

ll. 3–4. *Bourbon Charles*. Charles de Bourbon defended the Milanese against the German army of the Emperor Maximilian (1516).

ll. 5–8. *The monarch* . . . Francis I, who was engaged in a war with the Emperor Charles V. His enemies occupied Milan, which was being maladministered by the French.

45. ll. 1–4. Francesco Sforza II, grandson of Francesco I, was installed as Duke of Milan.

ll. 5–8. The French troops returned but were defeated by Federigo Gonzaga, Duke of Mantua, who defeated them and their Venetian allies on the Ticino (1522).

46. ll. 1–2. Federigo Gonzaga II, the first Duke (the title was conferred on him by Charles V in 1530), was 22 at the time of the battle.

l. 6. *The Lion's plan.* The strategy of the Venetians, allied with France.

Two marquesses. See Note to stanza 47 below.

47. *Both of one blood* ... Francesco d'Avalos, Marquess of Pescara, and Alfonso d'Avalos, Marquess of Vasto; cf. xv. 28 and xxvi. 52.

ll. 3–4. cf. stanza 33.

49. l. 1. *his Pescara cousin.* Francesco d'Avalos.

l. 3. *Bicocca.* A castle three miles from Milan where Prospero Colonna, commanding the imperial troops, defeated the Swiss and French, commanded by Lautrec (1522).

ll. 5–8. In 1524 Francis I attempted once more to regain Milan and sent another part of his army south to try to conquer Naples.

50–51. For the fickleness of Fortune, cf. xxvi. 47. 5 and Note. Francis believed he had 100,000 soldiers and the payments he had been making warranted this belief; but Francis was making merry in the Certosa of Pavia, while the money intended for troops had been squandered by corrupt generals and his forces were fewer than he realized. The cousins Francesco and Alfonso d'Avalos led the Spanish troops and contributed largely to the defeat of Francis at the battle of Pavia (24 February 1525).

54. ll. 1–5. *the other one* ... The army which Francis had sent to Naples, under the command of the duke of Albany, who returned to France.

l. 5. *The king returns alone.* Francis I, taken prisoner, was released by Charles V, leaving two of his sons hostage in Spain.

ll. 6–7. *New war.* Francis repudiated the treaty of Madrid and again invaded Italy (1526).

on his soil. France was being invaded in his absence (1526); but the invasions to which Ariosto here alludes have not been identified.

55. This stanza refers to the Sack of Rome by the imperial troops (1527).

l. 5. *the League.* Between the Pope, France, Venice, Milan and

Florence, formed for the defence of Rome. The army of the League was in Tuscany. When Rome was threatened, Guido Rangone was sent at its head to try to save the city; he withdrew to Otricoli and made no attempt to enter Rome.

56. Francis, in agreement with Henry VIII, decided to move to the assistance of Rome. He appointed Lautrec captain-general of the League (June 1527), but Charles V forestalled him and freed the Pope. Lautrec then marched to Naples.

57. ll. 1–4. The Spanish fleet set sail from Posillipo to bring aid to Naples.

l. 2. *the city of Parthenope*. Naples, so called because the siren Parthenope was said to be buried there. The fleet was intercepted by eight galleys under the command of Filippo Doria.
ll. 5–8. The French troops succumbed to plague and malaria. Of 25,000 men, only 4,000 survived. The siege of Naples was thus brought to an end.

61. l. 2. *my vow*. cf. his letter to Bradamante, xxv. 86–91.

66. l. 1. *the queen of Iceland's messenger*. Ullania.

l. 3. *three warriors*. The kings of Sweden, Gothland and Norway; cf. xxxii. 72–7.

l. 5. *The golden lance*. Astolfo's magic lance; cf. xxxii. 48. 2 and Note.

70. l. 4. *The golden shield*. cf. xxxii. 52–9.

77. l. 3. *her brother's name*. Rinaldo.

l. 5. cf. xxxi. 50 ff.

78. l. 3. *those two knights*. Rinaldo and Gradasso; cf. xxxi. 106–10.

l. 7. *Orlando's sword*. Durindana. It was given to Gradasso by Agramante after Ruggiero's combat with Mandricardo (xxx. 74).

82. Gradasso's armour is not enchanted in Boiardo's poem; cf. *Orlando Innamorato*, iii. vii. 46, 50.

85. cf. Malagigi's interference in the previous combat between Rinaldo and Gradasso (xxxi. 92).

86. ll. 1–3. The 'angry words' are not reported in the poem.

l. 4. *the Light*. God.

92. l. 4. *back to camp*. Outside Paris; cf. xxxi. 50 ff.

94. l. 3. *From the Far East*. Gradasso is king of Sericana, a silk-producing region of part of China.

95. l. 3. *twice already*. On a previous visit to France, Boiardo relates, Gradasso was defeated by Astolfo and departed for Africa. He returned to France to support Agramante.

96. l. 1. *the English knight*. Astolfo. For his journey from Spain to Ethiopia, see map on pp. 672–3.

100. l. 7. *Battus*. The founder of Cyrene.

l. 8. *Ammon's temple*. The temple of Jupiter Ammon; cf. xxix. 59 and Note.

101. l. 1. *Another Tremesin*. Tremisen in Nubia, as distinct from Tlemcen in Barbary.

102. l. 1. *Prester John*. A legendary Christian monarch of Asia. Originally believed to be patriarch of India, he appears in medieval legends and romantic epics as the royal presbyter of Ethiopia. The name Senapo may be a corruption of the name of the negus, Amda Syon (reigned 314–44), who was thought of later in the West as a crusader.

ll. 7–8. This belief is derived from Marco Polo, who mentions the Ethiopians in *Il Milione*.

103 ff. The legends concerning Prester John referred to the sumptuous splendour of his palace and the wealth of his realm. In the Italian romance, *Ugo d'Alvernia*, the hero visits Prester John and finds the Terrestrial Paradise situated near Ethiopia. In legends relating to Alexander the Great, he, like Prester John, tries to reach the Terrestrial Paradise and is punished for his arrogance. Phineus, a blind prophet, is visited by the Argonauts (Apollonius of Rhodes, *Argonautica*, ll. 178 ff.) who find him tormented by harpies which pollute his food. The sons of Boreas, Calais and Zetes, who have accompanied the Argonauts, drive off the harpies; in return, Phineus prophesies the further course of their journey. From these and other elements, both classical and medieval, Ariosto has constructed his story of Prester John (Senapo) and Astolfo.

123. l. 5. *his horn*. cf. xv. 14–15.

126. l. 8. According to legend, the Nile had its source on the mountain which has the Terrestrial Paradise on its summit.

127. In *Ugo d'Alvernia* (cf. Note to stanza 103) the entrance to Hell is situated at the foot of the mountain crowned by the Terrestrial Paradise.

l. 8. *Cocytus*. One of the rivers in Hell.

128. l. 4. *another flight*. To the Terrestrial Paradise.

CANTO XXXIV

2. l. 1. *He greatly erred*. The allusion may be to Ludovico Sforza, 'il Moro', who encouraged foreign intervention in Italy.

3. l. 3. *Lethean slumber*. Oblivion such as the river Lethe induces.

l. 5. *Calais ... Zetes*. The sons of Boreas who took part in the expedition of the Argonauts and freed Phineus from the harpies; cf. Note to XXXIII. 103.

4. l. 1. *The paladin.* Astolfo.

 l. 2. *his horn.* cf. XXXIII. 125.

5. ll. 3–4. Ariosto is following Dante's topography of Inferno.

9. ll. 6–8. This manner of addressing the soul echoes many such instances in Dante's *Commedia*.

11. Lydia's story is derived in part from the tale of the daughter of the king of Northumberland in *Palamedès*, and in part from the tale of Anaxarete in Ovid's *Metamorphoses* (XIV. 698 ff.). Ariosto may also have had in mind the story of Nastagio degli Onesti in Boccaccio's *Decamerone* (V. 8).

12. l. 1. *Harsh Anaxarete.* See Note to stanza 11.

 ll. 7–8. Ariosto seems to be poking fun at Dante in reversing the morality of *Inferno* (Canto V). Daphne, escaping from Apollo, was turned into a laurel tree; cf. Ovid (*Metamorphoses*, I. 452 ff.).

14. l. 3. *he who Medea grieved.* Jason.

 l. 4. . . . *left Ariadne.* Theseus.

 l. 5. . . . *abandoned Dido.* Aeneas.

 ll. 6–7. . . . *drove to deeds of blood/Prince Absalom.* Amnon (the first-born son of David), who raped Tamar, the sister of Absalom (David's third son by another mother). Absalom brought about the death of Amnon to avenge Tamar (2 Samuel xiii).

16. l. 1. *a cavalier.* Alcestes.

18. l. 1. *Pamphilia, Caria, Cilicia.* Provinces in Asia Minor, now Anatolia.

36. l. 8. *Hyrcanians.* Hyrcania was a province of ancient Persia on the south and south-east shores of the Caspian (Hyrcanian) Sea.

39. Ariosto alludes to eight tasks, five of which are among the twelve labours imposed on Hercules by Eurystheus, urged on by Juno. He refers to them by the regions where they were performed:

 l. 3. *Nemea.* A valley between Cleonae and Phlius, where Hercules strangled a monstrous lion.

 Erymanthus. A mountain from which a wild boar had descended into Psophis. Hercules chased it through deep snow and having thus exhausted it caught it in a net. (Some writers place the event in Thessaly.)

 Lerna. A place near Argos where a hydra lived in a swamp. It had nine heads of which the middle one was immortal.

39. l. 3. *Thrace*. Here Diomedes, King of Bistones, fed his horses
on human flesh. Hercules captured the horses and, having
killed Diomedes, fed his body to them.

l. 4. *Aetolian valleys*. Here Hercules controlled the course of the
river Achelous which ran between Acarnania and Aetolia and
frequently inundated these regions. (This is not one of the
twelve labours.)

  Numidian (valleys). In Libya, where Hercules killed the
giant Antaeus. (Neither is this among the twelve labours.)

l. 5. *By Tiber*. Hercules here killed Cacus, a giant, who stole the
cattle which Hercules had captured from Geryon. (This is
associated with, but not listed as, one of the twelve labours.)

  Ebro. A river in Spain, where Hercules captured the cattle
of Geryon.

46. l. 3. *pepper- and amomum-trees*. Ariosto calls them trees, though
they are shrubs.

49. l. 2. *jacinth*. The pale gold variety of the stone. This stanza
recalls Dante's description of the Valley of the Rulers (*Purgatorio*, VII).

50. This stanza recalls Dante's description of the Terrestrial Paradise (*Purgatorio*, XXVIII).

53. l. 3. *Daedalus*. See Note to XXV. 37.

l. 8. *The seven wonders*. They were: the pyramids of Egypt, the
hanging gardens of Babylon, the statue of Jupiter at Olympia,
the temple of Diana at Ephesus, the Mausoleum at Halicarnassus, the Colossus at Rhodes, the lighthouse of Alexandria.

54. l. 2. *An elder*. St John the Evangelist.

l. 4. *minium*. Red lead, from which paint was made and used for
illuminating manuscripts. The word 'miniature' is derived
from it.

58. l. 6. cf. John xxi. 20–23.

59. ll. 1–4. Ariosto seems to accept the belief that St John ascended
in the body, a belief which Dante refutes in *Paradiso* (XXV.
118–29). The fresco by Giotto in Santa Croce in Florence of
the Assumption of St John may have been commissioned as a
reply to Dante's refutal.

l. 2. *Enoch*. The son of Jared and great-grandfather of Noah.
According to Hebrew tradition he ascended to Heaven in the
body, cf. Genesis v. 24; Hebrews xi. 5.

l. 3. *Elijah*. He was carried up to Heaven by a whirlwind after a
chariot of fire had driven between him and Elisha; cf. 2 Kings
ii. See stanza 68, ll. 5–8.

l. 8. A reference to the Second Coming: cf. Luke xxi. 27.

60. l. 7. *our first parents*. Adam and Eve.
61. ll. 4–6. *Aurora . . . the fonder grows*. cf. XXXII. 13 and Note.
62. l. 6. *The wrong direction*. Orlando's obsessive love for Angelica.
64. l. 5. *a pagan maid*. Angelica.
    l. 7. *his cousin*. Rinaldo.
       twice. See Boiardo's *Orlando Innamorato* (I. xxvi; II. xx).
65. l. 2. cf. XXIII. 133.
    ll. 6–8. cf. Daniel IV. 33.
66. l. 5. *three months*. Ariosto here indicates the duration of Orlando's madness.
67. l. 3. *the circle of the moon*. According to Ptolemaic astronomy, the sphere of heaven nearest to the earth carried round the planet of the moon.
68. ll. 5–8. cf. stanza 59, line 3 and Note.
69. l. 7. *The sphere of fire*. This was believed to encircle the globe and had to be traversed in order to reach the heaven of the moon.
70. ll. 4–8. Ariosto here follows Pliny, who (*Naturalis Historia*, II. 11) says the moon is almost equal in size to the earth.
    l. 8. i.e. the moon has no water on it.
72. l. 8. Diana, the huntress, is the goddess of the moon.
74. ll. 7–8. Considered heretical by sixteenth-century commentators but the Holy Office never condemned these lines or the poem itself.
80. ll. 5–8. The reference is to the Donation of Constantine, by which the Emperor Constantine was believed to have endowed Pope Sylvester I with the western part of his Empire; cf. XVII. 78. For Milton's translation of these four lines, see Vol. I, Introduction, p. 82.
83. l. 6. *mad Anglante*. Orlando.
86. ll. 6–8. *Save for one error . . .* Ariosto speaks of Astolfo's one last error in the *Cinque Canti* (IV. 54–74). (It concerns his only amorous intrigue after his involvement with Alcina: the pursuit of Cinzia, the wife of Gaultier, an English baron.)
87. l. 6. *the apocalyptic book*. The Book of Revelation, of which St John the Evangelist was believed to be the author.
88. l. 4. *A white-haired woman*. One of the Fates; cf. Note to XXXIII. 1. l. 6.
89. l. 3. *another crone*. Another of the Fates. Ariosto here mentions only two; he does not name them.
91. l. 6. *an old man*. He represents Father Time.

CANTO XXXV

1-2. These stanzas are addressed to Alessandra Benucci.

3. l. 5. *a golden skein*. This represents the life of Cardinal Ippolito d'Este, the brother of Duke Alfonso I; cf. stanza 8.

4. ll. 6-8. Ippolito's birth (in 1479) will occur in the 1,480th year of the Incarnation, dating from the Conception, that is, twenty years before 1500 (MD in Roman numerals).

6. l. 1. *The king of rivers*. The Po.

l. 2. *A humble little town*. The town that will become the city of Ferrara. It is situated in the Po di Vomano, a branch channel of the main stream.

11. l. 7. *Lethe*. The classical river of oblivion, said by Dante to rise in the Terrestrial Paradise and flow down into Hell through the southern hemisphere.

13. ll. 1-2. These birds of prey are the courtiers satirized in stanza 20, ll. 5-8.

14. ll. 7-8. *Two silver swans*. These swans are true poets; there are only two, for true poets (cf. stanza 23) are rare.

   your / Proud eagle. The emblem of the Estensi was a white eagle on an azure field.

16. l. 2. *a fair nymph*. Fame.

20. l. 6. *ganymedes*. Court favourites.

22. ll. 6-7. *the benign / Augustus*. A generous patron of writers.

26. l. 2. *Virgil's epic clarion*. The *Aeneid*.

l. 4. *his proscriptions*. Octavian, at the time of the triumvirate, condemned many Roman citizens (including Cicero) to death.

l. 8. *If writers he had wooed*. D. R. Dudley, in the *Penguin Companion to Literature*, Vol. 4, 'Classical and Byzantine Literature', 1969, p. 121, writes: '. . . the revival of Latin literature in [Nero's] reign was a solid achievement . . . and probably owed more to his patronage and encouragement than his detractors allow.' (I am indebted to Miss Sylvia Bruce for this quotation.)

28. l. 4. *Vergilius was not her friend*. Ariosto means that it was in the poet's power to make or mar her reputation.

ll. 7-8. St John the Evangelist was believed to have written the Book of Revelation, as well as the Gospel and the three Epistles.

31. l. 8. *three monarchs*. cf. XXXIII. 66-9.

33. l. 2. *a damsel*. Fiordiligi.

l. 7. *Monodante's son*. Brandimarte.

l. 8. cf. XXIX. 31 ff.

35. l. 5. *her lover*. Brandimarte; cf. XXXI. 65–75.

41. ll. 5–6. XXIX. 3–25.

45. l. 1. *my African domain*. Algiers.

47. l. 7. *the golden lance*. Astolfo's magic lance; cf. XXXII. 48.

52. l. 1. *nothing more . . . was heard*. Until XLVI. 101.

54. l. 5. *Searching for Frontalatte*. Sacripante had departed in search of his horse; cf. XXVII. 84 ff.

56. l. 5. *home*. Cathay.

59. l. 6. *this horse*. Frontino.

67. l. 2. *Galicia's king*. Serpentino.

71. l. 6. *Rabicano*. Bradamante set out from Montalbano on Astolfo's horse; cf. XXXII. 48.

74. l. 1. *Lanfusa's son*. Ferraù.

CANTO XXXVI

2. ll. 5–8. In the war between Ferrara and Venice (1509), Cardinal Ippolito distinguished himself at the naval battle of Polesella by capturing many of the enemy's vessels, of which the pennants were hung in churches in Ferrara.

3. l. 4. *the Lion*. Venice. After the battle of Ghiaradadda on 14 May 1509 (cf. XXXIII. 38), the Venetians attempted to regain lost territories with the help of Slavonian mercenaries (l. 5).

4. In September 1509 the Venetians were besieged in Padua by the Emperor Maximilian. Alfonso sent troops to his assistance, led by Ippolito, who gave orders, it is said, that no such excesses as the Venetians had committed at Ferrara were to be repeated here.

5. l. 3. *this event*. On 30 November 1509, at Polesella, where the Venetians had built two fortresses, one on each side of the Po. Abandoning their ships, they withdrew to one of these strongholds. Ippolito pursued them and attacked the fortress with artillery.

6. ll. 1–2. cf. Homer (*Iliad*, XV).

ll. 3–8. Ercole Cantelmo and Alessandro Ferruffino advanced ahead of Ippolito's troops and penetrated too far into the fortress. Alessandro Ferruffino just managed to escape but Ercole Cantelmo was captured by Slavonian soldiers in a galley.

7. l. 2. *duke of Sora*. Sigismondo Cantelmo, the father of Ercole,

was fighting off the Estense troops. His son was decapitated before his eyes.

8. l. 8. *Tantalus*. He served up the flesh of his own son to the gods to see if they would be aware of its identity.

Thyestes. He betrayed his brother Atreus, who revenged himself by killing Thyestes' son and serving the father the flesh of his son to eat.

9. l. 3. *the Ganges' bed*. The Far East.

l. 5. *Anthropophagus*. Said by Boiardo to be king of the Laestrigons, cannibals (*Orlando Innamorato*, II. xviii. 37). In Homer, the king of the Laestrigons is Antiphates (*Odyssey*, x.).

l. 6. *Polyphemus*. Son of Neptune; one of the Cyclopes, he was also a cannibal (*Odyssey*, IX.).

10. ll. 6–8. *The Maid*. Bradamante; cf. xxxv. 65–80.

14. l. 3. *her cousin*. Either Orlando or Astolfo.

16. l. 1. *Marfisa*. She has gone to Arles to aid Agramante and has been tending Ruggiero while he recovers from his wounds; cf. XXXII. 6.

17. l. 2. *the daughter of the Montalbans*. Bradamante.

l. 8. *A phoenix*. cf. xxv. 97 and Note.

20. l. 7. *Aymon's daughter*. Bradamante.

23. ll. 7–8. *the lance*. Astolfo's; cf. XXXII. 48.

25. l. 1. *Troiano's gallant son*. Agramante.

31. l. 1. *the eagle*. cf. xxvi. 98–102.

42. l. 1. *a marble tomb*. This recalls the tomb from which Merlin speaks to Bradamante (III. 10 and 16–19).

43. l. 5. *Rabican*. cf. XXXII. 48.

54. l. 6. *an Erinys*. One of the Furies of Hell.

55. l. 1. *his blade*. Balisarda.

l. 3. *by enchantment*. cf. xxv. 15–16.

56. l. 7. *Hector's armour*. cf. xxx. 75.

58. l. 8. *A voice*. Atlante's; cf. IV. 29–32.

60. l. 1. For Ruggiero's descent, see Table, Vol. I, p. 734.

65. ll. 5–8. *Charon*. The boatman who ferries the souls of the dead across the Styx in Avernus. In Dante's *Inferno* (III. 76 ff.) he ferries them across the Acheron.

70. See Table, loc. cit.

l. 3. *Astyanax*. The son of Hector and Andromache. According to one tradition, followed by Virgil, Astyanax and his mother were taken to Greece as the captives of Pyrrhus; according to another, followed by Ovid, the Greeks threw the infant Astyanax from the walls of Troy.

71. l. 4. *city of the god of war.* Rome.
72. See Table, loc. cit.
    l. 7. *Agolant.* The father of Almonte, Troiano and Galaciella (Ruggiero's mother).
73. l. 7. *Beltramo.* Brother of Ruggiero II, the father of Ruggiero III.
74. l. 7. *six months gone with child.* She was to give birth to twins, Ruggiero and Marfisa.
81. l. 8. cf. xxx. 73–4.

CANTO XXXVII

This canto was inserted in the third edition of 1532; stanza 84 of Canto xxxvi was also added to serve as a link.

5. l. 1. *Harpalyce.* See Note to xx. 1. l. 5.
    Tomyris. Queen of the Massagetae by whom Cyrus was slain in battle, 529 B.C.
    the maid. Camilla; see Note to xx. 1.
    l. 2. *Hector's Amazon.* Penthesilea; see Note to xxvi. 81.
    ll. 3–4. *She whom . . . sailed on.* Dido, who left Tyre after the murder of her husband, Sichaeus, and founded Carthage.
    l. 5. *Zenobia.* Queen of Palmyra.
    ll. 5–6. *she who . . . warred upon.* Semiramis, Queen of Assyrians, Persians and Indians; cf. Note to xxv. 36. 5.

8. ll. 1–2. The four poets mentioned here were already dead when Ariosto wrote this stanza.
    l. 1. *Marullo.* Michele Marullo, who was Greek in origin, died in 1500. He was a distinguished Humanist.
    Pontano. Giovanni Pontano (1426–1503), a celebrated Humanist, originally from Spoleto, lived in Naples.
    l. 2. *Both Strozzi.* Tito Vespasiano Strozzi (d. 1505) and his son Ercole (killed by treachery in 1508) were known for their Latin and Italian poetry.
    l. 3. *Now Bembo.* Ariosto now moves to poets who are still living. Pietro Bembo, the Venetian Humanist, historian and poet, lived from 1470 to 1547. Ariosto submitted his poem to him for linguistic revision.
    Cappello. Bernardo Cappello, a Venetian nobleman and friend of Bembo's, died in 1565.
    l. 4. *the courtier's paragon.* Baldassare Castiglione, author of *Il Cortegiano* (1528).

8. l. 5. *Luigi Alamanni.* Author (1495–1556) of eclogues, satires, elegies and sonnets. His best known work is a poem on agriculture, *La Coltivazione.*

ll. 5–8. *the two . . . flood.* One is Luigi Gonzaga da Gazolo, called 'Rodomonte' for his daring and ferocity (1500–1532); the other is perhaps Luigi Gonzaga, son of Giampiero, who died in 1549. Endowed with both martial and literary skills, they were descendants of the Gonzagas who ruled Mantua, through which the Mincio flows.

9. Luigi Gonzaga da Gazolo married Isabella, the daughter of Vespasiano Colonna, despite the threats of Pope Clement VII, who had not forgiven Gonzaga for taking part in the Sack of Rome.

l. 3. *Parnassus.* Mountain sacred to the Muses.
Cynthus. Mountain sacred to Apollo.

11. l. 1. *well endowed.* Isabella, besides being endowed with virtue, brought a dowry of 20,000 ducats.

l. 5. *like a column.* A play upon her family name, Colonna.

12. l. 1. *New trophies.* Trophies of literature as well as of arms.
Oglio's shore. Gazolo is on the river Oglio.

l. 4. *Mincio.* The river which flows through Mantua.

l. 5. *Ercole Bentivoglio.* Bentivoglio (1506–73) was a friend of Ariosto. He wrote poetry in several genres, but excelled in satire.

l. 7. *Trivulzio.* Renato Trivulzio, a Milanese, wrote love poems in rhymed octaves.

Guidetto. Francesco Guidetto, a member of the Florentine Academy who collaborated on the 1527 edition of Boccaccio. There is a tradition that he assisted Ariosto in the revision of his poem.

l. 8. *Molza.* Francesco Molza (1499–1544), a poet of Modena, is known for his lyrics in the style of Petrarch.

13. l. 1. *Ercole, the duke of Chartres.* The son of Alfonso, later Ercole II, was created duke of Chartres when he married Renée de France. He wrote poetry.

l. 5. *My lord of Vasto.* Alfonso d'Avalos, Marquess of Vasto; cf. xv. 28 and xxxiii. 47.

14. l. 6. *Aganippe's fount.* The fount sacred to the Muses on Mt Helicon in Boeotia.

16. l. 1. *I will choose one.* Vittoria Colonna (1490–1547), daughter of Fabrizio Colonna and Agnese di Montefeltro, wife of Francesco d'Avalos, Marquess of Pescara (cf. xv. 28). She is among the best-known poets of the Italian Renaissance. Her poems to

the memory of her husband have rendered him immortal (ll. 6–8).

17. l. 1. *his fair sister*. Diana the moon.

l. 4. According to Ptolemaic astronomy, the planets were carried round the earth by the heavenly spheres once every twenty-four hours in an east–west direction; they each revolved in a west–east direction at varying rates of speed.

18. l. 5. *Artemisia*. Queen of Halicarnassus in Caria, wife of Mausolus. On his death she built the funeral monument called, after him, the Mausoleum. It was regarded as one of the seven wonders of the world (see Note to XXXIV. 53. l. 8).

19. l. 1. *Laodamia*. The wife of Protesilaus. When he was killed in the Trojan war, she begged the gods to be allowed to talk to him for three hours. Her plea was granted. When Protesilaus died a second time, Laodamia died with him.

Brutus' spouse. Portia, the wife of Brutus, killed herself after his death.

l. 2. *Evadne*. The wife of Capaneus. He was struck by lightning while scaling the walls of Thebes. Evadne cast herself into the flames which consumed his body.

Arria. The wife of Caecina Paetus, who was condemned to death, drove a blade into her breast and then handed the weapon to her husband to do the same (A.D. 42).

Argia. The wife of Polynices looked for his body and gave it burial and mourned him for the rest of her life.

ll. 6–7. *Lethe*. One of the rivers of Hell (see Note to XXXV. 11. 7).

ninefold shore / Of Styx. In the *Georgics* (IV. 480) and the *Aeneid* (VI. 439), Virgil says the Styx winds nine times round the world of the dead.

20. ll. 1–3. There is a tradition that Alexander the Great, visiting the tomb of Achilles, felt envy at the fame secured for him by Homer (the 'Maeonian poet').

21. ll. 5–6. *Marfisa ... her two comrades*. Bradamante and Ruggiero; cf. XXXVI. 84. 2.

26. l. 3. *three women*. Ullania and two handmaidens.

27. l. 1. *the son of Vulcan*. Erichthonius. Pallas Athene entrusted the child to Aglauros, who, against her instructions, looked at his serpent-like feet. He was said to be the first to use a chariot with four horses (*quadriga*).

28. l. 4. *Paestum*. A city of Magna Graecia (now destroyed) famous for its roses.

30. l. 1. *the Maid*. Bradamante.

l. 2. *her insignia*. cf. XXXII. 47.

30. l. 5. *the three kings.* cf. XXXIII. 66–9.

    ll. 7–8. cf. the humiliation of David's ambassadors by the Ammonites: 'Wherefore Hanun took David's servants, and shaved off the one half of their beards, and cut off their garments in the middle, even to their buttocks, and sent them away' (2 Samuel x. 4).

31. l. 1. *the shield.* cf. XXXII. 52–9.

36. ll. 1–7. Jason, who led the expedition of the Argonauts in pursuit of the Golden Fleece, disembarked on the island of Lemnos, where the women had killed all male inhabitants except Thoas, who was spared by his daughter Hypsipyle (Apollonius of Rhodes, op. cit.; *The Voyage of Argo*, trans. E. V. Rieu, Penguin Classics, p. 52).

38. l. 8. *A tyrant.* Marganorre.

45. l. 1. *his two sons.* Cilandro and Tanacro.

51. l. 6. *a lord and lady.* Olindro and Drusilla.

53. l. 2. *the lovely Greek.* She remains anonymous.

61. l. 8. *her land.* Byzantium.

86. l. 6. *their sire.* Phoebus, the sun-god.

92. ll. 1–5. *the great river* ... The Po, which rises in Monte Viso, into which the Ticino, the Lambra and the Adda flow.

96. l. 8. cf. stanza 33.

112. l. 8. *their vow.* cf. XXXIII. 75.

121. l. 8. *the ones who go towards Arles.* Bradamante, Ruggiero and Marfisa.

122. l. 5. *the lovers.* Bradamante and Ruggiero.

CANTO XXXVIII

1–3. cf. XXVI. 1–2.

2. l. 5. *Croesus or Crassus.* Croesus, King of Lydia, and M. Licinius Crassus, surnamed Dives, were celebrated for their riches.

5. l. 2. *His lord.* Agramante.

    l. 6. *Almonte's act of spite.* The attack upon Reggio; cf. XXX. 83, where Ariosto says that Ruggiero's father was killed by Troiano.

7. ll. 5–6. *where King Charles ... force.* Paris.

10. l. 4. *Pepin's son.* Charlemagne.

12. l. 3. *From India's sea* ... From the farthest eastern to the farthest western limits of the known world.

    Hercules' twin peaks. The rock of Gibraltar and Mt Abyla, now Jebel Hacho.

l. 4. *From Scythian snows* . . . From the far North to the far South.

14. cf. XXXVI. 58–66.

17. l. 1. *My sire*. Ruggiero II. For Marfisa's kinship with Charlemagne, see Table, Vol. I, p. 734.

l. 6. *Troiano's son*. Agramante.

18. l. 6. *Termagant*. See Note to XII. 59.

20. l. 8. cf. XVIII. 100–101 and Note.

21. l. 2. *Sansonet*. This is one of Ariosto's very few errors in the management of his enormous cast. Sansonetto has been taken prisoner by Rodomonte and arrives on the coast of Africa (XXXV. 53; XXXIX. 30).

l. 3. *Grifone (that imprudent boy)*. cf. XV. 101 ff.

ll. 5–8. cf. XXVI. 14–26.

22. ll. 2–3. These lines anticipate the care with which Charlemagne makes arrangements for Bradamante's wedding; cf. XLVI. 73–5.

23. l. 4. *lavacer*. Font (from Latin *lavacrum*).

ll. 5–8. cf. XXXV. 31.

l. 6. *the frenzied cavalier*. Orlando.

24. l. 2. *the highest point on earth*. The mountain crowned by the Terrestrial Paradise.

l. 3. *that precious phial*. cf. XXXIV. 82–3.

l. 8. *the king*. Senapo (Prester John).

25. l. 3. *Biserta*. The capital of Agramante's kingdom.

26. ll. 1–2. cf. II. 37–8; IV. 46–8.

27. ll. 3–4. *the blight / Of harpies*. cf. XXXIII. 125–8.

29. ll. 5–8. In the *Odyssey* (X. 1–100), Aeolus, King of the winds, encloses them in a pouch and gives it to Ulysses so that his voyages shall be calm.

l. 5. *Auster*. The south wind personified.

31. l. 8. According to the geographers of antiquity, the Atlas Mountains extended west as far as Cape Bon.

33. l. 2. *His mentor-saint*. St John.

43. l. 8. *Cambyses* (reigned 529–522 B.C.). The king of the Persians who sent his army across the Libyan desert to seize the temple of Jupiter Ammon. His troops were killed in the sand-storms which arose in the desert.

57. l. 5. *Four valiant cavaliers*. Aquilante, Grifone, Guidone Selvaggio, Sansonetto; cf. stanza 58, ll. 1–3.

l. 7. *his nephews*. Orlando and Rinaldo.

67. l. 8. *Mandricard*. cf. XXX. 68.

68. l. 7. *both the cousins*. Orlando and Rinaldo.

73. l. 4. *Melissa.* She has not intervened since XIII. 74–8.
74. l. 5. *lost his destrier.* cf. XXXIII. 89–92.
77. l. 7. *Two kings.* Agramante and Marsilio.
  he of Spain. Marsilio.
78. l. 3. *The helmet.* Won from Mandricardo; cf. XXX. 75.
  l. 4. *a greater poet.* Homer.
79. l. 7. See Note to I. 28.
80. l. 2. *him of Brittany.* King Salamone.
89. l. 1. They are fighting with battle-axes.

CANTO XXXIX

1. This is the only canto in which the action continues immediately without a prelude; but cf. XXXII.
3. l. 7. cf. XXXVIII. 48–64.
4. l. 1. *Melissa.* cf. XXXVIII. 73.
  l. 6. *dragon's hide.* Such as Rodomonte wears.
5. l. 2. *Troiano's doleful son.* Agramante, doleful because of Ruggiero's unsatisfactory performance in his combat with Rinaldo.
10. l. 8. *her sister.* Bradamante, Marfisa's sister-in-law to be.
17. l. 5. *Marios . . . Henrys . . . Karls.* The Italian, English and German troops.
18. l. 3. *Oliver's two famous sons.* Aquilante and Grifone.
  l. 6. *the two damsels.* Bradamante and Marfisa.
19. l. 4. *Astolfo.* cf. XXXVIII. 35.
  l. 7. *the Algazieran king.* Bucifar.
22. ll. 7–8. Ariosto is referring to Boiardo's *Orlando Innamorato* (II. xiv. 66), where Dudone is defeated in combat with Rodomonte. He is later (XV. 21) taken captive to Africa and handed over to Bucifar by Agramante just before he sets out for France.
23. l. 1. *The king of Sarza.* Rodomonte.
  l. 3. In the *Orlando Innamorato* (II. iii. 35, 36; XI), Rodomonte, impatient at Agramante's delay, crossed over into France with his troops. It was then that he defeated Dudone.
  l. 4. *Ugier.* Ugier the Dane.
  l. 6. *the commander.* Astolfo.
26–7. In *Mambrino* (XII. 4), by Il Cieco di Ferrara, Malagigi with the help of demons improvises a fleet which vanishes when it is no longer needed.
30. ll. 1–3. cf. XXXV. 44–5.

l. 4. *Orlando's brother* (*Oliver*). Orlando's wife, Alda, is Oliver's sister.

l. 5. *Sansonet.* cf. xxxviii. 21. l. 2 and Note.

31. l. 3. The vessel is blown east towards Biserta.

l. 8. Procne, the wife of Tereus, revengèd herself upon him for his ravishing of her sister Philomela by killing his son Itys. The gods in punishment turned Procne into a swallow, Philomela into a nightingale and Tereus into a hoopoe; cf. Ovid, *Metamorphoses*, vi.

32. l. 1. *the Imperial Bird.* The eagle.

l. 2. *The Golden Lilies.* The fleur-de-lis.

the Pards. As the son of the king of England, Astolfo has the leopard on his ensign; cf. xv. 75. These are the banners of the Empire, France and England.

34. l. 1. *King Otto's son.* Astolfo; cf. vi. 33.

36. l. 7. *a man so savage.* Orlando.

39. l. 5. *his cunning captor.* Rodomonte.

l. 6. *her love.* Brandimarte.

40. l. 4. *King Monodant.* Brandimarte's father.

41. l. 1. *Bardino.* In *Orlando Innamorato* (ii. xi. 46–7; xiii. 10–11), Bardino stole Brandimarte as a child to spite his father, Monodante, and sold him to the Count of Rocca Silvana. Later reconciled with Monodante, he went in search of Brandimarte.

45. l. 3. *the holy ancients.* St John, Elijah and Enoch; cf. xxxiv. 58–67. Only St John spoke to Astolfo of Orlando's state.

51. l. 6. *the son of Ugier.* Dudone.

57. l. 1. *the precious phial.* cf. xxxiv. 82–3.

60. l. 1. *Silenus.* The satyr and companion of Bacchus was found asleep by a nymph and two shepherds who bound him and stained his face with mulberry juice. When he awoke, he said 'Solvite me, pueri' (Virgil, *Eclogues* vi. 24).

The concern of the paladins to find clothes for the naked Orlando recalls his concern to find clothes for the naked Olimpia (xi. 59). It is strange that Ariosto should link this solemn moment of Orlando's return to sanity with the playful scene of the capture and release of Silenus. The satyr, on being freed, keeps the promises he made previously to sing for the shepherds and his songs surpass the music of Apollo and Orpheus. It is possible that Ariosto means that he too is released from the theme of madness and his poetry, like the rhapsody of Silenus, will attain unprecedented heights.

61. l. 4. *The one.* Angelica.

62. l. 4. *Ziliant*. The younger brother of Brandimarte; cf. *Orlando Innamorato* (II. xi. 48; xiii. 33).

l. 5. *the islands*. The kingdom of Monodante to which Brandimarte is heir is Dammogir; cf. XLIII. 163.

68. l. 2. *to avenge her father*. Agramante's father, Troiano; his uncle, Almonte; his grandfather, Agolante, were implicated in the injuries suffered by Marfisa's parents; cf. XXXVI. 69–77.

69. l. 1. *hunting pards*. In the Middle Ages, leopards were trained for hunting.

72. ll. 7–8. According to the tradition of the Carolingian romances, the tombs of the Roman cemetery at Arles (Les Alyscamps) were those of the warriors who died fighting in the campaigns of Charlemagne.

73. l. 8. *his paternal shore*. Africa.

74. ll. 6–8. In the *Cinque Canti* (I. 63, ll. 1–4), Charlemagne promises Navarre and Aragon to Orlando, who is about to drive out Marsilio.

80. l. 2. *the duke*. Astolfo.

83. l. 2. *ballistas*. Military engines for hurling stones.

l. 5. *Greek fire*. Missiles of bitumen and other combustibles set on fire.

84. l. 6. *His hand . . . clutching at the rim*. cf. Lucan, *Pharsalia*, III. 609 ff. and 661–9; Silius Italicus, *Punica*, 489–91. (I am indebted to Professor Claude Rawson for these references.)

CANTO XL

1. l. 4. *Herculean son*. Ippolito, son of Ercole; cf. I. 3. l.3.

ll. 5–7. *owls to Athens . . . pots to Samos . . . crocodiles to Egypt*. cf. 'coals to Newcastle'. The owl was the emblem of Pallas Athene. Samos was celebrated for its pottery.

2. Ariosto refers here to the naval battle of Polesella, in which Ippolito defeated the Venetians.

3. On 16 December 1509, Ariosto was sent to Rome to request aid for Ferrara from Pope Julius II.

l. 6. *The Golden Lion*. Venice.

4. ll. 1–4. *Trotto and Afranio . . . Zerbinatto*. Alfonso Trotto was the steward of Duke Alfonso. Afranio dei Conti di Pavia, Ludovico da Bagno, Francesco Zerbinato were courtiers. Alberto Cestarelli was Rector of San Clemente and San Gregorio.

Annibale Collenuccio was of the household of Ippolito. *Piero Moro* was also in his employ.

l. 3. *Three of my kinsmen*. They have not been identified with certainty. One may be Ludovico's cousin, Alfonso Ariosto.

4. ll. 5–8. After the battle, Ippolito hung the banners of the enemy and other trophies in the churches of Ferrara. It is reported that he seized fifteen Venetian galleys; cf. III. 57.

5. ll. 6–8. cf. xxxIX. 75–86.

8. l. 2. *Brigliadoro*. Given to Agramante by Ruggiero, who won him from Mandricardo (xxx. 75).

9. l. 2. Sobrino had advised against the war; cf. xxxVIII. 48–64.
   ll. 5–8. Orlando, now restored to his senses, is commander-in-chief of the siege of Biserta.
   the duke. Astolfo.

10. l. 4. *the armada*. Captained by Dudone.

11. l. 5. Astolfo's troops are Nubians.

14. l. 1. *The Imam*. The chief minister of a Mohammedan mosque.

15. The siege of Biserta balances the siege of Paris (xIV, xVI, xVIII).

18. l. 4. *'tortoises' and 'cats'*. Movable timber shelters for troops attacking fortifications.

21. l. 2. Astolfo.

31. ll. 1–2. *the stately king / Of rivers*. The Po.
    l. 3. *the fields of Ocnus*. The territory of Mantua.

33. ll. 1–4. This striking simile is drawn from Dante's image of the Stygian marsh which surrounds the walls of the City of Dis on the battlements of which stand the Furies (*Inferno*, IX. 11–48).

35. l. 6. *Folvo*. King of Fers.

39. l. 3. *King Pepin's son*. Charlemagne.
    l. 4. *Norandino*. King of Damascus; cf. xVII. 25 ff. His kinship with Agramante has not been mentioned before.

41. l. 1. Hannibal was handed over to the Romans by Prusias, King of Bithynia.
    l. 2. Jugurtha was handed over to the Romans by Boccus, King of Mauretania.
    l. 3. Ludovico Sforza, 'il Moro', was betrayed by Swiss mercenaries and handed over to Louis XII ('*Another Ludovic*').

42. l. 1. *the Pope*. Julius II. After the battle of Ravenna, when Ferrara was allied with the French, Alfonso relied on his own strength in his struggles against this Pope and, later, Leo X.
    l. 4. *his would-be champion*. The French king.

44. l. 3. *an island*. Possibly Linosa, which is not far from Lampedusa.

46. l. 3. *Gradasso*. cf. xxxIII. 95 and Note.

47. l. 1. *the Sericanian*. Gradasso.
    l. 2. *The Moor's*. Agramante's.

47. ll. 6–7. *The memory / Of Pompey*. He was betrayed by Ptolemy, King of Egypt, who offered him a refuge when he fled from Caesar.

48. l. 4. *your capital*. Biserta.

l. 4–5. *the son / Of Milo*. Orlando.

56. l. 7. *Durindana*. Given to Gradasso by Ruggiero after his combat with Mandricardo; cf. xxx. 74.

57. l. 5. *Almonte's horn*. Stolen from Orlando by Brunello, who gave it to Agramante; cf. *Orlando Innamorato* (II. xi. 8–9 and xvi. 13).

l. 6. *Brigliadoro*. Given by Ruggiero to Agramante after his combat with Mandricardo; cf. xxx. 75.

l. 8. *King Troiano's son*. Agramante.

59. l. 3. *The other two*. Oliver and Brandimarte.

l. 4. *the Sarzan*. Rodomonte.

61. l. 7. *the valiant Clairmont knight*. Rinaldo.

l. 8. cf. xxxviii. 88–90.

64. l. 2. cf. xxxviii. 87.

66. l. 8. *Montalbano*. Rinaldo.

70. l. 3. *the Dane*. Dudone.

71. l. 5. *seven kings*. They are named in stanza 73.

73. ll. 5–8. There is a discrepancy between editions of the poem as to the list of names. Instead of Baliverzo, Bambirago, and instead of Clarindo, Balastro, are mentioned in the editions by Pietro Papini and Cesare Segre. This translation here follows the edition by Nicola Zingarelli.

l. 5. *The king of Nasamona*. Puliano; he was killed by Rinaldo (xvi. 46).

l. 6. *Agricalte*. He was killed by Rinaldo (xvi. 81); so was Bambirago.

l. 7. *Manilard*. King of Norizia. He was struck down by Orlando and left stunned (xii. 84).

l. 8. *Clarindo*. African king of Bolga. Balastro was killed by Lurcanio (xviii. 45).

According to Zingarelli's edition, Ariosto resuscitates two dead men; according to Papini's and Segre's, he resuscitates four.

Rimedonte. African king of Getulia.

79. l. 1. *that iron club*. In Boiardo's *Orlando Innamorato* (II. xiv. 62), Dudone always fights with an iron mace.

80. l. 5. *her mother's side*. The mother of Dudone (Armelina) was the sister of Beatrice of Bavaria (wife of Duke Aymon). Bradamante and Dudone were therefore first cousins.

CANTO XLI

2. l. 1. *Icarius*. An Athenian who gave hospitality to Bacchus and was taught the cultivation of the vine. He was killed by peasants who had become drunk on wine which he had given them and who thought they had been poisoned.

l. 3. *the Celtic tribes*. The Gauls. Ariosto's source is probably Livy.

3. l. 5. *one*. Ruggiero.

6. l. 7. *seven kings*. cf. XL. 73.

13. l. 1. *Boreas*. The north wind personified.

15. l. 4. *The highest circle*. The Primum Mobile, beyond the planets and the stars.

24. ll. 4–5. *Beyond . . . side*. East of Biserta.

ll. 6–8. *Orlando . . . shore*. cf. XL. 60–61.

26. ll. 6–8. *How Falerina lost it . . .* cf. VII. 76, XXV. 15–16 and Notes.

28. l. 2. *Sericana's ruler*. Gradasso.

l. 4. Gradasso had captured Baiardo after his combat with Rinaldo (XXXIII. 89–95). Ruggiero gave him Durindana after his fight with Mandricardo (XXX. 74).

29. l. 2. *being enchanted*. cf. XII. 49.

30. ll. 3–4. This emblem may represent the pagan pride punished by God.

ll. 5–8. *his brother*. Oliver (Orlando's brother-in-law). The significance may be that Oliver lies in wait for his prey.

31. l. 2. *his father's sake*. Monodante has recently died; cf. XXXIX. 62–3.

35. l. 4. *the palace*. Presumably a palace in Biserta.

ll. 5–6. *the brave band / Of three*. Orlando, Oliver and Brandimarte.

l. 7. *the island*. Lampedusa.

36. ll. 5–6. The Christians will not have the rising sun in their eyes.

37. ll. 7–8. In Boiardo's *Orlando Innamorato* (II. xxvii. 46 ff.; xxviii. 1 ff.) Brandimarte, as Monodante's son, is the honoured guest of Agramante. Boiardo does not say that he accompanied the Saracen army to France, for he was already converted and baptized. Ariosto departs from Boiardo's account in this particular, implying that Brandimarte's conversion occurred after the arrival of Agramante's army in France.

40. l. 3. *Milo's son*. Orlando.

43. l. 5. *that dragon*. Satan.

48. l. 3. *The pact*. cf. XXXVIII. 87.

53. ll. 1–2. See Acts of the Apostles ix, 4.

54. l. 6. *his death*. cf. III. 24.

56. ll. 4–6. *The story* . . . See Matthew xx, 1–16.

61. l. 5. *Pinabello's death*. cf. XXII. 96–7.

    ll. 7–8. *Bertolagi's* . . . *death*. cf. XXVI. 13.

62. l. 5. *His wife and sister*. Bradamante and Marfisa.

    l. 7. *his offspring*. Ruggieretto.

63. According to legend, Este was founded by Phrygians or Trojans between the rivers Adige and Brenta at the foot of the Euganean Hills, rich in sulphur springs, where the Trojan Antenor founded Padua, so delighting in the region that he no longer missed Mt Ida, the river Xanthus, or Lake Ascanius in Bithynia.

64. l. 4. *new Troy*. Este.

    ll. 5–8. cf. III. 24–5.

65. ll. 1–5. The name 'Este' is derived from '*Ateste*'. Ariosto invents another origin: the Latin formula of investiture used by the Emperor: '*Este hic domini*' (Be masters here).

66. l. 6. *Pontiero*. Stronghold of the Maganzans.

67. cf. III. 25–62 and Notes. The hermit here replaces the pagan Atlante as Ruggiero's guide and mentor.

68. For this combat, see diagram, pp. 677–8.

    l. 5. *two other combatants*. Agramante and Sobrino.

71. l. 1. *The king of Africa*. Agramante.

72. l. 2. *the Sericanian*. Gradasso.

73. l. 2. *the black knight*. Brandimarte.

74. l. 8. *Falerina's sword*. Balisarda.

76. l. 7. *Milo's son*. Orlando.

80. l. 2. *Durindana*. In the hand of Agramante.

83. l. 2. *camail*. Chain mail attached to the headpiece protecting the neck and shoulders.

86. l. 6. *his lord*. Agramante.

88. ll. 3–4. Oliver is wearing the armour of Hector which Ruggiero won from Mandricardo; cf. stanza 29 and XXX. 75.

91. l. 5. *the son of Monodant*. Brandimarte.

    l. 6. *Troiano's son*. Agramante.

93. l. 8. *the other two*. Orlando and Gradasso.

CANTO XLII

2. ll. 5–8. Achilles thus avenged the death of Patroclus (*Iliad*, XXII. 395 ff.).

3–4. At the storming of the fort of Bastia (A.D. 1512) a stone fell on Alfonso's head. His soldiers, believing he was dead, destroyed the garrison; cf. III. 53–4 and Note.

5. Alfonso was storming Bastia to avenge the Governor, Vestidello Pagano, who was killed by the Spaniards after he had surrendered.

7. l. 6. *Falerina's brand*. Balisarda.

9. ll. 5–6. In Dante's *Inferno* the souls entering Hell are ferried across the river Acheron by the boatman Charon.

l. 8. *the Sericanian*. Gradasso.

18. l. 6. *Erebus*. The dark space under the earth through which, according to Greek and Roman mythology, the dead passed into Hades.

20–21. These stanzas are an example of Ariosto's playfulness. Federigo Fulgoso (or Fregoso), brother of Ottaviano, the Doge of Genoa, was an admiral who drove the pirates from the Mediterranean and defeated them near Biserta. He later became Archbishop of Salerno and a Cardinal. He is one of the characters in Bembo's *Prose* and Castiglione's *Cortegiano*. It would seem that he pointed out to Ariosto that no jousting could have taken place on the island of Lampedusa, which is rocky and mountainous. Ariosto ingeniously makes good his mistake by inventing the story of the earthquake.

22. l. 1. *Fulgosan*. The name Fulgoso means 'refulgent'.

23. l. 5. *who it was*. Rinaldo.

24. l. 4. *the vow*. cf. XXXVIII. 87.

26. ll. 1–3. cf. III. 9 ff.

32. ll. 1–2. In *Orlando Innamorato*, Malagigi was held prisoner by Angelica, who promised to set him free if he could bring Rinaldo to her (I. v).

35. l. 5. *the two fountains*; cf. I. 78–9.

38. l. 3. *young African*. Medoro.

42. l. 1. *the son of Pepin*. Charlemagne.

43. l. 7. *leaving Paris*. The Christians appear to have moved from Arles to Paris.

46. l. 8. *a monstrous female figure*. Jealousy.

53. l. 1. *A cavalier*. Scorn.

58. l. 2. *the Abyss*. Hell.

66. l. 4. *Blind Tobit*. He was healed of blindness by the Archangel Raphael, who instructed his son Tobias to apply the bile of a fish; Book of Tobit, Apocrypha.

67. l. 5. *Sericana*. The kingdom of Gradasso.

68. l. 2. *the Count Anglant*. Orlando.

70. l. 7. *a cavalier*. He is not named.

73. l. 2. *a palace*. Ariosto may be thinking of the palace of the Gonzagas in Mantua.

75. ll. 5–6. There is just such a ramped stairway at the palace in Mantua.

83. l. 2. *Lucrezia Borgia*. cf. XIII. 69–71 and Note.

l. 4. *her ancient namesake*. Lucretia. See Note to XXIX. 28. ll. 2–4.

l. 6. *Strozzi*. Ercole Strozzi wrote poems in Latin in praise of Lucrezia Borgia.

Tebaldeo. Antonio Tebaldeo, also a poet, was her secretary.

l. 8. *Linus*. The son of Apollo.

Orpheus. The son of the Muse Calliope.

84. Isabella d'Este, the sister of Duke Alfonso I and of Cardinal Ippolito, married Francesco Gonzaga II, Marquess of Mantua; cf. XIII. 59–61 and Note.

85. l. 3. *both Gian Iacopi*. Gian Iacopo Calandra and Gian Iacopo Bardelone, two poets of Mantua.

86. l. 1. *Elisabetta*. This is Elisabetta Gonzaga, the sister-in-law of Isabella, who married Guidobaldo I of Montefeltro, Duke of Urbino.

l. 2. *Leonora*. The niece of Elisabetta, who married Francesco Maria della Rovere.

l. 7. *Iacopo Sadoleto*. Bishop, and later Cardinal, of Modena and man of letters.

l. 8. *Pietro Bembo*. The celebrated Humanist and writer; cf. XXXVII. 8. l. 3 and Note.

87. l. 1. *A courtly Castiglione*. Baldassare Castiglione, author of *Il Cortegiano* ('The Courtier').

l. 2. *Muzio Arelio*. Giovanni Muzzarelli of Mantua; he wrote poetry in Italian and in Latin, and affected this latinized form of his surname.

88. l. 2. *Lucrezia Bentivoglio*. The illegitimate daughter of Ercole I, who married Annibale Bentivoglio of Bologna.

l. 6. *Camillo*. The poet of Bologna, Camillo Paleotti.

l. 7. *The Reno*. The river which flows near Bologna.

l. 8. *Amphrysus*. The river in Thessaly which heard Apollo

playing on his lyre when he was a shepherd of King Admetus; cf. Virgil (*Georgics*, III. ll. 1–2).

89. l. 1. *the town*. Pesaro.

l. 2. *the Isauro*. This river (now the Foglia) flows into the sea at Pesaro.

l. 4. *Auster*. The south wind personified.

ll. 5–8. *a double crown*. Guido Silvestri, called Postumo, was both a poet and a doctor. Athene, goddess of wisdom, and Phoebus (Apollo), god of poetry, place a double crown upon his head. Ariosto derives the name Pesaro (line 7) from the fact that there the Gauls, after the Sack of Rome by Brennus (390 B.C.), weighed the gold paid to them as tribute by the Romans (the Italian *pesare* means 'to weigh'; *aurum* in Latin, *oro*, formerly *auro*, in Italian, means 'gold').

90. l. 1. *Diana*. The daughter of Sigismondo d'Este who married Alberigo Sanseverino; she had a reputation for pride as well as beauty. She is among those who welcome Ariosto home (XLVI. 4).

l. 4. *Celio Calcagnin*. Professor at the University of Ferrara and a poet.

ll. 6–7. *the kingdom where | Monaeses ruled*. Persia. Monaeses, mentioned by Horace, is believed to be the same man as Surenas, the general of Orodes who defeated Crassus.

l. 7. *Juba's Africa*. The kingdom of Mauretania, ruled by Juba till his defeat by Caesar.

91. l. 1. *Marco Cavallo*. A poet of Ancona. His name in Italian means 'horse', which is why Ariosto compares him with the mythological winged horse, Pegasus, which struck water with its hoof from a rock on Mt Helicon or Mt Parnassus (the legend varies).

l. 6. *Beatrice*. This is Beatrice d'Este; cf. XIII. 62–3 and Note. She married Ludovico Sforza, called 'il Moro'.

92. l. 3. *Nicholas*. Niccolò da Correggio, author of a pastoral drama, *Cefalo*.

l. 6. *Timothy*. Timoteo Bendedei, a poet of Ferrara.

ll. 7–8. The river Po, where the sisters of Phaethon were changed into poplars and their tears into amber, as they wept for their brother who plunged into the Po; cf. III. 34. ll. 2–7 and Note.

93. l. 2. *The Borgia*. See stanza 83.

l. 3. *a tall figure*. Alessandra Benucci.

l. 6. *in black*. Alessandra's husband, Tito Strozzi, died in October 1515; however, Ariosto had seen Alessandra dressed in a black silk gown in 1513, when he first fell in love with her, as appears from his *Canzone* (1. 100–101).

95. l. 4. *One so uncouth*. Ariosto himself.

100. l. 6. *A pair of horns*. Traditional symbol of the deceived husband.

102. ll. 1–3. These lines in the original are perhaps a playful echo of Dante's line '*Io credo ch'ei credette ch'io credesse*' (I believe that he believed that I believed), *Inferno*, XIII. 25.

103. ll. 1–2. *the crest | Of Cornwall*. This is a literal translation of the original. (*Cornovaglia*, 'Cornwall', is a play on the Italian word *corno*, 'horn'. There may be also a reference here to King Mark of Cornwall who was cuckolded by Tristan.) The story of the cup which dribbles on to a husband's chest if his wife is unfaithful is derived from the Arthurian romance *Bret* in which a horn is sent by Morgain la fée to her brother King Arthur to test the fidelity of his wife Guinevere. It is taken instead to King Mark of Cornwall and there used to show the infidelity of Iseult. On this occasion the wine spills on to the wife's chest, for it is she who drinks from the horn, not her husband. The story is also told in *Perceval*, where the wine spills on to the chest of deceived husbands. It is likely that the dribbling horn (as symbol of the penis) signifies premature ejaculation, which would make a wife's infidelity more probable; cf. XLIII. 28.

CANTO XLIII

10. l. 1. *my evil counsellor*. Melissa; cf. stanza 24.

11. l. 1. *a city*. Mantua.

l. 2. *A river*. The Mincio, issuing from Lake Garda, forms a marsh round Mantua.

ll. 5–6. According to legend, Mantua was founded by the sorceress Manto, who fled from Thebes. Cadmus, son of Agenor and brother of Europa, slew a dragon and on the advice of Athene, sowed its teeth in the soil. There sprang forth armed men who killed one another, with the exception of five, who were the ancestors of the Thebans. Cadmus became the ruler of Thebes.

16. l. 8. *these eight*. cf. XLII. 83–95.

23. l. 3. *Helen*. Helen of Troy; cf. XI. 70.

ll. 3–6. *the offer made | To Paris* . . . The famous beauty contest in which Venus, Juno and Minerva were the competitors was judged by Paris, the son of Priam, who was guarding flocks on Mt Ida. He awarded the prize (an apple) to Venus.

24. *Melissa*. This story of Melissa's self-seeking use of her magic powers has led some readers to conclude that she is not the same sorceress as the one who devotes herself to the welfare of Bradamante and Ruggiero. (See Donato Internoscia, 'Are There Two Melissas in the *Orlando Furioso*?', *Italica* 25, 1948, pp. 217–26; Robert Griffin, *Ludovico Ariosto*, Twayne, 1974, pp. 107–11.) On the other hand, Ariosto has already indicated that Melissa went to Merlin for advice; cf. 111. 12. ll. 1–4. It is reasonable to suppose (and in keeping with Ariosto's control of his narrative) that Merlin instructed Melissa to use her powers for a better purpose than her own amorous gratification. The story related by Rinaldo's host refers, if this is so, to an earlier stage in Melissa's life. The departure of Melissa from Mantua (stanza 46, ll. 7–8) can be linked with her own words to Bradamante in Merlin's cave (loc. cit.). The theory that there are two Melissas and that Ariosto omitted to say so is less likely than that Melissa is a reformed sorceress, now exerting herself on the side of good.

28. See XLII. 103 and Note.

32. l. 1. *a city*. Ferrara, founded, according to legend, by the Paduans fleeing from Attila the Hun. Padua was said to have been founded by the Trojan Antenor.

41. ll. 4–5. At sunset.

46. See Note to stanza 24.

53. ll. 5–8. *Melara* and *Figarola* are towns on the left bank of the Po, *Sermide* and *Stellata* are on the right, to the west of Ferrara. l. 8. The Po divides into two branches as it nears the site where Ferrara was to be built.

54. ll. 1–2. One (the left-hand) branch is called the Po di Venezia, as it flows towards Venice; the other flows past Ferrara.

l. 3. *Bondeno*. At the confluence of the Panaro and the Po.

l. 7. *Tealdo*. A castle to the west of Ferrara built by Tealdo d'Este *c*. 970.

56. l. 3. *the isle*. See Vol. I, Introduction, pp. 17–18. Belvedere is no longer an island.

57. ll. 2–3. The astronomical year begins in March with the entry of the sun into the sign of Aries (the Ram). These lines mean that seven hundred years must pass from the time of Charlemagne until the period when Ariosto is writing.

l. 8. *Nausicaa's island*. Corfù, the kingdom of the Phaeacians, ruled by Alcinous, the father of Nausicaa; cf. Homer (*Odyssey* VI–VII).

58. l. 2. *the fair isle*. Capri, where the Emperor Tiberius had a palace.

l. 8. *Cyprus*. The birthplace of Venus.

Cnidus. City of Asia Minor on a promontory on the coast of Caria, much visited by travellers in the ancient world who went to see the statue of Aphrodite by Praxiteles.

59. l. 2. *care of one*. Alfonso I, Duke of Ferrara.

ll. 7–8. Alfonso was the son of Ercole I and the father of Ercole II.

61. l. 6. *thy lords*. The Estensi.

63. In the sixteenth century, the Po divided into two branches at Stellata; cf. stanza 53. One branch, the left, flowed towards Venice; cf. 54; the other flowed towards Ferrara. Nearer the estuary, it divided again; the left branch was the Volano, the right was the Primaro. At Primaro, six miles from Ferrara, there were two towers; the one to the left was called Gaibana, the other was Torre della Fossa.

l. 6. *San Gregorio*. A town near Ferrara.

66. l. 6. *Clarice*. She has been briefly glimpsed in xxx. 93, welcoming Rinaldo on one of his fleeting visits to Montalbano.

70. l. 7. *The city*. Mantua.

72. l. 3. *the flowing gown*. The academic toga.

l. 4. *Ulpianus*. A Roman jurist of the time of Alexander Severus (Emperor A.D. 222–235).

74. ll. 3–4. *that race of might*. Thebans; cf. Note to stanza 11, lines 5–6.

75. ll. 5–6. *the treasure of / Tiberius*. This may be a reference to Tiberius II, Emperor of Constantinople (A.D. 578–582). He was celebrated for his wealth. Tiberius, the successor of Augustus, was also famed for his riches.

79. ll. 5–8. The emblem of the snake is derived from the dragon slain by Cadmus; cf. Note to stanza 11, lines 5–6.

96. l. 3. *A damsel*. The sorceress, Manto.

97. cf. Notes to stanza 11.

98. This condition, which Manto implies is general to all sorceresses, has not been said to apply to Melissa.

101. cf. stanzas 78–80.

106. l. 3. *a dog*. Ariosto's contemporaries probably had no difficulty in recognizing in the dog the symbol of Adonio's penis. The urgings of Argia's nurse, and her own delight in the dog (stanzas 113, 115, 116), must have caused some earthy guffaws at the Estense court. The dog's ability to spray forth riches and jewels further confirms this interpretation, which has been

strangely missed by modern commentators, despite the well-known Freudian explanation of Aladdin's lamp. See also XXVIII. 67. l. 2; cf. Eric Partridge, *A Dictionary of Historical Slang*, under 'DOG'. (Adonio's dog is a descendant of Petitcreü, the magic dog which Tristan sends to Iseult; in this story the dog is probably the symbol of a dildoe though this does not seem to have occurred to editors of the relevant texts; cf. *Le Roman de Tristan*, ed. Joseph Bédier, S.A.T.F. 2 vols., 1932–5, Vol. I, pp. 217–31; and Louise Ghädinger, *Hiudan und Petitcreu*, Zurich, 1971.)

125. l. 4. *this river*. The Po.

132. l. 7. *My master's*. The boatman's master is the host who entertained Rinaldo on the previous evening.

145. l. 7. *Santerno*. A river which formerly flowed into the Primaro branch of the Po (it now flows into the Reno). *Argenta* (line 8) was on its right bank.

146. l. 1. *Bastia*. The fort which Alfonso's soldiers won from the Spanish garrison; cf. III. 54 and XLII. 3–5.

ll. 3–4. The inhabitants of Romagna will suffer the ravages of Alfonso's troops.

l. 6. *Filo*. A little town on the left bank of the Primaro branch of the Po, seven miles beyond Argenta.

l. 8. Ravenna was then a port, at Classe.

147. l. 7. *Montefiore*. Now Montefiorito, in the province of Forlì, south of Rimini.

148. It would seem that Ariosto sends Rinaldo via Urbino, rather than along the direct route south from Rimini, in order to pay this graceful compliment to the Dukes of Urbino: Federigo da Montefeltro, his son Guidobaldo, who married Elisabetta Gonzaga, Francesco Maria della Rovere and his wife, Leonora Gonzaga. Elisabetta and Leonora are two of the eight women represented by statues on the fountain; cf. XLII. 86.

149. l. 2. *Cagli*. Rinaldo descends the hill on which Urbino stands, and rides towards Cagli.

ll. 3–5. The river Metauro and its tributary (here called the Gauno, but probably the Candigliano) flow down from Mt Pietra Pertusa.

l. 8. *Trapani*. In Sicily, where Anchises, the father of Aeneas, was buried; cf. Virgil (*Aeneid*, III, end).

150. l. 1. *the island*. Lampedusa.

l. 3. cf. XLI. 68 ff.

151. l. 1. *Anglante*. Orlando.

l. 5. *the heir of Monodante*. Brandimarte.

158. l. 6. *the Maenads.* The Bacchantes.

159. l. 4. *the pagan monarchs.* Agramante and Gradasso.

163. l. 4. *Dammogir.* The capital of Brandimarte's kingdom.

165. ll. 4–6. *that mountain.* Etna; that is, they set out for Sicily.

166. l. 3. *the silent goddess.* Of the Moon.

168. l. 1. *Bardino.* cf. XXXIX. 40–41 and Note.

172. l. 4. *my lord and uncle.* Charlemagne.

174. l. 5. *the Decii.* Three consuls of this name who, according to tradition, died for their country: the father, in the battle with the Latins near Vesuvius in 340 B.C.; his son near Sentino in the war against the Etruscans, *c.* 295 B.C.; his nephew near Ascoli, in the war with Pyrrhus, 279 B.C.

ll. 5–6. *Curtius* . . . It is related that in 362 B.C. the earth in the Roman Forum gave way and a chasm appeared, which the soothsayers declared could be filled up only by throwing into it Rome's greatest treasure. Curtius, a noble youth, mounted his horse in full armour and, declaring that Rome had no treasure greater than a brave and loyal citizen, plunged into the chasm, whereupon the earth closed up over him.

l. 7. *Codros.* The son of Melanthus, and the last king of Athens. He sacrificed his life to save his country.

Argives. Greeks.

179. l. 8. *his limb.* Oliver's ankle is broken; cf. XLI. 68–90.

181. ll. 1–2. Ariosto seems here to be referring to the custom of hiring mourners (women) to weep at a funeral. Pietro Papini thinks these women are not the same as the genuine mourners mentioned in stanza 180, l. 8 (*Orlando Furioso a cura di Pietro Papini*, Sansoni, 1957, p. 606, Note to this stanza).

184. l. 4. *the Empress.* In the Carolingian romances, this is Galerana, daughter of Galafro, King of Spain, who became a Christian for love of Charlemagne. The historical Charlemagne had two wives: Ermengarda, daughter of Desiderius, King of Lombardy, and Hildegard the Swabian, by whom he had six children.

l. 5. *her father.* Fiordiligi is the daughter of Dolistone, King of Laodicea in Syria.

187. l. 2. *A hermit.* This is the hermit with whom Ruggiero has found refuge; cf. XLI. 50 ff.

189. l. 8. cf. XLI. 59.

192. l. 8. Sobrino, the only one of the three pagans to survive the contest on Lampedusa, has been cared for by Orlando; cf. XLII. 19.

197. l. 2. *Montalbano.* Rinaldo.

ll. 7–8. cf. XXXVIII. 88 ff.

CANTO XLIV

4. l. 1. *The holy elder*. The hermit who has baptized Ruggiero and healed Oliver and Sobrino.

6. l. 1. *Montalbano's lord*. Rinaldo.

7. ll. 1–4. cf. XXVI. 11–18.
   l. 2. *the king of Spain*. Marsilio.
   l. 3. *the princess*. Fiordispina.
   ll. 5–8. *both the sons of Buovo*. Viviano and Malagigi; cf. XXV. 72–6.

10. l. 3. *a splendid lineage*. Of the Estensi.

11. l. 2. *the son of Aymon*. Rinaldo.

16. ll. 5–8. Balisarda, Frontino and the armour of Hector were found by Orlando on the empty ship which beached on the shore of north Africa. It had been abandoned by Ruggiero and his companions in a storm; cf. XLI. 8–22 and 25–9. Ruggiero can in a sense be said to have lent aid to the Christian side on Lampedusa, since Orlando used Balisarda, Brandimarte rode Frontino and Oliver wore the armour of Hector.

17. ll. 1–4. cf. XXV. 15–16 and Note.
   ll. 5–6. cf. XXVII. 70–85.

18. l. 8. *the English duke*. Astolfo.

19. ll. 4–8. cf. XXXVIII. 27 ff.

20. l. 1. *The son of Ugier*. Dudone.
   ll. 2–8. cf. XXXIX. 26–9.

21. ll. 7–8. *Auster*. The south wind personified; cf. XXXVIII. 29–31.

24. ll. 7–8. St John's command to free the hippogriff has not been mentioned before.

25. ll. 5–8. *The magic horn*. Given to Astolfo by Logistilla; cf. XV. 14–15. Ariosto does not say what became of the book of counter-spells which Logistilla also gave Astolfo.

26. l. 5. *their belovèd friend*. Brandimarte.

27. l. 2. *Two kings*. Agramante and Gradasso.
   the third. Sobrino.
   l. 4. *a hero's rites*. The funeral of Brandimarte; cf. XLIII. 165–82.

28. l. 4. *the Saône*. The court has come south from Paris.
   ll. 6–7. *his own / Fair lady*. The Empress Galerana; cf. XLIII. 184 and Note.

29. l. 6. *Monglane . . . Clairmont*. These two names represent the two

principal families to which the most eminent of the French warriors belong.

30. l. 2. *Ruggier of Reggio.* cf. XXXVI. 70–74.

35. This is the beginning of a long passage inserted in the third edition, of 1532, extending to XLVI. 72.

39. ll. 7–8. Bradamante's will (to wed Ruggiero) is surrendered to Love.

53. l. 5. *Montalban.* Rinaldo.

  his cousin. Orlando; cf. stanza 9 ff.

56. l. 5. *her Trojan lover.* Paris.

  ll. 6–7. Pirithous attempted to carry off Proserpina from the underworld but was seized by Pluto and fastened to a rock from which (some authors say) he was never released.

60. l. 4. *The Greek.* Leone.

72. l. 7. *Rochefort.* A city on the south coast of France, originally a fortress.

76. l. 6. To cause him to be deified, because dead, a satirical allusion to the Romans' deification of their Emperors.

77. l. 7–8. *A unicorn* . . . A symbol of chastity.

79. ll. 5–8. This war between Constantine and the Bulgars is probably based on the historical conflict between that nation and Constantine V, Emperor of Constantinople from 741–775, and his son Leo IV (775–80). Leo's son, Constantine VI, was betrothed to Charlemagne's daughter, Rotrude.

95. l. 3. *the river.* The Sava.

98. l. 4. *neither rod nor sceptre.* The rod, or baton, is here the symbol of military command, the sceptre, of sovereignty.

101. l. 4. *a city.* Novigrad.

CANTO XLV

1. l. 4. *Polycrates.* Greek tyrant of Samos; at the height of his power, he was lured to the mainland by Oroetes, the satrap of Sardis, who had him seized and put to death, 522 B.C.

 l. 5. *Croesus.* King of Lydia (*d.* 546 B.C.), celebrated for his wealth, but later conquered and dispossessed by Cyrus.

  Dionysius. The tyrant of Syracuse (*c.* 430–367 B.C.), once rich and powerful, who was reduced to schoolmastering.

2. l. 7. *Servius.* Servius Tullius (sixth century B.C.). Of humble origin, he became king of Rome.

  Marius. A soldier of Arpinus who became consul; he lived from *c.* 157–86 B.C.

l. 7. *Ventidius*. A Roman consul and successful general, once a common soldier who eked out a living by selling mules; he lived from *c.* 91–*c.* 38 B.C.

l. 8. *King Louis*. Louis XII. As Louis d'Orléans he was taken prisoner by Charles VIII at Saint-Aubin and was in danger of being beheaded.

3. l. 5. *Matthew Corvin*. A prisoner of his predecessor, he was under sentence of death, but he became king of Hungary in 1458.

5. l. 2. *his rival*. Leone.

6. ll. 7–8. *The knight* ... The Romanian who has recognized Ruggiero's shield; cf. XLIV. 103–4.

11. l. 3. *Beletic*. It is not known what town Ariosto intended.

22. l. 1. *his promise*. cf. XLIV. 68–71.

39. ll. 5–6. *Procne* ... *Philomel*. See Note to XXXIX. 31. 8.

61. l. 8. *Paris*. Charlemagne and the court have moved north from Marseilles to Paris.

65. l. 6. *Galafron*. The father of Argalia and Angelica.

67. ll. 1–4. cf. IV. 48–9.

78. l. 1. *the edict*. The promise made by Charlemagne to Bradamante; cf. XLIV. 68–71.

92. l. 7. *Pegasus*. The winged horse, regarded as the horse of the Muses.

93. l. 1. *Cyllarus*. The horse of Castor (the brother of Pollux).
    Arion. The horse of Adrastus, King of Argos.

102. l. 5. *Nocturnus*. The god of night.

l. 6. *The Cimmerii*. A mythical people, mentioned by Homer; they dwelt in the far West, enveloped in mist and darkness.

CANTO XLVI

3. l. 5. *'La Mamma'*. A nickname given to Beatrice, daughter of Niccolò da Correggio, wife of Nicola Quirico Sanvitale.

    Genevieve (Ginevra). Either the daughter of Giberto da Correggio and Veronica Gambara (see following Note), who married Paolo Fulgoso, or the daughter of Giovanni Bentivoglio, who married Guido da Correggio.

l. 8. *Veronica*. The poet, Veronica Gambara, who married Giberto da Correggio.

4. l. 1. *Genevieve* (Ginevra). Perhaps the daughter of Veronica Gambara, who married a Strozzi.

l. 2. *Julia*. She has not been identified.

4. l. 3. *Ippolita the Sforza.* The daughter of Carlo Sforza and wife of Alessandro Bentivoglio of Ferrara.

l. 4. *la Trivulzia.* Domitilla, daughter of Giovanni Trivulzio.

l. 6. *Emilia Pia.* The wife of Antonio di Montefeltro; she is praised by Castiglione in *Il Cortegiano*.

Margaret. Margherita Gonzaga, who also appears in *Il Cortegiano*.

l. 7. *Angela.* This is Angela Borgia, the cousin of Lucrezia, who was the cause of rivalry between Ippolito and Giulio d'Este; cf. Vol. I, Introduction, p. 19.

Grace. Graziosa Maggi, wife of Enea Pio da Carpi.

Ricciarda d'Este. She has not been identified.

l. 8. *Bianca, Diana and their sisters.* Bianca and Diana d'Este are known to have had one sister, Lucrezia.

5. ll. 1–2. *the fair . . . Barbara of the Turchi.* Perhaps a member of the Turchi family of Ferrara.

l. 3. *Laura.* Perhaps Laura Dianti, mistress and later wife of Alfonso I.

l. 5. *Genevieve* (Ginevra). Perhaps Ginevra d'Este, sister of Ercole II, wife of Sigismondo Malatesta, lord of Rimini; or Ginevra Malatesta, wife of Obizzo of Ferrara.

6. l. 2. *conqueror of Gaul.* Julius Caesar.

7. l. 1. *My lord of Bòzolo.* Federigo Gonzaga. Bozolo is on the river Oglio.

l. 2. *Your wife.* Giovanna, daughter of Lodovico Orsini.

Your mother. Antonia del Balzo.

ll. 3–5. The Bentivoglii, Torelli, Visconti and Pallavicini families are here commemorated.

8. l. 1. *Julia Gonzaga.* Wife of Vespasiano Colonna the younger, considered the most beautiful woman of her time.

l. 6. *Her brother's wife.* Isabella Colonna, who married Luigi Gonzaga despite the opposition of Pope Clement VII; cf. XXXVII. 9 ff. and Note.

l. 8. *Anna of Aragon.* Daughter of Ferdinand of Aragon, wife of Alfonso d'Avalos, Marquess of Vasto; cf. XV. 28.

9. l. 3. *Her sister.* Giovanna of Aragon, wife of Ascanio Colonna.

l. 5. *Vittoria.* The poet, Vittoria Colonna, who celebrated her husband in her poems after his death; cf. XXXVII. 16–20 and Note.

10. ll. 7–8. *a knight, / Accolti.* Bernardo Accolti of Arezzo, called 'l'Unico' (the Unique) because of his talent for improvisation. He is among the characters in Castiglione's *Cortegiano*.

11. l. 1. *Benedict*. Benedetto Accolti, nephew of Bernardo, called the Cardinal of Ravenna, secretary of Clement VII.

l. 4. *Campeggio*. Lorenzo Campeggi of Bologna, lawyer and later Cardinal.

Mantua's Cardinal. Ercole Gonzaga, son of Francesco Gonzaga and Isabella d'Este.

12. l. 1. *Lattanzio and Claudio Tolomei*. Men of letters of Siena.

l. 2. *Paolo Panza*. A Classical scholar of Genoa.

Trissino. Giangiorgio Trissino, the poet, author of *Italia Liberata dai Goti*.

Latino. Giovenale dei Manetti, of Parma, was appointed commissioner of antiquities in 1534 by Pope Paul III.

l. 3. *The Capilupi*. Of these brothers of Mantua, the best-known were Lelio, Ippolito and Camillo.

l. 4. *Sasso*. Panfilo Sassi, a writer of Modena.

Molza. Francesco Maria Molza; cf. XXXVII. 12 and note.

Florian Montino. Florian dei Floriani di Montagnana married a lady-in-waiting at the court of Caterina Cornaro at Asoli. Her wedding is taken by Bembo as a setting for the dialogues of *Gli Asolani*.

ll. 5–7. *Giulio Camillo*. Giulio Camillo Delminio, author of *Teatro delle scienze*, a rapid guide to the study of eloquence.

Marco. This is Marco Antonio Flaminio, who wrote Latin poetry.

l. 8. *Sanga*. Giambattista Sanga of Rome, secretary of Pope Clement VII and author of Latin poetry.

Berni. Francesco Berni (1497–1536), who rewrote Boiardo's *Orlando Innamorato*.

13. l. 1. *Alessandro di Farnese*. Later Pope Paul III.

l. 3. '*Phaedra*'. Tommaso Inghirami of Volterra, called Phaedra after he had acted the part in Rome in Seneca's tragedy of that name.

Capella. Bernardino Capella of Rome, a Latin poet in the pontificate of Leo X.

Porzio. Camillo Porzio, of Rome, a poet.

Filippo. Filippo Beroaldo, Prefect of the Vatican, Latin poet and friend of Pope Leo X.

l. 4. *Maffei*. Mario Maffei of Volterra, Latin poet.

l. 5. *The Pierian*. Giampietro Valeriano Bolzani, called the Pierian because of his devotion to the Muses; tutor of Ippolito and Alessandro dei Medici, poet, prose-writer and archaeologist.

Maddaleni. Evangelista Paolo Maddaleni, Latin poet.

13. l. 6. *Blosio.* Biagio Pallai, of Rome, secretary of Pope Clement VII and of Pope Paul III.

Vida. Marco Girolamo Vida of Cremona, Latin poet.

l. 7. *Lascaris.* From Constantinople, he taught Greek at Rome and later went to the court of Francis I.

Musurro. Marco Musurro of Crete, Cardinal, friend of Pope Leo X.

Navagero. Andrea Navagero of Venice, librarian and historian of the Venetian Republic; he wrote poetry in Latin.

l. 8. *Marone.* Andrea Marone, improviser of Latin verses, friend of Ippolito d'Este.

Severo. A monk of Volterra and poet.

14. ll. 1–2. *Two other Alessandros.* Alessandro degli Orologi of Padua, and Alessandro Guarino, son of Battista Guarino and uncle of the author of *Il Pastor Fido*.

l. 3. *Mario d'Olvito.* Mario Equicola, called d'Olvito from his birthplace Alvita in Campania, secretary at the court of Mantua, author of a history of that city and of *Libro di natura e d'amore*.

l. 4. *divine Aretino.* Pietro Aretino (1492–1556); he called himself 'divine'. He is known as the 'scourge of princes' from his satirical attacks upon contemporary potentates.

l. 5. *two Girolamos.* Girolamo Verità of Verona and Girolamo Cittadini of Lombardy, both poets; the first wrote in Italian, the second in Latin.

l. 7. *Mainardo.* Giovanni Mainardi, a doctor of Ferrara.

Leoniceno. Niccolò Leoniceno, a doctor and professor of Ferrara and Bologna, translator of Galen.

l. 8. *Pannizzato.* Niccolò Mario Pannizzato, writer and Latin poet, professor of Ferrara.

Celio. Celio Calcagnini; cf. XLII. 90 and Note.

Teocreno. Benedetto Tagliacarne, called Teocreno, tutor of the sons of Francis I.

15. l. 1. *Capel.* Bernardo Cappello, poet of Venice, friend of Pietro Bembo; cf. XXXVII. 8. 3 and Note.

Pietro Bembo. The Venetian Humanist, poet and authority on the Italian language.

l. 5. *Guasparro Obizzi.* A Paduan, disciple of Bembo.

l. 7. *Bevazzan.* Agostino Bevazzano, Latin poet at the courts of Pope Leo X and Pope Clement VII.

Fracastoro. Girolamo Fracastoro of Verona, doctor and poet, author of *Syphilis sive Morbus Gallicus* and of *Naugerius, sive de Poetica*.

l. 8. *Trifon Gabriel*. A scholar and writer of Venice.

    Tasso. Bernardo Tasso, the father of Torquato, and author of the epic, *Amadigi*.

16. l. 1. *Two Niccolos*. Niccolò Amanio, poet, mentioned by Bandello in the first of his *Novelle*, and Niccolò Tiepoli, a Venetian patrician, Latin poet.

    l. 3. *Anton Fulgoso*. Antonio Fulgoso (Fregoso), of Genoa, poet and philosopher.

    l. 5. *Valerio*. Francesco Valerio, Venetian priest, possibly author of short stories; cf. xxvii. 137 and Note. He appears to have been attracted to women despite his better judgement. Lanfranco Caretti interprets this stanza differently, however, taking it to be *Barignan* (l. 7) who is being advised by Valerio. (See Lanfranco Caretti, 'Commento dell' *Orlando Furioso*', *Ludovico Ariosto, Opere Minori a cura di Cesare Segre*, Ricciardi, p. 1140.) Pietro Barignan was a poet of Brescia.

17. ll. 1–2. *I see . . . Pico and Pio*. Gianfrancesco Pico della Mirandola, grandson of the famous Giovanni, and his cousin, Alberto Pio da Carpi, a fellow student of Ariosto.

    ll. 7–8. *Iacopo Sannazaro*. The author of *Arcadia* and of *Egloghe pescatorie*, in which he wrote of sirens and fisherfolk, instead of nymphs and shepherds.

18. l. 2. *Pistòfilo*. Bonaventura Pistofilo da Pontremoli, secretary of Alfonso I, to whom Ariosto addressed one of his satires (VII) and several letters from Garfagnana.

    l. 4. *Angiar*. Perhaps Peter Martyr of Anghiera, poet and explorer; or the Humanist, Girolamo Angeriano.

    the Acciaiuolo family. Pietro Antonio, his son Iacopo and his nephew Archelaio, functionaries at the court of the Estensi.

    l. 7. *My cousin Malaguzzo*. Annibale Malaguzzi of Reggio, to whom Ariosto addressed two satires (III and v).

    l. 8. *Adoardo*. Poet of Reggio.

19. l. 1. *Vittore Fausto*. A professor of Greek in Venice and superintendent of the Arsenal.

    Tancred. Angiolo Tancredi, professor at Padua.

Machiavelli was disappointed not to find himself among the writers listed in this Canto.

    ll. 7–8. cf. xlv. 117.

22. l. 4. *the warrior of the unicorn*; cf. xliv. 77–9.

40. ll. 1–2. cf. xliv. 84–93.

46. l. 5. cf. xlv. 92.

49. l. 7. *Ruggiero's squire*. cf. xliv. 77–9 and 98–100.

59. ll. 1–5. Aegeus, King of Athens, at the instigation of Medea,

was about to hand a poisoned cup to his son Theseus, when just in time he recognized him by his sword.

62. l. 3. *her*. Theodora.

67. l. 1. *Monglane and Clairmont*. cf. Note to XLIV. 29.

ll. 3–8. Maganzans, enemies of the Clairmont line.

68. l. 1. *Montalban*. Rinaldo.

l. 5. *Pinabel*. cf. XXII. 96–7.

Bertolagi. cf. XXVI. 13.

77. l. 2. *a pavilion*. Compare Boiardo's *Orlando Innamorato*, II. xxvii. 50–61; pavilions embroidered with prophetic scenes were a feature of the Italian romances. Ariosto may also be remembering the sumptuous pavilion given by Duke Ercole I to Charles VIII in 1494.

78. l. 4. *the great Worm of Hell*. Satan.

82. l. 1. *by treachery*. Here Ariosto does not follow Homer but Dictys of Crete, who in *De Bello Troiae* (III) says that Hector was killed by Achilles in ambush.

l. 3. *Sinon's strategy*. Sinon, pretending to be fleeing from the Greeks, persuaded the Trojans to draw the wooden horse inside the walls of Troy.

l. 7. *Proteus*. Ariosto here follows Herodotus, who in *Euterpe* relates that Paris, sailing with Helen in the Aegean, was driven by storm to Egypt, where he was brought before King Proteus, who rebuked him and sent him away. Ariosto imagines that Menelaus gave Proteus the tent in gratitude.

83. ll. 5–8. At the battle of Actium, 31 B.C., Agrippa, the captain of Augustus, defeated Antony and Cleopatra.

84. l. 1. Constantine the Great, who by his alleged Donation endowed the Papacy with the Western Empire; cf. XXXIV. 80 and Note.

l. 7. *Apelles*. Greek painter; cf. XXXIII. 1. 4 and Note.

85. l. 2. *a queen*. Eleanor of Aragon, wife of Ercole I and mother of Ippolito; cf. XIII. 68–9 and Note.

86. ll. 5–8. The sister of Ippolito's mother, Beatrice, married Matthew Corvin, King of Hungary. Before he was ten years of age, Ippolito was sent to Hungary to visit his aunt; cf. XLV. 3.

88. l. 2. *the sceptre of Strigonia*. On his visit to Hungary, Ippolito was made Archbishop of Strigonia.

89. l. 3. *Tommaso Fusco*. The teacher and later secretary of Ippolito.

90. l. 1. He was made Cardinal at fourteen by Pope Alexander VI.

94. l. 2. *the unhappy Sforza*. Ludovico il Moro.

ll. 7–8. In 1499 he was driven from Milan by Louis XII. He was reinstated by the Swiss for a brief period but was finally delivered by them to the French (April 1500) and died a prisoner in the castle of Loches.

95. This stanza recalls Ippolito's part in unmasking the conspiracy against Alfonso by their two brothers, Giulio and Ferrante; cf. Vol. I, Introduction, p. 19.

ll. 7–8. Cicero was called 'the father of his country' for saving the Roman Republic from the Catiline conspiracy.

96. This stanza may refer to Ippolito's aid to the Pope in the war against the Bentivogli (1507), who were attempting to regain Bologna. With few and ill-trained papal troops, Ippolito defeated a superior force. The words of Julius Caesar, '*veni, vidi, vici*', are said to have been his report to the Senate of his victory over Pharnaces, King of the Cimmerian Bosphorus, (i.e. the Crimea), at the battle of Zela, 47 B.C.

97. This stanza refers to the battle of Polesella; cf. III. 57; XXXVI. 2; XL. 2 and Notes.

99. l. 3. *Atlante*. cf. VII. 62–3.

102. l. 2. cf. XXXV. 48–50.

l. 4. cf. XXXV. 51–2.

108. l. 6. *The marquess*. Oliver.

112. ll. 2–8. cf. XVI. 19–27.

119. l. 6. *the lady of Dordogne*. Bradamante.

135. ll. 5–7. cf. Shakespeare (*Coriolanus*, IV, V, 125–6): 'We have been down together in my sleep, / Unbuckling helms, fisting each other's throat . . .'

140. l. 4. *To Acheron's sad shores*. cf. Dante (*Inferno*, III. 76 ff.).

INDEX OF PROPER NAMES
(CANTOS XXIV–XLVI)

Ruggiero, 119; threatened by Rodomonte, 127; 135; 136; goes
on his way to Paris, 137; XXVII.2; tells Bradamante how
Ruggiero rescued him and set Viviano and Malagigi free, XXX.
87; tells her also of Marfisa, 88; 92; 93; XXXI.7; challenged and
unhorsed by Guidone, 8–10; hears Gradasso challenge Rinaldo,
98; XXXII.1; XXXVI.13; welcomes Bradamante, XXXVIII.8;
welcomes Marfisa, 21; XLIV.7

RICCIARDO, brother of Rinaldo: XXX.94; desires to avenge
brothers, XXXI.12; takes part in attack on pagans outside Paris,
55; welcomes Bradamante, XXXVIII.8

RICHARD: *see* RICCIARDO, RICCIARDETTO

RIMEDONTE: XL.73

RIMINI: XLIII.147

RINALDO: informed by Aldigiero of Lanfusa's barter with
Bertolagi, XXV.76; absent from Paris when Charlemagne is in
danger, XXVII.7–8; in search of Orlando and Angelica, 9–12; his
absence perceived by Satan, 13; 33; arrives at Montalbano,
XXX.90; has heard news of rescue of Ricciardetto, Viviano and
Malagigi, 91–3; forms band and rides to Paris, 94–5; story of his
expedition resumed, XXXI.7; encounter with knight in black, 8;
tries to dissuade Guicciardo from fighting Guidone, 11; under-
takes to fight Guidone himself, 12; combat with Guidone, 13–25;
suggests halt for the night, 26; gives Guidone new horse, 27;
learns Guidone's identity and discloses his own, 28–9; 30;
embraces and congratulates Guidone, 32–3; introduces him to
his brothers and companions, 34–6; recognizes and welcomes
Aquilante, Grifone and Sansonetto, 39–41; his grief at news of
Orlando's madness, 48; resolves to attack pagans before rescuing
Orlando, 49; leads troops during night, 50–51; attacks pagan
vanguard, 51–2; follows up attack, 53–4; his band of followers,
56–8; 77; 79; 82; vast number slain by him and his followers,
85–7; 89; Gradasso's ambition to win Baiardo from him, 89–91;
previous combat interrupted by Malagigi, 92; accused of coward-
ice and challenged by Gradasso, 95–7; rejects help of Guidone
and Ricciardetto, 98; refutes charge of cowardice and offers
explanation, 99–100; gives true account and calls Malagigi to
witness, 101–2; offers to fight Gradasso, 102; place and terms of
combat, 103–4; his knowledge of Orlando's madness and of
quarrels among pagans, 105; prepares for combat at dawn,
106–10; XXXII.2; 28; 49; XXXIII.72; 77; story of his combat
with Gradasso resumed, 78–82; interrupted by monster, 83–5;
pursues Baiardo but returns to camp, 89–92; 94; 95; XXXV.73;
XXXVI.14; welcomes Bradamante, XXXVIII.8; welcomes

Visit Penguin on the Internet
and browse at your leisure

◆ preview sample extracts of our forthcoming books
◆ read about your favourite authors
◆ investigate over 10,000 titles
◆ enter one of our literary quizzes
◆ win some fantastic prizes in our competitions
◆ e-mail us with your comments and book reviews
◆ instantly order any Penguin book

and masses more!

'To be recommended without reservation ... a rich and rewarding on-line experience' – Internet Magazine

www.penguin.co.uk

READ MORE IN PENGUIN

In every corner of the world, on every subject under the sun, Penguin represents quality and variety – the very best in publishing today.

For complete information about books available from Penguin – including Puffins, Penguin Classics and Arkana – and how to order them, write to us at the appropriate address below. Please note that for copyright reasons the selection of books varies from country to country.

In the United Kingdom: Please write to *Dept. EP, Penguin Books Ltd, Bath Road, Harmondsworth, West Drayton, Middlesex UB7 ODA*

In the United States: Please write to *Consumer Sales, Penguin Putnam Inc., P.O. Box 12289 Dept. B, Newark, New Jersey 07101-5289.* VISA and MasterCard holders call 1-800-788-6262 to order Penguin titles

In Canada: Please write to *Penguin Books Canada Ltd, 10 Alcorn Avenue, Suite 300, Toronto, Ontario M4V 3B2*

In Australia: Please write to *Penguin Books Australia Ltd, P.O. Box 257, Ringwood, Victoria 3134*

In New Zealand: Please write to *Penguin Books (NZ) Ltd, Private Bag 102902, North Shore Mail Centre, Auckland 10*

In India: Please write to *Penguin Books India Pvt Ltd, 11 Community Centre, Panchsheel Park, New Delhi 110017*

In the Netherlands: Please write to *Penguin Books Netherlands bv, Postbus 3507, NL-1001 AH Amsterdam*

In Germany: Please write to *Penguin Books Deutschland GmbH, Metzlerstrasse 26, 60594 Frankfurt am Main*

In Spain: Please write to *Penguin Books S. A., Bravo Murillo 19, 1° B, 28015 Madrid*

In Italy: Please write to *Penguin Italia s.r.l., Via Benedetto Croce 2, 20094 Corsico, Milano*

In France: Please write to *Penguin France, Le Carré Wilson, 62 rue Benjamin Baillaud, 31500 Toulouse*

In Japan: Please write to *Penguin Books Japan Ltd, Kaneko Building, 2-3-25 Koraku, Bunkyo-Ku, Tokyo 112*

In South Africa: Please write to *Penguin Books South Africa (Pty) Ltd, Private Bag X14, Parkview, 2122 Johannesburg*

A CHOICE OF CLASSICS

La Fontaine	**Selected Fables**
Madame de Lafayette	**The Princesse de Clèves**
Lautréamont	**Maldoror and Poems**
Molière	**The Misanthrope/The Sicilian/Tartuffe/A Doctor in Spite of Himself/The Imaginary Invalid**
	The Miser/The Would-be Gentleman/That Scoundrel Scapin/Love's the Best Doctor/Don Juan
Michel de Montaigne	**An Apology for Raymond Sebond**
	Complete Essays
Blaise Pascal	**Pensées**
Abbé Prevost	**Manon Lescaut**
Rabelais	**The Histories of Gargantua and Pantagruel**
Racine	**Andromache/Britannicus/Berenice**
	Iphigenia/Phaedra/Athaliah
Arthur Rimbaud	**Collected Poems**
Jean-Jacques Rousseau	**The Confessions**
	A Discourse on Inequality
	Emile
	The Social Contract
Madame de Sevigné	**Selected Letters**
Stendhal	**The Life of Henry Brulard**
	Love
	Scarlet and Black
	The Charterhouse of Parma
Voltaire	**Candide**
	Letters on England
	Philosophical Dictionary
	Zadig/L'Ingénu
Emile Zola	**L'Assomoir**
	La Bête humaine
	The Debacle
	The Earth
	Germinal
	Nana
	Thérèse Raquin

READ MORE IN PENGUIN

A CHOICE OF CLASSICS

Leopoldo Alas	**La Regenta**
Leon B. Alberti	**On Painting**
Ludovico Ariosto	**Orlando Furioso** (in two volumes)
Giovanni Boccaccio	**The Decameron**
Baldassar Castiglione	**The Book of the Courtier**
Benvenuto Cellini	**Autobiography**
Miguel de Cervantes	**Don Quixote**
	Exemplary Stories
Dante	**The Divine Comedy** (in three volumes)
	La Vita Nuova
Machado de Assis	**Dom Casmurro**
Bernal Díaz	**The Conquest of New Spain**
Niccolò Machiavelli	**The Discourses**
	The Prince
Alessandro Manzoni	**The Betrothed**
Emilia Pardo Bazán	**The House of Ulloa**
Benito Pérez Galdós	**Fortunata and Jacinta**
Eça de Quierós	**The Maias**
Sor Juana Inés de la Cruz	**Poems, Protest and a Dream**
Giorgio Vasari	**Lives of the Artists** (in two volumes)

and

Five Italian Renaissance Comedies
  (Machiavelli/**The Mandragola**; Ariosto/**Lena**; Aretino/**The
  Stablemaster**; Gl'Intronati/**The Deceived**; Guarini/**The Faithful
  Shepherd**)
The Poem of the Cid
Two Spanish Picaresque Novels
  (Anon/**Lazarillo de Tormes**; de Quevedo/**The Swindler**)